THE JACK WIDOW COLLECTION

BOOKS 7-9

SCOTT BLADE

Black Lion Media

ALSO BY SCOTT BLADE

SCOTT BLADE

A **JACK WIDOW** THRILLER

THE MIDNIGHT CALLER

Drifter. Outlaw. Hero.

Tom Clancy, in life you were a legend, a master, a true-blue snake eater. You are missed.

With Admiration,
—Scott Blade

PREFACE

FACT:
The first bricks of the Berlin Wall came down on November 9th, 1989.

1

JOSEPH McCONNELL, "Jo Jo" to his friends, left the meeting thinking that the right thing to do was to go to the FBI. But they weren't his first choice. His first choice would have been to go to the NCIS. But how could he do that?

He didn't know who to trust. The NCIS was risky. Homeland Security would be monitored. And the FBI?

He just didn't know. He needed time to think.

McConnell was a retired military officer himself. He hadn't retired with the highest rank for a man his age, but high enough. He was satisfied. Having low ambitions helped.

Never had he been anyone important. Nor had he ever aspired to be. He was happy in his former position. He had been satisfied with his accomplishments in the shadow of greater men.

There was nothing to be ashamed of. In the same breath, he also had nothing to be proud of, either. Not really. He lived a mediocre life because he was a mediocre man.

He deserved honorable mentions only for participation, not anything more.

Today, he lived a nice little life in the suburbs outside of Norfolk, Virginia, a well-established neighborhood called Brampton Heights, with sprawling sections of trees surrounding a mid-level golf course. It was quite the place to retire. Mostly, he had retired there not because of his accomplishments in the Navy, but for his silence. He knew things, dark things. And he had been rewarded for keeping his mouth shut.

The thing he knew now that he had learned today was too much, even for him. It was a secret that he couldn't keep.

This neighborhood was far above his pay grade, above his class. Most of his neighbors were well-to-do CEOs, retired congressmen, law partners in international firms, or members of the military who outranked him. Six four-star generals lived there. Soon to be five, because one was on his deathbed, although he had been for six months. Cancer.

Next door to McConnell, there were two retired admirals. He knew them personally. He was proud to have a relationship with each man. They were friendly with him, not in the "come over for cigars and a glass of bourbon every week" kind of way, but casual enough to where he had gotten invites to their homes for big neighborhood parties.

If either admiral had been interrogated, he would have acknowledged that he knew McConnell. And neither would have an opinion of him. He knew that. He had no illusions about that. He was forgettable.

McConnell knew many Navy personnel. That had been his branch of the military.

Not in twenty years of service did he ever stray. Never had he ever betrayed his commander's trust. Even though McConnell's rank wasn't as high as he would have liked, it was still high enough for him to know things. Classified things. Bad things. Sometimes illegal things.

Under normal circumstances, some things he knew would have made the most loyal dog bark. Whenever there had been a delicate mission in the past, he had been the guy to count on to oversee it, or at least to be a part of it.

Good Ole Jo Jo can keep a secret, they would say, or they would think. They must have, because they trusted him with secrets—dirty, dirty secrets.

McConnell stepped out of his town car and shut the door. He left it parked in the driveway because he used the garage to house the ten-foot-by-ten-foot model of the maritime battle of Midway, which he had spent the last six months constructing and piecing together, painstakingly. Many of the pieces had to be specially crafted from a hobby and craft shop on the edge of town. And others had to be ordered off the internet.

Before the meeting that he'd just left, he had gone to the shop and picked up a final piece. It was a model depiction of two fighter planes going up against a Japanese plane.

The piece was still in the box, sealed with plastic wrap. He was eager to pull it out and rig it up to complete the model set.

McConnell didn't know what to do about the subject of his meeting, but he knew that once he took out the set of planes and placed them in just the right place on his model set, he would be in a state of bliss. He could forget for a moment. He could ignore the danger that was coming.

McConnell closed the door to his town car and walked up the driveway. He left the vehicle doors unlocked. He hardly ever locked them because the car was controlled by one of those electric key locks, which he didn't like to use. He preferred regular keys because he considered himself to be old-school. He liked pressing the lock down, but he couldn't in this car because it just popped back up.

At his front door, McConnell paused and switched the brown paper bag containing the airplane models from his right hand to his left. He used his right hand to unlock the front door and push it open. He entered the house.

The outside light switched on automatically at about the same moment.

The house was completely dark except for a lamp that his wife had turned on before she left.

She was out with her friends, probably playing bridge, or mahjong, or some other game where she could lose his money. At least that was the common excuse that she gave him. Like he cared. He didn't. He always pretended to care about where she was and what she was doing to feign interest, usually in front of their children. He couldn't care less. She could leave and never return. He would find a way to live with himself. Of that, he was sure.

Luckily, he didn't have to pretend too often since their two kids were adults who had children of their own and lived in faraway states.

Suddenly, he wondered if that's why they had called him to the meeting. More than his reputation for being trustworthy, and that they needed him to set up contact with the Russian captain. The other thing was that he had no family here to worry about.

He didn't have to worry about what they were planning. He didn't have to worry about his family members being in danger. When the time came and the event that they were planning occurred, he could fly out to Colorado and see his son. He could be far away from the radius of damage that was on its way.

McConnell was all for returning to a better time. That's ultimately what the men in his meeting wanted. They were patriots, and they wanted to return to when the military meant something, when honor was still alive and well, when they had a clear-cut enemy unlike now, where the enemy wasn't a state with a flag.

In the meeting, the Listener had explained to him their plans. The Listener explained everything. And as with his wife, McConnell feigned he was calm and collected, that he could be trusted, but on the inside, he was terrified about what the Listener proposed—terrified.

But he listened and nodded and went along with it all. He acted like he understood, which he did. He was ashamed of the state of today's military.

Today's Navy had invisible enemies, unlike thirty years ago when times had more honor. Back then, they had Russia. They had the Cold War. They knew who their enemy was.

Politicians today used the Navy for spying and intel gathering like it was a spy satellite. And those pinheads at the NSA didn't respect what the Navy was for. They didn't respect the firepower that the Navy had.

What was the Navy doing with all their firepower now? Training exercises. Today's sailors and marines and SEALs hardly got much action. All they ever did was pretend.

It was all hogwash to McConnell and the Listener and the others. A disgrace.

To McConnell and the men in his meeting, the Navy wasn't a library or a tool for spying. It was a broadsword. It wasn't the transportation system that it had become for other branches to sail across seas. The Navy had the nukes. The Navy was the US military's atomic weapon. The Navy was the game-changer.

And now it was all being squandered.

Even though McConnell could agree with the sentiments of the small group of men that he had been speaking with, he wasn't sure about their plan.

He tossed his keys on the kitchen bar top and set the bag down with the models inside, carefully. He shivered a bit because the house was colder than usual.

Probably that time of year, he thought.

He opened the fridge and looked in. He cursed under his breath because his wife had thrown out the leftovers and had cooked nothing for him. Sure, there was food, but it was her duty to cook it, not his. That was how he was raised.

That was another reason he was glad she was out of the house all the tine. She had abandoned tradition long ago, the moment the youngest kid was gone.

They were living separate lives. They were roommates more than anything else. She had her room upstairs, and he had his downstairs, which suited him just fine.

It had all started with different drawers in a dresser and then separate closets and then different bathrooms. Before too long, she had taken over the entire second floor of the house, and he was evicted from it.

McConnell closed the refrigerator, went over to a cabinet on the opposite side of the kitchen, and took out a rocks glass. He wanted a snifter, but the only two he had were dirty, still in the sink. Another wifely duty being ignored, in his opinion.

He settled for a clean rocks glass and opened another cabinet above the bar and stovetop. It held a host of different liquor bottles. All dark. All whiskey or bourbon or a blend of the two or cognac, which was his favorite. He only took out the whiskey for special occasions when he wanted to get completely hammered.

He poured the cognac and swished it around in the glass. A strong scent floated out and caressed his sense of smell. He smiled, set the open bottle down on the bar top, and took a sip. Not bad.

He walked to a side door that led to the garage, scooped up the bag with the model planes, and took it with him on his way through the door.

The garage was dark, and colder than the inside of the house, but only by a degree or two.

He walked in, leaving the side door open so that a pool of light crept in enough to illuminate his path.

He set the bag down near the table with the model battle scene and turned to switch on the light. He flipped it, and the overhead light flicked on. The light was a single fixture with two bright bulbs. It didn't matter to him that the light wasn't enough to light up every nook and cranny of the garage. It worked perfectly as a spotlight on the table. Plus, he liked the atmosphere that the lower lighting created. It made the whole room feel like one of those cigar-smoking rooms you see in old movies.

The model table itself was lit perfectly. Shadows crept out and away from the pieces in just the right way.

On the edge of the model table was a glass ashtray, which McConnell was proud of because he had stolen it from the USS Missouri, which he had been stationed on during Desert Storm. Famously, it was the first battleship to launch Tomahawks into Iraqi-held enemy territory. He was always proud of that fact, even though he had absolutely nothing to do with it.

There was a half-smoked cigar resting on the ashtray next to a gold-plated lighter. It was his cigar. He had put it out the night before and saved it.

McConnell stood over the model table and smiled. He was about to complete another masterpiece.

Most of his fellow retired sailors could look back on their careers with great pride. McConnell was only content with his career. But creating these models was something he was proud of. It was sad to think that this was more of his life's work than his military record.

Still, there was one final piece to the puzzle.

He turned, still swallowing cognac, and returned to pick up the model pieces. That's when he came face to face with the man in black and the business end of a silenced SIG Sauer.

The man in black had a name, but McConnell didn't know it. He only knew who he was by reputation. The first time that he'd ever met the guy was over an hour ago at the meeting.

Even then, the man in black was silent.

Now he spoke. His voice was subtle and eerily normal, which was almost more frightening than the gun, strangely. Maybe it was the calmness in it. Or maybe it was the lack of humanity in it.

The man in black asked, "Where's your wife?"

McConnell didn't put his hands up to show surrender. He didn't drop his glass of cognac. He just stayed there, still, and said, "She's out."

"When is she coming back?"

McConnell shrugged.

"Where are your children?"

Without hesitation, he said, "They moved out years ago."

The man in black nodded. He believed him.

Just then, he asked a question that sent fear straight to McConnell's bones. It was the fear you feel the moment you know that you're going to die.

The man in black asked, "She knows about what we're doing?"

2

McConnell's wife drove up and parked on the curb because her husband hadn't pulled in close enough to their garage, again. She had nagged him about that before, many times before. So she knew he did it on purpose.

He did it so that she would have to park her convertible Mazda on the curb. She hated that because it was all white, and the neighborhood kids always stood out near it, every morning, waiting for the school bus. They spat on it and threw rocks at it. She knew it. Even though she couldn't prove it, she knew it in her gut.

And then there was the school bus. Every time that school bus passed, it kicked up dirt or mud or water from rain puddles onto her car. She hated it.

This time she was going to make Jo Jo come back out and move his damn car. She didn't care if he was tired or drunk. She didn't care about his models. She was tired of doing it herself. And she was tired of reminding him about it. She was tired of him.

She should have left him years earlier. She had her chance. Hell, she still could. But at this point in her life, why should she? What would she do?

Her husband was a bastard, but his retirement paid the bills, gave her a roof to sleep under, gave her the car she loved. Where would she go now, at this age?

She could get a job, but that thought made her chuckle.

She had quit her last job decades ago, after her first kid was born. She had done the loyal wife and loving mother thing for years.

No one would hire her. Not now. And even if some company did, what would they pay her?

She could take half of her husband's money, she supposed. But that wasn't much. She knew that. She knew what he took home as a retirement income. Although they had a nice house, there wasn't enough money coming in for her to make a separate life.

If she left now, she would be lucky to end up in a one-bedroom apartment. She would have to give up her car.

Martha McConnell shut the door to the car gently, not slamming it, which was what her instincts wanted to do, but she didn't. She was mad at her husband, not her car. Next, she clicked the button on her key to lock the car doors.

Unlike her husband, she locked her car every time she got out, even if she was only going a few feet away, like at the grocery store whenever she had emptied her shopping cart and had to put it away. She locked the car doors first, and then she pushed the cart to the nearest bin.

The alarm beeped once, and the lights flashed and shut off.

She stomped up the drive in her cheap Friday night pumps that she'd worn to her friend's house. She stopped at her husband's town car and waited for a low burp that passed through her throat and out into the air. She had a slight taste of chardonnay in her mouth.

She continued to the front door and opened it. It was unlocked, as usual. McConnell never seemed to care if their house was ever locked, which was another point that she constantly nagged him about.

Martha stopped in the doorway with the door wide open and reached in to switch the light on. She found the switch and flipped it. Nothing happened. She repeated the process—still nothing.

The lamp that she had left on was off as well. She suspected her husband had turned it off. He hated to leave lights on when no one was home.

Why was the foyer light not working? She wondered.

She tried it again—nothing. She flipped it a fourth time. Same results. Nothing.

The power wasn't out. She knew that because the light from the kitchen was on and working fine. The light was enough for her to see the silhouettes of her living room furniture and the dining room table and chairs beyond.

She cursed under her breath and stepped into the darkness. She closed the front door behind her. Her shoes echoed in the stillness on the tile floor in the foyer.

She dropped her purse on an end table near the door and stopped and took off her coat. She hung it on a hook and brushed their umbrella stand with her knee as she turned around.

Her footsteps were soon soundless as she stepped on the rug just after the foyer at the beginning of the living room.

The house was colder than she expected.

She said, "Jo Jo? Why is the AC running so low?"

No answer.

"Jo Jo, what's wrong with the lights?"

No answer. She walked into the living room.

"Jo? Where the hell are you?"

He must've been in the garage, clowning around with his precious models that she couldn't care less about.

"Jo?" she called out again. She called it out loud enough for him to hear her from the garage.

But there was no answer.

She set her purse on an end table near the door and stopped and took off her coat. She picked up her purse and turned around.

She dug around in her purse to find her cell phone. She swiped up on the screen and turned on the phone's flashlight feature so she could see.

The light was bright, but with a small cone of light that lit up the carpet in front of her first.

She used it to see where she was stepping, not to search the room.

She walked deeper into the living room, passing the TV, the sofa set, and the coffee table. But she stopped short of the armchair just before the kitchen because it looked like someone was sitting in it.

A second later, she was certain that someone was sitting there because she kicked a man's shoe. She twisted and turned to aim the cone of light onto the shoe and kicked it again. There was definitely a foot inside it because it was heavy to her kick, but the person didn't respond. No reflex response at all.

She kicked it again.

"Jo? Is that you?"

No answer.

Abruptly she was attacked by panic and then fear.

The light shook in her hand as she moved it up from a familiar pair of shoes and then a familiar pair of pants and then to a familiar white shirt, only it wasn't white anymore.

She saw his hands. They were duct-taped around the chair. The duct tape reflected the light with a blurry shine. It ran all the way around the man's lap in thick layers of tape.

There were violent waves and ripples in tape like the man had struggled hard to get free.

Martha moved the light upward. Next, she saw trickles of red, dried fluid that were more accurately described as garnet red, and blood.

The garnet-colored blood became more voluminous and syrupy and thicker as the beam of light shook in her hand, moving up from the man's lap to his shirt until there was no more white left in the shirt. That was when she saw only the garnet red color of blood.

Martha gasped at the sight of the neck that was also familiar, and then she saw the face that she knew better than her own. It was her husband.

His neck was well past the point of gushing blood because the blood he had in his body had gushed out much earlier. All that was left was a vicious-looking wound. It looked like someone had tried to decapitate him with a rusty hacksaw. Only he hadn't been decapitated. He had been garroted all the way to the bone.

Martha looked on at her husband's face. While she had known that face for many years, there was something brand new about it. It was his expression. She had never seen that expression on his face before. No one had.

His eyes were wide open, staring into the darkness behind her. Only not staring, because there was no life in them. Not even a sign that life had once occupied his body. There was no sign of anything but utter-terror on his face. It was unlike anything that she had ever seen before.

He was completely stone, like a marble statue made by some twisted sculptor.

The whites in his eyes were completely bloodshot, but not with the garnet color she had seen a second earlier on his shirt. This was a shade of purple that was almost eggplant. They looked like they were about to burst out of their sockets.

It was horrifying.

The phone trembled harder in her hand. She slowly reached out with her free hand. The tips of her fingers touched her dead husband's forehead. Immediately, she recoiled because his skin was so cold that it felt like touching ice.

Martha jumped back, but she was stopped dead in her tracks by a brick wall.

No, not a brick wall, a man. A powerful man.

She heard a subtle voice say, "Where are your children?"

A question that he already knew the answer to, but he liked to be reassured.

As if she were answering a game show question in the lightning round, Martha said, "They don't live here."

The man smiled.

She didn't turn around.

The man behind her asked, "When was the last time you spoke to them?"

Martha trembled even harder, which the man in black knew because the light from her phone danced across the wall, across McConnell's lifeless body.

"It's been at least a week. They're busy."

The man in black smiled in the dark. He didn't really need to ask her that question. He would know soon enough when he checked the phone log on her cell phone.

He liked the feeling that he felt just before she died. The anticipation before he killed her put a smile on his face. It was the best part. Other than the struggle his victims gave him, of course.

In a fast, violent, well-practiced exertion, the man in black whipped out a garrote that he had been holding, pulling it tight until the wire rippled and echoed lightly in the stillness. The wire went over her head to her neck and jerked straight back. The sharp edge of the wire nearly cut through the skin on her neck with little force. A second later, it broke the skin, and blood misted out as she tried to scream.

No sound escaped from her lips. No breath came out of her lungs.

Martha instinctively dropped the phone and grabbed at the wire around her neck with both hands. Desperately.

She fought violently to pull a fraction of slack out of it. But there was none to be had.

The man in black was too strong. He remained still, like a tree planted in the ground with roots dug down deep. Nothing would move him. Nothing would budge him.

She struggled and struggled. When that didn't work, she drummed on his gloved hands. And she gagged and retched and heaved dryly. She made all the faces imaginable under the circumstances, and then she duplicated her husband's dead expression.

The man in black still didn't move. He was much, much stronger than she. He breathed in calmly. This was his favorite part.

She fought and fought until she felt weak and suddenly feeble. She fought until fighting turned into barely moving.

The pain was beyond anything that she could imagine. It was worse than childbirth. It was worse than that time she'd nearly drowned at Lake Mead, a family trip, a better time.

She continued to struggle weakly against him until she was blind, until she could no longer move.

It made no difference.

3

THE MAN in black used his burner phone to call, but first, he dropped his garrote in the McConnells' kitchen sink. He ran cold water over the wire and the dual handles and watched as blood and skin and even bits of sinew washed off the razor-sharp wire.

Plenty of evidence was left all over the living room floor that the McConnells had been brutally murdered. It didn't take a forensic technician to see that, but he wasn't concerned with any of it. None of it would lead to him. And even if it did, it wouldn't matter after Sunday.

One thing that might lead to him, eventually, was the security gate that he had to pass through to get into the neighborhood. They had him on camera at the gate, where he pretended to be visiting someone who lived in the neighborhood.

The man in black had infiltrated maximum-security installations all over the western world. A minimum wage crew of security guards and the low tech of a rising boom gate wouldn't stop him.

The security camera had his face because he had to raise the visor on his helmet so the guard could match the photo on his fake driver's license with his face.

Normally, he would destroy the video from the camera somehow. But that didn't matter.

Once the operation that he was protecting went off, none of it would matter.

The man in black finished cleaning the garrote and then called the Listener, the person who had sent him to kill the McConnells. The Listener was the boss.

After he dialed the number, the phone didn't ring even once. The time counter for the call showed two seconds of connecting on his end, but there was already a voice on the other line.

The man in black said, "He's dead."

The Listener asked, "The wife?"

"Also dead."

"That's a shame."

"You wanted her dead."

"I know."

The man in black said nothing, but wondered how close the Listener had been to the McConnells.

The Listener said, "Get out of there."

"What next? How are we going to get to Karpov?"

"Farmer has found a way."

The man in black had no opinion on the guy named Farmer. He barely knew him. They ran in the same covert circles, with two very different occupations.

The Listener said, "It's quite brilliant. And simple. And a total act of fate."

"How so?"

"We found Karpov's daughter."

"Daughter?"

"She's in New York," the Listener said, and chuckled, which was audible enough for the man in black to hear him.

"Really?"

"And get this. She's a local operator for the FSB. She's been here under our noses."

The Listener had used the word "operator," which didn't mean the telephone kind. He had meant that she was a spy.

The man in black said, "You're kidding?"

He smiled and almost caught himself joining in the chuckle. It was quite a stroke of luck.

"Get to New York. We don't need you here anymore. We might need you there."

"Of course. I'll leave now."

"Good," the Listener said.

"What is Farmer's plan?"

"I'll explain when you get there. You're only going to be there for disposal and backup."

That was exactly what the man in black wanted to hear. Disposal was what he did best. All that espionage, intelligence gathering, and talking to people, making friends, earning trust. He was more than happy to leave that to the career schemers like Farmer. It didn't interest him in the least.

The man in black listened a little longer. The Listener spoke, telling him where to go and what to wait for.

The operation may not even need his services anymore, but it was better to have him around as a backup in case something went wrong.

After the Listener was done explaining things to him, the man in black said goodbye and hung up the phone. He took one more look over the McConnells' house, saw nothing left that needed doing, nothing left that needed his attention, and he walked out, down the drive and down the street to where he had parked his motorcycle.

He looked around casually until he was satisfied that no one was watching him. He slipped on his helmet, lowered the darkened visor, started the engine, and in a burst of exhaust, rode away into the darkening night.

4

THE CITY of New York or New York City?

He wasn't sure.

Jack Widow had heard it called both before. He knew one was the official title of the area that people sometimes simply called New York. With no "City" in the title. As if the state of New York didn't exist. Only the City mattered.

What was the official title of the city again? He couldn't remember, which was a scary prospect for a guy not old enough to have Alzheimer's disease. But grown-up enough to know the name of the City.

He didn't have amnesia. Did he?

No. Not quite. The reason that Widow couldn't recall the name of the City, not at that second, wasn't because of the five guys standing around him. Not all five, anyway.

It was because of only one.

The one that stood directly in front of him. The one with the massive bulk.

He wasn't the biggest of the five guys. But he was the one to worry the most about because he had that look on his face, like he knew how to throw a punch.

More than just the look on his face was his face itself. It wasn't a normal face and far from the kind of face that one would call attractive.

It was the kind of face that showed off the ability to take a punch. It showed that off because it had taken punches. Hundreds. Probably more, Widow figured.

The guy with the face wore a street cap, made from cotton or maybe wool. It was the kind of tattered street cap that looked like it came right out of the nineteen forties, just after the Great Depression.

It was the kind of thing that was cheap to find back then, and it kept the head warm. It was a functional garment. Not now. These days this kind of cap would go for a pretty penny in a department store in New York City.

The guy wasn't wearing it to stay warm. It was a fashion choice.

Times had changed. Certainly. The Great Depression. Another time. The nineteen forties. Or was that the nineteen-thirties?

Widow couldn't remember that, either.

The guy's face was rougher than a four-hundred-year-old map of the world and harder than the side of a tree. Widow saw the advantage of having such a face. On the one hand, it terrified most people, and intimidated even the most capable street fighters, like Widow.

There was a disadvantage about it, which Widow made the mistake of mentioning to the guy.

He said, "With a face like that, you must hear constant laughter from women every time you propose that one of them go to bed with you."

Not the drollest insult that Widow had ever hurled, but not the dumbest either. It did the trick, which was to piss the guy off—not a tactical decision on Widow's part. It was more of a need, the kind of need that Widow liked to have satisfied when he was squaring off with five guys with a woman and a gun present.

After the insult was hurled and the verbal shot was fired, you couldn't take it back. Suddenly Widow wished he could.

The guy with Map Face scoffed with an unintelligible grunt that wasn't even in the realm of sounding like an English word, probably because it was slurred out in a thick Irish accent. Widow didn't get the chance to decipher it because the map-faced guy punched him right in the cheek for the second time.

Hard. It felt like being hit with a battering ram, exerting enough force to bang through the castle doors.

Suddenly, the words "blunt force trauma" sprang to Widow's mind, and he blacked out, standing. It was only a second to the five guys and one woman standing around him. But to Widow, it felt like an eternity of black.

His mind wandered for that long moment. And his long-term memory seemed to work. He thought back to a long military career. Once, he had been undercover, working for the Naval Crime Investigative Services. He had been a Navy SEAL during the last stretch of that career. Although, not really because he was technically an NCIS agent, which is a civilian.

They assigned him to an undercover unit where he went on missions with the SEALs, as one of them. To them, he was one. No one knew he was really an NCIS agent.

He lived a double identity.

Most SEALs knew him as one of them. They trusted him with their lives. They treated him like a brother, but he wasn't one of them. Not really. Not honestly. He had always felt hollow inside knowing that truthfully, he was an undercover cop, sent to spy on his brothers. There was a word for that—rat.

And sometimes he felt like a rat. But only sometimes. Because the truth was ninety-nine point nine percent of SEALs and Marines were heroes—patriots. These were good men. It was lying to them that made him feel like a rat.

But then there was that point one percent. They were the ones who had stepped out of line. He had found that point one percent to be traitors, murderers, terrorist enablers, and even flat-out spies for foreign governments. And then there had been foreign agents who weren't in the US Navy or Marine Corps. Many of them he had to take down in his career. Taking them down was more satisfying because he didn't have to face an American who had gone too far over to the dark side.

At this moment, he couldn't remember any of them, not one face. He couldn't remember the official title of New York, and, for a split second, he couldn't even remember why this guy was punching him in the face.

Widow took the second punch to his right cheek, not as strong as the first one, which he had taken straight to his chin. That was the blow that rocked him.

The jaw and the chin are weak areas of the body. Get punched in the jaw hard enough, and you will go out. Every man has this weakness. It's only a matter of pressure and resistance, but get hit hard enough and it's lights out.

If being punched in the jaw could be measured on a number scale of one to ten, Widow guessed his number might've been a weak eight. But this guy's punches made him believe he had met a guy who could throw a punch that was a ten.

The only reason the guy had hit him in the chin was that, at the last second, Widow moved his face upward to avoid getting hit in the nose. He didn't want to get it broken.

Now he was thinking it might've been better than taking one of Map Face's monster fist punches on the chin.

Map Face had gotten him on the cheek next. A second blow that Widow hadn't agreed to.

* * *

FIVE MINUTES EARLIER, Widow had turned a corner in high spirits until he walked straight into this mess.

He turned the corner of Carbon and Seventy-First Street. It was night-time. Late. But the city always had enough light that he could still hear baby birds chirping in one of the growing trees planted near the sidewalk.

The leaves were still hanging on in the beautiful fall weather, but they had turned yellow about a week ago. Soon they would turn brown. This was the reason that he had come to New York.

What better place to spend his birthday?

He walked around the corner when he came across a man and a woman standing outside a closing Irish pub, which was abnormal on its own because Irish pubs didn't normally close before sunup, and that was far away.

He had noticed it because he was immediately sucked into the argument in front of him.

The woman was decked out in a leather half jacket, the kind of garment that barely stretched down to the small of her back. She had big brown hair, not in the eighties big perm kind of way, but not far off either.

She might've been about twenty-one years old. Although eighteen wouldn't have surprised him.

She was tall, too. Much taller than the man that she was fighting with. She looked to have an entire foot on him. To his credit, she was in large heels.

She wore a tight skirt, not quite a mini, but Widow figured it wasn't far off either. She held one of those small, shiny purses that were meant only for a cell phone, cash, credit cards, and keys, and nothing else.

Her top was a sequined silver thing. It showed her midriff was the kind that was more out of starvation over exercise. The girl's stomach wasn't the only thing on display. Her cleavage was out, and she wasn't shy about it.

The man had been wearing a three-piece suit, blue and wrinkle-free and dry-cleaned so crisp it looked right out of a flat press.

He wore more rings than he had fingers, which wasn't metaphorical. The guy was missing his pinkie finger on his right hand.

The rings were the size of Super Bowl rings but were more than likely bought from a class ring manufacturer because this guy would've never played in any sport. Ever.

From the looks of him, Widow would've thought he was too small to make it on a JV team in any sport.

The jewelry didn't stop at the rings. The guy had two gaudy necklaces on. They were gold plated, probably plated and thick. Nothing hung from them. He wasn't as blatant as one of those pimps from the seventies. He didn't have his name hanging from the end of one chain. Or anything like that.

Widow heard the guy screaming at the woman. All kinds of expletives and obscenities and invectives. Nothing that he hadn't heard before. And nothing that he had ever stood for before, not when directed at a woman, even if she wasn't dressed in the most innocent way. Not that he didn't approve of how she was dressed. As a man, he certainly liked it. As a citizen of the twenty-first century and America, he believed in *live and let live*. If she wanted to wear a wet trash bag and nothing else, it was none of his business. Naturally, her choice in clothes didn't warrant the kind of treatment that she was getting.

This was New York City, and people were mean to each other in all kinds of horrible ways on the streets and in public.

Widow couldn't stop and reprimand them all. It wasn't his place. He wasn't the manner police.

After turning the corner, his instinct was to assess and move on. No need to make a big deal out of it, as long as the guy wasn't physically abusing the woman or as long as she didn't request help. Then it was none of his business.

She makes her own choices.

Widow kept on walking in the direction that he had planned to walk, which was toward them and past them.

The girl had been standing with her back and left side to him, nearly a profile view.

Her face had pointed toward the man.

The moment that changed Widow's assessment from one of *live and let live* was when the woman's profile changed, and she looked in his direction.

So far, she hadn't said a word back to the gangster-looking wannabe. Instead, she had just taken the verbal abuse, like it was expected of her.

That changed when she heard or felt Widow's presence. She turned and looked right at him.

Her face was a mess of tears, muddy running mascara and bandages and swelling. She had white medical bandages on her nose. Her eyes were puffy, like she had been punched in both eyes. Her cheeks were so veiny that they looked like blue and red and yellow electrical wires running underneath her skin.

There was so much redness in her eyes that Widow wasn't sure if they were red from her crying for a week or if it was blood.

Something told him it was the latter.

Widow had always had a laissez-faire attitude, but there was a limit to that. His attitude had a second phase.

His first phase was to live and let live. His second phase was *do unto others*.

The woman had a face that was virtually broken. Obviously, this current situation had only been a follow-up to a worse situation. That had required her to go to the emergency room for a broken nose and swollen cheeks and probably two bruised eyeballs.

Widow saw this, assessed the situation, and immediately cranked into his second phase, *do unto others*.

The short guy had done something to another. And now it was time for Widow to do back unto him.

The gangster wannabe turned and looked at him and stared.

Widow was a tall man, and a dangerous-looking one at that. He hadn't known low self-esteem since he was in junior high, and back then it was only relative to women. He had never known self-doubt, not in fighting. Not anyone. Not anywhere. Not at any age.

But this guy's self-esteem must've been incredible because he looked up at Widow's face, which must have been ten-plus inches higher than his own.

And he asked, "What the hell you gawking at?"

Widow could've said something witty in return. He could have. But he didn't.

Instead, he stepped right up to the guy and, with his left hand, grabbed the dangling gold chains. He racked them down with enough pressure to hold the guy still, and then he threw a right jab. Hard and fast.

The bones in the guy's face, including his nose and probably his cheeks *cracked!!*

The gangster wannabe let out a cry that was louder than most dying animals.

Widow held onto the gold chains around the guy's neck, tight. He reared his right hand back, slow this time. He wanted the guy to see it coming.

After a calculation of power, because he didn't want to kill the guy or knock him out, Widow threw the second blow to the guy's face. He hadn't really made a plan. There had been no time for that. At that moment, he figured why not make the guy's face look like the girl's?

An eye for an eye was basically the same as *do unto others*.

Before Widow could execute a second horrific blow, the woman screamed, "What the hell are you doing?"

She latched onto his bicep, nearly hanging off it. She had moved so fast that she came out of her shoes.

"Let him go! Let him go!" she begged and pleaded.

Widow let the guy go.

He dropped like a tossed cinder block at a construction site; only he didn't crack open when he hit the sidewalk. That was only because he hadn't been tossed hard enough.

The gangster wannabe said something inaudible because his nose was broken and his cheeks were shattered.

He grabbed at his nose with both hands. Blood seeped out between his fingers and ran over his pale white knuckles.

The woman said, "What the hell are you doing? Why? Why?"

Widow looked at her, confused. It seemed pretty obvious why. This guy was beating on her, treating her like a dog.

He said, "What do you mean?"

"Why are you attacking us?" she shouted at him.

Attacking us? Us?

"I don't like men who beat women."

"He wasn't beating me. We were arguing!"

"What?"

"He didn't beat me!"

"Not this time. But what about in the last twenty-four hours?"

She looked up at Widow as she knelt, rocking the gangster wannabe. He cried like a baby.

"What the hell are you talking about, asshole?"

Widow looked at her. He was so confused. Was she this blind? Did she have Stockholm syndrome or something?

He had heard of abused women like this before. They defended the men who beat them. Some of them even let them do it. But he had never seen a woman who pretended that it wasn't happening, not when there was barefaced physical evidence.

Not like this.

She said, "Well?"

"Your face. Look at your face. You look like he's been beating you with a bat."

The girl stood up, walked right up to Widow.

She said, "These bandages aren't from being beaten! This is from plastic surgery! I'm a model! I had a nose job! And collagen injections!"

Widow looked at her, dumbfounded.

He had made a big mistake, and it was only going to get worse.

Right at that moment, a group of men walked out of the Irish pub. The door shut behind them like it had been attached to a squeaky metal door spring.

The four men who walked out were all big guys. They were dressed almost comically the same. Scruffy, threadbare casual suits. No ties among them. Some had vests. Some had dress shirts and slacks with suspenders.

Then the biggest guy stepped forward. He had been in the back like he was the anchor.

He was the guy with the map for a face.

The woman said, "You just beat up Vinnie, the Irish! Big mistake!"

Widow didn't know Vinnie. He had never heard of him. And Widow wasn't the smartest man who ever lived, but he had better than average common sense.

He knew that this was New York City. He knew he had been strolling through the town's only upper-class Irish neighborhood. And they were standing in front of an Irish pub that closed early on a Saturday night.

One of the few ways a business like that would close on a Saturday night, early, was if the staff had been given permission to by the owner.

Widow looked up, past the big guys, and stared at the sign.

It read: *Vinnie's Irish Pub.*

His face formed an expression of worry.

It turned out that Vinnie wasn't a gangster wannabe.

He was a gangster.

5

WIDOW FELT bad about his mistake.

The map-faced guy wasn't the spokesman for Vinnie. That job title turned out to belong to the third-biggest guy. He was also the only one who had all of his teeth, Widow had noticed. And he had the best facial features as far as being easiest to look at. He wasn't the ugliest one by far.

He stepped forward and asked, "Irene, what the hell is going on?"

"This idiot knocked Vinnie out. He thought he had been hitting me. 'Cause of the bandages."

The spokesman stepped up to Widow, and two of the other guys stepped around Widow in a circle. They didn't get within grabbing distance, which Widow also noticed. He noticed it because it meant that they weren't amateurs. Like he had assessed them, they had also assessed him. They knew right off the bat that he was no normal guy. He wasn't the kind of guy they usually set out to rough up.

Widow had a lean build, but he was hard as a rock. He had long arms and big hands that had more in common with sledgehammers than human fists.

The four guys all knew to stay out of his reach. Even the map-faced guy stayed clear of it.

They had the number advantage, and by the look of them, they had the experience advantage as well. Especially the map-faced guy. He was the one who worried Widow.

He worried him because not only did he look like he was their best fighter, he also looked a little familiar.

It took Widow a moment, but he was almost positive that he had seen the guy's face before. It was hard to forget, after all. Then it hit him. The map-faced guy was famous. Once the guy had a decent record as an Irish MMA fighter.

But he had retired from fighting in the ring. Widow wasn't sure why. Maybe it was because Vinnie paid more. Then again, maybe it was because he'd nearly killed a guy.

Whatever the reason, Widow didn't want to find out.

The spokesman stepped into Widow's view and asked, "You got a name?"

"Don't you?"

The spokesman smiled and said, "My name is Geoffrey."

He waited, and Widow stayed quiet.

He chuckled and said, "I know. It sounds like the name of an Irish butler. But that's my name. Real name too."

Widow nodded, kept his eyes on Geoffrey, but watched for motions from any of the other guys. If they moved, he moved.

Geoffrey said, "This is Big John. That's Little John."

He pointed at one of the other guys and then the next one. Widow didn't turn to look.

He said, "Guess we know which one is popular with the ladies then, don't we?"

Geoffrey smiled and said, "This one is called Laurie, which is short for Lawrence, which is short for Lawrence Holyfield. No relation to the famous boxer. Obviously."

Widow nodded.

"But you know why people often make that mistake?"

Widow said, "No clue." Although he knew.

"It's not because he's white. Clearly. It's because, like Holyfield, the American boxer, Laurie is a famous boxer. Kickboxer, actually."

Widow stayed quiet.

"Do you know what a kickboxer is?"

"A boxer who kicks?"

Geoffrey smiled and said, "Yes. That's it. But ole Laurie here can't kick for shit!"

Right then, three of them laughed a big, hearty laugh, all except for

Laurie. He looked at Widow with a death stare, like he wanted to kill him, which was probably true.

"Know why it doesn't matter that he can't kick?"

Widow said, "No. Why?"

"Because he never had to. He's more into the boxer part. And boy, let me tell ya. He can box."

Widow asked, "Why does it feel like I'm going to find out just how well?"

Geoffrey ignored that. He asked, "Now, what's your name, mate?"

"Tyson. Know what he did to Holyfield?"

Silence.

And then Geoffrey smiled and said, "Funny."

He looked around at the other three and then at Laurie.

"That's funny, Mr. Tyson. That's real funny. I can see that you've got some brains. So, I'm just gonna level with ya. This here is Vinnie the Irish. We're all Irish. Vinnie here isn't the boss or the boss's boss, but he's kin to the boss's boss."

Widow stayed quiet. Kept his fists down by his sides, but ready to go when action was called.

"See. Really, he's a pain in the ass. None of us like him."

Irene said, "What's taking so long? Kill him already!"

Geoffrey turned in a slow movement like he hated being interrupted, and he said, "Shut up, Irene! No one is talking to you!"

She froze like she was more scared of Geoffrey than she was of the others. This told Widow that he had been wrong.

Geoffrey wasn't the spokesman. Vinnie wasn't their boss. They were his babysitters. This meant that Geoffrey was some sort of top lieutenant, since he was the one doing the talking. He was probably charged with protecting Vinnie.

"Now, where was I?"

Widow tried a new approach. The silent stranger act that normally worked for him wouldn't work here. It was going to lead to him beating up four mobsters. And an ungrateful, crazy woman wasn't worth having mobsters on his back while he was in New York to enjoy himself.

He said, "Look, guys. I don't want any trouble. This is obviously a misunderstanding. I thought there was trouble here. Look at her face— simple mistake. I am truly sorry for busting up your friend. You're free to call the police. I'll stick around. Talk to them. I'll explain it to them."

Widow looked down at Vinnie, who was completely passed out at this point.

"And when your friend wakes up. I'll apologize to him. Maybe he'll want to press charges. I'll stick around for that. I am in the wrong here."

"No pigs!" Irene shouted.

Geoffrey shot her a look. Another way of telling her to shut up. And she did.

He said, "Like the girl said, we can't have the police involved. We're not those types of guys. We practice more of a street justice philosophy."

The apologetic approach wouldn't work either; Widow could see that.

Widow said, "Look. I apologized. Admitted fault. What else do you want? I don't have any money, guys."

Either Big John or Little John smirked. Widow wasn't sure which was which.

Geoffrey said, "I think that it's only fair that you take a beating. Like the one you gave Vinnie here."

Widow stared at him blankly.

"I'm sorry. But I can't have word getting back to my boss that we just let you go with anything less."

Widow smiled and said, "There's four of you. And you're all bigger than Vinnie. How am I supposed to fight four of you and call that even?"

"Fight? Oh, no, Mr. Tyson. I'm not saying that you have to fight all four of us."

Widow shrugged, and said, "What then? Just Laurie?"

"No. You're not fighting here. I said: 'take a beating.' I mean exactly that. You're going to stand still and let Laurie break your face. Like Vinnie's."

Widow smiled back at Geoffrey.

"I'm not letting anyone do anything like that. You can all come at me. At the same time. I'm not the type of guy to stand still."

Geoffrey said nothing.

Widow said, "And I've gotta warn you, fellas. You come at me; you're gonna lose a lot more than ears. You're gonna end up with broken bones and shattered faces. Maybe a couple of you will go blind when I mash your eye sockets to mush."

Right then, Geoffrey looked straight at Laurie, and then he looked around the empty street in a quick, scanning motion. He didn't look behind him, just in front, which was behind Widow.

Widow guessed that one of the Johns signaled to him that there were no witnesses on the street in the other direction because Geoffrey did the one thing that he'd need a street with no witnesses on to do.

He pulled out a Glock 19 and jammed it in Widow's face.

He said, "It's not up for debate. You're taking the beating, or you're taking a bullet."

6

"Not here," Geoffrey said, "Around the back. In the alley."

He was speaking to Widow with a Glock 19 pointed at Widow's face. Widow could have taken it away. Easy enough. A twist from the hips. Pivot on the left foot and a hand clamped down tight on the slide and trigger hand. Followed by a fast swipe down and away, jerking Geoffrey off his feet. Maybe he would break Widow's powerful grip and fire a round, but by that time, he would be aiming at the guy behind him. One of the Johns.

Widow thought about it. But in the end, he decided not to because Geoffrey knew enough to show off the gun quick, by pointing it in Widow's face, but then he knew to back away far enough, so Widow wasn't tempted to try a disarm move against him.

Smart guy. Well, smart enough, Widow thought.

Widow turned and looked toward a small street that led into the dimness of a small alley between the buildings.

Before he moved on, he looked left, looked right. Widow surveyed the street, to double-check Geoffrey's assessment that there were no witnesses. And there weren't, not at that exact moment.

But just then, a blue-and-white police cruiser rolled around the corner and slowed. The two cops in the front stared at Widow.

The car was a Nissan Altima model. It was a hybrid—some kind of move by the NYPD to seem more eco-friendly.

Widow wondered if they had to sacrifice speed and maneuverability and power for the PR stunt. Then again, New York traffic was usually too thick to worry about car chases.

Widow said, "Looks like you boys won't get the chance to follow through after all."

Geoffrey said, "Just wait."

Wait for what? Widow thought.

The cops rolled closer and studied Widow's face. They stopped about fifty yards away. Then Widow watched as they brought the car to a full stop and switched on their left turn signal and cut across the road and vanished down another street.

What the hell?

"The cops aren't going to help you. They won't be bothering us. I'm afraid that you're taking that beating whether you like it or not."

These guys were powerful enough to have the cops in their pockets. At least they had the local boys in their pocket.

Widow didn't even realize that the Irish mob had that kind of status in New York.

"Move it!" Geoffrey barked.

Widow moved on. He walked past one of the Johns and then turned the corner.

The other John stepped out in front of him and motioned for him to follow closer, which he did.

They led him halfway down the alley, past the garbage cans, to the back entrance of the pub.

The air smelled of disposed-food and coffee filters and half-empty beer bottles.

Steam drifted up from a grate on the sidewalk. There was one overhead outside light in the alley. It hung from a pole high above them. It buzzed and flickered.

The four guys stopped inside the yellow cone of light.

Vinnie came around the corner with Holyfield holding him up. He was awake.

Like he had done to his girlfriend, Irene, he was muttering expletives, only now they were about Widow. He tried to cut through his babysitters and march over to Widow. Only this didn't happen.

Holyfield picked him up from under his armpits and set him back where he was, like a rag doll.

Geoffrey said, "Shut up, Vinnie!"

Vinnie scuffed and grunted and mumbled, but he stayed where he was.

"Now, Mr. Tyson. This isn't a fight. You raise a fist; I'll kneecap you. Got it?"

Widow stood in the center of the cone of light. The backdoor to the pub was directly behind him, about five feet away. The two Johns stepped into the light. One to his right. One to his left.

Holyfield moved away from Vinnie and stepped up to the center. Geoffrey moved just behind him so that he could have a clear line of sight to Widow.

Vinnie was in the back, still sniveling.

Widow said, "You boys are making a mistake."

"Oh yeah, how's that?" Geoffrey asked.

"I told you I was sorry. I admitted fault. You don't want to make this worse."

"Worse for you. Not us."

"I beg to differ."

"How's that?"

Widow stayed quiet.

"You know what? Never mind. I don't care. Enough of the tough guy act," Geoffrey said, and then he looked at Holyfield. He said, "Do it."

Holyfield stepped closer. The most crooked smile that Widow had ever seen in his life flashed across Holyfield's map face. It was crooked and rigid, like a jagged knife had been used to open his mouth at birth.

Widow said, "I've been all over the world. And without a doubt, you're the ugliest person I've ever seen."

Holyfield's smile changed to an unrecognizable expression because of how uneven his face was.

But Widow recognized the giant fist that swung straight at him.

Don't fight back, or you'll take a bullet, had been the basic warning from Geoffrey.

And he didn't fight back, not at first.

He took the fist straight on the chin. It was hard.

Widow felt his jaw loosen, and his head whipped down in a violent jerk that could've sprained his neck for months. The punch was so powerful that it might've dislocated four of his vertebrae if he had taken it the wrong way.

7

THE SECOND AFTER the punch landed, Widow felt dazed to where he actually forgot things. His mind wondered about the official title of New York City and other things that didn't matter at that moment.

His jaw switched to feeling intense pain from the impact to feeling like his bones were on fire.

Widow had been rocked to the core.

Luckily, his vision was fine, and his mouth seemed to work with no problems because he made a remark back to the map-faced guy about being ugly or about hearing women's laughter. His mouth moved, and the words were coherent. But then he noticed he couldn't quite remember the map-faced guy's name. Not off the bat.

After he made a smart-ass comment about the map-faced guy, he saw another huge fist barreling down on him. He reacted. Fast. He moved his face back and looked right. He took a second punch on the cheek. This one wasn't as bad as the first, because Map Face's knuckles only brushed against his cheek. They didn't quite connect—a combination of a misfire and self-defensive maneuvers.

Although Widow forgot details, he remembered he wasn't supposed to fight back. However, that strategy wasn't working for him. He had enough.

Widow stayed where he was.

He shut his conscious brain off and let his instincts take over.

A flick of his eyes to the right. A flick of his eyes to the left and a quick glance at Geoffrey. No look at Vinnie.

Widow's only two concerns were Map Face and Geoffrey's Glock 19.

He knew that the other guys weren't armed, not with guns. They would've taken them out already. When your squad leader draws his gun, you draw yours—basic tribal gang practice. Widow knew that.

Geoffrey's Glock was the only one.

Map Face didn't have a weapon either. Why would he? He was probably designated by the state of New York as a weapon.

Widow was ordered not to fight back. He was ordered to take a beating, or he would be shot.

So far, he had been doing just that. It looked like he was taking a beating.

But Geoffrey never told him not to move. If a two-hundred-fifty-pound ex-kickboxer punches you, you move. That's a given. Naturally.

Map Face came in at him for the third time. This time he came at Widow from the left, which was what Widow had expected. It's only natural that after two rights, a boxer is going to come in with a left. Mixing it up is a major component of boxing. Any sports fan knows that.

When Geoffrey ordered Widow not to fight back, he meant with fists and kicks. He probably wasn't thinking about the forehead.

The forehead is another weapon that opponents often overlook.

Widow didn't have a forehead made of stone or anything, but he had a thick skull. A lot thicker than most. He knew this because of emergency room visits and numerous field medics and nurses over the years who always gasped at his x-rays and medical charts.

What's one thing that bones have in common with skin?

Bones heal and learn. Skin will heal and scar. Scar tissue is one of the strongest organic external tissues known on humans. Scar tissue can stop a sharp knife if it's bunched up and strong enough.

Widow's bones had built up many, many extra layers of calluses. His bones differed from most of the rest of the human population because he had beaten up a lot of opponents. And he had been hit in the head—a lot.

This had forced his skull to grow thicker and more rigid and tougher.

Widow couldn't remember how good a boxer Map Face had been, but he supposed that the guy's massive fists probably had never punched a forehead like Widow's before.

No one punches the forehead. No point. But Widow had head-butted enough people and been hit in the head enough times to know that his fore-head was like a rock.

As Map Face came at him, aiming for his right eye, Widow reared back in a fast, arching motion and catapulted his head straight down.

Map Face was fast and powerful. But he hadn't tried to be fast. He had thought that Widow was standing still like he had been ordered. He hadn't expected that he needed to move fast. This wasn't a fight.

Widow's head moved faster than Map Face's fist, and he broke the arc of the punch.

Widow's cement forehead whipped down and crushed Map Face's left hook. There was no crushing sound, not like Vinnie's face, but Widow felt the fingers dislocate and break and snap under the power and viciousness of his head.

Map Face's expression changed to one that he recognized—panic.

Widow's head wasn't the only thing working overtime. His feet moved and his body twisted.

As Map Face's knuckles were crushed, Widow used the boxer's momentum to shift him between Widow's body and the line of fire from Geoffrey's Glock.

Widow's right foot stopped and planted hard on the concrete, and he shoved the big kickboxer as hard as he could, straight into Geoffrey, straight into the gun.

Widow didn't stay in one place to confirm that his plan worked. He simply reacted as if it had worked.

Move. Shoot. Communicate. That was a SEAL mantra that he knew well.

Widow moved. Shoved. And now communicated that he wasn't going down. They were. He followed behind Map Face as he tumbled into Geof-frey, and the two of them went down. He wanted to stay out of the line of fire. And to control it.

Geoffrey didn't fire the gun. Not out of reflex, as Widow had suspected he might. Instead, he was taken totally by surprise, and he tumbled backward.

The Glock was the only thing that mattered at this point.

Like a football player losing the ball during a tackle, the Glock was out of Geoffrey's hand and sliding across the concrete, open to interception.

Widow wasn't the closest man to it. One of the Johns was.

Widow shifted priorities and ignored the Glock. He ran at John, who was so slow he didn't even go for the gun until Widow was three feet from him, which Widow anticipated.

The Glock had slid behind John, and he had to bend over to scoop it up.

Before his hand could get around the grip, Widow leaped in like a cat and swiped his boot up hard, and kicked John right in the ear.

The John toppled over. When the eardrum is busted or shattered, it's not normal to hear a sound. Not like a breaking bone.

But Widow did hear something come out of the guy's ear. There was a low *crack*. And thick red blood gushed out like a burst hose.

The guy screamed and toppled over and rolled onto his back, which was a mistake.

Widow didn't want to kill anyone, but these guys threatened his life. He didn't have any mercy for them. Not now. Maybe ten minutes ago, he could've let things go. But not now. No way.

He moved over the guy, fast, and stomped a massive boot down onto John's throat. He slowed it at the last second, realizing that death wasn't necessary. No reason to murder the guy. But if he died, no worries there either.

The guy forgot about his ear and started gasping and whishing. Which was good, in Widow's opinion, because if he was whishing, then some kind of air was getting in. He wasn't suffocating. He would need emergency surgery. But he would live if his pals took him to the emergency room fast enough.

Widow forgot about John and reached down for the Glock. But the remaining John intervened and wrapped two big, muscular arms around him. He jerked Widow back in a reverse bear hug. Which Widow thought was just insane. This wasn't a good tactical move, not in a fight against a guy like him.

Then he saw why John did that. The map-faced guy was getting up.

Geoffrey was still down. He was dazed. It looked like his head had hit the cement when he went down.

He probably had blurred vision, Widow presumed.

Widow's toes touched the ground, and he folded them in and pushed off as hard as he could. He launched up into the air a few feet, but a few were enough. He pulled his knees up and used his weight to make himself heavy.

The other John had no choice; he lost balance, and they both fell forward.

Widow tucked in and braced for the impact. It had little effect on him. The other John was mostly just stunned and not harmed.

With his right boot, Widow cracked him right in the face. Easy enough to not break anything, but hard enough to make the point.

John rolled in the other direction and held his face.

Widow didn't wait. He bounced to his feet. He wanted to go for the Glock, but he found that there was no time because Map Face was on him now. He was making his way to his feet, staying steady, standing enough to rush Widow.

Behind Map Face, Widow got another look at Geoffrey. He was scrambling to his feet behind the kickboxer but stumbling. Blood seeped over his left eye from a huge superficial gash across his brow. He clenched the eye closed and gazed around.

Widow ignored him and braced himself for Map Face, who stood up hunched like a linebacker and charged at Widow.

The common weakness of many professional athletes, especially boxers, is their egos. Often, they think because they are paid to play a sport, they can do anything. They think that because they've won a belt, have a crown, wear a gold medal, or hold the title of champion, that they are champions in real life, in the streets.

If Widow had been using his voluntary brain, if it had been working properly, at that moment, he would've recalled recently watching a program on a TV in a sports bar, down the road from a bus station in New Haven, Connecticut, where the Discovery Channel and ESPN were both covering a story about the famous swimmer Michael Phelps who was racing a great white shark in open waters.

To Widow, the whole idea was a ridiculous premise. A cash grab. And a perfect example of champion athletes thinking that they were the best at something just because they had won a competition in a safe, controlled environment.

Of course, the event was staged, and a computer graphic was used instead of a real shark. A real shark wouldn't have raced Phelps to the end. He would've taken a bite out of him instead.

Cage MMA fighting is a little better because at least Map Face had really been in some danger of bodily injury. But even in a cage match, there are rules, and a referee and judges and commentators, and both fighters were evenly matched in terms of weight and class, and they had teams of people behind them.

In the street, there are no rules. No referees. Nothing is balanced, unless by accident.

Plus, in the streets, Widow was fighting for his life, not for a trophy. Whereas Map Face wasn't fighting for his life.

He roared toward Widow, who didn't step right, didn't step left. He figured that Map Face might expect a sidestep. Instead, he stayed completely still until the last moment, and he flogged up his right foot and hurtled it out.

Widow booted Map Face right in the nuts. A hard, devastating attack. The blow hit home like a missile that rocketed straight out of a silo and hit a target seconds later. To Map Face, it felt somewhere between falling ten stories only to land on his groin and a shotgun blast to the crotch of his slacks.

Even though he was temporarily immobilized, Widow wanted to use the opportunity to take him out in a longer-term sense.

Map Face's street cap was dislodged and had slid to the side on his head, which was a bit of a surprise to Widow. Any other, lesser tough guy, and it would've flown off completely.

The guy could take a punch.

Widow scrambled forward to Map Face, who was still holding his groin but still awkwardly standing.

Widow grabbed the street cap and mashed it down over Map Face's eyes with his left hand. He fisted up his right hand and swung in for an uppercut to the guy's chin.

The blow probably wasn't harder or more powerful than Map Face's had been. But it certainly had been better executed and far more precise.

Down from the toes, Widow felt the energy surge up his body, and his fist cracked into Map Face's chin, rocked him, and knocked him straight onto his back.

And like that, his ticket was all but punched.

Widow knew that because Map Face let go of his groin and fell back limp. His mouth was open. His tongue hung out.

And Widow's fist hurt like he had just punched a brick wall, like an oncoming car that sped at top speed, intending to run him over.

His forward brain kicked back on and registered the pain. For a second, he was worried that he had broken the bones in his hand.

No time to speculate, he thought. And his back brain took over again, and he was back on his feet.

Geoffrey was also on him, but still struggling to see what was what.

That was obvious because he reached out to Vinnie, who stood off to his right, completely dumbfounded and half terrified by what he was seeing.

Widow registered another thought in his forward brain. He was grateful that Vinnie was a complete idiot. Any other half-competent mobster type would have gone for the gun.

Widow turned and saw that John, whose voice box was nearly crushed, was back on his feet, facing the other direction, but he wasn't going for the Glock either.

In fact, he was doing the only smart thing. He was running away, down into the dark end of the alley.

The girl, Irene, was a different story.

It turned out that she had been the threat that Widow should've kept his eye on because she wasn't just standing near the gun now. She was holding it fifteen feet away and pointing it straight at Widow.

"Freeze, asshole!" Irene shouted. Her voice cracked and whined. The New Yorker in her came out in her accent; only it was deeply nasal because of the swollen face and plastic surgery that she had undergone on her nose.

The whole combination made her sound kind of like some actress in a movie who picked up the gun and had zero knowledge of how to use it.

Widow stayed quiet.

Vinnie shouted, also in a nasal voice from his broken nose, "Shoot him, Irene!"

She didn't respond, but Widow could see her irritated with Vinnie bossing her around.

He stood up straight and looked her in the eyes. He held his hand out, palm facing Irene. It was in the gesture for the universal traffic symbol for stop.

He said, "Irene, you don't have to listen to them."

"Shut up!"

"Don't you tire of these guys pushing you around?"

"I'll shoot you!" she said.

She wouldn't shoot, Widow realized. Probably not.

He said, "Irene, you can come with me. I'll get you away from these guys."

"I'm serious!"

Widow saw Vinnie and Geoffrey moving toward her, which wasn't good.

He couldn't let them get to her because they would get the Glock. That was no good for him.

What else could he say? he wondered.

Just then, he got lucky.

The noise and the commotion had obviously been heard from inside the pub because a metal lock racked back, and the alley door swung open. A big Irishman with a hardy voice and an unlit cigarette tucked behind his right ear stepped out into the cone of light.

He said, "What the hell is all the noise back here?"

Sounds of pots and pans and dirty dishes clanking and racking into a sink somewhere echoed out from the open door.

Hot steam and bright light streamed out behind the Irishman.

Widow didn't wait. He took advantage of the surprise and lunged forward, in a half-crouch, with the bright light from the kitchen over his shoulder. He ran at Irene. He darted to the right the second that he knew she had seen him.

She fired the Glock.

The gunshot rang out loud and booming between the alley walls.

Widow didn't stop to check what the bullet hit, but he was sure it wasn't the Irishman, because the sound that Widow heard behind him was like a bullet hitting a brick wall.

He caught Irene completely off guard and knocked her back with a pop from his left hand, straight to her solar plexus. Not a hard hit. Not a game over knock-out strike. He didn't want to kill her or even hurt her. It was just enough force to drop her and pop the Glock from her hand.

Irene fell back on her butt, and Widow scooped up the Glock from the cracked pavement.

In a fast three-step movement, he backed away from her, swung back to the left, and pointed the Glock at Geoffrey and Vinnie and even the Irishman.

He saw the Irishman was simply a kitchen guy. He was decked out in an all-white, stained, and used uniform like a second-rate chef.

Widow wasn't worried about him, but remained cautious, anyway.

He said, "Listen up! You move; you get shot!"

Silence. They all stood still. The Irishman raised his hands up in the air, followed by Vinnie.

"You too! Hands up!" Widow said to Geoffrey, who paused at first, reluctant, unwilling to give up, unwilling to admit defeat.

Like Vinnie, Geoffrey also reverted to a position of primal submission. He hung his shoulders because he was beaten, and he knew it. But he didn't raise his hands.

Widow was impressed that his sense of pride outweighed the pain of his bleeding brow. But in the end, he submitted and raised his hands.

"All of you. Get on your knees."

They did, including Irene.

Geoffrey was the last to follow, probably because he was afraid of what was coming next. Yet he had no other choice. Widow had the only gun, and he had the distance. Geoffrey knew it wasn't a bluff.

"What are you going to do?" Vinnie asked, still nasally.

"Don't worry about that."

They all stayed on their knees and watched him. All of them trembled out of fear, except Geoffrey.

Widow corrected that.

He pointed the Glock at Geoffrey, made sure that he could see the muzzle pointed at him. He veered it to the right, just a hair, and squeezed the trigger.

Another loud gunshot echoed in the alley.

The bullet shot out and hit the brick wall directly behind Geoffrey. Shards of brick exploded, and a cloud of pebbles and dust hit him in the back of the head.

He flinched and hunched forward.

"Wait! Wait!" he shouted.

"Wait for what?"

"Don't kill us!"

"Why not?"

Geoffrey said nothing.

Irene said, "What are you going to do?"

Good question, Widow thought. He wouldn't kill them. He knew that much.

He said, "Close your eyes. All of you."

They closed their eyes.

"Count to five hundred. Out loud. Keep your eyes shut!"

He heard their voices start at *one.* They weren't in sync, but close enough.

"When you reach five hundred, get John to a hospital."

Widow backed away, slowly, out of the edge of the light. He backed into the darkness. He continued to watch and listen.

He waited for them to get to sixty, and he turned and walked away. He kept the Glock until he was out of the alley. There was a two-way street with a corner and a turn that headed east. He took the turn, kept checking over his shoulder to make sure that the John, who had run away, wasn't on his tail.

There was no one.

He found a dumpster, peeking out behind a green shutter, wrapped around a thin chain-link fence. He took out the Glock, ejected the magazine, and racked the slide. The chambered bullet ejected out. He pocketed the bullets and wiped the gun with the inside of his shirt.

Never letting his fingers touch it again, he reached over the shutter and lifted the lid of the dumpster. He tossed the gun in and dropped the lid.

He walked on and kept the bullets and the magazine for another two streets until he found a sewer drain to drop them in.

He thought about New York City, remembered that its actual title is City of New York.

Widow moved on into the night. He still had a headache from being punched twice, but his memory worked again. And he wondered what time it was.

9

FIVE TIME ZONES ahead of the City of New York, and more than twenty-four hours earlier, north of Greenwich, England, Captain Elon Karpov looked down at the tan line on the ring finger of his right hand, where his naval captain's ring normally was. It was a two-hundred-year-old silver ring, passed down from his great grandfather to his grandfather and to his father until it belonged to him.

By this time, he imagined the ring to be in his daughter's possession in America.

Karpov rubbed his head. It had been days since he shaved it, like he normally did every day.

Karpov had been an admired sailor in the Russian Navy. Not a legend or a famous hero or anything like that, but far from being looked down upon. He'd had a good career. His military records showed him as an above-average officer.

He was respected, but much more than that, he had been trusted. While being the captain of a nuclear submarine meant he had top security clearance and faith, it also meant that he had a background with the Main Directorate of the General Staff of the Russian Armed Forces or better known in English as the GRU or the Main Directorate Intelligence. The Russian version of military intelligence.

Karpov looked away from his ring finger and over at his hat. It rested on a metal panel near one of his crewmen. He felt more than ready to turn over

Russia's top-secret billion-dollar submarine technology to the Americans. Like in that American movie he saw, *The Hunt for Red October*. Which made him wonder if the Kremlin had considered that someone might steal that idea from the movie once it was obtainable to the public.

They hadn't taken it too seriously, as he only had to follow the same basic steps as Sean Connery's character had.

He wondered how bent out of shape his superiors had gotten when they learned how accurate the book was when portraying Russian sailors. The Russians still used a political officer as a way of keeping a close eye on their submarine captains, just as they did in the movie.

Karpov had such a political officer on board. Like most of the crew, he was still asleep. But Karpov knew how to deal with him. When the time came, he'd take a page out of Tom Clancy's book and just kill him.

He didn't figure that it would come to that. Most likely, the Americans would return him to the Russian government, like they would the rest of the crew members, who weren't aware of his plans.

Karpov remembered the first time he'd seen that movie. It was nineteen ninety. The Berlin Wall had just come down the year before. The Iron Curtain, as the West called it, was crumbling beneath their feet. Former countries of Eastern Europe were becoming countries of Europe again.

The communist states were falling over like dominoes. The Soviet Union was on its deathbed.

Back then, Captain Karpov wasn't a captain at all. Back then, he was a young man in a Russian state-sponsored university in Moscow. He remembered seeing American movies slowly making their way into his world.

But it was many years before the theatrical release of *The Hunt for Red October* would be available to the Russian population on VHS.

When the wall first fell, the copy that was available to people was edited to make Sean Connery look like the hero, but the defector stuff was all cut out. To most of the Russian viewing public, it appeared to be a story about a Russian captain who had saved the world from nuclear annihilation in the face of US intervention.

Karpov had thought how funny it was that people believed it.

He had seen the movie and realized that it was twisted into state propaganda. He knew that because his father had given him a copy of Tom Clancy's book in English. Luckily, his father had also insisted that he learn English as a boy.

Karpov read Clancy's novel and then watched the fake version of the movie and then sought out the original, which he found and traded a pair of baseball cards with another Russian officer who fancied the sport and had traded something else with a German who had the movie. It came as is. No subtitles.

Karpov watched it.

It was pretty good. Not as good as the book, he had thought.

It was a lot less technical than the book, a trend that he had noticed a lot in American movies. Often, they dumbed down the technical aspects of military movies.

He remembered thinking that Sean Connery played a brave sailor, not unlike himself. But he wasn't brave by fighting for the communist government. He was brave for escaping it.

Like Sean Connery, Karpov dreamed of the American landscape. He dreamed of freedom. He dreamed of escape from the Russian oligarch corruption.

Even though the Iron Curtain had fallen, and Russia was a democracy, he knew better. Russia had only been a democracy for about ten years until the only Russian president in Democratic Russia had turned over power to a young KGB officer and political administrator, Vladimir Putin.

That was when things changed for the country.

Karpov was a submariner by then.

He grew up in a military family. All seafarers. All proud. His father had been a famous Soviet admiral before he had died of pancreatic cancer.

Karpov remembered his father wanting to go to America when Karpov was a kid. An idea that Karpov's father had planted down deep in his mind.

Now, nearly three decades later, Karpov was at the helm of a top-secret fourth-generation Dolgorukiy-class nuclear submarine, known to NATO as a Borei-class nuclear submarine.

This submarine was special. It wasn't just the nuclear payload that was special. There was something else onboard—something more valuable, in certain eyes. That's why the American CIA accepted Karpov's deal. That's why they were going to grant him and his command crew asylum in the US.

In *The Hunt for Red October*, one officer dreamed of living on a Montana ranch. That sounded great to Karpov. He dreamed of owning a ranch and living the American life, far away from the ocean, far away from Putin's Russia.

But most of all, he wanted to achieve the dreams of his father.

"Captain, I see them," his first officer said. He looked through the periscope.

"Mr. Travkin, slow the approach. Ascend. Stay low. Stay quiet."

Travkin nodded and began relaying orders to the bridge crew.

Karpov gazed at his father's wristwatch and noted the time in his head, an occupational hazard more than necessity. He wouldn't document this meeting, not to his commanders. It wasn't a legal mission.

Sean Connery was a rugged Scotsman with a white beard and full head of hair in that movie. But Karpov looked more like Connery in real life. He was completely bald. The last time that he had seen hair on his head was probably nineteen eighty-nine. But he had the same white beard, with tinges of black in it.

Karpov looked at the skeleton bridge crew. The time was late night for them. Most of his crew members were in their quarters, fast asleep. The faces on the bridge were of men he trusted. And even some of them didn't know what his plans were. They trusted him anyway. He knew it.

Like Sean Connery, he had handpicked them.

The submarine hummed and the engines whined briefly and then slowed.

Karpov said, "I'm going up."

Travkin nodded. He knew it was one of Karpov's favorite things about being a submariner. He loved to ascend and stick his head out and watch the boat breach the waves.

Karpov waited to ascend the tower.

The nuclear pack droned, and the propeller slowed. The water rushed around the boat until the bow ripped upward and breached through the waters of the Arctic Ocean.

Karpov went up the tower and opened the hatch. He climbed past the cables connecting to the radio antenna and stepped up onto the tower.

He watched the waves spill over the bow and felt the icy night on his face.

Far off in the distance, blue and white lights lit up the night sky, outlining a vessel that looked like a deep-sea fishing boat.

Karpov smiled, pulled his collar up on his peacoat. He saw the lights of the fishing vessel and then pulled a small flashlight out of his coat pocket. He flicked the switch, and a bright, sharp beam came out.

He pointed the light at the fishing boat and pressed his hand over the beam, shuttered it three times like the CIA had told him to do. He waited a long minute and then got the response, which was four blinks of light back at him. He responded again with two more of his own. They responded again with three.

It was the CIA team that was supposed to take him and his crew from the submarine.

Travkin appeared behind him.

"Is that them, Elon?"

"It is."

"We're really going to do this?"

"There's no turning back now."

"We could."

Karpov said, "You want to?"

"Of course not! I'm with you all the way. I'm just saying that if you've changed your mind, the Americans will understand. I doubt the CIA will start anything."

"I've got no reason to go back."

Travkin nodded.

They stood together on the deck and waited for the CIA boat. They waited to make the transfer.

10

THE CIA BOAT was a deep-sea fishing vessel. It sped onward as the Russian submarine broke waves in the distance.

The man on the deck looked through a pair of binoculars equipped with night vision. He stared through the green colors until he saw the submarine moving toward them.

He called back to the skipper.

"Starboard. They're coming up."

The skipper nodded and ordered one of his men to slow the engine and take their speed down, just above a drift.

The boat had three sailors onboard, counting the skipper. It was a small crew, but all seasoned men. And all trustworthy. They were all glad to be well compensated for their troubles.

From a distance, the boat looked like it had eight crew members, because there were eight men on the deck. Everyone was dressed like a fisherman. They wore fishing waders and gloves and rimmed sea caps. The three real sailors wore similar outfits, only theirs were worn and tattered like they had seen years of sea damage. The other men looked to be wearing brand new fishing clothes, which they were.

They looked brand new because they had never been used before. The men in the new fishing gear had never fished on a commercial vessel in their lives.

The man on the deck holding the binoculars was running the whole show. Technically, the skipper oversaw the vessel, but this guy was the boss over all of them.

The man with the binoculars wasn't the only passenger. The other four men on deck, dressed like commercial fishermen, had been brought with him for this operation. They were four rough Special Forces guys, but not current Special Forces. They were all former operators, but the real fisherman and the skipper didn't need to know that part.

Technically, the man with the binoculars had handpicked them. He used them often enough. They were men he could trust, and this was a delicate operation. It was an off-the-books type of operation.

He looked over at one of them and said, "Get ready."

He saw them adjust their positions.

He said, "Guns low."

Which he hadn't needed to say because they already knew what they were doing. He said it more out of habit. He was used to giving orders.

The closest former Special Forces guy stood tall and lean. He was clean-shaven with short red hair. He didn't look like the kind of guy that a Hollywood casting director would think to audition for a role as a Special Forces operator, but that was one thing that made him deadly.

The other three men looked more like they were serious military types. They all had that rough, Spartan look about them.

They were a tight group. After the last of them retired from the Army, they all banded together for private contracting. They were partners in this endeavor, but the redheaded guy called the shots. He always had. Back in Afghanistan, their last deployment, he had outranked the rest of them.

More than being a tight crew, more than having shared interest in making money, they all had one more thing in common. Back in Afghanistan, something had happened to them. They shared a secret.

The redheaded guy had outranked them, but he wasn't always the team leader. There had been another guy, an officer with that good-hearted quality that none of the rest of them had.

The redheaded guy was his number two until he shot him in the back with a Taliban soldier's commandeered Makarov PM 9mm pistol.

The pistol had belonged to a Taliban prisoner that they were ordered to escort back to a forward operating base. They had two prisoners.

Instead of delivering them, as had been ordered by their actual commanding officer, the redheaded guy had conspired with the other three to shoot him in the back and blame the prisoners for it.

Of course, after they shot the Boy Scout officer in the back, they got to do what they had wanted to do. They tied the two prisoners up to a tree and used them for target practice.

Why not?

They wouldn't get caught. They only had to drag the dead officer's body back to base. No one would think twice if they said they shot the prisoners after they pulled guns on them and murdered their leader.

It all made sense. Simplicity was always key in these kinds of scenarios. The redheaded guy knew that.

The other three never questioned his plan. Not once.

And that had been a wise move on their parts because he had led them out of the Afghan mountains and into a prosperous life of covert operations for hire.

What wasn't to like about that life? They made money, took on contracts for the Pentagon and the CIA, and still got to kill people. It was all good to them.

The redheaded guy looked at the man on deck and nodded and signaled to the others with a half casual salute.

They approached the bow, kept the silenced Heckler and Koch MP5SDs down by their sides and out of sight. They stood in formation.

The air was cold and so crisp that it felt sharp on their skin, like tiny icepicks poking at them.

The regular fishermen were used to the air.

The redheaded guy stepped to the left and dropped to one knee. Slowly, the other three stepped away from the center of the bow and followed suit. They kept the MP4s down and ready.

11

Mr. Travkin stood behind Captain Karpov on the top deck.

"Where will you go first?" Karpov asked.

"What?"

"In America, when we get our freedom. Where will you go first?"

"I don't know," Travkin said.

The wind blew in shards of cold, wet ice around them. Travkin could feel the wetness in his beard. His eyes left the outline of the fishing vessel and broached across the horizon. Everything was black in all directions. The moon was nowhere in sight, which gave way to a sky full of stars. The stars lit enough of the black sky to give it a dark blue look.

The water crashed and streamed in steady, rhythmic waves.

Karpov kept his eyes on the fishing vessel.

Never had he and Travkin talked about Tom Clancy's book. He supposed that he'd never wanted to refer to it in front of anyone before. He didn't want to make it seem like he got his ideas from an American novel. It was a little embarrassing and very telling that he was enamored with the American lifestyle.

He thought, *what difference did it make?*

He spoke in English, even pronouncing Travkin's name in the Western version. He asked, "Edward, have you ever read *The Hunt for Red October?*"

Travkin looked back at him. He leaned closer to avoid eye contact with the two other sailors on deck.

He asked, "The American submarine movie?"

"I meant the book, but either. Have you seen it?"

"I saw it once."

"The real version?"

"Of course, not the propaganda one."

"Did you see where the captain said he wanted to go to Montana?"

Travkin said, "That's not what happened."

"It's not?"

"The first mate was the one who wanted to go to Montana."

Karpov tilted his expression and asked, "You sure?"

"Of course. I've seen it many times."

One sailor interrupted. He was a short man, no facial hair and pale white. He held a wired receiver in his hand. The cord stretched down and curled until it attached to a radio on his belt.

In Russian, he said, "The boat is approaching fifty meters, Captain."

Karpov ignored him, asked Travkin, "Why did you see it so many times?"

Travkin didn't respond.

"Captain," the crewmember said.

"Yes?" Karpov answered.

"The fishing vessel, sir. What now?"

"Now, we stop. Order full stop."

The crewmen nodded and called back the instructions into his radio.

They all heard the engine whine, and the propellers hum and the power of the track of waves splashed, and the water spray began dying down.

After several minutes, the submarine slowed to a stabilized drift along the surface of the ocean.

Karpov stopped asking about Clancy's book and said, "Mr. Ivanosky, any noise from the crew?"

He was referring to the sleeping men who didn't know about Karpov's plans to defect. But Ivanosky knew that, really, he was asking about the political officer, who was also asleep and unaware of any change in course.

Ivanosky said, in Russian, "No, sir, the men are still asleep."

Which was what Karpov had figured. Submariners could sleep through anything. Forty-plus days at sea on a huge, steel tube that vibrates everything will do that to a man. It's kind of like learning to sleep in a power plant or a manufacturing plant that runs twenty-four hours a day. At first, it's tough, but after a while, a man learns to sleep to the noise of humming engines and twisting turbines and wheeling cogs and the sporadic spray of steam. Karpov got so used to it he feared that once he was on land in America, he would never have a good night's sleep again without the echoes of machines nearby.

Of course, this was a problem that he looked forward to facing.

The submarine finally slowed until the surf, and the current pushed it along in a peaceful, improvised path.

Karpov smiled and waited. His freedom was only hours away.

12

THE FISHING BOAT approached slowly until the four Russian submariners on the deck were in clear view of the man who had been holding the binoculars.

He set the binoculars down on the roof of the boat and climbed down a ladder from what the skipper had called the bridge. A laughable title, but the man in charge and his Special Forces guys said nothing about it.

He walked up and stayed ten paces behind his guys. He didn't look down at them, but he knew that each had his MP5SD either hidden in one hand or within grabbing distance.

The MP5SD was more than a Special Forces favorite; it was designated with the "SD" in the model number because it stood for silenced. The MP5SD was specially designed to be suppressed. It was better than most suppressed weapons on the market for military units. Better because suppressors never really "silenced" a gunshot. When a suppressed weapon is fired, the gunshot is still loud. Instead of a *boom* it sounds more like a loud *pop!*

The MP5SD has a much-improved suppressor design. Instead of a loud *pop* there is a quiet *PURRRR!*

It is a much better weapon for when you need to kill a handful of Russian military officers onboard a submarine without waking the sleeping crew.

The man in charge looked over at the redheaded guy and nodded.

The redheaded guy said, without turning his head to his men, "Wait till they throw the docking plank down. I shoot first."

The other men all made verbal acknowledgments of the order.

The Russian on the deck waved. The man in charge waved back. He immediately recognized his Russian contact and smiled.

The submarine stopped, and the boat stopped. The Russian captain called out.

He said, "Omaha!"

Which was the city that the American in charge was born.

The American said, "Murmansk!"

The captain smiled. That was the name of the city in Russia where he was born. It was their greeting code to each other.

A moment later, a long, metal grated walkway sprang out of the bow of the submarine. It was a thin, long thing. It was automated and floated on the surface of the waves.

"Wait, behind me," the American said.

He knew Karpov trusted him, but there was no way that Karpov's men would let him walk out onto the bow of the submarine first, not out in the open. So, the American offered goodwill by stepping onto the sub first. He wasn't a seafaring man, so he struggled to balance as he stepped onto the cold, wet steel of the bow.

He was the only member of the fishing boat not wearing the right rubber boots. He had been wearing a pair of loafers, which now seemed the biggest mistake that he had made so far.

Even though the submarine wasn't moving, water still sprayed up over the deck and onto his shoes, making it hard to walk.

He managed and walked halfway up the deck when he realized that his stumbling about made the captain worry he might get swept out to sea.

Captain Karpov ordered something to his men in Russian, which the American knew must've translated as "let me down there. He's going to get blown off the deck." He knew that because the captain and his men were coming down to help the American walk.

He took a dive to play it up. He stumbled right and then left and then slipped completely on the deck.

He cursed as he felt the impact on his chest, which hurt a little. He stayed there and waited for the captain and his men to get to him. As they did, he nodded back to the redheaded guy.

The captain reached one big hand under his arm and helped lift him to his feet.

Their backs were all turned to the men on the fishing boat.

"Are you okay?" Karpov asked.

His English was as good as the American had been told it was. Only his accent was thick. He didn't sound the way the American imagined Russians to sound. He sounded more German. He had a real problem with the "th" sounds. He picked up on that when the captain said, "I thought you were fish meal."

The American realized he must have meant "fish food" and not "meal." Idioms were hard to translate and teach to foreign speakers. And English has tons of idioms.

The American said nothing as he was helped to his feet.

Within seconds, the Special Forces men were directly behind the Russians.

The redheaded guy had his MP5SD aimed right at the captain's head.

"What is the meaning of this?" Karpov demanded.

"Sorry, Captain. It's merely a precaution."

Karpov looked back over his shoulder, saw the silenced barrel inches from his face. He looked back at the American, stared in his eyes.

"It's unnecessary, Omaha."

"It's policy. Just until we make sure that everything is on the up and up."

"Up and up?"

The American said, "Everything is legit."

Karpov nodded.

The redheaded guy walked around, as did one of the other Special Forces guys. He said, "Hand over the gun, Captain."

Karpov was armed. He had a Navy-issued pistol holstered at his side. The American looked at the other three men.

The first mate also had one.

Karpov said, "What the hell is this?"

The American said, "Just do as he says, Captain. It's a precaution."

"We came here to get your help!"

The redheaded guy said, "Your gun, Captain."

Karpov reached for it. But one of the silent Special Forces guys stepped up and stopped him.

"I'll get it," he said, and he reached down and unsnapped the holster and pulled the gun out.

The redheaded guy said, "Take his too."

He pointed at Travkin.

THE MIDNIGHT CALLER   63

The guy stepped over to him and reached down and repeated the same process, unsnapped the holster, and pulled the weapon out.

"Let's get below, Captain," the American said.

Karpov looked at Travkin and said nothing.

He turned and led the way back to the tower.

"Down that way," he said, and pointed to the hatch leading down to the bridge.

The American said, "Where is it?"

Karpov's face molded into one of confusion.

"Where's what?"

The American said, "Don't play coy, Captain. The thing you promised us."

Karpov looked back at Travkin again.

"It's in my quarters. On a laptop."

"Show me," the American said.

Karpov pointed at the hatch and said something in Russian to one of the crew.

"Stop! What was that?" the American demanded.

"What was what?"

"What did you tell him?"

"I told him to go first."

The American looked at one of the Special Forces guys. He asked, "Is that what he said?"

The guy said, "He told him to go first, quickly, and to lock the hatch behind him. To make sure that we didn't get on board."

Karpov and the first mate stared at the Special Forces guy. They were surprised that he knew Russian. He was always amazed at how often Russians didn't expect him to speak their language, although he shouldn't have been. Most Americans don't learn a foreign language. He knew that.

The American looked at Karpov.

"Is that what you said?"

"You have guns. I can't allow you to board the submarine."

"You don't work for the Russians anymore. Remember? You want asylum in America. It's too late now."

Karpov said nothing.

"Are we going to have any problems when we get down there?"

Karpov said, "Return our guns. Lower yours, and we can board."

The American said, "Okay. Enough of this."

He looked at the redheaded guy, pointed at the first mate.

He said, "Kill him."

Karpov said, "No! Wait!"

It was too late. The redheaded guy squeezed the trigger of his MP5SD. He had the weapon selected for a three-shot burst.

The muzzle whipped up slightly, and the suppressor *PURRED!*

Three bullets surged out and burst into Travkin's chest and neck. Red mist sprayed out into the air.

Travkin never got a chance to speak because the impact made him lose his balance, and the wet steel made him slip. He went flying back off his feet. His head hit the deck and cracked, and his body bounced. Within a second, he slipped off the deck and splashed into the Arctic.

The current took him under, and he was lost in the blackness.

"You son of a bitch!" Karpov screamed.

The American pointed at one of the other crew.

"Him next."

"No!" Karpov shouted.

"Wait!" The American ordered.

The redheaded guy pointed the MP5SD at the other crewman. He didn't fire. A light puff of smoke wafted out of the suppressor.

The American asked, "Are you going to do what you're told now?"

Karpov breathed in and breathed out in heavy breaths. He repeated this process, again and again, didn't answer.

"Are you?"

"Yes. Don't kill us."

The American said, "Good. Now. Do you have any more guns down there?"

"Yes."

"Where?"

"They're locked up in the armory."

"And how many crew are on the bridge?"

"Just three more. Plus, us."

"Good. Good. See? That wasn't so hard."

Karpov had never been the crying type, but Travkin had been his friend for many years. And he had just seen him murdered in a split second.

He felt choked up.

13

WIDOW LIKED the double shot of black espresso he had ordered and consumed within the last thirty minutes, so much that he ordered another. Same amount. Same barista.

The espresso wasn't the only thing that he liked.

A barista named Montana, who might as well have been named Scarlett because she was the doppelgänger of the famous actress, waited on him.

Widow couldn't recall a movie that Scarlett the actress had been in. He didn't watch too many movies. He had no television. But he was sure that he had seen her in one sometime. Certainly, he had seen her in passing, on covers in gas stations or bookstores or somewhere.

Montana was younger than him. He wasn't sure how much. She was far from being a teenager, but under the age of thirty. If he had to guess, he would guess twenty-five, which made him feel a little weird; because today he turned a year older and he was well in his thirties.

Montana had smiled at him more than once. She had taken his order, and with a busy line of people who waited to order and go, she left her station just to bring him his espresso—a special trip.

Widow sat at a little round table near the window. His back wasn't in the corner, but a wall was behind him.

Before Montana returned to her post, she asked, "You sticking around a while?"

With nothing to say, Widow simply nodded.

She looked him up and down, quick. Not a lingering, flirtatious look-over, more like an inspection. She must've been curious, because he had nothing in his hands. He carried no backpack. No books. No smartphone. No laptop.

Obviously, he wasn't there to work on anything.

She said, "We sell newspapers."

"That's okay. I'll just sit."

"With nothing to do?"

Widow shrugged.

"Oh, you're waiting for someone?"

"No. Not waiting for anyone. Just sitting."

She looked at him a second longer and then turned away. Then she stopped and asked, "Sure, you don't want a newspaper? Maybe the *Times*?"

"Got a copy of the *Navy Times*?"

"What's that? Like a paper for the Navy?"

"That's exactly what it is."

"The Army has its own newspaper?"

Widow said, "It does. But the Army has one called the *Army Times*. The Navy is different."

"I know. I was just speaking generically," she said, and she paused a beat and took a breath and asked, "Were you in the Navy?"

"I was."

"Cool."

Silence fell between them for a moment.

Another girl behind the counter shouted, "Montana? Is there a problem?"

Montana turned back and said, "No problem. I'm coming."

She turned back to Widow, said, "I'll be right back with a New York Times."

He smiled. So far, his birthday was going pretty well.

A moment later, Montana had returned with a newspaper folded up, thick and wrinkle-free.

She placed it down in front of him.

"How much?" he asked.

"Don't worry about it."

"It's gotta cost something?"

"Usually, it does."

"What's the price? I'll pay. I insist."

"You don't have to. Don't worry. It's a day old. Can't charge you for a day-old newspaper."

He smiled and nodded—that made sense.

"Let me know if you need anything else. I gotta get back to work."

"Thanks, Montana."

She paused another beat. Widow saw the other two girls working hard behind the counter, and saw one of them look up with a bit of frustration on her face.

Montana asked, "What's your name?"

He looked at her and said, "Widow."

"Widow?"

"Yeah."

"What kind of name is that?"

"It's a name. What kind is Montana?"

She smiled again and said, "That's true. Enjoy your paper and espresso. Widow."

"I will."

She turned and went back to the counter, back to the grind of making coffee for strangers.

Widow picked up the *Times*, opened it, held it in one hand, and took a sip from the espresso in the other.

So far, so good, he thought.

14

THE TOP STORY in the paper was about a New York Stock Exchange Wall Street firm's main office that had been raided by the FBI over embezzlement, bribery charges, and a laundry list of other things.

Widow breezed through it, sipped his espresso. He skipped to the side panels and read a couple of interesting articles unrelated to Wall Street. But it was the second major story that interested him the most. It was given a huge panel underneath the top story, but there wasn't much to it because there wasn't much known about it.

Most of the panel space was the title of the article and two images. The first was an incorrect image of what the story was about. He knew that because the story was about a Russian submarine and the photograph was of an American Sea Wolf class submarine. He knew them all.

But the other photograph was legitimate, he assumed. It was a photograph, in color, of a Russian submarine captain. He looked Russian. But Widow had never heard of him. His name was Karpov.

The title of the article caught his eye. One of Widow's favorite things to do was read paperbacks, and one of his favorite genres was political espionage and mystery.

The title of the article was: *The Hunt for Red October Happens. For Real?*

Widow had read Tom Clancy's book long ago. Although it was fictitious, it remained a favorite of sailors all over the world.

The basic premise of the article was short but frightening.

A Russian nuclear submarine had gone missing somewhere north of Europe in the Arctic, beyond the borders of NATO's defense, but in international waters.

The Cold War was long over, but hard feelings remained. Some in Washington seemed to condemn the actions of the Russians using their stealth technology to subvert NATO radar.

Not to Widow. He saw nothing wrong with it. Sneaking around with submarines was sort of all about what they were built for. What's the point of a military vehicle that submerges underwater, out of sight? Subs are built for stealth operations.

American submarines were fitted with stealth tech. So were the Chinese and probably those of a dozen other countries.

The Russians even came forward and told us the story.

The article named "sources in the Kremlin." Widow knew there were no sources in the Kremlin. In Russia, that meant it came straight from the top. They didn't have a free press.

Widow hadn't read Tom Clancy's book in years, but he recalled the basic premise. A Soviet captain goes rogue, steals a billion-dollar nuclear sub with stealth drive technology, and tries to defect to the United States.

He remembered that in that book; the Russians didn't tell our boys about the missing sub for a long period. At first, they tried to sink it themselves. Then they claimed the captain stole it in order to nuke us, which turned out to be a lie, so that our subs would sink the Red October.

Good book, Widow thought.

The New York Times article painted a completely different picture.

The similarity to the story was that a stealth nuclear Russian submarine went missing more than a day earlier, and they believed the captain might've stolen it.

Those were the only known details. Everything else was fluff.

Widow wondered where it was. That part was a little terrifying.

Apparently, the US was sending much of the Atlantic fleet out to its last known location to find it.

The White House said the whole thing was a recovery operation. They said it appeared to have sunk.

15

THE LINE of people at the counter died down to three—all women. All office workers, obviously. They were talking and laughing, exchanging friendly banter, exchanging inside quips, and sharing in the same events of their day.

New York City lunch hours had ended for most of the suits who worked in the area. The tables emptied, and the people had cleared out, taking their trash to the can just outside the door. A few patrons stayed behind with open laptops and notebooks. Four of them sat together at one of two four-seat tables.

Widow assumed they were local students. They were young, in their early twenties, three young women and one young man. They wore laid-back clothes—baggy sweatshirts for the girls and long sleeves on the guy. They had that no-care attitude that college students often had about their current surroundings.

Widow took another pull from his espresso and found that it was the last. He finished it and set it down and looked out the window.

So far, he had spent his morning walking around Central Park. He rode the subway once, and then he walked the streets.

He would check out the MET later unless something more fun came his way. Maybe tonight he would take in an overpriced dinner and a show.

It was too bad that there was no sports game tonight, or he would see that instead. The two teams that he would like to see were the Yankees and the Knicks. Neither had a home game tonight. And he wasn't staying longer than tonight and Sunday.

Widow reached into his pocket and pulled out cash. He found a five and tossed it on the table for Montana.

Before he could get up, she was walking toward him.

"Widow," she said.

"Yeah? I'm headed out."

"Jack Widow?"

"How did you know that?"

He didn't remember telling her his first name. Then he remembered the first time he paid with his debit card. Maybe she had pulled it off there.

She stared at him and said, "There's someone on the phone for you."

He stared at her blankly.

"What?"

"The phone. At the counter. It's for you."

Widow stood up, took his empty paper cup with him. He walked past her toward the counter. They threaded in between tables and chairs. He stopped in front of the counter, away from a glass display case, on the opposite side of the line and cash register.

"Wait here," she said. Montana walked around to the cash register side of the counter and crossed behind one of her coworkers, who was ringing up a middle-aged man in a tracksuit.

Montana stepped out of sight behind a white wall for a moment and then returned with a portable, gray-colored phone that looked more like a remote control than it did a phone. She leaned across a side station, where customers were supposed to pick up their orders, and handed the phone out to him.

"Take it."

Widow took it and brought it up to his ear.

"Hello?"

He heard a voice and recognized it immediately, and smiled.

"Widow?"

"Rachel Cameron."

"Yes."

"What are you doing?"

"Technology is a wonderful thing."

Widow stayed quiet.

"The calendar on my computer popped up. Do you know what it said?"

"Today's my birthday."

Cameron said, "It said that today's your birthday."

Widow stayed quiet.

"Happy birthday, Widow!"

"Thank you."

"Know how I found you?"

"You're looking into my bank records, again? Saw my debit card used?"

"Have I done this to you before?"

"No. Last time you cleared out my account completely to get my attention."

A pause came over the line. He heard what sounded like a chuckle from Cameron.

Rachel Cameron was ten years older than Widow, but that wasn't something that he knew for sure. The only personal information that he knew about her for sure was her name, what she looked like, and that he could trust her. She had never led him astray, not without good intentions, anyway.

Cameron had been in charge of Unit Ten, Widow's old undercover unit with NCIS.

She was the voice in his ear. She was his handler.

"Ancient history now, Widow."

Widow said nothing.

"Got any special plans?"

"Just to walk the city and enjoy my day. Maybe take in a show."

The line cracked in Widow's ear. Another caller.

"Hey, Cameron. This is a business line. Their phone's ringing."

"Well, hey. I got you a present."

Widow paused.

"You did?"

"Yeah."

He looked at Montana. The thought had just occurred to him he had been in the state of Montana the last time that Cameron had interrupted his life.

The irony wasn't lost on him, but the belief of coincidence was. Now a feeling of suspicion crossed over him.

"What is it?"

"It's a surprise."

Widow looked away from Montana, shook off the suspicion. That would've been too much of a coincidence, even for Cameron.

Cameron said, "Go to The Plaza Hotel. Go to the front desk and give them your name. That's where your present is."

"Okay."

"And Widow, happy birthday!"

Cameron hung up the phone.

Widow clicked off and handed the phone to Montana.

"Thanks."

"Who was that?"

"Ancient history."

Montana gazed away from him in a slow movement, like she was searching for what to say next.

"Old girlfriend?"

Widow let out a laugh, just a quick chuckle. He said, "No. Old boss."

"Why's she calling you here?"

"I don't have a phone."

"You don't have a cell phone?"

He shook his head.

"How did she know to call you here?"

"She knows me too well," he said, not wanting to get into the long explanation of it all.

"I suppose you're taking off then?"

"Yeah."

Montana turned, but then she stopped and reached into her pocket and pulled out a folded slip of paper. She reached to Widow to give it to him, her hand trembling.

She said, "Take this. In case you get a phone. I hope you have a good day."

And she turned fast, walked back to the counter, back behind the register and back to work. She never looked up at him again.

Widow already knew what it was. It was obvious.

He didn't look at it. He just kept it in his hand and walked outside. He turned left, headed south.

He stopped in front of a garden supply store, not sure how much business they really had, being in the middle of Manhattan, but he didn't put too much thought into it.

He opened his hand, looked down at the folded piece of paper.

He knew it was Montana's phone number. What else would she give him?

Widow was no saint. He was no kind of idealist or religious man. And he liked women. Especially an attractive one. But Montana was young. *Too young for him*, he thought.

He didn't open the piece of paper because he knew he would memorize the phone number if he saw it.

Throwing it away had crossed his mind, but he wasn't ready to do that either. He wasn't blind.

A taxi blew by and honked its horn, which startled him for a second. It wasn't honking at him. He was on the sidewalk. It honked at a kid on a bicycle—a bike messenger, who flipped back the bird and turned the corner down a one-way street.

Widow stuffed the note into the front pocket of his jeans and tried to remember which way The Plaza Hotel was.

16

STANDING on Fifth and Central Park South, Widow was reminded of *The Great Gatsby*, a novel that he hadn't read in decades. He recalled a scene that had a confrontation between Gatsby and another character, whose name he didn't remember.

The Plaza Hotel was one of the city's oldest hotels and a historical landmark. One of those hotels with a history of celebrities, statesmen, and infamous people all staying there or walking through it at one point or another.

Widow passed through the park and turned on the street. He walked up the sidewalk and past yellowing hedges and huge planters.

There were expensive sedans parked along the street. A doorman stood up a flight of steps to the entrance.

Widow walked up and stopped at the double doors under a black metal awning.

He saw himself in the glass's reflection.

The doorman stayed quiet and looked Widow up and down. At first, Widow thought he was judging him on his attire, which was probably part of the guy's job description—keeping out the undesirables.

For over a year, Widow had lived like a drifter, going nowhere in particular, going everywhere for no reason.

He had often worn modest clothes and gone days without changing them. He got in showers every chance that he could. And sometimes, on the last day of wearing the same clothes, he looked more like a homeless person than he did a former Navy SEAL.

Luckily, this wasn't one of those times.

He wore a day-old set of clothes, including a blue sweater with the sleeves messily pushed up over his forearms, over a collared white button shirt, and a pair of gray chinos. He wore no belt.

The boots on his feet were the oldest part of his ensemble. They were a pair of black, quasi work boots, steel-toed. They reminded him of a pair of combat boots, only more stylish. He walked with the legs of his khaki-colored chinos pulled over them.

Perhaps to someone with fashion sense, they weren't very fashionable, but they were comfortable and clean—no reason to change them out.

The doorman said, "Good afternoon, sir."

He reached up for the door handle and pulled it open in a swift, flawless move like he had done a thousand times a day before.

A rush of warm air brushed across Widow's face. *The Plaza* was running a low heating setting.

It wasn't overly hot. Considering that it was November, the inside temperature felt just right.

Widow passed through the doors and into the lobby, which felt like traversing through a gateway to another dimension.

The word "grand" doesn't do the interior of The Plaza Hotel justice.

Widow had never been inside one of those royal Arabian palaces, but minus the Arabian part, this was probably as close as he would get. There were giant crystal chandeliers, soft pastel tones, a high ostentatious ceiling, and huge pillars stood at the opening to a dining area.

There was a huge skylight in the cathedral-style ceiling, along with good-size antique, Victorian-style tables, and oriental rugs and striking Italian tiles.

The restaurant was steadily full of travelers who were eating late lunches before they headed out.

Widow looked around the lobby, saw the desk to check in or check out. The air warmed up more around him as he approached the desk. To his right, a crowd of people stood around a politician. Must have been someone important too, because Widow noticed the Secret Service agents before he saw the crowd. Sixteen years as a Navy SEAL will do that.

There were only two visible. Maybe there were more hidden in the small crowd. Maybe they were already on the street, waiting with a car to chauffeur the guy around.

One guy stood, obvious, near the politician, facing forward, through the crowd of people. The other was behind him, standing with his back to the wall.

There were lights and a cameraman and a local reporter interviewing the guy.

Widow wondered who it was.

He watched for a moment until he could get a look at the guy. It was some gray-haired man, clean-shaven and polished. He wore a suit with no tie, as did the two Secret Service agents.

The mass of people was on both sides of the journalist and the politician.

After the journalist asked a couple of questions, which Widow couldn't hear, the politician shook her hand and then the hand of the cameraman and then made his way to the exit, shaking hands, waving, and smiling for quick pictures with smartphone cameras.

Widow didn't recognize him. The guy was probably a New York congressman or a senator.

The line to the lobby check-in desk moved up, and Widow was the next person.

A woman who looked more like a girl than a woman, regarding age, waved Widow forward.

The first thing that she looked at, blatantly, were the bottoms of his sleeve tattoos that were visible because of his pushed-up sleeves.

He wasn't sure if she was checking them out because it wasn't normal to see tattoos in a place like *The Plaza*, or if it was because she liked them.

In a polite, slightly automatonic voice, like she had been programmed or something, she said, "Hello, sir."

"Hello."

"Can I help you?"

Widow caught the crowd from the politician scattering, breaking up and moving on.

"Yes."

She smiled and waited.

"I was told that you might have a package for me?"

"What room are you in?" the girl asked and moved her hands into the typing position over a black keyboard resting on a brown, polished countertop behind the lobby desk.

"I don't have a room."

She paused, moved her hands away from the keyboard.

"We only hold packages for guests."

"Can you check anyway? I was told there'd be something here for me?"

"What's your name, sir?"

"Jack Widow."

The clerk moved her hands back over the keyboard and typed in his name. She stared at a computer screen that Widow couldn't see.

After a click of the mouse, a second click, and a pause, she said, "Here it is. Widow. Did you say that you don't have a room?"

"No room."

"It says you do."

Widow looked confused, said, "What?"

"It looks like you have a Terrace Suite."

"I do?"

"Yeah. It was booked for you this morning."

"It was?"

"Is there a mistake?"

Widow didn't know what to say. Rachel Cameron got him a suite at *The Plaza* for his birthday. And it was called the Terrace Suite, which sounded expensive. Then again, all the rooms in *The Plaza* sounded expensive. They could have called it the "Janitor's Closet," and it would have sounded expensive.

"The room is paid for?"

"Yes, sir."

"Then no mistake," he said, and smiled.

The clerk smiled back and returned her gaze to the computer screen. She hit the return key twice and clicked the mouse.

She turned around, walked over to a counter behind her, and opened a drawer. She came out with a key card and turned back to him. She swiped the card through a small black machine and smiled.

She took out a thin cardstock envelope and slipped the key card into a slit, folded it, and took out a black marker. She handwrote something on the side of the envelope and handed it to Widow.

"Take the elevator up to the ninth floor. Follow the signs. This is your room number," she said and pointed to the number that she had written on the envelope.

Widow looked down at the number. It was nine-eleven, which made him think of the terrible terrorist attack that had happened over a decade earlier—a natural thing to think of. In fact, he thought of it often because there had been many, many times that he would look at a watch or a wall clock and see that the current time had been nine eleven. An unfortunate, constant reminder.

He made no remark to her about it. Instead, he reached down and took the envelope and the keycard and thanked her, and turned to the elevators. He walked through the lobby, casually glancing, looking left and looking right, making no clear sign he was interested in anything.

The Secret Service guys and the reporter and the politician, whoever he was, had gone. But there was still a pair of guys left, sitting on a pair of expensive, antique leather chairs. They sat facing the entrance and the lobby front desk.

They wore similar clothes. Expensive Oxford shoes. Expensive chinos, one brown, one black. The guy on the left had a black knit sweater, sleeves pushed up like Widow's. The other guy had a white polo shirt under a black blazer; both looked expensive.

They wore silver watches, one with a traditional face, and the other with a digital face and loaded with buttons and probably diver features that were completely useless to the guy in real life.

Both guys were built a lot better than most of the men who walked through the lobby.

They spoke casually to each other, looking around, checking the entrance, and checking the elevators, and checking the fire door.

These guys were staking out the place. Widow knew that for sure.

They obviously weren't Secret Service, nor were they FBI or NYPD. Their outfits were too expensive for NYPD. And the FBI wouldn't stick two guys in the lobby, not so obvious. Not so close to each other. They would've had only one in the lobby, if that. Maybe they would've had a whole team outside, on the street. That would've made sense. They would've surveilled from a fake utility truck or a delivery van. They would've had a chopper in the air for a serious bust.

These guys looked government or former government. Widow considered CIA or NSA, which didn't seem legal since neither is supposed to operate on American soil, not in the stake-out sense.

And these guys weren't street thugs. Not in here. Not like the Irish guys that he'd already run into. No way.

They would never come into a place like this. Not in a million years.

The only other option remaining was private security, which made sense to Widow. A couple of clean-cut rough guys with blatant military backgrounds. That was a high probability.

Then again, maybe they were just a pair of veteran army buddies on vacation, hanging out in the lobby of a hotel in New York City, waiting for their wives. It could be true. Maybe the wives ran off to a local spa. Maybe they were getting their nails done, getting back massages, doing vacation things.

Widow was in *The Plaza*, led there by his former boss. She had led him astray before. She had manipulated him to do work for his old unit before. Had she sent him here for something other than a friendly birthday gift?

That was highly plausible.

And what were the odds that he had seen Secret Service in the lobby and now a pair of private-looking security guys, trying to blend in. Coincidence?

Could be. Stranger things had happened.

And really, was it that unusual? New York City is a major hub of all kinds of activity in North America. Just this summer, he had been there. He had been to the FBI headquarters.

Anything was possible.

Widow glanced at the two former military guys. If these two were some kind of private security, they weren't armed. Not that he could see.

There were no visible gun bulges in their waistbands. Not at their ankles. Not their pockets. No signs of holsters. No signs of handguns.

The one guy wearing the blazer might've had a gun tucked into his inside pocket. There was definitely no shoulder rig. Widow would've seen it because of the way the guy moved, checked his watch.

Widow's best guess was that they might have been sitting on their guns. They could have been tucked neatly away behind them at the smalls of their backs. Might have been carrying small handguns, the easily concealable kind.

Widow looked forward at the elevators. He reached them, stopped in front, and pressed the button, and waited.

He didn't look back at the lobby.

After a long moment, the right-side elevator came down to the first floor and stopped. The doors sucked open, and Widow waited for the occupants to unload.

Two young ladies stepped off.

Widow stepped on.

The elevator smelled of fresh daisies and perfume, and maybe a little cologne mixed in. That likely cost more than his whole wardrobe, not that expensive, because he had spent less than fifty bucks on his whole outfit.

Back in the United Kingdom, a long, long time ago, Widow had dated a

Dutch model. Not of the Victoria's Secret, famous runway variety, but certainly on her way. And she had tons of perfume. Most of it was probably free to her. A perk of the industry, Widow supposed. Kind of like how he got free bullets for being on a SEAL team.

Even though the stuff came to her free to use, Widow had looked at the price stickers, slapped on the boxes that the bottles came in, a force of habit.

Some of the prices on the perfume boxes were frightening.

Widow had never really been a man with low self-esteem. Life had enough tribulations without walking around feeling bad about yourself. But having seen the prices of things that model was used to getting for free sure made him feel like he had been put in his place.

He and the model were basically just having fun. But there was no future between them. He could never provide her with the luxuries that she had grown accustomed to.

He remembered having those kinds of doubts. The right thing to have done would have been to talk to her about them. Maybe she was above all that. Maybe she would have told him he was crazy for thinking she only cared about her lifestyle.

He never talked to her about it.

It turned out it wouldn't have made a bit of difference, anyway.

One day she had told him she was going to Paris for work. She never came back. He remembered reading about her later on. She had married some rich German guy with a famous last name. Not a celebrity name in the Hollywood sense, but in a wealthy family sense. They had old money, a lot. And this guy stood to inherit all of it.

Widow pressed the button for the ninth floor.

The doors paused for a long second and then closed.

17

THE HOTEL SUITE had a set of French doors that faced out over a courtyard. Not a Central Park view, but not bad either.

Soft music played low from the speakers of a smart television. Widow had searched for the music channels and left it on the first thing that he found, which was a station that catered to the light jazz crowd or simply the softer music people. He wasn't sure.

He wasn't an expert on music. Jazz was a type of music that no one claimed to like because most of the people who "liked" jazz always said that they "loved" it.

Jazz fans were mostly collectors and zealots. To Widow, it was okay.

The music might've been soft lounge music as well.

Whatever, he let it play. It was perfect for a quiet, tranquil mood.

He opened a French door and looked out at the balcony. There were two chairs and a little patio table.

He stepped outside with a bottle of champagne that he took from a small refrigerator and a rocks glass. No ice.

He popped the cork and poured a nice glass, stared out over the interior courtyard and the reflecting pool, left the bottle out on the tabletop. He didn't use the ice bucket.

It had been a long couple of days. Except for his run-in with the Irish mob wannabes, it had been a great two days. He had actually enjoyed himself.

The thought of going out for his birthday had occurred to him. He'd had nothing to eat since breakfast. He should have gone out to eat since a birthday only comes once a year. But he wasn't hungry. He felt more tired than anything.

Widow drank a glass of champagne and people-watched.

Across the courtyard, four floors down, he saw a handsome couple. They drank a bottle of red wine to the bottom and laughed and kissed every few minutes. They exchanged loving, soft touches and looks with each other between kisses.

The whole affair made Widow experience a sensation that he hadn't felt in a long, long time—loneliness. His was a life of solitude, a life uninterrupted. He couldn't imagine feeling beholden to someone else.

Widow enjoyed the company of other people. Especially the fairer sex. But he had never felt that *need* that he saw in couples from time to time. It was that obvious bond that lovers had; the kind of can't-live-without-someone sort of thing.

It was a beautiful thing. He admired it as much as any other lonely person did.

It was that thing called *love*.

On the flip side, that kind of thing was fleeting. He saw it every day, on trains, on buses, in parks, on the sidewalks, even in the company of the drivers who picked him up from the sides of American interstates.

The commonality of the thing called *love* that he saw in each one of them, and in the couple across from him, was that they were almost always in a honeymoon phase with another person.

Widow had never really been in love, not the imagined storybook version of the concept. Not the kind of thing where two people meet, fall in love, and wind up staying married until they grow old and die.

That sort of thing seemed almost impossible nowadays because of technology and culture. Widow knew that.

Still, seeing this couple made him a little envious.

Widow looked away from them and stared around the interior of the hotel.

He saw two men sitting a couple of rooms down from him. They too were on a romantic weekend in New York City. He saw that right off the bat. They kissed each other on the lips, not a loving, lustful, romantic embrace, like the two lovers across from him. It was more of the traditional *they had been together for a long time* kind of kiss.

Afterward, they peeked over at him. He nodded at them in a quick, polite gesture and turned his attention back to gazing around.

He drank half of another glass of champagne and started in to head to bed.

Widow got up from the chair, grabbed the half-empty bottle, and reentered the room. He slid the bottle back into the door shelf of the mini-fridge and left the glass on top. There was no sink or kitchenette in the room.

He left the window open because he liked the breeze that swept in. It was gentle, but enough to blow the curtains around in a slow-moving wave.

Widow turned down the bed, which was tucked tight. He stripped off his clothes and switched off the lights and dumped himself down.

In seconds, he was fast asleep.

18

Her wrists were bloody and bruised and hurt like hell. They would be black and red for days, maybe weeks, after she got free. If she ever got free.

Her vision was blurry, and she was dazed. It wasn't from being slugged in the face, but she had been twice.

She was dazed because they had injected her with something. She remembered that.

They had only gotten her twice, two days ago, and last night. Both times were around midnight, but she didn't know that. She only knew the first night was midnight.

They had ambushed her in her hotel.

She had checked into the hotel under a fake name, one of many that she had been assigned.

She wasn't sure what was going on. The only thing that she knew for sure was that she had been betrayed. Had to have been.

No one else knew where she was.

There was a slim possibility that her kidnappers were her own countrymen, dangerous guys from the agency that sent her, but she doubted that.

They wouldn't have ambushed her like this. Certainly, they wouldn't have locked her up in the bathroom of her hotel room.

And that was where she was. She was sure. Even with blurred vision and devastatingly disoriented, she knew where she was because she was lying in a spacious claw bathtub. It was unmistakable.

She knew they wouldn't move her from the hotel. One reason she had checked into it was because it was a popular destination—lots of witnesses.

That was the only way that she would meet with them. What she didn't understand was why they ambushed her. She thought her contact had good intentions. Her contact was a lot more than she bargained for. His intentions were less than honorable.

The woman in the bathtub was tall, five foot ten, and thin, which made her good for the spycraft because she was supposed to play the part of a model, living in New York, rubbing elbows with political leaders and people in the know.

She had been good at this assignment, another reason she doubted it was her own government that had ambushed her in her room.

The bad thing about being tall was that she was gangly, which made moving around in the tub very difficult. They had used zip-ties to restrain her hands behind her and tie her ankles together.

Then there was the headache, which felt more like a migraine. Her head pounded.

Every time that she fought or squirmed or shifted around, trying to escape her wrist or leg fetters, a sharp pain discharged through her head. It felt like fire. She didn't remember her attackers hitting her over the head. Why would they, when they had drugs to put her out?

The headache was probably a side effect of the sedative.

Her abductors had left the light on in the bathroom. She stared up at it and saw only the bright whiteness and fuzzy details of the ceiling.

She closed her eyes and tried to remember what had happened.

The first thing she remembered was checking into the hotel. Plenty of witnesses saw her. The hotel had been busy, a good sign. However, it also meant that she was forgettable among the crowd of tourists coming into New York.

She remembered going up in the elevator.

The woman in the tub paused, tried to remember anything before the elevator.

There were small crowds of people in the lobby and a line at the check-in counter, but there was one guy in particular she remembered sitting in the lobby. He was alone.

She remembered he was plain American, that was obvious, and had a demeanor of former military about him; only it was bred out. That was the first thing about him that stuck out to her. He looked not just former military, but like he had tried to lose the look.

He had brown hair, and a trimmed beard. He wore a sweater, sleeves shoved up, with sleeve tattoos. That was the sign that made her think he was former military. Not a guarantee, but a sign in the right direction.

The other thing that really stood out to her happened when she walked by him and pretended to be lost. Like she was headed for the elevator, only she went the wrong way.

She walked past him, stopped at the entrance to the restaurant, and looked around like she was searching. Then she asked one of the restaurant workers to point out the elevators. She even spoke in her accent, which she had found American men loved.

The employee pointed out the elevators, saying she had passed them.

She thanked him, turned, and walked back.

Both times that she passed the guy sitting in the chair, not once did he ever look at her. Not a glance. Not a quick peek. Nothing. And that wasn't normal.

He made no attempt to look at her backside, which never happened. Not in the tight dress that she was wearing.

She knew something was up with him.

She should never have gotten in that elevator.

She remembered opening the door to her hotel room. Then she remembered a gigantic, gloved hand swiping over her head and around her mouth and a muscular arm squeezing around her neck from behind.

One guy jumped her from behind, and the second stormed into the room after both of them. Within a few seconds, he had injected something into her arm. And then she was out like a light.

* * *

THE WOMAN in the bathtub opened her eyes and stared through the haziness and the mental fog at the ceiling and bright lights again.

How she got here didn't matter anymore. How she was going to get free was all that mattered.

She focused on nothing else.

She remembered that one of them, the second guy to enter her room, she figured, had injected her twice with the same sedative. The second time had been when she was confined in the bathtub. It had been around midnight; she figured, but wasn't sure.

She pushed off the tub with her butt and strained to see over the lip. Her sense of balance was off. Her brow barely cleared the lip.

There was a vanity counter, with a sink, crystal faucet, expensive-looking wallpaper and tiles, and a toilet.

She stared in the door's direction. She could see the basic outline and shade of off-white. The details of the hinges and the knob were still fuzzy.

It was shut.

A *mistake*, she thought. The proper thing to do would have been to leave it open so they could at least hear her in case she made noise, or be able to peek in with no trouble to make sure that she was still sedated.

Leaving the door closed left her with freedom of movement. At least it would if she could move.

The muscles in her lower back hurt and felt weak. There was a stinging sensation in her legs. A side effect of whatever drug they were sticking her with. She let go and slipped back down into the tub. Her skin squeaked against the interior.

She lay back, panting for a long second. It took a lot out of her just to make that little of movement.

She tried to relax, letting her lungs fill and expand. Then she let out each deep breath, slow and relaxed. Taking in one slow breath at a time and then repeating the process.

How the hell was she supposed to get out of this?

She had to figure it out, and there wasn't much time left. She had to get free before the guy came back in to inject her again.

There was no way of knowing the exact time in her head, not from waking up in a closed bathroom in a tub, but she figured it was around midnight. The guy had injected her with a sedative twice. She woke up groggy, which meant that she had slept a long time.

If they were using the same sedative, the same amount each time, then she probably woke up each time at the same hour. Maybe not dead on the minute, but close enough.

The woman in the tub concentrated. She didn't need to be calm, not in the Zen sense of the word. What she needed was her adrenaline to kick in.

Every day, every week, there were countless stories of women who looked like her being kidnapped, abducted by strangers. These women almost always ended up on the local news stations a couple of weeks after disappearing. Usually they had been tortured and raped, and were almost always dead.

Luckily, she was no ordinary woman. She had been trained. And she had been trained for this very situation.

She thought back to her training. The thought of suicide came to mind first. This wasn't her training, but she had learned that it had been the training of her predecessors from sixty years earlier.

The long list of women who came before her had been given cyanide capsules embedded in one of their back molars. This was the "way out" that they were trained to take.

Nowadays, this wasn't the answer for most of the women in her line of work. The institution she came from no longer cared if an agent was captured and tortured.

They didn't care because their agents weren't told anything. Secrets were typically kept away from agents like her.

Why should they care if she was captured?

If they found out that she had been taken, they would simply delete her records and disavow her status. She would be swept under the rug and forgotten.

And that was under the worst circumstances. Being captured in the United States by an American agency was a cakewalk for her. Her government knew that she would simply be returned to them.

No harm. No foul.

However, none of this was a comfort to her. It meant that her government didn't give a rat's ass if she lived or died. And for another, she wasn't sure who the hell these guys were.

The only thing she knew was that it wasn't typical of American agents to tie a woman up and dump her in a tub.

Her American counterparts were notorious for being more humane. Again, she doubted that these were American spies.

She closed her eyes tight, felt the adrenaline surge through her as much as it was going to, and popped her eyes open. She rocked up and then back on her butt and repeated it three more times until she could tuck in her knees and swing her hands up and underneath her. They brushed up her thighs and under the backs of her knees. Then she pulled them past her feet, and the zip-ties around her ankles until they were out in front of her.

Pain rushed through her shoulders from the fastness of it all.

She fell back and took a couple more deep breaths.

Then she rocked again as she had before, only this time it was to get on her feet. She finally stood up, reaching forward and grabbing the nozzle to the shower for balance.

She looked toward the door. She heard voices on the other side, distant, but in the hotel suite somewhere.

No one came, but she knew that soon one of them would come to check on her, probably with the needle in hand.

She waited another couple of long moments because she wanted to let her balance return for the next part.

After she felt confident that she could stand without falling over, she reached her bound wrists straight up in the air above her head, stretching them all the way out. Next, like a wild stallion's kick, she jerked them down as fast and as hard as she could.

It was one lesson that she was taught in her training.

The force and the speed of her action broke the zip-tie apart, and her hands were free.

* * *

IT TOOK several more breaths before the woman in the bathtub was ready to make another move after getting free from the hand restraints.

When she finally had her balance, she sat on the edge of the tub and draped her legs out and over the edge. She sat there for another minute, hoping that her vision would get better, but it didn't.

The little trick of getting out of zip-ties only worked on hands. Human legs aren't attached correctly for this to work. There was a method to do it, using the same properties of physics, same sort of movements, where the prisoner lies on her back and pulls her feet all the way back to her face, and then kicks straight up with both feet and jerks back at the end. But this method required tremendous strength and flexibility.

She had the flexibility part—that came from yoga twice a week—but the remains of the sedative coursing through her veins killed the chances of having the right amount of strength.

Besides, she was running out of time.

She stood up slowly. Blood rushed to her head, and she felt it. But she pressed on. Half-hopping, half-scooting, she made her way to the bathroom door.

She hadn't seen the suite, nor had she ever stayed in *The Plaza* before, but she had been trained well. Before she even checked in, she had memorized the layout of the Terrace Suite.

She was on the ninth floor. There was a balcony and a window overlooking an interior courtyard.

She closed her eyes and tried to picture the room next to the bathroom.

It was a bedroom. There should be a king-sized bed on the other side of the door.

There was a table with a lamp and an armchair. The next room after that was a living room, furnished with a television and a mini-fridge and hotel furniture.

Hopefully, the kidnappers would be in the living room. She knew that there were at least two guys. Maybe more.

She wouldn't get a better chance to make an escape.

She looked around the bathroom one final time. She had hoped that there might be a sharp object in there to cut through the zip-ties on her ankles, but she had no such luck.

No scissors left behind by the previous occupants—nothing in the trash.

Even if the previous tenant had left a pair of scissors or a nail file behind, the Plaza's housekeeping department was on the ball. They would have picked it up.

She reached out, grabbed the doorknob, and gently turned it. She peeked out.

No one was there.

She opened the door a little farther—nobody on the bed. No one sat on the chair.

She still heard voices. Then she squinted and looked into the next room.

The voices that she heard weren't her kidnappers. The television was on.

She couldn't make out the screen, but she could see the colors and hear the actors on TV talking.

It was a late-night talk show; she figured. Sounds of an audience laughing and a host telling jokes filled the room. It was turned up fairly loud, not enough to bother the neighbors, but enough to fill the suite.

At first, she thought that was a mistake because it might draw unwanted attention. It might have been because they were using a small crew to guard her and needed the noise to stay alert.

She couldn't see who was watching the TV. The sofa was out of her line of sight.

She ignored that and turned to the bed. She hopped over to it and used one hand to steady herself, and hopped as quietly as she could. She plopped down on the bed, partially because she'd lost the strength in her legs to sit down slowly.

She looked over at the open doorway. No one came.

She turned back to the bed and looked at the nightstand next to it.

On the nightstand, next to a thin gold-trimmed lamp, was exactly what she was looking for. She didn't find the number one thing on her list of items that she could really use right now. Nor was it the number two item. Number one would have been a loaded gun, and number two would have been a knife to both cut through her zip-tie and use as a weapon.

Instead, she had to settle for number three, which was a telephone.

A small digital clock sat next to it on the table.

She was close enough to see the time, blurry or not. She watched as three of the four displayed numbers changed over to the time. They went from eleven fifty-nine to midnight.

Her government trainers had taught her numbers to remember. One of them had been a local New York number to use in case of emergency, which this was, but the problem was that she couldn't call her contacts.

She was on a mission that wasn't sanctioned by her government. In fact, they would see her as a traitor for it. She was on her own.

The only thing that she could think to do was to call the local police. At least they would come for her. She could figure out how to get away from them later.

Chances were that her kidnappers didn't plan to let her live. At least the police wouldn't kill her.

The number for police in America was a short, three-digit number. That was one of the great things about Americans. They were good at streamlining things like that.

She scooped up the phone and put it to her ear. She dialed nine-one-one on the number pad, and the phone rang.

19

THE PLAZA HOTEL was an old hotel. They had old phone lines and old landline telephones in the rooms. Not rotary phones. They had push-buttons, but they were old. The phones were polished and kept clean. They looked like the original, out-of-the-box condition they were in the day they were all purchased.

Somewhere inside The Plaza Hotel, some years ago, it was determined that the phones would be maintained and kept for as long as they worked. It was a way of keeping a classy, uniform, antique look, which worked well with the motifs and the look of the hotel.

Back years and years ago, it was determined in the hotel industry that having a nine-eleven room was bad when most hotels have both an internal and external phone line system.

A person needs help. They dial nine-one-one, and instead of getting the police, they get the person staying in room nine-eleven.

To dial out, one must first dial nine—a universally known quantity.

The thing *The Plaza* did, instead of changing the room numbers and telephones, was they posted a card on the base of the phone that instructed the guests needing emergency services to dial nine-nine-one-one. A quick extra number, no big deal.

When this woman needing the police dialed nine-one-one, she got the room instead of the police.

* * *

Widow was sound asleep when suddenly his phone rang.

Widow opened his eyes abruptly, like he was way back in SEAL training and the instructors had just barged in, ringing dinner bells and sounding bullhorns in his ear.

He was facing away from the telephone, sleeping on his side.

He flipped over and grabbed the phone, nearly knocking over the lamp.

"What!" he said.

A pause. No one spoke. He heard breathing.

"Hello?" he said.

A low, sultry voice with a foreign accent said, "Help," in a whisper.

"Hello? Who is this?"

"Can you help me?"

"Who is this?"

"Are you police?"

Widow sat up and looked at the clock, saw the late hour, and asked, "Who the hell is this?"

"I need help."

"Where are you?"

"Are you police?"

"No. You dialed my room number," Widow said. He looked down at the base of the phone, read the note about emergency calls.

"You gotta dial nine-nine-one-one. Not nine-one-one."

He realized that was idiotic.

They should change his room number, he thought. He guessed even *The Plaza* was too cheap to change all the room numbers just to get rid of nine-eleven. He supposed they could have simply made a nine-twelve A or something.

"Help me," the woman's voice whispered.

Widow used his free hand and slapped it to his forehead, easy, and rubbed his forehead.

"Where are you?" he asked.

"I'm in the hotel."

"What room are you in?"

She paused a long beat.

Her accent, he thought, sounded Russian, or maybe Ukrainian.

"I cannot remember."

"Step outside and look at the number on the door."

"No. No. I cannot do this. No way."

"How can I help you if I don't know what room you're in?"

Silence.

"Ma'am?"

"I need help."

"Okay. Tell me what's going on?"

Silence again. Then she came back on the line.

"There're men. They kidnapped me."

"Kidnapped you?"

"Da. Da."

Widow automatically recognized the word as Russian for "yes," said twice.

"Okay. I can call the police for you."

"No! No!"

"Why not? You need the cops."

"No police. Please. You help me."

No police?

This sounded dubious.

Widow ignored that part, and he asked, "How many guys?"

"I don't know. Maybe two?"

"Okay. Did you get a look at them? They hurt you?"

"No. No look. Not really. They not hurt me so far."

"What have they done?"

"Just inject me with a drug."

Silence.

Widow asked, "They injected you?"

"Da. I mean, yes. Some kind of sedative."

Two guys kidnap a woman, in The Plaza Hotel, they inject her with a sedative, and they have not hurt her?

Sounded risky, Widow thought.

"Who are you?"

She answered, but then she said, "I cannot tell you."

"Why not?"

"Please. Just come help me?"

"Listen, ma'am; you need the cops. I'm just a guest."

"No! No! Police will be bad for me. Please, you help?"

Widow paused a moment.

Before he could answer, he heard a man's voice in the background.

The words were loud, short, and the accent was unmistakably American. Not Russian.

The man said, "What the hell are you doing?"

Then he heard another male voice. Far away, in the next room, maybe.

The second voice said, "How did you get free?"

"Ma'am?" Widow asked—a reaction.

"Help me!" she shouted.

He kept listening, didn't react.

He heard a scuffle. The woman attempted to scream, but it was cut short by a loud smacking sound.

One guy punched her in the face, Widow figured.

With his free ear, he had hoped that he would hear her scream, but she hadn't been loud or long enough to be heard. Plus, she could have been on any floor in the hotel.

Widow waited, listened.

The scuffle was over quick, but he still could hear voices, too low to be understood this time.

Then he heard scratching sounds like someone was picking up the telephone.

A brief silence and he heard nothing, and then a low sound that was unmistakably someone panting. Probably one of her kidnappers, listening for Widow to speak and trying to keep his loud breathing away from the phone.

Widow spoke first.

"Hello?"

No response.

"Hello?" he repeated.

The American voice, with low panting, said, "Sorry for disturbing you, sir."

"What's going on?"

"It's not your concern. It's my wife. She's had too much to drink. She gets like this sometimes. I apologize. Please, have a nice night."

The guy hung up.

Widow stayed where he was. He kept the phone to his ear and listened to the dial tone.

Was she telling the truth?

He was almost certain that she had been. Widow had heard a lot of lies in his life, and he had told a lot in his old life. The undercover cop life required lies.

This woman was telling the truth.

He should have called the police. She had begged him not to.

Why?

Widow hung up the phone and sat there for a long minute, trying to figure out what to do.

If she was telling the truth, then these guys wouldn't kill her. Not because she had gotten ahold of the phone. They hadn't gone through all the trouble of keeping her alive and sedated just to kill her for trying to escape.

Also, if these guys had access to sedatives that required injections as a delivery system, then they were more than just random street thugs.

Getting chloroform was a hell of a lot easier than getting expensive, fast-acting sedatives that required prescriptions.

Something bad was going on.

Widow stood up, still naked. He rushed over to the armchair and picked up his pants, slipped them on.

He walked into the living room. Left the lights off in case they were in a room across the courtyard and could see him.

He stood out of sight of the window and leaned just enough to peek out.

He saw nothing unusual.

The couple across from him was gone. There was only one woman sitting out on her balcony, smoking a cigarette, which Widow wasn't sure was allowed in the hotel or not.

He ignored her and returned to the bed, dumped himself down, and picked up the phone.

He dialed zero, listened to a whirring sound, and heard a click.

A hotel operator picked up and said, "Front desk, how can I help you?"

"Can you tell me what room just called me?"

"Is there a problem, sir? Someone bother you?"

"No. Nothing like that. Just a friend of mine. I forgot to get her room number from her."

"Would you like for me to reconnect you?"

"No. Just give me the room number."

Silence fell over the line.

Widow suspected the operator was reluctant. Maybe she wasn't sure if she could give out a guest's room number that easily.

"Look," Widow said, "The truth is kinda embarrassing."

The operator didn't answer.

"The woman who called, I met her tonight at the bar downstairs. She just called and asked me to come to her room to...finish our conversation. But like an idiot, I forgot her room number. I really wanna go visit her."

"I don't know," the operator finally said.

"Come on. It's my birthday. You'll really be helping me out here."

The operator clicked on the keyboard; Widow heard the punching of the keys.

"Happy birthday, sir. I guess I can do this for you. No problem."

Widow smiled.

She said, "You're in luck. The room is right around the hall from you. It's nine-twenty-one."

"Thank you so very much."

"No problem, sir. Anything else I can help you with?"

"You've done enough. Thank you," Widow said, and hung up the phone.

Nine-twenty-one was close.

He got up and jogged into the bathroom, turned on the sink, and ran water over his face, slicked his hair back.

Then he put his T-shirt on, left off the sweater. He put on his shoes, laced them up, left off the socks.

Looked around the room for a weapon to use in case he needed one.

There wasn't much that looked like it would be useful.

He opened the mini-fridge. There were bottles of beer. He considered emptying one, breaking off the neck, and using it as a stabbing weapon, but that seemed extreme. Besides, he didn't want to walk down the hallway carrying a broken bottle.

He'd already opened the champagne bottle, or he could have used it as a club.

Widow searched the drawers in the dresser. Nothing.

Then he looked in the drawers in the nightstands. He found a Bible. It was an old, thick hardcover, which was difficult to find. It must have been in the hotel room for ages.

The first question that he asked himself was, *Did they still keep Bibles?*

He flipped it open to a bookmarked page and looked at the bookmark. It was one of those Christian bookmarks offering a declaration of why he should immediately convert over. Then he stuck it back into the pages of the book at random and flipped back to the inside cover. The book wasn't stamped by The Plaza Hotel. It was stamped by a church on Fifth Avenue. Someone had left it. Probably someone from out of town, passing through and stopped at the church for a Sunday sermon.

Widow wondered if the church considered it *stealing;* if you take a Bible and leave it with the intention of someone else finding solace in it?

He closed it and shook it in his hand, slow, up and down, like a playground seesaw, and felt the weight. It was heavy and hard. As reading material, he wasn't interested. He had already read it before. But as a club, it would do nicely.

Widow took it and his keycard and left the room.

20

WHOEVER WAS WATCHING the girl with the Russian accent, whoever the kidnappers were, professional or not, they would wait for someone to come snooping around.

The girl had broken free and had dialed Widow's room. They may not have known whose room number had been dialed, but they would be cautious enough to expect him to come looking.

It was stupid to go straight for their room. An amateur would go there first. No, the right approach was to go to the elevator first. He wanted to check to see if one of them was watching the elevator.

It made sense to Widow that the two guys he'd seen in the lobby earlier might be related, somehow.

Maybe the guys in the room called down to the guys in the lobby. There might be two of them coming up. They might be armed.

Widow walked casually to the elevator. He held the Bible open and pretended to be reading the Book of Job.

As he turned the corner, he saw the elevator stop. The bell dinged. The doors opened. As he had expected, the two guys from the lobby stepped off, and the doors shut behind them. The elevator moved on.

They turned and looked left and looked right. The guy in the polo shirt and the blazer stepped to Widow's right. The other one followed suit and stepped back to Widow's left.

Widow ignored them, kept his face down, looking over the Bible. He kept his walk casual. At fifteen paces from them, he reached up and licked his finger and turned the page.

He noticed that both of them slowly moved their hands behind them. Both right hands. Both in the universal gesture that everyone understood as two guys with guns holstered behind them.

Widow walked forward, acting unshaken and unimportant, which was what he hoped they would see and back off.

Once he got within ten feet of them, he was at the elevator. He turned, reached out, and pressed the down button. He lifted his head from the Bible and acted like he hadn't even noticed them before.

"Oh. Hello, guys. Having a good night?"

The guy in the blazer stepped in closer, but stayed out of striking distance. He looked at Widow suspiciously.

He asked, "You staying here, sir?"

"Oh, yes. But I didn't pay for the room or anything. Can't afford it. I'm in town for a convention. Here in the hotel."

"A convention?"

"Yes. I represent the First Catholic Church of New Jersey," he said and showed them the Bible.

The two guys looked at each other blankly, almost dumbfounded.

Widow stepped closer, striking distance, and showed them the Bible's cover.

"This was my father's Bible. Are you guys religious?"

They shook their heads.

The other one, without the blazer, moved in two paces closer and stared at the inside pages of the Bible like he suspected it having a hollowed-out center where Widow was smuggling a gun.

He asked, "You're walking down the hallway, in the middle of the night, reading a Bible?"

"A Friday night," the guy in the blazer added.

"Of course. It never matters when you read the Bible. God's message is always welcomed."

They looked at each other again, a quick glance, speechless and obviously not buying it.

Widow determined within seconds that neither of these two was the leader. The one in the blazer was doing more of the talking, but he had also made more mistakes than the other guy.

It was common practice for Widow to take out the leader first, but in this case, both men were matched.

The one without the blazer was a little closer now, which made him a volunteer.

The one without the blazer asked, "What message is that?"

Widow could see his forearm muscles twitch and his veins pop. He was gripping and un-holstering his gun.

Right then, at the moment that Widow was calculating, the bell on the elevator dinged.

Both men glanced up and looked behind Widow, a fast set of glances, but slow enough for Widow to make his move.

He held his breath, pivoted from his left foot, and slammed the spine end of the Bible straight into the voice box of the guy in the black sweater.

It was a vicious blow, a little too vicious. A part of him hoped it wasn't enough to kill the guy. There was no need for that, not when he hadn't fully vetted them as bad guys just yet. He knew they weren't FBI or police, but they could have been CIA. That would have been highly unlikely and illegal, not that that had ever stopped them before.

The guy in the black sweater let go of his gun and tumbled back against the wall, wheezing. Which reminded Widow of the Irish John from the day before.

He was distracted for a split second by the thought.

The guy in the blazer was a lot faster than Widow had hoped. He didn't waste time trying to draw his gun. Instead, he rushed forward and pushed Widow straight back into the elevator.

The blow didn't cause any damage to Widow, but it got him off guard, and he went off his feet.

He was lucky enough to grab a quick handful of the man's blazer, and they both ended up hitting half of the elevator floor, half of the hallway carpet.

Widow kept the Bible in his other hand on the way down.

The two men hit hard. Widow took the brunt of it. He ignored the sudden pain because acknowledging it would give the other guy a second of advantage, which the other guy was expecting because he went for a gun with his right hand. Widow held the Bible in his right. He slammed his left hand, hard, and clamped down on the guy's forearm, holding his arm and gun hand locked behind him.

Instead of changing his tactics, the guy did exactly what he had expected Widow to do; he flinched, dwelled on his stuck hand.

Widow whipped his right shoulder back and up, flinging his arm as far back and as fast upward as it would go in the short distance between his elbow and the floor. He threw a short, but powerful right jab, using the spine of the Bible as a pair of knuckledusters.

The book hit the guy square on the bridge of his nose, cracking it, breaking it, making an obvious hole in the guy's face.

Blood gushed out like a runaway fire hose, like a cracked-open hydrant on a hot day.

Within seconds, enough blood sprayed out onto Widow's face to blind him if it had sprayed in his eyes, which didn't happen because he'd turned his face away enough.

The guy's right hand went limp for a split second and then jolted back to life and the guy fought to pull it away. Widow released it, and the guy grabbed at his broken nose or broken face. However he wanted to look at it.

Widow rolled him off and scrambled to his feet.

He kicked the guy over on his side and jerked the gun out.

It was an unusual handgun. He recognized it as a Maxim 9, which was a futuristic-looking gun because half of it, from the handle past the trigger, resembled a SIG Sauer Special Forces handgun, and the muzzle looked like a pulse phaser from Captain Kirk's personal arsenal.

He had never held one or seen one before in real life, only read about them in Forbes, as a new, expensive toy for collectors. The problem with that statement was that it wasn't available to the public, not as far as Widow knew.

The reason it wasn't available was that the boxy end part was a built-in silencer.

From what he could remember reading, it was whisper quiet, a great noise suppressor. Normally, they aren't silent at all. Normally, a .45 handgun like this, equipped with a suppressor, would sound like a loud cough when it was fired inside a place like The Plaza Hotel.

Not the Maxim 9. If the claims in the article by the manufacturer were true, then it was more like a quick hiccup.

The other thing that stuck out to Widow was the "unavailable to the public" piece of the article. So far, there had been only one buyer of this weapon that he knew of, and it was the CIA. The rumor, not mentioned in the article, was that it was being tested for wet work teams, which are essentially death squads run by the agency. These were Special Forces guys, with a little more bloodlust than the average soldier. And they were no longer military. These were guys who were privately contracted by the Pentagon, CIA, or held as exclusive employees, without the paperwork attaching them to the government.

The whole thing only meant that they weren't to be trifled with.

What the hell are they doing kidnapping a foreigner on American soil?

Widow didn't want to kill them, not without some answers.

Suddenly, he noticed the wheezing from the other guy had stopped. He turned to look and saw the guy was half-standing, his back to Widow.

The windpipe must have been okay, after all.

He reached for his gun and slowly drew it.

It was the same Maxim 9 handgun.

Widow could have shot him in the back, or even the leg. That would have put him down long enough for Widow to disarm him.

Instead, Widow hurtled the hardcover Bible at him like a major league pitcher. The book smacked the guy clear in the back of the head and hard. It was as hard as Widow could throw. If it had been a large rock, the guy would be dead from a crushed skull. But it was only a book.

The Bible bounced off his head and landed on the floor.

The guy tumbled forward and crashed first into the wall and then slid down to a cushioned bench. He didn't get back up.

Widow looked both ways up and then down the hallway, in case someone came out of a room to investigate the ruckus. No one came out.

Then he stuffed the Maxim 9 into the back of his chinos. It was a little loose because he wasn't wearing a belt, but it stayed put well enough.

He reached down and grabbed a handful of the trouser leg of the guy in the blazer and dragged him out of the elevator.

The guy squirmed and fidgeted like a snake, but with less power.

Widow dragged him over to the other guy. He stopped and reached down to check the guy's pulse. It was weak, but it was there. He was breathing, but he wasn't conscious.

Widow took his gun too and stuffed it into his front pocket. Then he hauled the first guy up by the arms and held him there by his collar.

"Who the hell are you?" the guy asked nasally, with a defeated tone.

"How many are in the room?"

"What?"

"How many guys are left in the room? With the girl?"

The guy paused a beat.

"You're the one she called? Staying in nine-eleven?"

Widow nodded.

"Just you?"

"I asked how many are in the room."

The guy didn't answer.

Widow reached up with one hand and grabbed the guy's nose over his hand, and pulled down on it.

The guy let out a nasal, pathetic screech.

"Wait! Wait!" he shouted.

"How many?"

"Two. There's two other guys."

"Thank you," Widow said. Before the guy could protest, he whipped his head forward in a violent arc and head-butted the guy right in the face. It wasn't the hardest that he could do, but enough to put the guy out, which it did.

One minute there had been somebody home, and the next there was not.

Widow lowered the guy to his butt and looked around once more—no sign of anyone coming out.

The elevator doors sucked shut, and he heard the low rolling sound of the cables. The elevator had been called and was on its way to another floor above him.

Widow saw a door marked as the fire stairwell.

He dragged the guy in the blazer across the floor and pulled open the door, hauled the guy through it, and tucked him away in the corner behind the door.

He went back into the hall and repeated the process with the other guy. In their pockets, he found wallets and IDs that looked fake, professionally done, but fake. He also found cellphones and cash.

Widow left the wallets, took the cash and the phones, left the Bible in the stairwell with them, and left both men behind.

He took the Maxim 9 from out of his front pocket and ejected the magazine, emptied the chambered round, and dry fired it at the floor. It worked.

He reinserted the magazine and scooped up the bullet that had ejected. He slid the bullet into his pocket and kept the gun out, ready to use.

Widow continued toward room nine-twenty-one.

21

One phone was passcoded, but the other was not. He tossed the passcoded one into a wastebasket in the hall and stuffed the cash into his pocket. A bonus.

He opened the home screen of the cellphone and pulled up the internet, searched for The Plaza Hotel. He found it and clicked the contact button, and waited. He saw the house phone number and clicked on it. The phone asked if he would like to call it. He clicked the yes button and waited. The phone dialed and rang.

"Hello, The Plaza Hotel?" a voice said.

Widow said, "Can you connect me to room nine-twenty-one?"

"One moment, sir."

There was another click and a dial tone.

Widow picked up the pace and walked on until he was standing outside room nine-twenty-one. He stayed out of sight of the peephole.

He moved the phone away from his ear, and slid it into his pocket, left it on speakerphone.

He heard the ringing on the other side of the door, and then it stopped. He heard a voice say, "Hello?"

In a wild, mad-dash scramble, he stepped out in the middle of the hall and charged forward and kicked the door as hard as he could. A lot of times, hotel doors are made hard enough to withstand the brute force of unwanted intruders' attempts to break-in.

Luckily, Widow applied the right amount of force, and the door wasn't deadbolted.

It slammed inward in a heavy swing.

One guy stood on the opposite side of it, looking through the peephole. The force of the kick and the blow sent him tumbling back onto the floor.

Widow barged into the room and pistol-whipped the guy square in the mouth, which had been a miscalculation. He had meant to hit the guy in the forehead, hoping to knock him out. Instead, he heard a tooth chip and crack, and the guy yelped.

The back of his head hit the carpet, hard, but not enough to knock him into unconsciousness.

Widow didn't go for a second punch; he didn't want to give the guy answering the phone time to react.

He pointed the gun at the guy and shouted, "FREEZE! FREEZE!"

The old cop voice came back like he had used it yesterday.

The guy froze. His gun was out, but it was on the tabletop. The room phone was in his hand, near his face, and his other hand was holding a corked syringe. The contents were clear and filled up to the halfway mark.

They had been about to sedate the woman, Widow figured.

There was something sickening to him about that kind of procedure versus the old-fashioned way of keeping a prisoner. Injections and sedatives and drugging and tranquilizing seemed clinical to him, almost inhumane.

It also confirmed in his mind that he was dealing with a group of bad guys who had some government ties or even backing.

He said, "Slow, stand up."

The guy stood up.

Widow stepped forward into the room and reached back with his free hand, shut the door. Only it wouldn't close. The inside door latch was cracked and splintered.

Keeping his eye on the guy by the phone, he used his foot to push it shut as much as it would go.

He stepped forward, stopped at the guy on the floor.

He was holding onto his mouth. Widow could see trickles of blood seeping out of his fingers, but nothing like the guy from the hall.

Widow looked down at him quickly, took aim, and said, "Sorry."

The guy's eyes looked up, wide.

Widow stomped down on his forehead with a heavy boot—another lights-out blow to the head, which worked like a charm. The guy's eyes closed, and he went to sleep.

Widow turned back to the guy in the chair next to the phone.

"Hang it up," he said.

The guy hung it up.

"Who are you?" the guy asked.

"Not important. Who are you?"

"Can't tell you that."

"Wrong answer," Widow said, and he squeezed the trigger of the Maxim 9.

It worked as advertised, almost. A bullet fired out and hit the telephone inches from the guy's hand.

The phone actually dinged once, like it had an actual bell inside, which it probably did. Expensive plastic cracked and shattered into small pieces, exploding all over the tabletop.

The guy flinched, covered his face with the hands.

"Okay! Okay!"

Widow waited, aimed the gun at the guy's center mass.

"We're a paramilitary group."

"Private?"

The guy nodded, which was exactly what Widow had suspected and also what he didn't want to hear.

"Government contract?"

The guy said nothing.

Widow closed the distance between them, stopped right in front of the guy, who had to look up to see him.

Widow lowered the gun, pushing the muzzle right on the guy's right kneecap.

"Are you working for the Pentagon?" he asked.

"No! No!" the guy said, trembling.

"Who then?"

"I don't know! I swear!"

Widow leaned his weight forward, intensifying the pressure from the gun down on the guy's knee.

"I'm telling you the truth! I don't know! I'm not in charge! I just take orders! We all do!"

"Who is in charge?"

The guy stayed quiet.

Widow said, "I'm not bluffing. Don't make me shoot you to prove it."

The guy trembled some more. His eyes darted back and forth. He looked at the guy on the floor and looked back at Widow.

"His name is Connors."

"Got a first name?"

"Danny Connors."

"He's in charge of your crew?"

"Yes!"

"He'll know the name of your contractor?"

"Of course! He pays us! He tells us what to do!"

Widow stepped back, moved the gun away from the guy's knees, and pointed it back at his center mass.

"What did he have you do here?"

"Babysit!"

"Where is she?"

"Bathtub!"

"Why her?"

"I don't know! I done told you that! We just are told what, not why!"

Widow nodded. He believed him. The guy was telling the truth. The good news was that these guys weren't CIA or contracted by the Pentagon. They were too much of an unknown, untested bunch. Widow could see that.

They weren't unqualified, just not professional enough.

They were good, but not good enough. Certainly not better than he was. Which was a high bar to reach, but the Pentagon would expect nothing less.

Out of all the contracts that private military groups could get, the US government was the best because they paid the best.

Someone else hired these guys.

"What's in the syringe?"

"I don't know," the guy said.

"You don't know?"

"I mean, I don't know how to pronounce it. It's written on the bottle," the guy said and gestured with his head where it was kept.

Widow didn't look.

"You think I'm stupid?" he said.

"What?"

"You think I'll look so you can charge at me?"

"No! I swear! I'm just telling you where it is!"

"Stand up!" Widow said, and he stepped back a couple of paces out of the guy's reach.

The guy looked puzzled, but stood up as ordered.

"Turn around!"

The guy slowly turned around.

Widow moved forward and switched the gun to his left hand while he scooped up the syringe with his right.

He pressed the plunger, squirting out a short spray of the contents.

He said, "Bend over.'

"What?"

"You heard me!"

The guy didn't turn around. He bent over as ordered, grabbed the rests on the chair to steady himself.

Widow stabbed the syringe into the guy's butt and pressed the plunger, emptied most of the contents into the guy's fatty tissue.

The sedative worked fast too because, within a minute, the guy was out. He toppled forward over the chair and sank forward in an uncomfortable position.

A few seconds later, he was actually snoring, in a cartoonish tempo.

Whatever was in the needle, it was powerful.

Widow used the rest on the guy on the floor—no reason to leave him to wake up before the other guy.

Widow tossed the syringe onto the floor and lowered the gun. He walked to the bathroom and opened the door.

Inside, he found the lights were already on, and he saw a woman's leg dangling over the edge of a claw tub.

He walked over and looked down.

Looking up at him was a beautiful Russian woman. She wore a tight, red dress, which was tousled and dirtied up a bit, but still on her body. Her shoes were at the bottom of the tub and off her feet.

She had long, dark brown hair that was disheveled and all over the place. It was thick enough to reject a motorcycle helmet.

Widow saw that her wrists had been double zip-tied. Which was overkill, he thought. And her feet were also zip-tied, but she hadn't been sedated yet. Her eyes were wide open and alert.

What he also saw was that she was stunningly beautiful, only with a look of terror on her face that would have made a cold-blooded killer uncomfortable. Which he realized was because there was a blood-covered giant standing over her, holding the same gun that the guys who had done this to her had been armed with.

22

WIDOW TUCKED the gun away and reached down to grab the woman by her wrists. She fought back and squirmed and kicked.

"Calm down," he said. "I'm here to help."

She stopped fighting and mumbled something that he couldn't understand because they had stuffed and duct-taped a rag in her mouth.

Widow said, "Hold on a minute."

He scooped her up, and out of the tub, sat her down on the toilet.

"This might hurt," he said. He grabbed the tape over her mouth and paused.

She closed her eyes shut like she was ready.

In one fast act, he ripped the tape off.

She didn't make a noise, but her expression turned to a quick, painful one. Then she spat out the rag.

"Who are you?" she asked.

"Not important right now. I'm the guy you called."

She nodded.

"Is there a knife here somewhere?"

She didn't answer.

"For the zip-ties."

She shook her head and said, "I don't know."

Widow stayed quiet.

She said, "Take me out of here first. We can find a knife later."

"Don't worry. I made a good amount of noise, busting through the door. Someone probably called hotel security by now. They can get you out when they get here."

"No! No! I can't be found by security or police. You must take me out of here."

"Take you out? Why no police?"

"Please! You must!"

Widow asked, "Where?"

"To your room. Let's go there first. Then we get me out of these, and then I go. No trouble."

Widow thought for a moment. Normally, he would just call the cops, but considering he beat up four guys who may or may not have ties to the Pentagon and his past, the last thing he wanted was to be involved at any official level.

He shrugged and agreed.

"How do we get back there? Are you going to hop there?"

She paused and looked him over from his ankles back up his torso.

"You are a big guy. Carry me."

"What?"

"Pick me up."

"Like over my shoulder?"

"Yes. Like caveman," she said and smiled, which made the terror that had been on her face sweep away at light speed, replaced by warmth.

Suddenly, Widow realized that the last time a warm-blooded, straight man had ever told her no was probably a decade in the past, more even. The last time that had happened was probably when she wasn't even a teenager, before her body was more developed.

As far as he could see, she had been blessed with the right amount of curves for a woman as thin and lean as she was. A second look at her told him that those curves were worked on. Her legs were muscular things, like a dancer's who did two shows a day, meaning that she probably incorporated squats into her daily workouts.

"Well?" she interrupted his boyish contemplations.

"Sorry. Yes. Let's go."

He knelt down and reached around her thighs, above her knees, and hauled her up over his shoulder carefully.

He walked to the door and opened it, peeked out into the hall. No one was there—no security guard.

Quickly, he took her out and shut the door behind him.

He walked at a fast pace, but not running or jogging, with her over his shoulder.

They passed the elevator just as it dinged, and the doors opened behind them, but they were well out of sight.

They made it back to his room. He set her down and opened the door with the keycard, and stepped in. He helped her hop in behind him.

The door shut, and he watched her hop over to the table where his hotel phone had been, and then she plopped herself down on the chair next to it.

"Let's get these off, please," she said.

And once again, he didn't say no.

23

THE LAST THING that Widow had expected to feel was hungover. But suddenly he did. He figured it wasn't the glass of champagne that he drank, but that he had been woken up from a deep sleep, had dredged up adrenaline and then had taken out four armed guys that caused his body to crash from the high. And now he felt hungover.

He opened the minibar and pulled out a couple of protein bars, offered one to the Russian woman, tied up, and sitting in his hotel room.

That thought made him smile.

"What's funny?"

She noticed.

"Oh, nothing. I'm not laughing."

"Why smile? This is serious situation."

"Sorry, it was just a thought I had from earlier. I was half asleep when you called. Still trying to get acclimated."

"Acclimated?"

"Reoriented."

She nodded.

Silence.

Widow asked, "You're Russian?"

She nodded.

"My name is Jack Widow."

"Anna Johannsen," she said.

"Johannsen? Is that Russian?"

She looked at him and smiled.

"Sorry, I meant Eva Karpov. That's my true name."

Widow nodded. She used an alias. Interesting.

"What the hell is going on?"

"First, get me out of these?" she asked, and gestured to the restraints.

"Of course," he said. He set the protein bars down on the table.

Widow looked around the hotel for a moment and then used the half-empty champagne bottle. He took it into the bathroom and over the sink, and considered breaking it on the countertop, but then thought about how expensive that looked.

He turned to the tub, dumped out the rest of the champagne, and used minimal force to break off the bottom of the bottle. One good, hard whack, and he had several fragments of sharp green glass and a whole bottleneck, still intact.

Widow dropped the neck into a wastebasket and picked up a sharp piece of glass.

He returned to her.

"This is all I can find."

She shrugged and gave him her wrists.

He sawed and tried to stay as far away from her skin as he could. The last thing he needed to do was cut her wrists.

After a lot of effort, the first zip-tie popped off.

"Stop."

She stopped him and motioned for him to back off. Then she repeated the same escape technique that she had done back in the other hotel room, the first time she got free from her zip-ties.

He was impressed.

"Where did you learn that?"

She didn't answer. She held her hand out and took the sharp glass fragment. She relaxed in the chair and pulled her feet up, and reached forward and started sawing the zip-tie binding her ankles.

"I learned it in the service."

Widow stepped away, picked up a protein bar, and sat in the other chair across from her.

"What about you?" she asked.

He stayed quiet.

"Where did you learn to take out armed professionals like that?"

"They weren't professional. Not really. More like semi-professional."

Karpov said, "I thought so. You are military?"

"No. Not anymore. Once."

"Thank you for helping me."

Widow nodded.

"I'll be out of your hair soon."

"Not so fast."

She finished cutting her feet free and then lowered them to the floor. Widow realized that he should have brought her shoes, too.

"What the hell is going on?" he asked.

She scooped up the protein bar, ripped off the paper like she was angry at it, and stuffed her mouth full. Apparently, her kidnappers hadn't fed her much.

She chewed and swallowed the first bite and put her hand over her mouth to cover her animal-like consumption.

"My name is Eva Karpov," she repeated. "I'm a rezidentura."

Which Widow recognized to mean resident. That's what the Russians called a spy who lived in a foreign country, a resident.

"You work for the SVR?"

"You know what that is?" she asked.

"It's the Russian Foreign Intelligence Service."

She nodded.

"I'm an agent."

"A spy?"

"Yes, but not anymore."

"What do you mean?"

"I quit."

"Quit? They let you do that and stay in America?"

"They don't know. Not yet."

"So, who are these guys? They're American."

"Yes. I don't know who they are."

Widow wasn't sure if she was lying or not. Normal people emit telltale signs that they are lying. We all do it. It's human nature. No one is immune, but some are better at hiding most of these signs than others. Especially a beautiful Russian agent with spycraft training. Widow had never known a Russian agent before, not a beautiful woman, anyway.

He had heard of them. They were legends in the intelligence world, myths. He had always thought that they were more myth than legend, more legend than fact. But there was one sitting in front of him.

"Sorry, but I'm starving," she said.

"Go ahead. That's yours," he said and pointed at the remains of his protein bar.

She didn't say another word. She scooped it up and devoured the bar like she hadn't eaten in days, which Widow realized she probably hadn't.

"Want something else?"

"Yes."

He returned to the minibar and opened it, and peeked in.

"What would you like?"

"Something big."

Most of the options were junk food.

He pulled out a bag of nuts, figuring that she needed the salt and the protein more than sugar from anything else that was there.

He handed it to her. She took the bag and started devouring them, too.

With her mouth half-full, she said, "Thank you so much for your help, Mr. Widow."

"Tell me what is going on."

"I don't think I should."

"Why not?"

"You could be in danger."

"I'm already involved."

She stayed quiet.

"None of those guys are going to forget me. When they wake up, they'll remember who did this to them."

She nodded and said, "We should leave the hotel too."

"Let's wait and see."

"Wait for what?"

"So far, no one has come to our door. No security. Which is usually what would happen. If we can stay the night here, that would be best. We could leave at first light."

"What if someone called the police?"

"We'll know that soon enough. NYPD is fast. If the hotel called them, they'll be here in the next ten minutes, I would think."

"What about the others?"

"What others?"

"You only knocked out two in my room. There are two others. In the lobby."

Widow smiled and said, "No, they're not. They're in the stairwell."

Eva smiled and asked, "Who the hell are you?"

"I told you. My name is Jack Widow."

"I mean, where did you come from?"

"I came from this room."

"What kind of soldier were you in the military?"

"I wasn't a soldier."

"I thought you said you were ex-military?"

"I was. I wasn't a soldier. I was a sailor."

Eva nodded, said, "You were Special Forces?"

"SEAL," Widow answered.

Her eyes lit up.

"I see. No wonder you can fight like that."

Widow stayed quiet.

Silence fell between them, and Eva ate the last of the nuts. She wiped her lips in a sultry way that Widow wondered was just second nature to her, because of the kind of training she must've gone through. He didn't want to bring it up, but he had heard that female agents were trained much, much differently from males.

Russians taught them to use all the wiles available to them. There are countless stories of Western politicians, generals, and even heads of state falling to the wiles of a Russian woman.

24

WIDOW WAITED another ten minutes on top of the first ten, making an even twenty, just to be safe. No one came to the door—no hotel security. No police.

Widow opened the door twice and peeked his head out into the hall.

He heard no commotion—no signs of police.

"That's weird. Right?" Eva asked.

He shook his head.

"Not really. It is a Saturday night, in New York City, and it's after midnight. Likely that whoever is staying in the rooms near nine-twenty-one is still out on the town somewhere. Either that or drunk and passed out in their beds, sound asleep."

He kept the door ajar and looked back at her.

She said, "Okay. But what about those men? They won't stay knocked out for long?"

"Except for the ones I injected."

"The other two in the stairs?"

"Yeah?"

"There's more of that stuff—the drug. There must be. You could knock them all out for the next twenty-four hours."

Widow said, "That's a good idea."

"I'll come with you."

At first, Widow wanted to tell her to wait, but the fear of her running away had occurred to him. After all, he still didn't know what the hell she was involved in. It might be in her best interest to sneak away, leaving him with four knocked out mercs.

"Let's go," he said.

They walked out of the room and side by side down the hall.

* * *

AT THE ELEVATORS, they stopped, and Eva looked down. There were small droplets of blood on the carpet, which were also matted down and disheveled and scuffed in several places.

She said, "Let me guess, this is where you fought them?"

Widow nodded.

She followed him over to the stairwell. They opened the door and found both guys still there. Still unconscious.

"Isn't it very bad to be knocked out for this long?"

Widow shrugged and said, "Didn't matter to me then. Doesn't matter to me now."

"Come on. Let's drag them back to the room."

Widow stayed quiet.

They both moved into the stairwell.

Eva shifted from one foot to the other because the concrete was freezing under her feet.

She watched Widow lift the first guy up from under his arms and drag him back to the door.

She went around and grabbed his legs, tried to pick him up like a wheelbarrow.

"Never mind that," Widow said. "Just get the door and then be the lookout. We don't want someone walking out to the hall now."

"You sure?"

"Yeah. Go."

She went behind him, passed him, and held the door open. She peered both ways and listened.

"I don't hear anyone."

Widow dragged the guy out onto the carpet.

Eva moved ahead of him and made her way to room nine-twenty-one. She didn't have the keycard to open it, but then realized that she didn't need it. It was still broken from Widow kicking it in.

She opened it and waited for Widow to drag the guy in. He dumped him down on the carpet.

They went back and repeated the process for the other guy.

After a short break, Widow found the supply of sedatives stuffed into a satchel under the bed.

He stopped and stared into it for a moment. He saw something that told him exactly what he needed to know about these guys and what they planned for Eva.

In the satchel, he found a bulky rolled-up sheet of plastic, black like a garbage bag. There was a box of surgical plastic gloves, and two pairs of hacksaws, and one very sharp bone saw that looked so crude it was almost obscene.

Widow took out the sedatives and closed the bag before Eva could see in.

He used the needles and the sedatives and injected each of the other guys, and re-injected the one who had only gotten a small portion earlier in order to equal it all out. He didn't clean any of the needle areas before injecting them. He wasn't concerned with sanitation, only their silence.

They checked around the room again for anything useful, found nothing but Eva's shoes, which she took this time.

"Damn," she said.

"What?"

"I had a bag. It's not here. What did they do with it?"

Widow looked at the pile of sedated guys and said, "We probably should've asked them that before we knocked them out."

Eva smiled and stepped out of the door first, back into the hall.

Widow came next and pulled the door as far shut as it would go, which took some effort. It dragged across the carpet.

Eva looked left and looked right.

Suddenly, she saw shadows and heard voices. Five young guys were walking down the hall toward them. They were talking loud and laughing. They looked like five guys coming back from a night out, clubbing, barhopping, having a lot of drinks on the town.

"Widow," she said.

He looked up and was holding the door shut. It kept jerking back from the hinges.

They were getting closer. Widow tried to close the door. He at least wanted it to shut.

Without hesitation, Eva took action.

She wobbled around, acted a little intoxicated, and scooped up two handfuls of Widow's t-shirt. She nearly ripped it, pulling it and him toward her so hard and fast.

She stood up on tippy toes and kissed him, hard and wet—a distraction.

Her lips were wet. Her tongue was ample, and she wasn't afraid to use it. That was obvious.

If Eva was a day over twenty-five, Widow would've been shocked. And if she had started her seductive spy training a day short of five years ago, he would've been doubly shocked.

She kissed him so hard; he was suddenly worried that even five drunk guys in New York City were going to complain to the hotel's management.

The guys walked, stopped talking for a long minute as they passed by. But they didn't stop and gawk. They kept on walking. Kept on laughing.

Eva didn't stop kissing Widow.

She kissed him hard and long. A good long time after the coast was clear.

She was damn good at her job. No question.

Widow suddenly doubted that the FSB would give her up under any circumstances.

After another long minute of kissing him, she stopped, backed down, and looked in his eyes for a moment. Then she asked, "Are they gone?"

Widow spoke, and for an instant, his voice cracked like he was a teenager all over again.

"Yeah. They're gone."

"Good. Let's get back."

She let go of him, but kept her hand locked onto the bottom of his fingers. She pulled him along, gently, seductively.

Widow wondered if she could even help it.

They walked back down the hall, past the elevators, staying close together.

Back in Widow's room, Eva sat back down on the same chair.

"What now?" she asked.

"Now, tell me what's going on?"

"Can I have something to drink?"

"What do you want?"

"Water, please."

"Of course," Widow said, and he reopened the minibar, took out two bottles of water, and handed her one. He joined her at the table.

Widow watched her screw the bottle open and take two long, deep pulls from it.

He did the same and waited.

"You don't have a cigarette?" she asked.

"I don't smoke."

She frowned, took another drink of water, and then she said, "Listen. I am grateful for your help, but you may not want to know about me?"

It was more of a question than a declaration.

"Tell me."

"My name is Karpov."

He nodded, knew that part.

She said, "I have been in America for three years. Working here in New York."

"Doing what?"

"Officially, I do modeling work and study at university."

"What do you do for the FSB?"

"I date who they tell me to date."

Widow nodded.

"It's not as bad as it sounds. I'm not a prostitute. They don't want me to do that. If I got arrested, it would be the end of my work here. I have a contact here, a handler, who tells me the name of someone and where to go to meet him. I arrange meetings and work my way into their circles. They give me information. I return that information to my government."

"Circles?"

"You know. Social things. Sometimes I date diplomats, lawyers, or whoever, and I work my way into knowing who they know and what they know."

Widow asked, "Married men?"

"Usually. But don't judge me."

"I'm not. Believe me. I'm sure I've done much, much worse for my country."

She said nothing to that.

Widow asked, "So why did these guys kidnap you?"

"They must be trying to stop me."

"From what?"

"My father. He's a submarine commander for Russia."

Widow drank another gulp and waited.

Eva said, "About a month ago, a man approached me. An American man. He is a CIA agent. They took me in and said they knew who I was. But they wouldn't turn me in if I helped them."

"What do they want?"

"I begged for this assignment. Here in America, I mean. Begged for it. Do you know why?"

Widow shook his head, even though she meant the question to be rhetorical.

"I love this country. I want to escape Russia. I hoped I could find a way out."

Widow stayed quiet.

"Of course, we all wondered about trying to escape to your country."

"What do they tell you?"

"Before we are sent here, we are warned not to run. If we run, they will do terrible things to our family."

"Like what?" Widow asked.

"They only pick girls who have parents."

Which was a surprise to Widow. He had heard that the Russians liked to use orphans. Girls who could disappear easily, without notice. No one left behind to worry about them.

Eva said, "They use the parents as leverage over us. If we try to...try to..."

She was struggling over a word.

She asked, "What's it called when a foreign citizen tries to request safety here?"

"Defect?"

"Yes. I want to defect."

"What about your parents?"

"I only have a father. He, too, wants to defect."

"Where is he?"

"That's why I'm here because he is the captain of a submarine."

Widow stayed quiet.

"A nuclear submarine."

25

Eva said, "A few months ago, I made a friend. More than that. He was another student in one of my classes. We hit it off, and I've been dating him."

Widow said, "Don't take this the wrong way."

"What?"

"This guy. He's a friend or a mark?"

"He's a friend. He's not government. Just a regular American guy. A chance meeting."

"Okay."

"We dated. I wanted to. It wasn't related to work."

Widow stayed quiet, listened.

"His name's Edward. He works as a fireman."

Widow noticed her face change as she spoke of him. Something in her eyes.

He asked, "You care about this guy?"

She nodded.

"What happened next?"

"Two weeks ago, he introduced me to this guy he knew, a friend. He said he used to work with this guy. So, I met with him—twice. The guy's name is Frank Farmer. He works for the government. After our first meeting, Farmer told me he was a CIA agent. And he knew who I was."

She stopped talking and looked down at the floor.

"What?" Widow asked.

"I was so stupid. They teach us not to have feelings for a man."

"Edward and Farmer aren't what they seem?"

"No. I trusted Edward and told him who I was. Who I really was. He told Farmer, and they both convinced me they could help me and my father get out of Russia."

"Let me guess. Farmer asked you to set up communications with your father?"

She nodded.

"What else did he promise?"

"Farmer promised he could arrange for my father and me to go under protection for the submarine."

Widow said, "Sounds like Clancy."

"Who?"

"You know. The book by Tom Clancy. The Hunt for Red October."

"Yes! I know this book! It's one of my father's favorites."

"I bet he knew that."

Eva said, "You think so?"

"Of course, CIA guys don't just show up by chance like that. They identified you before you and Edward even met. They knew exactly what they were doing."

She nodded, said, "Those are his guys that kidnapped me?"

Widow nodded.

She shook her head and said, "I feel so stupid."

"I wouldn't. You wanted to have a better life for you and your father. I can understand that."

She looked down in shame.

"You love this guy?"

"Yes. I think I do."

She had said it without hesitation.

Silence.

Widow said, "What exactly was the plan?"

"Farmer told me I was to go about my business for a week. Then I was to tell my father the plan and get his answer."

"He agreed?"

"Of course."

"Then what?"

"I was told to come here and wait. Farmer gave me coordinates to relay to my father. They were supposed to meet."

"Where?"

"The middle of the Arctic Ocean."

Widow said, "So, let me guess, the deal was this Farmer guy gets the submarine, and you and your father get your freedom?"

"Yes. And now I'm here."

"Why?"

"Why what?"

"Why the hell does Farmer want this submarine?"

She shrugged and said, "Because it's nuclear. I guess."

"No. We got nuclear subs. Better than yours. In terms of submariner warfare and technology, the US Navy has the best."

Eva said nothing.

"No offense."

She shrugged.

"Why the hell would the CIA want a Russian one?"

She didn't answer.

"There must be something else. What do you know about the sub?"

"Nothing. I know nothing about them. Just what I told you. It's nuclear."

Widow nodded and stood up. He paced to the center of the room and then over to the window. The drapes dangled and wafted slightly. He peered out and looked down at the courtyard.

"The good news is, no cops. They would've already been here. NYPD is pretty fast."

Eva asked, "So, what do I do now?"

"What about Edward?"

"What about him?"

"You know where he lives?"

"Of course. I've been staying there five nights a week for the last month."

"So?"

"So what?"

"So, where is it?"

"He lives on the Upper East Side."

Widow smirked and said, "Not bad."

"What's that supposed to mean?"

"For a guy who is a college student and a fireman, the Upper East Side is an expensive spot to live. Does he live with roommates?"

"No."

"It didn't strike you as odd that a guy on his dime can afford an apartment on his own?"

"It's a family-owned loft. Lots of people live here who have owned the same apartments forever."

Widow said nothing to that.

"You think I'm stupid?"

"Not at all. I think you had feelings for this guy."

She nodded.

"Love can be a real son of a bitch."

She nodded again.

"What about your handler? Who is he?

"He's a she."

"Who is she?"

"I can't tell you that."

Widow said, "I'm trying to help you."

Eva was quiet.

"Look, I'm not one of the bad guys here. Obviously. You called me. How could I have faked that?"

"Her American name is Sarah Walsman. She's a partner in a law firm down on Forty-Second Street."

"Is she American?"

"What do you mean?"

"Is she like you? She's here on a visa?"

"No. She's Russian born with American citizenship. She's been here most of her life."

"Do you know where she is?" Widow asked.

"Not at this time of night."

"No home address?"

"No."

"How do you contact her?"

"By a secure phone number."

Widow paused a moment, and then he said, "What about this Edward guy?"

"What about him?"

"You remember his address?"

"Of course."

"Then that's our next stop."

"Now?"

"Yes. We can't wait. I'd bet the guys who kidnapped you will probably have to check in with this Farmer guy, and when they don't, he will know something's wrong. We should go."

Widow stood up, finished his bottle of water, and said, "Want anything else to eat? We're not returning to this room again."

Eva drank the rest of her water, finished the protein bar. She got up.

"What about your stuff?"

"Don't have any."

She said nothing to that.

Widow carried both weapons, one still in his pocket and the other tucked in the back of his waistband.

Before they left, he picked up his sweater but didn't put it on.

"Here. You should wear this. It's chilly out."

"What about you?" she asked.

"I'll be fine for now."

She nodded and took it, which was fine with him since she was in a skirt that was barely there, and he still had chinos, boots, and a t-shirt.

They walked out of the hotel room and out of the hotel. No one noticed.

26

Widow stayed close to Eva as they stepped out of a random cab and onto the curb of East Seventy-Eighth Street, her directions to her boyfriend's apartment.

The wind blew between the remaining leaves on a single thin brown tree.

Widow heard sounds of cars whooshing in the distance on FDR Drive. He heard the ambient noises of a busy, dark city night.

"That's it. On the corner," Eva said.

Widow looked, casually, and then glanced around the street.

"Doesn't look like anyone is here, staking the place out."

Eva nodded. She'd done the same thing, only much more anonymously and, probably, with more thoroughness. She was a trained spy, after all.

"Okay. Let me go in first and check it out."

Eva said nothing.

Widow looked around and saw a 7-Eleven type of all-night convenience store less than a block away, toward the west.

"Over there. Come on. Let's go over to that convenience store."

"What? No way!"

"This isn't a time to argue. What if there's someone here somewhere? They'll recognize you."

She shook her head.

"Forget about it. I'm not your woman in distress."

Widow stared at her in disbelief. Had he appeared a chauvinist? He hoped not.

But he didn't apologize.

"I'm only trying to do this the right way."

"Look, this is my ass—not yours. If Edward betrayed me, I'm going to get to speak to him about this! Not you!"

Widow held his hands up in a universal "I give up" sort of way.

"Okay. Fine," he said.

"Good."

Although Widow's way was safer, he couldn't say that he blamed her. She had met a man, trusted him, and he had almost literally stabbed her in the back.

If a woman had done that to him, he too would've stepped up and confronted her. No question.

Widow headed toward the building on the corner that she had pointed to.

She followed him down the sidewalk. They stopped at a four-way intersection and crossed over the street.

They stopped at a side alley, too small for a dump truck, but wide enough for him to stretch his arms out and not touch both sides. Almost.

He gazed down it, his hand behind his back, fingers touching the butt of the Maxim 9 stuffed into his waistband.

There was a chain-link fence, about ten feet high, linked up the wall, blocking anyone from strolling into the alley. He saw various pipes and grates. There was one backdoor into the building that they were interested in, but it was padlocked.

The alley was empty.

They walked up the steps to the front door entrance. There was a key code lock—all numbers.

"What's the code?"

Eva didn't answer him. She just brushed past him and entered the numbers in a four-digit sequence.

"That's it," Eva said, and the front door made a loud, grating sound. She reached up and jerked the knob and pulled the door open wide.

Widow grabbed the Maxim 9, again ready to brandish it, but kept it hidden. He figured that the whole building probably wasn't CIA or whoever these guys were.

The inner lobby area of the building had high concrete ceilings and a long, white leather couch and a metal bookshelf, and various abstract paint-ings hanging on the walls.

There were a couple of thick concrete pillars half-embedded into the walls.

He saw a single thick, brown counter that wrapped completely around a guy sitting in a chair, leaning back like his feet were up on a desktop that wasn't visible from where Widow and Eva were standing.

He was looking down, playing on a smartphone, Widow figured.

Another one, he thought.

Suddenly, he pictured what would happen if one of his guys or team members had been caught playing with his phone back in the Navy.

The guard immediately recognized Eva and sat up straight, like he was at attention, and said, "Good morning, Miss Johannsen."

He knew her.

Another thing surprised Widow.

Suddenly, Eva Karpov spoke. Only any trace of her Russian accent had completely vanished. Her pronunciation of English had improved dramati-cally. It wasn't perfect conversational American. It still stood out that she was a foreigner, but where she was from was more of a guessing game.

If Widow had known no better, he would've guessed that she was British. Not that she was using a British accent. It was only because out of all the English-speaking people of the world; the Brits were the best at blending in with Americans. He had met a dialect coach once, a guy back in Glynco, Georgia, the NCIS training grounds, who had taught agents on various dialects and how to disguise them. At the end of the course, the guy revealed he was British, and they hadn't realized it the whole year.

When Widow entered the course, everyone in the class had presumed he was from Virginia. He had perfected that deep rural Virginia accent.

Eva said, "Hi, Gerald. How is it tonight?"

"Everything's been quiet. How are you?"

Eva nodded and said, "Good. I'm just going to go on up."

The security guard named Gerald gave Widow a look over, which wasn't the friendliest that Widow had ever seen. But he said nothing to the plus one that Eva had brought with her.

He simply nodded and waved them up.

Widow smiled at the guy and followed Eva around a corner and past several doors, generic and gray, until they reached an elevator.

"This is an expensive-looking building."

"I guess so."

Her accent returned.

"This whole industrial loft style isn't. Not anymore."

Eva asked, "So what?"

"I thought you said that Edward is a fireman? Allegedly."

"I didn't mean he is an ordinary one. He's an assistant deputy in the department. He works out of city hall."

"He's the next guy down from the top or something?"

"I think so."

"I didn't know they paid this well."

Eva shrugged and said, "Believe me. I looked into it. He makes a good salary."

Widow stayed quiet. He didn't know what to say to that. Truthfully, he wasn't sure if he believed it. But anything was possible.

They waited for the elevator. It came, and the doors sucked open. Widow followed her on, and she hit the button for Edward's floor.

27

THE ELEVATOR DOORS OPENED, and Widow and Eva stayed where they were, waiting, breathing.

Widow kept his arm out in front of Eva, blocking her path forward.

He took out the Maxim 9 and kept it back behind his thigh, out of sight of anyone walking past.

Eva whispered, "What?"

Widow said nothing.

After a moment went by, the elevator doors closed. He moved his hand out and blocked them. The sensors picked up the resistance, and the levers and gears turned back, pulling the doors open.

Widow stepped out into the hall. He looked left. Nothing was there. He jerked to the right and saw nothing there, either. No one was waiting to ambush them.

He tucked the gun back into his waistband and motioned for Eva to step off the elevator.

Eva said, "I think you've seen too many movies."

"Just being safe."

"You've done this before?"

"You can say that."

"Don't worry; this isn't Iraq. Or wherever you've been."

Widow stayed quiet.

Eva turned left and walked west.

"Which one is it?"

"The last one. On the corner."

Like the lobby to the building, the hallway had high ceilings, smooth concrete floors, and concrete walls. There was more abstract art hanging on the walls between the apartment doors.

The doors were these huge wooden things. No peepholes. No doorbells.

It was amazing how this industrial look had come back into style. Widow remembered seeing an old bullet factory in Ukraine once. It had been converted to a hotel. He couldn't remember the name, but the whole thing had a ton of roped-off photographs and old tank shells turned into art.

This building wasn't an old ammunition factory, but it had that same industrial look to it.

The major difference being that the old ammunition factory in Ukraine had once been a working factory. It had been designed that way for convenience, and it was cheap.

The owners of this place had probably paid out the ass to have the same look that cost nothing decades ago.

Strange what rich people will pay for.

The thought brought Widow to another conclusion. No way was this Edward guy just working for the fire department. Not with this kind of pad.

They continued on and stopped at the door.

"Should I knock? You stand out of sight?"

"There's no peephole. Makes no difference."

Eva shrugged and knocked on the door, flat-handed, three loud pounds. They waited.

Widow leaned into the door and listened. He heard nothing.

"Sounds like no one's here."

Eva reached out and pounded on the door again, two more times.

Widow asked, "How can we get in?"

"Can you kick it in?"

"No way!"

"You're a big guy. You can do it."

He said, "Besides all the racket it'll make, this door is solid wood. No one is getting in that he doesn't let in."

Widow reached out and tried the handle. It was locked.

"You don't know where he might keep a spare key?"

She paused, and then she said, "The front desk has one. He could let us in."

"Will he do that?"

"It's doubtful. But maybe."

"We could wait for him to get home."

"No. I can't wait. What if Farmer has already contacted my father?"

Widow thought for a moment, looked over her head, down to the end of the hall.

He said, "He probably has."

Eva said nothing, but a look of fear came over her face.

"You've been sedated for two days, right?"

She nodded.

"Then I'd say whatever this guy's plans were with your father; he's already well ahead of us."

"So, how are we getting in, then?"

Widow took stock again. He turned and headed back to the elevator.

"Come on," he said.

"Widow?"

"We'll convince the guard to let us in."

"How?"

* * *

BACK AT THE FRONT DESK, Eva stood and explained to the guard at the desk exactly what Widow had told her, a simple plan that usually worked.

"I have to get in there. We knocked on the door, and we heard him ask for help."

The guard looked at her. He was standing up.

Widow heard his fingers tapping on the desk behind the counter. He was waiting, listening hard for any sign that the guard was going to press a hidden security call button, like a hidden distress call he had seen in banks.

It was very doubtful that they had one that called the police. Why would they?

But if the security for the building was outsourced to a local agency, which it probably was, then they might have a call center, like a headquarters. They might have such a switch installed at all their building locations.

This was New York City.

The guard had a look of concern on his face. He seemed to buy the lie, but there was one problem.

Widow realized he was that problem.

The guard said, "I don't know."

Which was blurted out, like a reaction to the whole situation.

"Please! We have to get in there!" Eva said. She was good. She was really selling the whole concerned girlfriend bit.

The guard looked Widow up and down, fast.

"We should call the ambulance. I think."

Eva said, "No! We need to get in there!"

Silence. He wasn't buying it—not quite.

Widow thought of backup plans. He could just pull the gun on the guy and make him produce the key. They could lock him up in a broom closet and take away his cell phone. Or Widow could just knock the guy out. A swift, not-too-brutal punch to the face would do the trick.

However, he hated the thought of it. A security guard staying up all night on a long graveyard shift probably made minimum wage. He probably already had an inner resentment about having to guard a property that he couldn't even afford to live in, not even if his salary had been doubled or tripled.

Then Eva said something brilliant.

"Gerald, Edward is diabetic! He probably had an attack! The paramedics won't get here fast enough!"

Gerald stayed quiet, but the expression of disbelief in his eyes completely faded away, and the look of concern overtook him.

Eva said, "I know Edward! If the ambulance is called, his insurance will go bullets."

She had meant *ballistic*, not bullets, but Widow got it, and the guard named Gerald had as well.

Widow half-smiled.

She was good.

The thought made him terrified of what else she could convince a man to do. He figured with her training and mannerisms, plus her looks, she probably could convince a four-star general to leap off a ledge.

Suddenly, he wondered if she had ever done that.

Gerald said, "Oh, man! Come on! Let's go!"

Which wasn't the response that Widow had hoped. He had hoped that Gerald would turn over the key without going up with them. But he figured that was a long shot.

Gerald turned around and pulled a long drawer open.

Widow heard clanging metal, like a drawer full of keys would make.

Gerald pulled out a key fast, like he knew which one it was. It must've been organized into cubbies.

He put the key into his pocket and pulled his coat off the back of the chair.

Widow and Eva started walking to the elevator. Gerald came up behind them and slid his jacket on. The back of it said "Security" in generic lettering. There was no name of his company labeled anywhere.

Gerald had also scooped up a Maglite, which Widow figured was because of him. Maybe it was out of caution or simply second nature. Either way, it was a good clubbing weapon.

They all got on the elevator and rode up.

28

THE SECURITY GUARD SAID, "Did you call him? I should've tried that first."

Eva said, "Of course we did. No answer."

Widow said, "We're already here now."

Gerald nodded and pulled the keys out of his pocket, held them in his hand.

He tucked the flashlight under his armpit and held it there. He used his free hand and knocked on the door twice.

"Mr. Daniels? Are you in there?" he called out.

He listened. Widow and Eva pretended to.

No sounds.

He knocked again and again. He called out.

Eva said, "Come on! We've got to get in there!"

Gerald retracted his knocking hand and pulled up the keys. Widow noticed he trembled, which was a natural reaction when you think you're about to walk into an emergency where a guy might slip into a diabetic coma.

Quick and without hesitation, Widow reached his right hand back and grabbed the Maxim 9, ready to draw it. He placed his other hand out and just behind the security guard, in case he had to jerk the guy out of the way.

There was no telling who was on the other side of the door, waiting for him.

The door was heavy, and Gerald had to push it open. He did this slowly and knocked on the door.

"Mr. Daniels?" he called out.

No answer.

Eva moved her eyes side to side, scoping out the place. She had the advantage over Widow because she knew exactly the layout of the apartment. She knew where all the furniture was placed, where the bathrooms and closets were.

It turned out not to be that hard because continuing with the industrial design of the apartments, this unit was completely open and very spacious.

The door opened to a kitchen to the left. All stainless steel appliances. All new.

There was a large bar top that doubled as a cooking island. Three white stools were tucked in on the right side and cutting utensils and a stack of cutting boards and bar glasses were neatly placed on top.

Straight ahead of them was an open living room area with a twenty-foot ceiling and a metal stairwell that led up above them to a loft, which was probably the bedroom.

To the immediate right was a small half bathroom. The door was wide open, and the light was off.

With a quick glance, Widow saw the sink and the toilet. The room was empty.

To the right, past the bathroom, was the living room area. There was a huge television placed on top of a modest entertainment center, with a coffee table and two white leather sofas with three yellow leather chairs.

The apartment was dimly lit.

The television was on, but not to a program or a movie. It played a screensaver that kept changing between different earthly backgrounds.

There were two good-sized speakers on the floor.

Low lounge music that Widow didn't recognize hummed from them.

There were huge glass bay windows on the wall, with the best view of a combination of cityscapes and some of the East River that Widow had ever seen.

There was a glass door that led out onto a balcony. Edward Daniels wasn't out there. That was clear.

Nor was he upstairs, hiding, or simply asleep.

He wasn't in either of these places because he was lying on the flat of his back on the floor, near the back of one sofa. And he was dead.

His face stared up at the ceiling above, and his eyes were wide open.

His skin wasn't white as a sheet, as was often written in books or seen on TV.

He was as blue as the afternoon sky.

At least his entire face and head were.

The cause of death hadn't been diabetes; even Gerald could see that.

The cause of death had been strangulation and with a garrote. That was obvious.

Widow had seen a lot of deaths and murders in his career. Next to a gunshot wound, strangulation by a garrote was one of the most obvious ones because of the damage left behind.

Edward's neck was black and blue, and there were severe up and down lines left on his skin like he had struggled with a sharp piano wire, while someone who knew what he was doing nearly sawed his head off, trying to choke him.

29

"Oh, my God!" Gerald said.

In a mad dash, he ran straight for the body. Maybe he had never seen a dead body before. Maybe he thought the guy was still alive. Maybe he even still believed that Edward had an attack from diabetes and was only in a coma.

Running to the body wasn't Widow's first instinct. He had seen dead bodies before. His first instinct was to make sure that no one else was there, waiting to ambush them.

No reason to keep up the charade anymore. Widow drew his weapon.

Eva saw it first. She was smart. She didn't run to the body.

She stayed back in Widow's line of sight.

He took out the other gun and reversed it, one-handed, and offered it to her.

She took it, left-handed, and held it down and out that way. She clicked the safety off and racked the slide back, chambering the first round.

Widow shouted, "Gerald!"

He shouted, just to stop Gerald in his tracks.

The guard stopped and flipped around, saw the guns, and froze. He dropped his Maglite so fast and moved his hands straight up in the freeze position Widow was certain he had definitely seen a gun before. No question.

"Holy hell!"

"Keep calm," Widow said.

"What's going on?"

Eva motioned for Gerald to stay quiet, one finger over her mouth.

"Come back this way," she commanded.

Gerald moved back to them and stopped.

Widow said, "I'll check out the rest of the place."

Eva nodded.

Widow didn't wait to hear what she told Gerald about what they were doing. He imagined it was some kind of lie involving them being law enforcement or undercover cops.

Although a pair of undercover cops with high-tech, expensive handguns with built-in silencers was a stretch. Still, the guy would probably buy it. Why not?

Widow moved out into the kitchen and stopped. He saw a hand towel hanging off the oven door handle. He reached out and pulled it off. With the dead body there, it would be a good idea not to leave fingerprints, although the building had security cameras. But clear images of a person from a camera feed weren't the same as fingerprints or DNA. With an image, the only way to identify someone was actually to recognize his face.

He was pretty sure that his face wouldn't pop up anywhere to be identified.

He continued on, passed the body, but didn't look down at it.

He swept the corners of the room, which were shrouded in dark shadows, quickly. Then he pointed the business end of the Maxim 9 at the stairs, checked the darkness underneath. Nothing there but rows of sneakers and sealed moving boxes.

He looked up the stairs, followed the metal railing above. The room above him was black, but he figured that if anyone had been there, waiting, then they would've made themselves known with a bullet if they had a gun.

Widow stepped on the bottom step, which clanged like a rung on a metal ladder.

Luckily, he wasn't worried about being silent. They had already destroyed that tactic.

Widow climbed the stairs with giant steps, two at a time. Within seconds, he was at the top. He crouched, gun out.

It was one quick sweep, checking the corners, checking the bed, and checking the open doorway to the bathroom, which had a low ambient light on. It was one of those plug-in nightlights. Maybe it doubled as an air freshener, because there was the smell of factory-made lavender in the air, like a burning candle purchased from any grocery store or low-cost department store found all over America.

The dim light from the bathroom cut a cone of light out onto the bed.

It was a king platform thing. It was made. Unlike the cheap-smelling lavender air freshener, the sheets and the bedding and the bed itself looked expensive.

There was a modern-style headboard up against the wall. No footboard.

The thing about the headboard that Widow noticed, without trying to notice, like a reflex, like an involuntary instinct had looked for it, were the bruises on the wall behind the headboard. He had seen those kinds of scuffs before.

In the Navy, Widow had to room with guys, lots of different SEALs and sailors, and even Marines. Over the years, whenever he had been stationed dockside or wherever, it was rare that he got a hotel room all to himself.

Suddenly, he could recall all the socks that he had seen left out for him, tied around door handles. A universal indicator from one guy to another that the room was occupied for a while.

Widow was struck with a little jealousy. He didn't know Eva, and the feeling wasn't warranted, not on a logical level. She was basically a stranger and a foreign agent at that. But they had shared an intense first meeting. And there was something about her he felt drawn to.

Widow shook off the jealousy and checked the other side of the bed. No one was there hiding.

He flattened himself up against the wall, slid down to the corner of a massive walk-in closet. No door, but lots of darkness.

He saw a light switch, flipped it. He waited.

No gunshots. No one reacted to the light being switched on. No breathing.

There was no one there.

Instead, Widow looked on in awe at the collection of suits and ties and dress shoes, polished and neatly stacked on wooden shelves.

The bathroom was next to the walk-in closet, making it easy for him to take a peek inside, which he did.

He flipped on the light, but he didn't need it.

The bathroom was a big, square box room. There was a huge glass shower that looked more like an empty aquarium than a shower. There were towels neatly folded on metal shelving above the toilet.

The vanity was a plain, white thing with decent counter space for a single man, but not big enough for a woman to use effectively.

There was a single large mirror hanging above the sink and rising higher than necessary toward the ceiling, which made him think it was designed for a tall guy like himself.

There was a small, cube-shaped wastebasket, lined and half-full on the floor next to the toilet. Widow looked in and saw a red toothbrush tossed in. Underneath it was a woman's shampoo bottle, an empty pack of pink razors, and a crushed tampon box.

Widow lowered the Maxim 9, but kept it in hand, moved away and out of the bathroom. He returned to the closet and checked it.

There was a pair of matching suitcases on rollers pushed up to the inside wall.

On a shelf, next to a shelf with folded ties, was a good amount of expensive-looking jewelry. All for a man, he guessed. There were watches and bracelets and gold chains.

There was one empty shelf, which Widow wondered might've once been for Eva.

He left the closet and left the lights on for a moment.

Then he took a towel and wiped the switch, walked back to the bathroom and wiped that switch as well.

He hadn't touched the handrail on the way up the stairs, so he didn't wipe it on the way down.

At the bottom of the stairs, he saw Gerald was seated on the armchair, facing the kitchen and the body.

Eva stood near him.

She asked, "Anyone there?"

"No. It's empty. Whoever killed him is gone."

"We know who killed him."

Widow said nothing to this.

Gerald asked, "What the hell is going on?"

Widow said, "It's a need-to-know thing. Basically, we're the good guys. And the bad guys did this."

Gerald said nothing, but he didn't have to. The look of fear in his eyes said it all.

Widow walked close to them, kept the Maxim 9 down by his side, and the hand towel in his other hand.

Widow asked, "Who was the last person to come out of here tonight?"

"No one. You guys are it."

"He didn't have any other visitors tonight?"

"I saw no one."

Eva said, "He smells. Maybe he was killed yesterday?"

"Could be," Widow said. "You don't remember anyone coming in and out of here yesterday, either?"

Gerald shook his head, said, "I'm not the only desk guy. I mean, there might've been someone come out, and I wouldn't know. This ain't a bank or nothing. People come and go."

"Someone was here."

Eva asked, "What now?"

"Now, we leave."

"Go where?"

"Not sure, just somewhere else."

"What about him?"

Widow looked at the guard. He said, "Gerald, when's your shift over?"

"Four hours."

"I'm really sorry about doing this to you."

"Wha...What are you going to do?"

"Sorry, but we have to put you somewhere. We can't have you calling the cops when we leave."

"I won't! I swear!"

Widow cocked his head at him, but he said nothing.

"Is there any duct tape in here?" he asked Eva.

"Under the sink. There's a toolbox."

Widow nodded, tucked the gun into the back of his waistband, and went to the sink.

He used the towel as a glove, and opened the cupboard, pulled out the box, set it on the floor.

He popped the top and took out a roll of duct tape. He took Gerald to the downstairs bathroom without incident since he was terrified, and Eva still had her gun out.

He taped the guy up, bound his wrists and feet together, and then put one strip over his mouth. He checked the guy's pockets and pulled out the contents. He placed them on the vanity while he ran another series of tape strips around the guy's feet to the back of the toilet piping, to hold him in place.

Widow scooped and then carried the guy's possessions out to the kitchen and dumped them in the sink. He took the cellphone and held down the home button until the thing went off. He left it on the kitchen countertop.

He returned to the bathroom and shut the door.

Before shutting it, he said, "Don't worry. You'll be safe."

Eva asked, "What do we do?"

"Let's take off. And we can decide somewhere else."

"What about the guard? What if they come back?"

"They won't."

"How do you know that?"

"Would you?"

She shook her head.

They stepped out into the hall. Widow wiped down the doorknobs, both sides of the front door, and tossed the towel back inside the apartment.

He used the guard's key to lock the deadbolt behind them, slid the key into his pocket so he could keep it until he found some place safe to ditch it.

30

Captain Karpov's feet were killing him because he had been zip-tied with his hands out in front of him, and told to stay on his feet.

The submarine dove deep and would remain there for the rest of its mechanical life, right after they surfaced once more, but the captured crew on board didn't know that much.

They were nearing the time when they would surface soon, in a few hours.

Frank Farmer stood still, leaning over a console on the bridge of the submarine. Green lights reflected at him, washing over his face. He stood behind the only member of this team who spoke perfect Russian, as well as knew the controls of the submarine like the back of his hand.

Farmer had never even been onboard a submarine before. He wasn't even sure if he'd be able to handle it because of a slight concern for claustrophobia, but if he could overcome the fear of death, he could deal with a little claustrophobia. No problem.

Farmer stood back up and swiped his brow of sweat as relief overcame him. Which it had—tenfold, if he was honest with himself.

He had been feeling extreme stress because only a moment ago, they'd navigated deep under the surface of the North Atlantic through a cluster of US ships.

At this depth, and without breaking silence, he waited until his go-to submariner gave the all-clear from the scanning equipment of the US ships. Then he walked back to the captain's chair and dumped himself down.

He said, "Mister Kegler, you may take us back on course. We need to get there within the next few hours. Can you manage?"

"Why else would you have brought me along?" Kegler, the man at the screen, asked sarcastically. Sarcasm was a trait of many sailors that he had known in a past life.

Farmer had never been a sailor. He wasn't pleased with the sarcasm, but he ignored it anyway.

"Good. I'm leaving the command to you," Farmer said.

It really had been up to Kegler, to begin with, since Farmer's knowledge of helming a submarine was limited to what he had seen in movies.

"Where are you going?"

Farmer didn't answer him, not directly. Instead, he sat back in the chair for a moment and then got up. He waved at the redheaded guy to follow him.

They walked over to Captain Karpov and stopped.

Karpov had one black eye, swollen shut. Not from a fist, but from the butt end of the redheaded guy's MP4 stock. Two vicious blows to the face. Same eye. Within the same minute. All because Karpov had refused to instruct his crew to follow their orders over the intercom system on board the boat.

But like many of the enemies that Farmer had made in the past, the captain eventually gave in.

It surprised Farmer that it took them shooting his second-in-command and then beating him with the rifle, and then threatening his third-in-command. Who had been identified by Kegler, not just their submarine expert, but also their expert on all things Russian military.

Karpov, giving in to this threat, told Farmer everything that he needed to know about the captain. The way to get him to comply with demands was simply threatening someone else.

How noble! Farmer thought.

He was excited about the next person who he would threaten to Karpov —his own daughter.

"Let's go," the redheaded guy commanded.

Karpov stayed quiet but moved away from the wall where they had put him and walked ahead.

"Stop," the redhead ordered.

Karpov stopped.

Farmer said, "Take us to your quarters."

Karpov didn't argue or speak. He started walking, and they followed.

31

Outside on the sidewalk across the street, the man in black sat on a motorcycle, not one of those known as "hogs" from Harley Davidson, but a faster model from a Japanese brand.

The man was dressed in bikers' attire, no leather, but all black. A cotton-polyester blended jacket, black slacks, and a biker's helmet, with a tinted shield, pulled all the way down. It wasn't used for blocking out the sun, as there was no sun, not in the late-night hours.

The man in black also had a brown satchel that didn't match his fashion ensemble. It hung tight with one strap around one shoulder; the satchel part draped down the small of his back.

The satchel didn't match because he had taken it from Edward's apartment. Only because he needed to take Edward's laptop and smartphone and various memory sticks he'd found lying around.

Perhaps they contained records or notes leading the police, or whoever else, to Edward's connections to the CIA and, eventually, to the man in black and the person he worked for.

The bike's engine hummed and purred underneath him. The low, deep vibrations rattled through his thighs and bones. The bike was well made, but it wasn't made for idling. It was made for driving fast.

Right now, the bike was like a horse showing its rider that it was ready to move, that it was getting restless.

The man in black ignored the bike and waited, but he also felt the restlessness. A major part of his job was waiting. He didn't like this part, but it was necessary.

He was anxious because he had taken the stairwell in and out of the apartment building, disabling the security camera at the bottom of the stairs before he entered, of course. This wasn't a hard act to do, since the damn security was a joke.

Normally, he might've killed the guard behind the desk, but only if there was a threat of the guard being an eyewitness. Here there hadn't been.

The man in black kept his eyes on the entrance to the apartment building and his hands on the bike's handlebar, gripping the clutch, waiting.

He was about to take off after he walked out of the stairwell, because the stairwell's ground exit led straight to a fire door that opened out onto the other intersecting street, perpendicular to the entrance.

On his way out, he noticed a couple standing around the corner, chatting near the entrance to the apartment building.

He only glimpsed them. He stuck around and see if they came back out.

More than just the coincidence of their being there at that late hour was that he saw a bulge in the small of the man's back, a bulge that indicated a gun. Nine times out of ten, anyway.

Under the man in black's coat, in an inside pocket, was an expensive, simple piece of equipment that he used in his job from time to time, a razor-sharp wired garrote with two stainless steel cylinder handles.

It was a tool that was built for only one purpose, murder, and not just any kind of murder. The garrote is a stealth weapon. It's not as fast as a sharp knife to the throat or a bullet to the head or heart, but to the man in black, it was a hell of a lot more satisfying than a gunshot to the temple from a silenced gun, like the one he had in his pocket.

Normally, it was a shiny, clean weapon. At that moment, it was wiped clean, but still had stains of red, thick blood dotted along the wire and some spray on the handles. It needed a deeper cleaning, which the man in black would give it.

This wasn't that time.

He had only been given one target so far to take care of this time, but it had been relayed to him that there were to be no witnesses left alive. This gave him carte blanche to remove the couple as he saw fit.

Just then, he saw them step out, which made their presence more than a coincidence. However, they didn't qualify as eyewitnesses, not the kind that could identify him. So far, they hadn't seen him.

They may have discovered the crime scene. Not cause for panic, not to his mission. After all, it was going to be discovered, eventually. He intended for it to be found.

Edward was dead, and there was no trace of his involvement or sign of who Edward worked for in the apartment. He'd made sure of that.

The first thing that the man in black noticed about the couple who came out of Edward's apartment building was that the man was pretty tall, taller than he had noticed before, probably because the man in black's first instincts were to check for weapons on anyone and everyone new who came across his path, a call back to his training.

Even if this guy had no weapons, he still would be hard to take down, at least in a fair fist fight. But the man in black wasn't accommodating of the rules of engagement in fighting. He wasn't a fighter. He was a killer, which isn't the same thing. Snipers aren't trained to engage in hand-to-hand combat. They're trained to shoot and kill their targets with one shot from a distance. Sure, they're trained to fight up close if need be, but that's a last resort.

The man in black wasn't only an assassin, but this had been the focus of most of his training, which was why he felt pretty stupid that he'd failed to notice the woman first.

His instincts had led him to be a little misogynistic because, naturally, he thought the man was the threat. However, he realized that this wasn't the case after he got a good look at the woman.

The man he had never seen before in his life, but he knew the woman. And she wasn't where she was supposed to be.

32

Widow stepped off the bottom step first and looked right, looked left. He noticed a black van parked across the street. Being black made it suspicious automatically. But what made it stick out to him was that it hadn't been there on their way into Edward's apartment building.

He dismissed the van as nothing more than coincidence as soon as he saw the driver switch on the hazard lights and get out. The lights blinked, red in the back and yellow from the front.

The driver slid the side panel door open, revealing a steel setup with trays of plastic-covered food or baking ingredients, Widow couldn't tell, that were stacked on sliding metal shelves.

The guy was delivering early morning supplies to the back entrance of a corner bakery across the street, opposite the convenience store.

Widow ignored it, checked the rest of the streets and corners.

Steam rose from a sewer grate. A nearby lamppost hummed with electricity from the bright light above. Small groups of pedestrians walked on both sides of the street.

He saw a black shape in the shadows off on the next street. A dark silhouette that looked like a man on a horse to him, only for a moment, until he realized it was a guy riding a bike. Only the bike wasn't being ridden. It was stopped at the intersection—nothing to raise the alarm in Widow's head because the traffic light was red for the guy.

Even with the distance between them, Widow heard the foreign engine buzz and purr, ready to go, impatient by design.

The light turned green, and the guy on the motorcycle paused a long beat, stared at Widow, or so it appeared. Widow couldn't tell because the guy had a black motorcycle helmet over his head, with the shield down, which was the part that made Widow a little uneasy.

The primate part of Widow's brain didn't sound the alarms, but it was just below a code red. Caution was strictly enforced.

Widow kept his eyes on the guy. Even though he couldn't see the guy's eyes, he was certain that the guy was looking back at him as well.

After another long second, the light was still green, and the motorcyclist was still there, staring. Then he looked right, looked left, and turned left, headed away from Widow and Eva.

Eva asked, "What now?"

Widow watched the motorcyclist ride away and turned to her. Looking at her, it hit him why the guy on the motorcycle was staring so hard. Eva was still in that little dress, shivering, even with Widow's sweater over her. Although there was no way the motorcyclist could see the display on top, it was all covered. But he could see her legs. And these were no bony stumps.

Eva's legs looked as if they were strong enough to allow her to leap over parked cars. If she had been taller, she could dunk a basketball easily.

So, of course, the motorcyclist was staring at them. There was something to see.

Widow said, "We need to get some new clothes."

"New?"

"Different. Anyway. You're shaking."

"I'm fine."

"You're shivering."

She said nothing to that.

"Besides, the guys from the hotel will more than likely describe us from what we're wearing. Best to change out of these clothes."

Eva looked him up and down and said, "You think they'll describe you by what you're wearing?"

"No. But for you, they will."

Just then it seemed to dawn on her. She was noticeable. She knew that.

"Where are we going to find clothes at this hour?"

Widow shrugged.

"We could go to my apartment. It's far, though."

"Where?"

"Brooklyn."

Widow thought for a second.

"Nah. We can't go all the way to Brooklyn. Besides, whoever killed Edward probably knows where you live. We should avoid that for now."

"I wouldn't have any clothes for you, anyway."

Although Widow didn't know the exact time of night, he knew it was late, or very early, depending on your point of view.

"What time will your handler be in her office?"

"Probably, eight a.m., at the latest. But why?"

"I think we should have a talk with her. We can do it in the morning. We can stop and buy some clothes on the way. There's bound to be a department store opening somewhere by then."

"Widow, I can't go to her."

He stayed quiet.

"I've been gone for two days. Don't you think she'll want to know why?"

"Then, we tell her."

"I can't tell her I was held against my will."

"Why not? It's the truth."

"I am trying to defect, remember?"

"You don't need to tell her that part."

"What exactly do I tell her?"

Widow said, "We can figure that out. At least I don't see any other choice. Unless you know where to find Farmer, I think we are out of options. Edward is dead."

Eva shook her head and said, "I don't know where to find him."

Widow nodded, changed the subject, and asked, "You like coffee?"

"American coffee?"

He shrugged.

"Not really."

"I'm sure they'll have coffee from south of the border."

A confused expression came over Eva's face.

"South of the border? New Jersey?" Widow smiled and said.

"I like Turkish coffee."

Widow thought back to the last time he was passing through Istanbul. It had been a mission, like so many others. Undercover. And it included a stint sharing a hotel room with a pair of SEALs that he'd never met before, never seen since. They were doing something and waiting for something and passing the time with small talk, deep enough to be interesting, vague enough to keep their anonymity. All three had used names that were aliases, but Widow couldn't be sure about that. He knew for a fact that he had given them a fake name. He figured they had done the same.

He wasn't there to investigate them, but they all had the same mission. And they were told to keep it a secret.

While in Istanbul, he had the local coffee. He remembered they had to boil it in a pot. That was how it was made at home.

It wasn't bad. It wasn't good. To him, it was okay.

Maybe it was better at a café. He wouldn't know, because he never made it to any local cafés.

"Not sure we'll find that at this hour, but we should find somewhere. Get some breakfast and some coffee."

Eva shrugged.

"Let's get away from here."

"Lead the way."

Widow turned inward, left foot first, right foot followed.

Three paces forward, and Eva reached out, took Widow's hand. Hers was cold. He felt that and immediately figured she was trying to warm up. But he wasn't sure. Maybe she was trying to blend in. Her training might've kicked in and told her they should act like a couple.

By the end of the block, he was more confident that was her reasoning because she lifted his arm and ducked underneath it and came up on the other side. His arm draped over her, thick and hanging too long, like a gorilla hugging a spider monkey.

33

THE MAN in black sat on the motorcycle, a couple of blocks away from where he had driven after he had seen the large stranger that he didn't recognize and the woman that he did.

His helmet was off and under his arm. The bike's engine still hummed idly, and he was still sitting on it. It was on the side of the road in an empty parking space with a meter that still took quarters. Not something that was found too much in the city anymore because New York had pulled up those old metal meters and replaced them simply with a sign and a five-digit number intended to work with a smartphone application that allowed the commuter to open, type in the number and the time that he wanted to purchase. Then the app would charge a preset credit card for the amount.

The man in black didn't use such an app, nor did he have quarters for the meter. Nor did he intend to park there.

But he could see the couple walking together in the distance. He was close enough to see them, but far enough back to avoid detection should they look in his direction.

During normal business hours in New York City, he would've lost them easily. But during this time of night, on this side of town, he could keep up with them with little effort.

He set the helmet down on the fuel tank of the bike in front of him and unzipped his jacket. He reached in—right hand. He brushed past a gun in a shoulder rig, no silencer attached, but he had one squeezed into a tight pocket on the chest strap of the holster rig, in case he needed to be silent.

The jacket had two inside pockets. One was velcroed shut, made to hold a cell phone.

He unzipped it and jerked out his phone.

It unlocked as he pressed his thumb down on the home button and called the only number that he had used since he'd arrived in New York.

The phone rang and rang. The person who owned the number was asleep. So he knew it would take a minute before he got an answer.

On the fourth ring, he heard a groggy voice answer.

"Yes?" the voice said, not upset about being woken up, but calm and collected. Still, with surprise, because the call was unscheduled and the man in black was known for being punctual and methodical. He was a by-the-book sort if there was a book on killing people in a cold-blooded fashion, and one existed. He knew because he had been taught from such a book, back in his days of training and statecraft.

The man in black said, "Sorry to wake you."

"What's happened?"

"I'm not sure, but she's out."

"What do you mean?"

"Karpov."

The voice on the other line paused a beat.

"She's out? Freed?"

"Yes."

"You're sure?" the voice asked.

"I'm staring at her. Right now."

"Where?"

"Edward's place."

The voice asked, "What about him?"

"Eliminated."

"Does she know?"

"I'm sure she does. I watched them go in and come out."

"Them?"

"She's with some guy."

"What guy?"

The man in black breathed heavily over the phone, leaving an air of menace. The Listener, on the other end, heard him.

The man in black said, "I don't know. Just some guy. A big guy. Tattoos all over his arms."

"Russian tattoos?"

"Don't know. Don't think so. But I wasn't close enough to see them."

The voice on the phone said, "I don't know who that is. Must be some friend of hers or something."

"I don't know."

"How the hell did she get out?"

"Maybe her friend helped her."

"Maybe. That means she might know about what Farmer was planning."

The man in black stayed quiet.

"Where are they now?"

"Upper East Side."

"You know where they are going?"

"Only one place I can think of," the man in black said, and then he told the person on the other end with only two words.

"Eva's handler."

The voice said nothing.

"Want me to kill them?"

"No. Not yet. We need to know more."

"Want me to intercept them?"

The Listener said, "Not yet. Wait for now. See where they go. They may lead us to her handler. A bonus. Call me if anything changes."

The Listener hung up the phone, and the man in black slipped his phone back in his inside pocket, near his gun. He pulled down the visor on his helmet and watched the Russian spy and the stranger.

34

Eva held a coffee mug of cheap hot tea as if her life depended on it. Even with Widow's sweater pulled over her, the tight dress underneath didn't provide much warmth. Greasy spoons are notoriously cold all day, all night. Widow figured it had something to do with a happy staff over happy customers. The wait staff, the kitchen staff, and whoever else worked back there moved around a lot. They brought this out and took that back. They hauled heavy items from way back in the walk-in cooler and stocked items and took out heavy trashcans. Naturally, they were always hot.

Widow and Eva had originally gone on the search for a bakery or a doughnut shop that was open early enough for them to grab a doughnut and some coffee. Their search took them to an all-night greasy spoon first, which was just fine with Widow. He liked these places.

Nowadays, lots of doughnut shops and bakeries are parts of franchises. They were restaurants designed to look quaint, but truthfully they had bigger corporate faces—not all of them, but many, and many here in the city.

Widow was glad to find a diner locally owned instead.

Eva wasn't interested in coffee; she said it wasn't her thing. She asked the waitress for some kind of herbal green tea crap with three different names. All were plants that Widow had heard of before. All sounded healthy, in that overboard kind of way.

It was the last nail in the coffin of a fantasy that was birthed in his head about him being her kind of guy.

Eva was a refined woman and a Russian spy, which Widow wasn't sure meant that she had been trained to be refined or if she had been born that way, reared that way.

Either answer didn't matter, because she was refined now. And a refined woman wouldn't be interested in a man like him.

Widow said, "You sure you want nothing to eat?"

She looked up from her tea, and he stared into her eyes. There was something there. A sense of desperation, Widow figured. Like she was part scared, part worried, and part completely confused, all of it adding up to utter desperation.

She said, "No, thanks. I have no appetite."

"You really should eat something."

She stayed quiet.

"In the SEALs, we say if you want to eat an elephant, eat it one bite at a time."

She stared at him blankly, which was a better expression than her desperate look. He guessed.

"What does that have to do with eating?"

Widow shrugged and said, "Nothing."

"What the hell does it mean, then?"

"It's a metaphor."

"You mean idiom," she said.

He shrugged again, his shoulders fell, and he took a pull from his coffee.

"Same thing. I suppose," he said.

"So what does it mean? Idioms are strange to me. English has too many."

"I guess we have a lot of them."

"What's it mean?"

"It just means that if you want to achieve something, something huge, like an elephant, then you have to take small steps toward it. I guess. That's what I always thought it meant."

"Makes sense."

Widow took another large pull from his coffee and finished it, and put the mug down on the edge of the table. An old trick Widow had learned years earlier. Put the mug down on the edge of the table, and the waitress thinks it's empty, and she comes by to refill it, like a white flag of surrender. He figured.

Eva stared at him and looked away, toward a group of four older ladies who walked in from the cold. All white, grandmotherly types. All wore their Sunday best, which made sense because, to them, it was early morning. And old ladies across the globe often go to church on Sunday morning.

Right then, Widow realized something that he should have thought of an hour earlier when they were standing in Edward's apartment. He literally face-palmed himself.

"What is it?" Eva asked.

"Today's Sunday."

"Yeah?"

"Sunday."

Widow explained what he was thinking, but he didn't have to. She got it.

Eva said, "She won't be there today."

They had planned to go see her handler, a lawyer who worked near the United Nations building, but law firms aren't normally open on Sunday. That was basically true all over the world, not just in New York City.

"Shit," she said.

"Do you know where she lives?"

"Nope."

"She doesn't trust you very much."

"She doesn't trust anyone. She's been in America for a long time. I guess there's a reason for that."

"I guess so."

"What now?"

"Do you have a phone number for her?"

"Of course."

"I guess we call her then. Have her meet us somewhere."

"Okay. When do we call her?"

Widow looked over Eva's shoulder, searched the room for a wall clock, but didn't see one.

He saw a waitress look over at him while he looked around. She saw his empty coffee mug, and she stepped back behind the counter, picked up a pot of black coffee, and walked over to their table.

She stopped and poured coffee into his mug. Then she stepped back and picked up the empty plate that Widow had eaten a breakfast meal off. The plate looked licked clean, which he hadn't actually done, but he had used a fork to scoop, scrape, and shovel up every drop of eggs and hash browns.

The waitress asked, "Ready for the check now?"

Widow said, "We are. And what time is it?"

The waitress pulled a handwritten check out of her apron, placed it upside down on the tabletop, center edge. Then she fidgeted with a loose wristwatch and stared at it.

"It's almost five in the morning."

"Thanks."

The waitress walked away, and Widow took the check, studied the amount, and shoveled out the correct bills for it, as well as an additional five-dollar bill as a tip.

"It's too early to call now. Let's wait a little longer and call her."

"She's probably still not going to be awake."

"Doesn't matter. We'll wake her up. This is important. Besides, you're not going back."

"What do you mean?"

"You can't go back to your old life now. She's gonna figure out what you were planning, whether or not you tell her."

The look of worry overcame her other facial expressions.

She said, "Widow, they'll kill me. I can't tell her."

"You're safe now. Don't worry. You're not going back with her. She won't tell Moscow that you were planning to defect. Trust me."

"How do you know?"

"If she's been here for twenty years, then she won't want to be exposed. We threaten to tell that she's here. That she's a Russian spy."

She nodded and listened.

"And I don't mean we tell the Feds. We threaten to tell the *New York Times*. Her law firm must have a website. I bet she has a profile there with a headshot. She's probably got a LinkedIn profile too. We take her information and her photos and threaten to give them to the *Times*. They love stories like this. Her face will be blasted all over the place. The Feds will deport her. She'll be forced to return to Moscow, where she doesn't want to be."

Eva nodded, said, "That could work. I know for a fact she's terrified of losing her life here. She loves her status. In Moscow, they'll have her sitting behind a desk. If she's lucky."

"See. We can do this. We can figure this out."

"I'm not worried about me that much. I'm worried about my father. What if they have him?"

Widow said, "We don't know that for sure."

But he knew it for sure. If she had been abducted for two days and this Farmer guy was supposed to arrange a meeting with her father on board his submarine, it had probably already happened.

Farmer had already shown that he had the manpower. Four well-trained guys with high-tech equipment had revealed themselves to Widow already, back at the Plaza.

Plus, the dead guy that Eva had been dating, the turncoat. Whoever had killed him wasn't an amateur. Widow pictured Edward's dead body in his mind. The guy was shorter than Widow, but he had been no kind of slouch. He could pass as a New York firefighter, as he had pretended to be. His dead body showed that he had spent some time in the gym.

The killer had used a garrote. Widow was sure about that because of the deep wounds around Edward's neck.

Garrotes weren't the kind of weapons that could be bought at a hardware store or even a gun store or any store. Maybe it could be ordered off the internet. Or it could have been homemade.

Either way, the person who used it was strong and knew exactly what he was doing. Widow figured that the only way the killer could have strangled Edward like that was with a quick snag of the wire over Edward's head, from behind, then a fast turn from the feet and hips and a pull in the opposite direction, taking Edward off his feet.

The killer had wrenched him over his back, facing the opposite direction.

Strangling someone with a garrote is very difficult. Besides taking immense strength and coordination, it also has a huge risk factor when the victim has his hands and feet free.

Edward would've been flailing around and struggling to fight back. That's not what you want when using a garrote.

The killer would want him immobilized, and the only way to do that was to tie him up or to twist and hoist him over the killer's back like a guy with a meat hook towing a heavy chunk of beef.

Widow imagined the entire scene, and it was brutal. Edward had gone out with a violent death that Widow didn't want to experience.

Eva asked, "What are you thinking about?"

"I think we gotta get you into warmer clothes soon," he lied.

"I'm okay for now. I've worn less in colder places."

Widow smiled, and they sat there, waiting for the dawn.

35

THE WATERS off the Eastern Seaboard were cold, but the crew inside Karpov's hijacked Russian submarine hadn't known that by the sense of touch. They knew it from being educated about it because not one of them had ever been this close to the United States before.

Technically, they weren't breaking international law, which stated that the boundary between a nation's shores and international waters was universally accepted as twelve nautical miles. They weren't in violation of this law. However, the United States Navy was known for suspecting any foreign vessel that came anywhere within double that amount. And for Russian submarines, with nuclear-tipped missiles on board, the number of nautical miles was triple, if not more.

Farmer waited for his man to give the go-ahead, and then he climbed the ladder, past the tower, and up to the surface.

Karpov was still standing against an unmanned station on the bridge. The redheaded soldier had assigned one of his guys to watch over Karpov.

Karpov remembered the redheaded soldier saying, "If he flinches, shoot him."

Ever since then, the soldier watching him had done nothing else but blink a few times. Karpov knew for sure that's all he had done because he watched the soldier in exchange. He studied the man's patterns, trying to discern a rhythm to his standing there, breathing, and guarding Karpov.

Farmer had taken away Karpov's gun and his bridge crew's weapons as well. And of course, Travkin had gone overboard and was dead. But there was one last handgun that Farmer and his men didn't find. It was in Karpov's quarters. It was an old black-and-brown US Army issued Colt 1911. Supposedly left in Eastern Berlin by a US paratrooper on some covert mission that Karpov didn't know the details of.

The gun had been given to him as a gift by a now-dead Russian commander that he used to know.

He had the gun encased in a box with a glass lid. It was on display in his quarters, on the back wall. There were seven bullets lined up at the bottom of the case on the red velvet behind the gun.

Colt made good-quality guns. He knew that. If the origins of his Colt 1911 were true, then it was over seventy years old. Would it even fire after all this time? Under normal circumstances, probably not. But one of his favorite stress relievers was to take out that 1911 and polish it and clean it and oil it.

Although he had never fired it, not with live ammunition, he had dry fired it before—plenty of times. And it seemed to work.

If only he could get to it.

36

FARMER LOOKED AT HIS WATCH, which luckily was waterproof because the waves ripped and collided with the bow of the submarine, splashing over it with powerful, quick gushes of white-capped water.

In one wrong moment, a wave could have swept him and the redheaded soldier off the bow and into the Atlantic.

They both held onto the railing above the hatch that led down to the bridge. The water splashed hard enough to send droplets beating across their faces.

Farmer's blue windbreaker rippled around him from the intense icy wind blowing off the ocean surface.

He took several deep breaths, trying to adjust his lungs to the cold air.

Then he pulled a sat phone up from a long cord that hung around his neck. The cord secured it so that it wouldn't get blown away. With one hand on the rail and one hand on the keypad, he dialed a number from memory, starting the call that was slightly early.

Still, the recipients of the call would answer because they were already in play. And they worked for him. They had better be awake and waiting, even though in New York City it was early in the morning.

Farmer listened as the satellite phone whirred and rang. The connection was there, but the sound quality was closer to a CB radio than a ten-thousand-dollar phone stolen from the US military.

The phone rang and rang and rang. No one answered.

THE MIDNIGHT CALLER 169

Farmer waited, looked at the redheaded soldier.

No one answered.

He hung up.

"What?" the redhead asked.

Farmer shrugged and said, "No answer."

"Try again."

Farmer tried again. Same result. Same frustration.

"They are supposed to answer. They know that."

"What now?" the redheaded guy asked.

Farmer didn't answer. Instead, he dialed another number and put the phone to his ear, listened to the ring.

A voice answered that wasn't asleep. The voice sounded rested and awake, but frustrated as well.

"We have a problem," Farmer said.

"The girl is free," the Listener answered. The Listener already knew the circumstances.

"What?"

"She is free. Your boys messed up."

"How do you know that?"

"My guy. He saw her. On the street, outside Edward's apartment."

Farmer asked, "Why was he at Edward's?"

"Why do you think?"

A pause and a cold breath exited Farmer's lips.

He said, "You didn't need to kill him."

"Apparently, I did. I'm tying up loose ends. Your loose ends."

"How the hell did she get free? My guys aren't answering."

"She escaped."

"Impossible. She had four former Special Forces guys with her."

"She got away from them."

Farmer repeated the same protest of disbelief.

The Listener said, "She had help."

"What help?"

"I don't know. Some stranger."

"Who is he?"

"I just told you. He's a stranger."

Farmer said nothing.

The Listener said, "Don't worry. My guy is watching them."

"He needs to retrieve her. Now."

"We can't do that. She's out in the open, and we don't know who this guy is. What if he's FBI? We need to know who knows what first."

"Have your guy pick them both up. Interrogate him."

The Listener said, "Not that simple. It's New York City. There are witnesses everywhere."

"So, what then?"

"Don't worry. He'll get them both soon enough. They're bound to go somewhere more private."

"What about the operation? We need her to make Karpov cooperate."

"Does he know that we have her, yet?"

"I'm sure he's put it together. I wanted to have him hear her voice before I threatened him. Better impact that way."

The Listener said, "Time to change your tactics. Make the threat so we can stay on schedule."

"Karpov is a tough man. A smart man. He won't give up the launch code without proof of life."

The Listener said nothing to that. Instead, he said, "Just do it. My guy will have them soon, and we'll prove it to Captain Karpov if he so wishes. We have little time left. I want that missile in the air on schedule, Farmer."

"I'll have it done."

"Good. Don't give me your location over the line. But are you within the preferred striking distance?"

"Almost."

"Good. Get moving then."

"I'll call you back later."

Farmer hung up the phone.

The Listener clicked the cell phone off and laid it down on a desk, tried to relax. A yawn. A stretch. And the Listener was more alert again.

The operation had had a couple of hiccups, but it was going to happen. And no stranger or Russian was going to stop it.

37

Widow and Eva ended up walking around for over an hour. They had left the diner, and Widow had taken a full cup of coffee to go. He'd finished it long ago, and they had to stop once more at an early morning coffee stand on the side of the street to get another coffee for him.

Eva kept her hands free but had them wrapped up inside Widow's sweater.

She stayed close to him as they walked, partially for warmth, and partially for other reasons that he didn't completely dismiss, but also wasn't ready to believe were true.

The sun had come up, and usual morning activities had begun.

First, they saw the early risers hitting the streets. They saw the morning joggers coming out of their apartments. They saw the first shifts of first responders coming on and then the third shifts signing off. They saw fresh-faced cops driving their routes, getting coffee, preparing for the day.

They saw twice the number of stores and diners opening up. The street-lights switched off all at once, and the birds chirped.

Widow and Eva found themselves in the East Village, walking in circles after a while.

"Widow, I don't think department stores are open on Sunday morning. I think most of them don't open till noon, maybe eleven, but not this early."

"I'm sure we'll find something. Have faith."

Eva said, "You know we've walked this street before?"

"I know. See that van right there?"

She looked. There was a rented yellow panel van, parked in front of a small clothing store that looked half empty.

"What about it?"

"That's what we're looking for."

"What is it?"

They were coming up on the parked van from about ten yards away.

"It's an opportunity."

Widow led the way, and they walked over to a small store that was about the size of the First Lady's closet and not much bigger. The windows were tinted black enough to be the shades on a Secret Service agent's sunglasses. There was no visible sign for the store, only where it used to be above the door. There was the sun-bleached outline of letters. It was a name that Widow couldn't completely spell, because some letters were undecipherable. Not that he was trying too hard.

The name of the store wasn't important to him. What was important was what they sold.

"Widow?"

He pointed at a handwritten paper taped to the door and read it to her.

"They're going out of business."

"Do you think they'll sell us clothes?"

"I'm sure of it," Widow said, as they both saw stacks of open boxes with folded clothing hanging out.

They were greeted by a young couple. Both tattooed. Both had huge smiles on their faces. Both were busy moving things and packing things and telling two other guys to pack this or move that to the van. Hired help, Widow figured.

* * *

THE MAN in black circled past the parked van and the stranger and Eva twice. They had been in the store for almost an hour.

They were shopping for something. He knew that. But he was confused as to why?

He ended up parking down the street and waiting.

Finally, the stranger appeared first, and then Eva. And he knew exactly what they were doing because they both came out with new clothes on, which he figured was only a tactical decision for the girl. She hadn't been wearing any kind of field clothing, after all.

He watched them shake hands with a young couple, and then they left, headed for First Avenue and moving north.

The man in black started up his bike and followed as slowly as he could, staying back, staying way back because he knew the Russian was trained and obviously, the stranger must have been as well. At least he must have been dangerous.

He stayed as close to them as he could without being spotted until they came to the entrance to a metro station and ducked down the stairs into New York City's underbelly, which meant he had to follow them on foot.

He parked his bike, abandoning it in front of a fire hydrant. Illegal he knew, but what choice did he have? This was New York City. Sunday morning. The weather was crisp, but warming up with the sun, and early morning pedestrians were coming out to enjoy it. There was no parking available, and he would lose them if he searched for some.

He followed them down the steps into the tunnels of New York's subway system.

38

Eva wore all black.

They had told the couple that they needed some very comfortable clothes. When asked how comfortable, Widow had responded that it should be durable, comfortable, warm, and good for "night work."

The man had chuckled out loud to this comment, even though Widow was serious.

They played it off, and the guy helped Widow, while his wife helped Eva. It had turned out that the couple had moved to New York City with a dream of expanding their little shop into a franchise and a clothing brand.

The woman designed the clothes, and the man had obviously been in love with her about as much as Widow had ever seen in a married couple.

It also turned out that she was three months pregnant, and sales weren't going according to plan. However, the new addition to their family meant that neither of them was sad that they were being forced to close the shop and move back to Kansas or Indiana or wherever they had said that they were from.

Widow ended up in all black as well. Black jeans. Black t-shirt under a black hoodie that zipped up and had space in the pockets for one of the Maxim guns. The other he gave back to Eva, who stuffed it into a black bag that she had purchased.

The bag slung over her back like a backpack; only she had informed Widow it was a purse. He didn't argue.

They purchased their metro passes from a machine and entered the underground system.

"How do we get to the right street?" Widow asked.

She shot him a questionable look.

"What?"

"You don't know?"

"I'm not a local."

"Still, doesn't everyone know the metro in New York?"

"I don't. I've only used it once."

"What do you use, Uber?"

"I've used that once."

"How? You don't have a phone?"

"Someone else's phone."

"Old girlfriend?" she asked, and led him into the small crowd of commuters as they crisscrossed people going either.

"No. An FBI agent actually."

"FBI? Were you FBI?"

"I said it was someone else's Uber. She was an FBI agent."

Eva said nothing else about it and pointed down the tunnel.

"We're taking the sixth train. To Grand Central Station and then we'll transfer to head toward the United Nations."

Widow nodded and felt her warm hand take his. She led him farther, which distracted him, and he didn't see the man in black following behind them.

39

The Listener sat behind an office desk in a building that wasn't as busy as it was during the week because it was Sunday. The plan didn't include being in the office today. The plan had been to deal with everything from home since that was a quiet place with no family members around. No distractions. No significant other.

The Listener had no real friends here, anyway. Although there were plenty of colleagues who thought they held the title of friend. But to the Listener, that's all they were, colleagues—nothing more and nothing less.

It had been time for Russia to return to the good old days.

The Listener, the man in black, and Farmer, and the men at their command were dedicated to this.

The Listener had military training and counterintelligence training, and experience to boot. Most Americans that came and went throughout the Listener's daily life had no idea what it meant to live back when the Soviet Union was strong and powerful. Back when it and the United States were great enemies. That was when everything was great. That was the time to be alive. That was when it meant something to be a warrior, fighting for good, fighting for your country.

Today, globalization had changed everything. In today's world, the enemy was also your friend.

Russia and the United States were allies, who covertly waged war against each other, all at the same time. What the hell was that? What kind of state of affairs was this?

The Listener and the man in black and CIA agent Farmer were all on the same page on this front.

They were all tired of the world being so weak and gray.

The balance of power was gone. All three of them knew that. They knew that there was no more "balance."

The scales had been tipped in favor of the United States long ago. There was no enemy to fight. No opposition.

Politicians in DC and Moscow went on and on about terrorists. Terrorists were the new enemies. The militaries of both countries must fight terrorists. But what kind of enemy was that? What kind of war can be fought against so-called soldiers, most of whom can't even read?

It was a slap in the face to the Listener. It was a shot to the heart.

Experience told the Listener that most so-called enemy terrorists didn't even know the difference between right and left.

Afghanistan was a country that both the United States and Russia had fought in for decades. The Russians got there first, but both had been there for what seemed like forever. Fighting there was a complete waste of time. Most of the enemies they fought there knew nothing about warfare. They had little technology. They had no grasp of world affairs. They were below under-educated.

To the Listener and the rest of the operation heads, what they were doing was a necessary action.

The Listener looked at the clock and date on a cell phone screen. It was November ninth. It was a Sunday, and the time was nearing eight in the morning.

It was the day of the anniversary. It was the day of a restart of hostility between Russia and the US. It was the day that the Listener had been planning for a long time.

The Listener texted the man in black.

"Where are they now?" The message read.

A moment later, the message was answered with: "Going to subway. Headed to the United Nations is my guess."

The Listener read the message and took a sip of coffee from a mug on the desk. Then responded with, "No. They're headed to a law office nearby."

A moment later, there was another messaged response.

"You sure?"

The Listener typed back, "It's where her handler works. It's good. It means the stranger is a nobody."

The man in black typed back, "How so?"

The Listener responded with, "If he was a Fed, they wouldn't be going to the Russian spy handler for help. He has no backup. He really is a nobody."

And then the Listener paused a beat and sent another text that read: "Get a photo of them."

A couple of moments later, a message came back with three images attached. They weren't the best quality, all from a distance, with people moving in and out of frame. And all were taken with the zoom on a cell phone, which isn't the best resolution to begin with.

The Listener studied them. He looked hard at the stranger's face. A feeling of partial recognition, a stir of familiarity, and a sense of the kind of man the stranger was—came to mind. But he had no tangible memory of the stranger.

The Listener got more of a feeling of déjà vu. The Listener had never met the stranger. But something was identifiable about the stranger.

The Listener knew exactly what it was. The stranger had a long military career, possibly more.

Another text came through. It read: "Want me to retire them?"

The Listener typed: "Yes," but paused a beat and then backspaced and typed over it. The text read: "Forget them. We know where they're going. Go to the hotel. Wake up Farmer's men. We might need them. Be careful."

A moment later, the man in black responded with: "You too."

40

WIDOW AND EVA got off at the Grand Central Terminal, and Widow pointed out a payphone and reminded Eva that they should call her handler and get her to meet them. At first, the handler protested because it was a Sunday. In the end, she gave in and agreed to meet.

Afterward, Eva hung up the phone, and they exited the terminal and walked east down Forty-Second Avenue toward the river, where they turned at the United Nations building. Widow took in the row of flags and admired the building that had been built with good intentions. He was suddenly reminded of the cliché that the road to hell is paved by them.

Eva ignored it, probably because she had been there and seen that.

The temperature was warming up a little from light jacket to long-sleeve weather.

Widow asked, "Do you normally meet with her at her office?"

"No. I've been there before. People think she helps me with my green card. She helps a lot of Russians. She's an immigration lawyer. It's a perfect cover."

"Are all of her clients Russian spies?"

Eva smiled, said, "Of course. All of them are just like me. Beautiful seductresses here to take over your country."

Widow tittered but embraced the thought, anyway. He realized that if there were thousands of Russian spies that were just like her, the men in this city were in deep trouble.

They pressed on until they were close, but Widow never stopped checking the surrounding buildings, windows, entrances, and sidewalks. He looked at as many faces as he could of pedestrians, both on foot and on bicycles. He looked at the drivers of cars and at people sitting on benches, reading newspapers. He took particular interest in anyone using a cell phone. There was no one who stood out to him as out of place. No detectable surveillance. No men with earpieces. No dark, unmarked vans. Nothing.

Of course, in a place like New York City, Widow couldn't be sure. No one could. It was too crowded. Too many faces to vet. Vetting everyone that you come across on the streets of New York as a non-threat was impossible.

They came to the law offices, which were in a building complex with other firms and offices. The building was ten stories of brushed steel and shiny glass.

"This is it," Eva said.

"When is she going to get here?"

"Soon. She said twenty minutes."

"She must live nearby then."

"I guess. We wait then."

"Is there a café in the lobby?"

"There's a little cart thing."

Widow smiled, said, "Let's get some coffee."

"You drink a lot of coffee!"

He shrugged.

"Aren't you scared of a heart attack?"

"No. A beating heart isn't likely to have a heart attack."

"But isn't that coffee making it beat faster?"

"Better to beat fast than slow."

"Or not at all, I guess," she said.

They walked through a set of automatic doors and waved at a guard sitting behind a desk. This one was more alert and friendly than the one from Edward's building, which reminded Widow of the guard that they'd left duct-taped inside Edward's apartment. He wondered how long it would be before someone found him. He would have to remember to make an anonymous call to the NYPD about him when this was all done, if it was ever done.

They waved back at the guard, who seemed to recognize Eva, and smiled at her.

"He remembers me," she said.

"How could he ever forget?" Widow muttered under his breath.

"What was that?"

"Nothing. Where's the coffee?"

Eva pointed to an offshoot of the lobby, and they walked down it to grab a coffee and wait for her contact to arrive.

41

THE MAN in black kicked the guy that he knew to be in charge of the babysitting mission. The guy didn't budge. He lay on the floor, unconscious.

"Wake up!" the man in black said.

No movement.

One snored loudly. Another tossed and turned. All four of them had rapid eye movements, like they were in deep dreams.

The man in black went to the bathroom to find the team's black kit, which was where they kept the sedatives, needles, and smelling salts.

It wasn't in the bathroom. But he found signs of where the Russian girl had been kept. He wondered why they didn't have eyes on her at all times.

They were amateurs. For the first time, he questioned the Listener's logic in hiring them. Then again, the operation that they were running didn't lend itself to having a variety of options. They couldn't just ask any old mercenary to take part.

He searched the rest of the room and found the kit and, in it, the smelling salts.

He cracked the bottle open and shoved it under the nose of the man in charge of this group.

A loud gasp, followed by violent wrenching and coughing, erupted from the guy. His eyes darted open, and a look of utter confusion spilled across his face, which lasted for a whole minute. Then the realization hit him.

He sat up.

"Where is she? There was a guy. Some guy came in. He took us all down."

"Forget about that. I know all of it."

"Where are they?"

"At her handler's office."

The leader looked up at the man in black and didn't know him.

"Who are you?"

"I'm the one to set you straight. Now wake up the others. We don't have a lot of time."

"I'll make this up. We'll make it up."

"Don't worry. You'll have your chance. Now wake them up."

The man in black handed the rest of the smelling salts bottle to him. The guy took it and stood up, wobbly.

The man in black asked, "Where are your guns? Did he take them?"

The leader nodded.

"You got backups?"

"There are MP5s under the bed."

The man in black bent down and pulled out a large carry-on case. He unzipped it and found a stack of silenced MP5s. Right off the bat, he was embarrassed that they had them stacked inside the case with nothing holding them down. They looked used and worn and not very well maintained.

How unprofessional, he thought.

It took about twenty minutes to get all the men awake and on their feet and standing up straight.

The man in black messaged the Listener, "They're ready."

A moment later, the Listener messaged back with only an address and the name of a law firm. Then one more line of text. It read: "Take the girl alive. No witnesses."

42

THE INSIDE of the lobby was too cold for the weather outside the building, in Widow's opinion, but lobbies in emotionless steel office parks were like that in a lot of cities. They were faceless and callous and unremarkable. The management liked to keep them cold, so the workers didn't fall asleep. Office park management was like any other corporate management; it was all about productivity.

Suddenly, Widow didn't miss having a job.

Eva left him in a tight corner, near a generic plant and a small coffee table, to enjoy his coffee alone. She went to the restroom down the hall. So far, he hadn't enjoyed his coffee at all because it came in a little paper cup, and the damn thing was four bucks. That was more expensive than the Tall at Starbucks, which was the standard for overpriced coffee.

Whatever, he thought, and took a swig. Might as well drink it before it gets cold.

Eva was gone for more than five minutes. He'd nearly finished the coffee before she finally returned.

She stopped at the same café and bought a doughnut, which was a far cry from her previous statement of not being hungry. Apparently, she had been starving because she scarfed the entire thing by the time she sat down.

Widow smiled and asked, "Hungry?"

She laughed and smiled at him, mouth open. He saw nothing but white powdered sugar and her teeth.

"Was that a doughnut?"

"Yeah, a powdered sugar doughnut."

"Isn't that a lot of sugar?" he asked.

She shrugged and smiled so widely that powder was tumbling out of her mouth.

He reached over and handed her the napkin that he had been given.

"Here."

"Oh. Sorry." She took it and wiped her mouth.

Widow said nothing.

Eva finished chewing and swallowing, but kept the napkin handy. Then she asked, "So, Jack Widow, you married?"

"No way."

She made an audible, "Hmm." And a gesture like she was trying to think or make a life decision.

"What?"

"Why did you answer like that?"

"Like what?"

She said, "No way." Only she said it theatrically, like she was doing a dramatic reenactment of the whole thing. Then she reached across and poked him in the abdomen.

Widow didn't wonder if she was flirting with him. That was obvious, even to the one-tracked mind that he considered himself to be. What he wondered was if she was doing it on purpose, or if it was Russian seductress training.

He stayed quiet for a moment, and then he said, "I didn't mean it negatively about marriage. It was just a reaction."

"So, have you ever been married?"

Widow shook his head.

"Me neither."

They fell silent for a moment. Widow finished his coffee. He thought about a refill but saw a sign that said: "No Refills. Or Refunds."

He wouldn't shell out another four bucks for another little coffee that wasn't very good to begin with.

Just then, a woman a little older than Widow walked in. She wore a sweater that had a Russian university written on it, one that Widow couldn't pronounce because it wasn't in English. He knew it was a university sweater by the typical design. Although he supposed he could have been wrong. The sweater was red with gold piping and a single stripe.

The woman had thick, long hair, dark with thin gray streaks. It was pulled back. She had a dark complexion. No jewelry. No rings. No neck-laces. The only piece of jewelry was an expensive-looking watch with a plain black leather band and silver face that might have been real silver.

She looked straight at Eva and then right at Widow and waved them to come over.

Eva said, "Come on. That's her."

Widow stood up after Eva and stayed several feet behind to throw his coffee cup away. He caught up to them after the women hugged like old friends.

They spoke to each other in Russian, something that Widow didn't catch, nor would he have understood anyway.

Then Eva turned back to Widow and introduced him. She introduced the lawyer as Mina Putin, and then she insisted that there was no relation to the president of Russia.

Widow didn't doubt her claims, nor did he rule out that she was lying either. Putin was a common surname in Russia.

After a quick moment of shaking hands and smiling, Putin asked them to follow her up to her office. Before they could go to where the elevators were, Widow stopped dead in his tracks.

Eva asked, "Widow, what's wrong?"

He glanced at her and then at a large plastic doorframe that was hooked up to wires that vanished into the guard desk. It was set up between them and the elevators that they had to walk through in order to get there.

He stepped up and leaned into her and whispered, "Metal detector."

"Oh. Step over there. One second, Mina."

Widow stepped back to the lobby, and Eva followed. Then Eva passed him and headed back toward the bathroom, out of the line of sight of the guard at the desk. She surreptitiously drew the Maxim 9 out of her jeans and slipped it to him.

She said, "Take them to the bathroom and hide them behind a toilet tank. Then come up and meet us on floor six. It's the last office down the hall."

Widow nodded and left her and stepped into the bathroom to hide the weapons as instructed, which reminded him he was taking orders from Eva and not questioning them.

43

THE MAN in black stepped off his motorcycle, which was in the parking garage underneath the Russian lawyer's office park, alongside a white panel van. The doors to the panel van opened, and the four mercenaries working for Farmer hopped out. They were armed with four MP5SDs. They were cocked and locked and ready to go. A sight that the man in black was glad to see.

Even though that might have all been a little overkill, they had all been defeated by one man, so he could forgive their eagerness for redemption.

The leader of the mercs nodded at the man in black, and he led them toward a set of elevators. They almost made it to the elevators when a voice from down a few car spaces called out, "Hey. Who are you guys?"

The man in black turned to see a young security guard walking toward them. He had a flashlight in one hand. It was switched off, and the man in black wondered why he was even holding it. He must have intended to use it as a club if need be.

The man in black said nothing. He didn't talk their way past him. He simply reached in his coat and drew his SIG Sauer P220, not silenced, and he took aim, slowly and carefully.

The guard stopped and stared on.

"Wait! Wait!" he called out.

The man in black paused, closed one eye, and aimed down the sights. He wondered if he could still make a shot from that distance.

The young security guard dropped his flashlight and turned and ran, his boots stomping down hard, echoing in the underground garage.

The man in black waited until the last second and squeezed the trigger —one shot.

The bullet missed the bullseye, but not his target. He had aimed for center mass, an easier target from that distance with a handgun, but he had hit dead on the back of the guard's head. He knew that because a red mist erupted and brain and skull fragments exploded out from the other side. The bullet went clean through.

Not a bad shot, he thought, even with mediocre odds.

He pulled the gun back, wisps of smoke coiled out of the barrel. He paused for it to clear and holstered the weapon.

"Let's go," he said.

Farmer's mercenaries followed him to the elevator. He saw the security camera above the elevator. It was the only one.

He shrugged at it. It was no concern. He figured that the building was probably empty except for minimal staff and the targets.

He pressed the button to call the elevator and waited.

After the bell dinged and the elevator doors opened, and they all stepped on, he said, "Shoot to kill. Everyone but the girl. We need her back. Got it?"

Farmer's mercenaries all verbally acknowledged the order, and the man in black studied a sign behind a plastic panel with a list of all the offices in the building. He found the Russian lawyer's name and pressed the button for the sixth floor.

The doors shut.

44

WIDOW FINISHED HIDING the weapons and stopped to use the bathroom, since he was already in there. *Always take advantage of any situation,* he thought.

He washed his hands and dried them and headed back to the door. He stepped out of the men's room and turned the corner, back to the lobby. As he made eye contact with the guard behind the front desk, they both paused a beat because they heard a loud *BOOM!* that echoed from somewhere in the building.

Widow asked, "What the hell was that?"

The guard shrugged and said, "Car backfiring. There's a parking garage below us."

Widow nodded and stepped up to the desk.

"I'm going through now."

The guard looked at him, cockeyed, and said, "Okay. Go through. They're on six."

Widow nodded, stepped through the metal detector. It didn't buzz.

He walked over to the elevator and heard the motors humming as one elevator ascended the floors.

He clicked the call button and waited for the next one.

45

Eva remained standing in Putin's office, which she had been in a dozen times before. Usually, she sat across from her at the desk, without batting an eye. But this time, she stood because Putin kept a small silenced SR1MP pistol in her top desk drawer. The SR1MP was a lightweight pistol, popular with some Russian forces. It was good for covert operators because of its size and power.

Eva told her what had happened, but Putin stopped her with a hand up.

She said, "Eva. What have you done?"

Eva stayed quiet, and Putin sat alone.

"Yesterday, your father's submarine went dark and hasn't been heard from since. You have vanished for two days. I have tried to call you. I'm getting distressing questions from Moscow. What the hell have you done?"

Eva said, "I'm sorry. I had to help my father."

"What's happened?"

Before Eva could speak or explain, the door to the office slammed open like it had been kicked in by a SWAT team. Eva assumed it was Widow. She turned, and Putin stood up, fast.

"What is this!" she asked.

Five men came pouring into the office. They were armed with MP5SDs.

Like they were in sync, both women felt surprise and then terror. It wasn't the men with guns that scared Putin. For her, it was the fact that the MP5SDs were silenced. She had been in the US for twenty years, working successfully as both a lawyer and as a spy for the Russian government. She had been trained long ago. But one lesson that she knew for sure was that men with submachine guns and suppressors didn't have the best intentions. The local police didn't use suppressors. Neither did the FBI or any other law enforcement agency that she was aware of. Only two types of people would have them: soldiers and mercenaries. And soldiers wouldn't be barging into her office.

The reason Eva was terrified wasn't the guns or the suppressors. What terrified her was that she recognized the four men who had kidnapped her.

The man in black stepped forward and spoke.

He was a short man, not tiny, but for the type of men that she normally found herself in the company of, he was short. Maybe he was five foot eight, but he looked taller because he wore boots with significant heels. He wore all black, which made her think he was some kind of biker, only missing a helmet.

He had graying hair with black weaved in. It was thick and curly. He was white, but there was something else there. Maybe Latin. Maybe some kind of Native American, but whatever it was made up a small percentage of his ethnicity.

Even though the man in black was the shortest of the five, he looked amazingly strong. His chest was wide, but not overdone. It was like a cinder block, not a barrel.

Eva had never seen him before. But she recognized he was some sort of leader here. It wasn't Farmer. There was another man in charge. Right off, she recognized he wasn't the brains. He couldn't have been. He came off more like a weapon than a leader.

The man in black said, "Ms. Karpov. Ms. Putin. It's a pleasure to meet you both. Ladies, please sit."

The women glanced at each other and sat uncomfortably.

Putin asked, "Who the hell are you? How did you get in here?"

"Ms. Karpov, you've caused us grief. I've been chasing after you all damn night."

Eva said nothing.

The man in black looked at her. He looked at her fingertips. They rested on her lap. They trembled, which made him smile. Then he looked up at her arms; he noticed her muscular build. Then he traced the outline of her breasts inside her shirt.

She noticed and cringed, which was visible to everyone in the room. But the man in black didn't comment on it. He didn't falter from his staring.

Then he moved up to her neck. He stared at it. He savored the hint of veins and crinkles and flesh.

The man in black asked, "Where's your friend?"

Eva said, "What friend?"

The man in black smiled. He reached into his jacket and drew the SIG Sauer P220 out. He held it down by his side, one-handed. More like a threat than anything else. It was there to say, "I won't ask twice." But he did.

He asked, "Where's your friend? The big guy?"

"I don't know."

Just then, Putin bolted up from her seat. Back straight. Shoulders apart. It turned out that she had a gun under her desk, only it hadn't been in the top drawer. It must have been in a hidden compartment under the top, just above her lap. And it wasn't the SR1MP pistol. It was a Glock 17, unsilenced, which surprised Eva.

Time slowed down. Eva reacted as she had been trained to do. She leaped off her seat and ducked down in the back corner. There were no good options for cover in this situation. The office had one way in, and one way out, and the way out was blocked by the five armed enemies.

Eva wasn't sure if Putin was a good shot or not. She didn't know how much training Putin had with the Glock 17. All that didn't really matter much because the man in black was only seven or eight feet away, ten at the most. And even if Putin missed, she was bound to hit one of them.

It turned out not to matter how much training Putin had with a firearm. It didn't even matter how good she was, because the man in black was better.

Before Putin's Glock 17's firing line could near her target, he had raised his P220 like an experienced gunslinger from out of the pages of an old western novel. He didn't fully extend his arm like some kind of amateur.

In a gun duel between two cowboys, squaring off in the middle of town at high noon, the first mistake he always noticed in movies was the actors extended their arms all the way out. This was a mistake.

The proper way to be quicker, to be deadlier, was to practice firing from the hip, which the man in black had done a lot.

He drew from the hip and squeezed the trigger. Eva had missed that because she was staring at Putin, her friend.

The room filled and echoed and boomed with the sounds of dual gunshots.

The first was from the man in black's P220. The second one was from Putin's Glock.

Next, two things happened. The bullet from the P220 blasted through the air and blew a hole the size of a quarter straight through Putin's forehead. Red mist sprayed out behind her and splashed on the window and blinds with thick redness. She fell back into her seat and was dead. Eyes open, staring up and lifeless.

The man in black was faster than her. But Putin had squeezed off one shot. Only she didn't hit the man in black, as she had hoped. Instead, one of the other guys who came with him had been hit square in the side of his neck. He fell back against one of his friends and clung to life. He wrenched his fingers on his friend's coat and pulled at it, taking the friend down to the ground with him.

The others all stood around, setting their weapons down. They stood around, not knowing what to do. At least, that's what they wanted their buddy to think, even though he knew the truth. They had a procedure to follow if one of them received a life-threatening wound in the field. The procedure was simple. Let the man die. If there was nothing they could do for him on their own, without a hospital, then he was as good as dead. That didn't mean that they didn't care about each other. They were all friends. But that was the cost of doing business. They were involved in a highly illegal operation. There were nukes in play. They couldn't take him to the hospital.

By this point, the man was bleeding out profusely.

He knew he was going to die. He didn't cover his wound as he bled out, which was difficult for about thirty seconds, but after he lost a few pints of blood, facing death became much easier.

Within minutes, their friend was dead.

The man in black never took his eyes or the barrel of the P220 off Eva.

Finally, he asked once more, "Where is he?"

46

Gunshots echoed above him as he rode the elevator up. This time, Widow was certain it wasn't a car backfire. Not unless someone had parked a forty-year-old muscle car on the sixth floor.

He didn't have his guns anymore and had no time to get them, not if Eva's life was in danger. He couldn't make the elevator go back down to the lobby anyway, not until after the doors opened on six.

He was sure that he had heard two distinct handguns being fired. He wasn't sure about the make or models, but they sounded close to being simultaneous, which was only possible with two weapons. And one of them was louder than the other. It sounded like a .45 ACP, maybe. The second one was a nine-millimeter, no doubt about it.

Widow had enough experience to know that it was never a good idea to walk into a potential gun battle, unarmed and completely cold. He had to help Eva. That took priority over his fears.

Instead of riding up to six, he hit the fifth-floor button just in time as the elevator passed the fourth.

The elevator registered the change in the journey and stopped on the fifth floor. The doors shot open, and Widow stepped off.

He looked left and looked right. He prepared himself to dodge and roll back onto the open elevator if there had been a danger on that floor as well, but there were no signs of life.

Widow searched the signs above the doors in the hall until he saw the fire exit stairwell. He charged at the door and ripped it open in one heaving motion that would have torn a cheap door off its hinges. He took the stairs up, two at a time, and darted up two flights. He rounded the corner and stayed alert for sounds. There was nothing but the loud hum of the elevator, moving on to six without him.

He stopped outside the door to six and hugged the inside wall. His heart was racing. His blood was pumping hard. He stayed still and concentrated on his breathing. He breathed in and breathed out. He watched as his chest heaved up and then down. He waited, tried to slow his breathing, and thus, his heart rate. He needed to slow it all down so he could be as quiet as possible. He needed to recon the situation before making a move.

After a few moments went by, he knew the elevator was stopped because the humming had stopped.

He paused one last time, and then he turned and faced the door, crouched down and pushed the door open. He pressed the open bar slowly and then followed that with the door just as slowly. He cracked it open and looked down the hall. The elevator was behind him. But that was okay because what he was looking for, he saw a second later.

The door to Putin's office opened up wide. And there was Eva. She was alive, but she was bound. Her hands were out front, zip-tied together at the wrists. The look on her face was shock and terror all at once. She was being forced forward by four men, three of which Widow recognized from The Plaza Hotel. The fourth, he didn't.

The fourth man wore all black and seemed to be the leader. He was the only one who looked from side to side like he was checking the doors, checking the corners.

Widow heard him bark an order to the others.

He said, "Elevator!"

Widow slipped back and pulled the door with him, making sure not to click it shut. He didn't want the door to register a loud sound like most fire doors do when they are closed all the way.

He left it with a hair crack, just enough to make it look closed. He pushed his back to the wall and listened.

He heard footsteps, quick. The men were checking the open elevator. He waited until they had all passed. He heard Eva's footsteps and then those of the man in black. He knew Eva's because they were the lightest and sporadic, like she was being half-pushed forward.

Widow heard them pass and stop near the elevator.

The man in black asked, "No one there?"

The other said, "No. Nothing."

Silence for a long moment. Widow backed away and went up the stairs to the seventh floor. He stepped three at a time this time and tried to keep his footsteps silent.

He went up and not down because if they were going to check the fire stairs, most people looked down. Not up. It was stupid for an attacker to go up. Up was the roof.

Widow stopped two flights up on the seventh floor and crouched down out of sight, and listened.

He heard nothing, and he waited longer. Then he heard the sixth-floor door jolt open in one violent swing. He heard the clicking sound of a submachine gun being aimed around haphazardly.

He peered down with one eye over the edge of the cement. He got a glimpse of one of The Plaza Hotel guys, staring over the railing, looking downward.

Widow saw the back of the guy's head, and then he saw the MP5SD in his hand.

Widow slipped back slowly, in case the guy checked upward.

He paused and waited. The guy wasn't all that bad. He stayed there for a long minute until he gave up.

Widow heard him say, "There's no one here."

The words trailed off as the guy from The Plaza Hotel walked back through the fire door.

Widow waited until he heard the fire door shut. He descended back down the two flights until he was back at that door. He paused another beat, listening until he heard the elevator engine crank back to life and the cables humming somewhere behind the wall. They were on the move back down.

Widow charged through the fire door and checked the hall, fast. He swung right toward Putin's office, and then he swung left toward the elevator. It was indeed closed and moving down.

Widow ran back down the hall to check the office. He hadn't seen Putin leave with them, causing him to presume that she had been the recipient of one bullet he had heard fired.

The office door was open. Widow snapped in and snapped back out in case someone shot at him. But there was no one there to shoot him. Not alive anyway.

The first thing he saw was a dead guy on the floor. Blood still oozed out of a neck wound. The wound was so dark and covered with blood that Widow couldn't even see where the hole was.

He passed over the guy and saw the blood splatter on the window and the blinds. He saw Putin. She was definitely dead. There was a hole in her forehead, and Widow could see brain fragments on the window.

Shit, he thought.

He didn't wait. There was nothing else to see. He went over to the desk and saw that Putin had fired a Glock 17. He scooped it up, didn't need to test fire it. It looked like it fired just fine.

Then he turned around, but stopped because he saw that the dead guy on the floor was blinking.

Widow set the Glock down on the carpet, away from the pool of blood, and shoved his hand over the guy's neck, tried to stop the bleeding.

He asked, "Can you talk?"

The guy blinked.

Widow's hand found the hole in his neck, and he pushed hard.

"Speak!"

The guy said, "Don't wanna die."

His voice was weak, and his skin was cold, growing colder by the second. Widow was certain that his voice wasn't speaking with its normal tone because the bullet had scraped his voice box. It had to have because of the location. Widow was surprised he could even utter a recognizable word.

"Where did they take her?"

The guy said nothing. He just blinked.

"Where?!"

"Strike."

"What?"

The next word sent cold chills down Widow's spine.

The guy said, "Nuclear."

Widow heard: "nuclear strike." He changed course and asked, "When?"

"Today. The anniversary."

Anniversary, he thought.

The guy was dying faster and faster by the second.

"Where?"

The guy said something inaudible. Widow didn't understand. The guy's eyes rolled back in his head. Widow only had seconds left with him.

"Where did they take Eva?"

The guy coughed up blood. It splattered onto Widow's clothes and face. Then it trickled down the guy's cheek and mouth.

"Where is she?"

"Moreau."

Then he was gone.

Where the hell was Moreau? Widow wondered. But there was no time for that.

He picked up the Glock 17 and ran after them. Widow pressed the elevator button and watched for a second to see what floor it was coming up from. The second elevator answered the call. It was coming from the lobby, slowly.

He gave up on that and turned to the stairwell again. He ripped the door open just as hard as before, and he leaped from the flight of stairs down to the next landing. On the way down, he barely touched a stair. He was going as fast as he could. He knew they hadn't taken her back through the lobby. They had come from the parking garage below.

Widow went as fast as he could. But it hadn't been fast enough.

He burst through the door to the garage and caught the taillights of a white panel van traversing up the ramp to the street.

47

FARMER STARED AT KARPOV, who stood upright, mostly, with his hands behind his back. He was being held tightly by one of the guys who'd come on board with Farmer. The redheaded leader was standing behind Farmer.

Farmer held a roll of quarters in one hand. He stared at Karpov's bloody face and said, "Captain, I can keep hitting you, but we both know you're going to give me that passcode."

The Listener had clarified that the operation was going to go according to plan no matter what. He didn't need to say it. Farmer knew well enough.

Without Karpov's daughter, threatening him to give up a passcode was proving impossible.

The Russians had gotten smarter. Like the rest of the nuclear club with submarines, they equipped their nukes with not only two required turnkeys but also a failsafe passcode. It was a word that was required to arm the nuke. The missile could be fired without it, but the nuke wouldn't be armed without it. And a nuclear missile without the "nuclear" part is about as dangerous as dropping a Buick from the sky. Sure, someone could get hurt, but the damage was reduced to almost nothing compared to a nuclear blast.

Farmer had brought the roll of quarters just in case. One of the oldest tricks in the book. Can't afford brass knuckles? Use a roll of coins.

He stared down at his hand, which was turning red.

They had already tried to threaten the captain by shooting his men.

That proved useless because they had shot one in front of him, and nothing happened. He didn't give up a thing.

Farmer had suspected that much. Submariners swear an oath, just like any sailor. They won't give up such a dangerous thing as a nuclear passcode to the enemy. Not even for the lives of their fellow sailors. They had all sworn an oath, too.

They were prepared to die.

Farmer turned back to the redheaded leader and whispered, "This is getting us nowhere."

The redheaded leader nodded.

"We need to surface again. Call the Listener. We need Karpov's daughter. It's the only threat that seems to faze him."

Farmer left, and the redheaded leader followed but stopped to instruct the other guy to bring Karpov.

They returned to the bridge.

Farmer went over to his submariner and said, "Bring us to the surface."

The guy said, "Are you sure?"

"Do it."

"But we are likely to be seen? At least on sonar."

"Do it. I gotta call him."

The submariner did as he was told and barked orders at the crew in Russian. They followed his commands, all while the redheaded leader and one of his guys swept behind them, pointing and poking the backs of their heads with their MP5s.

48

Widow walked up the ramp to the street, pausing for a moment because he saw a dead security guard. He was sure the guy was dead because he could see the bullet hole in his head. It looked to be like the one in Putin's head and probably was. Probably the same gun. Probably from the man in black.

Widow continued out onto the surface street. He continued walking briskly in the direction that he had seen the van turn and moving away from the building. He was just in time to hear police sirens in the distance—screeching, blaring, and growing louder.

He figured that the guard at the desk must have called the police.

The white panel van was a far speck on the horizon, and then it was lost to sight.

Widow stopped dead on the sidewalk.

Pedestrians stared at him, avoiding him. Most moved to the other side of the street, or they turned around and walked away.

That was when he realized he still had the Glock out. He stuffed it into his waistband and then realized there was blood on his shirt and face. His shirt was black, but his face was white. Therefore, the pedestrians weren't staring at his shirt.

He turned away from the street and faced the buildings. He walked toward one, stared at a sign out front. It was one of those "You are here" maps of the office park. He waited for the sirens to pass.

A moment later, he looked over his shoulder and saw three NYPD spec cruisers pull up and stop dead on the street in front of Putin's building.

Widow saw himself faintly in the glass's reflection that encased the map. He pulled his shirt up and licked the tip of it and wiped his face.

Then he turned and walked casually, but hurriedly, away.

49

BREACHING the surface took a lot longer than Farmer and his men had thought, because they found out that there was a battle group nearby. Not on top of them, but within radar and sonar distance, for sure. It looked to be a US destroyer, along with an aircraft carrier and a couple of cruisers. They had also picked up a submarine coming toward the group from the south.

Farmer wasn't worried about it like his men were. But the reason he wasn't worried was that they were a part of the plan. He had known about the ships long before.

Still, they weren't ready to expose themselves just yet. So, he ordered them to move slowly away and out of range enough to surface.

The submarine was coming up, and the engines slowed. The waves broke over the bow.

"Let's go," Farmer said to Karpov.

The redheaded leader gripped Karpov by the elbow and hauled him onto his feet and over to the ladder and up it, staying behind Farmer, who climbed first.

On the deck of the boat, water sprayed in white and gray snarling waves. Karpov wasn't told where they were, but he knew just by listening to Farmer's commands and by the color of the water and the temperature. He knew they were near to the legal point of invasion into US waters. If he had to guess a more precise location, he would say that they were in striking distance of the major US targets, including New York City and Washington DC. The first target would certainly mean an all-out war with the US. But the second target would mean the crippling of the United States' centrally based federal system and, therefore, the nation's response time to the attack.

A nuclear strike on the US would mean a return strike on Russia. Probably from NATO, which meant a quick attack, which would mean the end of Karpov's friends who mostly lived in Moscow.

Karpov swallowed as he stared up into the blinding daylight above him.

Farmer was dialing a satellite phone and holding onto the guardrail near the hatch they had emerged from.

Farmer and his guys had already gotten the two turnkeys from Karpov and the political officer, who held the other one. That part was easy. The political officer had done little to hold out from volunteering it.

Karpov knew they needed the passcode, which wasn't widely publicized information—a secret code word that is entered a separate keypad on the bridge's computer. It had to be issued before the launch in order to arm the nuke.

There was no way Karpov was going to give up that code. But then he thought about why he was meeting Farmer in the first place—his daughter.

They had her. That's how they were going to get that code from him. The only person who he would give it up for was her.

He squeezed his eyes tight as he faced the sky. It was time to take away their upper hand.

In a fast spin, he turned and ran for the side of the boat. If he could make it to the edge, he could jump off. He could drown. He could save thousands of lives, maybe even millions. They might kill Eva, but at least he wouldn't have given up to the threat.

He shoved Farmer out of the way and ran to the edge of the boat.

The blinding light from the sun grayed a bit from the fast-moving cloud cover, making it almost impossible for Karpov to distinguish the exact edge of the submarine's bow, which was slightly curved anyway and painted to blend in with the ocean.

He neared it and ran at full speed. He didn't need to jump. He only needed to keep running. Eventually, he would fall right in.

As he neared what he thought was the edge, he heard a quieted *PURR!* It was a familiar sound. It was the sound of suppressed gunfire.

And suddenly, the metal deck in front of him sparked, and bullets ricocheted, and his instincts for self-preservation kicked in, overtaking him. He froze solid.

Funny how many suicides wind up being aborted at the last minute because of every animal's natural need to stay alive.

Karpov froze, and before he could force himself to continue forward, he felt strong arms grapple him and haul him backward.

The redheaded leader had wrenched him back off his feet and slammed him onto the hard, cold steel deck. The breath was knocked out of him.

The redheaded leader jabbed him once, hard, straight in the face.

"Don't try that again!" he shouted.

50

WIDOW HAD CONTINUED WALKING ABOUT AS FAR as he could go until he felt he was safely out of the reach of the NYPD's net, at least for now.

The lawyer was dead. There was a dead bad guy, who would probably come up as a John Doe for the low-level computer database of the NYPD, which might cause them to investigate with Homeland or the FBI, which might provide some better results.

Widow had no intention of being a part of their investigation. He had had his fair share of police lately. And there was a more pressing matter. The bad guy had said, "Nuclear Strike." Now the stakes were much, much higher, and Widow had to skip ahead. With such a threat out there, a credible one, there was no time for red tape and half-measures. He had to go over the heads of local law enforcement. And unfortunately, he had to set aside Eva's safety for the time being. A nuclear strike was more important. She would understand. But he intended to get her back alive.

Where should he go? Where to start?

The boyfriend, Edward, was dead as well. He couldn't start there. He had only the name Farmer, who was supposedly a CIA agent. No reason to doubt that was the truth.

But with the threat of a nuke, the thing to focus on for now was the stolen Russian submarine.

Widow walked back the same path that he and Eva had come, back to Grand Central Terminal. He had seen a payphone there.

Once he got there, he went underground and back to the phone. It wasn't being used, which wasn't a surprise. Most people had their own personal phones on them.

Widow picked up the phone before he realized he had no change. No quarters.

He didn't want to go searching around for a place to get change. So, he simply dialed one of those call-collect services he had seen advertised somewhere.

He waited and got the operator and requested to call collect. He gave her a number that he had used before that he knew from memory.

She asked him to wait while she tried to connect the call, and then he heard Rachel Cameron's voice answer. He was given a chance to say his name, which he did. Then he listened as Cameron was asked if she accepted the charges. She did.

"Widow? What the hell is going on?"

"I need your help."

"Okay?"

"There's a situation. A Russian submarine has been stolen. It's nuclear. I believe that they have a US target."

Cameron paused a beat, and then she said, "I heard about it."

"What? You know about it?"

"Why do you think I'm at the office on a Sunday? The whole unit is here. We've been working overtime with Norfolk and COMNAVAIR-LANT, trying to get hold of the sub's location."

COMNAVAIRLANT stands for Commander Naval Air Force Atlantic.

Widow asked, "Did you send me to The Plaza Hotel on purpose?"

"What? Of course I did. It was your birthday gift."

"No, I mean to get involved in this?"

"What? I don't understand?"

Widow took a breath. He was a believer in coincidences, only because he had been the victim of wrong place, wrong time, many times before. But this seemed suspect.

"You didn't send me there because of Eva Karpov?"

He could hear Cameron kind of snarl over the phone.

"Who? Widow, I don't know who the hell that is."

Widow said, "She was kidnapped while I was at the Plaza. She was being held for two days by a group of armed men. Supposedly they were part of a bigger operation."

"What operation? What's this girl gotta do with it?"

"I believe they wanted to hijack this sub."

"You know who's responsible then?"

"Yeah. Some guy called Farmer."

"Farmer? Never heard of him."

Widow said, "There's more. You already know that the Russian sub is nuclear, but do you know who the boat's captain is?"

"No. Who?"

"A man named Karpov."

"I've never heard of him either," she said, but then he heard her sigh. And she said, "That's someone related to Eva Karpov?"

"Her father. She says."

"This guy Farmer kidnapped her to get her father to turn over the boat?"

"Supposedly Farmer convinced her he'd help her and her father to defect. I don't believe that Karpov thought he was going to be turning over the sub to a bunch of terrorists."

"Wait, defect? Like in that movie? The one with James Bond?"

"Sean Connery, not Bond, but yes. Kind of like that movie. *The Hunt for Red October*," Widow said, and then he paused a beat and added, "It's a better book."

"This Karpov captain, he believed that this guy Farmer wanted to help him? Sounds naïve to me."

"Could have been. But this guy Farmer is supposedly CIA, which explains the manpower and the means and even the location of the hotel where they held her. The CIA love their expensive-ticket items."

Cameron ignored the quip about the hotel and simply asked, "CIA?"

"That's what she told me."

"I think we need to bring you both in. Where are you now?"

"I'm in New York still. At Grand Central Terminal, but she's not with me."

"Where the hell is she?"

"They got her. Again."

"How?"

"Long story. But there's a dead Russian immigration lawyer down near the UN building. We were attacked. They got away with her."

"Immigration lawyer? Wait, what did Eva do here?"

"She was a spy."

"A spy?"

"Yeah, the lawyer was her handler."

Cameron said, "This gets better and better."

Widow decided not to tell her about Eva's cover job as a model. The whole thing sounded more and more like an airport spy novel.

Instead, he said, "Send someone to pick me up, but Cameron, I can't come to you. This Farmer guy intends to use the sub to launch a nuke at us. I'm sure of it. It's the only thing of value on the sub."

"What? Why would he do that?"

"No idea. But we presume that's what they're planning. I need to get to Norfolk."

"Navy command?"

"I knew a guy who should still be there. Nick Ebert. We can trust him. Last I heard, he had been stationed there. He's in counterintelligence. Find him, will ya?"

"Okay. Stay there, by the phone. I'll call you back."

She hung up, and Widow did the same. He turned and looked around and found a bench along the nearest wall, within earshot of the phone. He took a seat and waited.

51

THE MAN in black punched Eva square in the stomach one more time. And she heaved forward as far as she could, tasting the doughnut that she had eaten earlier.

By this time, they weren't at their final destination, but they were already at the tip of Long Island, the northeastern side, on Highway Twenty-Five in Orient. They had pulled off the road and onto a dirt path. They drove for a while. Eva was gagged in the back of the panel van. She felt the bumps and knew that they had gone off road.

After the van stopped, the doors opened, and two of the men who had kidnapped her twice now got out and stretched their legs.

The man in black had hopped into the van with her and the third guy, who held her elbows back.

That was when the man in black punched her in the gut. He didn't speak a word to her, not one. No questions. No requests. He just punched her. And then he punched her again. Same spot. Same pain.

After she caught her breath, he pulled her chin up and ripped the gag out and said, "When I tell you to, you will speak."

She said nothing.

The man in black stepped out of the van, pulled out a satellite phone, and twisted his hand to see his watch. He waited.

They waited a long time, and finally, the sat phone rang.

The man in black answered it and said, "Yes."

He listened.

Said, "Yes," again. And then he listened some more.

Then he turned and walked back to the van, climbed inside, and said, "She's right here."

He reached the phone to her and held it in place for her. He said, "It's for you."

Eva listened and heard the wind blowing loudly in the background. Then she heard her father's voice.

He spoke in Russian, a simple, "Are you all right?"

But then he was struck by someone, she knew by the sound, and she heard a voice order him to speak English.

He asked, "Are you safe?"

She didn't speak in Russian.

She said, "I'm alive. In New York, somewhere."

Then she paused a beat and stared up at the man in black. She said, "Don't do whatever they want you to do, Papa!"

The man in black pulled the phone away and listened.

He heard Farmer speak, "That's enough. Hello?"

"It's me," the man in black said.

"Thank you for cleaning up after me."

"Don't worry about it."

"The Listener told me there was interference. Some guy?"

"Again, don't worry about it. We're back on track now."

"So, same schedule then?"

The man in black looked at his watch, then he said, "Yes. We keep going. Unless the Listener says differently."

There was a pause and a deep breath between both men.

Farmer said, "We're actually going to do this."

"Yes."

"Then, I'll see you at Moreau's in two hours?"

"In two hours. See you."

Then Farmer said, "If Karpov tricks us, kill the girl."

The man in black said, "In one hour, fire the nuke. If I don't see news of it by then, she'll be dead one minute later."

And both men hung up.

The man in black looked at Eva and smiled. Now that she knew they were actually going to fire a nuclear missile, she made that expression that he loved on the faces of his victims as he strangled them. It wasn't the same, but very close. She looked completely terrified.

Eva muttered something that the man in black pieced together. It was something like, "No. All those people."

He slid back out of the van, tossed the sat phone on the ground, and stomped on it over and over, violently until it was only shattered pieces of a phone.

Then he said, "No going back now."

Eva stayed quiet.

"Get her out and onto the boat."

The men who had kidnapped her hustled to it, pulled her out and dragged her along a smaller path between some brush and out onto a secluded beach. A military-looking zodiac was waiting in the shallow water.

She was thrown into it like a bag of bricks. A moment later, the men all climbed in, and the man in black followed.

They left the van where it was, alongside the man in black's motorcycle.

He sat right next to Eva and ordered one man to go. That guy climbed back out and shoved the boat farther out onto the water, where it was deep enough to use the motor. Then he climbed in, soaking wet.

He fired up the motor, and a moment later they were cruising along at high speed out around Long Island. They threaded through markers along the shoreline and weaved out until they were headed north and east toward nothing but blue horizons.

52

Karpov was hauled back down the ladder and through the communications tower to the bridge, with nothing but defeat on his face.

Eva was his little girl. She was all he thought of.

Farmer said, "Keep him standing."

The redheaded leader did as he was ordered.

"What's the password?"

Karpov looked at the floor panels and said nothing.

"Karpov, I won't ask again."

Karpov looked up, slowly, and stared at the faces of his men who were still on the bridge. They looked at him under gunpoint. Their eyes were all blank. They looked almost as defeated as he did. They looked hopeless. They knew they were probably all going to die.

In shame, he answered Farmer.

He answered with one word, "October."

Farmer smiled. He had the password. He had the keys. He had the nukes. Now all he had to do was wait one hour until the deadline.

53

THE PAYPHONE at Grand Central Terminal rang once, and Widow jumped up and walked over to it, catching it on the second ring.

"Hello?"

"Jack Widow?" a voice from the past asked. The sound behind the voice was familiar. It was a lot of ambient noise, like people talking and machines beeping and making sounds.

"Yep."

"It's Nick," the voice said, and then Widow heard a door open and wind noises.

"Hey, Nick."

"Man, you are all wrapped up in this mess?"

"I guess so."

More wind.

Widow asked, "Where the hell are you?"

Ebert didn't answer that. Instead, he said, "Listen, no time to chat over the phone. I sent you a car. Go out of the terminal back to the street. You should see it."

"What kind of car?"

"Don't worry. They know what you look like."

And with that statement, Ebert hung up the phone.

Widow hung up and turned and walked back out of the terminal and up the stairs to the street.

He didn't know what kind of car he was looking for. He saw a navy blue sedan, which was completely forgettable except for someone who knew better, and Widow knew better. It was a Navy vehicle. No doubt about it.

It didn't look like a police cruiser, but it was armored like one. There was no light bar on the roof, but that was only because sirens and blue lights were embedded in the grille.

There was an array of antennas planted on the back like little steel telephone poles.

The driver was leaned up against the vehicle. He called out from across the street.

"Jack Widow?"

"That's me."

"Hop in. We don't have a second to waste."

Widow scrambled across the street and opened the rear door out of habit. He was about to hop in when the driver said, "Sir, you can sit in the front."

Widow arched his eyebrow out of reflex. He wasn't used to sitting in the front of a cop car.

He shut the door to the back, opened the passenger front door, and dumped himself down on the seat, shut the door, and buckled up.

"Ready?" the driver asked.

"Ready."

And they were off to a destination that Widow didn't know. He assumed to JFK airport because, more than likely, Ebert was far away. Probably at Norfolk.

54

THE LISTENER LOOKED at his watch. Time was running out. Soon the entire world would witness the first and last nuclear attack on the United States, and they would blame the Russians for it.

So far, everyone was buying it. So far, everyone believed that a Russian submarine had gone quiet and was headed into Atlantic waters off the US coast.

They had reacquired the girl. The man in black had texted the Listener's phone and told him the good news that Karpov had given up the password, and now the nuke would be armed.

The Listener had considered pulling back on the operation. After all, many people that he knew would die—people blind to the world, blind to the uselessness of the current military.

They would die in less than an hour now. They would die in a fiery blast of nuclear clouds and sky and radiation.

The bums in Washington would have to listen then. They would have to return the state of the military back to its former grace.

The Listener wouldn't back out. No. He couldn't. Not now. Not even if he wanted to. Farmer was unreachable.

The Listener texted the man in black one last time before the planned nuclear strike and said, "Go dark. I'll reach out to you after the heat dies down. One more thing, wait for the strike, but don't wait for Farmer to make it. Just kill the girl. At your discretion."

The Listener waited, but there was no response. He figured that meant the man in black was already on his way to Moreau.

He stared down at his phone and selected edit in his messages app. He swiped to select all and swiped again to delete all. Then he did the same under call log.

He took his satellite phone, kept it in his hand. Then he slipped a coat on top of his uniform, walked out of his temporary office, and stepped out into the hall. He walked past sailors and other crew members, ignoring their salutes, and made his way to the deck of the USS Washington, which had once been a flag battleship until its decommissioning in nineteen forty-seven. It had recently been constructed once again, not the original ship, and not as a battleship, but a new breed of a high-tech aircraft carrier for the US Navy. They just reused the name, an unconventional approach, but worthy, the Listener figured.

The very existence of the new ship was another slap in the face to him and his cause to reestablish fear in the rest of the world. Why on earth does the government spend all this money on new tech that they never intend to use in battle?

The Listener walked out past flight crew members who worked on deck. Around his neck was a pair of binoculars, very expensive ones. He liked to walk around from time to time and observe the performances of the other ships in their vicinity. The sailors on board were used to it.

No one bothered him as he walked the deck.

He waited until he was out of sight of anyone around. He looked to starboard and back to port. No one was watching him. Casually, he leaned against the railing and held out the sat phone. He dropped it.

It tumbled off the side and was sucked under the water. It vanished just as quickly as it broke through the waves.

The Listener glanced once toward the US coastline in the distance, and then at the placement of Navy ships, which were there under the pretext of war games, but really they were hunting the missing sub.

Then he looked at the causeway between the farthest ship and the carrier. By this time, Farmer had already squeezed past them. The new Russian sub technology had an absorbent outer skin that actually surpassed their own. But that wasn't what made the boat so deadly; it was escaping detection. This new sub wasn't the world's only stealth sub that could escape detection, but it was probably the most advanced, for the moment. And the moment was all that mattered to him.

He couldn't help himself. He looked one last time at the precise location of where the Russian sub was supposed to be at the marked time. He glanced at his watch.

Forty-two minutes to go.

55

WIDOW WAS a little stunned because they weren't going to JFK. They went right back to where he had started recently. The driver took him to the United Nations building. The street was already shut down and closed off by NYPD. Because of the dead bodies in the lawyer's building, Widow was sure. But the driver showed his badge, which made him NCIS and not Navy. The officer controlling the flow of traffic let them pass.

"Where are we going?" Widow asked.

"Helicopter."

And that was all the NCIS agent had said. Widow made no remark to give away that he had once had the same badge. He simply sat back and watched.

They pulled up onto a drive and up to a guard station for the United States Department of State Diplomatic Security Service, which is assigned to guard the UN. The agent re-showed his badge, and they drove past the guards and into the compound.

After a few moments of driving and sweeping around the walls and posted security vehicles, they came to a clearing of concrete, where there was normally parking. The driver pulled to a stop.

"Let's go," he said and parked the car, left the keys in it, but turned off the ignition.

Widow followed him out and shut the door.

The driver walked around the hood and waited. He just stood there.

Widow asked, "Aren't we going in?"

He figured they were headed up to the roof, where there was a helicopter pad.

"No time," the driver called out. He had called it out loud, like he was preparing for it to be loud.

Then Widow looked up and saw a twin-engine Seahawk helicopter flying overhead, maybe four hundred feet above them. He recognized it as probably an MH60 or similar. It was gray and unremarkable as far as appearance, making it more unnoticeable to civilians, Widow guessed.

The chopper came down steadily, but not slow.

Widow looked around the ground and saw guards and diplomats who were outside, he figured, to stare at him like he was some kind of important figure to be getting a helicopter landing right in the parking lot in front of the United Nations.

And suddenly, he felt a little proud.

The Seahawk circled in, and Widow felt the pressure from the rotor wash growing stronger and more intense.

He watched as the machine came in and blew his hair up in powerful waves like blades of grass.

The Seahawk landed on its wheels and bounced once. The flight crew left the engines on, and the blades continued to turn above Widow.

The driver called out, "Come on."

Widow followed him onto the back of the helicopter, and they both buckled in—a Navy crewman who helped them get on banged on the roof twice, and cleared the pilot to take off.

They rose up and up. Once they were high enough, Widow felt the engines running harder and harder, and the helicopter tilted on the Y-axis, and they bolted forward at a much faster speed than the bird was used to traveling.

They headed out toward the Atlantic. Once Widow saw Manhattan vanish behind them, he called out to the driver, "Just where are we going?"

"To see Ebert."

"Yeah, but where?"

The driver said, "The USS Washington."

Widow sat back. It had been a long time since he had been on board a Navy aircraft carrier. A long time.

56

THE SEAHAWK FLEW under good weather, which made the trip faster and smoother. Widow had flown in helicopters many times before, but this may have been the longest trip on one that he could recall. He wasn't calculating the miles, and he didn't know the speed they traveled, but they had been flying over open water for thirty minutes or more. He didn't know the exact time. He didn't have a clock in his head. What an absurd notion that would have been.

He figured thirty to forty minutes was as good a guess as any.

They were flying to an aircraft carrier, so no need to worry about fuel. There would be plenty onboard.

The Seahawk came in over the Atlantic, and Widow scooted across the rear bench and leaned to see out the side window. He saw the aircraft carrier coming into range, and he saw a destroyer not far off, along with a couple of other ships too far away to recognize. What he did notice was their pattern. They were spread out in different directions but staying within sight range. They were hunting.

The wind picked up as they descended. The helicopter yawed and fell, and the rotors whooped and seemed to get louder.

After another five minutes of approaching, they were coming in over the new USS Washington.

Widow got up off the bench and moved into a position that allowed him to watch through the cockpit. He saw the ship come into view. He saw it grow bigger and bigger. He watched as the ground crew prepared for the Seahawk to land.

The bird landed on a clear helicopter-marked landing zone. Widow braced for the wheels to touch down and bounce, which they did. Not too hard. The pilot was a real pro.

The driver who had picked up Widow unzipped his windbreaker, and for the first time, Widow saw his nameplate. Hardy was his name.

Hardy said, "Follow me, sir."

Widow followed behind him as Hardy swiped open the side door and hopped out onto the deck. Widow did the same and immediately felt the wind blow across his face in slapping gusts. And a far-off, familiar feeling of life in the Navy came back to him.

Parked on the deck were dozens of fighter jets in different corners. They looked like EA-18G Growlers. Widow wasn't an expert on planes. Without checking out the call numbers up close, he simply trusted his gut.

Two of them were in the queue to dispatch at a moment's notice, one after the other.

Widow figured somewhere under the convoy was at least one American Seawolf attack submarine. Also waiting and hunting.

Hardy said, "This way, sir."

Widow followed him. They weren't headed below deck. They were headed up to the tower and probably to the bridge.

They entered through the bottom, passed officers and crew, and climbed upstairs until Hardy walked through an open hatch and onto the bridge.

The bridge was laid out bigger than the ones Widow had seen before. Normally, they were smaller than one would think. On a ship, realty space is a luxury. This one was huge in comparison. And high tech. There were new pieces of equipment that Widow had never seen, or at least never paid attention to. He washed his eyes over it all with a quick look. Saw everything, took in nothing.

There were up to ten sailors present, give or take, because every few minutes one would leave, and another would step on.

Widow's eyes went right to a familiar face.

"Jack Widow," Nick Ebert said. He was standing, middle of the bridge, facing the portal that Widow came through with his hand held out for a shake. Behind him were two other men, all wearing Navy-blue shipboard uniforms. All three men wore Navy caps. The two behind Ebert looked important. One was tall, lean, and older. He probably considered himself middle-aged, but he was more in his sixties. The man standing a little farther back and to the right looked ancient. He was short, thin, and had a professor's face. Like the kind who refused to retire and sometimes forgot where he was, but was also brilliant, in spurts.

Widow walked straight over to Ebert and took his hand and shook it. He looked at his collar pin. Widow said, "Commander now, huh?"

Ebert nodded.

"I wish we were meeting under different circumstances," he said.

"Me too. What's going on?"

"Cameron told us you already know."

Widow asked, "Any sign of the boat?"

Ebert turned to introduce the other two men.

"Widow, this is Captain Towdez," Ebert said, and the tall, younger man reached his hand out to shake. Widow shook it.

"And this is Admiral Kiley."

Widow paused a beat and took Kiley's hand and shook it.

"Admiral," he said. "I've heard of you."

Kiley reached out his hand in a slow upward movement that felt more like a crane was hauling it up rather than human bones and muscles and motor skills.

"All good things, I hope."

"Mostly good."

"So, what do you know, Widow?" Kiley asked.

Widow had never met Kiley before, but Kiley was the type of career sailor whose reputation preceded him by a decade and a thousand miles. To say that he had been around the block was an understatement. He had been around the block, and around again, and then had the block dropped on him.

The man was more of an institution at this point. He was the last of a dying breed of military man. Widow had figured that the man had retired long ago. Not that he had any prejudices against him. It was just that facts were facts. And the fact was that Kiley was old.

Widow was more than surprised that an admiral was taking part in this endeavor, which told him volumes. Then he remembered something about Kiley being *the* foremost expert on submarines, which was another reason he was probably there and not on a golf course somewhere.

"I think, Admiral, that you already know what I know."

"How do you mean, son?"

"Well, you're here."

"Come again?"

Widow said, "A famous Navy admiral like you rarely takes part onboard an aircraft carrier."

"I assure you that Captain Towdez is the commanding officer here. Not me."

"And yet, here you are."

Kiley smiled, probably because he didn't know what to say.

Widow moved on and said, "There's a hijacked Russian sub out there, and it has nukes. It's somewhere in the quadrant, and you're out here searching for it."

Captain Towdez and Kiley both nodded.

Ebert asked, "We knew that already. Of course. What don't we know?"

Widow asked, "How did you know about it?"

"One of our subs picked up unusual sound patterns two days ago in the Arctic," Kiley said.

"You knew it was a Russian sub?"

"No, but we picked it up again last night and again hours ago," Kiley said.

Ebert said, "And then, one hour ago. Just about."

Widow asked, "How did you pick it up and then lose it again? Weren't we watching it like a hawk?"

Ebert nodded.

Towdez said, "We think it's been surfacing."

Widow nodded and said, "To communicate."

Kiley said, "Maybe."

Ebert said, "That's what our intel guys think."

"Well, intel guys are only guessing. We don't know for sure, but it seems likely. That's why you're here, Widow. We think you might have the missing piece. Who they've been talking to. If they've been talking."

Widow nodded and said, "I know."

Just then, one sailor on-deck stood up from a machine that he had been seated at and walked over to them. He was average height, with a small gut. He looked Middle Eastern. He had a dark complexion, like he had literally just stepped out of the desert.

Upon closer inspection, Widow realized he wasn't Navy, not at all. His uniform was all wrong. His demeanor was all wrong. He didn't belong there.

He was an imposter.

57

THE IMPOSTER STOPPED a few feet from Widow and put his hand out, offered it for a handshake.

Widow asked, "What's this?"

"My name is John Ali, like the boxer Muhammad Ali. Only with John."

Widow stayed where he was.

Ebert said, "Widow, this is a state representative," which in slang terms meant a spook or a CIA officer. Often they claimed to be from the State Department. Which was a terrible cover because everyone knew it, but a great cover because it explained why they were wherever they were.

Widow simply cut to the chase and said, "CIA?"

Ali nodded, just a slight nod, but an affirmative, clearly.

Ali said, "I'm here as an observer."

Widow said, "No, you're not."

Ali said nothing.

"You're here because of your boy, Farmer."

Ali said, "You know about him?"

"I know he's the one who hijacked the submarine."

Ali nodded.

Ebert and Kiley and Towdez all said nothing, which told Widow that they all knew.

"So what are we doing here, fellas?"

Kiley said, "We're here to stop a nuclear missile from being fired onto the US."

"But why am I here? You already know about Farmer, apparently. You already know the sub is out there."

Ali said, "Frank Farmer went rogue a couple of weeks ago. He was..."

Widow held out his hand and stopped him. He said, "I don't care. I don't need to know his motivations or his terms or whatever. I get that you're here to represent the agency and to disavow the blame. I don't care about that. All I care about is stopping a strike and finding someone that Farmer has abducted."

"Abducted?" Ebert asked.

"Yeah, a girl."

"Who?" Ali asked.

Widow looked at them and said, "Karpov's daughter."

Towdez asked, "Who's Karpov?"

Which told Widow that things were worse here than he had thought. No one was talking to anyone, or the captain assigned to the ship hunting the Russian sub was a moron not to know the name of the captain of the very submarine that he was hunting.

The answer came to Widow just then—the captain was a moron. Because Kiley said, "He's the submarine captain."

"His daughter's been abducted?" Ebert asked.

Widow nodded.

Ebert looked at Kiley and said, "That means?"

"Farmer has the passcode," Ali said.

"The passcode?" Widow asked.

Ebert said, "The Russians use a two-key system to launch their nukes from their subs, but five years ago, maybe, they installed a passcode failsafe system."

Widow said, "The passcode arms the nuke?"

"Right," Ebert said.

Ali's face turned flush like he was worried for the first time. He asked, "How do we stop them?"

Kiley stayed quiet.

Ebert said, "We don't. Not unless we find them before it's too late. Let's hope they surface again."

One sailor called out, "I found them!"

58

THE RUSSIAN-SPEAKING soldier that Farmer had brought with him said, "They can see us now."

Sweat beaded on his brow as it did for all of them, including Farmer. Red lights flashed on the bridge. Everyone was washed over with the sudden realization of imminent devastation by the alert that the missile doors were opening. It was an automatic effect that Farmer didn't expect, but also didn't care about.

The reason that the soldier who spoke Russian knew the US ships could see their precise location was that Farmer had just ordered him to open the missile bay doors. The action of opening the port and flooding the chamber took some effort and time. Which, when you are about to launch a nuclear missile, can feel like an eternity.

Finally, after the door was open, and the missile prepped and ready, Farmer said, "Prepare to fire!"

The soldier who spoke Russian looked at Farmer and showed him one of the firing keys. He inserted it into the dash keyhole on one side of the bridge, and Farmer stood at the other with Karpov's key. He inserted his key into the opposite keyhole.

Farmer and the soldier who spoke Russian stared at each other.

Farmer said, "Passcode first."

The keyhole was near a computer terminal. The soldier who spoke Russian released his key and placed his fingers over the keyboard and typed in "OCTOBER" in all caps, in Russian as he had been instructed to. The computer whirred for a moment and accepted the code.

Then he called out, "Armed."

Farmer said, "Ready!"

The soldier who spoke Russian placed his hand back on the key and looked at Farmer. Their eyes locked, and sweat doubled on their foreheads.

Farmer said, "On three."

The soldier who spoke Russian said, "Ready!"

"One. Two. Three."

And both men turned both keys for a second that seemed an eternity. Right then, the submarine shook and flailed, and the hull vibrated like train rails singing.

At the top of the boat, near the control tower, they were close to the surface but still submerged.

The PC-28 Сармат or the Russian nuclear ballistic missile designated RS-28 Sarmat in English was more readily known by its NATO name which was SATAN 2. The missile is a liquid-fueled MIRV-equipped, super-heavy thermonuclear-armed intercontinental missile. Not the most efficient missile on the market, but there was a reason it was called SATAN 2. It didn't have to be the most efficient. It was unstoppable enough to get past missile defense systems, usually. And it carried with it a nuclear payload of nothing but fire and death.

The missile fired out of the silo as it was designed to and rocketed out of the water. It ripped into the air and roared high, high into the sky.

59

WIDOW WASN'T under anyone's command. Not anymore. And one perk of not being under command was freedom of movement. He had enjoyed this perk immensely.

But when he saw the RS-28 Sarmat fire from just under the water's surface about two miles away, several of the sailors on the bridge also had freedom of movement because they followed him as he ran out of the portal and onto the deck.

Ebert followed him out as well. Kiley and Towdez remained. True professionals.

Widow hit the deck running, followed by a small horde of sailors. They all stopped behind him like he was their leader. He stood on the deck and stared up as the missile rocketed into the sky. White exhaust smoked behind it. He saw the small fiery propellant at the tail, pushing it up and onward to a target unknown.

Widow was suddenly reminded of the shuttle Challenger. He had seen it explode on television when he was a kid, like the rest of the world. But before it tragically exploded, it looked similar to the RS-28 Sarmat, only bigger.

Widow watched with horror on his face and in his bones.

They actually did it, he thought.

Just then, he looked downward at the deck. Two flight crews of fighter pilots were scrambling for their jets.

Widow could do nothing. He watched until the missile was up, up, and then lost to sight.

60

WIDOW and the rest of the sailors cleared the way, moving back. Most of the crew started heading back to their posts. But not Widow. He had no post. He stood on the deck and watched.

The first pilot and his wingman strapped into their cockpit, fast, and within a minute, they rocketed off the deck into the sky, followed a minute later by a second jet.

That was enough for Widow. He turned and headed back to the bridge.

More fighter pilots and jets lined up and took off.

On the bridge, Captain Towdez was ordering the crew to do this and to do that. The whole ship was chaotic but in a good, old-fashioned sort of way, like ordered chaos. And it dawned on Widow that this was the first time since WWII that an American ship had seen this kind of act of war. Sure, they'd had Desert Storm and Vietnam and so on, but never with these stakes.

Widow looked around in awe at the proficiency of his fellow sailors. Strangely, he missed it.

Captain Towdez turned out to be a lot better under pressure than Widow would've guessed.

Ebert was with him, giving orders and checking over his shoulders.

Kiley stood still, watching, smiling.

61

THE PEOPLE WORKING onsite of the target went about their lives. Late afternoon. A fall day. The trees around were filled with red and yellow and orange leaves that looked more like painted watercolors than real life. Songbirds chirped and flew. The grass was freshly cut and kept as it always was, as was called for by SOP.

The people in the area lived a uniform life. They went to work. They were friendly with each other. They did their jobs well.

The Americans on the East Coast, in the target area, were well-trained and well-prepared. But nothing can ever prepare a community for a thermonuclear ballistic missile.

Although the people in the target area were always prepared, always vigilant, no one is ever truly prepared for what happened next.

Suddenly, the entire community was on high alert because they all heard the raid sirens at the same time. They were under attack.

Dozens of them ran out of buildings. Many of them were armed with assault rifles and handguns. Others, office workers, came to the nearest windows and looked out.

All of them wondered if this was a drill.

They could hear nothing over the sirens.

They couldn't hear the ballistic missile fly down through the clouds and wind. But some of them saw it.

The men and women nearest to the runway saw it best. They saw it best because it was coming crashing, screaming down on top of them.

Some others who could see it ran for shelter. Some piled in vehicles. Others fell to the ground and rolled underneath whatever they could find, thinking that would protect them from the blast. Others scrambled to whatever building was nearby and hugged the wall. Some of them fell to their knees and ducked their heads down.

The ones closest to the missile's likely contact spot did nothing. They just stood there, staring, watching, trembling. They didn't want to die.

None of them wanted to die.

The missile tore through the sky with raw, unstoppable force, and a moment later, it crashed, nose first onto one of the plane hangars on Norfolk Naval Base, crushing through the roof, collapsing it, and impacting with a malfunctioning C130 parked inside the hangar.

The nosecone smashed down into the unused plane first and exploded.

62

KILEY CONTINUED TO SMILE, and Widow saw it.

Just then, Ebert asked one sailor a question.

He asked, "Update?"

"The missile hit Norfolk Navy Base. That was their target."

Kiley said, "An act of war."

Towdez said, "Sir?"

Kiley said nothing.

"It's not an act of war. We know it was Farmer, not the Russians."

"Of course. I'm simply caught up in the moment."

Widow turned to ignore them both and waited for news. He looked at Ebert and nodded like he was psychically telling him what to say.

Ebert asked, "Confirmation?"

"I'm waiting."

Confirmation would have to come from somewhere else. If Norfolk were destroyed in a nuclear blast, they would have to get confirmation from as far away as the Pentagon.

Widow closed his eyes. He thought about the White House. He thought about Secret Service snatching up the president, violently shoving him down to the underground bunker for safekeeping. He pictured all the terrified people in the military and the government and the world, probably.

Then he pictured the missile. He pictured the nuclear blast. He had never seen one, not in real life. Few people had.

He thought about the one he saw on television from the old reel of nuclear testing in the Pacific. The blast from miles away. The shock-wave. The terror of it all. Then he thought about the mushroom cloud—that huge ominous cloud of death.

The mushroom cloud, he thought.

He opened his eyes and ran, full speed, right past a sailor coming in the door, almost knocking him down. He shoved past two others on his way back out to the deck.

Several of the fighter jets had already been scrambled out over the ocean.

He looked west, scanned the sky, waited.

Ebert and Ali both came running after him. Ali was short of breath. He tried to speak, but Ebert interrupted him.

"Widow? What is it?"

"The mushroom cloud," he said.

"What?"

Widow pointed at the southwest horizon.

"That's America!"

"Yeah. It's in that direction."

"There's no mushroom cloud! A nuclear blast would have a cloud! We would see it even from here! Small, but it'd be there!"

Ebert looked at the direction he pointed. They waited. But there was no cloud.

The sailor from the bridge came out after them, a young woman. She breathed in hard, chest panting from scrambling out so fast.

She said, "Commander."

He turned and waited.

"It was a dud!"

"A dud?" Ebert asked.

She shrugged and said, "It didn't explode."

"What?" he asked.

Gusts of cold wind beat across Widow's face.

"It exploded, but there was no nuclear blast. It wasn't much of anything."

Ebert asked, "You're sure?"

"Yes. We got Norfolk on the comms now. They're talking to Towdex. Nothing happened."

Widow asked, "Nothing?"

"The missile hit a plane hangar. It exploded like a normal missile, but it was a weak explosion. Might not even have been from the missile. Might have been from the fuel tank in the jet. They said it was being worked on. I don't know. But there was no nuclear blast."

Ebert said, "Get back up there. Order them to get HAZMAT out there! And clear that base!"

Ebert ordered it, but Widow was sure the base commander, whoever he or she was, had already started evac procedures. And he was sure that Ebert knew it as well. Still, saying it all out loud probably felt pretty good.

Widow smiled.

Ebert asked, "Wait! Any casualties?"

"Not so far. There's a fire."

Ebert nodded, and the woman walked off, back to the bridge. Ebert stayed behind.

Widow asked, "What about the sub? We gotta take it out now!"

Ebert nodded and pointed and said, "Over there!"

All three men turned and watched as two fighter jets flew off in the distance and fired missiles into the ocean. Then, from two hundred yards away, a swell went rushing through the water. It was a torpedo from the American sub.

Widow watched as the missiles and the torpedo collided in the same location. A fraction of a second later, there was an underwater explosion. Widow watched as water sprayed up and out like a volcano erupted under the surface and only shot out water and not lava.

Ebert said, "Looks like a hit. And the explosion means it's sinking. Out of commission."

Then he turned and headed back to the bridge.

63

BEFORE THE MISSILE ROCKETED AWAY, Farmer and the redheaded leader and the rest of his crew had docked the mini-submarine up to an empty torpedo tube and pressurized the tube to allow them to get into the sub. The fifth man in their crew had piloted the mini-sub to them from Moreau.

All four of them squeezed into it just after the missile was fired and noticed by the Navy convoy, and after they had shot Karpov's crew on the bridge, right in front of his eyes.

The redheaded leader was just about to shoot and kill Karpov when Farmer put his hand up and stopped him.

"Bring him. He may be useful," Farmer said.

Karpov felt nothing but shame for what he had helped transpire.

He didn't fight them. Weakly he had followed them back through the corridors of the sub, down the ladders, and through several hatches. He watched them shoot and kill every man who tried to interfere, and he did nothing. He had no strength left.

They entered the mini-sub and shot it out into the ocean.

64

WIDOW GRABBED Ali by the arm and said, "Wait."

Ali stared on at him.

Widow said, "You know what happened just like I do."

Ali nodded.

He said, "The passcode. Karpov gave them the wrong passcode."

Widow nodded and said, "We have to do right by him. We owe him that much."

"What do you propose, Mr. Widow?"

"His daughter is still out there."

"You know where she is?"

"I heard something about Moreau? That mean anything to you?" Widow asked.

Apparently, it meant something to him, because Ali's eyes lit up.

"What?"

"It's an old abandoned training facility for us."

Widow asked, "What kind of training facility?"

"It's a small town on an island. Used to be a fishing port a century ago or something. The government took it over after everyone left. The agency used it for different exercises. We're not the only ones either. The FBI used it for a time as well. The little town makes for a lot of cover for firefight exercises or whatever the FBI does for training."

"That's where they took her then."
Ali nodded, said, "What do we do?"
"Let's talk to Ebert."

65

Ebert suggested a SEAL team get her, take out the bad guys. But they didn't have a SEAL team onboard, nor did Widow want to wait for one.

Instead, he insisted on going alone or with a local team of whoever they had, but they had to go now. And like that, within thirty minutes, he was back in the same helicopter, only this time he was with Ali. Hardy came as well, and the same pilot crew. Ebert wanted to accompany them, but he couldn't. And he could spare no one else. Although he tried, either Kiley or Towdez had denied the request. Widow wasn't sure which.

He was sure that they made the same old claims that all COs made everywhere. Something about them still being on red alert, and they still had a mess to clean up, lots of red tape. The real reason being budget constraints or the fact that this was more of a federal law enforcement matter now. Moreau was an island belonging to the federal government, after all.

Widow didn't care as long as he got there. He was grateful for the ride and for the guns and body armor that Ebert insisted they take.

The three men geared up as they rode in the back of the Seahawk helicopter.

Widow figured the deck crew must have fueled the Seahawk up before they took off, as he had suspected, because they flew for even longer than the last time.

They flew north and west. Widow saw a blip of land far to the west, and then it was gone. New Jersey, he figured.

The three men were issued sidearms. Widow was happy to trade because a Navy weapon was always better than some Russian lawyer's weapon. Each of them got a Heckler and Koch .45 automatic. No suppressors. Ten rounds each. This was a fine weapon.

They each also got carbine M4 assault rifles. Widow kept his switched to single-shot. He had no idea what Hardy's was set to. And Ali actually rejected his weapon. He just took the sidearm. He claimed he wasn't much good with an assault rifle. Widow didn't argue.

After about ten more minutes, the pilot turned and called out, "We're nearing the coordinates you gave, Mr. Ali."

"Okay," he called back.

Ali turned to Widow and asked, "It's your show. How do you want to approach?"

"It's an island. There's more than a ninety percent chance we'll be spotted, no matter what. How big is it?"

"Not big. You can jog across it in forty minutes, maybe less. I'd guess like four miles. Not even."

Widow said, "Then let's just get dropped off wherever. Once we hit the ground, we hit it running. And we hunt them down."

Hardy asked, "Know how many hostiles we're up against?"

"At least four."

They both nodded.

Widow double-checked the Kevlar vest Ebert had given him, and then his ammo. He had a spare magazine for the M4 stuffed in his back pocket. That should be plenty.

Hardy had the same, and Ali had a spare for the HK45.

"We're dropping in now, boys. I don't see any hostiles so far," the pilot called out.

The Seahawk swung around the island and scanned it before touchdown. They saw a zodiac on the beach, abandoned, and they saw the abandoned town that Ali had told them about.

No people.

The Seahawk made its way back around to where the zodiac was abandoned and came down and landed on the sand. The rotor wash picked up sand and blew it everywhere.

Widow was the first man out. He ducked and rolled and came up ten feet away and crouched on his knees. Sand was flying around everywhere.

He looked through it and scanned the trees and dips in the topography. There was no sign of anyone.

Hardy and Ali followed. They ran off, following Ali toward the town. The Seahawk took off and continued to circle, staying high enough to see them and staying far enough not to get shot at by the enemy.

They trekked through a long path that eventually became a dirt road, surrounded by yellow shrubs and aging trees, with thick branches.

Ali said, "That way. Not far now."

Widow stayed quiet and followed closely. He took note that Hardy seemed to be a good wingman. The guy kept up the pace. He stayed low and held the M4 correctly.

They saw abandoned, rusted-out four-wheelers and one half torn-up boat on the side of the road. They passed a rusty old boat trailer with no tires left. They passed brick walls broken like a tank had driven through the area.

They came to the first structure of a house or just a building, Widow couldn't tell. It was empty.

They moved on, and Widow saw the town. They walked up a hill and could see the whole town. It was basically nothing. There were ten structures. All brick. None of them had roofs left. None of them showed any signs of people. The windows were all blown out. No glass was left anywhere. And there were thick weeds and grass growing all over everything.

Widow gave Hardy signals to go quiet, and they searched each building individually, which didn't take long because there was hardly anything to search.

After they were done, they came back out to the middle of the town.

Hardy asked, "Now what? There's no one here."

He dropped his M4 to his side and held it like he had given up.

Widow said, "Someone's here. That zodiac is new."

Hardy nodded.

"Where else is there?" Widow asked Ali.

Ali shrugged, said, "Maybe they're to the north. There are some rock formations and more trees. I don't know of anything else. I've never been here before."

Widow said, "Let's go."

And they hiked north.

66

THEY RAN out of dirt road about a mile later, and then they ran out of island.

They stood there on the edge of the island, wondering how they had missed the bad guys. Widow stood the closest to the edge of a rock cliff and stared out at the water.

"Where the hell are they?" he asked out loud to no one in particular.

And no one answered him. They just shrugged.

Then he looked down. The rock cliff wasn't that high off the water below, maybe ten feet. But he thought about how this end of the island was high, and the other was low.

"The elevation," he called back to the others.

They looked at him, and Widow turned left and started climbing down the rock cliff, stepping on one rock and then another until he was standing in knee-high water.

He inspected the cliff's wall and smiled.

There was no wall, only a huge opening to a cave.

"Down here," he shouted up.

Ali and Hardy climbed down.

"What is it?" Ali asked.

"It's an underwater cave," Hardy said.

Widow said, "Partially underwater."

Widow looked at the mouth and the ocean water that flowed into it.

He said, "It's deep in the middle."

"Yeah," Hardy said.

"How wide do you think this is?" Widow asked.

Hardy shrugged and said, "I don't know, maybe twenty yards?"

"Yeah," Widow said.

He ducked down and peered in. There was nothing but darkness ahead, and then the mouth opened up wider and curved right.

He stormed through the shallow water, which was the only part that could be walked on because there was a rock ledge. Then Widow realized it wasn't rock.

He said, "Ali."

"Yeah?"

"This walkway is manmade."

Ali looked and saw what he meant. It wasn't rock; it was metal.

"What the hell is this?" Ali asked.

Widow said, "It's an underground dock for a submarine."

67

Hardy said, "A small sub couldn't fit through here and then hope to get back out again."

Widow said, "Not a military one."

Hardy said nothing.

Widow said, "Ali, any chance that Farmer got himself a mini-sub? The deep-sea diving kind?"

Ali said, "Anything is possible."

Hardy said, "Do you think this guy Farmer escaped the Russian sub? Now he's here?"

"Maybe. Not all terrorists are martyrs."

Hardy said, "Those things are slow-moving. No way would he make it this far by now."

Widow said, "Maybe they didn't. Maybe they're on their way. Or maybe he had it retrofitted. They could have gotten their hands on one and dumped all the scientific gear out of it. Put on some extra propellers. Maybe an extra engine. A couple of thrusters. Expand the rotors.

"Hell, they could be here already."

Ali and Hardy said nothing.

Widow said, "Come on. Let's get wet."

They followed him down the metal walkway. Widow led the way and followed the walkway down the upper lip of the cave and on for another forty yards until it dipped up out of the water. They bent around the curve to the right and west, and then they came to an enormous cavern with dim lights strung up along metal rigs.

Off in the distance, about another fifty yards away, there was a platform with stacked equipment and a couple of utility poles. Beyond that was a set of stairs that climbed up and disappeared inside a small structure that could have been some kind of control room or something.

Widow noticed the cables snaking up under the stairs and going to the structure.

On the platform were two men that Widow had never seen before. They were seated on crates, talking.

Widow saw a third one, a redhead, pacing up and down the walkway, standing duty even though his buddies weren't helping.

Widow saw no one else. He assumed they were inside the structure.

The other thing that Widow saw was a black mini-sub, just like he thought. It floated underneath the platform. The headlamps were lit up like bright, glowing orbs. They cast more light on the inside of the cavern than any other light.

The sub looked empty, although he couldn't see into it to be sure.

"What now?" Ali asked.

Widow looked back at him. He said, "I'm not here to take prisoners."

Ali nodded.

Hardy nodded.

Widow led the way. They stayed crouched low in single formation. Widow crept along the catwalk, staying out of the light.

They came upon the redheaded leader first. He was walking the other way. Pacing half out caution, Widow figured, and half out of boredom.

He turned to come face to face with Widow. At about ten feet away, which was a shame because Widow wanted to keep the element of surprise, but he knew in such a limited space, a loud gunfight was inevitable.

He shot first.

Widow had the M4's stock embedded firmly in his shoulder. His butt touched his boot heel. He kept his elbow stiff, reinforcing the grip. He squeezed the trigger twice.

Two rounds exploded through the redheaded guy's center mass. He flew back and rolled off the catwalk and into the water. Dead.

The other two men on the platform turned to see what was happening. Before they could lift their guns, before they even stood up, Hardy dropped them both. Two single rounds.

The guy was a hell of a shot, Widow thought.

Now everything was loud. Widow jumped to his feet and charged up the walkway to the platform.

One guy came clawing up and out of the hatch of the mini-sub—no gun in hand.

Widow didn't care. He fired a round and hit the guy square in the face. Blood burst and red mist sprayed out. The guy dropped back into the sub, lifeless.

That's four down, Widow thought.

Just then, three more guys came running out of the structure above and saw the visitors and were met with a hail of bullets. They dropped as fast as their friends. One fell off to the side and rolled down the ramp, off of the structure, and the other was flung over the side into the water to join his dead friend, the redheaded leader.

The last just slumped back and landed on the ramp.

Widow didn't wait for more to come tumbling out of the structure. He ran up and took cover behind a wall to the opening. Hardy followed, and Ali stayed close.

Widow peeked in. The space ahead was crammed, but empty.

Widow said, "Stay back for a minute. It's small in there. Let me go first."

Hardy nodded.

Widow handed the M4 to Ali and went ahead with the HK45 instead. The space was too close-quartered for an assault rifle.

The space beyond was dark and didn't lead to a control room at all. Instead, there was a small hall that opened up into a large room with sofas and old armchairs, and some radio equipment that looked like the last time it had been turned on was during WWII. Off to one side was a string of long drapes hanging from the ceiling, like they were hiding a stage.

There was a coffee table near the sofas and an ashtray with two cigars still smoking.

A guy was sitting on the sofa. He was in bad shape. His face looked like he had been beaten within an inch of his life.

He wore a ripped-up Russian uniform. He was a submariner, Widow figured.

He stared at Widow, said nothing. Widow wasn't even sure if he could speak.

But his eyes were wide open and flicking to the left.

Widow rolled into the room, turned to the drapes, and paused. He figured someone was hiding behind it. And there was. He saw shoes underneath.

And a man jumped out. He fired an M9 Beretta at Widow. Widow suddenly felt bad for the guy. He was almost sure that the guy had never fired a gun before in his life. Only he was in the CIA; he must have.

The guy saw he had missed completely. He didn't readjust his aim to shoot Widow because Widow was looking back at him with the HK45 dead on target.

The guy dropped his gun, which told Widow who he was. Probably.

Widow asked, "Are you, Farmer?"

The guy nodded and started to speak.

Widow didn't let him. He squeezed two times. He put one through the heart and one through the guy's head for good measure.

Farmer tumbled back into the curtains, moving to one side, grabbing onto the other with his dead hand. His corpse pulled it down and off the ceiling. Widow looked beyond it to a stairwell that led up into the ground above.

Eva was nowhere to be seen.

Widow turned back to the man on the sofa. He walked over to him and asked, "Are you Karpov?"

"Yes."

"Where's Eva?"

Karpov stood up and must have been dizzy because he collapsed back over.

"Don't get up. Where is she?"

"He took her. Up," Karpov said.

"Don't worry. Stay here. My friends will get you. I'm going after her."

Karpov said nothing.

Widow ran to the stairs and climbed.

68

THE STAIRS LED UP and out of the cave to a wooden hatch that was so cracked and splintered Widow could see daylight. He was worried that it was a trap. That maybe the man in black waited for him above with that SIG Sauer he had seen earlier.

Widow took a deep breath, and with one fluid, fast action, he thrust himself upward, shoved the door open, and took aim, scanning in every direction. No one was there.

He saw lots of daylight and broken brick walls.

He pulled himself up and out. He was in an abandoned building. He walked out of it and saw he was back in part of the town. Trees surrounded only this part. There was no dirt road. He presumed it must have been an offshoot site.

He came out of the building, kept his back to the wall.

"Where are you?" he called out. There was no answer.

He looked through the buildings, and then he looked down and saw footprints in the dirt and grass blades stomped down. Widow turned to follow them.

The footprints led into a two-story structure with an old door hanging off rusted hinges. Widow entered and swept from left to right with the HK45. He saw nothing, but there were more footprints in the dust leading up the stairs. He followed slowly, carefully. He checked the nooks and corners. Checking the hidden areas as best he could. At the top of the stairs, there was a hallway with three open doorways. Past bedrooms, he presumed.

He walked down the hallway, following the footprints.

They led to the last room on the right, across from another room.

Widow was no fool. He had spent sixteen years as an undercover cop where bad guys would have killed him if they knew who he really was. So he was a cautious guy. Cautious enough. He checked the other two rooms before entering the last one. They were empty.

He stopped at the wall and hugged it before stepping into the doorway.

Like the other buildings, the roof on this one was mostly blown away. The sun was bright at the angle he was at. It beamed down through huge holes and was almost blinding.

Widow called out, "Eva?"

She didn't answer, not with a reply. Instead, he heard her making all kinds of noise. She must have been gagged. He peered in and saw her seated on a lone old desk chair. Her hands were zip-tied in such a way that it looked like she was stuck to the chair. The zip-ties went between her wrists and one of the chair's metal arms.

Widow looked around fast. No one was there.

He saw an open closet. It looked empty. There were holes in the floor big enough to fall through. He studied them. No one was down there, either.

There was a window behind her. No glass. He saw trees beyond it and nothing else.

Widow entered the room, confused. Where was the man in black?

He walked over to Eva slowly. She mumbled and squirmed. The chair's bottom was jammed into a hole in the floor like it was practically bolted there. She was flailing, trying to get free.

Widow said, "Okay. I'm here. I'm here."

He got behind her and looked at the chair's leg. He reached his free hand around her and pulled the gag out of her mouth.

Eva shouted, "HE'S BEHIND ME! OUT THE WINDOW!"

But it was too late. A second later, a razor-sharp garrote shot over Widow's face and came tightening around his neck.

69

THE MAN in black's garrote was deadly. He had never messed up with it before, and he had no intention of messing up this time. He had stepped out the window to hide on the ledge, but he also wanted the leverage because his target was a big guy.

His plan was to pull back and half drop over the ledge as best as he could to let his weight and gravity pull the target back to the window and strangle him that way—a perfect plan. At least it should have been. But he miscalculated the wire and Widow's neck and Widow's HK45.

The HK45 was jammed between the razor wire and Widow's neck.

Widow saw the wire at the last second and had jerked upward and shoved the gun between the wire and his face and neck.

The HK45 was twisted and turned and pointed left away from his face, which was good because a hair more inward and one shot would have blown a hole in his face.

The man in black was strong, not stronger than Widow, but at this angle and the way the guy was pulling him back and out the window, he had the advantage.

Widow struggled to pull him forward while the man in black wrenched backward.

Widow could feel his legs buckling. He could feel his shoulder muscles cracking and throbbing from pulling forward.

He didn't want to fire the gun so close to his face. And even if he did, what good would it do?

He tried to move, to shift away, and try to get free. But every move he made, the man in black was right there with a countermove.

He struggled and wrenched from one side to the other. The garrote wire was etching through the gun's hard shell. What was he supposed to do?

Eva struggled and bounced and tried to get free. She could help him if only she could get free.

That was when Widow decided the best thing to do wasn't to fight. The best thing to do was to give in. He felt the man in the black push off the wall outside the window with his feet, trying to pull Widow back to get him in a better strangling position.

So Widow shifted to the right and then spun left and jumped backward. His feet pushed off the floor with all of his power, and he took the man in black off guard and plowed into him. The two of them went back into the air, out the window, off the ledge, and into the trees.

They bumped into each other, and both fell to the hard ground below. Two stories. Not enough to kill them, but enough to break bones.

Widow landed on his left hand and felt two of his fingers twist and break. The pain hit him all at once. And instinctually, he let go of the HK45, which went flying into the man in black's face, snapped back at him by the garrote.

They both lay on the ground for a moment. Widow in pain from his broken fingers and the man in black with the wind knocked out of him and a bloody nose that could have been from hitting the ground or from the HK45 nailing him in the face.

Widow didn't care. He just wanted to get up.

He dug down deep and shoved himself up on his good hand and stumbled onto his feet. The man in black was up next, going for his SIG Sauer, Widow presumed, because he reached under his jacket to the shoulder holster. Only he came out with nothing because the SIG Sauer was up on the window ledge. And it wasn't alone.

The man in black and Widow both heard a voice.

Eva shouted down, "Hey!"

She was leaning out of the window. She was free from the chair, only not really because the arm hung off the zip-tie around her wrists. She had pulled the old rusted arm off. She held the man in black's SIG Sauer.

She called down to Widow.

"Are you okay?"

"I'll live."

"What about the missile?"

"Don't worry. It didn't explode," he said, and he looked at the man in black who looked shocked. And it dawned on Widow. They had thought it did. They had all thought they started World War III.

Widow said, "Karpov gave up the wrong passcode. Farmer entered the wrong one. The missile was nothing more than an oversized paperweight."

Eva asked, "Is my father okay?"

"He is."

She asked, "Want me to shoot him?"

The man in black's eyes sprang open. Blood trickled out of this nose.

And Widow said, "Do it!"

Eva squeezed the trigger, and for the second time in a day, Widow had blood sprayed across his face and neck and shirt.

The man in black's face was mostly still there. Mostly.

The corpse dropped to its knees and slumped over forward.

Widow called up to her. He said, "Let's get out of here. My hand is killing me."

70

THREE DAYS LATER, Widow waited outside of Admiral Kiley's office with his assistant, who was Widow's favorite person at the moment because she had brought him two cups of coffee, Styrofoam cup, back to back, as he waited.

The only thing good was the coffee, because so far, he was getting the silent treatment from the admiral, who had been in his office with Ebert for fifteen minutes. Widow didn't answer to them anymore, and they had told him he was a hero. But he still had to wait like everybody else.

Finally, Ebert opened the door and said, "Widow."

Widow stood up. He was in new clothes, black jeans still, but he wore a white sweater over a white t-shirt, which matched the cast on his left hand, also white. The hospital on Norfolk Navy Base was pretty good. They fixed him right up. One day, no waiting there, and they had set his bones and cast them up. He was supposed to keep his left hand above his heart. He had been given a sling to wear, which he elected not to.

Widow stood up from his chair and took his coffee with him. He walked into Kiley's office and shook hands with him, and then with Ebert.

Kiley said, "Widow, you did a fine thing for us. A fine thing. Your country is grateful."

Widow said, "I appreciate that."

"Have a seat then."

Widow looked down at the chair and said, "I won't be here long enough to sit."

Kiley looked at him, confused.

"Of course you will. The medal ceremony is this afternoon."

"Medal?" Widow asked.

Kiley said, "Yes. Don't you want your medal?"

"What medal?"

"The Secretary of the Navy is driving out. Or already has. He wants to shake the hand of everyone involved and present medals. I don't know exactly what yours will be, not a medal of honor or anything. But something you'll want."

"I don't want the medal."

"I'm sorry to hear that."

Widow kept smiling. He didn't want to seem ungrateful for the gesture. He looked around the room.

Kiley had quite a career, like the rumors suggested. The walls were littered with pictures of sailors that Widow didn't know. Some black and white. Some in color. There were awards and commendations and medals strung out neatly all over the place. Everything was chaotic, yet somehow organized, which reminded Widow of the aircraft carrier when the missile broke through the water, when Kiley had a smile on his face.

Then Widow noticed something displayed proudly on the table behind Kiley. Right in the center, there was a big, broken old brick. It was polished but was still worn and timeworn. Underneath it, there was a plaque with writing etched in gold.

Widow said, "You love this Navy stuff, don't you?"

Kiley said, "Of course! Don't you?"

Widow shook his head.

"I did once. But that was a lifetime ago. Not me anymore, Admiral."

Kiley said nothing.

Ebert broke the silence and said, "Widow, are you sure you don't want to stay?"

"No."

Kiley said, "One more piece of information that you will like."

"Oh? What's that?"

"Eva and her father will get asylum for their contributions to stopping Farmer."

Widow nodded.

"We offered to send them back, but they begged to stay. It wasn't up to me, of course. It was up to the State Department. But I'm sure that Ali had something to do with granting their request."

Widow thought of Eva. He asked, "Where is she?"

"I don't have the faintest idea. Their names are probably changed by now. They're being treated as if they're in witness protection. They're probably halfway to Oklahoma."

Widow stayed quiet.

Kiley asked, "Sure, you won't stay for the ceremony?"

"No."

Widow turned and walked back to the door.

Ebert walked with him.

Widow turned and said, "I should salute you, sir. After all, I was a SEAL, once."

Kiley seemed to like that statement. And Widow stood proud, head high, shoulders back, and saluted with his good hand. Ebert saluted as well. And Kiley saluted back.

Widow looked past him at the brick. The inscription read: Berlin Wall, November 9, 1989.

Widow dropped his salute and walked out.

Ebert followed and walked him back to the front of the building, and shook hands and said goodbye.

71

AFTER THE CEREMONY, and the shaking of more hands, and the salutes, and the drinks, and the cigars, there was dinner. And after all that, Admiral Kiley was exhausted. He said his goodbyes to Ebert and Towdex and the Secretary of the Navy, and God only knew how many other high-ranking officials. He lost track from all the pats on the back for a job well done.

He got in his car with a smile on his face and drove home.

On the way, he thought about McConnell, his friend. He hated that the man had to die. He hated that the man's wife had to die. Kiley didn't regret the man in black or Farmer.

He deeply regretted that the mission was a failure, really. War wasn't ignited. The nuke didn't go off. He had already been prepared to see it through. Destroying America's greatest Naval base would have done the trick. But it didn't happen.

It wasn't all a loss, though. There seemed to be a new surge of duty in the Navy now. He was proud of that. He could find another project to start things moving, to reignite honor and fight back into the Navy that he had loved.

He could find some warlord in the Middle East, to help or in Asia, perhaps.

Kiley pulled up into his driveway and killed the engine in his American-made Ford Taurus. He got out and clicked the button on his keys to lock the vehicle. He walked to his front door and opened it.

He stepped over to the alarm pad to switch off the alarm like he did every day. Only the pad wasn't counting down fifty seconds like it usually did. In fact, the pad looked totally different today because it was ripped halfway out of the wall. Wires dangled, and the plastic cover was in pieces.

He stared at it, dumbfounded.

Then he heard a voice from behind him in the dark in the doorway to his den.

Widow said, "All those people, Admiral."

Kiley spun around to see Widow standing there with one hand in a sling. And the other down by his side.

"Widow? What are you doing here?"

"You know you almost got away with it."

"What are you talking about?"

Widow said, "Come on into the den. I want to chat."

Kiley walked into the house. The den was where he needed to go. He kept his sidearm in the top drawer of his desk.

He walked past Widow and nodded politely, like some sort of English butler.

Widow walked behind him and sat down in a comfortable armchair across from the desk.

"Take your coat off," Widow said.

Kiley took off his coat and pulled a huge, leather-backed chair from his desk and sat in it.

He slid his drawer open.

Widow said, "I gotta know. Why did you do it?"

"Do what?"

"You know what."

"Indulge me."

"You orchestrated this whole thing. Farmer. Karpov. All of it."

"How did you know?"

"When I saw the brick from the Berlin wall in your office, I was sure. It told me you missed the glory days of war. Or some such nonsense. But the smile on your face when the nuke was fired. That told me first."

"This country doesn't appreciate its military," Kiley said, his tone changed to one full of confidence.

Then he thrust his hand into the drawer and grabbed for his Colt 1911 forty-five, only it wasn't there. And he looked up, terrified.

It was in Widow's good hand.

"How many people were going to die?"

"They're all nothing! They need to know what real war is like! They need to know honor!"

Widow stood up, pointed the 1911 at Kiley.

"Wait! Wait! I'm a patriot! I've saved lives!"

"You're not a patriot! Those men and women out there fighting every day! They are the patriots! You're a washed-up nobody!"

Then Kiley's face turned to one of something pathetic. And he begged.

"Please, Jack! No one has to know! No one really got hurt! The nuke didn't even explode! Remember?"

"No one got hurt?"

"Right!"

"What about Karpov's men? They're dead!"

Kiley shrugged and said, "So what? They're the enemy! They're Russian!"

Widow shook his head and said, "They aren't the enemy. You are."

He squeezed the trigger and watched as the familiar red mist exploded out the hole left in the back of Kiley's head. Blood and brain sprayed behind him across books on a bookshelf.

Widow saluted Kiley one last time with the 1911 still in hand. Then he walked over to the corpse and spit on it.

He turned and went to the kitchen, left the lights off. He found a dishtowel and grabbed it. Used it to pop on the light above the stove. He found a dishwasher and opened it, tossed the gun on the rack. Then he found soap and loaded the machine and started it on a heavy clean cycle, and left it.

He had touched nothing but the front doorknob and the alarm pad. He wiped both on his way out.

Widow walked down the driveway and out of the subdivision without being seen.

Thirty minutes later, he was back on a major interstate. The thumb from his good hand was out.

A semi-truck slowed and pulled over to the side of the road about twenty yards ahead.

Widow jogged to the passenger side, and the driver asked, "Where ya headed, guy?"

Eva and her father weren't sent to Oklahoma like Kiley had joked. Not that far away. But they had been given new identities and sent to Vermont, which Widow knew because Ali had told him.

Widow said, "Vermont."

SCOTT BLADE

A **JACK WIDOW** THRILLER

FIRE WATCH

A MILLION-SELLING SERIES

DRIFTER. OUTLAW. HERO.

1

A PRESCRIBED fire is a fire set deliberately. The fire that burned Molly's house to the ground was set deliberately.

Right then, her husband burned up in it, and she watched it happen. And she couldn't help but think about the raging California wildfires happening right then, farther south.

From outside the two-story, dark coastal house, she saw it all. The engulfing red-hot flames. The dark backfire. The plums of white smoke. And the clouds of black. It fumed together, killing off the oxygen in the air.

The smoke rose, blotting out the stars.

DeGorne's husband had been there. In the house. When it all started, she heard his screams. She would never forget. But that was all over now. He was dead.

She had packed a bag the night before—two of them. One was the same bag she packed every April 30th, every year, for the last five years.

Every year she packed a bag with what she needed for the next six months. She packed two pairs of hiking shorts, five pairs of short-sleeved tops, three pairs of cargo pants, five pairs of socks, five pairs of underwear, two pairs of long-sleeved tops, one raincoat, one warm denim coat, two knit sweaters, her basic hygiene and feminine products, two knit caps, two baseball hats, and a foldable toothbrush. Everything that she needed.

She had packed them all in one canvas backpack. It was packed tightly, but it was filled just enough to close. After five years of packing it every

April, she knew exactly how to do it. A man wouldn't have been able to pack so much so efficiently. She was much smaller than most men. Therefore, her clothes were more modest, more lightweight, and much easier to pack.

The second bag she had packed was a blue duffle, no bigger than her backpack, but a hell of a lot heavier. Heavy because it was packed with something else. Something that didn't belong to her. Something that she had found just the day before. The contents were the reason she had one black eye.

Neither packed bag was in the fire. Each was stowed away safely in the back of her truck. It was parked in a disconnected garage. It was away from the fire, directly behind her.

DeGorne stood shivering just off the gravel driveway. Out of sight. Off toward the woods. Out in front of the home that used to be hers half the year, she stood and gazed upon the life that used to belong to her. She wore her single black eye like it had always been there. He had done it to her. She wouldn't deny it. Not anymore. No more telling the neighbors that she tripped—no more telling the nurses and the emergency room that she had fallen down the stairs. No more lying for him.

Luckily, she hadn't had to lie to her parents for a long time now. They were already dead. Her father would never have stood for the abuse if he had known about it.

He was retired Army. Following in his footsteps, she had done four years herself, from eighteen to twenty-one. That had made him proud until she decided not to reenlist, until she married to start a family life instead. But family life never came. She never had children. Something about infertile eggs. Something about irreversibility, which was the news that started the abuse—the first time.

It was all around the same time, when her father got sick after her mother died, that she convinced her husband to transfer his job to Seattle. Part of which was so she could take care of her father. And part was to try again—a fresh start.

She threatened to leave her husband if he didn't go with her. She threatened to expose his secrets if he didn't transfer. Why? She couldn't honestly say.

Everything was fine for a while. She had gotten a great job, which allowed her space away from everything, which allowed her to run away from her husband once a year. It allowed her to run to the woods and hide, literally.

Last year was the hardest because that was when her father died. She had been away. Off in the forests of California for the summer. Doing her job, but missing her father's last moments of life.

When she came back from her job, she had to deal with her father's passing, his burial, and his estate. That was also when the abuse from her husband had started up again. Not as bad as before, but it was there.

Last night, it had gone on as it always had gone on. A drink too many. A push into a wall. A shove into a counter. Then a jab to the gut. And then a right hook to the face. Just like what he had done to her before. This time wasn't the first time, but it would be the last. This time she planned to do something about it.

However, last night turned out to be her husband's last time to do anything.

This time hadn't been the worst that she had ever had before. She had no broken nose. No broken cheekbones. No fractured ribs. She didn't need stitches to close torn eyelids. She didn't need to reset her teeth.

There was no dentist's appointment tomorrow. There was no emergency room visit—no paperwork to fill out. No lies to tell. She'd had worse. He had given her worse. But no more.

Her toes sunk into the gravel. She had thick, wavy blonde hair that cascaded down over her shoulders. It caressed her soot-covered body. She looked like she had woken up in the middle of the blaze. Her favorite t-shirt for sleeping hugged close to her small frame. She had no pants on. Just panties. Just the t-shirt and panties, and the soot, and the ash.

She had barely escaped the fire.

Goosebumps scuttled across her skin. The night was cold. Not winter cold, but cold enough. Stony and callous winds blustered off the Puget Sound.

Ashes wafted out of the fire. She thought about her bags. She had only packed the two, and both packed full enough—everything she needed and nothing she didn't.

Then her mind shifted. She thought about where she would go or what she would do, or how she would get through this. She couldn't go on to her job. Could she?

Her mind returned to nothingness, and she watched in horror as the house she had called home for five years burned to the ground, along with the marriage that she had known inside it.

She hadn't planned on burning her house to the ground. None of it was premeditated—none of it but the packed bags.

The flames rose into the night sky like a phoenix rising from the ashes. Fiery steeples jetted up and waved and sparked out like deadly solar flares rocketing off the surface of the sun. The heat was intense. She felt it on her face, even from fifty feet away. A three-thousand-square-foot house will do that.

The house was nestled in the woods, twenty miles north of Seattle. The closest neighbors were miles away. They would see the yellow-red torrents of blaze soon enough. They'd be calling the police and the fire department.

Within ten minutes, the nearest firehouse would receive the distress call of someone reporting the fire. Two minutes later, they'd dispatch a truck. And twenty minutes after that, the fire trucks would barrel down the dirt road onto the gravel driveway that led to her house.

The police would be there sooner.

The nearest police were actually the county sheriff, a pudgy, older guy named Portman. She knew him well. He had been a friend of her family her whole life. He and her husband weren't friends. He suspected the abuse. He had gotten a few reports from the hospital—nothing he could ever do about it because she always lied to him, too.

DeGorne stepped back off the driveway and planted her toes in the cold grass, barefoot. She did nothing. She said nothing. She thought nothing. She just watched and listened.

Trees surrounded her. The wind swayed the leaves in the same direction as the waving flames. She stood there until thoughts returned to her.

She thought. Her husband had been in the house. He had been in the fire. He was dead. But she was not. She was still here. She was still alive.

She froze in place, asking herself one question.

Should I run?

2

MORE THAN A THOUSAND miles to the south, in East Hollywood, Jack Widow hadn't showered in two days. He hadn't changed his clothes. He needed a haircut and a shave—badly. And he knew it. Everyone who passed by him knew it.

He wasn't unclean and rumpled by accident. It was on purpose. It wasn't because he was out of money. He could buy new clothes right now. He could pay for a haircut and a shave. No problem. He had the money to rent a motel room. Motel rooms had showers. That was a universal truth, in most cases. He could shower when he was ready to. There was no normal reason for him not to buy new, clean clothes or to get a haircut or to take a shower.

There were only two logical reasons anyone would look the way he looked. The first was that the person was homeless. Which was what he appeared to be. But that wasn't the reason he looked homeless. He looked homeless because of the second reason. It was on purpose.

Widow sat next to a pile of cardboard and garbage bags, in a doorway to an abandoned electronics store. The kind of place that thrived on selling stereo equipment three decades ago. It probably sold cassette tapes and Walkmans and ghetto blasters. The store was old. The whole building was old. It was a dump, like most of the street. The street was so rundown that half the streetlights were burned out.

The windows were barred. The doors behind him used to have thick glass windows. Now they were cracked, water-damaged planks.

Widow looked homeless because he was playing a part. He even had a used paper coffee cup from McDonald's out in front of him. Like a panhandler would have for spare change. Initially, he had purchased a coffee, intending to drink it. That was until someone came along and tossed spare change into it. At which point, he had gone back to the same McDonald's and bought a new one. The second coffee he actually got to drink before someone else walked along and dumped more change into it.

Widow didn't spend his daytime lounging in the doorway of the abandoned electronic store. Homeless people don't spend their entire days standing around the same place. They move around. They go places. They keep the blood circulating. And then they return to their nests.

He spent his days down the street, around the corner, and up another several blocks in a much better, much cleaner, and more respected neighborhood. The people there stared at him, gawked at him. And normally, they avoided him.

In the better part of town, he discovered an industrial plaza that had an actual Starbucks in it, not a closed-down one. The days were a little long and a lot boring, hanging around, waiting like he was. So, he found a used bookstore that might've been on its last legs. Widow liked books. He liked bookstores. The smell of the paper. The feeling of being around like-minded people. The organization of it all. It all made him feel at home in a small way.

Inside the store, he bought a John Grisham book, which he had read before, but had forgotten. He read it a second time that first day. Easy enough. He read it on a park bench, near an elementary school with two merry-go-rounds on the playground. One was old and boring. It was all metal, with no character. The second one was newer. It probably had a story about a city councilman wanting to upgrade the playground. And all they ended up getting was a new merry-go-round.

Widow also bought a book called Fire Season. Which was an interesting book about fire lookouts, a job that Widow had known before. But like the Grisham book, he had forgotten the details.

Way back when Widow was in his early twenties, before he joined the NCIS and rejoined the Navy, he had just returned from Afghanistan. His tour of duty had ended, and his time in the Navy was up. He didn't know what to do next. He needed time to think things over—an understandable proposition. He needed a little quiet time to look inside himself and figure out what he wanted.

It was the end of spring. Widow moved east, out of San Diego, following along the Rio Grande. He stayed in an interstate motel for a night and got a ride headed into New Mexico the next day. The guy who picked him up was a reporter who worked for the Wall Street Journal. They got to talking. It turned out the guy spent half his year in New York City writing for the paper and the other half working a very peculiar job. A job that Widow knew, but couldn't quite recall. And like a forgotten kiss, he felt a kind of familiarity to it, like déjà vu.

The job was fire lookout.

Widow rode on with the guy and skipped his planned destination. He sat in silence with the windows down. The scenery passed by like on a train. It took him a while, but he finally recalled where he had heard of a fire lookout before. It wasn't just hearing about it. It was reading about it in Jack London books when he was in the third grade. And then his memory brought back a long-lost fact. Jack Kerouac had spent sixty-three days as a fire lookout in the summer of 1956.

Widow thought, What was the name of the place? Desolation Peak?

Then he remembered a story that he had read before. There was a short tale of a fire lookout in Norman Maclean's A River Runs Through It, where the main character retold his experiences working as a fire watch one hot summer. Which was loosely based on Maclean's own life experiences.

The reporter was on his way to orientation to be a fire lookout again, at a place called Black Range. The reporter had already put in his time at another forest to the north. He had taken on a more full-time role and was moving to New Mexico to begin. Widow rode along and listened to the guy tell him stories about the beauty and solitude of being a lookout, which reminded Widow of being a Navy lookout, in a way. Once as a Navy lookout, it had been his duty to watch for ships and land and weather and everything that didn't belong on the ocean surface. The difference was a fire lookout watched for smoke.

Widow ended up taking a job as a lookout relief that June. He had sought it out.

June had been a great month. He moved from one tower to the next, giving the usual lookout time off, like relieving a sentry from his post.

Widow remembered he had six lookouts to relieve that summer. Three men and three women. All of them had been fascinating people. One woman had been there every year for twenty-eight years.

He enjoyed that month, and he had learned a lot.

Yesterday, he was amazed when he stumbled upon a paperback version of Fire Season, in a remote used-book store.

As Widow read on about the life of a fire lookout, he closed his eyes and remembered that June, long ago. He imagined that summer. He lived in six different towers. All of which were basically twelve by twelve rooms on stilts. He imagined seeing mountain ranges hundreds of miles away from his window. He remembered being high enough to see aplomado falcons diving for ground rodents or Bendire's thrashers soaring the southern skies. They were the most majestic views he had seen at that point in his life. He pictured himself walking through a forest canopy, stopping in meadows, taking in the grasslands. One time he spotted Konik wild horses grazing.

As Widow continued to read, he remembered the most important part of fire lookouts—looking for fires. He read on about crown fires and purging fires. He imagined how beautiful such a deadly thing was. He read about record-breaking fires that engulfed entire species of trees. Purging fires killed off trees that were once deemed to be plentiful by the US Forest Service. One moment there was a healthy amount of a single tree species. And the next, they had been extinguished by fire.

He learned that lightning strikes to a tree, in certain forests, were 30,000 times more likely than lightning strikes on humans.

He read about the history of apocalyptic fires—the horror of the destruction. But then he read about the life that came after. He learned it was in the nineteen seventies that scientists and firefighters and park officials realized fires were good for forests. After a deadly blaze swept over hundreds of square miles, the aftermath was blackness, at first. But then the local forests bounced back with great resilience—great rebirth. Streams sprung up again. Flowers bloomed. Once-dead trees were reseeded and grew back toward the sky.

As Widow read on, he got the picture in his head. The fantasy of living as a fire lookout once again, returning to a time that he had forgotten. He imagined living for months in God's country. Only having a dozen visitors in three months. Suddenly, Widow was in.

The only thing to do next was to figure out how and when. But that would have to wait. Right now, Widow sat in the same doorway two nights in a row, on purpose. He had a small mission to take care of. Something that he had to do. He didn't like injustices. And he had one to correct before he could leave.

Widow's clothes were tattered, secondhand, and thrift-store bought.

Blue jeans with holes in the knees and bare white threads sticking out like gutted sinews hanging on display. His hair was overgrown like weeds, not long, just unkempt—patches of whiskers stubbled out of his face.

His hair had already needed a wash and cut. That was just a coincidence. But two nights of rubbing dirt and dust in it helped to make it look dirtier than it would have been.

Widow was in East Hollywood, between a closed-down Starbucks and a hardware store that time had forgotten existed, in one of the worst parts of town, one of the most crime-ridden places that America offered. Not all of it was bad. There were a couple of streets to the west where things got better. And the daytime wasn't so bad, but none of it was safe at night. It was here that Widow had wandered into a little grocery store two days ago.

The area was bad, but the Korean family who owned the store had been there for years before other businesses moved out and moved on. They were there before the crime rate was so high. They held onto hope that one day it would flourish again.

And even if they wanted to leave, they couldn't go. Widow didn't know why. Maybe one of them was ill. Maybe they didn't have the money. Maybe they were stuck in a mortgage. Bills still had to get paid—crime or no crime.

Or maybe it had just been a matter of pride. They had no children that Widow was aware of.

If it hadn't been for his sense of justice, Widow would have left Hollywood, would have left LA. For the casual tourist like him, Hollywood was a city worth one or two days at most, like Boston or New Orleans or D.C.. Everything that you needed to see and do could be done in a day or two.

LA was more than a one-day place, but having seen it before, it was actually not a place he wanted to visit at all. But the life that Widow leads led him there. Like being guided by fate, if you believe in that sort of thing.

Widow had planned on leaving two days ago, until he wandered into this Korean grocery store on his way to a bus station. All of it by chance. He had walked a little too far down one street and turned on another, misread one street sign, and turned onto another wrong street, and before he knew it, he was in the bad part of town. And he was completely lost.

He knew the grocer was Korean before he set foot in the store. He knew because above the single open door was a sign written in both English and Korean. He recognized the letters. Before Widow was a drifter, he had spent sixteen years in the United States Navy.

The USN had a significant presence on the Korean peninsula. He had walked enough around Seoul and cities near Busan to know what Korean words looked like. He had no idea what they said, but he recognized the characters.

He walked into the grocery, looking to ask for directions. And maybe a cup of freshly brewed coffee for the road. But he got neither thing.

As he approached the entrance, he had to walk past an LAPD patrol car. The light bar was off. The engine still ran and hummed and smoked clouds of exhaust out of the tailpipe.

He heard the chatter of cop voices on the police radio. He heard cop codes. All was calm in a normal city kind of way, which was to say busy for a small-town police force but calm for a major city force. He heard familiar bandwidth static. And then the familiar humdrum of dispatcher voices. He listened and picked up a few things. He made out familiar radio codes and others that he could guess what they meant.

Widow ignored the codes and the dispatcher talk, and entered the store—his hands in his pockets, his face forward. He ducked his head an inch on his way under the low doorway. It wasn't a necessary act. It was just a habit that tall people everywhere shared. Right then, it happened. He was shoulder-checked by one of two cops walking out. It wasn't an accident. He knew that right off. The act had been on purpose. Widow knew that because it was stone hard—shoulder to shoulder in unadulterated, brutish gorilla fashion—no confusion there. Widow had been shoulder-checked before. He knew the act. It wasn't something he looked forward to, but it seemed to follow him everywhere he went.

The second cop closed the lid on a metal clipboard that he had been carrying. Next, he clicked and shoved a ballpoint pen into his shirt pocket. He stopped dead in front of Widow, who stayed still and stood his ground.

The first cop stopped.

The second cop stopped.

The first cop had spun around to face Widow.

Widow stopped inside the doorway. He stood with the first cop at the nine o'clock position and the second cop right there at his three.

He stayed quiet.

The first cop said, "Watch it, pal."

Widow said, "Sorry. My bad."

Apologizing, even without meaning it, was always the fastest way to deescalate a tense situation. Especially when the other two men involved were armed with Glock 21s.

The first cop rested his hand on his holstered Glock. Fingers loose like a seasoned gunslinger at high noon. He studied Widow up and down and back up again, slow like some kind of ancient lawman from those old East-wood Westerns. The same tired clichés of local lawmen and the new, rough-looking stranger who just moseyed into town. And the lawman who was going to warn him off.

The first cop said, "You're sorry?"

Widow stayed quiet.

"You got a problem?" the first cop asked.

Widow said, "Nope. No problem."

"That's Officer."

"What?"

"I said, that's Officer. You say, 'No problem, Officer.' Got it?"

"You serious?"

The two cops moved an inch to their right, in unison, like a pre-planned move of engagement. Which it probably was.

Widow stayed where he was. He didn't respond to the move. He didn't reply with an "Of course, Officer." Which was what the cop was waiting for.

Instead, he said, "Sorry."

Apologize, even when you did nothing.

All three men stayed quiet. So, Widow waited for a beat and added, "Officer."

The two cops nodded like they had taught a monkey a new trick.

The second cop looked at his partner and then back at Widow. He asked, "You got an ID?"

Widow stayed still.

"He's asking you a question, son!" said the first cop.

Son? Widow was in his thirties—not a young man in his own mind. The first cop looked like maybe he was in his late thirties. Calling him son was a little weird.

The second cop repeated, "ID?"

"What for?"

The first cop reached his left hand up to his belt and kept his right hand on his Glock 21. He stopped his left hand at what appeared to be a second holstered gun. Widow knew what that meant. The second gun in the second holster wasn't a gun at all. It was a department-issued Taser. Tasers were a safe alternative to shooting a suspect—a way of humanely rendering a man ineffective and compliant and docile. But Tasers had killed people before—many times. Unlike a gun, a Taser is a much more unpredictable weapon. You can shoot a guy enough times, and he's not getting up. With a Taser, you only get the one chance.

Being tazed was up there on Widow's list of things he didn't want to experience. Not today, not any day. He also didn't want to get shot.

Widow said, "I got a passport."

"Get it!" the second cop said.

The other one said, "Slowly."

Widow put his left hand up. It hung in the air. And with his right hand, he reached around to his back pocket, slowly, as instructed. He slid the tips of his fingers in and slid out a passport. He returned his hand to the front with the passport pinched between two big fingers.

The first cop said, "Take it."

The second cop nodded and stepped forward, and with a gloved hand, took the passport.

The first cop said, "Why don't you step out of this doorway here."

Widow stayed quiet.

The first cop backed out onto the sidewalk, motioning for Widow to follow. But that was where he had just come from. And he hated going backward—even just a little. Just the symbolism of going backward irked him. But what was he to do?

Widow followed the first cop out, slowly. Kept his hands visible. Palms out and open.

"Stand over there." The cop pointed with his right hand at the wall.

For a split second, Widow thought about going for the guy's Glock 21. This was his best chance. It was right there. The cop's gun hand had moved away to point him to the wall. He could lunge forward, one big step, and clamp down the guy's Taser hand with his own. Then grapple the Glock out of his holster. He could use the cop's body weight and his own momentum to spin them, so the first cop became a human shield against the second cop, in case he drew his gun fast enough.

The second cop had one hand occupied with Widow's passport. He stared at it. His eyes pointed down at the passport and off what was happening. And he was still back inside the grocer's doorway. Just enough to box him in and make his reactions smaller.

This was Widow's only chance.

But he wasn't in the habit of taking guns away from cops, not unless they deserved it. Right now, they may not have been acting as the best examples of police procedure, but they had a tough job. Tough neighborhood. Tough hours. Tough route.

Widow didn't envy patrol cops who worked in major American urban centers. Not one bit. It was a hard life. He had been there, done that. He had nothing but respect for them. He wouldn't trade lives with them for a second.

Widow did nothing beyond what the first cop was instructing him to do.

The second cop followed outside and stood to Widow's right. The first moved over to his left.

The second cop flipped open Widow's passport until he found Widow's photograph and pedigree information. He held it up and did a side-by-side comparison of Widow's face and the old photograph on his passport.

He said, "Jack Widow. Born November nine. Height six-four. Weight two-twenty."

The first cop looked at Widow with another up-down-up look over. He said, "You're a big guy. You think you're a big tough guy?"

Widow said nothing to that.

The second cop flipped through the passport beyond the ID page and kept flipping. He looked like his interest was piqued a whole hell of a lot by the stamped pages.

"McDiggs, look at this," he said and held up Widow's passport so that the first cop could glance at it.

Widow glanced at the second cop's nameplate over his breast pocket.

The nameplate said his name was Officer Jones. He took a glance back at McDiggs' nameplate and confirmed his name. Jones and McDiggs were their names.

McDiggs looked and squinted his eyes. Then he stepped closer. He kept his hand on his Taser, still holstered. He reached out with his gun hand and took the passport.

A second opportunity to take his Glock, Widow thought.

"What the hell is this?" McDiggs asked.

Widow stayed quiet.

Jones stayed quiet.

McDiggs asked, "Why you got so many stamps?"

"I traveled. A lot."

"I'll say," Jones said.

McDiggs said, "I've never heard of some of these places."

Widow shrugged and thought, Not my problem.

McDiggs flipped the page one-handed. He stopped somewhere between the first stamped page and the last stamped page.

He looked over at one country stamp and tried to pronounce it.

The sounds that came out of his mouth made no sense to Widow.

McDiggs spun his hand around and showed the passport page to Widow. He asked, "What the hell is this?"

Widow stayed still. He wouldn't step forward. That was a mistake. That was a trap. An old trick used by cops all over the world is to get the subject to step in, step forward in a sudden, quick movement that could be misconstrued, mis-characterized, misinterpreted, misdiagnosed, or simply used to make it look like an attack. Next thing, the Taser came out, and the cop tazed the perpetrator.

McDiggs would say that Widow lunged at him. Suddenly. What was he supposed to do? SOP called for action. And action meant a takedown.

The second cop would back up the story. No question. That's what good partners do.

Widow didn't fall for it. He stayed still and stared at the stamp from where he was instead. He said, "It's a stamp."

"Looks like Chinese. This supposed to be the date? Why the numbers backward?"

"They're not backward. It's the year first. That's how they write the date," Widow said. And it wasn't Chinese. It was Korean, stamped in Pyongyang. It was a North Korean travel stamp from a mission to the north, way back once upon a time when Widow had another life. An undercover cop life. An undercover SEAL life.

Widow figured it was best to omit the North Korea part.

McDiggs said, "It's backward."

He turned the page and looked at others, moving on. Widow breathed out.

He stopped on one and pointed it at Jones. He said, "That's a penguin."

And once again, McDiggs's facial expression showed that his interest was again piqued. He shoved the passport back in Widow's face and asked, "Who uses a penguin?"

"Polar bears have been known to eat them."

"What? Not eat them! Who uses them? What country?"

"Antarctica."

The two cops paused a beat and stared at each other.

Jones asked, "What the hell you doing in Antarctica?"

McDiggs said, "I thought that was all tundra and ice?"

Widow nodded, "Antarctica has about ninety percent of the world's ice."

"So, what the hell you doing there?"

"I thought only scientists live there. You a scientist?"

Jones said, "You don't look like no scientist."

"It's not just scientists. There are military there too."

The two cops looked at each other again. And back at Widow, again. McDiggs stared at Widow's arms. He saw the American flag tattoos on his forearms. He looked like he was about to ask if Widow got them in the service. Which he did, technically, but he didn't get them to fit in with his team or anything. He got them for other reasons.

McDiggs didn't ask because, just then, the radio squawked from Jones' radio rig over his chest and shoulder. He stepped back, took his eyes off Widow, and off of the passport. He stepped to the side and stopped. He reached up to the radio and clicked the button.

McDiggs stayed where he was and closed the passport. He kept his hand over the Taser and tilted his head in Jones's direction so that he could overhear the conversation.

They both listened to Jones talking back to a dispatcher. Listening. Talking again. And then responding with an "affirmative."

Jones clicked off the radio and stepped back over to them. He said to McDiggs, "Let's hit it."

McDiggs dog-eyed Widow one last time. He tossed the passport at him. It bounced off his chest and landed in his open palm.

Saying nothing, both cops turned and walked back to their police cruiser and slid in opposite sides—Jones in the driver's seat and McDiggs in the passenger's.

Widow listened to Jones slip the car's auto transmission out of park. He heard the accelerator igniting the engine and the tires taking a grip on the road. Without checking to see if anyone was coming from behind, Jones hit the gas, and they were away.

Widow stood still, watching the police cruiser fade away until it was gone from sight. He lowered his hands, pocketed his passport, and walked into the Korean grocery.

3

INSIDE THE KOREAN STORE, Widow found it to be much bigger than he had expected. There were dozens of aisles with shelves of snack foods and quick-grab items. There were stacks of food items out in the front aisle. In the first row were automobile items like lubricants and motor oils and windshield wiper blades and knickknacks that hung off rearview mirrors, and there was a shelf with actual rearview mirrors. Ready to grab. Ready to buy. Ready to glue onto a vehicle's windshield.

To his left, there was a long counter, half-barred for protection. There were cheap metal racks in the front of a single open window with no glass. There were various candy bars, and magazines, and condoms, and cigarette lighter packs, and various other impulse buys.

Widow saw the backside of a cash register. As he walked past, he noticed it was all the way open. It looked empty. Next, he saw a stool, also empty.

Widow stepped farther into the store. That's when he saw why the cops had been there. At the other end of the store, it looked like a torpedo had been fired into their glass coolers. The entire wall had built-in cooler doors with racks of beer and milk and water bottles and soda cans and energy drinks. Some of which Widow had never heard of before. The entire thing was destroyed.

There was broken glass everywhere, all over the floor. Widow saw broken beer bottles. Long, unbroken bottles rolled across the tile, over streams of spilled beer and milk and soda and energy drinks. All of it souped together, streamed down the cracks and trenches between the tiles of the floor.

Someone had come into the store and vandalized it. That was obvious. That was why the cops had been there. They had been called after the fact because they came out of the store with no one in handcuffs.

What were they going to do about it? Maybe something. Maybe nothing.

Then again, what could they do about it? In busy cities, vandalism wasn't high on the list of major crimes that cops focused on.

Off to the left, at the end of the counter, Widow saw two people hunched over. Sobbing and crying. She was speaking Korean. The tone was anger and frustration and a hint of fear; all rolled into one conversation. Widow could piece together the gist of it.

He walked in slowly. He made wide, heavy steps to help make his presence known. He stepped around the edges of spilled drinks and avoided the broken glass as best he could.

Maybe not the best time to be here, he thought. But sagacious curiosity and the need to know and a sense of duty guided him in moments like this.

He changed tactics and stepped directly on the broken glass, crunching it. It was loud in the silence. There was no avoiding it. It was everywhere. It looked like someone had taken a baseball bat to every structure built with glass. The floor was covered with it in all shapes and sizes.

He cleared his throat as he neared the two huddled people.

The woman was the first to hear him. Her head shot up, her eyes opened wide, and her jaw dropped open.

"Are you one of them?"

Widow asked, "One of who?"

The other figure kneeling on the ground was a man. He craned his head back and looked up at Widow. His nose was bloody, but not bleeding. His cheeks were pumped full of blood because they were flushed. He looked like someone had roughed him up, and good—not the worst thing Widow had ever seen. His nose had bled, but it didn't look broken. There were tears in his eyes, but no black eyes—no bruises on his face. No contusions. No discolorations.

Besides the blood-filled cheeks, there was nothing permanent. Nothing severe. The damage done here looked like a first-time warning, like a shot across the bow, like a first and only threat.

The woman said, "We closed now."

Widow nodded, and he almost retreated. But he stopped in his tracks. That compelling need to help froze him. That voice in his head of better angels nagged at him. There was nothing he could do to quiet it. He wasn't the kind of man who turned his back on people in need. No matter what. Just then, he was reminded of a SEAL motto, one of many.

The more you sweat in training, the less you bleed in combat.

The meaning of this adage wasn't created for this situation. It held meaning about training hard or being prepared. But like a lot of the SEAL mottos, he found deeper meanings all the time.

Here, his Jiminy Cricket brain was saying, "Hey! If you turn your back on people who don't train like you, they will be the ones who bleed for it."

Widow stopped and looked back at her. In a kind voice, he said, "I can help. What happened?"

The man started to speak, but the woman interrupted.

"I say. We closed now."

But Widow didn't budge. He watched her shoulders slump and sag like the fight was out of her. Like she had nothing left to push her to argue.

The man tried to get up. Widow stepped closer, his hands out, and palms exposed and friendly.

He stepped up to them and offered help to the man on the ground. The man took it and grabbed Widow's forearms. His nails were long and probably hadn't been trimmed in months. Widow felt them dig into his arm. He didn't protest.

He helped the guy to his feet, and the woman followed. She moved in and acted as a crutch for her husband to lean on. Although he may not have needed it, he took her assistance.

"I'm Chung. This my store," the man said. At full height, he couldn't have been more than five-foot-one.

The woman cleared her throat with a low sound that was intended for only the man to hear. A reminder to her husband that she was there.

Chung said, "This my wife. Su-jin."

Widow stuck his hand out and said, "I'm Jack Widow. It's a pleasure to meet you both."

She looked at her husband like she sought permission to shake his hand. He nodded—a slight gesture. She took Widow's hand and shook it. She was taller than her husband by about a half an inch. Which Widow figured was because the hair on the top of her head was thick enough to give her at least two inches, whereas Chung's hair was more inclined to travel down and away from a balding region on the top.

"What happened here?"

"Nothing," Su-jin said.

Silence for a moment. A car drove by out on the street, and the sound echoed through the store. It rattled a shelf of lightweight plastic cases near the front door.

"I saw the police here. They did nothing to help you?"

"They not help," Su-jin said.

Chung said, "Don't say that. He stranger."

Chung turned to look up at Widow. He added, "Not much they can do."

"It's okay. I met them outside. They weren't the friendliest cops I've ever met. I'm sure if they have something to go on, they will take action."

"We told them criminal name already," Chung added.

Su-jin interrupted and asked, "You want to buy something?"

"Actually, I came in for directions, ma'am."

Su-jin muttered something that was inaudible or Korean or both. Either way, Widow got the sense that it wasn't a sign of approval.

"I'm looking for a bus station. I believe I missed it."

They said nothing.

"I'm lost."

Chung twisted at his waist and surveyed the damage, pinched his nose with his right hand. He took a long moment to look over the store before he responded.

Su-jin said nothing. She stood next to him, waiting.

Chung spoke again, as if he was returning to the conversation. He said, "It south about a mile. You see it on left. One street over."

"Thanks very much. Is it possible to get a cup of coffee?"

"We got coffee," Su-jin said.

"Is it fresh?"

"It freshest around here."

"I can buy a cup from you."

She nodded.

Chung said, "There's a table. Back there. In corner."

He pointed at the back corner of the store, which was near a window looking out onto the street, near an aisle displaying motor oil and windshield cleaner.

"Sounds good."

Chung put his head up and pinched his nose, changing hands. Blood trickled out, but it wasn't much. He took precautions anyway.

"Su-jin, get him some coffee. I clean up."

Widow asked, "You want help cleaning?"

"Not the mess. We take pictures first. For insurance company. They cover damages."

"You have insurance for that?"

"We got insurance for everything."

"That must be pretty high?"

"It is high. Besides local hooligans pinching us for money, the insurance is almost as bad."

"Sounds like the real criminal here is your insurance agent."

Chung chuckled and smiled and pinched his nose harder because the laughing made it worse.

He said, "I clean nose and face. You enjoy coffee."

"Come talk with me after."

Chung said, "Sure. Okay."

Su-jin said, "You go there. I get coffee."

Widow didn't argue. He headed down one aisle and threaded over to the next one and stopped at a table.

It was a foldable metal table. Metal legs. Two metal chairs. He sat in one with his back to the wall. He could see the entrance, a clear view, and an old habit.

He waited, and a couple of minutes later, Su-jin came around the corner with a hot cup of coffee in her hand. It was a paper cup. No lid.

Widow saw the steam billowing off the top like smoke from a volcano on the verge of eruption. She placed it in front of him. It was black and hot and fresh—perfect.

He took out a wad of cash-money, slipped out a five, and handed it to her.

"I...," she spoke. But she sighed first, and said, "I no change you."

Widow thought back to seeing the cash register when he came in. The drawer popped open. Cash slots empty. They had no cash to change anything.

"Keep it. No change needed."

Su-Jin smiled and thanked him.

"Listen, what happened here?"

"No, sir. Don't think about that."

"Is there an ambulance coming?"

"Ambulance?"

"Yeah. For your husband?"

"No. He fine. We clean up. It all be fine."

She backed away and nodded and smiled. He watched her disappear around the motor oil. He sat back, stared out the window. That nagging little voice in his head might as well have been saying, "Do the right thing" —over and over.

4

SHERIFF PORTMAN WAS the first to arrive on the scene. His old patrol car was just about over the hill. It was a Ford Crown Vic. He knew he would probably die with that car. The county would bury him in it. No question. There was no way the county administration was ever going to buy him a new one. Not as long as the old thing ran. The only money that they would throw at his department was barely enough to cover new tires every five years. The ones that the car sported currently were about due for replacements. And even then, he didn't hold out hope that they ever replaced his tires with actual new ones. He was almost sure that all they did was replace them with used tires from LAPD.

Portman was fine with the old patrol car. He was fine with the low salary. He was even fine with only having two deputies under his command. The one thing that he wished was better was his pension. It wasn't good. It wasn't something to brag about. It was just good enough for him to stay employed because, at his age, what was he going to do? Start a new career?

Last year his wife left him, which surprised him. It surprised everyone. The whole department. The whole town. The whole county. No one saw that one coming.

One day she was there when he left for work in the morning. Then she was gone before he came home.

He knew why. It was because she had enough of their quaint little life.

Thirty years and they were in their thirtieth year. That was the icing on the cake for her. That was what pushed her to walk out on him. The same daily rituals, the same daily routines, had been enough for her. She couldn't take any more.

The reason she left was more than just his tiny little salary. It was more than their quaint life. He figured it out the day he came home. The whole thing was because she wasn't getting any younger.

They had stayed still for so long that one day she saw her future had shriveled and shortened right underneath her feet. She didn't want to spend another day standing still.

It wasn't anything to be mad about. He wasn't mad at her.

But they hadn't spoken since he came home two weeks ago to find her gone.

That hurt him the most. She hadn't called him. Not once. But she left a note, which was nice. He figured he would call her, eventually. Check up on her. He figured she was with her sister in Chicago or with her other sister in Miami or with her half-sister in Little Rock. Any of them was a good choice for her. Three cities. She was tired of rural life. She went to one of the three.

Portman got out of the old Crown Vic and shut the door behind him. He was the first to arrive on the scene, which meant no firemen. Not yet.

He pulled his car up into the drive, but parked it up between two oak trees, leaving plenty of room for the fire truck to pull in.

He stared at the structure engulfed in flames.

The smoke was thick and black. The stars above were completely blacked out.

His heart filled with dread when he realized whose house it was. He hadn't been out there for a long time. But he knew the owners. He knew them well. He felt bad for not realizing where he was.

He took a flashlight out of his car and jogged up the hill, past several thin trees and up to a safe perimeter far away enough from the fire, but close enough to search the house.

Parts of the exterior stood upright, still. They remained uncompromised by the intense heat.

Flames covered the entire first floor and the front porch.

He called out the names of the residents. A sense of worry filled him. He liked the wife. He had known her since she was a little girl. Hell, he had been the local sheriff since she was barely a teenager. She had been like a daughter to him. He was nearly her godfather. Not in actuality. Her real godfather had been an uncle that he had never met.

Portman walked counterclockwise, following the driveway. He stayed a safe distance. He wouldn't run into the fire. He knew that. There was no way to get in from the front, even if he was young enough or fit enough to dare it. The only way he was going in was if he got an answer from someone who was trapped inside.

He called out the wife's name. And waited. No reply. He continued walking up the drive, circling, angling his trajectory.

He called out her name again. Loud. No response.

The side of the house looked better than the front. It was less damaged. Less burned so far. He could make out window frames on the second floor. One of them still had the glass intact.

Just then, several huge balls of fire raged out of the several windows and landed on the roof. The shingles were seared and blistered. The smoke doubled and plumed.

Nearing the back of the house, he saw a detached garage. Slivers of fire burned in different parts of its roof. But, mostly, the garage was still safe. It still stood as if nothing had harmed it. He approached, hoping someone was alive. Hoping the wife was still alive.

Maybe they got out. Maybe they're in the garage. Maybe they aren't even home, he thought. He hoped.

The garage door was wide open. He saw a black Chevy Tahoe with government plates, parked nose in. Next to it was an old Ford Bronco. It looked like a 1970s model. It wasn't in pristine condition, but pretty damn close. The wax shone, like the owner had a lot of love for the car.

He called out the wife's name again. No answer.

He stepped into the garage and flicked on a wall light switch. A big overhead light pinged to life. The electricity in the garage still worked. He looked around. No one was there.

He called out the family name again. No answer. He turned back and walked out of the garage. He started toward the back corner of the house when he heard a low voice call back at him like a whisper.

The fire crackled and roared, drowning out the voice.

He heard it again, another whisper.

"Portman," the voice said.

He rotated ninety degrees and shone the flashlight over to the backyard woods behind the garage.

He saw a small figure standing there. It was a woman. Half-naked. She hid among the trees. She stepped forward and out into the beam from his flashlight.

She said, "Portman."

He called out the wife's name and said, "What are you doing in there? Are you all right?"

She whispered to him like she was scared. She said, "Is anyone else out there?"

"Come on out," Portman called back.

"Is anyone else there?"

Why did she ask him that?

"No, darling. I'm the first. No one else is here yet."

She paused a beat and asked, "You didn't see anyone else?"

"The fire truck is on the way. Nothing to be scared of now. Come on out."

"You didn't see anyone when you pulled in?"

"Who? See who?"

"Just. Anyone?"

"What's going on?" he asked.

She said nothing. Instead, she came forward a couple of paces and looked right, looked left. She ignored the fire and ignored the heat. She looked back down the driveway. She looked toward his car. She put her hand above her eyes like a visor from the intense light of the fire.

She asked, "You're alone?"

"I done told you. The fire truck is on the way. I radioed for paramedics, too. But you know they're thirty minutes out."

He paused a beat, and then he asked, "Where's your husband?"

She didn't answer that. She said, "No. I mean, did you see anyone else?"

Now he understood. She was scared, but not of the fire. She feared someone.

"Are you saying that someone else is here? Did someone do this? Did someone start this fire?"

He went for his gun, which was a Glock 17 in a belt holster, right side. He didn't pull it out. Not yet. He just unsnapped the safety clasp and readied the weapon. He rested his hand on the butt.

She slowly came out and walked over to him. Her bare feet stepped carelessly through the grass and the dirt until they trailed through hard gravel.

She grabbed at him. Her small hands rested on his shoulders. She said, "I need your help."

Portman looked at her. He looked at her soot-covered body. There were bruises on her arms and legs. She had a black eye on her face.

"Did he do this to you? Again?"

She stopped and stepped back away from him. He let her do it. She got about six feet away. She looked back over the driveway, down to his car, and back at the blazing house. Blasts of wind hit them both. Her body trembled, even against the fiery heat coming off the house.

"Did he do this to you?" Portman repeated.

The wife stayed quiet.

"Where is he?"

She looked up at him. Her bangs covered most of her black eye. She still didn't speak. She raised her right hand, pulled down on her shirt with her left. She pointed at the house, at the fire. She pointed at the second-floor bedroom, where she used to sleep.

"Is he dead?"

She nodded.

"Are you sure?"

"He's dead."

"What the hell happened?"

She didn't answer.

Portman took off his coat. It read *County Sheriff* on the back. He stepped over to her, slowly. He wrapped the coat around her. He pulled her close to him, hugged her.

She was a girl that he had known before she was even a baby.

He asked, "Did you kill him?"

5

Su-Jin returned to Widow after he had drunk one full cup of coffee. She smiled at him and asked if he'd like another. He didn't refuse. He never did.

After a moment, Chung walked over to the table. Su-Jin followed and dropped off the coffee. She bowed her head at them both and walked away, saying nothing.

Chung's nose had stopped bleeding. Widow saw makeshift nose plugs stuffed up into each nostril. They looked like two halves of the same cotton ball.

Chung asked, "Can I sit?"

"Sure."

Chung pulled out the metal chair across from Widow and sat.

"You are stranger here?"

"I am."

"You want job?"

Widow shook his head.

"I'm retired."

"You young."

Widow said nothing.

"You retired from what?"

"Navy."

"You were soldier?"

"Sailor. Navy has sailors, not soldiers," he said. Then he asked, "Why aren't the paramedics here?"

"No hospital."

"Why not? Didn't those cops call them?"

Chung looked down.

"Why didn't they call them?"

"They no call. We ask them not to call. Ambulance company almost as bad as insurance company."

Widow nodded. The guy didn't want to pay for an ambulance ride and an emergency room check-in. He understood that.

"Who did this to you?"

Chung said, "Bunch of hooligans."

"Who?"

He shrugged.

"I don't know their names. Not exactly. Just street names like Capone."

Widow had seen this kind of thing before. A lot of cops have. Robbers don't bust up cooler doors and break glass inventory. Robbers get in, take what they can take, and get out. It wasn't just a robbery. There was a clear message being delivered. The message was, "pay up or else." This had been a shakedown.

Widow said, "I can help you."

"I thought you retired?"

"Just because I don't want a job doesn't mean I don't want to help you."

"How you help?"

"Tell me who did this? What hooligans?"

"I shouldn't say."

"Don't be scared. They won't know it was you."

Chung paused a beat, and then he said, "What you do?"

"I can take care of it."

"It not that simple."

"Tell me."

Chung adjusted the half cotton balls in his nose. He winced as if he had hit a tender spot. He said, "It's these guys. Local guys. They work this neighborhood. They're just junkies. Drug addicts. They not real problem."

"Junkies?" Widow asked. In his experience, junkies were usually the bottom of the barrel. They weren't organized enough to do any real crime other than desperate, half-ass things like mugging people. They certainly weren't organized enough to operate a shakedown operation.

"Who's the main guy? Who's the real problem?"

"Their leader is real problem. He is some mob guy. Only not really. He joke. Everybody know it. But people around here are scared of him."

Widow listened.

Chung said, "He just some guy who think he mob. He dresses in suits and fancy secondhand clothes. Like ties and cufflinks and fancy hat. He talk like a gangster too, but he no gangster."

"He talk like gangster? Like from the 1940s?"

"No. Not like impersonation. He talk tough. But he no tough."

Chung leaned in closer. He mustn't have wanted his wife to hear him. He said, "There more. Not just drugs. He also run girls."

"Girls?"

"Yes. Rumor is they young. Not good. Not good person. He no tough gangster, but he bad man."

Widow didn't like guys like that, tough or not. He asked, "What's his name?"

"They call him Capone."

Widow looked at him, cockeyed. He asked, "Capone? Like Al Capone?"

Chung nodded.

"Whatever. Where is he now?"

"I don't know. Maybe street people know. But not me. I don't associate with his friends."

"Someone knows. What are street people?"

"Homeless people and junkies. Tweakers. They might tell you. Maybe."

"These tweakers. Where do they buy?"

Chung shrugged. A car passed by on the street, followed by a second one going the other way. More city street sounds wafted in through the open door. Widow looked out the window.

He asked, "How many junkies came here and did this?"

"Two of them. But next time they bring more guys. They say I not pay enough. They bring more. They probably bring all of them."

Chung stopped. He looked back over his shoulder for his wife. Then he leaned in again and said, "They say next time, we don't pay, they break Su-jin nose. Time after that, they break her fingers till I pay."

"How long have these guys been shaking you down?"

"This second time. They used never to come down this street. They must have territory somewhere north. Now they expanding.

"First time they come month ago. They threaten me. They say we have one month to pay. I told them get out of my store. I told them I call cops."

"What did the cops say last time?"

"They come. They take report. Then they do nothing."

Widow nodded.

"I met the cops. Outside. Are they the same ones that came last time?"

Chung nodded and said, "Same cops. Every time. This the edge of their neighborhood. They okay. But they do nothing until..."

He paused. Then he said, "Until I dead."

Widow sat back, took the last pull of his coffee. He asked, "When are these hooligans supposed to come back?"

Chung said, "Two days from now."

6

A BLACK CHEVY TAHOE with government plates waited across the street from the visitor parking lot of Sheriff Portman's station house, which was about a thirty-minute drive from the fire, including one long, barren road.

The station house was farther inland and farther away from clusters of suburbs closer to the ocean. It was built closer to the more rural areas— something about fairness.

Time had passed, as time always does. It was midafternoon now. The sun charioted across the sky. Cloud formations fanned out like a five-finger spread. The station house visitor parking lot smelled of gun barrel smoke. The driver of the Tahoe had gotten bored waiting around and passed the time. He patched a suppressor onto an untraceable Glock 19 that he had for emergency situations. He used it for target practice at the sheriff badge logo mounted on the outside wall. He didn't go overboard with shooting at it—no rapid fire. He knew that there was at least one deputy posted inside. But he was too good to be speaking to a low-level deputy.

The Tahoe driver stood at the opposite side of the Tahoe's hood, set his elbows and arms over the hood, took aim, and squeezed the trigger. He wound up using two full magazines before giving up.

The fire had burned all night. And the Tahoe had been parked there since the early morning, waiting for the Sheriff to bring the wife in for questioning. The Tahoe had been parked there like the driver knew about the fire in advance. The driver had been waiting the whole time, like a stakeout. Only the subject was a rural county sheriff.

The Tahoe's cab was empty. After doing target practice, the driver of the Tahoe stood out front, smoking a cigarette, still waiting. No rush. Not really. He was calm and patient and collected. He had to be in his line of work. There was no real margin of error.

It was easy to be calm in a place like Washington State, even dealing with rural lawmen like Portman. It was far less pressure than dealing with the kind of men that he dealt with regularly. Just about every day he had to deal with unpredictable men, the kind who would just as soon put a bullet in his head rather than hear an excuse.

A moment later, a puff on the cigarette later, and he spotted movement coming from the road leading up to the station house. He saw Portman's old Crown Vic driving up to the lot. Portman drove past at first. He went out of sight like he was headed to the rear entrance. He was about to pull into his secure lot, but saw the Tahoe and realized it was the same one that was parked in the garage of the burning house, only it couldn't be the same one. That one, he had one of his deputies move to another location, along with the Bronco.

Portman let out a long, exhausted yawn. He had been up all night because of that fire. He had found only one survivor. He had taken her into custody, and he had listened to her story. He locked her up in cuffs, in line with his better judgment, but against his better angels. But the law was the law. Everything was preliminary. But she looked guilty. It looked like she had set her house on fire on purpose. An unhappy marriage. A violent spouse. A black eye. The two packed bags. It looked like she had killed her husband.

Before the fire crew arrived, she had sat in the back of his squad car and begged for him to release her. Portman was a good cop. He was the Boy Scout type. Never in over twenty-five years of public service had he even considered breaking the law, looking the other way, or abusing his authority. Not once. He never even thought about cutting in line at the local grocery store. Not ever.

Not even when his wife had gotten a speeding ticket from the highway patrol one time, and he could have. It was a pretty common practice to call in favors. He could have picked up the phone, called the chief of the Washington Highway Patrol, and requested a little favor. But he didn't.

The law was the law. And he wasn't above it. No one was.

But the wife that he had known for so many years, she was once the little girl that he had known. He had been close to her family when they were still alive. Her father had gone to Vietnam with him. They had served side by side. Once, he had even saved Portman's life. Nothing dramatic. He hadn't taken a bullet for him or anything like that. It was just a case of being under fire. And her father had told him to duck at the right moment. One second later, he'd be dead. He never doubted it. And her father had never brought it up. Not in decades of friendship. Not once.

When they returned to regular life in the States, Portman never forgot it. How could he? The Army didn't give his friend a medal for it as they should have. But Portman wouldn't forget. No way. As far as he was concerned, he owed a life debt.

Now, her father was long gone. Over a year ago, he had died from cancer. Portman wasn't even sure that the daughter knew about the debt he owed her father. To her, there was no debt. He owed nothing.

Only he did. He owed her more than the debt. He owed her the same thing that he owed everyone in his community—protection. So, he listened.

She had told him a story that he couldn't believe. But he listened.

Just in case she told the truth, he took her Ford Bronco. He had one of his deputies move it. Not to the impound, which was standard procedure. He asked him to move it to an abandoned parking lot in front of an abandoned oil change hut close to the Sheriff's station house. It was out of sight enough not to be seen by passing cars, but close enough to grab in case her story panned out.

Right then, she was handcuffed inside his station house, not in a cell. She was handcuffed in his office.

He had left her there earlier that morning. Last he saw, she had laid down on his office sofa and closed her eyes.

One of his deputies was in the bullpen, doing every day desk-work: answering phones, typing up reports, and standing guard.

His other deputy was out on the road, patrolling the community. Everyday police work had to go on—fire or no fire.

It wasn't until he saw the man standing in front of the Sheriff's station house he believed her. She might have just been telling the truth. Why else would the guy be there so fast?

Portman turned the steering wheel, and the police car scooted up onto the gravel lot. He drove over to the man at the Tahoe. He rolled down his passenger-side window.

"Can I help you?"

The man took a drag off his cigarette. He blew out the smoke.

The guy had a completely shaved head, not from Mother Nature or bad genetics, but from a portable electric razor. The guy had facial stubble, neatly groomed. It wasn't until Portman had gotten close to him he saw he had a teardrop face tattoo. It wasn't anything dramatic. It was right underneath his right eye. It was small and colored blood red, like a blood droplet and not a teardrop.

Portman had never seen that before. Not a red one. He wondered what it meant, if it meant anything at all.

The guy was wearing light blue jeans with small holes ripped out at the knees. He wore a long-sleeved black knit shirt. The sleeves were rolled up sloppily over his elbows. His skin gleamed a natural dark, like he had at least one Hispanic parent.

A pair of Ray-Bans covered his eyes with wide black lenses. He took them off down the front of his shirt.

Portman noticed he wore an expensive watch. It was silver and big and shiny. He also had a huge cowboy belt buckle. It was exposed from under the bottom of his shirt. The buckle showed a pair of crossbones—black and metal, no skull, like on warning labels for poison. It was just the crossbones.

None of that was the thing that Portman kept his eye on. Those were just details. The main thing that made Portman nervous was a Glock 19, out in plain view, in a pancake holster on the guy's hip.

Wearing a gun in the state of Washington wasn't an illegal act, not with the right permit. And he might've had that permit. Plus, this was the country. Odds were he didn't need the permit. Odds were this guy was exactly who the wife said he was. Odds were he was licensed to carry by the federal government.

Still, Portman kept one eye on the Glock.

Portman repeated his question.

"Can I help you?"

The guy put the cigarette back in his mouth and pinched it with his lips. He reached down and grabbed the bottom of his shirt, to the left of his buckle, and he pulled it up and over to reveal a police badge.

Portman looked at it. No, it wasn't a police badge. It was a DEA badge.

Portman saw a gold eagle, huge on the top. Underneath were the words: Department of Justice, the DOJ. And underneath that was a star with the words US Special Agent and the Drug Enforcement Administration wrapped around it.

He was DEA.

The guy pulled the cigarette out of his mouth and spoke with a hint of an Irish accent, which didn't throw a monkey wrench into Portman's theory of one Hispanic parent. Not necessarily.

The guy said, "Danny Ryman. DEA SWATters. A special ops unit of the DEA."

"Portman. Local Sheriff."

Ryman smiled and offered his free hand for Portman to shake. He offered it through the window.

Portman took it and shook it. Ryman had a big hand, a strong grip. He seemed more military than a cop, which meant that he was Special Ops. The DEA wasn't like other civilian law enforcement agencies.

That's because the drug cartels weren't like most criminals. They operated on American soil every day. They had elaborate drug operations. And they were headquartered in foreign countries. Most other law enforcement agencies dealt with Americans committing crimes on American soil. Not the DEA. They fought a losing battle with foreign entities. Some of these entities were governments. And all of them were ruthless. And many of them had small armies to fight back.

The cartels were equipped better than some armies of small countries. They had better weapons, more manpower, and endless supplies of cash. The DEA was under-funded, out-manned, and outgunned.

The DEA was more like a paramilitary law enforcement agency. It had to be just to keep up the fight.

Ryman looked like he was more a part of that military side than the civilian side.

Portman asked, "SWATters? What is that?"

"It's like SWAT, only worse. We are like special ops for the DEA."

Special Ops for the DEA sounded more like black ops.

"What can I do for the DEA?" Portman asked. He kept one hand on the wheel, obvious. It was his right hand, his gun hand. His department-issued weapon was in plain view, in a holster on his right hip. Ryman could see it. And he looked directly at it. He didn't hide his gaze. No discreet look around. Nothing casual. He just looked right at it.

Portman noticed. But it wasn't Portman's only weapon. He had a backup weapon, a German revolver. He kept it tucked down in an ankle holster on his left boot. And right then, his left hand was out of sight from Ryman's view.

Portman inched his left hand down his leg, slowly. He kept it within grabbing distance of the backup gun. One quick but concealed reach and tug, and he could have it out and ready to fire.

He was probably acting stupid. The wife's story was probably a lie, but he felt safer this way.

Ryman took his hand back and placed it on the window frame. He leaned against it.

He said, "To tell you the truth, Sheriff. I'm distraught."

"Why's that?"

"Because my brother is dead. I think you know that."

Portman nodded and said, "You're partners with Mike Lee?"

"Not partners. He was one of my men. A new member to our team, but still a brother."

Portman said, "I'm very sorry for your loss."

He knew about his partner's death quickly, which made Portman inch farther toward his gun.

Ryman nodded.

"What can I do for you?"

"I want justice, Sheriff."

Portman stayed quiet.

"I heard Lee burned to death in his house, and the wife survived?"

Portman nodded. He couldn't deny that part.

"She killed him."

"We don't know that. We'll know more after we've investigated."

"We? There's no 'we' here, Sheriff. I can see that. You guys are way out here in the sticks. The only one doing the investigating will be you, right?"

"And the county fire investigators. First, they have to rule it a homicide and arson. Then we'll coordinate with them to investigate."

Ryman shook his head.

"Cut the crap, Sheriff! You know who I am. We'll coordinate this investigation."

"Excuse me?"

"Lee is one of us. One of our own. You know something about that? Don't ya?"

Ryman took another long drag off the cigarette and exhaled another puff of smoke up into the air over the police cruiser.

He asked, "How many investigations you handle like this? Way out here?"

Portman stayed quiet.

"I'd bet the answer is none. Zero."

Portman stayed quiet.

Ryman changed the subject. He asked, "How many guys you got here?"

"Enough," Portman said.

"I got an idea."

"What's that?"

"Why don't you turn her over to me? We'll take care of it. I got more guys than you. More resources. And we can get this over with quickly and neatly and quietly."

Portman said nothing to that.

Ryman said, "This is a small community you got here. My understanding is that Mrs. Lee grew up here. You might not be impartial. You might've known her."

"I guarantee you that justice will be served for your guy. Don't you worry about that."

Portman's hand hovered over his ankle gun as close as he could without making it obvious.

Ryman leaned in a little closer. He stopped, his face just outside the window. He half-whispered, "Let me have her."

"You know I can't do that. We got procedures here too. You'll just have to wait for the conclusion of our investigation."

Ryman paused a long beat, kept his stare on Portman. Then he moved back out of the window. Stood up straight and eased away from the cruiser.

He smoked the rest of the cigarette.

He asked, "She here? In your jail?"

Portman couldn't quite reach his ankle gun without bending forward more, which would've been obvious to a seasoned agent like Ryman because it would've been obvious to anyone. He knew that.

He said, "She's not here. We don't have a jail cell here."

"No cells? You serious?"

"Not for women, I mean. We don't get a lot of women criminals out here. Mostly drunk men. You know, bar fights and all."

Ryman took the cigarette out of his mouth, held on to it.

"We couldn't throw her in the cell with a couple of drunk guys, now could we? That wouldn't be very respectful of her civil rights and all."

"So, where's she at?"

Portman thought about it. He almost told him he couldn't answer that. But Ryman wouldn't be satisfied with that answer. Instead, he said, "County. The women's prison. Of course."

It sounded right. County bureaucracy and regulations and all. As a DEA agent, surely, Ryman knew a lot about bureaucracy and regulations.

Ryman nodded. He eased away, stepping back, one foot at a time. He kept his eyes locked on Portman, all while walking backward until he got halfway back to the Tahoe. There, he spun around. He put his Ray-Bans back on, tossed the cigarette out onto the gravel, and left it.

He opened the Tahoe and hopped up into the driver's seat. He fired up the engine, backed out, and drove away. Portman watched and waited.

After he was sure that Ryman was gone, he returned his left hand to the steering wheel and took his foot off the brake and wound around the lot. He drove back onto the street, orbited around the station house, and parked in the secure lot.

He shut off his car and got out. He unsnapped the buckle on his hip holster, just to feel safer. He walked in through the back police entrance, threaded past an empty desk, and waved at the one officer in the bullpen.

The deputy said, "You're back. Finally."

The deputy looked at his wristwatch and said, "I've been here all day. I was supposed to go on a break three hours ago."

"I've been dealing with the fire."

"Can I go now?"

Portman stopped halfway back to his office. He said, "I need you to stay overnight. Maybe."

"Another double?"

"I only got the two deputies. I need you. Unless you want me only to have one deputy?"

The deputy's arms slumped down to his sides. He said, "Can I at least take a break now?"

"Yeah. Go. Be back in an hour," he said, but he knew it would take him longer. He counted on it.

Portman waited for the deputy to leave, and then he looped around a couple of empty desks to his office and opened the door.

The wife was awake now. She stared up at him, silent. Her black eye didn't look bad. It had settled into a dark bruise curved into her eye socket.

Portman said, "You might be telling me the truth."

7

WIDOW LEANED his back up against the inside wall, inside the abandoned storefront's doorway. He was growing tired of waiting around.

On his left side, he had a to-go coffee cup that he had bought at the Korean store this time. Not the McDonald's. He drank it all down. He didn't want to keep going inside the Korean store for coffee, in case he missed his chance to see the thugs. He didn't want to be inside the store when they returned. That would give him a disadvantage. So he just waited.

Widow hadn't been on a stakeout in a long time. Doing a stakeout, like sniper-work or sharpshooting, was a perishable skill. But his skill hadn't perished. Not yet. It was still right there in his arsenal.

He had seen multiple cars drive the street. He had seen pedestrians walking, stopping, turning, and moving on. He had seen actual homeless people passing by. Some stopped and checked him out. Others ignored him.

One guy held up a sign showing that he was a World War II vet, which could have been possible. Maybe. If the vet was a hundred, which this guy wasn't—clearly. He looked fifty years old, at most.

Later, Widow saw another guy walk by holding a Vietnam vet sign, which looked plausible. At least the age matched up. And then there were two separate Iraq vets. One of which was a woman—all of which he didn't doubt.

None of them spoke to him. They all passed right on by. Widow wasn't sure if this meant that he was doing a good job blending in or a terrible one.

The homeless in the area seemed to be territorial, like salesmen. This spot was theirs, but no one said a word to him.

He waited.

The sun was up in the sky, not high like noon, but somewhere between four or five p.m., he figured. Probably closer to five than four.

Widow listened to the city sounds of distant honking cars, a barking dog, and blips indicating that the blind could cross the nearest intersection safely.

He looked right, down the street, and saw one of those low-rider cars coming by for a second time. It had big chrome rims, a front grille to match, and obnoxious fire red paint. It slipped past him. He watched.

The car was older than the driver and the passengers it carried. But it was better kept than all of them combined.

It looked like it was waxed weekly. It was loved. It was taken care of.

The stereo system inside must've been that aftermarket crap with double everything. Double speakers. Double woofers. Double bass.

The thing thumped and bounced up and down the street. Widow could hear music that had so much bass in it he couldn't discern whether it was rap music or heavy metal or simple African drums, just cranked all the way up. Full bass.

The car was a two-door sedan. It was all metal, from the last generation of muscle cars still made of metal. Maybe it was a Monte Carlo or a Cutlass or whatever. The only things that Widow noticed that concerned him were the three bullet holes in the trunk lid. All three were lined in a tight parameter. The metal turned outward, which told him that someone had shot them from inside the trunk.

He studied them as the car passed again for the third time. This time, the driver slowed just in front of Widow and looked his way. Looking him over and clearing him of being any kind of cop. Technically, he wasn't. Not anymore. But the guy wasn't totally off.

Widow looked away. Kept his eyes half-closed like he was drifting off to sleep. Something that homeless people did anytime, anywhere.

The car moved on and stopped on the diagonal, just down the street, in front of the Korean store. Widow watched the driver park the car. He stayed in his seat. The engine ran idle. The passengers all got out. Three big but scrawny guys, all sticks and bones, popped up and out of the passenger door, one after the other. The first one had to bend the seat forward so the other two could climb out of the back.

Widow watched.

Two of the men were pale white, one of them almost lily colored. The other man was a black guy, covered in tattoos. The driver was behind a window of black tint. Widow could see the top of his head because he had left the window cracked while he puffed on a cigarette, or maybe a marijuana blunt. The smoke peeked out and swirled up over the car.

The smell wafted and carried across the street.

Marijuana. No doubt about it. Weed had a distinguished odor that Widow knew well. Not because he smoked it. Only because he had worked in the Navy. After all, some guys smoked it recreationally. He didn't approve. He didn't disapprove. It wasn't his place to judge. Live and let live had always been his personal motto, with one caveat. Live and let live, unless you aren't letting live; then he might just have to retaliate.

The three men walked into the Korean store. Each of them with a stupid swagger Widow had heard called *gangsta*. Whatever that meant.

He saw at least one gun bulge in the back of the only black guy's blue jeans. It was stuffed into his waistband. It was probably a Glock, and definitely a nine-millimeter. No way was he going to be sporting anything bigger. And Widow could clearly see a magazine lip sticking out of the butt of the gun.

Desert Eagles had magazines, like other Magnum firearms. And these gangsta types liked Desert Eagles just as much as third-world warlords did. But this guy was too scrawny, and his jeans were too baggy and loose to be carrying a gun like that.

A Desert Eagle, fully loaded, would've pulled him to the ground. Certainly, his pants would've dropped to his ankles, belt or no belt.

Widow didn't want to engage these guys inside the Korean store. He didn't want to cause more damage than they already had. He also couldn't let them cause any kind of serious harm to the owners. He got up from the doorway and kicked off some dirty clothes that he had piled over his legs like blankets for extra effect.

Feeling that he had no choice, he crossed the street. He stuffed the paperback of *Fire Season* in his back pocket and left behind the Grisham book. He was done with it.

Widow took his empty paper coffee cup with him.

* * *

THE DRIVER LOOKED FORWARD and then back to his left. The homeless guy who had been sitting in the abandoned storefront back down the street was gone.

The driver looked in his rearview, saw no one. There was just a single car down the street. Left turn blinker was on. It flickered.

Then he heard a rapping on his driver's side window.

He leaned forward, changed his blunt from his left hand to his right, and rolled down the window manually. He rolled it down all the way.

A tall homeless guy stood there, waiting for him to roll the window down. The guy had a paper cup out in front of him. He was mumbling incoherently.

The driver said, "Beat it, homeboy!"

Widow said, "Change. Got any change."

He hobbled around and fidgeted like he was drunk or coming down from a bad high or was missing most of his marbles, or all the above.

The driver repeated, "Beat it!" He reached into the front of his waistband, right hand, and pulled out a Glock 17. The blunt was tucked between his fingers and the Glock's custom grip.

The whole gun was customized. Not in a way Widow respected. Most of the original exterior parts had been replaced with identical parts in fire-red colors. The grip, the slider, the sights, even the trigger were fire red, like the car.

That was enough to make Widow vomit. Which helped because he inched back to the rear of the car, retreating the way he had come. The driver watched in the side mirror as Widow stopped at the rear bumper and dropped his hand on the trunk lid like he was steadying himself. Then he heaved over the back of the car like he was hurling.

He made all the usual sounds.

The driver cursed and dropped the blunt into the car's ashtray. He popped the door open. It creaked on old hinges. He hauled himself up and out and walked back to the heaving homeless man.

"Hey, bro! This my car!"

Just then, with movements so quick they looked like real-life quick edits, Widow pitched forward and then back upright with a right hook he had already been preparing down out of sight.

His fist jammed right into the guy's teeth, which had been covered over by a chrome grille that matched his car. The grille broke and cracked and shattered and tore apart. Instead of reinforcing his front teeth, like a consumer who bought it because a dentist said it was required to fix his teeth would probably expect, it was the grille that ripped his two front teeth out by the roots—no protection at all. It resulted from the right amount of pressure and torque and the size of a big fist, Widow figured.

The driver dropped his Glock and bent over like someone had dropped a cinder block on his head. He heaved blood and teeth and grille fragments. Widow thought he saw gum particles.

"Oh, man! Oh, man! My teeth!" was what he had tried to say. Only it came out all fragmented and stuttered and robotic and garbled like the letters were out of order. But Widow had gotten accustomed to understanding guys who had terrible articulation. Some of them even had the same trouble as this guy had.

Widow stepped down on the Glock, a big foot in a big shoe that wasn't budging.

He grabbed a tuft of the guy's hair, which wasn't much. He jerked the guy's head back and looked him dead in the eyes.

He asked, "You Capone?"

"Nah, man! He back at the church!"

"The church?"

"Yeah, man! Church! The throne room!"

Throne room? Widow thought.

"Where's this church?"

"It's over on Ninth Street. Everybody know the church!"

Chung didn't know it. Then again, Chung wasn't a criminal.

Widow asked, "Is it an actual church?"

"Condemned! Old place."

Widow smiled. Then, in one violent motion, he slammed the guy's face right into the side of the car. All-metal. Last of its kind. American made. A better generation of cars.

The driver bounced off the metal, hit the street and the blacktop. He was out cold.

Widow grabbed the guy's head, moved it and his neck so that he wouldn't drown on his own blood. Widow didn't want to kill the guy, although he wouldn't lose sleep over it either.

Live and let live, unless you don't do the let live part; then he had to retaliate.

He picked up the Glock 17, which made him embarrassed to be holding a fire-red gun. Then he ejected the magazine. He checked the load out and checked the chamber. It was empty. He dry-fired the weapon. It worked. He returned the magazine and chambered a bullet.

He checked up and down the street. No one came running. No backup. No cops. No witnesses who cared. No sound of sirens. Nothing.

He turned and went to the Korean store. He put his back to the outside wall and pivoted on his foot and peered in through the open door. The three thugs were inside and pushing Chung around. Widow couldn't see Su-Jin.

One guy said, "Where's ya ole lady?"

Another said, "She back there somewhere?"

The third one said, "Don't make us check it out."

The black guy pulled his Glock out and waved it around. He didn't point it at Chung, which was good. But it added a dangerous element that Widow was hoping to avoid. A gun out raised the stakes much, much higher.

Widow saw nothing had gone a step too far. Not yet. At that moment, the gangster wannabes were poking and prodding at Chung for the money that they felt was due them. But they hadn't gone far enough as to shoot anyone. Not yet.

Widow figured that Su-Jin was in there, hiding back in the stockroom or the office or the ladies bathroom. Or maybe she had wised up and run out the backdoor. It wasn't optimal to take the fight inside. Not with guns involved.

Widow walked back to the Monte Carlo. He circled around the rear and scooped up the driver by bunching up his collar. He dragged the guy back to the open driver's door, hauled him up, and dumped him down on the seat.

Blood trickled out of his mouth and down his chin.

First, Widow pulled the gear into neutral and popped the parking brake. Then he thumped the driver forward. The guy's head flopped forward, honking the horn. A loud, obnoxious sound blared out from under the hood. He let it continue.

Widow grabbed the top half of the door and put one hand on the roof of the car. He heaved and pushed and rolled the car forward. He reached in and turned the wheel. He ran with the car for a moment, and then backed off, letting the car roll on its own. The car rolled and turned to the right. He backed away and let it roll off the street, over the curb. It rammed a fire hydrant. The hydrant ruptured, and water rushed out of one nozzle. Slow at first, and then it burst into an explosion of spray.

The hydrant stopped the car from rolling forward.

Widow stepped back to the sidewalk, backing away toward the wall, out of sight.

A moment later, all three gangster wannabes came swarming out. All three faced the car. All three ran up to it exactly where Widow wanted them to be.

"What the hell, man!" one called out.

The second guy called out the driver's name.

"Carlos!"

Widow waited for the black guy, who was the last to run out. Then he sprinted after them, staying low, staying as close to a crouch as he could, which turned out to be easy. The blaring horn covered the sound of his steps. Plus, these guys were dumber than the actual dummies he used to shoot at, back at Seal Beach.

He came up behind them and stopped. He was close enough to where he didn't need to use the commandeered Glock. Probably.

The three gangsta wannabes looked at the car, shock on their faces. The first one ran to the passenger side door. He jerked it open and slid in. He reached over and shook the driver. He pulled him up and back from the steering wheel. The horn stopped. The driver's head flopped back like a rag doll onto the headrest.

The guy called back out.

"Carlos was attacked! His teeth are gone."

But the warning was too late.

The black guy spun around, his Glock in hand, but it was still pointed back at the Monte Carlo.

Amateur, Widow thought. And he let the guy know by clamping down on it with one hand, squeezing and locking it down, making it impossible for the guy to shoot it.

With a massive right jab, he punched the guy right in the jaw. Widow heard cheekbones cracking and bones shattering and teeth rattling. The guy flew off his feet, slumped forward, and tripped off the curb.

He released the Glock. Widow took it.

He pointed it at the other two guys. And right there, two things were confirmed. First, these guys were unarmed—no doubt about it. Neither of them reached for any weapons of any kind. And second, they were amateurs.

"Hey, man!" one said.

The other said, "Take it easy!"

"Who the hell are you, man?"

"What are you, a cop, or something?"

Widow stepped forward, closing the gap between them and keeping the black guy on the ground in front of him.

He said, "I'm the guarantor." He couldn't help himself.

One said, "The what?"

"The underwriter."

"The who?"

"The minder."

"The what, man?"

"I'm the guardian. The bouncer. Like in an exclusive, nice club. You boys ever been to a nice club?"

Silence.

"Sure we have," the second one said.

"This is kinda like that. See this grocery," he asked and pointed back at it with his free hand.

"This place is off-limits to you boys now. I'm the bouncer. To enter this place, you boys need a membership. If you don't got a membership, then you don't get in. And Chung here says you boys ain't got a membership. Got it?"

They were silent for a beat. Widow moved the Glock up to the first one's center mass. He asked, "Got it?"

The guy said, "It's not up to us, man!"

The other said, "We're just doing our jobs."

Widow saw that the second one had needle holes all over his inner forearms. Heroin would have been Widow's guess. But these days, who knew? Junkies shoot up anything.

"So who's your boss? Capone?"

They looked at each other, and the first one said, "Of course."

The second said, "He runs everything in this neighborhood. Everybody knows that, man."

"And he's at the church?" Widow asked.

"Yes. Of course."

"Where else would he be?"

"He's always at the church."

Widow said, "Take me to him."

They looked at each other.

Widow asked, "You both know where the church is? Right?"

"Of course."

"Good. Then I only need one of you," he said, and he pointed the

Glock at the second one. Next, he went to the black guy. Then back to the first one. And round and round again. He mumbled the words, "Eeny, meeny, miny, mo..."

The first one said, "Wait, man!"

"We'll take you."

"I don't have to shoot you?"

"No way!"

Widow said, "Oh good. Saves me some bullets."

Then he took a moment and looked at the trunk. He thought about the poor bastard who had shot out of it. He wondered if the guy got out. He hoped so. Then he looked back at all three gangster wannabes and smiled.

"How many bodies does that trunk hold?"

8

THE TRUCKS WAITED in Portman's county, parked in a circle in the woods. They were parked less than a football field away from his station house. They kept out of sight and quiet until they were sure the coast was clear. Seven men congregated in a single, uneven semicircle. Some stared over shoulders. Others were right in front and could see The Leader's iPad, that he held over the hood of his truck. He used it to guide them, and to discuss tactics, to plot out the plan of attack.

On the screen was a real-time video, taken from a small, tactical spy drone. Which was being held in a holding pattern, circling around the target area until one of them, piloting it, used the app on his smartphone to return it to where they were.

"It's all straightforward. There's two armed cops inside. Maybe three," The Leader said.

"Maybe there's an office worker or two. But maybe not. This place has no funding."

He showed a satellite photo of Portman's station house.

"Looks like overkill to me," one guy said.

"Better we do it like that than one guy going in alone," said The Leader.

"I can just go down there. Take them out alone," said another, zealously. Perhaps overconfidently.

"I told you. Better this way," said The Leader.

One guy said, without thinking, "I don't know. Why make all this fuss over one woman?"

The Leader stepped back, away from the hood of his truck. He set the iPad down on the hood. And he turned to face the insubordinate member of his team.

"What?"

The guy realized his mistake and said, "Nothing."

"What did you say?"

"Nothing. Sorry. I didn't mean nothing."

The Leader, like the rest of his men, had a LAR-15 assault rifle strapped to his chest. But he ignored it and drew a Glock 19 with a tactical light. No suppressor. Not yet.

He walked over to the insubordinate guy. The other five men stepped back and away. They knew better than to cross him. They had worked with him before. Not the insubordinate guy. He had been pulled from another department and added to the team, kind of like a promotion, which meant that it was a trial thing. Like all promotions, it comes with an understood probationary period. In that period, if he crossed the line, there would be a penalty. In some trades, that only meant a verbal warning. In others, it could mean termination. In his trade, it could mean a bullet, unless you were related to someone important, like a powerful family.

The new, insubordinate guy was related to no one. But The Leader was. He was related to the only one who mattered, his boss.

"I'm sorry. I meant nothing by it," the insubordinate guy said. He backed away. Slowly. There was nowhere to run.

The Leader stayed quiet. And then quickly, he pulled out a weapon suppressor and screwed it into his Glock. He racked the action and chambered a bullet.

"You know what I hate more than anything?" he asked.

"I didn't mean it! Come on, man!" the insubordinate guy said, and reached for his Glock, which was stuffed into a pancake holster at his hip. He touched the butt. That was as far as he got.

The Leader said, "I hate disloyalty! I hate traitors! Are you a traitor?"

He raised the suppressed Glock and pointed it at the insubordinate guy's center mass. Then he slowly raised it to the guy's neck. A target that would bleed—a lot. And it would be very painful. The insubordinate guy knew that.

"I'm no traitor!"

"Are you questioning my directive?"

"No! Of course not!"

"Are you questioning my plan?"

"No!"

"Are you questioning my leadership?"

"No!"

The Leader got that look in his eye. A look that all the guys, except for the insubordinate guy, had seen many times before.

The insubordinate guy had only seen it once before. Recently. A look like a primal animal, like an ancient meat-eating creature, had—a reptile look.

One of the other men stepped up and put his hand on The Leader's shoulder and said, "He's just tired, sir. He's with us."

Then he looked at the insubordinate guy and asked, "Right?"

"Yes! Of course! I'm not a traitor! Not like Mike Lee!"

The Leader lowered his Glock and started chuckling. Like the whole thing had been one big joke, a hazing.

"I'm just kidding with you!"

Sweat beaded off the guy's brow. He said, "Of course! I knew that!"

The Leader said, "I wouldn't shoot you like this."

"I knew it was a joke," the guy said nervously.

"Nah, it'd be better if you got shot out there," The Leader said, and he pointed the Glock south, toward Mexico.

"One day," he continued, "we might be out on a mission. Maybe, you get shot by one of those bangers. Or maybe friendly fire. Happens all the time."

The insubordinate guy said nothing.

"You gotta watch your own back. You know? Amigo?"

The Leader reached out with a big, gloved hand and patted the insubordinate guy on the shoulder. He smiled and backed away, letting go of the insubordinate guy's shoulder. He holstered his weapon, which took an extra second because of the suppressor. Then he motioned for the other six to fall back in line.

* * *

THE SEVEN ARMED men watched the visitor parking lot. The sun had started its nightly descent to the west but hadn't gone all the way down. The last wisps of light spilled out over the distant waterscapes and thickset green treetops. They hadn't seen a vehicle come by the station house in over thirty minutes. Not one. Not one passed by on the street.

They counted the vehicles in the rear lot. The deputy had gone. He hadn't returned. Not yet.

The Leader clicked his earpiece, switching it on. He said, "Check. Everyone. Check. Respond."

He waited and heard affirmatives from all six men. They were split into two teams. A normal formation they had practiced and implemented in real scenarios before. Keep it simple was the way The Leader ran his team.

Both teams were split up into three men each, including The Leader. One man stayed behind, controlling the spy drone.

The Leader said, "Eagle Eye, confirm the layout."

The man controlling the spy drone looked down at the screen on his smartphone. He saw a clear picture of what the drone's camera picked up. The grounds, the parking lots, the roof, the exterior of the station house, and the woods surrounding it were all illuminated in heavy-duty greens—night vision.

"Eagle Eye here. All is clear."

The Leader said, "Affirmative. Team Two, are you ready?"

"Team Two. Ready."

"Okay, guys. Stay frosty. On my mark. Go!" The Leader ordered. Less than thirty-five seconds later, the teams were posted at their designated breaching positions on either end of the station house.

The station house was a normal setup. It had a front door for walk-ins from the public. And a rear door for just the cops and cuffed prisoners.

The Leader waited behind his team's breacher, who had an easy job because they were at the front of the station house—not much chance of being shot breaching the front. The sheriff would expect people to walk in from the front. No surprises there. No reason to open fire on three guys coming in through the front doors.

Team One's breacher didn't have to set up breaching charges or use a battering ram or shotgun to blow out the hinges on the front door. It was already open, naturally. Instead, he jerked the door open and backed away.

The point man took over and rushed inside. The Leader followed.

They fell in line, one after the other, right into a tiled area with a long reception counter and corkboard signs posted to the back wall. Everything that a receptionist needed was there: office machines, faxes, two telephones, a computer, and an office chair. It was all empty. No one was there.

The Leader took point, his LAR-15 out in front, his finger in the trigger housing, ready to fire. He stopped and covered an open area to the right that led behind the counter and beyond to a full-length wall of concrete.

The point man crouched low and swung around the counter and entered the bullpen beyond. The breacher came up on The Leader's back and pinched his shoulder, giving him the ready signal.

The Leader moved forward, following tight to the point man. Within minutes, they covered the entire bullpen and came face to face with Team Two.

To the back of the station house was a row of cells, only three. Inside there was only one prisoner. A drunk. A man. He was fast asleep, snoring loudly.

"What the hell is this!" Portman said. He stood in the doorway of his office, a coffee mug in his hand.

"Freeze!" the point man of Team Two called out.

Portman stood there, frozen. The last thing he expected was to see six armed men with black ski masks pulled over their faces, storming into his station house. He inadvertently dropped the coffee mug. It crashed on the floor, shattering. Hot coffee spilled over his shoes and the bottoms of his pants. Instinctively, he backed away.

"Stay right there, amigo!" one of the masked men commanded.

The Leader lowered his LAR-15 and stepped past his guys. The other five men had Portman dead to rights in their sights.

"Sheriff Portman, you've got a prisoner that we'd like a word with."

Portman had his hand near his gun. Another thing that was instinctive. But it was too late. And he knew it.

* * *

PORTMAN'S DEPUTY came back from his meal break a little late and a little fuller than what he was comfortable with. He squared his car in a space in the secure lot. He switched off the music player on his phone. He listened to it at full volume when he drove because the radio in the patrol car had been busted since the atom bomb was dropped, he figured. No way was Portman ever going to shill out taxpayer dollars for a new one or to repair this one. He knew that. Portman was a good, solid cop. But he was a cheap bastard.

The deputy throttled the gear into park, switched off the vehicle and climbed out. He left two fast food bags on the seat. The second one still had a half-eaten sandwich inside. He would save it for a snack. In case he got hungry later. All he had to do was tell Portman he was running out to his car to grab something. Then he could eat the rest or smoke a cigarette or both. Which he knew would happen.

That wife, who burned her husband alive, was locked up in Portman's office. So the sheriff wasn't going anywhere—not tonight. He'd stick around all night. He had some kind of special relationship with her daddy or something. None of that mattered to the deputy. The only thing that concerned him was that it meant that he'd need a midnight snack and a midnight smoke.

The deputy swirled his keys around his index finger, letting the keyring twirl, and hitting his knuckles on the way down. He sauntered to the backdoor, passing Portman's car, passing their dumpster, which smelled like it needed to be picked up soon.

In the distance, he heard wind whooshing over the hills and through the trees above the station house. Then he stopped a few paces from the backdoor. He heard a strange sound. It was faint, but not too distant. It wasn't like just the sounds of wind. This was more like helicopter blades, only softer. Like amplified butterfly wings. Like a hummingbird on steroids.

He looked around, checked the lot, and checked back up to the trees. He looked in all directions at eye level. He saw nothing. Then he gazed up toward the sky above him. He saw something black and mechanical hovering over the roof of the station house.

"What the hell?" he said to himself.

It was some kind of drone with a pair of dual rotor blades. They looked serious. It had no lights on. He couldn't tell the size of the thing. But it looked military-grade, no question about it. Like it was for local tactical reconnaissance. It looked like the kind of thing he had seen in *Call of Duty*, his teenage son's favorite video game.

The deputy slowly gazed forward. He looked at the backdoor again. Only this time, he saw something was off-kilter about it. Something was different. He hadn't noticed it before. The door was ajar. But it was more than that. It was hanging open.

No! It was broken. He saw that the frame of the door had been bashed in. The lock was completely shattered. And the ends of the door were split and splintered. It looked like someone had used a small grenade on it or a mine.

What was it that the game his son played called it? A breaching charge?

The deputy reached for his gun. He unsnapped the safety buckle and brandished his Glock. He chambered a round and aimed it at the backdoor.

He reached up to his shoulder mount and scooped up his radio.

He clicked the button and said, "Ramas! Come in!"

Ramas was the other deputy who was still working the county in his patrol car, or he was napping, parked somewhere secluded. Either way, he wasn't off the clock. No way.

The deputy waited. There was no answer. He tried again. No answer. He tried a third time. No response.

This time, he heard a strange signal echoing back at him from the radio, a cacophony of radio sounds. It sounded kind of like when he called up to the station house, and someone was using the fax machine. Like a whirring, static sound, only a little abrupt. A little more aggressive. And very annoying.

He clicked the button on the radio again.

"Ramas! Come in!"

Nothing.

"Ramas!"

No answer.

He looked back up at the drone above. It hovered a little higher. It moved back over the lot. He thought about shooting it.

He watched. The drone wasn't hiding its location. It was right there in the open, in plain view.

Suddenly, a thought passed through his mind, a thought that turned into fear. And he felt his heart pumping. His blood pressure spiked.

He asked himself one question. What if someone was using a radio jammer?

Why not? He had already seen evidence of a breaching charge and a military spy drone.

He decided not to wait any longer. He burst through the backdoor, pushing through the shattered wood and the splintered metal shards from the lock. He swept the back entrance. He saw no one. He walked over more broken wood from the backdoor. He stepped past a series of unused lockers, past a set of long benches. And he turned a corner to see the bullpen.

He came face to face with four masked men and Portman.

Portman was on his knees. He was restrained by two of the men, while another stood in the dead center of the room. The fourth sat on the sheriff's desktop. His feet dangled off the edge.

The man standing in the center of the room, in front of Portman, held a black leather SAP, which was a vicious blunt weapon, similar to a blackjack, only flat and crafted with leather.

It was a weapon that wasn't too big, and easy to conceal. In the right hands, it could do massive damage to a man's skull.

This one was thick on the beating end. It looked worn, like it got plenty of frequent use.

The guy holding it must have pounded Portman on the top of the head with it more than once because dark violet bruises were welling up all over Portman's forehead and face.

Blood dripped off the end of the thing.

All five men, including Portman, stopped and stared at the deputy. He pointed the Glock at them. He trembled, and the barrel shook in his hand. They could all see it.

"Freeze! Let him go!" he called out, without dithering.

The guy holding the SAP stopped, turned, and faced him.

"Drop the weapons!" the deputy said. He looked at all four of the men and saw what he thought to be AR-15s and sidearms. They were well equipped.

The guy holding the SAP didn't drop it. And neither did the others. None of them even attempted to make it look like they were even considering it.

"Take off the masks!" the deputy called out.

The man holding the SAP reached up slowly so as not to get shot, and with one hand, he pulled his black ski mask off, revealing his face.

He was Hispanic.

"Drop your weapons!"

The guy holding the SAP was The Leader. He said, "Where's Molly Lee?"

"Who?"

"Your prisoner! The wife who killed her husband in the fire! Where is she?"

The deputy noted The Leader spoke with a Mexican accent.

He looked at Portman's office, a natural, involuntary look. The Leader followed his gaze. He said, "So, she was here. Thank you."

"Drop your weapons! Let him go!"

Just then, The Leader spoke in Spanish, which was his native language.

The deputy was debating on whether he should just shoot. But that was quashed because right then, he realized The Leader was speaking Spanish to two other guys who stood behind him. He knew this because he felt the muzzle of a gun on the back of his neck. It was pressed hard. The muzzle hole was unmistakable. Suddenly, he was overcome with images of bullets. And the trembling became worse.

"Drop the pistol," The Leader said.

The deputy paused a beat, but then he felt a gloved hand clamp down on his gun. The second man stepped up and forward and took his Glock away. He jerked it out of his hand and stepped back.

The Leader barked out a command, again in Spanish. And the deputy felt himself being shoved forward. He stumbled over to Portman.

"All we want is the wife. We don't want you. We don't want to kill cops."

"She was in there!" the deputy said. He pointed at Portman's office.

"Shut up!" Portman shouted at him.

The Leader smacked him, backhanded with the SAP. Portman spat blood and a single tooth out of his mouth.

Then The Leader folded up the SAP and stored it in one of the cargo pockets on his pants. He un-holstered his Glock. The suppressor was still attached. The deputy looked at it. For an attachment that was manufactured to be silent, the reality of seeing it was deafening in the station house.

The Leader smiled at the deputy and said, "You know. You're the lucky one."

"What?"

The Leader shot him in the gut. The muzzle flashed. A reverse cone of fire spit out, followed by a single bullet.

The bullet tore through the flesh and organs in the deputy's gut. Blood the color of oil gushed out. And the deputy toppled over, clutching at the bullet hole.

He screamed in pain.

The Leader stayed where he was. In Spanish, he ordered the two men behind the deputy to lift him and drag him closer. They did.

The Leader grabbed a tuft of Portman's hair and jerked his head up.

"Look at him," The Leader said.

Portman looked.

"He will bleed out slowly. Unless you tell me what you did with her."

The deputy cried out.

Portman said, "Go to hell!"

The Leader said, "I'm from hell. It's our home. Amigo."

Portman stayed quiet.

"You may not care about your cop. But eventually, we'll find someone you do care about."

* * *

NOT TOO MUCH EARLIER, Portman had watched DEA Agent Ryman pull away in his Chevy Tahoe from his Crown Vic. Then he pulled around to the back of the station house. He picked up a brown paper bag from off the seat and walked inside. He kept the bag folded up underneath his arm. He told his deputy to take a break. He waited for the deputy to pull away from the station house and drive off.

Portman went into his office.

Molly Lee sat on a black leather sofa, parked along the sidewall. She had been cuffed out in front of her.

Portman unlocked her handcuffs and returned them to his belt. He handed her the paper bag.

"Get dressed. We don't have a lot of time."

She looked up at him. Hope in her eyes. She asked, "You believe me now?"

She had told him the whole story. The DEA. The fire. All of it. At least, he hoped all of it. She had told him the truth about what her husband was into. She didn't think that he would believe her, but he did.

"I just got a visit from a DEA Agent."

Lee's face turned to one of complete fear.

"Who?"

"A guy named Ryman?"

"He was Mike's partner."

"That was your husband's partner?"

She nodded.

"Is he into what Mike was into?"

"I think so. Probably."

"I believe you."

"Why?"

"There's no way he would get here this fast unless he was already here waiting. Like he already knew about Mike being dead."

"What am I going to do?" she asked.

"First, get dressed."

"Then what?"

"Just get dressed," Portman said.

He left the room and paced the bullpen, waiting. He tried to come up with a plan. But it was all happening so fast. And there was no time. If he was going to protect her, then he had to act. How was he going to get her out of there? How would he explain it? How much time did he have before Ryman drove out to the prison and saw that there was no Molly Lee turned over to them by his station or that there was no one with that name even incarcerated?

The more he thought about it. The worse it played out for him. No matter what he did, he was going to get in trouble for it. He couldn't turn her over to the FBI, the DEA, or the US Marshals. Not now. If Ryman was dirty, if what she told him was true, then there was no telling who would monitor his communications, or his next moves. So far, no one suspected him of helping her. He had to act fast. Had to act now.

Molly Lee walked out of his office. She was wearing her own clothes, a long-sleeved cotton knit shirt, a pair of cargo pants, and a winter vest, not too thick, just some random stuff he had grabbed out of her backpack. She had told him not to get anything out of the duffle bag. She had told him that her backpack had more appropriate clothing. The duffle was filled with feminine items and personal items that she had packed the night before, when she had planned to leave Mike, and not planned on him being killed.

"What do I do?" she asked.

"Is there anywhere you can go away for a while? Someplace safe?"

She thought for a moment and said, "I've got cousins. Up north."

"No. That won't do. That'll be the first place they'll look."

Silence.

Portman asked, "Where were you planning to go before the fire? You said that you were going to leave him. You packed a suitcase."

"I was going to leave him. Like I told you. I was just going to go to my summer job."

"What job?"

"Years ago, I took a job to get away from Mike. To have some peace to myself."

"What?"

"Every summer, I work as a fire lookout."

Portman said, "Did Mike know that?"

"Of course."

"And he was okay with it?"

"He didn't care what I did."

"What about Ryman? Does he know?"

She thought for a moment and shook her head.

"Are you sure?"

"Why would he? Mike never talked about us. I'm sure of that. And I don't go by my name there. I use my maiden name."

Portman thought for a moment. And he said, "I don't see that we have any other choice for the moment. We have to get you somewhere safe."

"How long can I last working out there? Won't he find me through a government database or something?"

"No. The government isn't that efficient. The FBI could do it, but let's hope he doesn't have any contacts at the Bureau. "Besides, I'll get you under protective custody by then."

She nodded.

"Do you have any identification with your name on it?"

"You mean Lee?"

"Both?"

"I have two driver licenses. I have one that says: *Molly Lee*. And I still have an old one."

"Where are they?"

"They're both in the truck."

"What about a passport?"

"That burned up in the fire."

"Give me your license."

"It's in my suitcase. What about my Bronco?"

"I moved it. It's in a safe spot."

"My license is there."

He nodded and said, "Okay. Let's go."

They walked out the back entrance and over to his patrol car. She got in, and he followed. He fired it up and drove off.

THEY MADE it to the interstate and drove south for five miles until they came to a state-run rest stop. Portman drove down the off-ramp and lined up past two semi-trucks and circled around the lot one time to make sure that there were no prying eyes.

Cars zoomed by on the interstate. Some driving south. Some speeding north.

He parked the car right next to the old Ford Bronco and slipped the gear into park.

Portman looked left and looked right.

"It looks safe. You should get going. I need to be back before anyone walks into the station house. Or in case the nine-one-one dispatcher's office calls."

"I don't know what to say."

Silence fell on them for a moment.

She said, "I'll be at the..."

"No. Don't tell me where. In case they try to pressure me, I won't be able to tell them the exact truth."

"But won't they figure it out? DeGorne is my maiden name. Someone will figure out that I'm using it."

"Don't use your passport. Don't register anywhere. No credit cards. No swiping. No filling out your real information. Not until I talk to you. We can probably get you into some kind of witness protection or something. You just need to keep your head low for a few days. I doubt it'll take longer."

"What will you do?"

"Tonight, I'll do nothing. I'll give you a good head start, make it whatever direction you're going. Then tomorrow, I'll make some phone calls."

"Who will you call? Who can help us? The Feds?"

Portman shook his head and said, "No. The Marshals. I'll call them when I figure out which of them I can trust. They'll know what to do. Give me three days, seventy-two hours. And then call me directly."

He unbuckled his seatbelt, hitched himself forward and dug down into his back pocket. He looked like a bear trying to reach an itch. He pulled out a thick, worn brown wallet and opened it up. He took out a cheap business card on white stock and handed it to her.

He said, "Call my cellphone three days from now. Directly. Got it?"

She took the business card and looked at it. His cell number was typed on it.

She wrenched forward uncontrollably and hugged him.

"Thank you!" she said.

He thought back to Vietnam. He thought back to her father.

"It's my job. To protect is part of the serve and protect."

She pulled away and smiled at him. A single tear welled up in her eye. He leaned forward again, reached his left hand down his leg for the second time that afternoon. He brandished his backup weapon, a silver snub-nosed revolver. He balanced it in his hand and showed it to her.

He asked, "You still remember how to use this?"

"Of course."

He reversed it and handed it to her.

"Don't use it unless it's absolutely necessary. Got it?"

She stared at it and took it. With his index finger, he pushed the barrel away from him, pointed it toward the dashboard.

"Keep it hidden."

She nodded.

"Okay," he said, and looked at his watch. "You'd better take off. Don't trust anyone that you don't already know until you hear from me."

DeGorne looked at him and felt afraid. She enjoyed being alone out in the wilderness, but here, among people, she felt a little afraid. She still had to make the drive to her post in northern California.

She turned and got out of the patrol car.

He shook the keys to the Bronco at her and said, "Here. I took them out of the car."

She took the keys.

"Give me your license that has Lee on it."

She nodded and went into the Bronco and opened up the glove box. She placed the revolver in it and sifted around for a couple of seconds for her license. After moving around the registration and two envelopes stuffed with maintenance receipts, she found both licenses. She looked at the most recent one and then the old one. The old one was expired, but she could still use it for an ID. And if the cops stopped her, they'd be looking her up in a database. She'd just drive carefully.

In case she got pulled over, then at least she would have it for the cops to look at.

She came back out of the Bronco and handed her new license over to Portman. He slipped it onto the console in his cruiser.

"Okay. You'd better take off."

He paused a quick beat and then said, "You'll need cash. Plenty of it. Don't use credit cards."

He pulled out his wallet and stared at what he had, which wasn't much.

She smiled for the first time all day and said, "Don't worry. I have plenty of cash."

He looked at her, puzzled.

"I was planning on leaving him. Remember? I took out all of my cash and packed it away. I have more than enough."

"Are you sure?"

She nodded.

"Okay. Wait for me to leave, and then you take off. Call me as soon as you can."

"Like when?"

"At least in the next seventy-two hours."

She said, "Okay. Thank you!"

Portman said, "Molly, your father was proud of you."

"He was proud to be your friend."

Portman nodded, took the gear out of park, switched it to drive, and took off. She waited until he was gone from sight, and then she fired up the Bronco. The gas gauge was full. She turned around in her seat. Her eyes scanned the rest stop around her. No one was watching. She pulled up one of her packed bags and unzipped it just enough to see in.

It was all still there. Portman hadn't opened it. Luckily, he had opened only the backpack, which had her clothes packed tightly in it.

The duffle had inside it a black garbage bag and inside that were stacks of cash—all hundreds. All banded together just the way she had left it, which was just the way she had found it.

She didn't tell Portman about the money. She figured it wouldn't look good if there was an element of stolen money in her story.

9

Widow rode up in the Monte Carlo, riding in the backseat with one Glock in his hand. The other still in his pocket. The muzzle of the first was jammed to the back of the gangbanger's neck through the gap between the headrest and the seat.

The gangsta drove, slowly, down a one-way street and turned left onto another until he stopped the car right alongside an actual church.

Widow looked up at it. He was part amazed and part dumbfounded.

He said, "It's a real church?"

The guy said, "Yeah, man!"

"Capone's in there?"

"You got it, man."

"Put the gear into park."

The gangsta did as he was told.

Widow said, "Turn off the ignition."

The gangsta turned off the ignition.

"Get out. Slow."

The gangsta opened the door and slipped out. Widow followed with the rear door. He stood up, tall, and kept a dead stare at the gangsta. They were the only two riding in the car's part that was meant for passengers, except for the original driver, who was still out cold on the passenger side of the front bench.

The gangsta said, "What now?"

"How many guys he got in there?"

"None."

"None?" Widow asked.

"Yeah. We, it. We the whole army."

"Who else am I gonna find in there?"

"No one. Just the Greecers."

"Greasers?"

"Yeah."

"Like mechanics? Guys who like cars?"

"No, man. Greecers. Like the country. They just customers that hang around Capone. Most of them are girls. They get so blazed we call 'em Greecers like they up there, with the gods, man."

Widow shook his head.

"You guys are weird."

"Now, take the keys. Walk to the back of the car."

"Why?" he asked.

"Do what I say!"

The guy walked to the back of the car. He crept. He went, knowing that he was going in the trunk with the other two guys, which Widow had thought of. And that thought put a smile on his face. Jamming three big gangbangers into the trunk of a Monte Carlo wasn't the worst idea in the world. But he didn't think there would be enough room. Not for all three of them to be stuffed in there. Lid closed. And still be alive the next morning, or however long it took for the cops to find them.

Instead of shoving the guy into the trunk, Widow gave him a solid blow to the back of the neck. The medulla oblongata. All the wiring for the brain. The important stuff.

First, he told the guy to open the trunk. This put the guy in front of him, bending at the waist, shuffling forward. Waiting like he knew something was coming and not being able to do a thing about it.

Next, Widow reversed the Glock in his hand, repositioned it as a clubbing weapon. Not the best gun to use a tool, but combined with Widow's sledgehammer fist, it would do a pretty good job.

With one devastating blow, like Paul Bunyan slamming down an ax, he hammered the gangbanger right in the back of the brainstem, crushing the power box to the brain.

The guy launched forward like he was catapulted off his feet and slammed his face into the car's trunk lid. He hit teeth first. Between the four of them, these guys had lost a lot of teeth. Which Widow figured they wouldn't really mind. It seemed like they were meth heads. And the two things that meth heads didn't seem mind losing were their money and teeth.

Widow looked around. He looked up the street, and then back down it. He looked in front of the church, checked the windows, and checked the alley on the side.

He saw a trashcan fire in the small courtyard of the church. There was a wrought-iron fence surrounding it. But no people. No guards. No homeless people. No one.

He stepped back and waited for the gangbanger to slide off the rear of the car and down off the bumper. Then he stepped forward and rolled the guy under the back bumper of the car with his foot.

The gate to the courtyard wasn't missing, but it was stripped off its hinges and sprawled out on a concrete sidewalk that ran out in front of the church.

Widow read the church sign on the way in, hard not to. It was big and posted to the front entrance to the church at the top of wide concrete steps. Whatever the denomination had been, that part of it had long been stripped away. In its place was the word "Capone" in all capital letters. It read: CAPONE CHURCH, which should have been CAPONE'S CHURCH or CHURCH OF CAPONE. But Widow wasn't there to give this guy a grammar lesson.

Widow shook his head as he passed the sign. This guy, Capone, was about the biggest joke he had ever seen as far as criminal enterprises went. If the gangbanger had been telling the truth, then there wasn't much to his organization. There were the four street guys, who only had two guns between them, and a bunch of stoned idiots waiting inside the church.

Not much to it at all, which might've explained why the cops ignored this, for now. They might've had bigger fish to fry, bigger concerns to worry about, than some two-bit hoodlum who fancied himself to be a crime lord from the nineteen-twenties.

Widow didn't bother looking for a back entrance to the church. He walked right in. No problems.

The inside wasn't much of any kind of house of worship, almost as much as it wasn't a suitable place for a self-respecting crime lord to live. The inside looked more like an abandoned community center that was refurbished into a crack house.

Only a few pews remained. Most of the floor was exposed. Along the walls and corners, he saw bodies of people lying around, talking, whispering. He saw drug paraphernalia. Most of the people along the inside of the church were rail-thin. There were women, men, some teenagers. It was hard to tell exactly because the only light was candlelight. Only Widow noticed as he walked in. It wasn't candlelight. It was more closely related to torchlight because there were no candles. There were only barely controlled fires set around the corners of the church in trashcans.

Widow looked around, studied the people as best he could. He wasn't sure that every one of them was even alive. The place didn't smell the best. And many of them weren't moving. That was probably because they were passed out, high, or both. But he wouldn't have been surprised if some of them were dead, and no one around them realized it.

The ceiling was high. Maybe twenty feet off the ground, maybe twenty-five.

Stained-glass windows adorned the upper walls of the church. Widow looked up, saw that each window depicted a scene from the Bible. All the Jesuses had their faces shattered, like someone took to throwing bricks through them. There was broken glass all over the floors underneath them. The only faces in the panes that remained unbroken were of the devil. That was obvious because of the red skin, the goat hooves, and the horns on a human face.

The church was Capone's own little slice of hell.

Widow walked farther in, through the church doors, which were wide open. He stopped dead in front of a long pathway. It was the only thing not littered with used drug needles and broken crack pipes. On the left side of the pathway, Widow saw why it was clean. There was a scrawny man with a broom. He was virtually shirtless because his shirt had been torn to shreds. He walked barefoot. And he was mumbling to himself.

The church was essentially a junkie's paradise. Everyone had to be somewhere.

Widow had never been addicted to drugs. Although, if it was anything like coffee addiction, then he could empathize. He could see how someone might fall prey to such a life. He had seen it in the military. He had seen it in foreign countries. When you lived under a dictatorship or a theocracy or an oppressive regime, and you had no source of legitimate income, no way out, then drugs were the only cheap way to escape.

Widow walked up the path, keeping one Glock in his hand, being mindful that the other was in his front pocket. He kept his face forward, chin down. His eyes scanned from left to right and back, checking the corners, checking faces. He was stopped right there in the middle of the pathway by the junkie with the broom.

"Who...who are you?" the guy mumbled.

"I'm looking for Capone," Widow said.

"And who...who are you?"

"Where is he?"

The guy jittered and danced from foot to foot. He started scratching his bare forearms, which were the size of spatulas, and just as breakable.

He asked, "What is...What is this regarding?" Like a receptionist taking a phone message.

"Where is he?" Widow asked. He stretched his neck out and stood up as tall as he could go, like he was a bear showing off its size and stature to a trespasser on its territory. At six-foot-four, he towered over the junkie. He towered over most people.

Fear overcame the junkie's face. That was obvious. And he said, "I'm not...not supposed to let anyone pass. Boss is with a new girl. No...no one interrupts when he's with a new...new girl."

In a fast, violent movement, Widow racked the slide on the Glock in his hand, and the chambered bullet ejected out the top. It flew up into the air. No spin. He caught it almost as fast as he had racked the slide. With his right hand, he slid it down his palm until it reached his index finger. He pinched it between his index and middle fingers. He showed it to the junkie.

He said, "See this?"

The junkie swallowed hard.

"I see...see it."

"This is a nine-millimeter parabellum."

The junkie stared at it with a kind expression of both recognition and finality on his face.

"It's a bullet."

"I know...know it's a bull...bullet."

"Good. Then you know the thing about bullets, right?"

"Wha...what?"

"There's a bullet for everybody."

The broom junkie swallowed hard, again.

"This one is for you."

The junkie swallowed one last time and backed away; only there was nowhere to back away to. Not unless he planned to turn and scramble up ten feet to the nearest window and jump out it, which wouldn't be as fast as a bullet in the ass. Any right-minded person would know that. But junkies weren't right-minded people, not in Widow's experience.

Which was why he kept his guard up, kept checking his six, even though he outweighed this guy by double digits, maybe triple. Drugs made people do many crazy things, especially heavy drugs like meth, which seemed to be the drug of choice for most of the church people. Widow could see it on his skin, on his teeth, or lack thereof.

Widow asked, "Where is Capone?"

The junkie looked at the nine-millimeter bullet, and then at Widow. He said, "Priest bedroom."

No stutter this time.

The junkie turned back to the altar, up the middle of the path, and pointed at a door in the back wall.

"Thank you!"

Widow pocketed the bullet in case he needed it, which he doubted. He had plenty more in the magazine. He knew. He had checked. But he racked the slide and chambered the next bullet in line.

He left the guy there with the broom. The broom junkie returned to sweeping, with no real plan or order to his madness.

Widow walked up the pathway, up to the altar. There he saw a huge broken crucifix, erected on metal legs at the bottom, like a Christmas tree. Most of the bottom half was undamaged, unharmed.

The top half was broken off at the arms. The top half lay on the floor.

Widow ignored it and passed it. He headed straight for the door. When he got there, he didn't knock. He grabbed the knob and turned it. Slow. The knob moved. No lock. He opened the door and walked through a dark passageway, treading down a couple of steps. His shoe touched down onto a thick red carpet at the bottom.

The interior of the room was huge. It looked more like a king's throne room rather than a clergyman's bedchambers. The thick red carpet continued. There was crown molding on the ceilings and a huge stone fireplace at the back wall.

The fireplace looked like an afterthought. It wasn't a part of the original priest's dwellings. But it had been nicely added on, which was weird. Like Capone, or whoever had run the clergy out of the church, had then hired a contractor to come in and install it.

The rest of the room was also lavish and gaudy. There were two wooden dressers lined up on one wall. There were two plush sofas and two armchairs. There was a bar cart parked in one corner, fully loaded. One open vodka bottle was half empty.

In the fireplace, a fire blazed on, not roaring, but enough to light the entire room dimly, just well enough to see. Dark shadows danced in the lower corners from the fire.

At the center of the bedroom was a huge Victorian bed, all wood and blankets and sheets. Drapes hung from lofty bedposts made of wood and decorated with abstract carvings. In the softly lit room, Widow saw what looked like a pile of bodies on the bed. Not dead, but piled in a heap.

Widow saw soft-moving limbs and joints and human appendages. He saw skin. And he heard hot breathing and panting.

Then he heard a man's voice.

"Who the hell is there?"

Widow walked over to the bed like a monster in a nightmare. His eyes adjusted to the dimness quickly. His eyes had been trained to adjust fast in darkness. In his military career, he had spent a lot of time in the dark.

Widow saw a naked man and a half-naked woman. The woman wasn't talking, but her eyes were moving.

Widow switched the Glock to his left hand and reached out, slammed his right hand onto the sheets around the naked man. He jerked the guy off the bed and onto the floor.

"Hey!" the guy screamed.

On the floor, Widow could see him better. He was a white man. No visible tattoos. No visible scars. He looked about forty. Partially balding in the front. He didn't have a grille in his teeth like one of his guys had.

If Widow had seen him on the street, he would have never pegged him as a guy that anyone would follow around and call their boss. Certainly, he didn't look the part. He didn't look like any kind of criminal mastermind.

Widow asked, "You Capone?"

"Oh God! Are you her father?"

Her father?

Widow didn't look back. That could be a trap, a ruse. He knew that. Capone didn't look like any kind of threat, but that was exactly how he had gotten to be a local crime boss, probably. The guy was low level and slap-dash, but still a crime boss.

Widow had seen it before. Cops and criminals, and almost everyone else, could easily be fooled by a guy who looks like he belongs in the suburbs but not running a small drug territory in a small neighborhood in Hollywood.

Widow reared his foot up and crashed it down on Capone's inner right thigh. A severe attack. The guy cried out in pain. Then Widow repeated the attack for good measure. He used the same heavy foot in a thick shoe, the same relentless force behind it. If Widow dialed it up one more degree, he'd be snapping bone and probably ripping through a major artery.

Capone screamed and wailed in agony.

"Are you Capone?" Widow asked again. His voice steady. His demeanor calm.

The guy rocked on his naked butt, clutching his inner thigh. Tears welled up in his eyes.

Widow aimed the Glock at the guy's inner thigh, the same bruised spot he had crushed with his shoe. The guy stared up at him.

Widow fired a bullet into the floor, inches away from the guy's thigh. The gunshot was deafening in the stony priest chambers. It echoed and bounced off the walls.

"I won't ask again."

"Yes!" the guy said. "I'm Capone. Who the hell are you?"

Widow reversed his position and circled around Capone so that his back was to the fire and not to the door. He didn't want to get any surprises, like armed guards he didn't know about.

A wide shadow fell over Capone.

Widow looked at the woman on the bed. She moved, but slowly, groggily. Her small hands grabbed at a single sheet and pulled it up to her chin.

After getting a good look at her face, he noticed something about her he hadn't before. She wasn't a woman. She was a girl.

Widow asked, "Are you okay?"

The girl shivered and said, "I think so. Yes, sir."

"How old are you?"

"She's old enough!" Capone squealed.

Widow jackknifed another vicious stomp onto his right thigh. The same place. Same heavy shoe. Different stomping position.

Capone screamed again.

The girl whimpered and said, "Eighteen."

Widow frowned, furrowed his brow like he did when he wanted the truth from someone.

"How old are you, really?"

She looked down at Capone, like she was seeking approval from him. Like he would tell her what to say. But Capone said nothing. He knew better.

She looked back up at Widow with terror in her eyes. She said, "Sixteen."

"How old?"

"She said she was sixteen!"

Widow popped Capone in the back of the head once with the Glock.

"I wasn't asking you!" he said, and looked back at the girl in the bed.

"Where are your parents?"

"I don't know."

"You don't know?"

"They're home. I guess."

"Where's home?"

She told him the name of what sounded like a suburb, probably outside the city.

Widow asked, "Are you drugged?"

She didn't speak.

"Did he give you something?"

She nodded.

"Cocaine?"

"Crystal," she answered.

Meth, Widow thought.

Capone writhed and retched around. He said, "My leg. I think I need a doctor."

"He gave it to you?" Widow asked, again.

"Yes, sir."

"Your parents. They know where you are?"

She shook her head.

"No. I left."

"You ran away?"

She nodded slowly.

"When?"

"I don't know. Maybe two weeks ago?"

"I want you to get dressed. You know where your clothes are?"

She nodded.

"Get them and put them on."

Widow waited.

The girl slowly got up and out of the bed. She looked at him, bashful like she wanted to ask him not to look at her, but Widow had to look. He had known plenty of cops who had been fooled by decency, by youth, by innocence.

She seemed like a lost girl, like a nice girl, who ran away from home. She seemed like she had just gotten mixed up in something that she shouldn't have gotten mixed up in, which was probably true.

She seemed like a girl who was in way over her head, but she might've also been a junkie, not like the broom guy, but not far off either. Just around the corner and down the street, really. Going from a first-time user to a full-blown junkie was all relative for everyone. It came with different degrees. But in the end, meth usually won. Users, more often than not, turned into addicts before they knew it.

Meth was a drug that seduced the impressionable. Teenagers are impressionable. And runaways are even more so.

A teenage junkie can still hide stabbing weapons, the same as anyone else. Widow didn't watch her dress. He stared down at Capone as she dressed. But he kept her in his peripherals enough to know what she was doing and where she stood.

He waited, and she dressed. He said, "What's your name?"

"Samantha. But I go by Sam."

"Sam, wait for me outside. Just by the door. Don't talk to anyone. Don't go off anywhere. Okay?"

"Yes, sir," she said, and she stumbled past him and out of the bedroom. No shoes. He figured she had lost them.

Widow waited till she shut the door, and then he looked down at Capone.

"Take the girl. You can keep her," Capone said.

Widow stayed quiet.

"Keep her. Seriously, man! I'm done with her, anyway!"

Widow stayed quiet.

"Hey, man! It's all good! Do what you want to her! I'll even give you some free samples, man! She loves the stuff!"

Widow stayed quiet.

"Talk to me, man! What? She's not enough for you? You want another? I can find one, man!"

Silence.

"What? You want younger?"

Widow said nothing.

"I can get you younger, man! What do you want?"

Widow said, "To be honest, I came here to show you the error of your ways. I came here to set you on the path to being a better person."

"What?"

"I came here to tell you to stop pinching hardworking people for their money."

"What the hell are you talking about?"

Widow shook his head and said, "I thought you were a two-bit gangster. Taking money from hardworking people.

"But I gotta tell you. Now, I really wish that's all you were."

Capone said, "What, man?"

"I'm not happy with what I've found here. Not at all. I thought you were a wannabe gangster type, like your four boys. But you're something worse. Something beneath that."

Capone scrabbled away like a rat.

Widow said, "You're a lowlife piece of shit!"

"Hey, I'm just doing what the system allows, man. You know? Trying to get mine! That's all!"

Widow thought for a moment, and then he asked, "I got a question for you."

"Yeah. Sure, man."

"I want a straight answer."

"Anything."

"Your life depends on it."

"Anything! You name it!"

"Why don't the cops bust you up?"

Capone shrugged, "They don't mess with us."

"But why? They know you're here, right? They gotta know. You're about the dumbest criminal I ever saw."

"They know I'm here. But they don't dare come here. Nobody here is worth their time. They got other fish to fry, I guess."

Widow thought about it. He wasn't happy with the answer, but it wasn't new. American cities had their problems. Crime was high these days. Higher than the bums in Washington liked to admit.

"What are you going to do?"

Widow looked down at him, smiled, and shot him. Right there. Not a flesh wound. Not a warning shot. Not a shot to a limb. Not a shot in a shoulder. That would've been a waste of a bullet, no reason to waste a perfectly good bullet.

Ten billion bullets are manufactured in America every year. One billion of those are fired. Forty thousand of those are used on human targets. Twenty-five thousand of those kill people. And the most common bullets are nine-millimeter.

A bullet for everybody. Certainly one for Capone.

Widow shot him right between the eyes. Maybe it wasn't the most heroic thing he had ever done. But it felt good. It felt right. He wouldn't lose sleep over it.

Widow had no idea how many other girls had ended up like Sam, or how they ended up after they had been used and discarded. But he had a pretty good picture of it.

He looked down at the dead gangster wannabe, who used to be named Capone, and then he looked back at the door. He walked to it, stopping at the fireplace. He ejected the magazine and the bullets. He disassembled the Glock's parts quickly, and he tossed them into the fire, keeping the bullets out.

He looked over the carpet, near the body. Blood pooled around the head, soaking into the red fabric. He kept his shoe prints out of it. He found the brass from the bullet and scooped it up. He slid it and the magazine into his pocket.

Outside the door, he found Sam waiting there. Her eyes were wide, like she knew what he had done. And she knew. He turned back to the knob, took out the bottom of his shirt, and wiped his prints off.

He took Sam by the hand, and they walked back down the pathway. Most of the junkies were so stoned that they didn't look up to see what the gunshot was. Or they were used to it. Or they just didn't care. That was the nature of the urban jungle.

Widow trudged past the junkie with the broom—Sam behind him. The guy looked like he was going to protest, but in the end, he stayed quiet.

Widow led Sam to the Monte Carlo. He told her to wait on the curb.

She looked on at him in complete shock as he popped open the passenger door and dragged out one of Capone's thugs, laid him on the sidewalk. Then he walked around to the trunk, opened it, and hauled out two more guys. Both were unconscious.

He dumped them behind the car, where she saw another guy, unconscious and already sprawled out on the concrete.

Widow rolled them all away from the rear bumper and closed the trunk. He wiped his prints off with his shirtsleeve, and walked around to the driver's side, opened the door. He looked over the top of the car at her and asked, "What's your address?"

She told him, a little slow, a little hazily. But accurately, he hoped. They both got in the car and drove away.

Widow drove the speed limit, stopping at traffic lights, making complete stops at stop signs. Following the road signs and the local traffic laws as best he knew them. On the way out of the city, a couple of blocks later, Widow saw a police patrol car, which gave him pause. The car drove by. The light bar was lit up on top. They seemed to go in the church's direction. He saw on the front bench of the cop car, McDiggs and Jones, the two cops from the Korean store. The whole neighborhood must've been their usual beat.

He hoped they would do a better job this time. He also thought that it might be good to get out and stay out of the city for a while. They wouldn't throw up roadblocks for a two-bit, child-molesting gangster, like Capone, or would they?

Where should he go next? Where was a good place to hide out?

The answer didn't matter, not yet, because first, he had to bring Sam home to her parents.

10

Special FBI Agent Joanna Watermoth pulled up in an airport-rented Chevy Caprice, blue exterior and a clean white interior, which was all that mattered to her. She parked the Caprice on the street. The visitor lot was blocked off.

Several cops from the neighboring two counties were hovering around. A forensic team was taking photos, and two plain-clothes detectives were standing around waiting. She killed the ignition and got out of the car, walked over to the crime scene.

It was a county sheriff's station house, north of Seattle, in the country.

One detective, in plain clothes, walked over to her.

"You the FBI?" he asked.

She reached into her coat, inner pocket, and pulled out a leather billfold, flipped it, and showed her FBI ID behind glossy plastic, and her badge. He looked, read her name, read that she was a Special Agent.

"Ms. Watermoth, I'm Detective Collins. With the state police," the closest detective said. He was a young guy. Probably only been at the state police for one, maybe two years. He had a mustache, nicely kept. He immediately struck Watermoth as some kind of hotshot.

"I recognize your voice, Detective, from the phone. So, what have we got here?"

She walked past him, tucking her badge and FBI ID back into her pocket. She had done this many times before. A woman, in her early forties or not, was always going to get resistance from the local cops. They were normally always men, and they normally always had a pissing contest with her about jurisdiction and state rights and blah, blah.

Her FBI male counterparts assured her it wasn't a sexist thing. The local boys did the same thing to them. But her male counterparts weren't females. And they didn't know that the local boys always tripled their pissing efforts when it came to a woman coming around and taking charge and stepping all over their toes.

Watermoth offered her hand to Collins, which he noticeably hadn't done to her. And they shook.

She asked, "Who's your partner?"

"That's not my partner. I'm here alone."

"Then who the hell is he?"

She looked at a tall, built cop, his back to her. He was in plain clothes, albeit expensive clothes. He had his back to them. She had seen Collins talking with the guy when she pulled up. She assumed he was also a detective.

"Let me introduce you. Truth be told, ma'am. I'm not sure who is in charge here."

"Why do you say that?" she asked, but she found out as soon as the cop-looking guy turned around.

He had a pair of Ray-Bans hanging from the top of his button-down flannel shirt. His sleeves were rolled up over his elbows. And he definitely had a sidearm. It was a Glock 21, holstered at his right hip in a pancake holster.

She also noticed a blood-red teardrop tattoo, small, but noticeable, on his cheek, just under his eye.

Collins said, "This is Ryman. This is Agent Watermoth."

Ryman looked at her. He chewed on a toothpick. He stuck his hand out, offered it for her to shake.

"Nice to meet you," Ryman said.

"Who are you exactly?"

"Why don't you have them fill you in first? Then I'll tell you who I am."

Watermoth said, "I am filled in. Dead sheriff's deputy and some poor bum in the cells. The sheriff is missing. I got that. Why don't you tell me who you are?"

"Sure, my name is Danny Ryman. I'm a member of SWATter," Ryman said, and he lifted the bottom of his shirt to reveal the same badge that he had shown Portman six hours earlier.

Watermoth looked at him, then moved her eyes down to the badge.

"DEA?" she asked, shaking her head.

Ryman smiled and dropped his shirt. He fingered the toothpick with one hand, poked at the gap between his front teeth.

"What the hell is the DEA doing here? This drug-related?"

"It is. In a way."

"How's that?"

"Today, I came by here."

Collins said, "You were here? You never said that to me?"

"Sorry, mate. I'm not at liberty to share information with pigs."

Collins moved his hand to a Glock holstered at his left hip. He didn't touch it. He didn't put his hands on it. Just made the gesture out of habit, Watermoth guessed. Like when some criminal calls him a name, then he goes for the gun to show them who's boss.

A hotshot and a hothead, she thought.

But she wasn't the only one to see it. Ryman saw it too; only he didn't react to it. Not aggressively.

He said, "You going for your gun, lad?"

Collins shrugged it off like he was just adjusting his coat.

"You go for your gun; you'd better be ready to use it, boy-o!"

"I wasn't. I was just taken off-guard. You shouldn't be calling cops pigs."

Ryman stared at him. Something sinister in those eyes. Watermoth had been at the FBI long enough to know the type. Only usually they were on the other side of the law. The only guys she'd ever met with those kinds of eyes who weren't criminals were DEA agents. Which made sense, she supposed.

The DEA was basically fighting a losing war. And to be in that world, you had to have one foot in the mud.

She said, "Chill out, guys. You're both on the same team, so act like it."

Ryman smiled at Collins.

Watermoth said, "Now, come this way." She motioned for Ryman to walk and talk with her.

Ryman left Collins standing alone and followed her.

"What's this about, you being here? Why is the DEA here?"

Ryman's eyes changed right there in front of her. Mister badass had become mister sensitive.

He said, "Last night, there was a fire."

"Okay. Where?"

"West of here. Inside the county. A man died in it. And a woman was taken into custody. His wife."

"The sheriff arrested her?"

"Yes."

"Go on."

"It looks like the wife either killed her husband and then tried to burn their house down, cover up the murder..."

"Or?"

"Or she burned the house down with him inside it to kill him and cover up the murder."

Watermoth asked, "And the wife, husband thing is drug-related?"

"The husband's name was Mike Lee."

"Yeah?"

"DEA Agent Mike Lee."

"Oh."

"He was my partner, lass."

Watermoth said, "I'm sorry for your loss. So, you're here to see about that?"

"I came here earlier to see Molly Lee, the wife."

"And what happened?"

"Sheriff Portman. The sheriff here. He told me she was checked into county prison. He gave me some nonsense about he couldn't keep her locked up here because they don't have women's facilities. He said she'd be there, where they had women's facilities."

"Was she there?"

"Portman told me right to my face, lass. I drove there. And no, they didn't have her. She never arrived there."

Watermoth looked around the outside of the station house.

"She never checked in?"

Ryman shook his head.

"Portman lied to you."

Ryman nodded.

"What happened next?"

"Next, I came here and found the deputy dead, gunshot to the gut. A prisoner in the jail cell, dead. Shot in his sleep. Back of the head."

Watermoth looked at him, then up to the sky.

"So we got a missing sheriff, missing prisoner who's a murder suspect. And now somebody shot up the station house."

Ryman nodded, took the toothpick out of his mouth.

"You think this Portman killed his own guy? Killed a prisoner? And then took off with Holly Lee?"

"Molly. Her name is Molly Lee, lass."

Watermoth said nothing to that.

"That's a plausible theory. This is a small community. Big region, but small community. Best I could tell; Molly is from here. She's a local girl. And Portman is a local boy."

"What about your partner?"

"He's not from here. He only moved here to keep her happy."

"What's a DEA agent doing working and living way out here? You guys work out of Seattle, I presume?"

"We do. And the answer to your question is Canada."

"Canada?"

"Yes."

"I thought most of the drug wars were fought in Mexico?"

"The drugs come up out of Mexico. That there is a fact."

"But?"

"But the US is only one of two markets the Mexican cartels sell to."

"Are you saying that you guys operated out of Seattle to fight the Mexican Drug cartels before they crossed over into Canada?"

"Something like that."

Watermoth rolled her eyes involuntarily, but she did it.

"Hey, Canada has a major drug problem, too. But the DEA doesn't give a rat's ass about Canada. But we care about Alaska and taking out the cartels everywhere. Mike and I hit the cartels down in Mexico all the time. But we also monitor the traffic of methamphetamines crossing our border into Canada.

"The cartels take a more lax approach when they ship to Canada. We don't take out the ones crossing over, but we watch them. It helps us to track them back to Mexico."

She nodded. It made some kind of sense. With everyone else watching the Mexican border, the bad guys wouldn't be so uptight at the Canadian one.

"How bad is it?"

"It's not US bad, but it's bad. It's freezing in much of Canada. Cold weather leads to bored teenagers, who take to narcotics. Most of it is cannabis, which they can get themselves. But the best meth is still cooked south of the border."

Watermoth asked, "You mentioned Alaska? How bad is it there?"

"Real bad. Alaska is freezing."

She nodded again. She had to take his word for it, she supposed.

"Why did Molly Lee kill your partner?"

Ryman looked away. He looked genuinely upset.

He said, "They didn't have the best marriage."

"What happened?"

"Marriage stuff."

"She having an affair?"

Ryman shook his head, said, "No way! Mike would've never allowed that."

"He'd never allow it?"

"I mean. He wouldn't have stood for it."

Watermoth asked, "He abuse her?"

Ryman said nothing.

"He beat her up?"

"Sometimes. Honestly, I didn't approve, but it was his marriage."

Watermoth nodded.

"He was my partner. You know? My brother."

She nodded again. She knew what that was like. Currently, she didn't have a partner. They tended not to stick around. The FBI kept saddling her up with some new guy, but within months, she'd drive him away.

"Well, Mr. Ryman."

"Danny. Please."

"Danny, it sounds like you should know that this isn't a DEA case, then. There are no drugs. Nothing related to drugs or Mexican cartels, not so far. That makes this an FBI case."

He nodded, said, "I know. I just want to be a part of it. I'm not here to tell you what to do or boss you around."

"I don't know."

"No offense, lass, but it's not up to you."

"Excuse me?"

"Like I said. No offense. The DEA has already authorized me to be here. You can call your SA. They should already know. Agent Lee may have been handling sensitive information."

SA stood for Supervisory Agent. In Watermoth's case, that was John Smith, which was his real birth name, or as he liked to put it, his "Christian name." She would call him to confirm this news. But only because she was a thorough type of agent. She already knew that Smith would go along with it, even if he didn't confirm it. He was that type of agent. He was a yes man, a team player.

"What kind of information?"

"The sensitive kind."

She looked away.

"I'm with you until we find her, whether you like it or not."

Watermoth said, "Come on. Let's look at the crime scene."

"No need. I already saw. You won't find anything in there about Lee or Portman."

"What about Portman's car? Did they take it?"

"That's good thinking. It may be in the back. I don't know."

"So, you're not going to be much help then?"

"I'm not here for help. I'm here to find out why my partner is dead," Ryman said, and he put the toothpick back in his mouth. He shoved his hands into his pockets and smiled. That primal, sinister look returned to his eyes.

Watermoth wasn't sure about him. She stepped away. She had a job to do, with or without the help of her new, unwanted partner.

* * *

Two MINUTES LATER, Watermoth stood in the rear security parking lot of the station house. She had walked around through the building. She saw the two dead bodies, but she stayed back and out of the way of the state forensic team. They would do a good enough job that she didn't need to call on her own.

She walked out of the backdoor and stared at the lot. Only one parked cruiser. Collins met her out back. He walked up behind her, made himself known.

He said, "That guy's a real piece of work."

"Forget about him. What do you make of that?" she asked. She pointed at the backdoor.

Collins reversed and stared at it. There was one forensics woman standing on the other side of it. She measured the broken door with a yellow measuring tape. Then she wrote the measurements onto a clipboard.

Collins looked at the door, up and then down. He said, "Looks like someone broke through it."

"That's obvious."

"Then what are you asking about?"

Watermoth stepped closer, pointed at the hinges, the shattered lock, and the doorframe.

"What's that look like to you?"

Collins knelt and took a closer look. He touched nothing.

"Looks like a breaching charge?"

"That's exactly what it is."

"What the hell does that mean?"

"It means this station house was raided."

"By who?"

"Someone with access to police equipment."

Collins said, "This is the country. Everyone out here has probably got access to explosives and charges."

"Not breaching charges. Breaching charges are designed to be as quiet as possible. Plus, they are designed not to inflict harm on people on the other side of the door you want to breach. They're for hostage rescue. This is police equipment."

"You think Portman breached his own station house?"

She ignored that stupid question.

"This was done by more than one person. No one breaches the back alone. Not when you can just walk in the front door. No, this was more than one person. Probably a small team of people to get the drop on two armed policemen."

Collins didn't bring up Portman acting alone again. He said, "That means someone took Portman with them and killed the other two. But why?"

"They didn't want Portman. They wanted Molly Lee."

"Why?"

"I don't know."

Silence.

Watermoth said, "Can you excuse me? I need to call my SA."

He looked at her, dumbfounded.

"My boss."

He nodded.

She stepped away and took her smartphone out of her pocket, dialed Agent Smith.

The phone rang, and she heard his voice.

"Joanna. You got there okay?"

"I did."

"What d'ya think?"

"It's strange. It's still preliminary, but strange."

"Enlighten me."

"There are two dead bodies. Both males. Both shot with .45 autos."

"What else?"

"One man shot is a sheriff's deputy."

"Where's the sheriff?"

"He's missing. Taken, I believe."

"Taken?"

"It looks like someone raided their station house."

"Raided?"

"Yeah. There's evidence of breaching charges on the door. And they took down a sheriff's deputy. Plus, the sheriff himself, we have to assume they overpowered him. Probably, they drew their guns first. Took them both by surprise."

Silence fell over the line.

Watermoth could hear Smith breathing and then the clicking of keys on a keyboard.

Smith said, "Don't jump to conclusions. That being said, you be careful down there. I don't have to tell you we must presume the sheriff is alive and being held against his will."

"I know, sir."

"Good. Get to it then."

"There's one more thing."

Smith said, "Yes. The DEA agent?"

"Yeah. So, then he's legit?"

"You play nice with him. But Joanna."

"Yeah?"

"Keep an eye on him. I don't trust him."

"You know him, sir?"

"No. But my contact at the DEA told me to watch him."

"Can I get a file on him?"

"That might take some doing. But I can tell you what my guy told me."

"Which is?"

"Apparently, this Ryman and Lee were a part of a special ops team called swatters, like SWATters. Like they swatted bad guys or some such nonsense."

"I see."

"He's not Investigation. Neither was his partner. They were mostly undercover and SWAT. These guys operate with a certain amount of impunity."

"Impunity?"

"Not the legal kind. It's more of a turn your cheek and look the other way kind."

"How's that, sir?"

"My guy tells me the SWATters are more into take-no-prisoners than making arrests. Got it?"

"Yes. I'll keep an eye on him."

"Like I said, be nice. But be smart."

"Just so we agree. Am I supposed to look at him as a hostile?"

"No. I'm not saying that. I'm saying he may be hostile but not a hostile. Just play nice for now."

Watermoth said, "I got it, sir."

"Anything else?"

"Yes, the wife of the DEA agent who's dead. Apparently, she killed him. Maybe. And now she's missing. In fact, she's not even in the system."

"You think someone came for her? Maybe some local good ole boys?"

"Maybe. But what I need to know is, can you get me a file on Lee?"

"The same rule applies here. About DEA files. But I'll do my best."

"Not Mike Lee. I need something on Molly Lee, the wife. She's not DEA. You should be able to get something on her."

"Sure, I'll have someone get that."

"Send it to my phone, okay? Thanks. I'll be in touch."

She clicked off the phone and went back to Collins. He was inside, looking over the dead bodies.

"So, what now? You want me off the case?"

She looked at him and said, "Off the case? No way. I need you and your guys on. It's just going to be me here. No need for more agents."

"What about Ryman?"

"He stays. For now."

"So, what's our next move? Want to hear about the bodies?"

She looked at the dead deputy on the floor, at the pool of blood, at his lifeless eyes.

Coldly, she said, "What for? We won't learn anything here. No. But what I do need are roadblocks."

"Roadblocks?"

"No," she said, and then she told him about the dead DEA agent, his missing wife, the missing sheriff, and that Ryman was his partner.

Then she said, "We've got a manhunt and a probable abduction. So, call up your guys. Tell em to be alert, but no roadblocks, too much ground to cover. Make it happen. It's been seven hours since this all went down. If she's got wheels and is going interstate speed limits to avoid being pulled over, that gives us a radius of five hundred miles."

"But five hundred miles. She could be in any of the surrounding states by now."

"So?"

"I work for the state of Washington."

"Call whoever it is you call and use my name. Tell 'em that the FBI is insistent. Got it?"

He nodded. She wondered how green he was.

11

Less than five hundred miles south, the north stretch of Highway 101 going through northern California was dark and barren and isolated and abandoned. It was cold and wet and stark all in the middle of the night—all at the edge of nowhere.

Even though it was nighttime, Widow could see a blazing wildfire. It had gone on for weeks. The middle of California was on fire. He saw it all the way up from LA.

When he dropped Sam off at her parents' house, he stayed long enough to see them open the door, to see the recognition for their daughter on their faces. He watched the father drop to his knees, to wrap his arms around the daughter that he thought he'd never see again.

Widow saw the mother come running out behind them. She screamed and cried tears of joy. It was hard to peel himself away from watching something so satisfying as returning a lost child to her mother. But Widow had road to cover. So he backtracked several miles to a junkyard that he had noticed off the highway. He pulled in and left the Monte Carlo wedged up tight between several junked cars. He wiped down everything that he had touched with a car rag he found under the seat.

He carried the second Glock and the magazine and the bullets with him for forty-one minutes, until he found a bus station. He dumped the magazine and bullets down a rushing sewer drain. The Glock he disassembled and pitched into a dumpster, where it would be picked up by a trash truck, dumped in with other neighboring trash bins, and taken out to a city land-fill. There it would be lost forever.

Widow took a bus until he reached San Francisco. There he walked twenty minutes until he found a diner. He enjoyed one cup of coffee, a plate of eggs, and crisp bacon. There he met a trucker who couldn't pay his bill. So Widow volunteered to pay for it as long as the guy gave him a ride.

He carried the paperback book in his back pocket the whole time.

On the way north, Widow said something that upset the guy. He wasn't sure what, but suddenly the guy grew hostile. He kicked Widow out, right there. The guy had picked him up, and his truck spat him back out.

Widow was left dumbfounded, watching the truck's taillights fading away.

Forty minutes earlier, he had a nice, cushy ride north. Now he found himself discarded like litter on the highway, and alone.

He walked on the side of the road, off to the shoulder, which was practically a small cliff over a deep ditch. He looked north, looked south, saw the distant towering forest fires, still blazing, still demonic and jaw-dropping.

He looked west and looked east. He was alone in the blackness, and the faint, distant firelight. He was alone in all directions.

12

Four miles later, Widow's boots and pants were dry on the inside but still covered in mud on the outside. But he wasn't mad anymore. Not at the trucker. Not at himself. That was life. Life was full of coincidences and outcomes and unforeseeable incidents.

Widow put it behind him and walked on. Even though the temperature had dropped, and it was slightly colder than he would have liked, it didn't matter because the scenery more than made up for it.

In fact, it made him smile. The forestry of northern California was a far cry from the urban desert lands of LA.

Widow walked north through pitch darkness in terms of no city lights, or manmade towns, or streetlights, or even headlights from passing cars. However, there was a dim light. Part of it came from the faint blaze hundreds of miles south of him. And part of it came from the stars in the sky and the full white moon. The night sky to the north wasn't cloudless, but the cloud cover was sparse enough to allow most of the stars up there that shined down on Earth to do just that.

Blackness shrouded the surrounding trees, but he could see their outlines and silhouettes. They looked more like terrifying monsters than naturally growing trees. They were vast and gigantic and colossal. Widow had never seen trees this big before that he could remember.

He couldn't see much vegetation or plants, but he figured they were there as well. And they were plentiful. Had to be.

The road wound and looped and curved on for long stretches. He saw mountains in the distance to the right. And as he rounded one long stretch of the highway, he saw the ocean off to the left. Suddenly, there was even more lowlight. The ocean looked calm from that distance until he stared harder at the shoreline. Then he saw cliffs and rocks. The water line was white and crashed up against the shore in long, measured intervals. Up close and personal, he imagined it to sound loud and rugged and majestic at the same time. From this distance, he couldn't hear individual waves crashing. He could only hear the faint crashing of all of them at once. The sound was calming and soothing and peaceful.

He was reminded of early explorers, crossing the vast American landscape, not knowing what was ahead. Many of them dying on the trail. Many of them leaving their dead loved ones behind. And then finally approaching this scene. All except for the highway. He imagined the way it must've looked to them.

He wondered if it was all worth it.

He was glad to be out of that guy's cab and on foot in such a beautiful place.

He walked on and finally came to the first sign that man had discovered this piece of land before he had, other than the existence of the concrete from the highway.

There was a large green sign posted among the trees, but unobstructed by nature. It was up high, maybe fifteen feet off the ground because the ground beneath it dropped below the highway.

The sign was green and reflective so that road vehicles could see it as it reflected their headlamps back at them.

It was ten feet wide, maybe more.

It read: Gray Wolf Redwood National Park.

Automatically, he searched his brain and couldn't recall that name anywhere from any roadmap that he had seen before. He couldn't recall it from any conversations or newspapers or whispers or rumors. He had never heard of it.

In smaller letters, under the title, the sign read: Gray Wolf Mountain Observatory: one mile ahead.

Usually, an observatory meant a lodge or office structure, and had a visitor center with park workers. This time of night that would all be closed. However, national parks were under the jurisdiction of the National Parks and Wildlife Service, which had a twenty-four-hour staff of law enforcement rangers. And the chance of there being a ranger station onsite at the Gray Wolf Mountain main campus was practically assured.

Widow walked past the sign and saw his first headlights coming toward him and going the other way. The lights came up on him, and he slowed his walk. He shifted over as close to the lane as he could without being in the road to let the driver see him plainly, which they must have because the vehicle slowed to a crawl as it came up on him.

It was a white pickup truck, full-sized, with a rear bench. The driver and a passenger looked at him. They seemed like they were going to stop.

It was a couple—possibly early forties, probably married, and potentially had kids in the backseat who were lying down, fast asleep on the rear bench, which would mean no room for him, anyway.

The wife tugged on the man's sleeve. He said something and looked right at Widow with worry on his face, which Widow presumed to be about him. And then he saw the worry on the wife's face that definitely looked to be about picking up a hitchhiker in the middle of redwood wilderness, someone who wasn't the most enticing ride-along companion.

Widow waved at them. Other than being a little cold, he was happy to continue on with his current path. It was relaxing and calming, and he felt a little pull to it, like the book in his pocket.

The couple didn't stop. Instead, the truck sped up and continued on its course. Widow shrugged. He didn't look back.

13

As WIDOW CONTINUED, he forgot all about the truck. The night breeze turned into gusts that felt more like a winter giant blowing down on him than a natural event.

Widow walked the winding, mountainous highway until he came to an off-road track. It was paved, but had long since needed a facelift. A sign posted above an entrance on two high poles with the sign crossing over indicated it was the path to the Gray Wolf Mountain Observatory and Ranger Station.

Widow turned onto the road and glanced back one more time to look for any signs of cars, but there were none.

He didn't have to walk long before he saw two vapor lights set up high on poles just inside the trees. They cut cones of yellow light out into the darkness. Moths, and probably other insects, collided and crashed and danced around at the lights' origin.

A loud howl cut the ambient silence in the distance and then another and then another. Widow's first thought was that it had been a coyote, but then he realized it was a wolf's howl.

Gray Wolf Mountain Observatory.

About twenty seconds later, there was a fourth howl, followed by a fifth and then a sixth—the animal kingdom's version of Public Service Announcements, perhaps.

There's something about hearing the howls of wolves in the wild at night. Even though Widow was a big guy, it still sent chills down his spine.

Farther up the road, he came to a fork. One way led off into the darkness, toward deeper forests and hills. The other path led only a hundred yards ahead. The second had more vapor lights up on poles and more cones of yellow and more insects. The track was wide and drivable.

At the end of the road stood one small building built of wood that appeared to be cabin-inspired, but two stories and narrow. A second building loomed behind it. It was much bigger, with wooden planked catwalks and big bay windows. It was built from wood and brick.

The second building was also two stories, but much larger in terms of area. The second building looked completely void of life. Everything was dark. Even the vapor lights around it were dead.

The first building had a stone chimney climbing up out of the rear. Smoke trickled out. Widow saw a large antenna raised and fanned out above the rooftop. It had three intersecting poles, thin and triangulated up toward the sky. A serious radio antenna, he presumed.

There was a short sign out front, staked into the grass—ranger station sign, most likely. He couldn't read it, not yet.

Widow could see a light on. It came from a small window on the front door, behind a thin curtain.

As he closed the distance, he saw a ranger truck parked along the opposite side of the hut. Nose faced out. The truck was parked with the tail backed in.

He walked up the track and was right. The sign read: Ranger Station. A station call number was printed at the bottom.

The porch lights plunged on, dousing him with more yellow light, and the front door swung open. A giant holding a .45 caliber Smith & Wesson Magnum stepped out onto the porch.

14

"Stop right there!" the giant said.

Widow couldn't see much of the giant's face because of all the light blasting from behind him in the open doorway, blinding Widow. It looked like the giant had switched all the lights on in the hut along with the porch light when he saw Widow approach. They must've been all on the same panel inside the door, mounted on the wall, most likely.

The giant stood just a couple inches shy of seven feet tall, and he was as thick as a tree trunk. His shoulders were broad enough to take down a brick wall. Each of his legs was like a barrel from a tank. The guy's arms were huge. His fists were like mailboxes, and his forearms were about as thick as mailbox posts. He didn't need the gun.

Widow was a big guy, but this guy was like the monster that gave him nightmares.

The giant stepped all the way out to the end of the porch, stopped just at the end of the first step down.

He said, "Step closer now."

The only detail that Widow could make out was the silver gleam of the barrel of the gun. He had fired a Smith & Wesson before, plus plenty of other .45 calibers, but Widow had never been shot by one. And he didn't intend to start now.

Widow stepped forward, slowly, and raised his hands to the surrender position. Universally known.

He said, "Calm down. I'm not a threat."

The giant said, "Who are you?"

"Jack Widow."

"What the hell are you doing here? It's the middle of the night."

"Actually, I'm looking for you."

"Me?"

"Not specifically you. But a ranger station."

The giant said nothing.

"You're a ranger, right?"

The giant stepped down off the front porch. Every single board squeaked under his weight with the personification of utter relief.

"I'm a park ranger," he said, and lowered the gun, but kept his finger near the trigger housing.

Widow got a look at him. He was older than Widow by about twenty years, but had plenty of muscle and bulk to him. Widow didn't want to be in a position where he'd have to fight the guy for that gun. Something told Widow that the odds weren't in his favor.

The giant was dressed in a park ranger's uniform—brown button shirt, dark pants, and a hunter brown windbreaker. He had a full beard with silver streaks in it. His face was worn and slightly blistered. It was a memorable face. It probably would haunt his nightmares.

The giant looked more like a mountain man than someone born of this time. He was out of place in that uniform, but in his natural habitat with the silence and isolation of a grave-shift park ranger.

He said, "What you doing out here? Your car break down or something?"

"My ride ditched me. Back on the 101. I tried to catch another, but no one's out this time of night. I saw the signs. And came here."

"Why'd your ride ditch you?"

"He was disagreeable."

The giant nodded and said, "You can use my phone."

Widow shrugged and asked, "Where's the nearest town?"

"There's a coastal town south. About seven or eight miles. But it's tiny. Not much of a twenty-four-hour kinda place. The closest city is Eureka. That's far."

Widow said, "I doubt a taxi will come this far out."

"I doubt it."

Silence fell between them. They stood there for a good long minute until another wolf howled and broke the silence. The giant looked around and peered north.

He said, "Well, I can't have you wandering around out there all alone. I guess you'd better stay here until morning."

Widow nodded.

The giant kept the .45 in his hand. At first, Widow thought it was because he still saw him as a threat, but then Widow saw the giant wasn't wearing a holster.

He said, "Come on in."

They walked into the ranger station. The first floor had a sofa, two armchairs, a fireplace, and a kitchenette with a round eating table. The floor was made of long, wooden planks that creaked in regular intervals under the giant's weight, which made them already worn in for Widow. To the right was a split-level that stepped down through an open doorway. Inside, there was a set of office desks and business machines. The walls were postered with wildlife images, maps, and two calendars. One was old but still hanging, maybe to take up wall space.

There was a makeshift mudroom area near the entrance. The giant stopped there and looked down at Widow's feet. Looking for mud, he guessed.

Widow stomped his boots until they were as clean as they were going to get, and then he just slipped them off. He picked them up and held them in his hand. He didn't want to leave them behind. Two things you didn't want: to be caught with your pants down or your shoes out of reach.

The giant turned to a wall of hanging coats. Suspended from one of the empty hooks was a gun belt, black leather, and creased. He pulled it off the wall and holstered his weapon, but didn't return the belt to the hook. He took it with him over to the armchair closest to the fireplace and dumped himself into the seat. He strung the gun belt across his lap. He craned his head over his shoulder and asked, "You hungry?"

"No."

"Well, don't just stand there. Come in. Make yourself at home."

Widow walked deeper into the station, feeling a little like he was in the principal's office.

The giant said, "Sorry about the gun. I'm out here all alone tonight. It's unusual to get a visitor coming down the track."

"Don't you have campers out here?"

"Sure we do, but not this time of year."

"Why not? It's a beautiful land."

"Oh, it's gorgeous, but no one comes this time of year. Hunting season is over. Camping season ends tomorrow."

"You have a camping season?"

"Of course."

"I never heard of that before."

The giant said, "You're not from around here, are you?"

Widow shook his head and said, "I've never even heard of this place before."

"Few people have. It's the most unknown of the parks in the area. You got Crater Lake and others within proximity. Why would you come here?"

"Why is this one separate?"

"Because of the gray wolf."

"The gray wolf?"

"Yeah. A section of this park doubles as a sanctuary for them. You know one of our number one priorities as wildlife officials is conservation of endangered animals."

"Is the gray wolf endangered?"

"Not really. But hell, to those bleeding hearts in Congress, they're all endangered. But don't worry. We got plenty of them here."

"So why does camping end tomorrow?"

"First day of summer."

Widow shrugged.

"Out here, like a lot of national forests, the temperatures and the winds and the humidity get just right for wildfires."

"So campers aren't allowed here in the summers because they might set off a fire?"

"Not "might." They will set one off. We have them almost every year."

"Every year?"

"Sure. That's just a part of nature. We get a lot of purging fires. They come once a year, normally. The firefighters will come out and monitor them."

"Monitor them?"

"Yeah. They don't put them all out. They usually set up a controlled fire to keep them contained. They only put them out if they get out of control or are headed toward civilization."

"I didn't know that."

The giant said, "You don't have to stand around. Make yourself comfortable."

Widow joined him and sat on the sofa across from him.

In case the giant forgot, Widow said, "My name is Jack Widow."

"Mine is Gordon. Henry Gordon. Sorry again about the gun."

"No sweat. It's understandable."

"I was sleeping when you knocked. I don't normally do that. It's my last night. I'm retiring tomorrow."

Widow looked around the room. None of his coworkers were there to throw him a party. Widow didn't know the SOP for retiring professionals for the Wildlife Department. But he knew about camaraderie and fitting in. Wildlife rangers weren't that different from regular cops. He was surprised that no one there surprised the guy. The giant seemed bummed out about it.

He must've guessed what Widow was thinking because he said, "They're forcing me out. It's a long story that boils down to they want to portray a friendlier image to the public. And I ain't that image. I'm the last of the old staff to go. They've brought on all new guys."

Widow nodded along like he understood and agreed, like he was saying, "Yeah, the man is always doing that to us."

Widow realized it wasn't exactly what he was saying. He saw the reason they were forcing the giant to take his retirement. The giant pulled out a black flask and twisted the top off, carefully, painstakingly slow, because his fingers were far too big to be operating it. It was like watching someone using heavy building equipment to build a dollhouse.

Finally, he got it open and took a swig. He offered Widow some without a word.

"No, thanks."

"What? You don't want to celebrate my retirement either?"

Then Widow thought about Gordon's gun. He thought about the unknown factors about Gordon.

Widow shrugged, reached his hand out, and took the flask. He took a sip. It was whiskey. He had drunk whiskey before. He had been in the Navy, after all.

After another moment, Widow tried to lighten the mood.

"Is that hand cannon government issued?"

Gordon chuckled, tapped on it with his fingers.

"Old Mary here is from my private collection. Of course, we're allowed to carry personal weapons. In fact, we have to have something. Like I told you, I'm from an older generation. This is the gun for me."

Widow nodded.

"Wanna know why I named it Mary?"

"Why?"

"Mary Tyler Moore."

He chuckled again and said, "She was my muse. You know what I mean?"

"I do."

He looked at his wristwatch and said, "Hey, look, Jack. You're a good guy. If you want to catch some sleep. I understand. We got rooms upstairs. There's beds. All clean. Use the one down on the end. It's got a shower in it."

Widow stayed quiet.

"Hey. It's not a four-star hotel or nothing. But beats wandering along the highway this time of night."

Widow shrugged.

"Go on. Go ahead. I'll wake you in the morning. There's two more coming."

"Two more what?"

"Fire lookouts?"

Fire lookouts? He thought. That was exactly the book he had been reading. It was the job he had all those summers ago. Suddenly, he felt fate. He got that rare feeling that he was on the path he was supposed to be on, like destiny giving you a glimpse of a road sign.

The giant said, "Oh yeah. It's a cool gig. If you like the wilderness and complete isolation."

"I know. I did it once."

"Did you?"

"Yeah, I worked as a relief. One summer."

"That's a strange coincidence. Most people have never heard of it."

Widow stayed quiet.

The giant said, "You know, today was the first day of the fire season. We're actually missing two lookouts. They're supposed to come tomorrow. Or they don't get paid."

Gordon yawned, rocked, pressed his hands on the arm of the chair, and hauled himself up. Then he stretched a moment and said, "Look here."

Widow got up off the sofa and followed him. He led Widow down two steps, carpeted, and into the office, which was also carpeted.

On one wall, underneath a huge window that faced the observatory station, there was a table with a chair and a large CB Radio. The radio was on, and the gauges were lit up. All that came over the speakers was static.

Gordon walked over to a desk in the corner and plopped his gun and belt down on the top. He went over to a bulletin board on the wall, turned his back to Widow. He jerked a pamphlet off the wall, thumbtack and all.

Gordon handed it to him.

"Take this upstairs with you."

Widow looked it over. It was a pamphlet about the position of fire watch. It looked all official. It was marked with the seal of Wildlife and Rescue on the back.

"Thanks," Widow said, even though he already had the book. Then Widow said, "Guess I'll take you up on that room then."

Gordon agreed to it because he wanted to go back to sleep on the sofa.

"Sure thing."

Widow walked back to the main room and looked left, looked right.

"Where's the stairs?"

Gordon pointed to a door in the corner.

"Through there."

Widow nodded and walked to it, opened it. There was a short hallway that led to a staircase.

"Go on. I'll wake you up at seven a.m. When the last two arrive. Then I'll drive you into town."

Widow nodded and walked up the stairs. He shut the door.

Widow flicked on a light at the top of the staircase and went to the last room, as Gordon had instructed him to do.

All the doors were open, and moonlight trickled in through the windows. The last bedroom was small, but larger than the other two.

He flipped on the light and found a made-up cot with a thick wool blanket neatly stretched across the top and two pillows underneath.

He dropped his boots onto the floor.

The room was warm from heat blasting in through floor vents.

Widow locked the door, just in case. Gordon didn't seem like someone he would trust in normal circumstances.

Widow went to the bathroom, flipped on the light. It was a simple enough setup. A shower and tub. A basin. A circular mirror. And a toilet. All he needed.

He stuffed the pamphlet into the book like a bookmarker, tossed them both on the bed, and went back to the shower. He turned the knob and listened to the pipes sing and strain. Then a mist of water sprayed out of the showerhead, followed by a strong enough spray. Widow wrenched the knob until the dial was all the way in the hot direction. With two fingers, he gauged the temperature. It was cold. He left the bathroom, left the water running to heat, and pulled off his clothes.

He slipped his socks off first, setting them at the foot of the bed, then a pullover he'd just bought, a black undershirt, and last his pants. He folded them all neatly and left them in a pile on the bed.

He turned down the covers about halfway and returned to the shower.

There was a toothbrush, heavy-duty-looking thing. It was still in a package, resting on the corner of the sink. There were two of them. And a tube of toothpaste. No razors.

There was one bar of soap.

Towels were folded and piled behind the door.

Widow grabbed one and wrapped it around his waist. He felt the shower again, still too cold.

He went back to the bed and looked over the pamphlet.

What a coincidence? He thought again, like he couldn't help it.

The pamphlet was an advertisement for the job of a fire lookout. There were neat photos of a watch tower that looked like a cabin built on sturdy legs—three flights of stairs wrapped around the base of the tower to the loft above. From the watch tower, there were panoramic views that were breathtaking, which would make sense.

Can't be an effective lookout if you can't see three hundred sixty degrees.

The watch tower had everything a man needed to survive in the wilderness for long periods of time. There was a wood-burning stove, a refrigerator, navigational devices like he had seen in the Navy. Only these were lower-tech, but he got the gist.

There must've been a generator somewhere outside the tower.

There was a desk, a cot, a table, and lanterns. The whole venture seemed appealing. He thought about it. He was a tourist, going from place to place. He wondered if he could even stay still for four months.

Widow left the pamphlet on the bed. The shower was finally hot, and he took one. Afterward, he toweled off and decided that they could spare one toothbrush, since he didn't have one of his own anymore.

He brushed his teeth, tossed the towel over the shower, and returned to the bed. He moved his clothes to a chair and got under the covers.

He leafed through the pamphlet again. He thought about the paperback book. He thought back to his brief experiences as a summer fire watch.

It was an appealing proposition. Technically, he would be trapped in one location for four months, longer than he was comfortable with. But he would be miles away from the nearest human being, who would be another fire lookout. And he would have all day to roam and explore the wilderness. No people. No city sounds. No rushing around. No buses or hitching for rides. No junkies. No meth heads. No people like Capone.

He deserved to get away. He deserved a break from people. But if he remembered right, he'd have to fill out forms, pass background checks, and jump through bureaucratic hoops just to get the job.

He closed his eyes and drifted off to sleep.

15

Widow woke in the morning to the sound of tires on dirt, a truck motor, and a static voice. He could hear the voice pleading. It sounded almost electronic.

Gordon hadn't come to wake him up like he had promised. Widow got up and quickly put his clothes on, struggling with the pant legs.

He hopped over to the bathroom and ran cold water out of the tap, splashed his face, slicked back his hair, and sipped water from cupped hands. He turned it off and left the bedroom, walked down the stairs.

The voice he had heard was coming from the CB radio. A radio transmission. A commanding voice blared from its speakers.

"Gordon! Pick up! Gordon!"

Widow looked around—no sign of Gordon. His flask was empty and lying on its side, abandoned on the coffee table. Widow guessed he didn't care who saw it, since he claimed that last night was his last night.

Widow called out his name.

"Gordon?"

No answer.

"Ranger?"

No answer.

"Hello?"

Nothing.

Widow didn't bother a fourth time. He figured Gordon was outside waiting for the approaching vehicle. Maybe new rangers.

He stepped farther into the living room and heard the CB radio's voice go off again. It was a man.

"Gordon! Come in!"

Widow walked into the office and looked around. In the daylight, he noticed the rifle cabinet. He hadn't noticed it the night before because it stood up against the inner office wall, opposite the CB radio, behind the doorway.

Gordon had left the cabinet unlocked. The glass door was ajar. He walked over to it, professional curiosity, and opened it. There were five slots for rifles or shotguns. But there were only two rifles. Both scoped. Both Henry Long Rangers. Both good for a national park like this. They could defend a person against a bear attack within one hundred yards.

There was a box of shells, closed and stored underneath.

There was also a can of bear mace. Suddenly, Widow realized that there must've been black bears roaming around the park. Gordon had already told him that there were gray wolves. He had walked right in off the highway, middle of the night, in the emptiness, and hadn't even thought that he might run into a bear.

Widow closed the door to the cabinet all the way and walked to the window. He peered out. In the distance, he saw dust kicking up from the dirt drive. He saw a blue Ford Bronco climbing up over the rugged road, on course with the ranger hut.

The CB went off again, called for Gordon.

Widow thought Gordon was out there, waiting to greet the driver of the Bronco, but he saw no sign of him.

Widow turned and decided that he might need to know whatever message they were trying to give Gordon. It might be important. So, he picked up the CB receiver and clicked the button, held it. He was silent at first. It had been a long time since he'd used a CB radio. He tried to think if there was some vernacular that park rangers had different from sailors. He had no idea. He just said, "Hello."

The voice on the CB said, "Hello? Gordon?"

"Negative. This isn't Ranger Gordon."

"Who is this?"

"My name is Widow."

"Widow?"

"Yeah."

"Who the hell are you? Where's Gordon?"

"I'm not sure where he is. Maybe meeting a vehicle that's coming up the drive."

There was silence for a moment. Then the voice said, "Who are you?"

"I'm Jack Widow. I'm nobody. Ten-four."

Widow remembered saying ten-four was a universal thing. Then he remembered it wasn't "ten-four." It was supposed to be "over."

"What are you doing answering for Gordon?"

He wasn't saying "over" because he guessed CB talk for park ranger was more casual.

"Sorry. I was here, and you sounded urgent. I answered."

Static.

"Are you a friend of Gordon's?"

"No. I told you. I'm nobody. I wandered in from the highway last night. Gordon let me crash here for the night."

More static and silence.

"Mr. Widow, is Gordon there?"

"I told you. He must be outside, waiting for the truck. It's just coming up now."

"Mr. Widow. Do me a favor. Go outside and look. Grab him if you can."

Widow held down the call button and said, "Okay. I'll check."

The voice said nothing to that.

Widow set the receiver down and went back through the station to the front door, opened it, and went out. He walked the width of the station, along the front porch, and turned the corner. As he made it around the side, he saw the blue Ford Bronco still coming up the drive, making its way to him.

Then he scanned the forest, the trees, and the observatory, which was still dark, still quiet.

Widow turned back and looked at the road coming in. He saw dozens of tracks merged. Then he saw tracks leading away from the station. He remembered the truck parked on the side, Gordon's truck. He walked back to the front of the station and checked. It was gone.

He went back in, returned to the CB, and picked up the receiver.

"Hello?"

A moment of static.

"Hey. Yes. Where is he?"

"I think Gordon took off."

Silence.

"He took off?"

"I guess. The station truck is gone."

More silence. Then a click. Then the voice said, "You're probably right."

He stayed quiet.

"You said a truck was coming?"

"Yes."

"How many people?"

"One. A driver."

The voice asked, "Who is it?"

"I don't know yet. Looks like a woman."

"That's Molly. She's a fire lookout."

Widow stayed quiet.

"Listen, Mr. Widow. I need you to do me a big favor."

"What?"

"My name is Tate. I'm in charge of this region. Gordon was one of mine. He was retiring. Being pushed out, to be frank."

"Yeah. He mentioned it."

Widow could've mentioned the drinking, but what for? Not his business.

Tate said, "At any rate, he's out. And my next ranger isn't arriving there for another two hours. The observatory staff won't be there before that either. I'm in a bind here. We need to get all the fire watch towers filled. You know there's a major fire headed this way. From the south. I'm sure you've seen it at night, right?"

"I saw it. But I didn't know it was heading this way."

"Yep. So far."

"Isn't it like a hundred miles south?"

"A hundred twenty miles south, but it's moving fast. A lot faster than people predicted."

"Why hasn't the fire department put it out? Too big?"

"It is big. But that's not why. It's what's called a purging fire. They'll let it burn as long as it's kept under control, although a lot of it is not. Clearly."

Widow stayed quiet.

"At any rate. It won't come to where you are. Still, we need every post filled. Part of it is a logical thing. Part of it is a political thing. We can't have empty fire watch towers. Not when all eyes are on us now."

He paused and waited like he was waiting for Widow to acknowledge.

"Go on."

Tate said, "One of the fire watch crew members had a heart attack yesterday."

Widow stayed quiet.

"I need you to tell Molly to go on without him. They were supposed to ride out together. Tell her that the Lincoln Ridge Tower will have to go empty. She'll have to check in on it herself."

Widow paused and clicked the button, said, "I can do that."

"Good."

Then he paused another beat and thought about the pamphlet. He thought about the book. And he thought about that summer, long ago. He remembered the romance of it. And then he thought about Capone, and city streets, and how he had just had enough of it all for the moment.

He thought about fate, about destiny. What could be a clearer sign? He had been thinking about fire watch, and life had delivered him an opportunity.

He clicked the button again and said, "Mr. Tate."

"Widow?"

"What if I do it?"

"Do what?"

"What if I stand in for your guy? Until he gets better? Or you replace him?"

Silence. Tate said nothing for a long beat. And then he said, "You want to do that?"

"It's no problem."

Tate stayed quiet.

Widow said, "Actually, I have experience. I worked as a fire lookout once."

Tate waited. Then he came back on and said, "I appreciate the offer, Mr. Widow. But I can't do that. I know nothing about you. There is a hiring process in place. There are background checks and references, and interviews."

"Listen, you need someone temporarily. I can help. I'd love to get away and stay out in the wilderness for a week."

Tate said nothing.

"If you're the guy in charge, then you can hire whoever you want, right?"

"I do, but..."

"You seem shorthanded. I'm offering my help. It's only temporary. Like a stand-in. Like a substitute teacher. You know? Until your man gets better.

You'll know if he's going to recover inside of a few days—a week, tops. That'll give you time to find someone else. And you'll know that I'm out there watching whatever sector he was supposed to watch."

Tate said, "It gets lonely out there. Boring."

"I live that way now. I'm always alone. I'm a nomad."

"You running from something?"

He thought about Capone and the cops. They might look for him, but he doubted it.

"No. Just a life choice."

"Nah. I can't, Mr. Widow. Like I said, I know nothing about you."

"Listen, what rank are you?"

"Rank?"

"What's your federal rank? You guys are labeled GS10 or whatever. What's yours?"

Tate was quiet for a moment. Then he said, "We're all GSs. Mine is high."

"Okay. And you guys are law enforcement?"

"Technically. That is a part of who we are."

"So if you have a high rank and you are law enforcement, you must have access to federal records? Law enforcement records?"

"Naturally."

"Can you access NCIS records?"

"I can't access them like you think. But I can request specific records from the D.o.N."

"How long would that take you?"

"Requesting them would take a couple of minutes. Getting them back might take some time. Why?"

"You got contacts over there?"

"Sure. I know a guy."

"You friendly with this guy?"

"Sure."

"He normally answers you fast? Or does he put you on the back burner, get to you whenever he feels like it?"

Tate said, "I know the guy. Personally."

"Good. Get off the radio and call your guy. Ask him if he can access records of personnel. Ask him to look me up. And call back after."

"Okay."

16

Outside the station, Widow heard footsteps on the porch. They were light. He heard a knock on the door and a female voice.

"Gordon?"

He walked to the door and opened it.

A woman stood in the doorway on the porch. Her stature was small, but her presence was far from that. She had toned arms, not a bicep to brag about, but defined enough that Widow knew he wouldn't want to feel a direct jab to the nose, not from her.

She looked magnificent. Avocado eyes stared back at him over the tops of dark sunglasses. Although there was a trace of a black eye on one of them. It was healing fast. But still noticeable.

She had long tresses of golden hair, not the kind out of a bottle, but natural. It was all braided back over her head and down the tops of her shoulders. Widow believed the style was called a Dutch braid, or something like that. He had seen it before. Hers was like a long tuft of rope, thick enough to support an anchor from a small ship. And definitely dense enough to climb, in case she was ever abducted by a witch and kept in a tower.

"Hey," he said.

"Who are you?"

Widow reached out his hand, presented it to her to shake, and said, "I'm Jack Widow."

She shot a nervous smile at him. It was friendly, but nervous. They made eye contact. Her eyes were glassy, like she had been crying, which might explain the extra brightness to her cheeks and the strained look on her brow. But not the black eye.

She had no make-up on, although she had no need for it. Not in Widow's opinion. Her skin was pale and smooth and inviting. Her lips were full, with a bare pink shade to them.

Her voice furthered his hypothesis that she had been crying somewhere, sometime, because when she spoke, her voice had that undertone of someone who had shed a tear, and had sniffled, and had almost wiped it all away.

She reached out and took his hand.

"Who are you, Jack Widow? Where's Gordon?"

"That's a funny story," Widow said. "I just met the guy last night. He told me it was his last night. He seemed bent out of shape about it. And this morning, he was gone."

"Gone?"

"Yep."

"Who are you?"

"Jack Widow."

"No, I mean, who are you? You said you just met him. Are you a new ranger?"

She looked at him from top to bottom and reversed it.

She said, "You don't look like a ranger."

"I'm not."

"So, who are you?" she asked. The nervousness was still there.

"I'm nobody. I was lost, and I wandered in from the highway. Gordon let me crash here. This morning I woke up, and he was gone, and now you're here."

"You're just some guy who drove in, and he let you stay?"

"I didn't drive in. I walked in."

"Your car break down on the 101?"

"I don't have a car."

She stared at him.

"How the hell did you get lost way out here?"

"I lost my ride. I hoped that the ranger here would let me call a taxi, but he said they don't come out here. He offered to drive me today. And I took a cot upstairs. That's all I know."

"Maybe he went out to the park?"

Widow shrugged and said, "Maybe. He took the truck."

"Have you tried to call him?"

"You get cell service out here?"

"No. On the radio?"

"I haven't, but a guy named Tate has been calling for him over the CB."

"Tate. Did you talk to him?"

"I did."

She asked, "What did he say?"

"He thinks Gordon bailed. The guy was borderline drunk when I last saw him."

"Did you try him on one of the long-range walkies?"

"I didn't see any."

She said, "Guess that wouldn't matter, anyway. He's got a CB in the truck. He would've heard Tate."

Then she reached up and grabbed the door. Widow let go of it and backed into the room.

She walked in, back through the living room, past the kitchen, and down into the office area. She swung to the right and walked over to a thin door that Widow assumed was a closet. She swung it open. Beyond it was no room, just a built-in shelf with all kinds of extra ranger gear. On the floor were several pairs of hiking and climbing boots.

About three feet above that were hooks that hung two firefighter jackets and two regular winter coats. The shelf above had four flashlights, two flare guns—unloaded—with a box of flares next to them. There were some rolled-up pairs of socks, and folded t-shirts, and folded cargo pants. The top shelf had a battery-charging station with slots to plug in long-range walkies. There were about a dozen of them. All the slots were filled. All the radios were jacked in, and the charge light on each was solid green, showing they all had full charges.

She said, "Damn. He didn't go out with a radio. He would have never gone out into the park without a radio. No way. He was reckless, but not stupid. He must have quit."

Widow shrugged.

She walked back into the room, and out into the living room, looked around again. Then she returned, holding the empty flask.

She held it up and said, "Looks like you're telling the truth, Jack."

The way she held the flask, Widow could see Gordon's name inscribed on the side. Then she turned it upside down and shook it with the cap off. Nothing came out.

"That idiot!" she exclaimed.

Widow stayed quiet.

Just then, the CB crackled to life.

Tate's voice said, "Mr. Widow? Come in?"

He looked at the woman and said, "That's Tate. We already spoke."

He picked up the receiver again and answered, "Tate, I'm here with your fire lookout."

"Molly?"

She stepped closer to the radio and said, "It's me. Molly DeGorne."

"Good. DeGorne, listen up. I have bad news."

She braced herself.

Tate said, "Ellis had a heart attack."

"Oh, no!"

"Don't worry. He seems okay. He's in the hospital. Obviously, that means that we are short a fire lookout. And it's sector Two Twenty-One."

Widow looked at DeGorne. He had no idea what Two Twenty-One was. But the look on her face told him that maybe it was an important sector or a dangerous one or both.

Molly stepped forward, put her hand on Widow's, and took the receiver. He didn't fight her.

She clicked the button and said, "I can take it. I guess."

Tate came back on and said, "No. That won't be necessary. We got a temporary replacement."

DeGorne asked, "Who?"

"Mr. Widow."

She looked at him.

She said, "Tom, who is this guy?" Then she lowered the receiver and mouthed the word, sorry.

Widow shrugged.

"Molly, we're in a bind here. We need someone to watch Two Twenty-One. It will take a week or two to get someone vetted."

Silence fell between them.

"You got any better ideas?" Tate came back over the radio.

"What about Jerry?"

"Corman is retired. You know that. He couldn't hike through that terrain, and you know it."

"What makes this guy qualified?"

The CB squawked, and Tate came back over, sounding annoyed. He said, "Molly, this isn't a debate. I checked him out. He's got a service record that speaks to his qualifications. Now, let me speak to Widow for a minute."

DeGorne handed him the receiver like it was a hot potato. She smiled and left the room, left the ranger hut.

Tate asked, "Widow?"

"Yeah,"

"My friend said that he could only get part of your record. Said the rest of it was redacted. I gather you must have been some kind of black ops guy."

Widow stayed quiet.

"He told me you looked like a do-gooder. But I have my concerns."

What are you getting at? Widow thought.

"A lot of guys get PTSD when they come back," he said and paused a long beat.

He said, "Do I need to spell it out for you?"

"You wonder if I got Post Traumatic?"

"It happens. Especially to SEALs."

"No, it doesn't happen to SEALs. Not any more than anyone else. In fact, I'd guess it happens a lot less to SEALs. These guys are the best of the best. The number one qualifier to becoming a SEAL, other than the love of country, is mental fortitude. They can train us to do the rest. But you gotta come with strong mental facilities already."

Tate said nothing.

"Are you worried about me getting out there and going crazy? What, like Rambo?"

"It's a serious thing, Widow. We've had our share of crazies living out there in the park."

Widow stayed quiet.

"Anyway, my guy in the DoN said you were the real deal. Considering the bind that I'm in, I don't see any other choice."

"You don't have to worry. I'm sure I can handle it."

"So you'll be in sector Two Twenty-One, which isn't so bad. Molly has it worse. A harder terrain. We've had fires there before. Some areas are still burned up."

"What's so tough about it? The terrain?"

"That's part of it. So, I have to ask you a dumb question. Do you have any climbing experience?"

"Of course. SEAL stands for Sea, Air, Land."

"I figured. How good is it?"

"Good enough. I'm not an expert or anything."

"That'll be fine. You may need it. At any rate, DeGorne will be the closest neighbor you have. She can help you with questions. You may not even need to worry about too much."

"Okay."

"Everything good? Got it?"

"I got it."

"Okay. You'll ride in with DeGorne. Remember, she can show you the rest. It's easy. There are daily duties you'll have to perform, easy enough. The rest of the time, explore and be safe."

"Sounds good. I'm sure it'll be fine."

"One more thing. I'll need to get your bank information so we can direct deposit your money."

"Money?"

"It's a job, Widow. You want to get paid, right?"

"Sorry, I didn't even think about it."

He hadn't gotten paid for work in ages.

"You do want to get paid?" he repeated.

"Sure."

"Good. Go on then. You got a ride to catch."

"You said that Molly will help me?"

"Right."

"Okay then. Ten-four," and Widow let go of the receiver, placed it down on top of the radio, and memorized the channel, in case he needed to know it.

He left the office and walked out of the station.

17

THE TIME WAS SEVEN A.M.

DeGorne waited outside of the ranger hut in the Ford Bronco that Widow had seen her driving up in. The truck was old, well-kept, and well-maintained. It had clear headlight covers, no dirt or grime, except for the loose dirt that she'd acquired from the drive up.

She sat close to the steering wheel, her fingers over the wheel. Elbows bent. The bottoms of her forearms rested neatly up against the steering. The Bronco's front windows were both rolled down. There were dual roll bars spiking up and out of the middle rear.

DeGorne glanced forward for a moment and then turned her head back to Widow, but kept her body where it was, facing the front. She looked right at him.

"You coming?"

He smiled and said, "Let's go."

"Hop in."

He glanced at the road ahead, an act of pure instinct, and not at all on purpose. Then he turned and gripped the handle, pressed the button, and pulled the door open.

Before he slid in, he gazed over the backbench. He saw a duffle bag and a backpack, both packed full.

Widow got comfortable and buckled his seatbelt. He looked around. He liked the interior. He didn't have to duck his head. He didn't get that feeling of the ceiling being right on top of him.

They drove off. DeGorne accelerated hard, like she was in a hurry. With the early morning wildlife sounds, the hard wind, the rustling trees, and the tires bouncing over the terrain as the dirt track got narrower and rougher, they had to raise their voices like they were talking over helicopter rotor blades.

"Where we headed exactly?" Widow asked.

"Our towers are close together. We're headed north and veering west."

"They're close together?"

"Ten miles apart."

"That's close together?"

"Out here, it is."

They continued on for a long period with short bursts of conversation, of small talk, getting to know each other. She had asked him where he was from. What his name was again? What was he doing walking along the side of the road? And where was he headed?

He said, "My name is Jack Widow. I'm from Mississippi, originally. And I'm headed nowhere."

She looked over at him, said nothing.

"Right now, I'm headed to tower Two Twenty-One. With you, I guess."

She asked, "And what were you doing out on the road?"

"Walking."

"I know that, Jack Widow. I mean, why?"

"That's how I travel—sometimes."

"I mean, why walking? No car?"

"No, ma'am. No vehicle."

She paused a beat, slowed the Bronco. There was a dip, then another, and some rugged patch of track. She drove it like she knew it was there.

"You drive this a lot?"

"Every year."

"How far we gotta go this way?"

"First, we drive this for about two hours. Then we hump another six miles."

"Six miles? Humping through the wilderness?"

Just the two of us? he thought.

"Six miles for me. Eight for you."

"Eight?"

"We don't walk together. You go one way. And I go the other."

Widow watched ahead. He saw a deep gulch, checkered with erratic rock formations, surrounded by trees. Everything was surrounded by trees.

DeGorne said, "I'm Molly Lee. By the way."

"Lee? I thought it was DeGorne?"

She nodded fast and said, "Yes. DeGorne, I meant. Sorry. It's an old habit."

He looked at her ring finger.

"You married?"

She turned pale, stared straight ahead for several seconds. Then she said, "I was."

"Ah. Sorry to hear that. You mind if I ask? Does it have something to do with that eye?"

She looked into the rearview, pushed her shades all the way back, covering her eyes.

"Sorry. I didn't mean to pry. It's none of my business."

"It's okay. We're gonna be neighbors. We'll talk a lot. So, you married?"

"Me? No, ma'am."

"You military or something? What's with all the 'No, ma'am's'?"

"I was. Once upon a time."

"What did you do in the military?"

At that point, Widow didn't see any point in lying to her. For all he knew, he'd be out there with only her to talk to for a week, maybe more. He didn't want to tell her the whole truth, that he was an undercover cop. So, he said, "I was NCIS."

She fell silent. Her jaw didn't drop, not literally, but it looked like it was going to.

She automatically looked in the rearview again, looked at her duffle bag.

"You're like a federal agent?"

"Was. A long time ago."

"But not now?"

"No. Now I'm nobody."

She was quiet for another mile. Widow stared out the window. He saw a clearing and a low valley, covered in green bushes and grass. In it, he saw horses running free, dozens of them. They had thick manes and looked huge. From that distance, they blended together in shades of brown and black and white.

"Horses," he said.

DeGorne leaned to the right, stared out over the dash.

"Wild horses."

"You have them out here?"

"Sure. This is the west."

"I never saw wild horses before."

"They are something."

They were quiet. Widow watched the running horses. DeGorne saw he was looking and stopped the car, switched off the engine.

She said, "Listen."

Widow listened. He could hear their hooves stomping and clomping down on the hard ground.

They stayed there for a long moment. Then she fired the engine back up and moved on.

DeGorne said, "So, what is a cowboy like you doing this far from home?"

"Home?"

"Yeah, where are you from?"

"Mississippi. Originally."

"Why so far from there?"

Widow said, "Mississippi's not home, though. It's just where I was born. And I never met a cowboy there. That's more Texas or Montana."

"Where is it, then?"

"Mississippi? It's in the Deep South. Between Alabama and Louisiana."

She glanced over at him. Her sunglasses slipped down again, and he saw those avocado eyes peering back at him from above the rim. The glassiness in her eyes had dried away. A gust of wind beat across her face, whipping thin strands of loose bangs down on her forehead.

He said, "Or it's between Tennessee and the Gulf of Mexico, all depending on your perspective. I suppose."

With the glassiness gone, her cheeks had returned to their normal color, and she seemed like a different woman, like whatever had been weighing on her had suddenly become void, or at least forgotten.

For the first time, she smiled at him.

"I know where Mississippi is. I meant, where is your home?"

She looked back at the track ahead again. She slowed down because they were coming up on a hill and a curve. She braked, and the Bronco engine continued to hum as it dipped over and took the curve. Good and steady.

"My home is right here," Widow said, placing his right hand on his chest.

She glanced over at him one more time, and then back at the road.

"What?"

"This is my home."

He patted his chest.

"Hilarious. If you don't wanna tell me. That's fine."

"What I mean is my body is my home. Where ever I am is where I live."

She kept facing forward, staring ahead, and staying quiet for another mile. Then she asked, "So, you're homeless?"

"Nope. If I was homeless, then I would be dead."

"Come again?"

"I would be body-less. If my body is my only home."

She looked over at him.

Those avocado eyes again.

"You're weird, Jack Widow."

"Aren't all the good ones? And just call me Widow. No one calls me Jack."

"Okay, Widow. Guess I'm weird too."

She smiled, like he expected, and continued driving.

They drove on for another forty-five minutes. And then another hour. The ride was slow going because it was all dirt roads and off-road tracks. She handled the Bronco like a champion bull rider, and Widow realized she was the cowboy here, not him.

The roads wound around and meandered and threaded through the park. Widow stared out the window at the passing trees and sunlit grass. Occasionally, he saw herds of horses, flocks of birds, once a murder of crows, and a distant pack of wolves running up the side of the mountain. They were still far away, but they looked huge.

"The gray wolves here, are they endangered?"

"No, but they are protected."

"Is there an issue of hunters killing them?"

"Yes. I call them poachers. But really it's trophy hunting. They come into the park and kill them. They take them to be stuffed like trophies. It's sick."

Widow nodded.

DeGorne turned on a CB radio attached below the car stereo. She thumbed the knobs. Static filled the interior.

"You looking for something?"

"Just checking for any chatter. Sometimes you can pick up one of the other towers."

She turned the dial to the station and sat back. They listened, but there was nothing but static.

She said, "So you were a fire lookout before?"

"Yes. Long time ago. I worked as a relief."

"Good. Then you should be right at home."

"Maybe."

"If you need any help. Just call me on the CB or a walkie."

Widow nodded.

* * *

AFTER TWO HOURS, right on the nose, DeGorne pulled into a small clearing where there was a tall metal carport. They saw two vehicles already parked underneath it. Both were four-by-four trucks. Both were covered with tarps.

"This is the end of the line. We gotta walk from here."

"If we split up here, then how do I know where to go?"

"I have a map. You can take it," she said, and leaned over to Widow, one hand on the wheel. Her breasts angled and curved, pushing the limits of the demarcation of her top. No bra. That was obvious. Although she had been dressed somewhat conservatively, in plain hiking attire, some things weren't hidden away so easily.

Widow caught himself leering. Her long hair fell forward across her back and shoulder and brushed across his arm.

She said, "Sorry."

She reached out with her hand and popped the button on the glove box and jerked it open. She sat back behind the wheel and righted herself.

"Look in there."

"What am I looking for?"

"A map. You can take it. I know the way."

Widow reached into the glove box and searched for the map. He found it easy enough. It was folded up, smaller than a road map. He pulled it out, but right there underneath was something else.

He found a revolver, fully loaded.

18

THE REVOLVER WAS MANUFACTURED by a German company called Weihrauch. Once Widow had known a German Special Forces crew. He worked with them on a co-op mission in Afghanistan. He got to be good friends with a guy named Jürgen, who liked to be called Eric. He wasn't sure why.

Eric was also a cop of sorts for the German military. He and his guys were very helpful to the NCIS in busting up a gunrunning highway system made up of mostly random Russian trucks, which were used to navigate through various countries until they passed through Ukraine and then into Russia, where they would lose the shipments they carried across Asia into various places.

Back in 2005, when most of the US was focused on Iraq, the USN was having many problems in Afghanistan. Everyone knew how the Taliban was getting AKs. No surprise there. Most of them were left over from the Russians, but now they also had other guns as well. The Navy had seen newer weapons showing up. Some German, which explained Jürgen's department's interest in the whole affair.

There was a Taliban lieutenant, not a top boy, but important enough to be on the USN's radar. He had a lust for Weihrauch guns. He liked the .38 Special, in particular. Widow didn't know why. Maybe he watched American cop shows as a kid, or maybe he liked the old black and whites of the forties and fifties, where guys like Bogart pulled out a police .38 on the bad guy.

Jürgen had told Widow about the Weihrauch Windicator. Only in English, it was pronounced Vindicator, which seemed like a good name for a gun.

The .38 Special in Molly DeGorne's glove box was a cheap gun to get. It had a two-inch barrel and held six rounds. This one had a nice black finish to it. The whole thing was probably less than three hundred dollars landed.

Cheap didn't mean weak. A .38 Special was a .38 Special, no matter the cost, and Germans knew how to make a quality gun. It wasn't a preferred weapon of choice for any serious SEAL anywhere. But in the civilian world, it would get the job done.

Widow pinched the map between his index, middle finger, and the rubber grip of the .38, and pulled both out at the same time.

He said, "That's a serious weapon."

DeGorne looked over at it. Her expression, for only a moment, was one of fear and recognition, like she had forgotten the gun was there.

"That's for protection. This is the middle of nowhere," she said.

"You keep it loaded?" Widow asked. He weighed it in his hand over a flat palm. The map underneath.

"It's no good to me unloaded."

He shrugged and said, "I'm not arguing with you there."

Widow could see that she was nervous that a stranger she'd met just two hours ago was handling her gun. He reached forward and returned it to the glove box, barrel facing out and away from both of them.

"No! I'll take it. It won't do me any good if I leave it here."

Widow handed it to her, grip first. She took it and slid it into one of her cargo pockets.

Widow lifted the glove box lid and snapped it shut. He pocketed the map into his back pocket.

DeGorne walked to the rear bench of the Bronco and took out both bags. She slipped the backpack on and dragged the duffle on the ground.

Widow had gotten out and walked over to a folded tarp. He covered the Bronco like he saw the other vehicles.

"You need help with that?" He nodded to the duffle.

"No!"

Widow stayed quiet.

"Sorry. I mean, I got it. You can cover my truck. If you don't mind."

"Sure."

Widow pulled the tarp all the way up and over. He checked it and tied it down with some bungee cables he found and walked around it. It looked secure.

"Okay."

"Let's go. We're walking up a trail. Through those trees over here."

DeGorne pointed. Widow nodded and stayed close to her.

After a minute of dragging the duffle bag, she stopped and said, "You know, it would be cool if you can carry this for me."

"No problem."

She dropped the straps to the bag, and Widow grabbed them. He heaved it over his shoulder.

"This is heavy."

She said nothing.

"What the hell is in here? Bricks?"

She smiled and chuckled. Then she said, "A million dollars in cash."

Widow laughed too, but for a moment; he didn't doubt she was joking.

19

The Leader stood in the door. Five of the seven members of his team were still asleep. All of them shared a house with a "for sale" sign stuck in the yard out front. The house had been on the market for seven weeks. No one would come by, not while they crashed there.

The members of his team were asleep because he had ordered them to sleep. They did whatever he ordered them to do. And tired soldiers were only half as good as well-rested ones.

The Leader and one other guy, one of his most loyal, had their masks off —no reason to hide their identities from Portman now.

The two of them were downstairs in the cold basement.

Sheriff Portman was naked. He lay on his back across a cold metal folding table. His eyes were bloody. His nose was broken and reset and then broken again and then reset again. Now, he had duct tape strips across it, keeping it together.

He hurt everywhere. But he hadn't given her up yet. He hadn't given DeGorne up.

They tried to get it out of him. But he told them nothing.

The Leader spoke in Spanish to his guy, who didn't speak English at all. He said, "He is a tough old bastard."

"What do we do now?"

"We keep at him."

The guy yawned and said, "I should get some sleep. You should get some sleep."

"You're right. Of course."

"We can try again after the morning."

The Leader said, "I don't want to let him rest." He added, "Let's go for one more hour. Then, if he holds out, he deserves a break."

The guy nodded.

The Leader said, "Let's mix it up a bit."

"What do you have in mind?"

"Wet Willy."

The guy looked at him and said, "Will that work?"

"Why won't it?"

"He's American."

"So?"

"Wet willy as a torture technique is a cartel thing."

"And who the hell do you think we work for?"

"Cartel, I know, but will that work?"

The Leader looked down at Portman.

Portman was whispering to himself, over and over. He said, "I held out. I held out."

Then he said some nonsense about Vietnam. And something earlier about a debt.

The Leader said, "We give him the American version of Wet Willy."

The guy smiled. The Leader smiled.

The American version wasn't what Americans thought of when they heard Wet Willy. The American version was what the US military called water-boarding.

20

WATERMOTH WOKE up early in a motel room that looked like all the motel rooms the FBI had put her up in a hundred times before.

She was on the second floor, a non-smoking room. She knew that because the FBI insisted on non-smoking rooms.

She slept in a short t-shirt and a pair of pajama bottoms. A gift from one of her nephews, which meant it was a gift from one of her sisters. They hated she was single and slept alone and slept in her underwear. They always had hated that about her. She was the oldest, and they had all shared a bedroom until she was in junior high. Back then, she had slept in her underwear.

Watermoth jerked the covers off the bed and jumped up. She was groggy. She needed a cigarette. She went searching for one in her briefcase. She found a pack of half-smoked Newports. She took one and a lighter, and went into the bathroom. She folded the top seat of the toilet down and plopped down on it. Then she got back up and flipped the bathroom vent switch on.

The vents kicked on.

She returned to the toilet seat and lit a Newport.

She inhaled two long puffs and exhaled in relief.

Just then, her smartphone rang. She hopped up and ran into the bedroom, grabbed it.

It was Collins; she guessed because it was a local area code. And no one else had her number.

She answered it.

"Collins? You're an early bird?"

"Yes, ma'am."

"Collins, just call me Watermoth or Joanna. Not ma'am."

"Yes. Joanna."

"What the hell do you want?"

"We got the report back from forensics."

"Go on."

"Both victims at the station house were killed by the same bullets."

"Which are?"

"Nine-millimeter parabellums."

"The most common bullet known to man. Great! Did you call me this early just to tell me that?"

"No, ma'am."

She took another drag from the Newport.

"Sorry, Joanna."

Watermoth said nothing.

"I have some good news."

"Yes?"

"The shrapnel from the blast through the rear door."

"Yes?"

"They isolated the pieces."

"And?"

"They separated the wood from the door, the metal from the lock, the grease from the lock, and the explosive parts."

"And?"

"You were right, and you were wrong."

"How so?"

"The tests came back to identify the pieces used in the breaching device as military-grade, but not police grade. Nor is it used in either."

"What does that mean?"

"It means it's not the kind used in either police departments or the US military."

She shook her head, took another drag. She inhaled it and exhaled it.

"But."

"But?"

"But, I took it upon myself to go further with my investigation."

"Jesus, Collins, you sound like a television cop. Just spill it already."

Collins said, "Yes, ma'am. Joanna. I found that it's not the US military or police force. And it's not because it's outdated. I looked a little further into it, and the types of explosive breaching charges that are still built with this material are still used in Mexico."

Watermoth's eyes lit up.

"Mexico?"

"Yeah, by both the Mexican Army and the Federals or Fedlospollos?"

"The Federales?"

"That's the one."

"That's the Mexican Federal Police."

"Yeah."

"You did good, Collins."

He started to speak, but she hung up.

She smoked the rest of her cigarette and thought about the Federales. Someone had their equipment. Someone who took Portman, raided his station, killed a cop, and was out there. What the hell did they want?

21

RYMAN SLEPT three rooms over from Watermoth. He was fast asleep when one of his two phones rang. It was the only one that had the ringer turned on.

He opened his eyes, didn't stress about being woken up. He stressed little about anything. A skill that he had learned on the job.

He sat up in the motel bed and tossed the sheets off. He planted two bare feet on the tile and walked over to the table. He picked up the burner phone.

"Hello?"

A voice spoke in Spanish.

"It's me. You alone?"

"Yes."

The voice switched to English.

"Good. Any news?"

Ryman said, "Not yet."

"What about the cops?"

"They sent the FBI."

"Already?"

"Yes."

"We gotta get her first. We gotta get that money."

"You're the one who left it behind!" Ryman said.

He heard The Leader breathe, heavy over the phone. He breathed out. The disappointment in his voice was unmistakable. But Ryman didn't care. He wasn't one of The Leader's men that he could just order around.

The Leader said, "Careful how you speak to me, Agent Ryman."

"You don't scare me. This whole thing is your fault."

"How you figure that?"

"You forgot the money! How could you forget the money? That's what you were there for."

"We asked Mike where it was. He didn't know."

"You believed him?"

The Leader paused and looked back at the basement door from the kitchen of the house he and his men were squatting in. He said, "I've had plenty of experience interrogating people. Trust me."

"Maybe you were too easy on Mike?"

"Easy? He stole money from me! From us! It was difficult. I shot him. I lit him on fire. He told us where the money was. It wasn't there. What were we supposed to do?"

"I don't know. Find it before you killed him and set his whole house on fire?"

"You're the one who told us he was alone in it."

"He was supposed to be. The wife was supposed to have moved out. He told me she was leaving him. At least, he thought she was."

"Sounds like you're the one who made a mistake."

Ryman said, "It doesn't matter now. Now we have to find her."

"Any idea where she is?"

"Not yet. But I'm embedded with the FBI agent. I'll find her."

"Good."

"What about Portman?"

"That's why I'm calling. He has told me something."

"What?"

"He swears he doesn't know where she is. He's telling the truth. He probably told her not to tell him. But, he said she would call him."

"When?"

"Tomorrow."

"You got his phone? We didn't find it."

"We have it."

"Good."

"Ryman, stay with this FBI agent."

The Leader clicked off the phone.

Ryman tossed it onto the bed. He dropped back down onto the mattress and closed his eyes.

22

WIDOW'S LOOKOUT was set high, built up on a long, tall ridge connected to the mountain. The highest peak was separated by jagged cliffs and rock formations and green and red plant life. The sun beat down hard on the mountain several hours out of the day, nourishing the plants and trees with its light and killing them with its heat.

He had separated from DeGorne just as she told him, and went uphill. She took the duffle bag and dragged it behind her. Widow walked up to the base of a trail that led up to Lincoln Ridge Lookout.

At the start of the ridge, he was standing on the upward slope, where he found an obvious trail that led into packed trees. Behind him was an incredible view of rolling valleys and grass and brush and trees.

He stopped and stared out as far as he could see, more than once.

Gray Wolf Mountain to his back, he could see one hundred eighty degrees in a western direction. Although he couldn't see the ocean, he knew it was there somewhere. It was too far away. But it was there.

He was miles from anywhere, in the middle of nowhere. Miles from nowhere, even.

Then a thought occurred to him. He had only the clothes on his back. If he ended up staying there for more than a week, he'd have to wash his clothes every few days in a river or whatever. Which was no big deal, he guessed.

The sun was positioned in the sky around the ten-thirty a.m. position, he figured. He was far from the 101. That was for damn sure.

Widow turned to stare at the trail leading up the ridge. There were two wooden signs posted and staked into the ground—each with an arrow pointing in opposite directions. One read "Nickel Lake" and pointed one direction, and the other read "Lincoln Ridge Fire Lookout," which was his —the Two Twenty-One.

Widow started up the path to the Lincoln Ridge. The path led on, flat for a good long walk, more than a football field, maybe one hundred fifty yards. There was a section where he had to climb up and over some rock formations. Not a big deal. It involved grabbing onto ropes that were already fastened into the rock face and pulling himself up using manmade foot indentations. Once he got over the rocks, the rest of the trail was merely an inclined slope upward.

Widow came to a grassy area, half-red, half-green, with many tall trees. They looked like Bishop pines, with low branches curving out and up. Pinecones were scattered under the branches of each. They had some thinning green on top, like a receding hairline.

Most of them were tall.

Widow walked through them until the area opened up to a big clearing on top of the highest point on the ridge. And there it was: Lincoln Ridge Lookout, Two Twenty-One.

A sign staked near the bottom of the camp confirmed it.

Without realizing it, Widow called out. A habit of good manners, he figured.

"Hello?"

No answer.

"Is anyone there?"

No answer.

The tower was like the last one he had been in years ago, only it had more stone involved in the construction. There was a stone base at the bottom. It led up to a staircase that wrapped around wooden stilts like the other one had.

The stones were painted white. Underneath the stilts was a small wooden structure with a door that was padlocked. The lock appeared to be old and slightly rusted, but sturdy.

A single cropping of wires taped together led out of the structure from the back. The same wires were connected to a series that ran up the tower to the station on top. Widow followed the other end, which led east. It was

held up off the ground by short telephone poles. High enough to keep crit-
ters from chewing on the wires, but low enough for him to reach by going
up the climbing rungs without fear of falling to his death.

The rungs were there in case he needed to work on the wires; he
supposed.

His eyes followed the wires until they stopped at a small structure about
fifty yards from the stone staircase. Next to the structure was a gas-powered
generator. There was a tank already hooked up to the back. And probably a
couple of spares in the structure at the bottom of the tower.

The structure next to the generator confused him for a moment, until
he realized what it was. It was an outhouse, which made sense. The fire
watch station wouldn't have indoor plumbing.

Widow turned and went up the staircase. As he climbed, he stopped
periodically to see the views from his elevated position. It was all pretty
breathtaking.

Then he noticed a glimmer of light to the southwest. He squinted his
eyes and saw it was DeGorne's lookout station. She was pretty far, but not
too far. Her station was just high enough above the tree line to be visible
with the naked eye.

Widow continued heading upward on the staircase. At the top platform, he took another view over the horizon. It really was a majestic sight.
He saw trees in the distance, some thick, maybe redwoods. He saw low
mountains and one tall mountain, Gray Wolf. He saw the sunbeams spray
across everything.

He turned to the station on the top level. The windows were all
boarded up, which was probably a precaution they did every year when
they closed up shop. The deck wrapped around the entire station. The
boards creaked under his weight, like they had gotten stiff from being
unused for the last six months.

Widow tried the doorknob. It was locked.

Now what?

They had forgotten to give him a key. Maybe the guy who had the heart
attack, who usually lived there, had it still in his possession, expecting to
return here for the summer.

Widow thought, Where would an older wilderness type hide a
spare key?

There was a welcome mat. He tried underneath it. No luck.

The door had a glass window on it. He guessed he could break it if he
had to.

He reached up and felt the top frame of the door. Nothing there. He tried to picture all the places that people left spare keys. Unfortunately, he didn't know the usual guy at all. He wouldn't be able to guess where he would've hidden a spare key.

Widow walked around the deck, checking underneath the railing. There was an off chance that maybe he duct-taped a spare to the bottom of the railing. That's what he would've done.

He studied the station house for nooks and crannies that might be good places to hide a key. He saw nothing. Then he walked back down the stairs, looking under the previous stairs for a hidden, duct-taped key.

Nothing.

He stopped at the bottom step and surveyed the perimeter. He saw a cluster of head-sized rocks. He could easily use one to break the window. He wanted to avoid doing that because he already knew that the nights out here could get chilly. And an open window was bound to put him at risk of a cold. The last thing he needed was to get sick way out here in the middle of God's country.

But he also wasn't seeing much choice. He figured that if he really wanted to, he could find his way to DeGorne's lookout. There was probably a trail, probably signs that pointed the way. How far was that? Ten miles? More? He wasn't about to walk that far just for a key.

Instead, he walked over to the cluster of rocks, stood over them for a long minute, like he was picking out his weapon just before an arena-style gladiator match. He bent down and scooped up one rock. It was smooth and cold to the touch. He let it sit in his hand. It was heavy enough to break a man's skull open like an eggshell. Certainly, it would do the job on the window.

Then he stopped for a moment and looked to his right. He saw the outhouse and again thought, *Where would a wilderness type hide a spare key?*

Widow dropped the rock and headed over to the outhouse. He tried the door. Unlocked. Why wouldn't it be?

Then he opened it.

It smelled clean but musty and stale, like it hadn't been opened in six months, which it hadn't.

The toilet was right there in the center. It wasn't porcelain, but plastic. It was open and cleaned. It was embedded down into a wooden bench, which probably covered the tank beneath. He wondered if cleaning it was like cleaning a latrine? He didn't see why it would be any more advanced.

There was a light switch on the wall, which surprised him. He flicked it. Of course, nothing happened because the generator was off.

Still, part of the ceiling was a thin, white plastic piece cut into the wood. It allowed light to come in. Widow took a quick look around and saw on the back of the door was a spare key, right there, duct-taped, just like he'd thought.

A good hiding place. Obvious enough for someone to find, but still hidden in an unconventional place.

Widow took the key and shut the door. He walked back up the hill, back up the stairs, and to the station house. He used the key and entered.

It was dark inside. He looked to the right and saw a thick green button on a metal electric box near the door. A handwritten label on it read: Generator.

He pressed it, and down below, he heard the faint rattle and compression of the gas generator kick-starting to life. He leaned back out and watched it. The generator rumbled at first, and thin smoke puffed out, and then it calmed into a steady hum.

He immediately saw the CB radio station, pressed up against the opposite corner, snug, facing northeast. It must've been switched off because it hadn't crackled to life with the power generator.

He wanted to check it before he did anything else. He needed communication. He walked through the room, shaded in darkness because of the boarded-up windows. He stepped to the right to let the sunlight from the open door light up the knobs and switches on the radio.

He found the on/off switch and flipped it, turned the volume knob all the way up. No sound. He turned it all the way down. Nothing. He flipped channels. Nothing. He tapped the gauges, an instinct action not backed by any kind of mechanical experience. Nothing happened.

The radio wasn't working.

Great, he thought.

23

WIDOW FROZE in place for a long moment, wondering what else he could do to get the radio to work. If the heart attack guy was competent, and Widow figured he must've been, then the radio would've been reported as broken or malfunctioning before he left last November.

After double-checking all the knobs and switches and the cords to the outlet and then the outlet itself, Widow did the one thing that he could think to do. He banged on the top of it. Not pounding his fist hard enough to dent metal roofing, but a good solid wham!

Nothing happened.

He stepped back and shrugged. Maybe the fire lookout didn't care about the CB and just used the walkie.

He turned and scanned the room in the daytime darkness. The lights in the station stayed off. Probably because he hadn't flipped their switch on, but the power-on light on the charge station for the walkie lit up green. The charge station was back toward the door, on a wooden writing desk. He followed it and saw the light switch near the door. He flipped it, and the lights kicked on. There was a single heavy overhead bulb that provided a wide cone of yellow light, splashed over the Osborne Firefinder table, and a single desk lamp on a jointed metal arm. The two provided just enough light to find his way around.

He was surprised that the walkie had charge after so many months without power. He snatched it up quickly and inspected it.

It was old. A bit nineties-looking. It was bulbous and round and bright yellow. There was a thick antenna towering out of the top, next to a channel knob, and a volume dial that doubled as the on/off dial. He switched it on and turned it up all the way.

He left the channel on the one it was on when it was shut off. He figured that was probably the only channel that DeGorne and the heart attack guy ever used.

Widow clicked the call button and said, "DeGorne? Come in?"

He waited. No response.

She was probably still lugging that duffle bag up miles of wilderness. What the hell she needed it for, he didn't know.

He left the walkie on a desk near the western window and looked around the station house.

It was one large octagonal room. A mini-fridge hummed but was empty, of course. There was a box with canned food that still looked edible. There were two stacks of bottled waters still wrapped in the plastic case. He wondered if there was a well nearby.

There was another big box full of MREs, which he was very familiar with.

In the middle of the room was a square island made of wood and cabinets. On top was a round table with a map in the center and anglers on two sides. It was a device that he had seen before.

It looked like an ancient sundial; only this one wasn't meant to tell time. It was an Osborne Firefinder. He had seen it before, over a decade ago. He couldn't remember how to use it. He'd have to ask DeGorne.

Widow stepped away, inspected the rest of the tower.

Along the wall with the mini-fridge was a low double shelf, with more jarred food products and more MREs and some canned soups. On the other side of the mini-fridge was a small oven with a two-burner stovetop. Guess he wouldn't have problems eating well way out here.

On the desk was a laptop, old in terms of computers, but new in that he had hardly ever used a computer. He didn't even remember ever owning one. At least, not one that the Navy hadn't provided.

A thick jump drive stuck out of one of the USB ports. The laptop was plugged into a wall socket. The jump drive hummed to life when he powered on the generator.

Not sure what he would use the laptop for. Guess they might want him to log things, keep records, and whatnot, which he wouldn't do.

Behind him, there was an AM/FM radio with a single antenna already sticking up, extended all the way. He wondered if he could even get any stations out here. Maybe.

There was a cassette player as well. And a stack of cassettes next to the radio.

He studied the tapes. They weren't music. They were books on tape. Mostly Agatha Christie and various classic mysteries.

Also, there was a stack of paperbacks strung across the windowsill by the cot. They, too, were mystery books. Some he'd heard of, and some he hadn't. They were all airport reads, which reminded him. He took out his paperback book and tossed it on the desk. It might still come in handy.

Suddenly, the walkie crackled, and he heard DeGorne's voice.

"Widow?"

24

"DeGorne," Widow answered.

"It's me. Of course."

Widow stayed quiet.

"I guess you made it inside. I didn't realize it until I got in mine that you didn't have a key. Did you break the window?"

"No. I found the spare."

"Oh, good. I was worried."

"I managed. And don't ask me where he keeps it."

DeGorne said nothing to that. Instead, she paused, and then she came back on. "Okay. I won't. Listen, there's a lot to go over. But I can't sit here all day and train you. I've got my own stuff to do. So how much of it do you remember?"

Widow said, "It's familiar, but a rundown wouldn't hurt."

"Just grab the checklist and go through it. That's really the hardest part of the job, minus a fire. Of course."

Widow smiled, even though she couldn't see him.

"I see that the walkie works. What about the CB?"

"Nothing from it."

"That's not surprising. Danvers never liked to talk on it. He always used the walkie. I was the only person he ever talked to. I guess. I think it even broke years ago, and he never replaced it."

"Is that the guy's name?"

"Yes. Danvers. Great old guy."

Widow said nothing.

DeGorne said, "Most of this gig is gonna be inventory and observation. You should find a manual there somewhere. It'll stick out. It's thin, rung together in a binder."

Widow looked around, saw the manual right there on the desk, underneath the laptop.

"I found it."

"Good. You don't need to memorize it or anything. It's more of a reference book. In case you run into an issue, it can help you decipher what to do next."

"I don't need to read it?"

"I didn't say that if Tate asks. But no. There's a chapter, the third one, that talks about the Osborne Firefinder. You should look over that part."

"I recognized that."

"Oh, good. Then you know how to use it?"

"Not really."

"It's easy. Just look it up. It finds fires."

"Yeah, I got that part."

Widow paused a beat, changed gears, and asked, "What about a gun? I don't see one."

"That's why I bring my own."

"Right."

"Don't worry. If you need a gun, just call me. I'll save you."

Widow laughed.

"What do you think you'll need one for? I'm a tiny, little woman out here all alone. You're a big guy. No reason for you to fear anyone."

"What about bears? They're not afraid of me."

DeGorne laughed, but then she said, "We shouldn't make jokes. Really. We got black bears out here. And hikers and campers have been attacked before."

"Really?"

"Oh yeah. Every year. Several times."

"Anyone killed?"

"All the time."

"That makes me feel good."

"Don't worry. The chances of one of them climbing up the stairs of your tower are pretty slim. Unless you leave food out on the ground. Remember, pick up after yourself."

"What about when I'm hiking? What do I do if I encounter a bear? Am I supposed to play dead or something?"

DeGorne laughed. Widow was glad to hear it.

"Sure. Play dead. See what happens."

"What will happen?"

"The bear will probably try to eat you. He'll think you're dead."

Widow said, "I hope not."

"If I were you, I wouldn't worry. You don't look very appetizing."

"I don't?"

"No. The bear would have to be starving to death to wanna eat you."

They both laughed.

DeGorne said, "Thanks, Widow."

"For what?"

"Making me laugh. You don't know how stressful my life has been lately."

He said nothing to that.

She said, "Seriously, there's a can of bear mace in your pack."

"My pack? I didn't bring one."

"There's already one in there. Somewhere. All the lookouts have a pre-packed back up in the tower. Look for it. There are goodies in there you'll need when you venture out. Including a map."

"So, do you need me to return yours to you?"

"Sure. No hurry."

"I'll search for the pack. Anything else I should know?"

"I wouldn't worry about the bears. The wolves are more dangerous. The bears here avoid people like the plague. The wolves are different. They travel in packs and feel brave because of it. Most of the wolves stick to a part of the mountain, near Wolf Creek."

"Wolf Creek? That's aptly named."

"Everything here is aptly named."

"Why Lincoln Ridge?"

"You didn't see it?"

"See what?" He asked.

"The ridge you're on. When you get the chance, look at the ridge from the tower. To the south. It's a peak and a cliff that looks like...well. You'll see why it's called Lincoln's Ridge."

"Okay. Anything else I need to know?"

"Not that I can think of. Call me if you need anything."

I asked, "What about emergencies?"

"Same. Call me. Foreman has a phone in her station."

"Foreman?"

"Our closest neighbor. She's like the unofficial regional manager for all of us. To the east, you'll find telephone poles with single wires on them. They hook up to her lookout. So, if you need anything, anything emergency-related, then you call me, and I get her on my CB. You won't be able to get her on your walkie. Too far."

Widow paused a moment. Then he asked, "Ever run into people out here?"

"Oh, sure. There are going to be teenagers who come out here hiking. They usually need our help because they don't know what they're doing. Sometimes, we'll get hunters sneaking in even though it's the offseason. Same with fishermen."

"What do I do to them?"

"You do nothing to them. Just ask them to leave. In particular, look out for fireworks and campfires."

"People shoot fireworks out here?"

"Why do you think teenagers come out here?"

"To get wasted?"

She said, "They do both."

Widow was quiet.

The radio crackled again, and DeGorne asked, "Anything else?"

"I can't think of anything."

"Look over the checklist and the manual. I'll call you later. And keep your walkie with you at all times."

"Okay. Got it."

"Good to have you here, Widow. It makes me feel safer."

She had said it like she really meant it, like a woman on the run.

Widow waited, listened to the static on the walkie, and realized she was gone.

25

WIDOW KEPT the walkie clipped to the back of his cargo pants waistband like a gun holster.

The great outdoors took on a whole new meaning out here. It was quite something. And right off the bat, he felt the risk of fire. The sunlight had warmed the entire mountain within minutes. A thermometer was posted by the door so that it would be at eye level every time he walked out. He read the temperature to be pushing one hundred degrees already, and the summer had just started.

The good news was that it didn't feel that hot. There was enough wind at this altitude and proximity to the Pacific Ocean that the heat was more than bearable. It was pleasant.

It turned out that Danvers was a methodical man; not only did he have the certified NPS checklist, but he also added in nearly twenty more things to check for newcomers.

Widow went through the checklist, plus Danvers' added requirements. It all made sense. It was all a normal thing for him. He had come from sixteen years of military and police service. He had filled out many check-lists and reports. He knew how to do such bureaucratic things.

He had completed the checklist by the time early afternoon was turning into late afternoon. Luckily, little of the checklist was something he would have to do every single day. Next, he took some time to read through the manual. Most of which he found to be like every other government document—tedious, wordy, and unnecessarily complicated. It was a committee document that started with maybe one person with any fire experience. Then it made its way to higher-ups, who sent it to the legal department. A team of overpaid government lawyers redlined it and regurgitated a needless document that protected the NPS from litigation and made it possible to blame the fire lookouts in case of fire.

Widow wasn't sure if the others had read deep enough to see the fine print of that. Being a former NCIS agent sent undercover with the Navy, he had double experience reading through documents and manuals. Which made the thought occur to him he should've gone to law school, but he quickly shut that notion down. Law school and the profession of lawyering would've made him kill himself. He was sure of that.

After he read the manual, he reread the section about the Osborne Firefinder, just in case. He got the gist of it.

Widow looked over it for a while. It seemed to be, as DeGorne had said, simple enough. He picked up the manual again and thumbed to the diagrams and explanations of the Firefinder.

At first glance, it was basically a map of the region under a glass top on a round table. Following the instructions in the manual, he found the thing rotated and slid on a track built underneath, and it tracked along with all four points on a compass. There were two metal measuring tools that stood up vertically: one measured elevation, and the other helped to pinpoint the distance of any fire that was spotted.

Widow spent some time experimenting with the Firefinder and discovered that the basic mechanism of it was the same as a rifle. You could look through the hairline crack of the distance ruler to spot the fire, right off. Then double over to the elevation finder, stare through a hairline crack in its center and use the distance finder to line up with the fire out the window.

It was one of those old technologies that worked and was simple enough, not unlike the scope system of a rifle.

If it ain't broke, why fix it?

26

TIRED OF BEING COOPED up in the fire tower all morning, it was time for Widow to check out his designated watch area, the Two Twenty-One.

Which made him wonder what his exact area was. He was tempted to call DeGorne, but he was a big boy. He could read maps. He'd figure it out.

First, he grabbed the backpack near the door and zipped it open, took a gander inside.

He found a neatly folded pullover hoodie, a folded map, and a small square device that looked like a smartphone, only it was a little wider and all screen. He shook it. Nothing happened. He felt along the edge and found a single button. He pressed it, and the screen lit up with a generic powering-on icon. And then a home screen came on with a map of the area. It was a GPS device with real-time positioning. That would be handy. He guessed the map was backup. The battery on the GPS was low. Deeper in the pack, he found the wall charger for it. He plugged it in and leave it behind. There was no lighter or matches, which he expected, but there was a pack of glow sticks. For cave exploration, he guessed.

There was a survival knife. Standard. The blade was sharp enough to cut, but dull. It was worn and probably a decade old, or more. Widow unscrewed the cap and found nothing inside. He imagined that the original packaging came with a fire-starter or a knife-sharping rock. Either way, now it came with nothing.

There was an empty canteen and one last item—a set of keys, two on a ring.

Widow already had the key for the fire tower from the outhouse.

He returned everything to the pack, minus the keys and the canteen. He ran water into the canteen from the sink, which worked fine, and cleaned it and filled it. He packed it into a side pouch on the backpack and left the fire tower. He used the key from the outhouse to lock the door.

He headed down the stairs. But he remembered what DeGorne had said about Lincoln Ridge. He stopped and leaned over the rail, looked to the south. He saw nothing but majestic vistas and mountains and trees and fields. Then he saw the smoke in the distance. The California wildfire was still raging on.

He took a deep breath of the cool, crisp air. He looked down at the ridge. And he saw exactly why it was called Lincoln Ridge.

The ridge to the south, from a high view, looked just like Lincoln's top hat. There it was: a long top and round rim, and it was all dark in the shadow of trees like it was a gentlemen's black top hat.

He chuckled to himself.

Widow turned back and headed down the spiraling staircase, stopped at the bottom, and tried the keys on the padlock. There were only two on the ring, and it turned out the second one he tried, worked.

Where did the extra key go? Maybe it was for a supply box somewhere? That would make sense.

Widow hooked the key rings together so that all three were on the same ring and slipped it into his pocket.

He opened the shed door and walked inside. A light bulb dangled from a wire above and a short chain underneath. He pulled the chain, and the light clicked on. It gave little more light than was already beaming in from the sun through the open door behind him. At night, it was probably very handy.

The shed had a single wall with tools hung up on nails and a stack of two-by-fours, probably extra wood for boarding up the windows. There was a workbench with another sink next to it and a cutting board on the table. Immediately, Widow figured that was for scaling and cleaning fish. Next to it was a fillet knife, sharper than the survival one, and a fishing pole leaning against the wall.

There was a small tackle box on the ground.

On a different wall, he saw something that was more interesting. The other wall was designated for storing climbing gear. There were two sets of bundled up rope, a hanging flashlight that clipped onto clothing, and an ax with its blade covered. He slipped off the cover to see the terrifying-looking blade. The ax was a combination of an ax and an ice pick. It was white and silver, with a black rubber grip around the base and handle.

Widow recognized it, but couldn't remember the exact name of it. He believed it was called an ice ax or a mountaineer ax.

It was a violent-looking thing that was used for climbing ice or rocks. He'd bet it was more applicable for ice. It could hack into the ice. The serrated edges of the blade would set into the ice, making it reliable for climbers to hack their way up the side of an ice wall.

There were no ice walls in the park—not this time of year. Maybe in winter, the mountains could be high enough to have snow and ice.

Widow didn't intend to use the ax for climbing, but it would come in handy if he ran into a bear or a pack of gray wolves. So, he took it. He felt safer.

He snugged the leather sheath back onto the ax and slipped it into the backpack. The handle stuck out a bit.

Widow shut the shed door and locked it.

27

Widow spent the day hiking from west to north to east to south in a clockwise direction, starting from the eight on the dial, and trekked around toward the six. He never made it to the six, to the south of Lincoln Ridge, or to the east, because the north was expansive enough, more than he had expected.

He only cracked open the map once, at the beginning of his day. Widow had a pretty good memory. He committed the map to memory, or so he liked to believe, but there were several times he almost stopped to consult it. He almost cracked it open again.

But something deep inside him forbade it, like men are built not to stop and ask directions. Once, he had read a paper on that. It was a scientific thing, like something you'd find in college publications. He read it because it was convenient, back in some place in his life. Only, he couldn't remember where, which made him suspect that his memory wasn't as good as he thought. Or it was just a part of getting older.

Widow stared at the mountains, hiking through huge redwood trees near the foot of Grey Wolf Mountain, learning the terrain, and enjoying every minute.

The great outdoors was taking on a whole new meaning for him.

Widow never considered himself an outdoorsy type of guy, not in a mountain-man, survivalist kind of way. But he was no homebody either. He was a good outdoorsman. Good enough.

He walked a manmade path and followed it up a winding ridge until he was on higher ground. The terrain ahead fell flat, sloping off to the north until the horizon was set as a backdrop to a valley of redwood trees. The trees went on as far as the eye could see.

Even before he reached the mouth of the valley, he saw the trees were huge, like dinosaurs from another era.

Standing underneath them, he could no longer see the horizon. Not over them, that was for damn sure. And not between them.

The redwoods were so massive that it looked like someone could've built a thousand treehouses in them.

There was plenty of room to traverse between them, but there always seemed to be a tree blocking the view of what was beyond. Navigating them was easy close-up, but impossible for knowing the direction you were headed in.

At the base of the path that led into the trees, there was another sign staked in the ground: *Gray Tree Valley.*

Where did they come up with these boring names? He wondered.

But he learned soon enough where. The clouds seemed bigger out there. A sky full of clouds merged and overcast the sky, like soldiers committing a coup d'état on the sun.

The trees turned gray. The path turned gray. The grass turned to shadow.

Suddenly, the name made sense.

Widow walked on for nearly half an hour into the redwoods when he encountered another gray phenomenon.

Since he could no longer see the sun in the sky, he couldn't tell the time. He wondered what it was. He didn't have a watch, and he had left the GPS behind to charge. So, he pulled out the walkie, which was when he realized it was switched off.

He wasn't sure if that was an accident or he had forgotten to turn it on. He switched it on and checked a small digital screen, like a calculator's. It told him the channel, the signal strength, and the time.

It was ten to five in the afternoon. Almost evening. Almost sundown.

Abruptly, the walkie vibrated in his hand, and DeGorne's voice came on over the single speaker.

"Widow? Widow? Come in?"

He clicked the button and responded.

"Yes. I'm here."

"Where are you?"

*Without hesit*ation, which translates in the Navy, to: *without thinking.*

Widow said, "In Green Tree Valley."

Static, and silence, and then DeGorne said, "No you're not. You're in Gray Tree Valley."

"Right. Gray Tree Valley."

He felt dumb for the mistake of misspeaking.

"What the hell are you doing all the way up there?"

"I was reconning."

"You're what?"

"Looking around. You know surveying. That's our job, right?"

"No. It's: *observe and report.* But, hey, while you're there, you know you're about a mile away from it."

"From what?"

"The second-best view in the park."

"Second-best?"

"The first is from the summit of Gray Wolf."

"I see. So, where do I go for the second-best view?"

"Head out of there and go northwest."

"What am I looking for?"

"You'll know when you get there."

"Okay."

DeGorne said, "Start heading that way."

"I will. Question. Which way is northwest?"

"Oh my god," she said and chuckled again. "Are you lost?"

"It's just that it's very hard to get your bearings in here. The sky is grayed over. The trees are enormous. I don't see the sun anywhere."

"What branch of the military did you say you were in again?"

"Navy."

"Were you a submariner?"

"Funny."

"Okay, let me ask you something."

"Yeah."

"Did you take the pack with you?"

"Yes."

"Inside. Did you find a survival knife?"

"Yes," he said. He knew exactly what she was driving at. The butt of the knife was a compass.

He said, "I know. I know. I forgot."

"Okay. So, buzz me when you get there."

"Got it."

They both got off the walkie, and Widow used the compass on his survival knife to find northwest. He followed the direction, traversing through the redwoods, avoiding a channel of muddy ditches that looked natural.

After forty-five minutes, not his best time in hiking just over a mile, he made his way out of the forest of trees. He walked through treeless foothills until he heard rushing water. It grew louder and louder until finally he reached where he was supposed to be. He stood over a ravine. To his right, there was a crisp, magnificent waterfall. It was wide. The water was crystal clear. It rushed over the side of the ravine and flowed down into a stream below. He let his eyes follow the rushing stream.

The ravine was so clear of trees and natural obstructions that he could see for miles. The stream rushed violently until it became a river, and then it poured into a huge lake.

His walkie crackled.

"Widow?"

"Yeah."

"You see it?"

"I see it."

"That's Nickel Lake."

"It's really something."

"That it is."

"Can you see it from there?"

"No. I'm too far. But I like that view at sunset."

"I see why," Widow said. And he saw why. The sun went down, and the colors from the sunset filled the ravine. They reflected off the top of the lake.

"That's what I wanted you to see."

"Thanks for telling me about it."

"No problem."

They said nothing.

"Hey, Widow."

"Yeah?"

"I'm glad you're here."

"Me too."

"Why don't you call me later on."

"You got somewhere to be?"

"I'm starving from humping up here. I'm going to cook an MRE."

"Okay. Talk to you later."

And he clicked off the walkie. Widow looked around, found a flat-topped boulder, and planted himself there. He enjoyed the sunset, which was one of the best he had ever seen. Not as good as one from an aircraft carrier out at sea, where the sun looks gigantic over the ocean, but pretty damn close.

28

TWENTY MILES NORTH OF SEATTLE, Watermoth walked among the remains of the burned house. Collins was nearby. They weren't speaking. Collins looked at burned wood on the ground and studied the crumpled roof. He didn't know what he was looking for. He was studying Watermoth, studying her process.

Watermoth held her smartphone in her hand. She traversed over broken planks of wood, charred brick, and ash that she couldn't distinguish as wood, paper, furniture, or plastic.

She held the smartphone in case she needed to make a video. So far, there was nothing to make a video of.

She stepped through the dirt and soot without worrying about her shoes, which were expensive. But that was part of the gig. Expensive dress shoes. Expensive suits. All a part of keeping up the FBI's professional image. No choice.

Watermoth found nothing interesting in the remains of Lee's house.

Ryman smoked a cigarette and stayed back with the Tahoe.

Collins waited for a beat. Then he walked out of the house's remains. He circled the grass and stopped ten feet from the edge of the house. He waited for Watermoth.

Eventually, she walked out of the house and joined him.

"I don't mean to bother you, Joanna, but what the hell are we looking for here?"

Watermoth turned on her left heel, faced Collins.

"We're looking for clues. You know, Collins, police work."

"I mean, everything is burned to ash. What are we going to find here?"

Watermoth pointed, using her smartphone clung in her hand, and said, "What about that?"

She pointed to the garage.

She said, "Come on. Walk with me in the garage."

His guys had already searched the garage, the house, and the perimeter. They'd found nothing. But he didn't question her.

She looked in the garage, and he stood five feet behind her.

"We're positive that one vehicle is missing?"

"I told you that already."

"Don't take that tone with me."

"I'm sorry. I didn't mean it to sound that way. I just wonder what else are we going to find out here?"

"What is the missing vehicle?"

Collins paused, took out his phone, and scrolled through a couple of screens until he was at a digital copy of the police reports. He read through it and found the vehicle information.

He said, "A blue, 1971 Ford Bronco."

"And the name on the registration?"

"Michael D. Lee."

"Not her name?"

"No."

"What about the insurance carriers?"

Collins scrolled up, pinched his fingers, and zoomed into the document. "Same."

"What about the wife? She's on it, right? It was her vehicle?"

"Molly April Lee. She has full coverage."

"Molly April Lee."

"That's her name."

Watermoth stepped around the empty parking spot. She looked up at the ceiling high above. The fire from the house had burned hot enough to send sparks flying up and away, far enough to hit the garage's roof. There was fire damage done to the garage's roof, but minimal.

"And your guys questioned the neighbors?"

"Naturally."

"No one said anything about her?"

Collins shrugged, and said, "Just typical small-town stuff."

"Like?"

"Molly Lee was a beautiful woman. She was liked by the neighbors."

Watermoth looked back at him and asked, "But?"

"But, they say she was quiet. Kept to herself mostly."

"And she grew up here?"

"Sure, but she moved away as soon as she turned eighteen."

"And?"

"And then she met Mike Lee. They married. They returned here. Now he's dead."

Watermoth nodded and said, "Why did you mention she was beautiful?"

"That's what some neighbors pointed out. Like it was the first thing they noticed about her."

"It was the only thing they noticed about her?"

"Like I said, she was quiet. Kept to herself."

"Let me ask you something. Was it just the men who said she was beautiful?"

Collins said, "I don't know. I didn't ask them. I'm just giving you a general statement from what I see in the report, here."

"Did you see her photo?"

Collins touched the screen, exited the document, and pulled up a jpeg file. He stared at it and flipped it, so Watermoth could see it.

It was a digital copy of Molly Lee's driver's license.

"She's good-looking."

Watermoth didn't look.

"I've seen it already."

Collins put his phone down. Then he slipped it into his pants pocket.

"Joanna, what're we really doing in here? You got access to all this already. I know an agent like you has probably already seen it."

Watermoth walked back to the open garage door. She looked out, saw Ryman smoking, leaning up against his Tahoe.

She turned back to Collins and pointed at Mike Lee's vehicle.

"We're not here looking for clues about Lee."

"What are we doing here?"

"Notice anything strange about Ryman?"

Collins shrugged and said, "He's an asshole."

"Yeah, that he is, but what else?"

"I don't know."

Watermoth waited.

Collins said, "He doesn't seem to be interested in looking around here for clues."

"More than that. He has shown zero interest in it."

"So what? He's a DEA SWAT. Those guys aren't into police work as much as they are a tool for capturing and raiding meth cook houses."

Watermoth asked, "You got a partner?"

"I do. But our department is stretched thin. He's on something else right now."

"You been with him a while?"

"Four years."

"You like him?"

"He's a pain in the ass. But he's okay."

"You got his back?"

Collins said, "Of course. He's my partner."

"What if someone murdered him?"

"What about it?"

"What would you do?"

"I'd want to get them!"

"Arrest them or kill them?"

Collins paused a long beat, and then he said, "Both. Either."

"That's why we're here."

Collins said nothing.

"Ryman's partner was murdered by his wife two nights ago, and he doesn't seem to even care about looking for clues at the crime scene."

Collins looked back out the door at Ryman.

"You think he knows something? Was he involved?"

"Maybe. I'm just saying we're not just here for clues about Molly's whereabouts. We're here to see how Ryman behaves."

"He's not doing well so far on that front."

Watermoth nodded and said, "So far, he hasn't even come up to the house. Like he feels guilty."

"What do we do?"

"I'm telling you because I need your help."

"What do you want me to do?"

"Just have my back. And watch him."

Collins said, "You got it."

29

AT NIGHT, Widow stayed in his tower and watched the wildfire burn farther to the south. He had Turkish coffee brewed out of a pot of boiling water. Not bad. He ate an MRE of Chicken Alfredo and two rolls. He and DeGorne talked on the walkie until the battery died. He plugged it into the charger, and walked along the balcony around his fire tower.

He saw the light from her lookout coming from the east. He found a pair of binoculars and watched her. She paced and watched the fire from the south. Eventually, he saw her kick back in bed. She read for a while, until she seemed to have fallen asleep.

Widow thumbed through the field manual until ten o'clock at night. He called it lights out and crashed. He briefly woke up at midnight. He had to go down to the outhouse. Afterward, he was trekking back up the spiraling staircase when he noticed DeGorne's light was on.

His walkie had powered up. He checked the time. It was ten after midnight. He grabbed the binoculars and looked over at her. He found her looking back at him through a pair of her own binoculars. He waved at her. She waved back.

His walkie crackled.

"Can't sleep?" she asked.

"Couldn't hold it."

"Couldn't hold what?"

"You know."

"Oh. Yeah."

Widow said, "It sucks having to get up out of bed and walk down fifty-one stairs and a hundred feet to the bathroom.'

"You counted it?"

"I counted the stairs, not the feet. I guessed that part."

"Weirdo."

Widow smiled. He wondered if she could see it from there.

"You don't have to go down to the outhouse. You know?"

"I don't?"

"No. You don't."

"How you figure?"

"Widow, you're a man. This is the middle of nowhere. God's green woods. You can pee anywhere."

"I didn't think about that."

"Next time, just go over the side. That's what I do."

"You do?"

"Duh. I'm a woman. But I ain't no lady."

"How do you do that?'

"Do what?"

"How do you go over the side?"

"I thought you were smart?"

"I never claimed to be."

"You knew an awful lot about my gun, earlier. You seem to remember the protocols of this job well enough."

"Yeah, from like a million years ago."

"Still, you remember it, right?"

"Some of it. I don't remember being neighbors with a beautiful woman."

She said nothing to that.

"Danvers must be killing himself that he's missing time out here near you."

"No pun intended? I hope."

"Nothing intended."

"We got along well. He's a nice old man. Loves nature. Not much of a nighttime companion."

"What do you mean by that?"

"He was always up at the crack of dawn. He's a grandpa, you know?"

"What's that got to do with nighttime?"

"You know. Morning people are morning people because they go to sleep early at night."

"And not you?"

"Not me. I wake up halfway through most nights. I stay up late. And I wake up late. What about you?"

"I sleep whenever I can. Daytime or night. Makes no difference to me."

"Is that because of the military?"

Widow shrugged to himself. He said, "I guess so. They teach you to sleep when told. They teach you to be awake when told. You're even told where and when to piss."

"It sounds awful."

"It wasn't. It was fantastic, actually."

"Why did you quit?"

"My mom was killed."

"She was? That's horrible. I'm sorry."

"It's over now."

"How long ago?"

"Only a few years. But it seems like she's been gone forever."

He heard a wolf howl in the distance, like the first night at the Ranger Station. And then he heard another.

"Those wolves. They sound close," he said.

"They're not."

"How do you know?"

"I don't. They might be close. I just didn't want you to have nightmares."

"Funny."

"They come out at night. They usually stick near Hooters."

"Hooters? There's a restaurant out here?"

She laughed over the walkie. Widow listened. There was something about her laugh. He liked it. Then he noticed something else. It was the sound of suction, the sound of glass clinking, and the sound of liquid pouring.

DeGorne said, "Hooters is west of you, south of Nickel Lake. It's not really called that. It's a combination of Two Mule Hill and Screech Point."

"These names. Screech Point?"

"Because it's a forest with a dense population of Western screech owls."

"So why do you call it Hooters? The owls?"

"No, I call it Hooters because there are two big hills out there that look like boobs."

Widow smiled and said, "Danvers was missing out."

"How so?"

"You're hilarious, DeGorne."

"Thanks. I think so."

They were quiet for a moment. Widow held the binoculars down at his side. Then he heard the radio crackle again, and the glass clinking sound, and DeGorne drinking something.

"What's that?"

"What's what?"

"Are you drinking?"

"You caught me. Yes. I'm having a drink."

"What is it?"

"Vodka."

"You drinking it with ice?"

"Yes. I put a cup of water in the freezer and crack ice chips from it."

"Clever."

"Tell me something, Widow. Why aren't you married?"

"I don't know. Guess it just never happened for me."

"It's not worth it. Trust me. You're better off."

Silence.

Widow asked, "Mind if I ask you something?"

He heard her take another drink. And she must've finished it, because then he heard her pour another glass.

"Shoot," she said.

"How did you get that black eye?"

More silence. This time it seemed to last forever. Widow picked the binoculars up to his face and looked at her tower. He saw her drinking out of the glass, staring off in the distance like she was lost in thought.

He said, "Sorry. I didn't mean to get personal."

She said, "My husband did it to me."

"I'm sorry. I hope that's why you left him."

She took another drink. He listened to her breathing, then swallowing.

"I leave him every summer to come here. But it is why I started taking this job five years ago. And I've been doing it every summer since."

"He knows where you are?"

"He never knew. I told him I had a job, but I lied about the *what* and *where*."

"Did you leave him this time for good?"

"I'll never see him again. I'm sure of that."

Widow said nothing.

DeGorne said, "He wasn't always that way. He used to be a good guy.

But he got mixed up with the wrong people. You were in the NCIS. Maybe you can relate. He worked in law enforcement too."

"I knew guys who couldn't handle the pressures. Sure."

"You don't strike me as the type of guy to hit a woman. Especially one you love."

Widow told the truth. That's what he always did.

"I'd hit a woman, under the right circumstances."

"What circumstances?"

"She was trying to kill me or someone I loved."

"You're talking about self-defense, no-choice scenarios. I'm talking about like in an argument or just for kicks?"

"No. I'd never do that. I was raised in the south by a single mother. Believe me, that kind of thinking would never even cross my mind."

"I knew you weren't like how he was."

Widow listened.

He asked, "Was?"

DeGorne stayed quiet.

"You talk of him in the past tense."

DeGorne stayed quiet.

"Did something happen to him?"

"I'm tired now. I'm going to hit the hay. I'll see you tomorrow."

And she was gone.

30

WIDOW WAS certain that he wasn't supposed to be fishing in Nickel Lake because he'd read in the field manual that it was required to have a fishing license. And he did not. But he couldn't help himself.

The next morning, he woke up bright and early, and took Danvers' fishing rod and tackle box, along with the pack full of gear and the ice ax, on a fishing expedition.

He caught five nickel trout and threw back five nickel trout. As was required, even if he had a fishing license. After fishing, he set out to explore the west and south and planned to end his day in the east.

That morning, he skipped breakfast, but when noon rolled around he stopped and ate beans out of a can. Afterward, he wrapped up the empty can in a brown paper bag with his dirty fork. He returned it to his pack to throw away later.

He drank two bottles of water by midafternoon. By then, he'd already passed through the west and the south. He had explored the creeks, a basin, and a valley. He'd found an open cave, and he followed the winding manmade trails until he was in Thunder Gorge, which threaded beyond the eastern foothills of Gray Wolf Mountain and led straight to DeGorne's fire lookout.

Along the way, he found several lockboxes—all numbered. All locked with a combination lock. The lockboxes were listed in the field manual. It was for the fire watch crew to leave supply items for each other. However, mostly he found letters left to future fire watch crewmen. Previous fire look-outs had used them as time capsules to communicate with people from the future. They began with the date each message was handwritten. The oldest one he found was from way back in nineteen thirty-two.

It started with an introduction of the author and ended with a riddle. That riddle was later answered by the next fire lookout and replaced with a riddle of his own making.

Widow liked to ignore the answers and try to answer them himself.

By nightfall, he was in the east, and he had hiked to five miles away from DeGorne's fire lookout.

They had radio silence until the late afternoon.

"Weirdo. Are you there?"

She said *weirdo* like Widow. She made it sound similar—a pet name. Widow wasn't sure how he felt about that.

"I'm here."

"How is your day?"

"Great," he said, and he told her all the things he had done. And all the exploring he had done. Starting from the west, turning to the south, and heading east, until he was basically five miles away from her.

"Wow! You did a lot!"

"I wanted to see as much as I could today."

"Glad you didn't waste any time. How come yesterday you didn't make this kind of progress?"

"I looked at the map this morning. Planned out what I would do. I memorized it."

"Good. Did you remember to do the checklist? That's important."

"I did."

"Well, I wish I was that productive. I didn't even get out of bed until nearly noon."

"How can you sleep in out here?"

"I had some help from a Russian friend."

"I know. We spoke last night."

"We did? Oh, God! What did I say?"

"You don't remember?"

"Not really."

"It's all good."

She was quiet for a beat. Then she said, "Where are you now?"

"Thunder Gorge."

"You're very close to me."

Silence, again.

"Did you plan that?"

Widow stayed quiet.

DeGorne said, "Do you want to come over? Can I whip up a home-cooked MRE for us? For dinner?"

"I'd like that a lot."

She was quiet another beat, like she was considering what she was getting herself into by inviting him over to her place.

She said, "Yeah. Come on. I'll take another aspirin, and we can hang out, watch the fire tonight. From here, it looks huge."

"Sounds like a plan."

"So come on."

She clicked off the radio. Widow smiled and looked to the east. He could already see her tower. It was small and seemed farther away than his own lookout, but it was there.

He continued down the trail.

31

WATERMOTH AND COLLINS drove to Seattle, and Ryman followed. He stayed behind them and stayed within range. He never let them out of his sight, which was fine by Watermoth. She had strong suspicions of his motives ever since she first laid eyes on him. But she had been told to play nice. Also told to keep her guard up.

She could have ordered Collins to speed up, to flash the light bar on the roof of his Washington State Police Ford Escape, but she didn't. She didn't want to lose Ryman. She wanted to keep him at arm's length. But in separate vehicles. This way, she could speak with Collins without worrying about Ryman overhearing.

They drove into the city. It was twenty-one minutes past six in the evening. The California Wildfire was all over the cable news stations, the local news, and the radio. The fire had raged on for weeks. Over two hundred thousand acres of land burned. National Wildlife and Forest Fire-fighter teams had let it rage on as a controlled fire, necessary to purge and start over.

The anchors on Collins' radio said that Wildlife authorities feared the fire was headed far north into California Redwood country.

Plenty of kindling there for it to burn, Watermoth thought.

Collins said, "We're almost to your field office. Anything you want to say while Ryman can't hear you?"

"Not much to say. The DEA won't give us much on him or his function in the SWATters exactly. And Molly Lee seems to be a ghost."

"We asked everyone we can think of. No one knows much about her other than she lived there."

Watermoth shrugged.

She asked, "And you're sure your guys found nothing at Portman's house?"

"Nothing. House was empty. Ramas claimed his wife left him. Not too long ago."

"And where's she?"

"I told you. She's in Miami. With her sister."

"Sorry, been a long day."

"She hasn't heard from him. She sounded worried, though."

"Have Miami PD monitor her."

Collins turned the wheel into traffic, merged into the fast lane, and glanced at the rearview mirror. Ryman was tight behind him.

"He's good."

"DEA. They do a lot of tailing."

"I always thought their job was pretending to be buyers to bust drug dealers."

"Ninety percent of their job is probably surveillance. They are good at it."

"You think? What's it like being an FBI agent?"

"Ninety percent of my job is paperwork."

"That's basically my job."

"Not much difference."

"You sound like you don't like it?"

Watermoth said, "I love it. I'm sorry. It's not really all paperwork. That is a lot. It's ninety percent details. We spend a lot of time combing over details."

"Details, huh?"

He slowed and stopped at an intersection.

"You know how they say the devil is in the details?"

Collins looked over at her. She was staring back at Ryman in the passenger-side mirror.

"I've heard it."

"With the FBI, the case is in the details."

Just then, her phone buzzed and vibrated in her pocket. She pulled it out and pointed at the radio. Collins took it to be a signal for him to turn it down. He pressed a button on the steering column, and the radio's volume went to a low hum.

Watermoth looked at the caller ID. It was Smith.

"Go ahead, sir."

"Are you alone?"

"No. I'm with Collins."

"Who?"

"State Police."

"He trustworthy?"

"Yeah."

Smith said, "Fine. Where is Ryman?"

"He's in his own car. Why? What's going on?"

"I tried to dig into Lee and him. I called over to the DEA. I called the head of their department."

"And?"

"They're giving me the runaround."

"What else is new?"

"No. I mean, like the runaround. I've never had so much backlash for asking questions. They're giving us zero cooperation, at the same time telling me they'll cooperate fully."

"That's interesting."

"Tell me about it. And get this. I called above me. I asked my boss to request files on Lee."

"And?"

"The FBI director called me."

"What?"

"Our boss's boss's boss. You know. The guy who signs our Christmas cards every year?"

"He called you?"

"Yeah. He told me he'd take it as a personal favor if we'd stop asking questions about the SWATters and their crew."

"Really?"

"Yeah."

"Anything else?"

"He told me that the FBI's official tasks here are to find Molly Lee and recover Sheriff Portman, if possible. And to find and arrest the guys who raided his station house."

"How do we do that without investigating the connection with the SWATters?"

Smith said, "Then he told me unofficially that the SWATters might engage in covert missions over the Mexican border."

"What? Can they do that?"

"They can, with the assistance of the Mexican Federales. Apparently, they engage in assaults and raids on drug farms and compounds over there all the time. From what he told me, they aren't exactly by the book over there. Then again, over there, they're going by Mexico's book, which ain't by the book either.

"They play by dirty rules. They have to. The cartels aren't going by the Geneva convention."

"What kind of ops are the SWATters pulling over there?"

"If I had to guess, I'd guess everything from illegal interrogation to illegal surveillance, to assassinations."

"Assassinations? Of who?"

Smith paused a long beat. He said, "Watch what you say in your present company."

"Of who," Watermoth repeated.

"Of criminals. I hope. Anyway, it's not our business. But it could be connected."

"What if it is?"

"For now, Molly Lee is our main suspect and our only lead. It looks like she burned her house to the ground and escaped custody. Stick to her for now."

Watermoth wasn't satisfied with that answer. She stayed quiet for a second, and then let her better judgment speak for her.

She repeated, "What if it is?"

"Joanna, you see smoke, you smell fire, or you feel the heat, you get the hell out of there. You drop it. Got it?"

Watermoth stayed quiet.

"Listen, I got something else for you. It's a real lead."

"What is it?"

"Our guys pulled all the records on Molly Lee. Something interesting was that she filed her taxes separately. Or rather, a separate version was filed for her."

"What do you mean?"

"Turns out she's a federal employee. Which means the IRS already knows what she's paid. They're sent copies of her W2 and her paystubs. Well, it's already online for them to view."

"No one here has said anything about her having a job."

"Well, she did."

"What department?"

"United States Department of Agriculture. The United States Forest Service."

"What the hell does she do there?"

"I don't know. But it turns out that she wasn't using her married name. She goes by her maiden name."

"Which is?"

"DeGorne. Molly DeGorne. Look at her records. I sent them over to your office."

"We're almost there now."

"Good. Keep me updated," Smith said, and he clicked off the phone.

Watermoth slipped her phone back into her pocket.

32

WIDOW AND DEGORNE finished their dinner, which was an MRE, as DeGorne said it would be, and they stayed up sitting on the balcony of her fire lookout for two hours before he realized the time had passed.

They sat on a pair of matching, foldable lawn chairs. Widow's legs and feet stretched out so that his toes nearly hung over the side of the deck. DeGorne was far from having the same problem.

A wolf howled in the distance.

Widow asked, "How many damn wolves are out here?"

"I got no idea."

"It seems like every night they're up howling at the moon. And they're everywhere."

"It only takes one or two to howl enough for you to hear it constantly. You ever own a dog?"

"I like dogs."

"I asked if you ever owned a dog?"

"Once. When I was a kid, we had a dog."

"It has a name?"

He smiled and said, "Ronald."

"Ronald?"

"Yeah."

"As in McDonald's?"

"As in Reagan. You know, the fortieth President of the United States?"

"Why not call him Reagan then?"

Widow shrugged.

"I was only five years old when we got him."

"Anyway, Weirdo. Did he bark a lot?"

"Can't remember. Probably."

"That's what dogs do. They bark. Wolves. They howl."

Widow pulled a tin coffee mug up to his lips and took a drink from the rest of his third cup.

"Do you want more coffee?"

"Sure."

"You love coffee, don't you?"

"I do. Yours is better than mine."

"Danvers liked some kind of Egyptian coffee."

"Turkish. He has Turkish coffee. It's good, but not this good."

DeGorne rocked back once, pulled herself up to her feet with her momentum, and said, "I'm going to have something stronger. You want to share? Instead of the coffee?"

Widow stayed quiet, thought about her offer.

"I'm not much of a drinker."

"Look out there," she said and pointed out over the land to the distant wildfire.

Widow looked.

"How often will you have time to have a drink with a woman like me out in the middle of all this?"

"That's a good point."

She smiled and went indoors. A minute later, she came out with two rocks glasses. Both had three ice cubes. Both had vodka poured over the ice. She handed him one.

He took it, and said, "Can't say I ever drank vodka over rocks before."

"You sailors probably just shoot it, right?"

"In my youth."

"You're young now."

"Not like I used to be."

She raised her glass and offered it to him for a clink. He mimicked her gesture, and they clinked glasses.

"Cheers," she said.

They each took a sip.

Widow said, "That's stout."

"Oh, what? You can't handle it?"

"I was a Navy SEAL. I can handle it."

"You were NCIS and a SEAL? How does that work?"

"I had a long career."

DeGorne looked away, stared off over the balcony at the fire. She took a couple more sips and finished her drink.

She turned back to Widow.

"Want another?"

He said, "I'm still sipping this one."

"I'm having another."

She got up and went back into the tower. He listened, sipped his vodka. He heard the same sounds of ice, glass, bottle cap coming off, and new sounds.

First, he heard something coming off. Shoes, he figured. Then socks. Then he heard something soft. Something cotton. Something different. Like fabric dragging across the floor.

Behind him, the light in the interior of DeGorne's fire watch switched off.

A moment later, she came sauntering back out with a new drink in one hand and a thick, knit blanket in the other, casually dragging half behind her across the wood.

She reached her drink out to him.

She said, "Hold this."

He reached up, and she set it down on the palm of his hand like it was a tray. Then she grabbed her chair and dragged it over to him. She slid it armrest to armrest. She turned around and flicked the blanket outward. She let the wind pick it up. She sat down next to him, close. The blanket floated down on top of them both.

She tucked her knees up and in. She took the vodka drink from him, curled up next to him. She said, "Take your shoes off. Get comfortable."

He did as she commanded.

She said, "This is nice."

"It is. Very."

They stayed there for long, quiet moment. He listened to her breathing. He heard her heartbeat, felt it on his chest. He felt one of her hands on his leg.

They stayed there even longer, not talking, just sipping, and watching the stars, and watching the fire.

She said, "It's getting pretty late."

"Yeah."

Silence.

She said, "It's a long walk back to your tower."

"Yeah."

"You should stay here."

"You want me to?"

"I do."

Another moment went by. Another wolf howled in the distance.

She finished her drink and set it on the floor. She turned toward him. She took his glass away and set it next to hers. Then she stood up. She took the blanket with her.

"Are you coming?"

He stood up, cold, and shuffled into the tower behind him.

She waited in the middle of the room. The blanket was wrapped around her. Something wasn't right. Something was off. Something that wasn't bad. Just off.

Then he saw it. She was moving and shifting under the blanket.

He waited. He stayed quiet.

She stepped back, gently, toward the cot. He saw her pants and her top and her panties. They were on the floor. She moved behind the Osborne Firefinder. She stepped over to the side of the bed and tossed the blanket back like a bullfighter's cape.

She was completely naked and spectacular. Absolutely flawless.

She whispered, "Do you like it? Do you like it, Jack Weirdo?"

Widow nodded.

"I would stare at you over a million wildfires," he said. And he meant it.

"Come here?"

He came over to her. She sat back down on the bed. She reached over to him and used her fingers to undo his belt buckle. She took her time. She fought with his pants but got the zipper, the button, both undone. She slid his pants down to the floor.

Widow breathed in and breathed out.

She looked up at him, whispered, "Take off your shirt."

He did as he was told.

Her soft fingertips crawled back up his body. She explored every part of his skin, and he let her.

She stood up on tiptoes and whispered, "Kiss me."

Widow embraced her. He spanned his hand across her belly. He smoothed his hands around her waist until he was caressing her back. He pulled her into him and kissed her.

Her mouth was wet. He felt her tongue. He felt her hands move down his back, clawing him, gently.

They kissed for a long, long time.

Next thing he knew, he was on his back, on the bed, and she was on him.

The California wildfire raged on farther to the south.

33

WIDOW WOKE up naked in a beautiful woman's bed, and he didn't mind—
not one bit.

DeGorne was snuggled up to him, tight. She held onto him like no
other woman had before. He held her back. Out there, in the middle of
nowhere, it felt unlike anything he had ever felt before. She was
incredible.

He let the fingers on his one free hand brush her hair. He listened to her
breathing.

He must've watched her for forty minutes before she woke up.

Outside, he heard birds chirping, leaves rustling in the distance.

DeGorne's avocado eyes opened, slowly at first. Then all the way. She
stared at him—a slow tear formed in her eye.

"What?" he asked.

"Nothing," she said, and smiled up at him. "Good morning."

"Good morning."

She sniffled, and another tear formed out of her eye. It streaked slowly
down her face.

He brushed it away.

"What is it?"

"I haven't been with another man before."

He stared at her and asked, "Like a virgin? I thought you were married
before?"

"No!" she said, and laughed. "I mean with another man other than my husband."

"Oh."

"It's a good thing, Weirdo!"

She poked at his chest.

She stretched in his arms, fanned herself out over his body. Her feet didn't even reach his ankles, and her head barely reached his chin. She yawned a loud yawn. Then she leaned in and kissed him, a long, passionate kiss. As good as the night before, if not better.

Then she sat up and took the blanket with her.

Widow dragged his legs out of bed and stood up, tall. He stretched out his joints and bones and muscles. He felt the bones in his neck and back crack. He yawned—a big bear yawn.

He walked away from the bed, passed the Osborne Firefinder toward the sun in the east.

DeGorne watched him go.

She stood up and walked over to him. Her feet cracked as she walked across the floor. She dragged the blanket with her.

She stopped behind him. She stopped cold and stared at his back. She pawed at three small circular scars at the top and center of his back. They formed an uneven triangle, if connected.

She asked, "What's this?"

"That's nothing."

"What is it?"

"Scars."

"I see. But from what?"

"They're from a long time ago."

She was silent for a long moment. DeGorne had been told to shut up many times before by her husband. She was afraid to push. Afraid to ask questions.

But Widow wasn't like her husband. He was different. He was a good guy. She knew it. She felt it.

She said, "They look like bullet holes. Are they?"

He turned around to her, grabbed her, pulled her into him, tight.

"They are bullet holes."

Silence.

He said, "They were bullet holes. Once. A long, long time ago."

"You were shot? Three times? In the back?"

He stayed quiet. He didn't nod. He didn't blink.

"How are you alive?"

"Molly, it was a long time ago. And a long story."

She nodded and hugged him, squeezed into him. She couldn't reach her arms all the way around him. He squeezed her back.

"I feel safe with you."

He stayed quiet.

"Hey, what shall we do today?"

"Work?"

"We got all summer to do that."

He wouldn't argue about it. He asked, "What do you want to do?"

"I have one thing I need to do later. I have to go over to Forman's tower. I need to use the phone."

"Okay."

"You want to come with me?"

"Sure."

Silence.

Then he asked, "What should we do till then?"

She reached up to him and whispered, "I know what I want to do."

She kissed him, and they shuffled back to the bed, back to doing what she wanted to do, what they both wanted to do.

34

RYMAN HAD his feet up on an empty desk in the Seattle FBI field office, which was a place that he never imagined he'd be. His eyes were shut. His head back against a wall.

He sat at an empty desk in an unoccupied office cubicle. His Glock 21 stuffed in his pancake holster, but off his belt. It was resting on the desk in front of him. He wasn't pretending. He was asleep.

Collins was fast asleep on a sofa in an empty office. His suit jacket draped over him like a blanket.

Watermoth was awake. She was the first to wake up this time. And she liked it that way.

She was in her own office but could see the other two because most of the whole floor was nothing but offices and business machines and desks and a conference table, and all of it was separated by nothing but thin walls and glass windows.

Watermoth had woken up early because she had set her alarm on her phone to wake her up at five in the morning.

She wanted to wake up this early because the main office for the United States Forest Service's main headquarters opened at eight in the morning, and it was in DC, which was on East Coast time.

She made the call and waited and got an office line with an operator.

"The United States Forest Service?" the voice said. It was a woman's. Pleasant, and no-nonsense sounding.

"This is Special Agent Joanna Watermoth with the FBI out here in Seattle."

"Yes? How can I help you?"

"I need to inquire about one of your employees. It's urgent."

"Oh, dear. I hope everything is okay?"

"I'm sure it is. But I need to know what her job title is? And where she might be located?"

"I'll do my best," the operator said. "The office administrator from her specific branch will know better than I."

"Can you look her up and find out what branch?"

"Sure thing. What is her name?"

"Molly DeGorne."

The operator took a moment. And Watermoth heard typing on keys and clicking on the return button, and then several clicks of a mouse. She waited patiently.

The operator came back on and said, "Hold, please. And I'll transfer you."

Without a chance to respond, Watermoth was on hold and being transferred. Several minutes later, she got a voice.

"Mr. Tate's office."

"Tate?" she asked."

"Johnathan Tate of Forest and Parks?"

Then Watermoth took the time to explain everything all over again. Who she was, where she was calling from, and who she was looking for.

"No problem. Let me patch you through to Mr. Tate."

Another instance of not being able to protest a transfer. Then a male voice came on the line.

"Tate. Who is speaking?"

"Joanna Watermoth of the FBI."

"Good morning, Agent Watermoth. What can I do for you?"

"I'm looking for an employee. I need to know what is her job title and where I can find her?"

"Name?"

"Molly DeGorne."

"Molly? Is something wrong with her?"

"Do you know her?"

Tate said, "I've met her once. I speak to all of my fire lookouts at some point."

"Fire watch?"

"That's her job title. She's good. She's been with us for five years. I think."

"Is she at work this season?"

"She is. I think."

"Where can I find her?"

Tate said, "She's in California. North part. Working in Gray Wolf Mountain Park."

Watermoth said, "Thank you, Mr. Tate. You've been very helpful."

"Wait, Ms. Watermoth."

"Yes?"

"The park is hundreds of miles big. Don't you want to know which tower she's in?"

"Yes."

"Hold on. I'll look it up," Tate said. And he was gone for a moment. She heard the same rattle of fingers to keys and mouse clicks.

Tate came back on. He said, "She's in Tower Two Twenty-Two. Do you need me to send you a map? It'll list all the towers and their call numbers."

"Yes. That'll be great," she said. She gave him her email address and told him to send it there.

Then Watermoth asked him, "She got a phone out there?"

"No. There's a phone in the next tower over. Do you need me to call for her?"

"No. Please don't. We don't want anyone to know that we're coming. Can you give me the number for the nearest ranger? We may need his help."

"The only ranger who worked anywhere close to her has quit. I'm afraid."

Watermoth said nothing.

"I can scramble another one to meet you out there, but it'll take several hours to get there. A lot of my guys are embedded south because of the fire."

"Right, the wildfire. How is that fight going?"

"Bad. I'm afraid."

Watermoth said, "Send someone to meet us. We'll be there soon as we can."

"I can reach you at your Seattle office number?"

She gave him her cell number, and he wrote it down.

"Thanks, Mr. Tate."

Watermoth clicked off the phone and waited for his email.

If DeGorne was working out there as a fire lookout, then she wasn't going anywhere.

While waiting for the email, Watermoth balled up her suit coat and placed in on the desk. She laid her head down and fell asleep.

35

By noon, Sheriff Portman was nearly dead. And by thirty minutes after noon, he was dead. He had withstood hours of torture and waterboarding. The Leader was about to quit, about to give up on him, until the sheriff told him about the phone call.

The Leader walked up, out of the basement, and stood outside on the front lawn. He looked up and down the street. There were children riding bikes. He heard water sprinklers going off, spraying hedges, spraying flowerbeds at the neighbor's house. He heard dogs barking, and cars driving slow. And he heard the ambient chatter of every suburban neighborhood anywhere in America.

He took out his smartphone, saw that he had a missed call from Ryman.

He redialed Ryman's number.

"Yeah?" Ryman answered the phone.

"I got something," The Leader said. "Portman is talking."

The Leader told Ryman about the reckless plan that Portman had slapped together to help DeGorne. He told him about the life debt he felt he owed her dead father. He told him about the phone call he was expecting from DeGorne. He even told Ryman about her maiden name.

"That's good that you got Portman to spill the beans. But I got something better."

"What's that?"

"Forget about the phone call. I know where she is."

The Leader asked, "Where?"

"The FBI has found her. She's working as a fire lookout. In Northern California."

"She's a firefighter?"

"Not a firefighter. She's a fire lookout," Ryman said. He was driving, following Watermoth and Collins in his Tahoe. He stayed close behind them.

Ryman explained to The Leader what a fire lookout was.

The Leader asked, "Where are you?"

"I'm in traffic. We're headed to the airport now."

"Airport?"

"The FBI has a helicopter. We have to fly to where she is."

"Where is she?"

Ryman relayed to him the fire tower designated number that he had spied from a fax that Watermoth had received back at her office.

"Good work. I guess keeping you on the payroll has proven to be useful after all."

Ryman had no chance to respond because The Leader had hung up the phone. He looked at his watch. He calculated the time in his head. They would be better off attacking at night, but the FBI was already headed to pick up DeGorne.

But by the time they got a helicopter and made it six hundred miles south, it would be close enough to nighttime. So, he went back inside the empty house and told his guys to gear up. They were headed to the nearest airport, which was SEATAC. That's where they had flown to themselves after picking up the sheriff.

The Leader already had his own helicopter. It was parked at SEATAC Airport.

He told one of his pilots the coordinates that they were headed to. And then he remembered Portman.

The Leader walked through the kitchen and down to the basement, where Sheriff Portman was handcuffed to a pipe. He was shirtless and still wet from either the waterboarding or sweat or both.

He said nothing.

The Leader took out his Glock and suppressor and attached it. He pointed the gun at Portman, who looked up and stayed quiet.

The Leader shot him in the head.

36

Widow and DeGorne spent the next morning having coffee, having breakfast, and going over her tower's checklist. They showered together and went hiking to the south, where DeGorne showed Widow different caverns that Native Americans used as way-stations seven hundred years ago.

DeGorne told him that a couple of neighboring tribes would meet there for treaty negotiations and neighborly celebrations. He wasn't sure if the story was true or completely made up by someone who passed it down to someone and so on until she heard about it. But there were signs of ancient peoples using the caverns. There were ancient rock carvings and cave drawings that seemed to back up her story.

By the end of the day, Widow and DeGorne were on a wide trail headed farther from her tower.

DeGorne's mood had changed to a more serious one as the day went on.

Widow noticed she kept looking at her watch, and he asked her about it. She said, "I told you. I have to make an important phone call."

He didn't press her about it anymore.

They walked uphill and then down, crossed over a gulch, and found a shallow river. They hiked another two miles, following close to it. Then Widow saw a fire tower in an open field. There were phone lines he had seen earlier, but these crossed through trees and ended up on a telephone pole, and then wired right up to the fire tower.

"This is it," she said.

DeGorne sprinted up ahead and climbed the stairs to the tower.

The fire lookout who worked in this tower came walking out with a towel in her hands like she had been caught doing the dishes.

She came out and greeted DeGorne; Widow saw them hug. He walked up the stairs.

"Hello," she put her hand out to greet him.

"Jack Widow."

"Christine Forman," she said. He took her hand and shook it.

Forman was an older woman, in her sixties, at least, but she was healthy and fit. She wore khaki pants and a green sweater with a thin scarf around her neck. She had a straw hat on her head. She wasn't washing dishes. Widow could see she was painting the vista to the north.

There was an easel, a half-painted canvas, a coffee mug stuffed with paintbrushes, and a mixing palette of various colors. The rag she held was dirty from wet paint.

"You're a painter?" Widow asked.

"Yes. I am. Are you an artist, Mr. Widow?"

"Me? No. I probably couldn't even follow color by number."

She laughed and said, "So, you're the replacement for Danvers?"

"No, ma'am. I'm not replacing anybody. Just a stand-in. For now."

DeGorne looked at her watch again and asked, "Can I use the phone?"

"Sure, dear. You know where it is. Jack and I will stay out here and talk."

DeGorne went inside.

She closed the door behind her and went over to Forman's desk. She sat down and pulled up close, like she did when she drove. She picked up the phone, which was an old white landline thing. It wasn't a rotary phone but from the same era.

She dialed Portman's number from memory.

She waited for the dial tone to ring. It did.

She stared out the window to the southwest at the fire.

The phone rang and rang and rang.

No answer.

She hung it up and waited. Then she tried calling again.

No answer.

She felt her knees buckling and her stomach twisting.

Portman. Where are you? Where are you?

She set the phone back down on the receiver and waited another five minutes. Then she picked it up and called again. This time she let it go to voicemail.

DeGorne said, "Portman? Where the hell are you? It's been three days. Today is when you are supposed to answer me? I'm getting nervous here."

She paused a beat and listened to the silence. Then she said, "Call me back at this number. Tell the woman who answers that you want to speak to me. Tell her it's an emergency. And then wait for me to call you back!"

She hung up the phone and buried her face in her hands.

37

At Fire Watch Tower Two Twenty-Two, Widow and DeGorne sat out on the deck, quiet, finishing two more MREs. Chicken and rice this time.

Widow said, "Everything okay?"

"Yeah."

"You're quiet."

She said nothing.

"You've been quiet ever since we left Forman's. Did you get bad news?"

"No."

"Who did you call?"

She didn't answer.

He finished his chicken and rice and set them aside. He left the plastic fork and plastic knife in the bag.

He stood up and went over to her. He walked behind her and placed his hands on her shoulders. He rubbed them.

"You can tell me anything, Molly."

"I...I can't."

She stared off over the horizon, maybe at the fire, maybe at the coming darkness. Or maybe just into space. None of these options would've surprised Widow. She was acting like she had just gotten bad news and didn't want to tell him.

He said, "Is it your husband?"

She craned her head and stared up at him.

"What?"

"Your husband? Is it about him? Did he tell you something bad?"

She looked into him, anger in her eyes. He could see it. He had overstepped his bounds, maybe.

She jumped up and said, "Why did you bring him up?"

Widow shrugged and said, "I just thought..."

"You thought what?"

"You haven't said much about him. I thought that's who you were calling."

She turned away, placed her hands on the railing, and looked down over the side. For a moment, Widow thought she might jump. He had seen it before. But it would be stupid. A two-story fall probably wouldn't kill her. She'd break her legs or ankles or feet, but she'd live through it.

It wasn't a smart way to go. Then again, most people who committed suicide didn't use their brains to begin with, or they wouldn't do it.

He said, "Look, I'm sorry. I didn't mean to pry into your business."

She didn't speak.

"We slept together," he said and instantly regretted it.

Great, Widow! He thought.

"What? Why would you say that?"

"I'm sorry. I didn't mean to say it like I was throwing it in your face. I just meant that I deserve that you talk to me. I just want you to talk to me, is all."

She turned back to the horizon.

"I think you should go."

"Molly?"

"Just go. Leave me alone tonight. Okay?"

Widow shrugged. He sat back down on the lawn chair and put his socks and shoes on. Then he stood up and asked, "Can I use your toilet first?"

She waved him off and didn't answer. She didn't care. But he wanted to ask it, anyway.

He picked up his pack, readjusted the ice ax, and made sure the ax's cover was closed. He walked down the stairs and didn't look up at her. He stepped to the outhouse, left his pack outside, up against the wall.

He didn't really need to use the toilet. He wanted to splash water on his face. He stood over the sink and twisted the knob, got a handful of cold water, and splashed it on his face. Then he ran his cold, wet fingers through his hair, slicking it back.

He dried his hands with a towel and looked in the mirror. He saw the duffle bag jammed between the sink and the wall.

He figured she'd left it here because it was too heavy to drag up the stairs. Or it contained her personal items that she needed when she used the sink. Only her shower was around the other side. So why not leave the bag in there?

Curiosity got the best of him, or it was an old habit or his defenses. Whatever the reason, he opened the duffle. He stepped back, jaw dropped.

Inside the bag, he saw the money—lots of it. It was taped together and stacked into bricks of equal denominations. There were fifties and hundreds and nothing else.

He dug his hands into it, checked the middle and the bottom of the bag. It was all money, not money piled on top of something else. It was all money.

He zipped up the bag and lifted it and hauled it out of the outhouse.

DeGorne was standing there on the trail. She stared at him like she knew he would come out with it.

He said, "Molly, what is this?"

Then he noticed she wasn't empty-handed. Down by her side, in her right hand, was the Weihrauch Revolver.

38

"Put it down!" DeGorne said. She raised the revolver and pointed it at Widow.

He set the bag down.

"Molly. What is this?"

"You won't believe me," she said.

"Try me?"

"No! You won't believe me!"

"Molly, tell me!"

"I want you to go!" she screamed. "Just leave!"

Widow stayed where he was.

"I'm not going to hurt you. I want to know."

DeGorne stayed put. The revolver shook in her hand.

Widow stepped closer. He reached out and showed her the palm of his hand.

"Give me the gun, Molly."

"No!"

He stopped.

She said, "I want you to go!"

"Let's take a breath. Okay?"

She stayed quiet.

"That's a lot of money. Why do you have it out here?"

"It's mine."

"Okay, but why in cash? Why is it in a bag? Way out here?"

She stared at him. Tears rolled down her cheek. She lowered the revolver, took her finger out of the trigger housing.

She said, "I'm sorry."

He didn't move.

She said, "It's a long story."

"You can tell me. Whatever it is, I can help you."

She thought about it for a long, long second. Then she said, "I want to trust you."

"Trust me, Molly. I won't let you down."

She was quiet. And then she said, "I want to be alone. Just go back to your tower. I want to be alone tonight. I'll radio you later."

Widow wasn't sure what to do. He stayed there, staring at her.

"It's okay. I'll radio you later. I'm not going anywhere. We're miles and miles from anywhere. I'm staying here. I'll radio you later. I promise. Just let me be tonight."

Widow picked up the duffle bag and said, "I'll put this back."

She nodded and watched him do it.

He came back out of the outhouse and said, "Are you sure you don't want me to stay?"

"No. Just go back."

"Okay. Radio me. Whenever."

He turned and reluctantly left her.

39

WIDOW WAITED for DeGorne to communicate with him. He regretted leaving her alone. But what was he supposed to do? When a woman asks you to leave, you leave. Still, it didn't feel right. He wanted to call her. He wanted to go back there, talk to her. Hear what she had to say, but he figured she would tell him the whole story when it was right.

He spent the rest of the night going over the checklist that he could go over at night. Everything was good, as he expected.

Widow played with the Osborne Firefinder for a while, sliding the ruler around, peering through the slits in it. He aimed it at the wildfire to the south.

After he got bored doing that, he sifted through the audiobooks that Danvers had. He stuck one into the cassette player on the desk and cranked the volume. He heard a familiar voice that he had heard before, but he didn't know the name of the performer.

The book was one of Agatha Christie's. He listened for a while and then switched it off. He paced around the fire watch tower's balcony until he saw something that stuck out. In the distance, he saw something indistinct, shadowy, and dark, hovering in the air like a dark, flying machine.

He saw it yaw and ascend and circle around in a long, oval flight pattern. It might've been a helicopter. It was.

It was an NPS Papillion Helicopter. The words: *National Park*

Service was printed along the side. The helicopter hovered over his tower, and a spotlight switched on. They shined the light down on him directly.

He stared up at it. Then he saw a woman staring back at him from the cockpit, passenger side. She signaled something to the pilot, and they took off, switching off the light. They looked lost.

He watched them ascend and vanish over to the east.

* * *

THREE AND A HALF MINUTES LATER, Widow saw another helicopter, only this one wasn't a National Park helicopter. This one was a military Black Hawk. A UH-60. This one had no blinking lights, like the last one, like all helicopters were required to carry and turn on at night.

It had one headlamp on, dousing the forests with a cone of yellow light.

This helicopter did as the other. They yawed and hovered above his tower. He saw dark figures staring down at him. Then the helicopter realized he wasn't who they were looking for, so they took off.

He watched them, also heading east.

What the hell is going on? He thought.

Maybe they were searching for someone. That's what it appeared to be. But it wasn't him.

Just then, he looked to the east. DeGorne's tower, that was the direction they were heading.

He scrambled over to the walkie. It wasn't in the charger. He looked on the desk. It wasn't there. He searched the cabin. There was no sign of it. He looked in his pack. It wasn't there either.

He closed his eyes, tried to remember where he saw it last.

It was on the desk in DeGorne's fire tower.

40

WIDOW RAN EAST AS FAST as he could. He had to cover a lot of distance. He had snatched up the pack as he jetted out of his tower. He practically leaped down the staircase.

Halfway to DeGorne's tower, he had stopped to take a breath. His chest hurt. His legs hurt. He couldn't remember the last time he had to hump a pack through rough terrain like this at full sprinting speed. It must've been a decade in the past.

He grabbed a water bottle out of his pack and drank it down, crumpled up the bottle, and ditched it. He wasn't worried about littering. Then he took off again. He ran and sprinted as fast as he could without overheating.

The helicopters were both out of sight. He ran through trees. He ran for more than an hour. Then he came through a clearing and saw it.

He felt the heat first. Then he saw the fire.

DeGorne's fire lookout was up on the hill. It was engulfed in violent, powerful flames.

41

WIDOW WAS COMPLETELY out of breath by the time he reached the trail to DeGorne's fire tower. He stopped, saw the burning fire tower from over the trees. He saw the glass had blown out. The shutters dangled low on broken splinters of wood. They raged in the fire. The roof started caving in. The balcony was on fire. The stairs. All of it except the stone rock at the base.

Widow heard loud voices. He heard helicopter blades humming, slowing. He continued up the trail and stopped ten feet behind the outhouse. He stayed in the darkness. He slipped the backpack off, ditched it. He slid out the ice ax. The blade was a tool, but it could be a deadly weapon. Tonight. If he needed it to be.

He crouched low, knees bent. Elbows bent.

Silently, carefully, he stepped up the path behind the outhouse. He stopped, stayed out of sight. He heard the voices, muffled over the fire.

He peeked around the corner.

He saw the green NPS Papillion helicopter parked on its landing skids, out in front of the tower. The flames high above made the rotor blades shimmer as they twirled, reflecting the firelight.

Widow saw five people. They were cops—had to be. There were two men in plain clothes. One man in a park ranger uniform, like the one he'd seen Gordon wearing, only regular size. And there was a woman, early forties, athletically built. She was the best dressed of the four. And she was FBI. No doubt about that. Widow had seen enough cops and feds to know the difference. The FBI had a standard of how you dress and how you carry yourself that hadn't changed in nearly a century. Not really.

The park ranger was standing near the cockpit like he also flew the helicopter. Widow guessed he did, because there was no one else to be a pilot.

DeGorne was also there. She was alive, which was good news. She hadn't been in the fire tower when it exploded. But there was bad news too. The bad news was the FBI agent had her in handcuffs, stuffed in the helicopter's rear.

The voices Widow heard were them trying to arrest her. They argued with her and ordered her to surrender.

Why was the fire tower on fire?

And just then, Widow got his answer.

The Black Hawk flew overhead, fast, like it was making a pass. A pass like a bomber would make.

Widow witnessed the rear door slid open all the way. He saw two men in all black, like SWAT team gear. They hurled out two objects. They were round like baseballs. They had rugged, jagged edges etched into them, not like a knife's serrations, but more like in jagged rocks.

The baseballs flew to the ground. One went flying into the trees, just beyond the fire lookout—the other hit right underneath the nose of the parked Papillion helicopter.

The FBI agent screamed, "Look out!"

She turned and grabbed DeGorne by the underarm. She jerked her out of the helicopter, violently. Both women went tumbling backward to the ground.

Widow saw them roll out of sight, into the trees and the brush.

Just then, the first baseball turned out not to be a baseball at all. It wasn't a baseball because it exploded in a ferocious blast of heat and fire that was so hot it had blue outer edges and a white-hot center.

42

THE FIRST EXPLOSION lit up the trees, igniting them like they were nothing but kindling. Within seconds, fire consumed two whole trees and the brush below. Within minutes, it would consume twenty feet of forest.

The second baseball exploded, and it confirmed what Widow suspected. These weren't fragmentation grenades. They were incendiary grenades, which explode in a massive fireball. Flames are sent out in all directions, burning and fuming and killing everything.

The second grenade erupted fire all over the parked helicopter. The windshield exploded, and the glass shattered. The rotor blades continued to spin, but fire flew off the tips. The outer shell was all lit up, all of it blazed and raged, and a second later, black smoke plumed up over the trees and the clearing in front of DeGorne's lookout.

Widow lost track of the two women.

He scanned the surroundings for the three men. He saw one of them, the pilot. He was on the ground, bleeding around his neck and face. The helicopter had exploded right behind him.

Widow saw the other two men to the right. One of them was dressed like a detective. The other, he wasn't sure what he was. But the guy had a blood-red teardrop tattoo.

They had both been thrown by the exploding helicopter.

Widow listened. He heard the *whap, whap!* of the Black Hawk. It was coming back over for another pass. He rose and sprinted as fast as he could to the pilot. He scrambled across the field. No one saw him. Not yet.

He held the ice ax down low, right hand.

He made it to the pilot.

"Can you stand?" he shouted.

The pilot's eyes were shut tight. Blood soaked around his sockets.

"I can't see! I can't see!" he shouted.

Widow looked up, saw the Black Hawk returning. The same two men were hanging out the side—the same baseballs in their hands.

"We gotta move!" he shouted.

He grabbed the ranger by the back of the waistband of his pants, hauled him up to his feet, and shoved him forward to the trees. They ran past the fiery structure that used to be DeGorne's fire tower, past the outhouse, and into the dark trees beyond.

Behind them, Widow heard two more explosions. He felt the rush of heat spraying out behind him. He leaped into the trees, knocking over the pilot. They both hit the ground hard. The wave of blue fire barely missed them.

Widow said, "Stay down!"

The pilot didn't argue.

Widow looked back. The outhouse wasn't on fire. Flames ate their way to the generator next to it. Ten seconds later, like it was on cue, the generator exploded into a fireball of gasoline.

The rest of the outhouse exploded next. The wood crackled and splintered and burned.

And Widow saw the two other men who came with the FBI agent. They were next to each other, staring at the outhouse. Both of their jaws dropped.

Widow's jaw didn't drop because he had already known what was inside the outhouse—the money, which was now floating through the air and raining back down to Earth. There was lots of it. And it was all on fire.

43

THOUSANDS AND THOUSANDS of shreds of exploded, fiery cash rained down over the clearing. Widow didn't know how much had been in DeGorne's duffle bag, but he knew it was a lot. And it was all ruined now.

He also knew that whatever this was, whatever these two opposing teams of people with guns were, they were all here for that money. No question.

Maybe DeGorne stole it. He had no idea, but it didn't matter. Not to him. Not then.

What mattered was that the Black Hawk helicopter was landing. He watched it through the smoke. The machine came down.

The rotor wash sped up the falling money until now it looked like a huge whirlwind of cash. The money twisted and wound around and around, up into the air.

Widow shouted to the pilot, "Stay put!"

He didn't wait to listen to the pilot's objections. Instead, he reached down to grab the guy's gun off him, but there was no gun, just an empty holster. He must've dropped his gun in the explosion.

Widow picked up the ice ax and started running through the trees, staying in the darkness.

He didn't know exactly who anybody was. But he knew that the Black Hawk passengers were enemy combatants.

He slowed as he neared the landing zone. He stayed back in the trees and waited.

The helicopter stopped on three landing wheels, and seven men stepped out, including the pilot. They were dressed in SWAT gear from head to toe—all black. All wore lightweight Kevlar vests. They each had earpieces for close and quiet comms.

They had their faces painted. Black waves with dark green waves criss-crossed in between.

Widow waited. He listened for them to speak.

One of them did—The Leader. He spoke Spanish. They all did.

These guys were Cartel. Had to be. Widow had been in a firefight with cartel guys once. Not an experience that he had wanted to repeat. He had been down in Colombia. A Navy SEAL mission. A lifetime ago.

He remembered some of the intel from the briefing. The cartels had small armies. Everyone knew that. But they also had the best that money could buy. Mercenaries, mostly. And they provided them with major equipment. And drug cartels had a lot of connections.

If Widow had to guess, he'd wager these guys snuck into the country and then were given the Black Hawk from a military post somewhere. Maybe an Air Force mechanic looked the other way. Maybe they were only supposed to borrow it.

Whatever.

The seven men were armed with LAR-15s. And Glocks in side holsters. Serious weapons. Then Widow noticed something else. He hadn't noticed it before.

On the side of the Black Hawk were three letters, only they had been painted over.

He saw the remains of the letters: *DEA*.

44

WIDOW WATCHED as the Team Leader walked casually, the six men at his back. They walked over to where the two cops were. The two men came out of the path up ahead. The younger, clean-looking one was out front. He had a Glock in hand. The one with the teardrop tattoo stood behind him. Also, with a Glock.

They needed help. Widow had to do something.

The younger one held his gun up and shouted at the seven men.

"Freeze! Drop your weapons!"

The seven men kept walking toward him, their LAR-15s in hand, but pointed to the ground. They kept walking like they weren't afraid of getting shot. Not afraid at all.

Something was wrong.

The fire raged high above them, and the tower's legs buckled and crackled. Just then, the lookout tower broke at one stilt, and the whole thing came tumbling, crashing down to the west. It fell just twenty yards from the Black Hawk.

The team leader barked orders back at the last man in formation. He was the pilot, Widow figured. Widow's Spanish was basic, but he understood The Leader was ordering him to take the bird up and out of the path of the flames. They didn't want to be stranded out here.

The pilot turned and ran back to the bird, and Widow slumped back into the trees, staying low. He followed the pilot.

As the pilot reached the Black Hawk, Widow looked back. He saw something he couldn't believe.

The other cop, the one with the teardrop tattoo, shot the younger cop in the back.

45

WIDOW DIDN'T MOVE. He didn't shout or protest. He stayed in the dark. But he heard someone protest. He heard a woman shout from the forest. It was the FBI agent. He saw her. She was with DeGorne. Only DeGorne was still handcuffed. She looked terrified.

The FBI agent opened fire on the men. They started shooting back.

Widow couldn't help them empty-handed. He snuck up to the Black Hawk and hopped in the rear. The pilot was in his seat. He was flicking switches and checking gauges. The rotors hummed as they swung above. He was getting the bird ready for takeoff.

Widow didn't know how to fly. He thought for a split second maybe he should keep the guy alive. They might need him to fly them out of there.

But he shrugged and reared the ice ax all the way back. With all of his strength, he swung the ax forward. The blade stabbed right through the guy's pilot seat, right through his Kevlar. It ripped through leather, and springs, and bone. It burst through the guy's spinal cord, punctured his right lung, and broke through his ribcage.

Widow jerked it back out and watched the pilot flung forward. Blood spurted out a huge hole in his back. But the pilot didn't scream. He was already dead.

Widow was certain because his blood stopped spurting after several seconds. It just leaked out instead.

The guy's heart had stopped pumping.

Widow kept the ax in his hand, but he scooped up the guy's LAR-15, checked the weapon, checked the magazine. He also took the Glock 21 and checked it.

He stuffed the Glock into the waistband of his pants. He slung the LAR-15 around his shoulder and back with the strap. He wanted to keep the element of surprise. They were still seven guys strong, counting the teardrop guy who was a turncoat.

Widow slid out of the Black Hawk.

He saw the seven guys scattering into the trees ahead. They were chasing the FBI agent and DeGorne.

46

FIRE from the scorching tower and the trees burned and merged. Soon the fire would grow enough to be a major concern for the National Fire Service.

Black smoke fogged the ground. Widow stayed back in the trees and in the smoke. He kept the ax in his hand. He heard gunfire ahead, followed it.

He walked for five minutes into the smoke until he found a trail. He crouched low and listened. Occasionally, he'd hear gunfire up ahead. He heard the loud, echoing sounds of gunshots from LAR-15s, and then he'd hear the *pop, pop* of a Glock.

The FBI agent, he figured. Had to be.

How many rounds did she have left? How much longer could she fight back?

Widow kept going. After two more minutes, he reached the edge of the smoke. He saw a figure up ahead. Not one, but two. Two-man formation. They were separated from the group. They looked professional—trained men. But they weren't trained well enough, because they made one fatal error. They forgot to watch their six.

Widow crept right up on them. He got close to the one on the left. He reared the ice ax back and then heaved it forward like he was sledgehammering a nine-inch nail into concrete. The blow pounded right into the back of the left-hand guy. He didn't wait. He planted his foot on the guy's back as he went down and ripped the ax blade out. Blood splattered across Widow's chest and neck and face.

The right-hand guy spun around. He'd heard the cracking of bone and the wet sound of blood splatter. How could he not hear it?

He shone a flashlight attached to the end of his LAR-15. The beam washed across Widow's face.

The guy might've had time to react. He might've had time to get a shot off. It would've saved his life too. But he wasted his last seconds of life screaming. He saw Widow's face and screamed in utter horror.

Then he was dead. The ice ax cut his chest wide open. Widow left it planted there. The guy fell back. He was dead before he hit the ground. He had to be. There was far too much blood for him to have any left in his body.

Widow looked back at the left-hand guy. He smiled because he saw one incendiary grenade clipped onto the guy's belt.

Widow took it. He jerked the ice ax out of the right-hand guy's chest, and he continued forward.

He changed his route and stepped over between two huge redwood trees and walked the same direction as before. He saw lights up ahead. They were from the flashlights under the LAR-15s.

He heard more gunfire. It sounded like the Glock. It came from less than a hundred yards ahead. Maybe even fifty yards. Widow saw the muzzle flash over some hills, past more huge redwoods.

Widow sprinted forward faster. He panted. His body was worn and tired, but adrenaline surged through his system. He wasn't stopping.

He sprinted on until he got close to another guy. He could hear radio chatter. It was muted and quiet, like it came from an earpiece. By now, The Leader must've realized some of his guys weren't answering him.

Widow stopped and saw three figures in the dark. He crept closer, closing the gap between them. He got close enough to know it was the enemy. He saw the LAR-15s. The flashlight attachments. The black gear.

They walked in a three-man formation like the points of a perfect triangle.

Widow looked at the incendiary grenade and smiled. He pulled the pin, tossed it right in the middle of them. Then he whistled to get their attention. He ducked behind a tree.

They opened fire at him. But they got few shots off because five seconds later, they exploded in liquid fire. Skin ignited. Bones burned. The heat was so intense; he had heard of victims having their eyes explode in their sockets.

He wasn't sure about that. He peeked out from behind the tree and saw one guy still all in one piece. Still alive. He danced around like he could escape the fire. But he couldn't.

Widow took the ice ax, reared it back like a professional knife thrower. He threw it at the guy, hard. The ax blade tore right into the guy's fiery center mass. He went flying back off his feet.

Widow left the ax right where it was.

He took up the LAR-15 and left it in single-fire mode.

He stalked through the trees. He counted the paces in his head. Then he counted the dead bodies. The pilot, the two he killed with the ax, and the three with their own grenade. That made six down. And two left.

Widow stopped and squatted on his feet. He looked around, waited. Everything was quiet. Then he saw gunfire from a Glock. Then it stopped, suddenly. She was out of bullets.

47

Widow sprinted downhill. He ran between more trees and over foothills. He heard a wolf howl in the distance, off the mountain. He realized this was as close to the mountain as he had been.

He moved on until he lost the last position of the gunfire. He squinted his eyes and scanned the area—nothing.

He waited. Then he heard voices. He heard shuffling feet.

He turned and followed it.

Forty-seven seconds later, he was hugging close to a redwood. He looked around it and saw the FBI agent, her hand up in the air, surrendering. He saw DeGorne on her knees, her hands still handcuffed behind her back. Tears streamed down her face.

Both women were trapped under a high gorge. Tall trees hung thirty feet above them.

The FBI agent's Glock was on the ground at her feet. The chamber exposed. It was fired empty.

DeGorne pleaded and begged for her life.

"The money! You can take it! Take all of it! I should've never stolen it!"

The FBI agent stayed quiet.

Two men stood over them. Both armed with Glock 21s. The Leader had a LAR-15 strapped to his back, but he wasn't planning to use it. Not in close quarters.

DeGorne said, "Please, Danny! Please! Let us go! We won't say anything!"

The FBI agent stayed quiet, stayed still.

The Leader spoke into a receiver pinned to his collar. In Spanish, he said, "We got them."

Which Widow understood well enough.

But he got no answer.

Then he said, "Pedro! Come in!"

No answer.

Widow wouldn't get a better chance. He set the LAR-15 down against the tree and drew the Glock. He stepped out, aimed. But just then, The Leader turned around, saw him.

Several fires burned behind Widow, lighting him up from the back.

"Danny!" The Leader shouted in English.

The Leader fired his Glock in Widow's direction.

48

WIDOW DROPPED TO ONE KNEE. He heard wood from the tree splinter behind him. Several shots rang out from the Team leader's Glock. The bullets exploded bark from the tree behind him on impact.

Shooting guns at live enemy targets wasn't about speed. That was a factor, but it was low on the totem pole of what was important. What was important was staying calm and breathing and staying steady and being accurate.

Widow wasn't the fastest shooter, but he was calm.

He aimed at the team leader. He squeezed the trigger twice. *Bang! Bang!*

Both bullets hit The Leader right in the neck and face. He tumbled backward in a heap.

The one called Danny didn't shoot back. He was a different man. He thought on his feet, only he thought about protecting himself, like a coward. He leaped forward and spun around DeGorne. He grabbed her by the hair. He got a handful of her long locks and jerked her to her feet. He held her close to him like a human shield.

Widow moved his arms, aimed at the one called Danny.

"Ryman! Let her go!" The FBI agent shouted.

"Shut up! Shut up! You should be dead! All of you!"

Widow rose to his feet, slowly. He stepped forward.

"Stay right there! Or I'll put a bullet in her! I swear!"

Widow stopped dead, fifteen feet from them.

"Danny, listen to me! No one knows what you've done here! No one but us! You can still get out of this!" The FBI agent said.

She was good, Widow thought. She was brave.

"Drop your gun!"

Widow stayed still, aiming through the Glock's sights. He saw Ryman's forehead, ducking, shaking, trying to stay behind DeGorne.

DeGorne stared at Widow. Her avocado eyes were huge with fear.

He stayed quiet.

"Drop it!" Ryman shouted, and he made a mistake. He made the mistake that Widow hoped for. He jerked DeGorne's hair. That long, Rapunzel hair. He pulled it so hard that her head whipped back with it. Her shoulders tightened, and her head ducked down, and Ryman's face became a bigger target over her shoulder. It was only a second, but it was good enough.

Widow squeezed the trigger, and the Glock fired. The muzzle flash was bright in the darkness. The bullet rocketed through the space between them and hit the dead center of Ryman's teardrop tattoo. It blew a small, dark hole into his face. The bullet never came out the back of his head. And he never said another word because a split second later, he was on his back, dead in the dirt, in the middle of nowhere.

A man that Widow had never met, never spoke to, never knew, was now dead by his hand. And he didn't give him a second thought.

DeGorne ran straight at him, her hands still handcuffed behind her.

Widow held her close.

"It's okay. You're safe now," he whispered.

She didn't move. She just stayed there, her face buried in his chest.

The FBI agent walked over to him.

"I'm FBI Agent Joanna Watermoth. Who are you?"

Widow said, "Me? I'm just a guy. I'm no one."

49

Special Agent Joanna Watermoth was called and apologized to and congratulated by the director of the DEA himself. On the phone, of course.

He told her that Ryman was a bad egg. And not to judge his guys based on one rogue agent. He told her that the SWATters had always been a bad idea. They had become corrupt, but the corruption stopped at Mike Lee and Danny Ryman.

Apparently, they had been getting kickbacks from the cartel. They were paid to look the other way, at first. Eventually, the payments got bigger, and the crimes got worse.

The DEA director swore to clean up that department. They disassembled the SWATter team and reassigned all the agents. By the end of the year, Watermoth heard the director had resigned. It was all over the papers. It was scandal related.

Agent Watermoth was promoted to her old SA's job. And Smith was moved to a new field office, the same job.

* * *

As for Jack Widow, only one person knew where he was. After the last bullet was fired, the authorities were notified by a fire watch lookout named Forman. She had seen the explosions from her tower, and she had the only telephone.

When the FBI arrived and took in Agent Watermoth, they also took Widow and DeGorne. They were all choppered to a hospital in Sacramento.

Widow and Molly DeGorne vanished from the hospital. It was like they never checked in.

They did checked in somewhere, just not in the hospital. They checked into a hotel on Bay Street. And they didn't check out for three whole nights.

SCOTT BLADE

A **JACK WIDOW** THRILLER

THE LAST RAINMAKER

DRIFTER. OUTLAW. HERO.

AUTHOR'S NOTE

A decade ago, Hong Yeoja, then a young girl of fourteen, fled the clutches of a horrifying reality in North Korea. But her journey only began there. She trekked across miles of frozen river, evaded armed North Korean border patrols, desperately bartered with corrupt Chinese officials, evaded human sex traffickers, and endured through despair and consuming urges of suicide.

It took her, her sister, and her mother two years to escape to the United States.

To freedom.

Currently, she is alive and well with a husband and son.

Hong Yeoja isn't her real name. It means Jane Doe.

I thank her for sharing her story with me and leave her in peace.

1

THE SNIPER'S scope was trained on the target at an incredible range. Impossible for ninety-nine point nine percent of the world's population, with an infinite number of nines after that.

Not for James Lenny. He was a man in the most elite sniper club imaginable.

Lenny was British, mostly. He had some Irish in there and some Scottish on his mother's side. Maybe there was some Welsh, but British was how he identified himself.

He was a little worn around the middle, not much, but a little. He considered himself to be in decent shape for a man his age. His fifty-fifth birthday was only five days away. He wasn't looking forward to it.

He stood six feet tall, only not then, because right then he wasn't standing.

Lenny lay prone on a worn, heavily threaded sniper mat that had seen a lot of action, a lot of wartime, a lot of desert floors, and a lot of other various types of dirt.

His legs were apart, feet apart—an open scissor position—elbows planted in the dirt, feet and toes turned awkwardly so that the arches were flat against the ground. Bright orange earplugs jammed in both ears. He wore a hunter-green camo Castro hat turned around backward to keep it from obstructing his aim. He wore camo pants to match and a black T-shirt under a dark canvas jacket. A pair of sunglasses were folded and stored in a case on the edge of the mat.

The sun beat down from high above him. He didn't worry about it interfering with his target.

Woodland sounds surrounded him, calm, atmospheric, almost hypnotic. Old-world flycatchers cawed in the distance. Their wings fluttered in the wind. Leaves blew and quivered. Clouds were sparse in the sky above. There were no signs of rain—not yet, which was good for a cool, Irish spring day. The green of the land was everywhere, to the point of being all-consuming, nearly overwhelming, enveloping, like being inside of an emerald.

Lenny's body was completely still, his left hand wrapped around his right shoulder, where the stock of an Arctic Warfare Magnum rifle was nestled, a measure of reinforcing the sniper shot.

He was ready to take the shot. Ready to squeeze the trigger. Ready to explode his target into a million wet, red, fleshy pieces.

The AWM, also known by its technical designation as the L115A3 sniper rifle, was Lenny's rifle of choice. Nothing beat military instruments manufactured from the UK, in his opinion. Snipers are notoriously brand-loyal, patriots are country-loyal, and he was both.

The Americans also made pretty good weapons, he thought. *Sometimes.*

For military munitions, the Americans were among the best. Right there with the Germans. Both second to the British.

He would never admit that to any of the American soldiers he knew, of course, or to the Germans. And he certainly would never disclose that opinion to any of the guys from his old sniper unit.

Not that any of them took his phone calls anymore.

He could understand why. His post-traumatic stress disorder made him socially awkward, a little hard to be around. He could see that. It wasn't lost on him.

He tried not to focus on that. It was pointless now. He focused on the thing he loved most in the world, his rifle.

The AWM was a bolt-action sniper rifle, great for extremely long-range shooting, and completely wasted at any other range.

His AWM was chambered with a Magnum round. The Magnum bullets made the weapon system more terrifying to his enemies than regular bullets.

Sure, a regular bullet fired from his rifle would kill a man. But a

Magnum would destroy him. It would blow a target apart. It would make identifying the body nearly impossible.

Imagine the destructive force of a Magnum combined with the extreme range of an AWM rifle. The combination of the two made survival after getting hit by one round a miraculous act of God. A man who walked away from such a devastating shot was nothing short of immortal. Plain and simple. No one survived a bullet like that.

No one.

Superman couldn't survive a bullet like that. Man of Steel, meet the bullet that tears through steel.

Lenny and the mates from his old unit used to have a running joke.

Only God survives the bullet from one of their rifles.

Something like that.

The thought made him smile. Made him nostalgic for the good old days.

The AWM was his favorite for those reasons and a few others. But mostly it was because he had used the same gun, the same weapon system, way back in his military days. It was like an old friend.

It got him an impressive kill count—the best in the world once upon a time, a limited time.

It was his favorite possession in the world.

The most important thing in combat was his rifle. The most important thing in his life was his rifle.

The second most important thing?

His boots.

He wore a brand-new pair of combat boots. Unlike the rifle, he liked to update his footwear regularly. Nothing destroys your chances for success in the field like broken-down, worn-out, faulty footwear. He had learned that the hard way ten years ago in Afghanistan. Not personally, but one of his squad mates, his best friend, had been complaining about his boots sticking him in the bottoms of his feet.

The guy was always rubbing the soles of his feet at night before bed.

One morning, at sunrise, he jerked the insoles out to make them more comfortable, more accommodating for their mission.

Later that morning, his unit was clearing out a cluster of abandoned structures, and the guy got himself shot because he turned a corner and inadvertently stumbled down a hidden incline. He had no grip in his shoes, so his feet were slack inside.

The combination of loose gravel and no grip led him to his death. He ended up on his back in a circle of concealed insurgents, five guys in total.

All armed with AK-47s abandoned way back in the eighties by fleeing Russian armies.

He found out the hard way that AK-47s were every soldier's worst nightmare in that part of the world.

The AK was a reliable weapon, a very reliable weapon. Lenny had heard stories about Afghan fighters discovering them buried in the sand. They had dug them up after twenty-plus years. Ten times out of ten, they worked the same as the first day off the factory floor, making the Kalashnikov family one of the most powerful weapons manufacturers in the world.

They had no equal.

Before Lenny and the rest of his squad could get down to their teammate, the guy was dead, filled with countless 7.62 millimeter boat tail bullets and countless bullet holes.

It was a massacre.

Lenny could never look at Swiss cheese the same way again.

Of course, his unit took care of the insurgents in a take-no-prisoners kind of way. They killed them all. British ammunition. British weapons. British fingers squeezed triggers and left the enemy lifeless—the British way.

Directly behind Lenny's boots was an unmanned spotter scope set up on a tactical tripod. The tripod's legs were extended all the way out and planted firmly in the dirt between lush green blades of grass.

At the base of the tripod, there was a clipboard and an expensive pen. The clipboard was covered with technical information about the shot, the target, the direction, and the wind—all nice and neat.

The technical info was in Lenny's handwriting.

The spotter scope was unmanned, and the writing was all his, because Lenny was all alone out there, the way he liked it. This made his shooting take longer than it would if he had a spotter with him. But it also made the range much more challenging. That was what he looked for—a challenge. He wanted to recapture a long-distance shot that he had made once before. Only once. And only back in Afghanistan.

No, he wanted to surpass it. He wanted to beat the new world record. It was rightfully his.

It should've been his. He used to be seen as a hero. The guys in his elite sniper unit used to look up to him. They had worshipped him. He was the guy who shot the world record. He was a king. A god. A man who deserved to be up on the wall.

That had all faded away. That was all crushed.

At first, they acted like they felt sorry for him. At first, some of the new guys still looked up to him.

Now they had forgotten him.

Lenny had no one to spot for him. Besides, part of him wanted to do it without the help of a spotter, unlike the current record holder, who used a military spotter.

And he wanted the world to know it. That was why he also had two Canon XA11 high-definition video cameras on tripods. One was planted to the right of the AWM's barrel, about a meter away. It was on and recording and focused on him. His face, the weapon, and his body from his knees up were visible and in frame.

Then at the end of the range, focused on the target, was an identical camera. This one was angled behind the back of the target so that the muzzle flash from his shot would register with the actual explosion of the organic target.

Everything was set. The only issue Lenny had now was that his mind continued to wander, which was part of his PTSD. Ever since being discharged against his will, he'd had a problem keeping his mind on the task at hand.

He had been married once, but that hadn't worked out either. Now he was alone.

He shook off the regrets of the past and stared through the scope, his safe place. He watched the target. He took long, deep breaths until he slowed his heart rate. He was in no hurry.

The wind blew, lighter than normal. He was positioned in high, lush grass on the apex of a hill, which was the only way to be accurate at the great distance in front of him. He needed the hill, the downward slope, and the curvature of the Earth to make a shot this far away.

Most of the terrain around him and between him and the target was grassy. There were mountains far to the west which started with groups of pebbles that turned into stones that turned into boulders over the course of two thousand–plus yards. There were trees to the west, the south, and the east. Behind him, about two hundred yards, was a cluster of thick trees just beyond the gravel road.

The road was the only way in or out. Lenny's four-by-four truck was parked between him and the road, about fifty yards back.

Lenny watched the target, held his breath. His index finger on his right hand squeezed the trigger back slowly. Then he felt the powerful kick of the gun as the .338 Lapua Magnum round rocketed out of the muzzle. A devastating long-range bullet, and his favorite.

The AWM bucked and kicked hard, and the bullet was off.

The gunshot *cracked!*—echoing across the landscape like a thunderclap.

Lenny watched through the scope at the target.

The target was a ten-pound overripe watermelon, with a huge bullseye spray-painted on it in red. He had trucked it in the bed of his pickup, trucked it down the range on a dirt motorbike, also in the bed of his truck.

Nine other melons remained stacked in a crate, waiting their turn. He planned to shoot only eight more today; the last one he was going to take home and enjoy—a celebration for accomplishing the unaccomplishable.

To be honest with himself, however, he had attempted to break the current record many, many times before. And each time, he had gone home with a watermelon that he couldn't enjoy. Symbolic. He'd ditched the watermelon out in the street, leading to his house. The neighborhood dogs got plenty of watermelons to eat year-round.

This time, he felt, would be significant. This time he would get the bullet on target.

Lenny breathed out, forgetting that he had been holding his breath for a moment.

The bullet had traveled a distance of more than twenty-seven hundred yards, and it missed. Not surprising. Just disappointing.

He looked once again through the scope and checked the watermelon, checked the red-painted bullseye. He could see the melon stuck on a six-foot stake in the ground. He saw the curved green shell, the red paint, the bullseye. He saw the stake. Nothing had been hit by the bullet. All of it swayed in the wind but remained whole and intact.

He racked the bolt on the rifle back, withdrew the brass, rested it back in an open box of .338 Lapua Magnums beside him. He never left them out in the field, even if it was his personal practice range. He believed in recycling. Besides, he was taught not to leave a trace of where he had been. Not that he was up to no good at the moment. But old habits die hard.

Lenny racked the bolt again. The magazine sprung the next .338 bullet up and into the chamber. Lenny moved his head away from the scope for only a moment and removed his left hand from embracing the stock. He let the AWM rifle slope back; the barrel tilted up on the bipod and faced the sky in a forty-five degree incline. He never let go of the stock. He used his left hand and grabbed an open bottle of water, took a pull from it, and placed it back down on the northwest corner of the mat. Then he returned to his firing position.

He breathed in deep and breathed out slow. He repeated this once again. Then he slowed his heart rate again.

Adjusting the scope's elevation and parallax and focus knobs, he saw something else.

Sudden. Unexpected.

It popped out at him, startled him.

The watermelon and the stake were dug in at the foot of a two-hundred-eighty-yard slope, with a dirt wall more than twenty yards behind them. A standard safety precaution to keep the bullet from traveling beyond the intended target and accidentally hitting a pedestrian, which would've been bad on many levels, primarily because the bullet would kill the person.

Lenny had never heard of anyone surviving a .338 Magnum round before, not once. The best-case scenario was getting an arm or a leg blown off without damaging the center mass. A center mass hit was a kill shot, guaranteed—no walking away from that.

The second worry that Lenny had, just as loud in the back of his brain, was that his rifle was illegal in Ireland. Although, he was way out in the countryside, about fifty miles west and slightly north of Cork, Ireland. He was in a rural area, where the authorities were more likely to overlook the possession of an illegal firearm, being that every family within fifty square miles had firearms on their property. Still, it wasn't a legal weapon. Not for him. Not with his PTSD.

He couldn't help but feel the fear of getting caught with it. War hero or not, he would get jail time. No doubt.

Lenny moved his finger away from the trigger in case the movement he saw was another human being. He didn't want whatever it was to startle him again. He might squeeze the trigger accidentally. And kill someone. He didn't want that. He had enough problems.

Another strange thing was that he was far from the nearest village and at least five miles from the nearest farmhouse. So who the hell would be out here?

He looked through the scope, adjusted it again. He repeated all the same steps to bring it into focus. He veered the rifle up and stared over a ridge into the trees beyond. It must've been almost four thousand yards. Farther than he had ever fired accurately before.

He saw a sparkle of light flash. It was quick, like someone was signaling to him with a flashlight or a mirror. Then he saw it again. It was not a flashlight. It was a reflection, maybe a mirror.

What the hell? he thought.

He adjusted the sights and the zoom and the focus again. Something came into focus. He saw a figure lying above the lip of the ridge, behind the watermelon, far in front of the tree line. Someone was lying prone on the ground, looking back at him.

How the hell had he not seen him before?

The figure was blurry. He adjusted the scope again until he could see more detail.

He saw the shadow of the figure on the ground, like a heap. It was small and tight. Then he saw the reflecting surface that flashed at him. He saw it clearly. It was the glass end of a rifle scope—the wrong end.

It flashed a reflection at him once again. He breathed in heavily.

He saw one last flash from the rifle; only it didn't come from the scope.

Seconds later, maybe less, he would never know for sure. He would never know, because right then, James Lenny's rifle scope exploded, and a bullet ripped through it and blasted out the back of his head. His skull exploded. Deep red mist sprayed out along with parts of the front of his brain that had mashed into the back of his brain.

From a bird's-eye view, Lenny's clothes and back and a couple of feet past his sniper mat—everything was painted red.

His head had been blown back by the force of the bullet in one quick whiplash, and then his neck muscles had whipped it forward like it was spring-loaded. His empty right eye socket beat against what remained of the scope and stayed there.

* * *

THE SNIPER, almost four thousand yards away, stayed down for a long moment, watched through the scope until there was no sign of Lenny getting back up.

The sniper stood up slowly, picked up a pair of field glasses and zoomed in on Lenny's position, saw the damage, saw the red mist wafting in the air like a smoke plume that wouldn't die.

The sniper smiled, then turned back to the rifle and disassembled it in seconds. The rifle fit neatly into a black backpack—the stock, the weapon system, the magazine, the bolts, the barrel, and a box of ammunition, all of it. It all had a place in the backpack because the backpack and the rifle were built and designed together.

After it was all reduced to smaller parts, the sniper zipped up the backpack, rolled up the sniper mat, took off a pair of black shooting gloves, and set off to the kill to take a photograph of the dead body for a keepsake.

2

FOUR THOUSAND MILES away and twenty-five miles southeast of St. Mark's Memorial Hospital at the center of Minneapolis, Jack Widow rode the Empire Builder, a long, historical passenger train, departing from Seattle first, then easing away from the Emerald City, mostly threading parallel with the Canadian border and winding along only hundreds of miles from it. The train passed through the Cascade Mountains, raged across heavy tracks over the Columbia River Gorge, twisting through Glacier National Park, baking across sandy low and high deserts, barreling through endless grassy fields in Big Sky Country, and traversing the plains of North Dakota.

Remnants of a long, cold winter persisted for half the trip out of Seattle, and finally relinquished a little of their hold on the land at the last leg of Widow's forty-six-hour trip from Seattle to Chicago.

Widow had walked the train several times, eaten in the dining car, slept twice in the sleeping car—two full seven-hour cycles—gone to the bathroom several times, and showered twice—the second time in his clothes, to clean them. After the last shower, he stepped into the sleeping car in the daytime to avoid sharing a car, and hung his clothes over the side of an empty bunk across from him to dry. He lay down on the opposite bunk and closed his eyes.

When he woke, the car was still empty. No one had entered to bother him. Perhaps the sleeping car attendant had checked on him once or twice without him noticing. Normally, Widow wouldn't have believed that anyone could sneak up on him in his sleep, but after meeting the staff, he knew differently. They were professionals. The sleeping car attendants were as quiet as church mice.

They should teach classes in Navy SEAL school, he thought.

Widow had served with top-notch SEALs who made more noise on covert raids.

After his clothes had dried enough, he put them back on and returned to the spot where he'd spent most of his thirty-eight hours so far—the Sightseer Lounge car.

Widow sat in the same chair most of the time. It was in the back corner, south side, which gave him a good view of things coming and cut it off after they passed.

He drank coffee, which wasn't the best in the world, but probably the best he had ever had on a train. It ranked up there with the best he had ever had in his life regarding freshness. It was like they made a fresh pot every time he wanted a refill, which was a lot because the cups were these dainty, white ceramic things, which probably cost fifty bucks apiece. They looked more like fancy British teacups than coffee mugs. Widow seemed to remember a similar design and pattern and trim when he'd visited Buckingham Palace once in another life.

The grip was so incredibly tiny that Widow could barely fit his pinkie finger through it, joint to fingernail, before it got stuck. These were clearly designed for smaller people.

The lounge car attendant served the coffee on little saucers to match. They clinked when the coffee cups contacted the small circular surface. The lounge car was relaxing and quiet, in the way a café can be relaxing and quiet. All he heard were the ambient sounds of clinking coffee cups, the tinkling of stirring spoons, and the low murmur of surrounding conversations.

The car wasn't full, but it wasn't empty either. Widow would guess that it was nearly half full of like-minded passengers who'd rather spend their time staring out the window, sipping coffee, and sharing life stories with fellow passengers over sitting back in coach.

Widow knew little about train design or train engineering or train construction. He considered himself a layman in terms of details of the processes involved in building a train like this one. But he wasn't completely in the dark about the Empire Builder. He liked to learn things. Life is boring without constant new information.

Widow had read a thick booklet about the Empire Builder that the lead attendant had retrieved for him. It was a courtesy gift.

The lead attendant had told him so. He had told him he was free to keep it, but if he wouldn't keep it, then he should return it when completed. It turned out that Amtrak used to hand them out like candy, but most people trashed them or left them behind or used them as coasters, leaving coffee rings on the cover. The booklets were expensive to make, expensive to maintain. So when the publisher hiked up the prices and Amtrak started losing business, maybe ten years ago according to the lead attendant, corporate had no choice but to limit the books to purchase-only. The lead attendant kept a handful of them to loan them out. It was an extra little touch that he added to the experience. He said that occasionally he met a passenger like Widow, who was alone, who took the train more out of tourism than travel, and he would offer the booklet if the passenger showed interest.

Widow set the Empire Builder booklet on the tabletop in front of him. He sat in the Sightseer Lounge, stared out the panoramic windows to the south, watched rolling hills in the distance, saw storm clouds a few miles after that, and swiveled his head to the north, looking past empty seats and empty tables, and out the large windows.

He had noticed that most of the people who were in the lounge car stayed away from him. He wondered about it for a moment, and then he let it pass.

Widow was a tall guy, six foot four, and two hundred twenty pounds, all natural muscle. He had dark features, short dark hair, and a slight beard to match. He had been told that his eyes were both welcoming and terrifying. They were ice blue. To be honest, this was something that he used to his advantage when the situation called for it.

Like back in California when he'd met a woman named Molly DeGorne. With her, he had used his eyes to portray trust, intimacy, and friendliness. But with his enemies, he offered a different look. A look that wasn't friendly. But he wondered if his eyes were a factor in why the other passengers had sat far away from him. Maybe they did. Maybe they didn't. Maybe it was because he had taken off a black leather bomber jacket and rolled up the sleeves of a blue long-sleeve knit shirt to reveal a pair of sleeve tattoos. Both arms. Both colored in red, white, and blue—American flag designs draping over his forearms and wrists. Tattered, ripped, and torn flags. They represented battle flags from a lifetime ago.

To the onlooker, they were tattoos. To Widow, they were symbols, like scars, in a way. He saw both his tattoos and his scars as symbols. They were reminders, mementos of past lessons and past friends.

It was reasonable that the other passengers avoided sitting near him because of the way he looked, his size, his tattoos, or his eyes—whatever it was. He understood all of it. People judge other people by the way they look, books by their covers and all. It wasn't just an American thing; he had been judged all over the world.

No big deal.

Widow stared down at his watch. The time was eleven past midnight. The wristwatch reminded him of a woman because he had picked it up, secondhand, at a military consignment store back in Seattle, after saying goodbye to Molly DeGorne.

He had stuck around with her for a while after the events at Gray Wolf Mountain National Park, after the cops told her she could return home.

But she had no home to return to. It turned out that it had been burned to the ground before he met her. So they rented an apartment north of the city center, a nice area, overlooking the Puget Sound. DeGorne seemed happy for a time. Widow was happy for a time as well. Before they knew it, a week had gone by, and then two more days, and then the inevitable happened.

The honeymoon was over. Reality slapped them in the face like a crack from a baseball bat. Widow had experienced it several times before, but it took him by surprise every time. It shouldn't have.

He was a nomad. By definition, Navy SEALs are violent nomads. It's one of their common nicknames. They trained to embrace the life of being far out in the field for long stretches of time without support, without communication, without orders. And Widow had been an undercover NCIS agent, embedded with the SEALs, the first of his kind. He had endured very long stretches of being out in the cold.

It was hard at first, but by the time he retired from the SEALs and quit the NCIS, it had become a lifestyle that he couldn't let go of.

DeGorne had to reboot her life after she lost everything. At first, she wanted Widow to be in it. But the reality had caught up to her too.

Her husband had died. Her house was gone. She was reborn, making a fresh new start. She didn't want a man to take up a significant portion of it.

She wanted her freedom. She'd told Widow that, the night before he boarded the Empire Builder. He was already thinking about leaving. Her anxiety about starting a new life with him in it had been a blessing for him. It had been a way out. It had been an escape hatch that she opened for him with the red carpet laid out. He could leave her guilt-free.

He took it. He didn't apologize. He stopped her from apologizing. He remembered kissing her one last passionate time. He remembered her latching on to him like she was saying goodbye to an old friend, like she was on the docks, watching her sailor sail away to war, never to return.

Widow hated goodbyes like that, but it was unavoidable. And it was necessary. It helped with closure. He wasn't a robot, after all. He had a heart. He knew he would think about her from time to time, but like relationships he'd had before, he would move on.

Widow brought his coffee up to his lips, recalled DeGorne's lips. Then he took a drink and finished the coffee.

He set it down on the tabletop and stared out the window.

Then suddenly, the train hissed and roared. Time seemed to slow down. He saw flashes of light out the north window. He felt the surrounding air fill with tense sound waves, like violent ripples.

Metallic sounds surrounded him, echoing at first; then, they turned into fierce metal singing and then to brutal screeching. He heard people around him screaming and saw them moving, even running. He heard the horrendous sound of the train brakes squealing in the cars ahead of him. They squawked and wailed.

Widow saw the attendants running up the aisles. He saw the people at the far end of the train fight to stand up. They piled on top of each other to stare out the window to see what was happening farther up the rows of train cars.

One last attendant, the one who had waited on him, started running up the aisle until a sudden ripple of metal and torque and booming that started at the nose of the train undulated back through the tailing cars and impacted theirs.

The train derailed in front of Widow's eyes. He knew it derailed because a second after the booming sounds and the piling of passengers to the front windows, the running attendant had come up off her feet and slammed into the roof of the Sightseer car.

Instinctively, Widow grabbed a safety rail at the base of the nearest windowsill and held on tight with his right hand. His left hand went up into the air, as did the rest of him.

Outside, the train car tore up off the tracks and plowed into the back end of the car in front of it, and the lock bolts ripped off. The front cars had derailed at an overpass and plowed into each other, one after the other.

Cars passing under the overpass below the train tracks were crushed into scrap and shrapnel as the front train cars came piling down. They scattered across the highway below.

Fires exploded out of the front train cars, and two gas tankers were crushed when the train overturned.

The Sightseer Lounge car erupted off its couplers and tore forward and pulled the cars behind it, veering off the tracks, crashing through trees, and leveling empty warehouses.

Widow's left arm crashed into the glass of the window and broke instantly. He heard the bones crack internally and felt the intense pain shoot up to his brain. He curled into himself as best he could to minimize any more damage.

He tried to protect his head the most but was limited because he knew that if he let go of the safety bar, he would go flying and tumbling like everyone else, which happened right then. The Sightseer Lounge car came up again, ramming through a warehouse wall and tumbling over once, twice, twisting free from the cars behind it.

Widow saw the passengers at the front of the car tumble through the air, somersaulting like clothes in a dryer. Tables and chairs banged around. Dishes and saucers and the dainty coffee cups shattered into small pieces. Hot coffee spilled out of the attendant's bar area.

The last thing that Widow saw was the attendant who waited on him, the one who had run forward to help the passengers only seconds ago. She slammed into the roof, banging her head, cracking her forehead open. Now she rolled around, unmoving.

The instincts that protected Widow while everyone else tumbled around inside the rolling train car betrayed him at that moment because they told him to help her. He let go of the safety rail, tried to scramble over to the attendant, and that's when he realized the train car wasn't done rolling.

It rolled one more violent cycle, and he went flying into the air. He held his broken left arm against his stomach, but he kept his eyes forward on the attendant.

The last thing that Widow would remember was that he flew up, head-first, into the ceiling, not unlike the attendant.

He heard a *crack!* He felt pain in his head that would be described by a medical examiner as blunt force trauma. The last thought that ran through his mind, after wondering if the attendant was still alive or not, contained five words, words that he had heard many times before but never about himself.

Medical examiner. Blunt force trauma.

3

WIDOW HEARD BIRDS CHIRPING. He smelled grits cooking. *Like Mom used to make*, he thought. Until he opened his eyes and remembered that his mother was a terrible cook. She never cooked grits. At least, he never ate them, which was why he learned to cook on his own as a fourth grader. Back then, he only did mac 'n' cheese or simple things like that. He remembered reaching fifth grade and thinking that he could transition to culinary excellence by cooking some kind of complicated Mediterranean thing that he'd never heard of and couldn't identify today in a police lineup if he were asked to do so.

The whole experiment was contingent on two important things. The first was his mom not being present. She never let him cook on the stovetop because of the gas. His mother was working another long night shift, which ticked the first contingency box.

The next thing was that he had to not burn down the house. That second contingency ended his chef career early.

He remembered the fire. He remembered it getting completely out of control, too much for a ten-year-old boy to handle on his own. He remembered trying to put out the flames with an extinguisher. And he remembered feeling completely stupid when he learned later that you're supposed to pull the pin out of the extinguisher before it will work.

And how could he forget his sheriff mother coming home to see the town's only fire truck parked in front of their house? At ten, Widow burned a hole in their roof, and his mother beat his butt for it. He never started a fire again, not unintentionally, anyway.

Widow lay back in a bed. He knew that much, that he was in a bed.

His vision was fuzzy and bright and filled with blurry images of white light. Tears watered his eyes like he was opening them for the first time, and the exposure of light was too much for them to handle. He closed them again. The light was too bright.

Instead, he listened to the birds. He listened carefully, making a long examination of his surroundings by taking in the sounds, trying to determine where the hell he was.

His first thought was he was outside, but why would he be in a bed?

The birds were chirping. The bright light was like sunlight, but he felt cold. There was no sunlight on his face or his skin. He moved his hands, starting with his fingers. He moved his right hand, index finger first and then middle and ring and pinkie. He made a fist. It felt good. Then he tried his left hand. He started with his index finger, then the middle, then the ring, and then the pinkie. Everything moved. Everything was right. Then he tried to make a fist.

Suddenly, burning pain shot through his palm and his wrist. He jerked his right hand over to grab the left. It was instinct. But the right hand stopped three inches from its horizontal position. He heard a clanging sound, metal on metal. He pulled at his right hand again and got the same results. He heard the same clanging sound.

He opened his eyes, looked down. Everything was still blurry, but he didn't need to see clearly to know what caused that sound. It was handcuffs. Widow was handcuffed to the rail of a bed.

He looked around the room, tried to make out the blurry objects. He let his ears help him. He listened for the birds chirping, craned his head in that direction. It was up about twelve feet above him. He could make out a green blur with a brick texture.

Must be a wall, he thought.

He looked up toward the sound of chirping birds. The sound changed to two people talking. He realized it wasn't birds, not real ones. He was staring at a television, hung up high in the corner of a room with green walls. He looked around the room. He could make out blurry pieces of equipment. Some were lit up. Some were beeping and purring quietly.

He was in a hospital room and a hospital bed.

He squinted and strained his eyes. His eyelids blinked heavily and violently, trying to clear the tears from his eyes, trying to focus his vision.

Another burning spasm of pain shot through his arm. He craned his head up and down, looked over his chest at his left arm. It wasn't handcuffed to the bed like his right arm, but there was something else. Something heavy was on it.

He felt weak. He must've been drugged.

He dug deep and used his left shoulder to pull his arm up higher. The feelings in his arm and fingertips were there, but the arm felt strangely numb, like he had just woken up from sleeping on it.

Widow heaved it up and held it above his chest for five seconds, long enough to see what was so heavy about it. Then he saw it.

From two inches below his elbow, stretching for ten inches to his wrist, stopping where his palm started, was a brand-new white cast.

The pain returned and shot again through his wrist, up into his forearm, and up his bicep. And he had to let the arm drop. It fell and landed on a small pillow that someone had stuffed underneath it.

One or more of the bones in his left forearm were broken.

4

WIDOW'S VISION returned as the first person he had seen all night walked into the room to check on him. It was a nurse.

She was a young black woman. Maybe twenty-seven or twenty-eight. She saw Widow's eyes open, and she walked over to him.

"Where am I?" he asked.

"How are you feeling?"

"Fuzzy. My arm hurts."

She said nothing to that. She just stood near him, out of reach, and looked him up and down.

"The doctor will be in shortly," she said, and she turned, said nothing else. She vanished back through the doorway.

* * *

NEARLY AN HOUR PASSED before a doctor came into his room. And she didn't come alone. A man in uniform escorted the doctor. It wasn't hospital security. Widow's vision was still not one hundred percent, but he knew that much. Hospital security guards don't walk the way this guy walked. They don't carry themselves the way this guy carried himself. They don't stand at attention the way this guy stood at attention. He could've been a cop, Widow guessed. Maybe.

The doctor came in close to Widow, stood on the handcuffed side of the bed. She held a metal hospital clipboard with a metal cover to prevent damage to the paper. It was stuffed under her left arm. She stopped and stayed where she was. Then she took out the clipboard and opened it, looked over the first sheet, and flipped it to the second one.

She also held a thick manila envelope. It was sealed. There were markings on the front. Widow couldn't make anything out.

She smelled like maple syrup, which led Widow to believe it must've been in the morning, either that or she'd just eaten her breakfast and was on the graveyard shift. He had been there before. Breakfast, the most important meal of the day, didn't have to be eaten in the morning. Technically, there were two types of mornings: the actual time of day, and whenever you woke up.

Maybe she worked the graveyard shift. Maybe it was one o'clock in the morning.

The doctor got in close enough for Widow to see more details. She had brown, curly hair, the kind that women everywhere would pay to get. Widow didn't think she paid for it because it was pulled haphazardly back in a ponytail away from her shoulders. That kind of hair costs a lot of money for women with straight hair to get. He didn't see someone spending three hundred bucks for curly hair just to yank it back like that.

He squinted his eyes. Still couldn't see, but that didn't stop him from trying to read her name badge, which was clipped to the bottom lapel of a white doctor's coat. She wasn't wearing scrubs underneath, but regular brown khakis and a black top.

Widow noticed a wedding ring, gold, worn. She had been in a long marriage.

He squinted again. Still couldn't make out her name. Or the hospital that he was in.

She spoke with a hoarse voice, as if she had just overcome being sick herself. "Mr. Widow?" she said, looking at him from over the clipboard.

Widow stayed quiet. He felt a draft wash over him. The air conditioner had kicked on and was blowing down from a vent at the top corner of the room near the TV.

"Mr. Widow? Do you know where you are?"

"Aren't you supposed to ask if I know my name first?"

She was quiet for a beat, and then she asked, "Do you know your name?"

"Jack Widow."

"And what about where you are?"

"I'm in a hospital."

"Do you know what city?"

Widow stayed quiet.

"Do you?"

"I'm not sure."

"Do you know why you're in here?"

Widow thought for a long moment. Mostly, he was waiting for his eyes to adjust. He stared at the doctor, who shifted from one foot to the other patiently. Then he tried focusing on the cop behind her, then the TV, which was now playing a show about renovating houses. He realized he could see the people on the screen, the house torn up in the background.

He looked back at the doctor. She was slowly coming into focus. She was younger than he thought. Maybe his age.

"My name's Jack Widow. I was born in Biloxi, Mississippi. I'm thirty-six years old. Birthday is November 9. I was in the NCIS and the Navy for sixteen years."

Till my mom was shot by some asshole back home, Widow thought.

"I returned home one day. My mom died. I took care of what I needed to take care of."

"And?"

"And I never went back to the Navy."

"You went AWOL?"

"If I went AWOL, I'd be in prison. I wasn't military anymore. Technically, I was a civilian."

"Thought you said you were in the Navy?"

"I can't tell you any more than that. Classified."

Widow had been part of an undercover unit with the NCIS while he was in the Navy, which meant that he was ostensibly an officer in the Navy SEALs, but actually a civilian because NCIS is a civilian investigation force.

"I'm not here to ask you about that, anyway. I just need to know if you remember how you got here."

Widow closed his eyes, imagined the scenery he'd spent thirty-five-plus hours watching. He pictured seeing the Empire Builder for the first time. He imagined the two GE Genesis P42 locomotives, half a dozen sleeper cars, a single baggage car, and several passenger cars. He remembered how impressive the machinery was. There was something seductive about it. Then he remembered the moment he was dropped off at the station. He remembered kissing DeGorne goodbye and good luck.

"Train wreck."

"What do you remember about the wreck?"

"All of it."

"All of it?"

"I guess the parts I was conscious for. I remember sitting in the lounge car. I remember flashes of light out the window. I remember loud sounds like metal and screeching. I remember it felt like an eternity. I remember seeing people tumbling around. I figure the train must've derailed and flipped."

"That's right. The train derailed, and your car separated from the car in front of it. And it tumbled through the warehouse district."

"What about the attendant?"

"Attendant?"

"The Sightseer Lounge car? She was blonde, young. She hit her head pretty bad. That was the last thing I remember."

"I'm not sure about her. Not exactly. But there were some casualties."

"How many?"

"Ten. So far."

"What the hell happened?"

"There was a car parked on the train tracks. The engineer didn't see it in time."

"Car?"

"It was a suicide by train."

"The police are sure?"

She said, "Yes. That's what they said in a statement."

Widow looked up at the ceiling for a moment. Then back at her. He said, "Last I remember, we were in Minnesota. This must be Milwaukee?"

"Minneapolis."

"I know. Was joking."

"We're in St. Mark's Memorial Hospital. My name is Karen Green. I'm your doctor."

"Doc, why am I handcuffed to the bed?"

"I can't speak to that. I'm here to talk about your condition."

Condition? Widow thought.

"You mean my arm?"

Green paused a beat and fumbled with the clipboard. She glanced at it quickly and back at Widow. "Your left arm was broken at the ulna bone. It's in the forearm," she said and showed him on her forearm.

"I know where it is."

"Does it hurt?"

"It does when I move it."

"I'd recommend minimal activity until the cast comes off."

"When's that supposed to be?"

"Well, normally I'd say four to six weeks. But in your case, it could be more like ten."

"Ten?"

"Yeah," she said and closed the clipboard and set it down on the blanket over Widow's shins. She took out the manila folder, undid the metal clasps holding it shut, and walked over to a wall-mounted X-ray board. She clicked on a switch, and the board hummed to life. A back light lit up the board's white surface.

She pulled out an X-ray and stuck it up on the board. "Can you see that, Mr. Widow?"

Widow craned his head and stared in her direction. "I can," he lied.

She took out a pencil and pointed at the X-ray. "See, your ulna broke, clean, when you had a sudden traumatic impact. Probably against the window in the train car because you had dozens of shards of broken glass lodged in your arm. We got them all out. Luckily, none of the gashes required stitches. Plenty more glass cut up your face as well. Again, lucky that it's all superficial. No permanent scars."

She paused a long beat. Widow was eager for her to cut to the chase.

"The thing is that after we X-rayed your arm, we found your arm has been broken before."

"I know that."

"Mr. Widow, it's been broken in five places before. See, right here?" She tapped the pencil tip to the screen and traced it along the bones. "You've got rugged healing scars from each place."

"I know. I was there. What's your point?"

"While you were out, the orderlies had to remove your clothes. Put you in a gown."

Widow looked down, realized that's why he'd felt the draft earlier. He wasn't in his clothes. He was in a green hospital gown. Then he saw the ID bracelet on his right arm, just above the handcuff.

She continued, "They saw your back."

Widow was dumbfounded for only a moment. Then he remembered what was on his back.

"They saw the bullet wounds."

Widow stayed quiet.

"You've got three wicked scars on your back. The only discernible thing is that someone shot you three times. So we did X-rays. There're no signs of bullet fragments or even massive penetration from a bullet in your organs. Most of the damage back there was surface level, some major nerve damage, and it looks like four badly fractured ribs, all of which healed a long time ago."

She stared at Widow like she was waiting for a response that would answer the bubbling questions she had in the back of her mind.

Widow stayed quiet.

"So, naturally, we became concerned about who you are. We ordered more X-rays and found a lot of healed bone scars."

"What about it?"

"Have you ever heard of Evel Knievel?"

"Of course."

"It's like him."

"No way. Knievel was a crazy daredevil who had four hundred broken bones over a long career of doing stupid things."

"Four hundred thirty-three broken bones."

"I don't have that many."

"No. Maybe not. We don't know because we stopped counting at two hundred fifty. And some of those we couldn't rule out aren't double infractions."

"Infractions?"

"Some of your bone scars overlap."

Widow said, "I was in the military. Been around. I told you that."

"I wasn't in the military, but I called around. First, to the Marine Corps here in the city. They transferred me around a while, until I got patched over to McCoy, spoke to a surgeon there. He's never encountered a soldier with half as many broken bones as you."

McCoy, Widow thought. That's in Wisconsin, not Minnesota. Then again, he really was fuzzy on details that normally he knew well. "So?"

"So, I'm concerned. I looked on the internet, and there are people who've had a lot of broken bones."

"So?"

"The most I could find were with Knievel and several champion karate fighters."

"Karate?"

"MMA or whatever."

"And?"

"And you rank somewhere in the middle. My initial thoughts were that you were involved in dangerous criminal activity. The bullet scars. All the broken bones. So I told the MPs over at McCoy."

Widow said, "The guy standing behind you. He's not police, is he?"

Green looked back over her shoulder at him and said, "No. Well, yes. He's military police."

"He from McCoy?"

"The Lakes. I think. I don't know. He'll tell you that in a moment. First, I need to explain something to you."

Widow waited.

Green took down the X-rays of his broken arm. She tucked them neatly back into the manila folder like they were precious records that couldn't be damaged under any circumstances. She took a breath and seemed to calm down a bit, like she had been on pins and needles before. Perhaps she was a little afraid of who Widow was exactly.

She took a new X-ray out of the folder. She whipped it gently to straighten it out, and then she slid it into the frame of the white X-ray box. She repeated the whole process with a second X-ray. This one was a profile shot of the same part of the body—Widow's skull.

He stared at it. He stared at both of them. He realized that the good news was his vision was syncing up properly. The bad news was that he was staring at two X-rays. One was his skull from the top. The second was the side of his skull. It showed the starboard point of view.

Widow's vision was almost back to normal, which was to say it was still not perfect, but he could see details again. His far vision was worse. The X-ray box was within twelve feet of his bed, which was close enough to see discoloration on the starboard side of the skull, like the outer shell of his skull was hit so hard that it almost cracked.

Green pointed the pencil back at the X-ray. She pointed at exactly the spots he was staring at.

"Do you know the difference between a mild concussion and a severe one?"

"One is worse than the other?"

"Yes. Of course. But do you know what that means exactly?"

Widow shook his head, noticed that some bruises he had seen on the skull moved with his vision. Those weren't bruises at all. They were vision spots. But the major bruising didn't move.

Now, he was a little afraid. Brain injuries were no joking matter.

Green said, "Because there are only two classifications of concussions, there is no classification for a moderate concussion. But that's what you have. Technically, you have a severe concussion. But I've seen much worse."

Widow stayed quiet.

"I tell you this so that you know not to worry. But you have a severe concussion toward the lower end of the spectrum."

"I've seen concussions before. What can I expect?"

"It all depends on each individual case. You've experienced a blackout. Very common with this type of injury. You said you remember the events of the train wreck, but you seem to have forgotten some things. You weren't out the whole time. When the paramedics brought you in, you were conscious and speaking."

"I was?"

"Yes. So you don't remember that, which is normal. You may never remember it. That's okay. The rest of your memory doesn't seem to be affected. What about vision?"

"It's spotty."

"You can see the X-ray?"

Widow nodded.

"How was your vision before?"

"Twenty-twenty."

"Then it will return. No worries there. How does your head feel?"

Widow stopped and intuitively tried to reach his forehead with his right hand, clinking the metal of the handcuff again and feeling frustrated by it.

He said, "It's not that bad. I've got a headache."

Green nodded. She added, "You may not experience many of the symptoms till later on. It is my understanding that this officer is going to explain things to you and take you into custody. So you'll be active. I'd rather you stay in bed, but I don't think that's an option."

She craned her head, reversed her position, and stared back at the guy standing at the opposite side of the room. Widow followed her gaze and saw the guy was coming more into focus.

The guy looked to be about forty years old, probably closer to forty-five. He was one of a thousand guys Widow had seen before. The kind of elite sailor or soldier or Marine who took extra steps in his fitness and diet regimen to make sure that his body was as young as it could be for as long as it could be.

The guy stayed where he was. He didn't give a nod or say a word. He wouldn't give out any information, not in front of Green. She was a civilian. Whatever he was there for was for Widow's ears only. That was obvious.

Green said, "Okay, Mr. Widow. I'm giving you this bottle of Extra Strength Tylenol. I want you to take them as needed throughout the day. Don't exceed six in twenty-four hours. Only two at a time. Try to drink plenty of water."

"How long will I have the concussion?"

Green shrugged and said, "Could be a few days. It could be several. It depends on you. Try to get plenty of rest. And don't get into any more train wrecks."

Green smiled, took up the X-rays, and inserted them back into the folder. She tapped Widow once on the leg, picked up the metal clipboard.

"Take care, Mr. Widow," she said, and she walked out of the room.

* * *

THE OFFICER who came in with her waited a full second after she left, until the door sucked shut behind her, and then he stepped forward.

He looked to be six feet flat. He wore a navy-blue blazer over street clothes, a pair of green chinos, a black leather belt exposed only over the buckle, a white polo shirt, untucked, and black oxford shoes. Everything neat. Everything polished, even the leather of the belt.

Widow could make out a very slight bump on the guy's right hip. A gun, no doubt. It was probably a Beretta M9 or a SIG Sauer P228 M11 pistol. Widow figured that because of what the guy's official department was, only because Green had said that he came from the "Lakes," which meant the Great Lakes. Had to be NAVSTA Great Lakes. NAVSTA just meant Naval Station. He was from the Naval Station Great Lakes, which meant that he was Naval Police, which was officially called master-at-arms. The Navy loves to be different.

The guy said, "Commander Widow. My name is Crews. I'm here to transport you."

He reached down and raised his shirt, which revealed an M9 Beretta holstered in a paddle holster, nicely concealed. He snatched a badge off his belt, fast like a draw. It clipped off, and he approached, put it directly in Widow's face.

It was a gold badge with an eagle at the top and wings draped around the outer top edges, connecting with two olive branches on opposite sides of the bottom of the badge. There was a single bold black star stamped into the bottom center. An anchor with a rope looped and hooped around it occupied the middle. Widow knew it was a master-at-arms badge because it said so right there on the badge's surface. It had four letters, spaced slightly apart: C M A A, which meant, "Chief Master-At-Arms."

Widow asked, "You a chief warrant officer?"

Crews nodded but didn't give his exact rank.

"Wanna tell me why I'm in handcuffs, Chief?"

Crews rubbed the stubble on a two-day-old shaved head and said, "Mister, not Chief, okay? And you're only in the cuffs as part of the story."

Widow had called him Chief, knowing full well that it would irritate him, at the very least. Not as a sign of disrespect, but more like making himself feel better for being handcuffed. Since he had done nothing wrong, nothing that the Navy knew about.

Petty, he knew, but being handcuffed for doing nothing, for a cover that hid some mysterious reason the Navy wanted him back wasn't good enough a reason to be handcuffed.

"Part of the story? What story?"

"We need you back, Commander. I wasn't told why. I was only told what the cover was to prevent the doc and hospital staff or reporters from asking questions."

"There are reporters here?"

"Yes. There was a major train accident. They love train accidents. Two major networks are outside. All the local boys and CNN and MSNBC."

"What? Nothing coming out of the White House to cover today?"

Crews smirked a little. Widow figured he had jabbed at the guy enough. Better to have him on his side. Apparently, he was going somewhere, and he had no say in the matter.

Crews added, "Plenty coming out of the White House. Plenty of scandals. You know how it goes."

Widow nodded and asked, "Wanna tell me what this is all about?"

"My orders are to escort you back to the airbase in Minneapolis–Saint Paul and put your butt on a plane."

"A plane? What the hell is this?"

"I honestly couldn't tell you, sir. I'm only a messenger."

"A messenger without a message."

"You're the message, Commander."

Widow said nothing to that. He pulled his head up and adjusted his elbows so that he could rest on them.

"I got a choice in this?"

"Sure. You could resist."

"I doubt that'll come out in my favor."

"Doubt it will too, sir."

"Guess I'm coming with you then."

"Guess you are."

"Does the concussion make a difference?"

Crews shook his head, said, "I was told if you were walking and talking, then your butt's flying."

Widow took a deep breath and asked, "Wanna get me some pants, then?"

5

IT TURNED out that Crews was deadly serious about keeping the cover intact because he rolled Widow out of the hospital in a basic metal wheelchair with Widow's right hand cuffed to the arm of the chair and his left in a cast in a sling around his neck. The handcuff clinked and clanged all the way down the corridors and to the elevator, and back through more corridors because one wheel wobbled all the way. Widow figured it was a backup chair because the hospital seemed almost overrun with patients from the train wreck.

The halls echoed the sounds of chattering voices, both from conversations one-on-one and from radio chatter because there were a lot of police around, probably to keep order.

Crews took Widow down back halls, through a kitchen, and through a laundry. White steam rose from heavy washing machines against the back wall.

"Can you tell me who exactly sent for me?"

"Can't tell you that. I don't even know who. I know it came from Washington."

"Is that where I'm going?"

"Could be."

Crews rolled Widow down a ramp and out the service entrance of the hospital. Bright sunlight bathed over Widow's face, and his vision went from getting better to blinding whiteness, which lasted for several moments and then passed.

Crews rolled him out to a navy-blue sedan parked in the alley behind a delivery truck.

Widow said, "You can let me out of this chair now. I think the cover is maintained."

Crews stopped the chair just in front of the driver's side back door. He took out a handcuff key and undid Widow's cuffs, opened the door for him. Then Crews paused for a moment like he was considering putting the cuffs back on Widow. He didn't seem to know what the right call was in this situation. Widow wasn't a prisoner.

Widow saw him working it out in his head. He didn't let Crews get the chance to put the cuffs back on. He hopped into the back seat and buckled up.

Crews shrugged, returned the cuffs to a holster on his belt and shoved the wheelchair away from the car. He closed Widow's door and slid into the driver's seat.

The engine fired up, and they were off.

* * *

CREWS TOOK Widow to exactly where he'd said he was going to take him. They pulled up at the guard gate to Minneapolis–Saint Paul Air Reserve Station. They traversed through the gate with no problems. Then Crews wound through the streets and buildings and Widow realized Crews was no longer driving on roads. He was weaving between airplane hangars.

They came to a stop in front of a parked C-20B. It was mostly white, with blue trim along the bottom. It had a designated tail number and two twin engines mounted above and between the wings and the tail.

The plane looked like Air Force One, only one-third the length. That's when Widow knew he was in deep because the Air Force C-20B is basically a civilian Gulfstream jet that's been converted, reinforced, and armored to shuttle government officials from place to place. The problem with that was most government officials flew commercial. The ones who needed an Air Force jet weren't ordinary government officials. They were DOD people—important DOD people—like the Secretary of Defense, for example. This meant that whoever was racking up taxpayer dimes to pay for the flight was someone important, someone with clout, someone with a much higher pay grade than Widow was when he discharged.

Crews accompanied Widow to the staircase leading up to the plane's entrance and stopped. He put his hand out for Widow to shake.

Widow turned back and stared at him.

"You're not coming?"

"No, Commander. You're on your own from here."

Widow took Crews's hand and shook it.

Before he boarded the plane, Crews saluted Widow and said, "Try to keep yourself from getting any more broken bones, Commander."

Widow said nothing to that, just climbed the stairs and boarded the plane.

Onboard, he was greeted by a steward, or possibly the pilot. He wasn't sure. Not until he stepped into the aisle and the guy said, "Have a seat anywhere, sir."

Steward.

Widow picked a spot in front of the wing window seat. The interior was all butterscotch leather and walnut veneer and pristine white carpets and white walls. There were no overhead bins or other clutter. There was a nice-looking kitchenette area in the front, stocked with bourbons and expensive vodkas.

This was a private jet for the rich and famous—only the rich and famous were members of the DOD, the Pentagon, maybe, and whoever else.

The steward said, "Sir, buckle in. We're taking off right away."

"Where are we heading?"

"We're going into the sky, of course."

"Of course," Widow said, and sat back. The steward stood around for another long second, waiting for Widow to buckle his seat belt, which he did.

The steward returned to the front of the cabin and sat in a jump seat near the cockpit hatch and strapped himself in. When the steward had said they were taking off right away, he wasn't exaggerating. Thirty seconds later, they were on the runway. A minute after that, they were climbing into the clouds.

6

IT WAS HALFWAY into the flight that the steward informed Widow he was Air Force, along with both pilots, whom Widow never saw, not once. They never came out of the cockpit.

The steward brought Widow a coffee in a foam cup with one sugar packet and one creamer and one stirrer. Widow hadn't asked for any of it, but was grateful for one part of it. He drank the coffee, black, which was better than nothing, far worse than the coffee on the Sightseer Lounge car of the Empire Builder, which made his mind wander back to the near two-day trip and back to the blonde train attendant who he'd tried to help. He wondered if she was going to be all right. Within a moment, he forgot whether he had asked Green about her. He also realized that he had asked no one how much time had gone by since the train wreck.

How long had he been out?

Admittedly, he'd find out, eventually. Then he thought about DeGorne for a moment. She'd be in her apartment, thinking, planning her future.

Another thought occurred to him: he'd better call her when he got the chance. Crews had said that there had been a lot of news coverage about the accident. Good chance DeGorne might've seen it. She dropped him off at the train station. She knew of his plans to get on a train. She might've known about his plans to head east. Then again, he might not have even had plans. He couldn't remember.

His vision was getting much better by this point. He had stared out the window for one hour and forty minutes, and seen everything below with no problems. He watched a couple of Great Lakes and lots of blue-collar states pass under the plane.

It was clear where they were going. He'd known it way back when they headed over Lake Michigan. They were going to Andrews, which is a joint base for the branches of the military. It's a major base.

The C-20B adjusted and started decelerating before the pilot came over the intercom and informed the steward that they were landing. Fifteen minutes later, they were on the ground for a total flight time of five minutes less than two hours, twenty-five minutes faster than Widow had calculated in his head, which was both good and bad. Meant that his calculations were off, although they were usually right on; it also meant that he was calculating things.

Better than losing that part of my brain, he thought.

As they landed, Widow stuffed his empty coffee cup into a cup holder near the arm of the chair and left it. The plane taxied off the runway, and the steward got up off the jump seat.

Widow took this as a sign to get up. He tried to stand, but felt light-headed. Not a severe thing, but annoying enough. He remembered the doctor had given him a bottle of Extra Strength Tylenol before he left the hospital. He reached into his front pocket, pulled out the bottle, popped the top, pitched a pill down his throat, and swallowed it.

Widow hated taking pills, but it was better than forcing an Air Force crew to have to half-carry him to wherever he was headed.

He stepped out into the aisle and walked to the front of the plane. He stood next to the steward, who said nothing, until the aircraft stopped and the hatch opened to blinding sunlight.

Widow stepped out onto a portable staircase on wheels and climbed down, using the rail the whole way. He couldn't cover his eyes from the sun and use the rail, not with only one hand available, so it took him several seconds longer than it should've to reach the bottom step.

Another CMAA warrant officer met him with a navy-blue sedan, only this WO was in uniform blues, and the sedan was a military police car. The WO had the light bar going off. Blue lights circled around and around.

No siren.

Widow walked up to him, didn't bother checking his name patch, partly because he couldn't make it out just yet and partly because he didn't care. Truthfully, he was over meeting new military people, learning their names, and having them keep him in handcuffs.

Luckily, this guy didn't even offer, and better yet, he didn't refer to him by his last known rank.

The guy said, "Jack Widow?"

"That's me."

"Glad you're not too beat up."

Widow stayed quiet.

"Come on. I'm driving you."

Widow nodded and stepped to the passenger door, but the WO cleared his throat and signaled to the back door.

Widow wasn't surprised. Warrant officers were usually boy scouts. They followed the rules to an insane amount of loyalty. Andrews Base's official policy for civilians riding in police vehicles was that civilians always ride in the back seat.

Widow didn't argue, and slung himself down onto the rear bench. Twenty seconds later, they were off.

Widow stared out the window. His eyes adjusted to the sun, and he watched the buildings. Long-forgotten memories of countless meetings, conversations, and undercover investigations that involved or took place at Andrews came flooding back into his mind. Some occurred at the very buildings he passed, which promptly triggered the replay of the memories. Then he wondered how many of those actually happened at Andrews. He wondered if any of them were memories misplaced by his concussion.

Minutes and several turns later, they were parked in front of a low building that Widow didn't recognize.

"This is your stop," the WO said.

Widow waited for the WO to get out and open his door because, like civilian police cars, military cars don't open from the inside of the rear bench. Like civilian police cars, that's where criminals and suspects go.

Widow climbed out and walked forward, and stopped.

"Here. Clip this on. Outside your jacket. Make sure it's always visible."

The WO handed him a name badge that had the word VISITOR in all caps, boldly across the front of a photograph. The photo was one that Widow hadn't seen in years. It was the last photo on his official Navy ID. Black and white. His head shaved to the stubble. No smile.

He took it with his right hand, fumbled with the clasp, and clipped it onto the outside of his bomber jacket. He had to readjust his coat because it nearly fell off his left shoulder. His cast was in a sling, tucked underneath the jacket. The left sleeve hung empty.

"You coming?" Widow asked.

"No, sir. Just you. My rank stops me here."

Stops you here? Widow thought.

"Just head through those doors. Stare into the camera. They'll buzz for you. Someone will tell you where to go."

The WO saluted Widow after all and turned and drove off in his car. He didn't wait to make sure Widow didn't get cold feet and take off in another direction. Then again, where the hell else would he go?

7

THE WHOLE PROCESS seemed like overkill. By the time Widow arrived at what he had guessed was his destination, he had gone through two electronic checkpoints, without armed guards, until he finally arrived outside a door that led up a bland staircase. At that point, there was one sentry—a military MP. Army, not Navy.

The MP asked him to stay still for a pat-down. Which surprised Widow. They were on a major military base, and he had been escorted by a warrant officer, straight from the hospital, straight to a plane, and then straight here.

The MP patted him down, checked his cast, all his pockets, and even the inside of his empty jacket sleeve for any weapons. Afterward, the MP asked him to take his shoes off.

Widow said, "You serious?"

"'Fraid so, sir."

Another "sir." What the hell was he getting himself into?

Widow sighed and pushed his boots off with one foot and then the other. He didn't want to use his one good hand because that would've meant that he would sit on the floor. He stepped back out of the boots and stood there. The MP bent down, picked them up. Widow wondered how important security was to them. The MP bent over right in front of Widow. If he had wanted to, a fast knee to the guy's head, and Widow could've taken him out cold.

There was no need for any of that.

The MP finished checking his boots and then picked them up. He handed them over to Widow.

Widow took them with his good hand and switched them over to his left. Just kept them in his left. He stayed in his socks.

"Go on up, sir."

Widow stayed quiet and walked through the open door, stepped onto the bottom step. He felt the cold metal through his socks.

The top of the stairs opened straight up into an unused set of military surveillance equipment, counterterrorism stuff. There were dozens of TV screens lit up. Some were playing American news channels; others played foreign ones. They were all muted and had English captions turned on.

The whole floor was dark except for the light from the monitors. He checked them out as he passed.

Other monitors showed surveillance video from around the world. There was some CCTV stuff. As Widow stepped out past a set of unmanned cubicles, he saw multiple rows and aisles of the same thing. This was some kind of counterterrorist unit or plain old counterintelligence, he guessed.

There was no one in sight, but Widow heard voices at the other end of the floor. He looked and saw an open door. A bright artificial light beckoned him to it.

He threaded the aisles and rows of cubicles and electronic equipment and stepped into the room.

It was an Army conference room, which meant that the walls were painted green. The carpet was green. And the long oval table at the center was plain wood.

Huddled at the table were three people—two men and one woman.

One man and the woman were in dress uniforms. They were Army.

They both turned and faced him as he walked in. The man was an older guy. Probably close to sixty. He was tall and had a sense of refinement about him, like a man who came from poverty, got paid, and discovered the better side of life.

He was a one-star general. Widow saw that from his patches.

The woman was a sergeant. She held a notepad in her hand, clamped shut, with a ball-point pen in the other. She had a pair of black-framed glasses on and was thirty years younger than the general, easily. Widow assumed she was his assistant or desk sergeant or whatever.

The other guy was the only one, besides Widow, to wear street clothes.

He faced the other direction. He sat on the edge of the table, one leg waving under him, slowly.

All Widow could make out about him was that he was of average height, medium build, and had thick, curly hair, which looked more like wool than human hair. The light reflected countless curls of gray mixed in with jet-black hair.

In front of the room, a large TV monitor and a camera on a tripod faced them.

The general said, "Ah, Mr. Widow."

The man with the wooly hair stayed where he was, but Widow sensed he became suddenly uneasy. His shoulders tensed under a sleeveless zip vest, black. The guy didn't turn around.

"My name is Sutherland. Tom Sutherland. This is my assistant, Sergeant Andy Swan. We're both US Army."

Widow stayed where he was.

"Come on in, Commander." Sutherland summoned him with one hand. But the other, his left, rested on his belt, near a holstered M9 Beretta.

The firearm was loose in its holster. It was pulled up higher than it should have been, which meant that either Sutherland was a poor excuse for a man who had access to an Army-issued weapon, or he had just slipped it back into the holster, not pushing it in all the way.

Widow guessed it was the latter, because the holster's safety snap was undone.

Widow's vision must have cleared up because he could see the red indicator dot on the side of the M9. The safety was off. The hammer was pulled back. The gun had a chambered round. It was set to single-action fire mode and ready to roll.

Brigadier generals rarely carry firearms, not walking around their own office.

The M9 was there because of Widow. Had to be. The sentry from below had radioed up, told them that Widow was on his way. Sutherland drew his weapon and disengaged the safety. Then he readied a bullet to fire.

"Come in," Sutherland repeated.

Widow stepped in, kept one eye on the M9, an old habit with or without the knowledge that it was there because of him.

He walked in about five feet, smelled hints of cigar smoke. Probably from the general's uniform.

"Commander, I hate to be direct, but I need to ask you if you're going to be civil."

"What the hell is this about?"

"Just answer the question."

Widow said nothing.

"Please."

"I've been dragged out of a hospital bed, flown all the way out here. Not to mention, I was in a train wreck. I've got a broken arm. I'm concussed. And a little irritated that I'm even here. I'm as civil as you're going to get, General."

Sutherland nodded and said, "Fair enough. I guess."

"So just cut to the chase?"

Sutherland glanced over at the face of the man with his back to Widow. He nodded.

The wooly-haired man stood up from the edge of the table, slipped both his hands into the pockets of his vest, taking them out of sight, and turned around slowly.

Widow stood still, questioning his eyes for a long moment because he was staring at a man that he'd once warned.

Never let me see you again, he had said to him.

"Hello, Widow," the wooly-haired man said with a hint of a Spanish accent.

Widow said nothing. He glanced at the M9 Beretta in its holster, safety off, ready to fire. Ready to kill. But was Sutherland ready to use it?

They had gone through a lot of taxpayer-expense and trouble and manpower to get him out here, not to mention jet fuel.

Would Sutherland really pull that gun? Probably. But would he shoot an unarmed man for doing what Widow was about to do?

Only one way to find out.

With his boots in his left hand, Widow's face gave nothing away. Not that it would've mattered, because it would all be over in a second and a half.

Widow stepped forward, left foot, his socks sliding a bit, but not enough to kill his momentum. He twisted at the waist like a pitcher gearing up to throw a fastball. His right hand bunched up into a massive fist. Doctor Green had mentioned all his broken bones and scars and doubled bone scars. She never mentioned the ones on his hand and under the skin on his knuckles. He had calluses bunched up like a set of natural-formed knuckle-dusters.

He lunged with devastating force and whipped forward from his shoulders and plowed a thunderous right hook straight at the wooly-haired guy's face.

It wasn't enough force to take out an eye or push a nasal bone up into the guy's brain, but it was enough to break bones—no doubt about that.

The wooly-haired guy was expecting it. He anticipated it like he knew from the second Widow walked into the building that Widow was going to break bones in his face.

He expected the attack, but he had underestimated the speed. Maybe he assumed Widow was older now. Maybe he assumed Widow was out of practice. Maybe he assumed Widow was weakened from the crash, from the drugs. He was wrong on all accounts.

There was no time to dodge. No way. He was getting punched in the face—no question about that.

The next best thing was to moderate the power from the blow, to alleviate the damage. His training was all he had to rely on.

The wooly-haired guy moved as fast as he could. He tucked his chin down and threw his arms up to absorb the impact of the punch.

It half worked—sort of.

Widow's fist punched straight through, but it impacted the wooly-haired guy's left forearm first. Then the jumbled mass folded back into the wooly-haired guy's face. He went tumbling back over the table.

Widow wound back, fast, ready to step forward and stomp on the wooly-haired guy's throat while he lay on the ground.

But that was all put to bed instantly, because Sutherland had drawn the M9 Beretta after all. He shoved it in Widow's face.

"Hold it, son! I'll shoot you where you stand!"

Widow looked up in the general's eyes. He saw two things. First, there was terror. Not the kind of terror that a non-soldier experienced when confronted with an assaulter. That was the kind of fear only untrained citizens experienced.

This was the kind of fear that a seasoned one-star general experienced only one or two times in his career. It was the kind of thing he got when facing down a madman.

At that moment, Widow was that madman.

The second thing that Widow saw was that the general wasn't bluffing. He would shoot him.

For the first time in a long time, Widow had to ask himself a serious question.

How far would he go to kill a man he should've killed twelve years ago?

8

WIDOW STOOD over the wooly-haired man, ready to stomp down on his head and break his nose, or stand on his throat and break his voice box. Whichever he could get away with first. The throat would've killed him. Instantly. If Widow wanted.

The head wouldn't kill him. Not when Widow was still in socks. But it would hurt like hell. He could break the wooly-haired guy's nose. He could shatter the guy's cheekbones. Maybe he could dislocate one of his eyes from the socket. Maybe even crush it.

But Widow had to ask himself: *Do I want to kill the guy?* The simple answer was that he didn't know. Not for sure. He was thinking.

Another question: *Am I willing to die just to kill him?* The answer to this question was not complicated. No, he didn't want to die. Not here in a conference room on an Army base. That was a newspaper headline that he didn't want to be written. Not about him.

"Widow! Hold it!"

Widow put his foot down, consciously, just now realizing that he had it hiked up, ready to stomp down violently. His body had already made half the choice for him.

Andy Swan had stepped way back, making plenty of room between her and the madman. Some might say she was overly cautious. But that's because they didn't know about Widow. They hadn't read parts of his file. She had. To her, it was not cautious enough.

She pushed her back against the wall. She had dropped the notepad and the pen during the commotion. They lay on the floor.

Widow took a deep breath, held it. Waited a long second and let it out. His brain relayed signals to the rest of his body, telling him to stand down, which was repeated at that moment by an Army general. Verbally.

"Stand down, sailor!" Sutherland said.

Widow stepped back away from the wooly-haired guy and repeated the deep breathing. Once. Twice. And a third time.

He said, "You're not in the Navy, General."

"Technically, neither are you."

"There's no reason to call me sailor. I haven't been a sailor in years."

Sutherland retreated from a shooting stance, slowly, and lowered the M9 down to his hip. He didn't holster it.

The muzzle, the barrel, and the front sights were all targeted on Widow. Staying where they were. He had no intention of changing that.

Accuracy from the hip was harder. Widow knew that. But not at a range of two yards—less even. Widow knew that, too.

"Are you okay?" Sutherland asked the wooly-haired guy without glancing at him.

"Yeah. I'm fine. Goddamn it, Widow! Was that necessary?"

The wooly-haired guy stood up and picked carpet fibers out of his mouth and off the stubble on his face. He had the beginnings of a cylinder-shaped black ring around his eye. It formed at the base of his left eye socket. Widow watched it in real time.

The wooly-haired guy's cheek was already swollen and mottled and bruised. The blood gathered and painted half his face the color red, like the flag itself.

"I warned you. I told you what would happen if I ever saw you again."

The wooly-haired man stood up. He was trying to act like he was not afraid of Widow. An act that everyone saw right through. And he twisted at the waist like he was stretching after a judo match.

No big deal, guys. His body posture was attempting to say.

Sutherland ignored the wooly-haired guy and said, "Andy, come back over. It's okay."

Swan walked back into the room, picked up her notepad and pen. Stopped at the edge of their circle and stared at Widow like he was some kind of mountain man come out of the woods, a look he had seen so many times. He expected it when he met new people.

Sutherland said, "Commander, you're right. Neither of us is Navy. But we both wear a uniform. I expect you to act accordingly."

Widow stayed quiet.

"Can I holster my sidearm?"

No answer.

"Will you play nice?"

"Can't make any promises."

"Widow, I need an affirmative acknowledgment of the order given."

Widow turned his gaze and stared at him, said, "You're not in my chain of command. You don't give orders. No one gives me orders. Not anymore."

"Commander?"

"I'll be good. Put that gun away."

Sutherland paused a quick beat, thinking it over. Then he clicked the safety switch. The hammer was uncocked. He slid the M9 back into the holster by degrees, like a shuttle using rockets to slow its landing.

Sutherland didn't button the safety latch on the holster.

"It's apparent that you know Benico. So let's skip all that. Have a seat."

Widow stared back at Benico Tiller, who was cupping the left side of his face.

"Andy, can you grab me a pack of ice?"

Swan nodded and set her stuff down on the table. She took off through an open door, into an office break room, Widow figured.

He stepped back, set his boots down on the edge of the table, and dumped himself down in the closest empty chair. He kept Tiller and Sutherland in his line of sight.

"Will you just get to it?" he asked.

Sutherland said, "Widow, you're here against my better judgment."

Tiller said, "I asked for you."

"You? What the hell for?"

"For this," Sutherland said, and walked over to a table below the TV monitor. It was hooked up to a MacBook, some kind of connector cable plugged right into the back of the TV from the front corner of the laptop. Sutherland clicked and patted the trackpad with his index and middle finger.

The TV monitor burst to life. First, the screen was black, then it blipped, and then it displayed the MacBook's screen.

On the screen, Widow saw a topographical map, satellite view. Google Earth, he figured. It was over a two-mile patch of land that he recognized immediately, like no time had passed since Tiller had shown it to him once before, twelve years in the past. And he was reminded of what had happened right there. It was a mission gone terribly wrong. The reason he hated Tiller. The blame that he placed on himself. All of it. Right there.

"I can tell by the look on your face—you know where that is?"

Widow nodded.

"He knows it," Tiller said.

Swan returned with a bag of frozen peas in one hand and a plain white mug of hot coffee in the other. She handed the cold bag to Tiller. Desperate to keep the swelling down, he immediately crammed it against his cheek and under his left eye. He was brazenly superficial, just like every CIA operator that Widow had ever known, minus a few exceptions. The first thing he cared about was how he appeared. These guys were all about taking credit when things were good and obfuscating when they were bad.

Swan handed the coffee mug to Widow, who didn't offer to take it with his hand. He just waited.

Swan set it down on the table in front of him. She said, "I read in your file that you like coffee. Hope that's right."

"That shouldn't be in my file."

"It is."

Widow didn't know what to say to that. Apparently, his file extended beyond his years in the Navy. Someone's been keeping tabs on him. Apparently, it covered much, much more. He wondered what exactly was in there. But he didn't ask.

He smiled and nodded a thank-you for the coffee. He pulled it close and studied it.

"It's not poisoned," Sutherland said.

Widow took a fake sip, just in case. "So, what do you want me to do in North Korea?"

"China."

Widow stared over at Tiller.

"Technically, that's China. Not North Korea."

Widow pointed at the side of the map and said, "That part's North Korea."

"True."

"I'm not going back there. If that's why you brought me all the way out here, you're wasting your time. You could fly me first-class all the way there. Private jet and all. Even if it was on Air Force One, I'm not going."

"It's not why you're here."

Widow listened.

"Not precisely. It's more like, proximate to why we brought you here."

Sutherland clicked the trackpad on the Mac again. He stayed standing near the TV. A new photo came up on the screen like a slideshow, only on a TV monitor instead of from a slide projector.

The photo was of a sniper in field gear. His face was weather-beaten and sandblasted. He had a serious tan going on. A combat helmet covered his head from the sun. He had shades on. But the rest of his face was visible. He was posing for the camera.

There was an L115A3 sniper rifle, a serious weapon, cradled across his chest, pinned there by one of his gloved hands. The folding stock and the handguard matched the desert-brown bulletproof vest he wore underneath. Everything was desert camo; only it wasn't American camo. The patterns were slightly different. He was British Army.

Widow guessed he was a corporal of horse in the cavalry by his uniform and patches. The COH was the basic equivalent to a sergeant in the army in any other part of the world.

The guy was a sniper, obviously. Take out the big sniper rifle, and you were still left with a sniper stance, a sniper way of carrying himself, that translated through the photographs.

Widow had seen his kind before. Many times. Take a trained soldier, throw him into intense sniper school training, and this was what you'd get— a guy who stood like him and posed like him. Snipers held their rifles like an extension of themselves, like a lover and a child all wrapped into one. They held their rifle like it was one of their severed limbs off a battlefield, and they clinched it close, desperate to reattach it.

Widow was also sure about the terrain in the background. The guy was in Afghanistan. Widow knew the desertlike mountains in the background. He had been there. Not that exact location, but close enough.

"Do you know who this is?"

"A British sniper."

Tiller asked, "How did you know that?"

"He's holding an L115A3 rifle."

Sutherland asked, "How do you know he's British? His flag is covered."

"His teeth."

"Be serious, Widow."

"Those aren't US Army fatigues. He's a sniper in Afghanistan. That's obvious. Must be a ten-year-old photo. So I'd guess Brit."

"You're right."

"His name is James Lenny," Tiller added, pushing the frozen peas harder into his cheek. He turned and stood up from the table and stepped away from Widow.

"Is that supposed to mean something to me?"

"Does it?" Sutherland asked.

"Never heard of him."

"He used to hold the record for longest confirmed sniper kill in the world."

"Used to?"

"He got that record back in 2009."

Sutherland added, "About eight years later, his record was completely shattered."

"What was it? His record?"

"Twenty-five hundred meters."

Which was about twenty-seven hundred yards, or a hair over a mile and a half. Widow stayed quiet, but his face registered his shock at the number.

"That's a hell of a lot of yards," Sutherland said.

Widow nodded. "What's the new record?"

Sutherland and Tiller looked at each other.

Sutherland said, "Thirty-five hundred forty meters."

"Bullshit."

"It's true. Someone came along and shattered his record. Literally. A record that never existed before, and it was destroyed eight years later."

Widow stayed quiet. He converted the meters in his head and then calculated the miles for a grand total of three thousand, eight hundred seventy-one yards, or two and a quarter miles, almost.

He caught himself after the fact, but he still muttered it. "Two miles."

Tiller nodded, said, "Over two miles."

"Who broke it?"

"That's part of the mystery. We don't know."

Silence.

Sutherland continued, "It was a Canadian. Canadian forces have a great sniper team. They hold five out of the top ten longest confirmed kills."

Tiller added, "They're really one of a kind."

"Why is there no name?"

"They claim their sniper is still enlisted. Still in. They don't want his name out there."

"Protecting his safety?"

Sutherland nodded.

"That's part of it. They're worried about enemy forces taking steps to find him and eliminate him. Beating that record at a thousand more yards is like putting a target on his back for enemy snipers all across the world. Some people would see him as a trophy kill. Like a challenge. They'd love to take him out."

Widow took a drink from his coffee, letting go of his fears of poisoning. Realizing it was stupid. The Army doesn't poison. They use bullets and bombs. The CIA, however, that's a different story. But they wouldn't do it like this. He hoped.

He took his time, swallowed. He said, "This is all fascinating, but why am I here?"

Sutherland clicked the trackpad again. Another photograph came up. This one was of a sniper, dead in the dirt. His head was blown apart. Blood was everywhere, covering everything. The soil. The long, overgrown blades of grass. The dead man's clothes. Everything.

"Who is it?"

"It's James Lenny."

"He was killed in combat? So what? Part of the risk."

"This isn't combat, Widow. Lenny was discharged from the Army back in 2014. His file cites he had PTSD. Badly."

"Where's this?"

"This is from three days ago."

Widow stayed quiet.

"This photo is from a patch of land in Ireland. Where Lenny is from. Apparently, he still shoots. This is a makeshift range out in the middle of nowhere. He's been shooting out there for years."

"Someone shot him?"

"That's the thing, Widow. Someone shot him from the other side of the range."

Tiller added, "While he was target practicing."

Widow stood up slowly. He kept the coffee in his hand and walked over to the screen. He stared at it. He stared at the gaping hole in the back of Lenny's head. Noticed that it was empty of blood. Noticed the huge exit wound, could tell that the entrance was Lenny's right eye.

Widow looked closer.

"He was shot through the scope?"

"That's right."

Tiller said, "Straight through the scope."

Sutherland said, "No damage was done to the windage, parallax, illumination, or magnification knobs. Only the focus was scratched up."

Tiller added, "A bit."

Widow stared back at the bloody mess on the screen.

Sutherland said, "The bullet traveled straight through the scope and barely touched anything until it exploded out the back of Lenny's head."

"You said it was fired from the end of the range?"

"It was fired from over Lenny's target."

Tiller said, "He had it all set up to match his record. Twenty-seven hundred yards."

Sutherland said, "He was trying to beat it. The sniper who murdered him shot from far behind it. Making him a much better shot than the second-best shot that ever lived."

Widow's jaw dropped. He turned, faced Sutherland, Swan, and Tiller, mouth opened wide.

Sutherland said, "We're working with the Brits on this."

"And the Koreans," Tiller said.

"Technically, it's a case for the Irish, but they're hitting some walls. And they don't want to implicate anyone outside their own jurisdiction. Not yet. Plus, there's the obvious thing that the killer is very good. And that's a terrifying prospect."

Widow remained silent.

Sutherland continued, "Imagine a sniper out there with this capability. Imagine what he could do. Imagine how easy it would be for him to kill a head of state. He could simply wait for the US president to give a stump speech in a field in Iowa or on the back of a corn truck in Nebraska or on an outdoor stage at the state fair in Indiana. Hell, he could take out the president while the president was giving a speech to the troops on the runway onboard a docked battleship. And he could do any of it from two miles away. No one could stop him."

Widow pictured it.

"This sniper just made the US Secret Service completely obsolete."

Tiller squeezed the bag of peas harder again, took a deep breath, and just stared at Widow like he was waiting for something to click.

Widow said, "Who did it? The Canadian?"

"That was everyone's first thought."

"But?"

"There are some obvious implications to that since the Canadians claim he still works for them."

"Has Ireland reached out to them?"

"No. But MI6 has. They didn't tell the Irish. Assorted feelings of jurisdiction and all. Plus, their priorities aren't to solve a murder but to spy for their government. They've reached out to us."

"Is MI6 working with Ireland at all?"

"It's gray."

"But a joint effort with the CIA? That's not likely."

Tiller said, "We're playing nice these days. You've been out a while."

Widow nodded, didn't believe it. In his experience, you can always tell when a government spy is lying, because his lips are moving.

"What do you need me for?"

"There's another possibility," Tiller said.

"What's that?"

"It wasn't the Canadian. It was someone else."

Widow paused, stared at Tiller with cold eyes.

Tiller had seen that look before. He nodded and said, "That's right."

"No one believed me twelve years ago. Now, you believe me?"

"Don't be angry with Tiller. He told us about your ghost sniper. Back then. Back in China. And he's the one who suggested we find you now."

Widow closed his eyes. He saw the nightmarish faces of ghosts, but not one of them was a ghost sniper. He saw something else. Nine faces. All in a row, standing one by one over each other's shoulder. They were aligned like they were posed by some unseen photographer who had one goal in mind— to haunt Widow for the rest of his life.

9

IGNORING the faces of the dead as best he could under the circumstances, concussion and all, Widow didn't acknowledge them. He looked ahead like they weren't there. He closed his eyes tight but faced the direction of Sutherland and Tiller. He was reminded of the mathematician John Nash, a guy who made significant contributions to game theory and modern economics but was more famous because he saw imaginary people.

They talked to him every day like real people, almost pushing him to the brink of insanity.

Widow opened his eyes and said, "So what? Now you believe me?"

No one spoke.

"I told the truth all those years ago. I always did. Now someone else is dead. It's on you!"

Tiller said, "It was the Pentagon who didn't believe you. Not me."

Widow paused, took a breath, and looked at Sutherland. "Is that true?"

Sutherland said, "It's true, Widow." He paused a beat, walked over to Tiller, placed his hand on the CIA agent's right shoulder like he was defending a nephew. He said, "Tiller fought for your side of the truth. He went to bat for you. Don't put the blame on him. I'm sad to say that it was my office that let you down. It was my call to ignore your story."

"You?"

"Yes. I oversaw the op. I gave the okay. I approved it. Not Tiller. The

CIA can't conduct military actions without the military part. You know that."

Widow asked, "Why was a government desk jockey giving orders involving Navy SEALs in the first place?"

Silence.

"General? You guys got your own snake eaters for that."

Widow threw out SEAL slang that he hadn't meant to. *Snake eater* is a generic term for USSF operators such as SEALs, Green Berets, Rangers, and others.

Sutherland didn't seem to notice. He ignored the quip and said, "I was leading a committee overseeing ops on the Korean Peninsula. We had an admiral in the loop, and the Air Force and the Marines. My authority over you was tethered to the admiral."

"Why isn't he here instead of you?"

"Back then, that would've been Admiral Holland. He's long retired by now. I believe."

"No, he's not. He's dead," Widow said.

Tiller said, "Dead?"

Sutherland asked, "You knew him?"

"Yeah, I knew him. He died. Natural causes. Years ago, now."

"Sorry to hear that."

"Don't be. He was a tool."

Sutherland said, "You show little respect for the military, don't you, Widow?"

"Is that a joke? I respect the military more than you'll ever know. But with the politicians, not so much."

"Holland wasn't a politician."

"Course he was. He wore a uniform, sure, but he began his career as the son of a politician. He went to college on the Navy's dime. Started playing politics with the lives of his men. Found how easy it was for him to move up. He was no sailor. He was a bureaucrat."

"Why did he stay in the Navy? It takes decades to reach the rank of admiral."

"Guess he got so good at playing the game with the higher-ups that he saw a better future for himself inside over the one he'd have in the private sector. Why give up the huge paychecks the higher-ups make? He would never see an actual battle."

"You were an officer. Are you lumping us all in together?"

Widow shook his head.

"I'm not like Holland. The only time that man ever fired a service weapon was in boot camp. Far as I know. I'm just calling it like I saw it, General."

Sutherland nodded and said, "That's pretty much how I remember him. That's why he didn't say no to sending in a SEAL team instead of my guys. Not to defend him, but we really thought that six would be enough."

Silence.

Swan cleared her throat quietly. Tiller lowered his hand, and the frozen peas with it. He reached up with his free hand and touched his cheek. It hurt. He winced, returned the frozen peas slowly.

Widow said, "Tiller made the call to leave the others behind. He was the one there. Not you. Or Holland."

No one spoke.

"Five of them were our guys. Since when does the US military leave men behind?"

"They were dead," Tiller said.

Widow didn't respond to that.

Sutherland said, "Take deep breaths, Widow."

Widow did as instructed. He breathed in and breathed out.

Tiller said, "Don't you think I regret that?"

Widow stayed quiet.

"I see a lot of dead faces, Widow. Just like you, I'm sure. More than my fair share. That's counterintelligence life. Right there. That's life in the field. Soldiers die."

"They weren't soldiers."

"Sailor then. Whatever. I am still haunted by their faces. Plus, a half dozen others. I've had a long career."

Silence.

"Ops go bad."

Sutherland said, "You ever heard the saying, 'What's done is done?'"

"Of course."

"It applies here. I'm a soldier and a commanding officer in the US Army. I've sent a lot of people to their deaths. Mostly young boys. I can't linger on it. It's already done."

Widow said nothing.

"Instead of being pissed off at me or at Tiller, why don't you redirect that anger at the men responsible? The Rainmakers."

Widow stared at Sutherland, said, "The Rainmakers?"

"That's what they're called."

"Who?"

"They're snipers," Tiller added.

Widow looked at Tiller and back at Sutherland. Apparently, they believed him after it was all too late.

Tiller said, "After what happened twelve years ago, the DOD noted the possibility of your ghost sniper being real. They buried it. But they didn't ignore it. Not completely."

Sutherland said, "There's a file in Fort Bragg."

Fort Bragg meant that the file on the Rainmakers, or whatever they were, was deeply classified.

Tiller said, "The Rainmakers is a name they got from locals. There's a Korean word for it. Basically, it translates as 'men who make rain of fire fall from the sky.' Catchy, right?"

"Who are they?" Widow asked.

"As you know, we don't know a lot about North Korea."

Sutherland added, "All we know is what we get from the South. And their intel isn't the best."

Widow said, "And what you see on satellite and drones."

Sutherland nodded, said, "For decades, the North's had ambitions of nuclear proliferation."

"That's why we were there twelve years ago."

Sutherland nodded, said, "But building nuclear weapons is only one aspect of their military ambitions."

Widow stayed quiet.

"They also formed a sniper team. Very elite, Widow. Apparently, they spent a fortune to build it up. And the intel that we've gathered was that the applicants were only given so many chances before things got bloody."

"Bloody?"

"First, the government would threaten members of the sniper's family. They cut off the fingers and limbs of their children. Things like that. If that didn't work, then they just killed the sniper."

Widow nodded.

"That made quite the incentive to be the best of the best."

"Why would anyone join this group?"

"They weren't volunteers. They were volunteered. The military tested soldiers for aptitude and..."

Widow said, "If you could shoot, then you were automatically a volunteer?"

"Right. North Korea's whole goal for getting nukes is to be taken seriously and to instill fear among the rest of us. The fear that they could strike."

Tiller said, "Anywhere."

"That's why they formed the Rainmakers. Possibly the world's most elite snipers. Imagine it. The Rainmakers were meant for covert assassinations."

Sutherland paused for a moment, took a breath. Then he said, "Did you see on the news, last year, the assassination of one of the North Korean dictator's brothers?"

Widow nodded and said, "I remember. He was poisoned. Some kind of nerve agent or something very high-grade."

"That's right."

"They caught the assassin."

Sutherland nodded, said, "They did. But what you didn't see on the news was she killed herself. Right in the police jail. Cyanide pill in her tooth. After she was caught. She had been trained to kill and then trained to kill herself when caught."

"Cyanide tooth? That's a real thing?"

Tiller said, "It's real."

Sutherland said, "Imagine it. The Rainmakers are sent abroad and trained to kill from ungodly distances. They'd never even be caught if they played their cards right. Imagine the terror around the world."

Widow nodded. It sounded like a terrifying scenario.

"Anyway, they never deployed the Rainmakers. Not before now. They've been stationing them along the borders. Often, they wait for defectors to cross over a mile of frozen river and terrain, and then they shoot them. Each time trying to get better. Each time trying to shoot farther."

Tiller said, "There's only been one encounter—that we know of—that they've ever shot over two miles and killed with deadly accuracy."

Sutherland said, "It was your op."

Widow said, "That sniper killed nine people in that encounter. I'd say he's proven he can shoot ridiculous distances."

Sutherland and Tiller both nodded at the same time.

"Now you want me to catch him?"

Everyone paused a beat.

Sutherland spoke first. He said, "You're not in the Navy anymore, Commander. But we'd sure like your help."

"With what, exactly?"

Sutherland said, "Twelve years ago, you went on a mission. An op that was so covert only a small SEAL team was spared to take it."

Sutherland didn't have to say their names. Widow knew it. Concussion or not.

Sutherland clicked the trackpad again, and the photo changed. It was an aerial view photo of Lenny's corpse, taken by a small drone, Widow figured.

Sutherland clicked it again, and the photo changed again. The next one was of the target area that Lenny was aiming at. There was a tall, wooden stake stabbing into a green watermelon.

"Interesting target," Widow said.

Sutherland nodded, clicked the trackpad again, and another photo from the drone came up. This one was farther back and above where the target had been. It was a higher elevation, which made sense. Lenny would've been firing in a downward slope. Partly because of the range. And partly because he didn't want to shoot someone on the other side of the target accidentally.

Sutherland stopped on the photo.

Widow studied it. There wasn't much to see. There was heavy grass, collapsed and bent over.

He said, "That's where the sniper who killed him was."

Sutherland said, "The Rainmaker. We believe."

"What is it I'm supposed to see here?" Widow asked.

Tiller said, "Widow, we know you were really an undercover investigator with NCIS."

Widow shrugged, said, "You're CIA. And you're Pentagon. I know you know. So what?"

"We need you to investigate."

"Secretly," Sutherland added.

Widow took another pull from the coffee, stood up, kept it in hand, and walked over to the screen. He looked hard.

"Nothing to see here that's not obvious."

"Indulge us."

Widow looked again. He switched the coffee over to his left hand, set it down, bottom in his palm like a space shuttle landing, and held it there. His left hand hurt from the effort, but he knew that broken limbs fell under the principle of "use it or lose it."

He pointed at the screen with his right hand, traced over the outline of the crushed grass. "This is where the sniper lay prone and killed Lenny. He used a sniper mat. That's why it's shaped like a rectangle."

Sutherland and Tiller nodded. Of course, they knew that part.

Widow said, "Can you zoom? Make this section bigger?"

He pointed at the top corner of where the mat would've been laid.

"Yep," Sutherland said, and pinched and clicked his fingers on the trackpad. The whole process took a long second.

The screen was filled with grass.

Widow looked hard. He saw broken and crushed and destroyed blades of grass. It started at the center, where it was destroyed, then moved up in a direction that Widow guessed to be east because of shadows on the ground.

Widow traced the variations of grass with his index and middle fingers. He said, "Yeah."

"Yeah, what?"

"Nothing."

"What is it?"

Tiller said, "Anything is better than what we got."

Widow said, "I'd guess you got two killers here."

"What makes you say that?"

"The grass. It's not just pushed down. It's crushed. It's destroyed here and here," he said and pointed.

Swan interjected for the first time. A natural, involuntary act, like being sucked into a story by a stranger involving a monkey and saying, "What happened to the monkey?"

She said, "And there too." She pointed at the third section of grass destroyed. Not pushed down. Destroyed.

Widow looked at it and nodded.

Tiller said, "A single person could've done that."

"Not likely."

"Why not?"

"First, the guy would have to be more than two hundred pounds. Probably two-twenty or more."

"Plenty of guys are two hundred twenty pounds."

"Sure, but not snipers."

Sutherland said, "I've seen guys out at the range that heavy."

"Maybe at a civilian range. Maybe retired snipers. But not an elite sniper. Not a North Korean."

"'Cause Koreans are smaller?"

Widow said, "On a general level, sure, they are smaller than us. But that's not what I mean. They are underfed. North Korea doesn't provide for its people. I'd be surprised if the military gets three squares a day. Elite snipers or not."

"What's the second thing?"

"The second thing is that this guy would've had to have been rocking around to make three different destroyed grass patterns."

Tiller said, "So?"

"Snipers don't move. Not a sniper who got this good. He'd be silent and still. Very. This guy would have to be like a Shaolin monk. I'd be shocked if his breath would even register in freezing temperatures. To be that good."

They all nodded, staring at Widow.

Sutherland asked, "Two snipers? You're sure?"

Widow said, "There's another thing."

They waited. No one spoke.

Widow said, "I don't think it's two snipers. I think it's one sniper and one spotter. Snipers in the military use spotters. I'm impressed that Lenny could shoot that far on his own. Must've taken him a long time to set up the shot and zero his aim that close to target."

"Then we're looking for two Koreans. Both light. Both well trained."

"That'd be my guess. If they really are Rainmakers."

Sutherland nodded. He stared at Tiller, who nodded back. "Widow, before we go any further, we'd like for you to work with us on this."

Widow stayed quiet.

"We need you. We have to stop these guys before they do irreparable damage in the world."

Tiller said, "Next, they might shoot someone who matters. You know? On the world stage."

Widow stared down at his coffee.

"What do you say?"

"What exactly are my parameters?"

"You'll answer to Tiller, who will report to me."

Tiller added, "Our goal is to find and capture—if possible."

"And if not?"

"Then we dispatch the targets."

Widow took a deep breath. He said, "If this is the sniper team from twelve years ago, I'm not interested in capture."

They said nothing to that.

"I'll do it. But know that for me, it's not about putting to bed any fears that some politicians might have. For me, it's about a thirteen-year-old girl."

Tiller nodded. He knew exactly what Widow was talking about. Sutherland nodded eventually. He caught on. Swan didn't know what he meant by that.

10

THE STEWARD FROM THE C-20B—WHO had flown with an unlogged, unmanifested, unkempt giant of a passenger from Minneapolis–Saint Paul Air Reserve Station all the way to Andrews Air Force Base just ninety-eight minutes ago—finished up his daily checks on the interior of the plane. Then he gathered his paperwork and flight check-ins and collected the little trash that had been produced from the two flights—one empty paper coffee cup from the recent one—and he stowed everything away and rechecked that it was all in its place. A place for everything. Everything in its place. One of the Air Force credos.

After he finished, he stepped off the plane and out of the hangar. He pulled his carry-on suitcase along the pavement as the hard plastic tires jerked across the tarmac.

He looked at his watch. The time was fifteen minutes past four in the afternoon.

He walked past flight crews readying to board a nearby C-130 and stepped into the crew center. He walked past more crew members. Only one recognized him. He nodded at her and moved on.

He passed one officer who outranked him, and he stopped and saluted. Then he continued until he was in front of the crew center. He waited at the sidewalk for a base shuttle to take him to his car.

He stared at his watch again and looked at a posted sign with shuttle times and routes. According to the posted schedule, he was going to be waiting for ten more minutes before the shuttle arrived. He figured this probably meant twenty minutes. It was the later part of the afternoon, which meant that the military day shift would be looking at the clock, waiting for five o'clock so they could scramble to their cars and fight Maryland traffic for thirty-plus minutes before they could get to their homes and kick off their shoes.

He had just flown from Minneapolis to Andrews, not a long flight, but before that, he had already been on a six-hour, twenty-five-minute flight from Andrews out to Davis-Monthan Air Force Base in Tucson. Right at landing, they were ordered to fly to Minneapolis–Saint Paul to pick up some VIP, another three-hour, fifteen-minute flight.

All things considered, he was in a pretty good mood but dog tired. He was ready to go home and get some sleep.

To kill time and to earn a couple of bucks, he decided it was time to call a journalist friend he had at the *Washington Post*. No one special, just a low-level researcher. Which was her official title, but it didn't mean that all she did was write briefs and summaries by reading articles on Wikipedia or by interviewing willing witnesses. Some people she interviewed, called sources, were people she had to pay to buy information.

The more valuable the information, the greater the risk. The greater the risk, the higher the price tag.

The steward pulled out his cell phone and dialed her number.

It rang once, twice, and on the third ring, she answered.

She said his name and a hello. He said her name and hello back. Then he asked her how much she wanted a tip about a top secret VIP transport package.

She said, "Depends. What are we talking about here?"

"Something very valuable."

"How valuable?"

"Plenty."

"Specifics?"

He said, "I want to get paid first."

"I'll send money by PayPal. Per usual. Tell me the info first."

"No way. You send the money. And if it's high enough. I'll tell you the intel."

Silence.

The researcher said, "Give me a minute."

She put him on hold. No warning.

A minute and ten seconds later, she came back on the line.

"Check your account."

The steward said, "Okay."

He took the phone out of his ear, clicked the screen and swiped, and opened an app to his PayPal account. *You received a payment.*

He smiled, saw the number, and smiled bigger.

"Is that enough?" he heard her ask, even with the phone away from his ear.

"It is. That works."

"Give me the intel."

He told her all he knew. He told her about the urgent turnaround from Davis-Monthan to Minneapolis–Saint Paul Air Force Reserve Station and waiting, and how the pilots told him they weren't logging the flight in with the tower nor reporting the secret passenger who had gotten on the jet.

She said, "Is that all?"

"We took him to Andrews. Some kind of top secret thing."

"What else?"

The steward was quiet.

"Who was he?"

"I don't have a name."

"This isn't enough. What's so strange about this guy? The unlogged flight is unusual, but no one here is going to be interested in a phantom flight."

"I can tell you what he looked like."

She was quiet.

"He was a big guy. Like *Terminator*. And he wasn't military."

"What was he?"

"I don't know. But important. They sent a Navy MP to escort him, and we dropped him off at Andrews. An MP picked him up. My guess is he's some kind of secret agent or a CIA assassin. Maybe. He wasn't a normal guy we pick up."

"Is that all?"

"That's what I got."

"Okay. Thanks. If you think of anything else, call me."

And they disconnected.

* * *

SECRET AGENT, she thought.

The researcher at the *Washington Post* was good at her job. She had worked there for three years, right out of college. A lot of competition went into securing a job there. Once she had gotten a foot in the door, she taught herself the ropes. The thing about the ropes was learning that the news business was cutthroat. In order to maintain her position in the ranks, she had to be cutthroat. When she couldn't dig up a story, sometimes she had to take extreme measures. She had to stir the pot and see what came to the surface.

And sometimes, she just liked to make a little money on the side herself.

She couldn't do much with the intel she had paid for. But she could make a little money off it herself. She could always use it if more to the story ever developed.

She ignored the landline on her desk, pulled out her cell phone and dialed a number that she had written in her notes, not logged as a contact.

She waited and listened to the number dial.

A voice with a Chinese accent answered the phone. It was a man. He said, "Chinese Consulate. This is Lu Er."

The man on the line wasn't a secretary or even a desk jockey at the Chinese Consulate, but he was there. Probably. He was a midlevel official. She didn't know his job title but knew that it was just a generic title like "agent." It could mean many things.

His real name wasn't Lu Er, as no one in China was really named that.

In America, John Doe was the standard name for a man unidentified. The Chinese put a common name together with a number, like John Four or Joe Two.

The man on the phone's name was Lu Er, which just meant Lu Two. Nothing too clever, but Americans never caught on. Neither did almost any other person from any other continent.

She said, "It's me."

Lu said, "Hello."

"I've got a story for you."

And she told all the parts she knew. She told him about the man flown in top secret. The jet. The covert nature of it all. She told him about all she had so far. She didn't know what it meant or if it even applied to the Chinese government. Random chance it was.

Technically, what the Air Force steward had done wasn't illegal, not in the civilian world. It may be a court-martial offense in the military world. She had no idea. Not her problem.

But what she was doing, selling military secrets to a foreign government, might be a breach of federal law, but only if she was selling privileged knowledge to a foreign government, like spying. Theoretically, she wasn't telling him anything that she was privileged to. She didn't work for the US government. She wasn't in the military. She wasn't the Air Force steward. If he had sold the information directly to Lu, that would constitute a felony.

To her, right then, it didn't differ from her selling information to a newspaper, like the *New York Times*. That would have been a fireable offense since they were a competitor to her organization. But it wasn't illegal.

Lu listened and took it all down.

She asked about payment, which, normally, she would've done up front, but that's not how the Chinese government does business. They want to know the information first, know if it's valuable, and they decide the amount of payment based on that.

They were good for it. She knew that. She had sold information to them in the past. It was just a way to make some extra money. Living in DC was very expensive.

They used none of her information anyway, she figured.

Lu told her the payment was being sent. Then he paused a long, long beat. It was so long she had to ask if he was still there.

He answered he was, and then he did something out of the ordinary. He said, "Never call me again. Good luck to you." And he hung up the phone.

She took the cell phone away from her ear and stared at it. *That was odd*, she thought.

11

An hour later, the local time was fifteen past midnight when the woman got off a plane at Dublin International. She had flown China Southern Airlines from Beijing with a layover in Amsterdam, which pissed her off because it was only two hours, and she had never been to Amsterdam. She'd caught her connecting flight with KLM and had just landed without delays.

She walked softly across the linoleum floors in the terminal like it was carpet and she was gliding on bare feet. She stepped lightly because she was light. Her hair was pulled back, a no-nonsense ponytail, and she wore no makeup. Not on a flight. She flew a lot for her occupation and had learned long ago not to wear makeup when she didn't have to. To the men in her profession, it sounded like a meaningless topic. But among the few women who worked at the high level she worked, it was a topic of heated debate.

Wear makeup; get noticed by men for being attractive. Don't wear makeup; get noticed by women for not following the rules of engagement deemed by social norms.

Ultimately, it was a case-by-case kind of decision to make. Here, she chose not to. Mostly, she chose not to because she had to endure a thirteen-hour, fifty-minute flight over eight countries with commercial carriers. At least she flew first class. That made things a little easier. A little more bearable. At least she could sleep since they had reclining seats with one hundred percent horizontal tilt capabilities, which was good.

She got to sleep on a portion of the flight. Enough to make her appear to be awake enough when she met with her Irish counterparts.

The only thing about flying first class was that even though she could skip putting on the makeup, she had to dress the part. She couldn't wear comfortable workout clothes. She had to look like she belonged. Official policy from China was to not draw attention to herself needlessly.

She stepped off the plane wearing a dark-green pantsuit with a Chinese collar, notched. She believed the fabric was part bamboo and part cotton. It was comfortable. The single-breasted jacket had sleeves hastily pushed up over her elbows. It was part of the Western style. She had been told it'd be fashionable in Ireland.

She hauled a carry-on behind her. It was a small thing with an extended arm for pulling across the ground. Unlike the Air Force steward's, her wheels weren't jerking.

She walked out through the local customs area, where she had shown her passport and been given a stern look-over, partially because she was a foreigner with a Chinese passport. Not a lot of Chinese people in Dublin, she figured.

She stopped at the last point of international land before she was officially on Irish soil. And she glanced down at the official line at the airport. It was one of those "you're crossing over into a new country" lines.

A frown came over her face because she had expected it to be green. But it was a red line. She stepped over it and out into the general population, into Ireland.

After following the signs to arrivals and taxis and passing the baggage claim area, she walked out the front doors, where normally there would be a line of limo and taxi drivers waiting to pick up arriving passengers. But this time of night meant that only one guy was standing there.

He was one of the other people in Dublin with a Chinese passport.

The only difference between them was that she was not Chinese. Not by birth. Only by citizenship. She was Asian by birth from one of China's neighbors. Most people couldn't tell. She looked Chinese enough.

No one in her adopted country ever guessed that she wasn't. Why should anyone in Ireland be any different?

The man wore an all-black suit. Black jacket. Black pants. That was the first thing she noticed, naturally. The second was that he was armed. He had a Glock 17 in a pancake holster at his right hip. It was well concealed, but not to her. She had been trained. She knew what to look for.

The last thing she noticed was that he held up a sign with her name on it. It was her real name. No need to use aliases. Not here. Not when the name was written in Chinese.

Who the hell here was going to read that?

She stopped out in front of him. He smiled at her, gave a nod, and spoke Chinese.

They made introductions. They shook hands. And then he told her she was going to her hotel first. Nothing they could do tonight. They'd have to take another flight first thing in the morning to a city called Cork.

She didn't know why she was there. Not yet. In Beijing, they hadn't told her anything. She just knew that she was going to Dublin first because there was a Chinese embassy there. That's where they would update her.

That's where she'd learn that her assignment wasn't a regular assignment. That's where she'd learn that it was personal.

12

SUTHERLAND AND TILLER finished their sales pitch with Widow and wrapped everything up. Tiller took the bag of peas, handed it back to Swan, who must've thought to return it to the freezer right then because she got up and walked out of the room.

Sutherland scratched his belly over his uniform shirt, moving his gun hand out of drawing distance for the first time.

Widow noticed but said nothing—did nothing.

"I want to remind you of a couple things. First, you report to Tiller. Second, we don't need any collateral damage. Got that?"

Widow nodded.

"Third, remember you were granted top security clearance once upon a time."

Widow nodded again. He remembered.

"Remember the paperwork that you had to sign to get that security clearance?"

"That was like a hundred years ago."

"But do you remember?"

"I remember it. How could I forget? Two lawyers came to see me. Made me sign a book worth of documents."

"In that book, some clauses grant us the right to have you locked up until you turn old and gray if you violate any of the stipulations in that agreement."

"What's that got to do with anything?"

"It means you can't tell anyone about what we have told you here or what happens in this investigation."

Widow said, "That agreement still holds water?"

"It does."

Widow nodded.

"Last, don't get caught. If you get arrested in a foreign country, we can't help you."

"Am I going to another country?"

"Of course."

Tiller said, "Lenny was a Brit. Shot in Ireland. As far as we know, the Rainmaker is still there."

"I won't get caught."

"Good," Sutherland said and closed the MacBook. "Tiller will take it from here."

Widow nodded and watched the general walk to the door, heading off in the opposite direction that Widow had come from. He paused in the doorway, turned, and looked back. He was contemplating whether to leave Widow alone with Tiller. That was obvious.

In the end, he did.

"What now?"

Tiller said, "We get started. Let's get out of here."

They went down the same elevator that Widow had come up in. The whole time Widow couldn't help but have thoughts of doing more damage to Tiller. But he held back.

They went down the same corridor, passed the same guard station, and passed under the same security cameras on the way out.

This time, there was a black Escalade parked on the street. Engine running. Two men inside. A driver and another guy in the back seat.

The guy in the back seat got out and waited for Tiller to step up. He opened the front passenger door for him like a chauffeur. Only the guy looked more like a Secret Service agent. He was not.

He didn't open the door for Widow. Widow got in the back seat on his own, one-handed, all the way. He could feel the warmth.

Tiller introduced the two guys as part of his team. Widow forgot their names two seconds after learning them. His impression of them was that they were the muscle and nothing else.

After everyone was in and buckled up, the driver took off, and the Escalade was on the road. Five minutes later, they were back at the runways. Thirty seconds after that, they were parking at a jet hangar. Not the same one that Widow had come in to.

"What are we doing here?"

Tiller turned around from the front seat and looked at him. "We're going to Ireland. You got your passport, right?"

Widow dug in his pocket, pulled it out.

Tiller looked at it, shrugged. "You won't need it."

"I will in a foreign country."

Tiller said nothing to that. Instead, he swung back around and got out of the Escalade. The muscle got out after him. Widow followed.

He followed them out onto the tarmac. There was a Lockheed C-5 Galaxy parked around the corner on the edge of the tarmac in what used to be grass and was later covered with gravel and then repurposed with filled-in concrete.

The engines were on.

Widow followed as Tiller and the two muscle guys boarded the plane. They climbed up wobbly portable jet steps and entered.

They fumbled in past the cockpit and into the belly. They stopped just before the cargo area. There were four seats stacked and plain and all metal. No cushions. They folded out of the wall like the jump seat Widow had seen the Air Force steward sit on.

In the cockpit, Widow saw two pilots and an airman, who was set to fly with the plane to watch over the cargo.

In the back of the plane, there were stacked crates and boxes and various packages. There was one military Humvee locked in place by tire boots, jacked into the floor on a track. The Humvee was empty.

Tiller sat in a jump seat, followed by both muscle guys. They were just like Rosencrantz and Guildenstern, two characters from Shakespeare's *Hamlet* who were so indistinguishable from each other that Hamlet was always confusing them. Only these guys were worse because they were like puppets who followed Tiller around with no original thought between them.

In *Hamlet*, the prince ended up leading Rosencrantz and Guildenstern to their deaths, but only because they were supposed to trick him and betray him and lead him to his execution. He outsmarted them.

The thought of tricking them into stepping into their executions crossed Widow's mind.

Widow looked at the last seat with disdain. He didn't want to sit next to Tiller, and he didn't want to sit on a metal seat, taking off in an overstuffed metal box. The days that he had to fly bare-bones were long in his past. He had hoped.

In that instant, Tiller saw him eyeballing the jump seat. He put a hand up and spoke. "Not here. This is for the crewman."

Widow looked over at the third airman and back at Tiller. "You serious?"

"Sorry."

The airman walked out of the cockpit toward the jump seat.

"Am I supposed to sit on the floor?"

The airman reached out to touch Widow's arm but decided not to.

He said, "Sir, you can sit in the Humvee."

Widow looked over at the Humvee. "Are you serious?" He looked at Tiller. "Is that legal?"

Tiller said, "This isn't LAX, Widow."

The engines echoed throughout the hull and the fuselage and the nose, loud and brassy. The vibrations and the noise rattled through the metal and through Widow's legs and his bones and his broken arm and his skull.

He remembered being in Humvees. Hundreds. Maybe thousands of different ones in his past. Not one specific memory came to mind. It was more of a military blur.

Widow shrugged and walked back past more metal and cargo nets and stacked boxes and various Air Force equipment. All of it boxed up or stowed away in containers. And all of it strapped into countless pockets and netting.

The airman was right behind him, offering a hand getting into the Humvee. Widow shoved it off and maneuvered around strapped-down cargo and the hood and two of the big tires, and opened the passenger door to the vehicle. He pulled himself up and dumped himself down on the seat.

He decided not to get behind the steering wheel. The passenger seat offered more legroom.

"Buckle your seat belt."

Widow wasn't used to doing that in a Humvee. The Navy didn't require it. The Army did. The Marines, he was pretty sure, didn't. He didn't know the policy of the Air Force regarding wearing a seat belt in a Humvee.

He buckled in and nodded at the airman. The guy nodded back and walked away.

At least Widow didn't have to sit next to Tiller on the flight over the pond. And at least he was in a cushioned chair instead of a crappy jump seat. So he smiled.

A few moments later, the C-5 Galaxy was up and off the ground and airborne. About five minutes into the flight, the captain came over the intercom, which was blasted out of back speakers behind the cockpit.

The crew wore crash helmets with headphones in their ears. The speakers were only for non–Air Force members' benefit.

The captain introduced himself, announced the flight time of five hours and some change, and said they were flying to an American Air Force base in the UK called Lakenheath.

Widow never heard of it and had never been there. He wasn't sure how it worked. Was it a British installation with an American unit? Did the US Air Force have a continuing contract with the government? Or was it US soil, kept after World War II?

He wasn't sure.

He had no window view, only military ordnance, and the inside of the cargo plane, and Tiller's group, which he really didn't want to look at or think about.

Widow took a moment to fumble with his pill bottle and pop the top. It took him a long moment to get it open. It reminded him of a pressurized hatch on a submarine that won't open. He suspected the bottle lid was his mortal enemy. Finally, he popped it open and downed another pill. He returned the lid to the bottle, the bottle to his pocket.

Widow stared at the lifeless dash on the Humvee for the first twenty minutes. His gaze never moved. He did this until he closed his eyes and drifted away into a nightmarish sleep. A memory that he had locked away had been rattled loose by a train crash and a concussion. Like he had it all squared away in a lockbox in his mind, but now someone had broken the lock.

He thought back to a pair of volcanic eyes he would never forget.

13

Her volcanic eyes stared up at him. She held his hand tight. He could feel her grip through the Navy-issued tactical glove, which was white and thin and tough and durable. The best material. It protected against harsh weather, and overheating from firing rounds from any assault rifle or submachine gun systems.

Widow had needed them. They did their job—protection against anything.

Only there were some things in the world that they couldn't protect him from.

One was those volcanic eyes.

He held her hand.

She was the last one alive. The last man standing. Minus himself.

He stared into those volcanic eyes. He watched the life slip away. She was out in the snow. The mist hung around her like dust settling. Only it never did.

The surrounding snow had been white only seconds before. Now it had turned to a deep, deep red. The way he imagined a giant vat of ruby-red lipstick would look at first in a huge metal container on the factory floor of a lipstick company.

The red was blood. She was bleeding out. Shot. She wouldn't make it. No way.

He moved his eyes to her lips. They faded to pink and then to gray.

He stared into those volcanic eyes.

He watched her die.

14

The Navy spared no expense training the men who crossed through BUD/S, or Basic Underwater Demolition/SEAL training, and Widow had delivered more than twenty-five missions by that point.

Twenty-five covert missions were in one of Widow's files, locked away in Virginia at the Department of the Navy. But another dozen or more were locked away offsite in Quantico, in the secret basement offices of Unit Ten.

His double life.

The border between China and North Korea was primarily composed of two rivers fused together as one. Plus, there was the rugged mountain terrain to deal with.

From west to east, the waters of the Yalu River swallowed the violent torrents that flowed south out of the Paektu Mountains and the Tumen River. The rivers divided the two countries.

To the north, there was one main bridge connecting nation to nation over the Tumen.

In the summer months, it helped to expedite importing and exporting between a city in China and a main village in North Korea.

But in the winter months, it was frozen completely over.

Widow and the other SEALs on his team were there in the dead of winter. A snowstorm had blown through only a day before.

They had used the day after the passing storm to achieve their mission.

This winter, the river waters rose to near flood levels, and the drawbridge was raised, and the ice froze over the road top, leaving both sides of the drawbridge gaping open. They stood up out of the ice at thirty meters apiece, like they were the saber teeth of some unspeakable horror that lived below the ice.

A dense and heavy mist rose from the top of the ice and plumed up into wafts of thick white fog. The skies were gray in the early morning hours. The sun must've been up somewhere because the far-off recesses of the sky were white, but nothing was blue. No blue in sight. Only the grayish blue of dreary gloom.

Widow's boots sank into the drifting snow, as did those of the five SEALs that brought up his rear. Widow was leading a SEAL team on a secret mission.

Widow was nearly out of breath when he reached the middle of the distance between North Korea's last steppe, just before the rocky ice on the frozen river and the edge of the highway in China.

Before crossing the river, Widow had to wait and look in all directions. He had to make sure that no one was around, watching him and his guys. The last thing they needed was to be seen by Chinese natives who might call the cops. The local police doubled as soldiers. They'd send a guy out in a patrol truck with snow tires to check out the foreigners who didn't belong. Maybe they'd send cops.

Once the cops saw that Widow and his team weren't Chinese, they would bring out the sirens and spotlights and guns. They would cuff them, throw them in the back of the truck, and haul them back to headquarters. If this happened, it wouldn't be good. It would be bad for Widow and his team, and bad for the US. And that was the best-case scenario.

They would know Widow and his guys were special operators just by the weapons they carried. Widow was armed with a SIG Sauer P226 Legion RX edition, which was the same as the standard, only better. His SIG Sauer had a red-dot sight and other features he didn't care about. He liked the Romeo sight. It was great for nearly guaranteed accuracy.

Besides the SIG, he and his guys were armed with Heckler & Koch MP5SD submachine guns. The MP5SD came suppressed. This was an SMG made for covert ops, and they were engaged in a covert op. No question.

This was a CIA black op. Widow knew that because he had met the guy in charge—a shady agent named Benico Tiller.

When one of the other guys in his op, a lieutenant named Lyn, asked Tiller in a five-minute briefing if this op was against regulations, Tiller responded, "Regulations are regarded more like guidelines when it comes to special ops."

Widow shrugged. He didn't respond to that.

The snowfall had stopped an hour earlier, which was good because he, Lyn, and the others were getting worried.

The mission was to rescue and extract a North Korean civilian—a scientist. The man knew something about the regime's nuclear program. Which the pointy-heads at the Pentagon were still hoping to curtail.

Widow never knew exactly what the guy's function or knowledge was. It wasn't mission-critical. Widow was on a need-to-know basis. And the details didn't need to be known.

The scientist's name was Kweon. Widow didn't know Kweon's first name. Not important. Not for identification, because the guy would defect from North Korea by crossing over the frozen river at the coordinates that Tiller gave Widow.

They were given the place. They were given the time. And they were given the number of defectors.

The defector was taking his family out with him. They were getting asylum in America. A good deal for them. They'd get relocation money. They'd get new names. They'd get new passports and new identities.

Widow imagined they'd be put up somewhere in Indiana or Oklahoma or Kentucky or Kansas or whatever state was deep in the middle of the country. They would relocate to a small town and given monthly allowances and education, and probably a small business. They'd have a good life, a real change from the horrors of living in North Korea. Especially for a guy like Kweon.

Widow could only imagine that Kweon, being some kind of prominent scientist, was under a big-brother type of surveillance. From what he knew of important people in North Korea, of guys critical to the success of the nuclear program. If they weren't cooperative, then they were forced to take part.

Widow could only imagine what Kweon must've gone through on the other side of the border to get all the way to the edge and cross the barbed wires and the fences and the armed patrols.

It must've taken a lot of CIA funding to get known North Korean diplomats and maybe border guards to look the other way for a small window of time, while Kweon and his family hiked across miles of rugged, snow-covered terrain to make the final leg of the journey to cross a dangerous, frozen river.

Widow had been briefed on countless failed attempts by previous non-agency important defectors.

But it wasn't until that moment when he saw dead bodies frozen in the ice below that he realized how often people died trying to escape.

Widow stepped slowly through the snow and over the ice. He paused a beat about two hundred feet from the edge of China's highway. He had seen movement and small figures on the horizon through his field glasses back at the checkpoint.

The checkpoint was two klicks behind him.

That's where Lyn and Reyes waited. They were posted on the roof of the only structure within ten square miles. It was part of the remains of a hardware store. It had been closed, abandoned, and looted a decade in the past, like the rest of a small enclave on the side of the highway. Initially, it was a lived-in small town on the route to the next city. Now it was abandoned and long forgotten. Perfect for Widow's SEAL Team to set up camp the night before.

Reyes acted as backup for Lyn, who was in Widow's ear on a tiny wire receiver. The wire was tucked away behind Widow down his back, down to a small radio rig strapped to the side of his rucksack.

Widow and his team were decked out in all-white-and-blacks to camouflage them with the terrain and the snow.

Their faces were painted in camo blacks.

Lyn watched him from the checkpoint through a rifle scope. Reyes knelt over Lyn's shoulder.

Lyn took his fingers away from the trigger housing and squeezed the talk button on his laryngophone—a mic rig that's circular and fits around an operator's throat—also known as a throat microphone. It's ideal for covert work in harsh weather.

Lyn said, "Scorpio, do you see them?"

They were using zodiac animals as call signs for the mission. Widow had been born in November. Therefore, he was Scorpio.

Widow pulled down a bandana that was covering his mouth and nose so he could breathe in the icy winds. He glanced from one side to the other. On his left, there was a SEAL he'd worked with before named Clery. On his right, there was a SEAL he'd only just met named Hollander. Pulling up the rear was another SEAL called Slabin. Widow made eye contact with Clery, who nodded and then at Hollander, who also nodded. He didn't look back at Slabin.

Widow took a breath and pressed the talk button on his laryngophone.

The transducers kicked to life and picked up his voice, crisp and bright against the harsh, icy wind.

Widow said, "No. I can't see a damn thing out here. Just lots and lots of white."

Silence.

Widow asked, "You got them still?"

Lyn said, "Affirmative. I see them. About sixty, maybe fifty yards ahead."

Widow let go of the MP5SD and let it fall back on a sling over his back, out of the way. He held one hand up over his eyes and scrunched it into the shape of a makeshift visor. He stared off into the gloom.

Widow waited.

He clicked his throat mic and said, "I see nothing."

Static fired over the receiver in his ear. And then a long pause. He heard Lyn breathing like someone about to say something but holding onto the last breath.

Lyn said, "About twenty-five yards now. To the northeast. Over the snowbank."

Widow turned and looked in the direction Lyn indicated and paused. Then he heard noises. Frantic. Like heavy breathing. And whimpering.

Widow clutched his talk button and spoke.

"How many?"

"Four. Yeah. Four. Two are small, like children. That's gotta be them."

"Okay. I'm going to meet them at the bottom of the hill."

Widow clicked off, and Lyn said nothing.

Widow glanced at his team again. He gave them hand signals, informing them what positions to take. The other men took their positions, guns at the ready. Then, Widow stepped forward, leaving the bandana loose on his neck. The wind batted against his face. Gusts slapped hard several times. He felt his breath ripped out of him.

After seven minutes of carefully stepping and sliding through snow and ice, the Team made it to the bottom of the hill. They set up there, awaiting an ambush. A necessary precaution.

Widow planted one boot in the snow and went down on one knee. The Team followed suit. Widow held his MP5SD up and out. Kept the muzzle pointed down at the four o'clock position. He didn't want to accidentally shoot whoever was walking over the snowbank. Or scare away the family he was there to rescue. He didn't know if they knew who they were meeting. He didn't even know if they spoke English.

A mistake just hit him. He clutched at his throat mic.

"Chicken. Come in."

"Rooster" was Lyn's technical zodiac animal, but not his assigned code name for this op. His code name was the American calendar year's counterpart.

Since he was Chinese and born in the right month and right year for it to apply, January 1982, Widow was just having fun with him.

Widow heard static. And a puff of air, like exhaling. And Lyn's voice. "It's not Chicken. It's Capricorn. We're using American astrology signs."

Widow said, "I didn't know we'd decided on that yet."

Lyn ignored that and asked, "What is it? You see them?"

"Not yet. But I just realized, why am I down here, leading the extraction and not you? I don't speak Korean."

Lyn was Chinese, but he was a polyglot. He spoke Chinese, Korean, English, and Japanese, which made him a damn valuable member of the SEALs.

"That's because you studied no other language."

"So why am I out here instead of you?" Widow repeated.

"Two reasons. First, you're expendable and I'm not. And second cause you can't shoot a sniper rifle for shit."

The other Team members chuckled around Widow. He shot them a stern glance, one for each of them. They all went back to being quiet.

Widow said, "Seriously?"

"Ten seconds. You'll see them."

Widow stared up at the top of the hill. He slipped a quick hand into his coat pocket and slid out a device that looked like a cell phone. Only this one cost about ten grand. It was a military device. Like a cell phone, it was also a multifunctional device.

He clicked on the home screen and thumbed to a photograph of what Dr. Kweon looked like. The photograph was dated. It was taken in the eighties—a close-up of a class photo. In order to learn the trade of nuclear weapons and technology, Kweon had to go outside of North Korea. He attended school in China.

The image was black and white. Widow had to tack on decades in his mind. But he had a clear picture of what Kweon should look like today.

Widow reversed the device and held it up and showed the photograph to Clery and Hollander and then to Slabin. They all took a look and memorized the face and nodded back to him when they each had it.

Widow took one last look at it, memorized it for himself, and slipped the device back into his pocket and returned his hand back to the MP5SD.

Lyn said, "Just repeat to them what I tell you. It'll be fine."

Widow stayed quiet.

Just then, he saw them.

Four figures climbed up over the snowbank. Panting and sweating and breathing hard, like they had been running for their lives, which they had.

First, Widow saw a tall figure. He checked his mind's photograph of Kweon and waited. After a moment, the tall figure came closer and into view. It was the father, Kweon.

He wasn't tall by nature. He looked tall because he was holding a young girl. A teenager. Thirteen. Maybe.

She was latched on to his back like she was playing a normal game of piggyback. Like they were a normal family at the lake. Minus the ice and snow and a six-million-man paramilitary stretched over the country behind them.

Widow studied the other members of Kweon's party.

He saw a woman, about five years younger than Kweon. She was his wife, the children's mother. He also saw a teenage boy, about fifteen—maybe. The boy was helping his mother. They were holding hands. He helped her climb the hill.

Widow saw them. He made eye contact with the father, who then glanced over the other SEALs. They ignored him and scanned the terrain around them for hostiles.

Widow called out the guy's name.

"*Kweon bagsa?*"

Kweon was the guy's name. And *bagsa* was the word for *doctor*. Widow knew that much Korean. Or he thought that was right. And Lyn heard him say it and didn't correct him. So he assumed he pronounced it all well enough.

Silence.

Widow repeated it. "*Kweon bagsa?*"

There was no answer. No response.

Widow raised the MP5SD, a precaution. He hoped. Clery, Hollander, and Slabin did the same.

Finally, Kweon called out to them. He asked, "American?"

Widow answered, "Yes."

"I am Kweon. This family," the Korean man said.

Widow nodded and lowered the MP5SD but didn't release it altogether. The other SEALs kept their guns up, not pointed at the Korean family walking towards them, but not pointed far away either.

Lyn said over the radio, "Sounds like he speaks some English."

Widow clicked the throat mic and said, "Affirmative, Chicken."

The Kweon family got close, within earshot. Kweon let the teenage girl slip off his back, then he asked, "What is chicken?"

He panted, but seeing Widow seemed to boost his spirits. And then the other three followed suit.

Their eyes opened like they had been wakened by shots of adrenaline right to the heart.

Their postures changed. They stood erect. And their shoulders straightened. The mother seemed ten times stronger.

She was the second one to speak. She spoke to the doctor in Korean.

Lyn came on over the radio. He said, "Get in closer. Press your mic button. I'll translate."

Clery, Hollander, and Slabin moved outward around them and guarded the perimeter. They kept their heads on a swivel, scanning the horizon and peering through the thick white fog.

Widow stepped closer to the Kweon family. He got about three feet away from the doctor and clicked his throat mic.

The mother continued speaking, and the doctor listened.

Widow studied them. The teenage girl moved closer to her brother. She squeezed his hand and stared at Widow with huge volcanic eyes. They were brown. And deep. There was a fiery quality to them. Like they were blazing right in front of him. Right inside of her eye sockets. Like swirling brown lava. Like the center of a hurricane at night. Circular and unrelenting and completely hypnotic.

Growing older, she'd have to deal with the local boys of wherever she ended up. They'd bust down her door trying to get her to go out to the creek or the fields or the abandoned railroad or the school after closing hours or the dying shopping mall or wherever kids hung out these days.

Her father was going to have a hell of a time keeping them in check.

Maybe Widow could give him pointers if he had to sit on them for several more hours until they could get the chopper to extract them.

He'd have to play it by ear. Not because of the North Koreans. But because of the Chinese. The Chinese had the technology and the know-how to catch the SEALs' Black Hawk on radar. Caution was required and would be taken.

The Pentagon would play it like they were running exercises out of

South Korea. Apologize for inadvertently popping up on Chinese military monitoring devices. Believable enough unless they were spotted on the ground.

Kweon said, "We all here. We ready to go."

Widow said, "I'm Lieutenant Commander Widow."

Then, Widow introduced the others quickly. Kweon glanced at them, but looked confused. He wasn't a military man. The designations meant nothing to him.

Widow said, "Just call me Widow."

Kweon offered a shivering hand, and they shook. Before he shook any of the other SEAL Team members' hands, he said, "We go now. They might be behind us."

Widow looked up and back—a long-held, innate instinct. Clery and Hollander reacted the same. Slabin kept his gaze on the rear, at the road.

Widow waited and stared at the horizon, behind the Kweons, past the frozen lake, and into North Korea. He paused in case there were troops rushing behind them. But he saw no one. No enemy troops. He saw nothing but white mist and snow.

"I don't see anyone," Lyn said in his ear.

Widow said, "Affirmative. Follow me. Stay close."

They turned and trekked back through the snow and over hills and across the ice. Widow led the way. Clery and Hollander took up the flanks and Slabin stayed at the rear.

Kweon said little about himself, but he did try to speak to Widow along their trek back to the road. Kweon had a lot of questions about where they were going and if they would be protected from their *Supreme Leader*. This was exactly how he said the man's title every time he mentioned it. Like a mustered-out Catholic making the sign of the cross every time he passed by a church, even though he had long since converted to atheism. Old habits die hard.

You can take the servant out of servitude, but not the servitude out of the servant, Widow thought.

They continued for another twenty minutes, but they were slow-moving, hiking only a mile across the snow and ice.

Halfway forward, Lyn came on over Widow's earpiece and said, "Scorpio."

"What is it?"

"The mother is limping."

Widow looked over at her. She was limping. The son was half-carrying her. And he seemed exhausted. Clery reacted first, but Widow put up a hand and stopped him. Widow gave him a signal to continue taking up the right flank. Then Widow slung his MP5SD across his back and offered to take over, helping her walk. The son was happy to let him.

Widow helped her walk for another half mile. The mother thanked him in broken English.

He smiled at her, and they continued.

"We go there?" Kweon asked. He pointed in the direction of the road up ahead.

"Yes. We go there," Widow said.

Kweon seemed half-scared of the road and half accepting that it was their destination.

He feared Chinese patrols. That was Widow's guess. They were almost as bad as North Korean patrols. At least the Koreans would've just shot them on sight. The Chinese had clear shoot-to-kill orders for illegals crossing the border, but they were more famous for trying to make a buck, which made the fates of any defectors worse.

Widow had been briefed on the corruption and illegal activity that occurred for most defectors who had been caught by the Chinese. They weren't known for their compassion for prisoners. Especially in that region.

Underpaid border guards had to make a buck. They were notorious for selling off the women to Mongolian sex traders. If they couldn't bribe the defectors to pay them to look the other way, and no sex traders were interested in who they had captured, then they'd just shoot them.

What if they caught a group of Navy SEALs extracting illegal aliens through their territory?

Widow didn't want to think about what would happen then.

The SEALs and the Kweons pressed on. They crossed around a frozen and overturned boat left abandoned in the river. The ice had twisted it and overturned it and captured it, where it would stay until the spring.

They followed a path beyond it. It led them the rest of the way. It wound and twisted until they stepped over the last patch of ice.

Widow saw Kweon breathe out. The breath came out cold and frosted. Widow said, "We're almost there."

Kweon nodded and smiled.

They approached the road, which was half-covered in snow and ice. Plenty of areas were shoved away by car traffic over the course of the day.

Widow looked both ways, a habit and a precaution.

He saw nothing in the gloom. No traffic. No headlights. Nothing but drifting fog and yellow vapor lights. He could see them for a long distance in both directions. They were above the low mist.

The lights shone hazy and bleak and high in the air. Most of them were on. Many of them flickered and gleamed like extinguishing firebugs in the dark. Some spots where he expected lights to be were black.

The air was growing wet, like rain might come at any moment, or more snow.

He motioned for the SEALs and Kweon and his family to follow. He led them across the dark highway. Everything was still. Clery stopped on the road, faced the south, and watched for oncoming traffic. Hollander did the same to the north. And Slabin maintained the rear.

Widow saw the girl with the volcanic eyes look around. Not with fear in her eyes, but a kind of bravery. He recognized it. He had seen it countless times in the eyes of sailors and marines. Common among the military. Rare for a little girl.

The highway was like a road out of a post-apocalyptic future—the last road made by man to survive the inevitable nuclear war.

Vast sections of concrete exposed in the snow and ice were cracked and broken.

The trees on the other side were white and dead. They climbed up over rugged hills and down into valleys.

Widow looked in Lyn's direction, toward the highest of a cluster of abandoned structures. He couldn't see Lyn or Reyes in the dark. But he knew they were there. Lyn was behind the sniper rifle. And Reyes was his lookout.

Widow looked back at Kweon's face, which was frozen. His body was frozen. The boy had stopped. The girl with the volcanic eyes had stopped.

Lyn came back on Widow's ear receiver. "Truck! Truck!"

"Where?"

"From the north!"

Widow froze in place, looked north, and saw Hollander staring ahead. He had already seen it. Widow focused and tried to see it too. Then, he saw it. Faint headlights appeared in the mist. They were coming on. Fast.

"Got eyes on the driver?" Widow asked.

Lyn said, "Affirmative."

Widow asked, "A passerby?" But he already knew the answer. Lyn didn't need to tell him.

Widow knew because after he saw the headlights, he saw blue and red lights rotating from a police light bar.

15

"Military," Lyn said.

Widow hand-signaled to the SEALS and the Kweon family to stop in their tracks. The SEALs responded first. Everyone froze. Clery kept an eye on the south. Hollander aimed his weapon in the direction of the oncoming headlamps.

Widow stayed quiet. The other SEALs stayed quiet. The Kweon family stayed quiet.

No one moved. They were frozen in place, like the countless dead people in the frozen waters behind them.

Widow waited.

The vehicle was headed right for them. Maybe it was two or three klicks away.

Widow asked, "Headcount?"

Lyn said, "Can't tell. More than one."

"Okay."

Lyn said, "Back! Get back!"

Widow waved the other SEALs and the family back off the road and into the snow and ice, back toward the river.

The Kweons may or may not have understood the words, but they understood the urgency.

The son took the mother and helped move her away. The father and the daughter followed close behind. Widow stayed in the back. He waited until they were out in the darkness, then he waited behind, five meters out of earshot.

Lyn said, "We can't get compromised here."

Widow said, "I know."

"I should take them out. If they stop."

"No. Sit on it. I repeat, observe only."

Silence for a moment, and then Lyn said, "Affirmative, Lieutenant."

Widow looked back at the family. They were behind a snowbank. Slabin stood back to their rear and Clery guarded them from the south. Hollander was further to the north, watching the moving vehicle, awaiting Widow's orders.

Widow remained on the road, watching, waiting. Then, he turned and ran toward the family and the SEALs. He blazed through the snow and dipped down behind a dead tree stump. It was frozen over, like everything else.

Widow sat back against the icy, lifeless wood and called out to the SEALs over his throat mic. He said, "Guys, stay back and down, but stay frosty. We have to protect the Kweons at all costs."

Each SEAL responded by clicking their throat mics as acknowledgement of the order.

Widow was the closest to the road. He kept himself between the Kweons, his guys, and the headlamps. He watched the oncoming vehicle's lights. The blue and red lights strobed and grew larger in the mist. The beams vapored and washed over the road.

The vehicle was coming on fast. The slipstream echoed and cracked in the wind. The tires rolled and crunched on the pavement. The engine thrummed in the silence.

Lyn said, "Ten seconds."

Widow clicked the MP5SD to full auto. He pulled the bandana up over his mouth and nose, in case he was spotted. A white man in northern China on a guarded border would be more easily identifiable than the abominable snowman, despite having painted black camo on his face.

He waited and breathed slowly.

The vehicle approached.

Lyn said, "Five seconds."

Silence.

Lyn said, "They're slowing."

Widow whispered, "Shit."

Lyn said, "They're stopping. Side of the road. One on the dial."

Widow stayed quiet. He pushed off the stump and faced the direction of the headlights. He peeked around the stump.

The vehicle was a Chinese police SUV. It was ancient but well maintained. Some kind of Mitsubishi, Widow figured.

The vehicle brakes hissed and the tires skidded slightly in the snow. The police vehicle came to a complete stop. The engine idled. Widow didn't hear the driver slip the gear into park. But he heard the passenger door open. He heard voices. They spoke Chinese. It was too far from his throat mic for Lyn to pick up what they were saying.

It didn't matter anyway.

Widow understood the context. They suspected something in that vicinity.

There were maybe thirty miles of abandoned highway along the frozen river.

Did the North Koreans call them? Widow wondered, but he had no idea.

Lyn said, "Two. Three. Four guys. All armed."

Widow stayed quiet.

Lyn said, "Three on foot. The fourth is still in the cab. Behind the wheel."

Widow glanced at Clery, who was the closest SEAL to him. He raised his MP5SD and aimed down the sights at the vehicle ahead of Widow. But stayed hidden. Widow glanced at Slabin and Hollander. They nodded at him. They were ready for anything. Widow looked at the Kweons. He saw the girl with the volcanic eyes peering from over the snowbank. She looked right at him. Pleading. Afraid.

Then her father appeared behind her. Low down. He put a hand on her shoulder and whispered to her—a comforting word from a concerned father.

Widow was struck with wonderment about what it must've been like to live under North Korean conditions.

He imagined it was horrifying.

Widow returned his gaze to the parked police vehicle. He pulled the MP5SD up, slipped his finger into the trigger housing, and readied himself.

Widow called to the others over his throat mic. He said, "Clery, Slabin, and Hollander, you guys stay down. Keep the Kweons safe. The mission is to get them out."

Clery said, "Sir, we can take them out together."

Widow said, "Negative. Stay on mission. The mission is the Kweons. Not me."

Hollander came on the mic. He said, "But, sir..."

Widow interrupted him. "That's a direct order. Keep them back. Don't engage unless absolutely necessary."

The SEALs went quiet.

Lyn said, "Lieutenant, they're drawing weapons."

Widow heard it. Right then. All sidearms.

Lyn said, "Wait. One of them just took out a rifle."

"What kind?" Widow asked.

The Chinese police are good, but they have old military ordnance, especially way out in the rural areas of the huge country, like this stretch of road. Some of their rifles and weapons were the same ones they had carried for five decades or more, unless these guys were special units, which was why Widow had asked about the rifle.

Lyn said, "It looks like a QBZ-95."

Not the ideal answer, but better than something else. The QBZ-95 was a bullpup-styled assault rifle. It was effective in the right hands. Widow assumed that if only one guy had it, then he was the right guy for it.

Widow asked, "What else?"

Lyn said, "The sidearms are all revolvers."

Widow breathed a sigh of relief. Not intentional. Just by instinct. Chinese police with revolvers meant they were front men or beat cops. Basically. Although, these guys might've been a little higher up the food chain than ordinary foot patrolman. They were still assigned to the border, which meant they were a little better than the average rural cop. They also could've been some kind of highway patrol equivalent.

Either way, it was better than going toe-to-toe with special units.

Widow said, "Lyn, keep your scope trained on them."

Lyn said, "Roger."

How did they see the Kweons? All the way out here? Widow wondered.

They had crossed the frozen river. In the dark. In the thick mist.

Widow glanced back out over the river. He saw faint light. Maybe two miles away. Nothing was coming their way. Not a truck or a helicopter or a snowmobile. There were no North Korean patrols or vehicles of any kind. There was nothing back across the frozen river.

All Widow saw were the same rural lights that had been on for most of the night.

He assumed they were border security lights.

Lyn said, "Widow?"

Widow said, "Yeah?"

"The SUV is backing up without the three guys."

Widow waited. He scooted up to the stump and peered an eye through a crack in the top. He saw the SUV and saw the three men. They stood out in front of the SUV in a triangle formation. The front man had the QBZ-95. They looked in all directions. They were definitely searching for something.

The men were thirty-five yards away. The SUV was ten yards behind them.

Suddenly, the point man called back to the driver. An order. Clearly.

He was the leader, which could've been good or could've been bad. Chinese military and police were notoriously corrupted. If he was the group leader, Widow could conclude two reasons for him to have the assault rifle. One, he was the best with it. And the best in combat, which was why he was designated with the better weapon.

Second, he possessed a superior weapon because he was the guy in charge. A simple case of outranking the other three. And therefore, he got to pick the deadliest weapon.

Widow took a peek at the revolvers. They were basic nine millimeter weapons. Small. Almost dainty. He couldn't recall their designation. A fact he wouldn't want to admit to Lyn or the others.

He knew Norinco manufactured them. They were Chinese-made and cheap. It wasn't an opinion. It was a fact. They were terrible firearms.

But they fired bullets effectively enough. That was all that mattered.

Widow couldn't help but wonder if they would work in the extreme cold.

He wasn't planning to find out. But he was ready to find out, if necessary.

Just then, the orders that the leader barked at the driver became clear.

The SUV had a standard door-mounted spotlight on it.

The light came on. A bright beam coned and spotlighted a big area. It was a small light. But in the vast flatness of the frozen river's surface and emptiness, the spotlight might as well have been mounted on a Black Hawk helicopter and been ten times the size. It was quite effective.

The beam was everywhere. Even in the early morning hours, it did the job that the sun couldn't against the mist.

The point man called out into the gloom in Chinese. Widow pressed his throat mic. Let Lyn listen in.

Widow listened for a long minute until he realized the guy was repeating words. Widow picked up that the guy was repeating the same commands over and over.

Widow asked, "What's he saying?"

Lyn came on over his ear mic and said, "He's calling out to them. He wants them to come out, slow, and to turn themselves in. Then he promises they will be safe."

Widow said, "That's what we didn't want to hear."

Lyn said, "It gets worse."

"How?"

"He used their full names."

Widow was quiet for a long second. He listened to the repeated Chinese commands. Then he heard it. Right at the end. The commander said, "Kweon."

Right there.

Widow muttered, "Shit."

Lyn heard it over the throat mic and said, "Yeah. Shit. Lieutenant, they know who the Kweons are."

Widow stayed quiet.

Lyn asked, "Think they know about us?"

"No way. We'd be surrounded by Chinese paramilitary by now."

"They could be on their way. Maybe they got a warning about the escape from the North Koreans."

Widow took another look back. The frozen river. The snow. The gloom. The far-off lights.

Maybe, he thought.

Lyn said, "What do you want to do?"

Widow didn't know. The second to last thing he wanted to do was engage with members of the Chinese military. But the last thing he wanted to do was get captured by them. Undoubtedly, they'd be imprisoned for espionage and never seen ever again.

Giving up wasn't an option. SEALs don't give up. And they wouldn't outrun them. Not out here on the ice.

"Widow, they're moving in."

Shit, he thought.

Kweon looked up over the bank at Widow. And the girl with the volcanic eyes did as well.

Widow signaled for them to get down.

Lyn said, "I can take them. Should we engage?"

Widow said, "Not yet." And he backed onto his feet and stayed low. He looked back. He looked right and looked left.

No choice. They'd have to take the Chinese police down. The only other option was to make them give up, which was not likely.

If he and the SEALs engaged, maybe they could wound them. Leave them alive. But even that seemed unlikely. In the special operators' world, one dead foreign adversary was as good as ten or twenty or five or four. If they killed one, they already crossed the line of engagement. It didn't matter to the Chinese government how many they shot. One dead was as good as a hundred dead.

The thing that mattered at that point was leaving witnesses.

"Lieutenant?" Lyn asked.

Widow asked, "You got clean kills?"

Lyn paused a short beat and said, "Affirmative."

Widow said, "Take out the point man first. Then light up the others. I'll go for the driver."

"I've got them."

"Go."

There was a loud *crack!* It was the gunshot from Lyn's sniper rifle. The sound was muffled by the suppressor. Even without the muzzle flash and the full sound, the muzzled shot echoed over the trees and the snow and the ice. It must've carried on to the edge of North Korea and beyond.

Widow leaped out from the side of the stump just in time to see the point man's head explode into a red cloud of brain and skull and bone. An eyeball burst forward and blew out of the guy's head, like it had been flung out of a slingshot.

The body collapsed forward and slid down the snow. Blood sprayed everywhere.

The two standing soldiers looked stunned.

Shock and awe.

They looked at each other. Fast.

Widow had expected them to turn around toward the gunshot and stare at the trees or the abandoned structure. He expected them to pinpoint the origin of the sniper that killed their leader. A natural thing to do for any person—soldier or otherwise.

But they didn't look. They didn't search for the sniper. Not in the first and last seconds of their lives.

They didn't look at Widow either. They must've sensed he was there. The spotlight from the vehicle was bright. It shone in his direction like it was waiting for him to leap out.

But they still didn't look in Widow's direction. Instead, they stared at each other.

Widow knew what they were doing. Each was looking at the other to see if they were in agreement on what to do next. They were thinking about giving up. Their leader was the head of the snake and he was dead.

Against their training. Against their SOP. They were already considering giving up. Obviously.

Widow hated to shoot unarmed men. Taking prisoners was out of the question. And he couldn't leave witnesses behind. *No witnesses* was SOP for covert engagement. That was clear. These guys had to go.

Better to do that now rather than give them false hope of survival.

Widow aimed the MP5SD at the SUV. He squeezed the trigger, took out the spotlight. It exploded. Glass shattered and sprayed in tiny fragments across the Mitsubishi's hood.

Widow saw the driver react. He raised his hands to cover his face. He knew what came next.

Widow shot him in the face.

A look down the iron sights. A brace of his feet. A held breath. And a squeeze of the trigger. Three rounds sprayed out. One after the other. Fast.

The windshield exploded and shattered, leaving behind three gaping holes. Glass spider-webbed in cracks around all three. And red mist and blood filled the space in the vehicle where the guy's head used to be. He was dead. Instantly. No question.

The two remaining men turned fast, towards Widow. They raised their revolvers, but not to give up. They raised them to fire back.

They realized they wouldn't get the chance to surrender. They realized it was a take-no-prisoners kind of situation.

They aimed at Widow.

They had no time to squeeze the triggers because right then, the head of the guy standing on the north side exploded. Less than a second later, maybe a half a second later, the next guy's neck exploded. Both were thrown forward off their feet.

One.

Two.

The same muffled *crack!* echoed and rattled, and rang out over the trees, over the snow and over the ice. The echo tapered off somewhere behind Widow.

The north guy's head was gone. But the revolver was still gripped tightly in his lifeless hand. Index finger on the trigger. A fraction of a second away from squeezing it.

Widow had a split-second fear that he still might fire it.

The south guy had let go of his revolver. It slid down the snow and stopped on a patch of ice.

The guy gripped his neck.

Widow walked over to him and stared down at him.

Terror hadn't filled his eyes yet. Mostly he still looked like he was in the shock-and-awe phase, just before he realized he was a dead man.

Widow readied his weapon for a mercy shot to the head. There was no reason to leave him to suffer. But it was unnecessary because the guy stopped staring at Widow. He stopped clutching the huge bloody hole in his neck.

He was dead. Blood seeped out and blanketed the snow. It left a macabre image of crimson red over paper white snow.

Lyn spoke into Widow's ear.

He said, "Better check the driver."

Widow looked up. The driver's side door was still closed. The red mist was still settling over the headrest.

He looked back at the SEALs and the Kweon family. They stayed hidden. Clery stood up and started to edge out of hiding like he wanted to join Widow before he went any further. Clery wanted to back Widow up, but Widow threw up a hand and gestured him to stay where he was. Clery nodded and stayed put.

Widow turned to the SUV. He walked back up the river bank and up the hill and onto the highway. He looked both ways: north and south. There were no new headlights, no sirens, and no flashing light bars.

Widow checked the misty horizon. Both north and south. No signs of helicopter beacons or drones. He looked east and west. Same thing. No sign of any kind of backup. Not yet.

He stared into the SUV driver seat. Then he gripped the throat mic. Widow said, "The driver's dead."

Lyn came back on and said, "We're all clear from up here. I see nothing."

For the first time, Reyes joined the conversation. He said, "There's no enemy radio chatter, boss."

Widow said, "Come on down. Both of you, and meet us. Bring the gear. We gotta get out of here."

Lyn said, "Affirmative."

Reyes repeated the same response.

Widow dropped the MP5SD to let it rest in the sling behind his back. He opened the SUV's door and reached in and grabbed two handfuls of the dead driver's police uniform. He hauled him out—all the way. The legs came out last.

Most of the guy was still in one piece.

Widow turned the dead guy over and grabbed him from behind. He dragged him, shoulders first, off the road, down to the river. He dumped him down the bank and watched the dead guy roll down the hill like a bag of rocks.

Then he called out to the other SEALs and got Clery and Slabin to help him. He ordered Hollander to stay with the Kweons and keep them from coming out. He didn't want the children to see what he'd done. No need to give them nightmares.

Widow, Clery, and Slabin made their way to the three sniper kills and did the same to them as Widow had to the driver.

Widow wasn't concerned with burying them or hiding them in a hole. Leaving them just off the highway out of view was good enough. He and the SEALs and the Kweons would be up in the air and out of there in twenty-five minutes, Widow figured.

By the time Widow and the other two were done disposing of the bodies, Lyn and Reyes had shown up on the road. Lyn's rifle was in his hand. He held it down in a safe trail-carry position. Reyes carried his MP5SD in the safe trail-carry position also.

Lyn walked past the SUV, up to Widow, and patted him on the bicep, congratulating him. A gesture used by SEALs all over the world. Reyes did the same to Widow's other bicep.

Widow said nothing.

Lyn said, "Nice work, Scorpio."

"Back at you, Chicken."

Reyes moved on to join the others in the snow, off the highway. He introduced himself to the Kweons.

Lyn remained on the road with Widow a beat longer. And then he nodded and walked over to the edge of the highway, leaving Widow standing there to stare to the north in the direction the Chinese police had come from. The road was dark and quiet.

Lyn kept his rifle in one hand and used the other to wave out into the gloom. He shouted something in Korean to the Kweon family.

A moment later, Clery, Hollander, and Slabin emerged with the Kweons in tow from out of the mist. They came up out and around the dumping ground for the four dead soldiers. The Kweon parents kept their hands over the children's eyes while they passed the dead.

The SEALs went first, then the father led his family. He climbed up the edge of the highway first. Lyn helped them. He held his free hand out to help bring Kweon up. Lyn repeated the same gesture with the daughter and then the boy. He had to step down a little farther to help the mother up onto the highway. Reyes helped. Clery, Hollander, and Slabin scattered around Widow and around the police vehicle. They checked out the vehicle and the surroundings.

Lyn spoke to the mother in Korean.

He said something about medical attention, Widow figured, because he started inspecting her like a combat medic doing a quick once-over as he would for a wounded soldier.

Afterwards, Lyn said something else to her in Korean. Then he offered her help, and he helped to guide her up the edge of the highway. They all gathered in front of the lights of the SUV.

Widow joined them.

Lyn made introductions in Korean. He introduced each of the SEALs, and himself and Widow last.

The girl with the volcanic eyes glared at Widow, a bit of terror in her eyes. He could only imagine how he appeared to a child. She was maybe five feet tall and weighed less than a hundred pounds, maybe ninety pounds soaking wet.

Widow was six foot four. But he weighed more back then. He was in the Navy, on the SEALs team, and had to lift regularly. And he had to eat a lot. He had a lot of gym-muscle mixed with real-world muscle. He might've been pushing two-forty to two-fifty, all muscle, all heavy muscle.

The girl moved back out of the light. She hid behind her father, who joined his wife to speak with Lyn and the others.

Lyn noticed the girl's uneasiness when looking at Widow. He spoke to her in Korean as well. She stared at Widow and whispered something to Lyn. Using context alone, Widow was certain she had a compared him to some kind of Korean bogeyman, like the American Bigfoot.

Lyn laughed out loud and pointed at Widow. The other SEALs joined in on the laughter, even though they had no idea what she was saying. Lyn bent down and whispered to the girl with the volcanic eyes.

She giggled and stepped half out from behind her father. She looked at Widow and said a word, but she said it in English.

The girl with the volcanic eyes said, "Chicken."

16

Twelve years later, Widow woke up in the passenger seat of the Air Force Humvee secured to the bed of a Lockheed C-5 Galaxy.

He squinted. His vision was still iffy.

The Humvee and the plane and the surrounding cargo rattled as the plane changed its flight pattern to a descent. He heard the landing gear crank and lower. It resonated throughout the plane until he was sure the plane was coming in for a landing. He braced himself.

The engines were louder just before the plane's wheels hit the concrete. The Lockheed C-5 Galaxy was on the ground seconds later.

It landed on the edge of an airstrip at the Royal Air Force base of Lakenheath. Which he had guessed was where they were landing.

Tiller unbuckled, and his two guys followed him. He moved to the cargo space and told Widow to come out.

Widow unbuckled, stepped out of the Humvee.

They left the C-5.

The jet wash from the slowing engines breezed through Widow's hair. No big deal. His hair was short, but Tiller was a different story. His hair was thicker than the brush he must've used in it. Widow was amazed at how much it blew around and, yet, whipped right back where it was after he distanced himself from the C-5.

They walked twenty-five yards away from the landing spot and met a local airman in another Humvee. This one blue, like the last. But this one seemed smaller, lighter, thinner. Widow figured it wasn't armored as heavily, which made him wonder where the other one was headed. He figured it must've been slated for Iraq to continue the fight with ISIS or to Syria to help the rebels, all while pretending not to be fighting the Russians when actually they were basically fighting the Russians there.

The airman was a staff sergeant. His nametape said Meter, which made Widow think of the British measure close to a yard. But the staff sergeant introduced himself, pronouncing it *met*-er. Not *meet*-er.

Tiller introduced himself and Widow, and no one else. Not his guys. They didn't complain.

They piled into the Humvee, Tiller in the front passenger seat, Rosencrantz and Guildenstern on the window seats in the rear bench, Widow squeezed in the middle, crammed like a sardine in a can. He didn't complain. His arm hurt. His head hurt from the air pressure. He was feeling jet-lagged, even though he'd slept on the plane. And he felt double jet-lagged because he had part of the nightmare of the memory of twelve years ago, and he had been ripped out of it.

He stayed quiet.

Meter drove them out to the front of the base, where they stopped in at the main office. Tiller got out alone and met an Air Force officer who stayed too far away for Widow to see his rank or name. But he was sure the guy was an officer in charge of something. Maybe the base. He knew that because the guy walked like an officer, stood like an officer, nodded like an officer, and shook hands with Tiller like an officer. All of which was a bureaucratic nature and demeanor. Widow had seen it a million times before. Perhaps he was a guy who had started out with ideas in his head and love of country in his heart, but over years, he had gotten swallowed up and beaten up and molded and transformed into the system's version of a good military citizen, someone who goes along to get along. Not a boat rocker. A simple yes-man.

Widow didn't care what they were saying, but he could imagine it was something about their being there. And a lie about their goals and another lie about where they were going.

After words were exchanged, Tiller walked back to the Humvee and dumped himself down into the front passenger seat. Meter drove off, took them to the main gates. He drove through and nodded to the guards, who were already expecting to see them come through—a prearranged phone call from the bureaucratic officer, no doubt.

They drove out of the gates and onto the main streets. They drove for thirteen more silent, uncomfortable, sardine-squeezed minutes before Widow spoke.

He asked, "Where are we going now?"

Tiller spoke, didn't look back. "We're going to the airport."

"We just left the airport."

"That's a military airport. We need to fly commercial."

Widow didn't ask where they were headed. He already knew. He dreaded another flight, even if this one was a shorter trip than the last two.

After fifty-nine minutes of driving the English countryside, partially suburbs and partially cityscapes, they arrived at Norwich International, where Tiller had everything already prearranged, as a CIA agent often does —part of why Widow never trusted him. Constant preparation at his level of operations equaled a man who planned, schemed.

They got through ticketing and local security. Tiller gave Widow a boarding pass, which read, "Cork, Ireland," as the destination. He was in economy class with one guy. Either Rosencrantz or Guildenstern, he still didn't know which, and he still didn't care.

He got a window seat this time and got comfortable and stared out the window, hoping to see one of his favorite views out of all the flight paths he had seen, the greens of Ireland. He knew he wouldn't be able to because it was night outside. He wondered what time it was. He had lost track of time from the flight from Minneapolis to Andrews, the international flight from Andrews to Lakenheath, and now another flight from Cork.

Plus, he had lost his wristwatch. He pictured an orderly back at St. Mark's Memorial Hospital finding it and keeping it. It's an occupational hazard.

The last captain he had flown with had mentioned the time in an announcement. He was an Air Force pilot. No need to mention it.

Widow shrugged to himself in his seat. Rosencrantz or Guildenstern, whoever, looked over at him as he did it.

Widow moved the fingers on his left hand, felt pain in his broken arm under the cast from the movement. Then he turned, stared out the window at the night stars, not the green views he had hoped for, but he was satisfied with them.

17

THE WOMAN from Beijing told Lu what to do, and he did it. Why wouldn't he?

She waited in the car in the back alley behind Cathery's Pub.

Everything was as green as Ireland was famous for. All the clichés of the local dialects were there. All the clichés about the men and the drink were also apparently something they took literally.

Lu went into the pub alone. No backup. She was his backup, but he wouldn't need it, she figured.

She heard a crackle of thunder in the sky. She leaned forward from the passenger seat of a rented black two-door Lexus, made by Toyota. Not the official choice for a person in her position in her line of work. Not something that she'd advertise back home in Beijing.

Her coworkers wouldn't approve. After all, they were Chinese, and it would embarrass them to have one of their employees renting a Japanese car. They weren't fans.

She figured they wouldn't care because there was no other option on the lot that was Asian. And Lu wouldn't say a word about it, not to her.

Just then, lightning flashed. She saw it. High to the west. A jagged flash cracked and spider-webbed across the sky, lighting up the gray from copious cloud cover. Then came a thunderclap, echoed by rumbling.

The rain came next. It started as a drizzle for about ten seconds, and then it was a full-on downpour. The drops bounced off the windshield. She looked over at the keys hanging in the ignition where Lu had left them. He had left the engine running. He had left the headlights on. She sat in the passenger seat. She leaned across the seat and the console, reached around the steering column, and clicked the switch for the wipers. They fired on and wiped at a medium pace. The water cleared for fractions of a second and then returned and cleared and returned. It repeated in a predictable pattern. Soothing. In a way.

She sat back up and heard gunshots—two of them.

Cathery's Pub was not open yet, naturally. The time was too early in the day. It wasn't an all-night establishment. Although she figured it could've been. All the other clichés about the Irish had been proven in her mind.

She looked back and around. Saw no one coming. No one heard the gunshots. And if they had, they'd ruled them out, chalking them up to thunder.

The back door to the pub, right there at the top of a flight of stone steps, one o'clock from the hood of the Lexus, came slamming open in a single violent arc, like someone had kicked it open from the other side, which was almost true.

What actually happened was that Cathery himself came flying out the door.

He rolled and bounced off the bottom step. He rolled again on the dirt and cobblestone in front of the car. He stopped right in front of the car, about a yard in front of the grille.

He got up slowly on one knee. Then on both.

The woman from Beijing saw blood on his face. He had taken a beating. Nothing too serious. Nothing fatal. Nothing hospital-worthy. Not so far. Outpatient maybe. That's all. His nose was broken. That was obvious. It was black and blue and gushing blood. One of his eyes swelled.

Lu appeared behind him, standing in the doorway, top of the steps. He looked both ways up and down the side street. He saw no one watching. No one was coming.

He had a Glock 17 in his hand, held down low. Smoke exhausted out of the muzzle.

She decided it was time to get out, play her role, play good cop, only without the cop part, which would've made both of them dangerous, deadly, not to be trusted.

Hopefully, Cathery wouldn't figure that part out.

She looked up at the pouring rain and looked to the side of the pub near the stone steps. There was an awning, but it was too high and far from Cathery to be an effective interrogation point. She was going to have to get wet. She looked around the car's interior and checked the footwells in the front. She checked the back seat and smiled. Lu had brought an umbrella. She grabbed it and got out.

She popped the umbrella and stood under it.

Rain drops sounded over the top and echoed underneath the umbrella's dome. She walked out in front of the headlights.

Cathery was up on both knees. Face bloody but not serious. He could talk. He could answer questions.

"Who are you?" he asked and spit blood, far. The projectile hit her shoes.

She looked down and sighed. Guess good cop was out.

She raised her boot, like she was inspecting it, and in a swift, vicious blow, she kicked him right in the same broken nose.

If it hadn't been all the way broken before, it was now.

The remaining unbroken bones in it snapped and cracked and split. The sound was loud, like a habitual knuckle-crack in a dead-silent church. It was so loud that the woman from Beijing looked around instinctively for more thunder.

Cathery grabbed at his face and howled in pain. "What the hell do ye want?" he shouted.

Lu walked down the steps into the rain. He circled around Cathery like a predator.

"I dun told ye that I don't work for the Chinks anymore."

Lu tapped the guy on the top of the head with the Glock's barrel. A hard tap. The sound was audible, not the metal-on-skull sound one would expect to hear, because the Glock 17 was constructed mostly out of a hardened polymer, but it was loud enough.

"Mr. Cathery, that kind of talk isn't necessary."

Lu brushed the barrel of the Glock against the guy's ear. A reminder, in case he forgot the last one, that there was a gun present. A reminder that he had already fired it into the guy's ceiling—twice.

The woman from Beijing said, "I'm not here for the matter of unearned wages that you took from my government, and that you, so far, haven't held up your end of the deal. In fact, I don't even know exactly what they would want with a flatfoot like you."

He stared up at her.

"What I want to know, which I'm sure that Lu has asked you already, is about a stranger."

"The only strangers here, lass, are you!"

He spat more blood in defiance. But not on her boots. He had learned that lesson, which meant that he could learn. That was good. That was going to keep him alive.

She said, "Mr. Cathery, if you don't cooperate, I'm going to have my associate shoot you."

"You won't do that. This is Ireland. You can't get away with that here."

The woman from Beijing laughed. "Of course I can."

"No way, lass. If you shoot me here, you better kill me here."

She smiled at him, bent down, stayed out of grabbing distance. The umbrella came with her. The whole move was a dramatic thing. She knew that, but these things were about shock and awe. He had gotten the shock part. Now it was time for some awe. Theatrics.

She said, "What do you think I meant when I said he was going to shoot you?"

Cathery said nothing.

"He'll shoot to kill. We don't waste time. We don't have time to waste. You don't tell me what I need to know, we'll just shoot you dead. No problem. You think the Gardaí will give a shit? They'll find your dead body out here in the trash. And when they do, they'll search your pub and discover that you're an arms smuggler. They'll think you were killed in a deal gone bad. That's all."

He stayed quiet and spat more blood. Not at anyone, just out on the ground. "What do you want?"

"I told you. A stranger bought a weapon from you."

"I don't sell to strangers."

"You must've. You're the most prominent arms smuggler within fifty kilometers."

"A hundred," he corrected her, smugly.

"A hundred. You must know who it is."

"I didn't sell to any strangers. But might've been one of my guys."

"You already know who I'm talking about. Don't you?"

Cathery's thin hair was soaked. The rain ran the blood down off his face. "It'll cost you."

She looked back at Lu, who nodded.

"It'll cost me? It'll cost you if you don't tell us."

"Come on, lass. I'm a businessman. I can't give up one of my guys without some form of compensation."

Selling out a colleague isn't an Irish stereotype, but a common criminal one, she thought. "Give me the name, and I'll make it worth your while. Fair enough?"

"Reestablish the payment arrangement I already had in place with your people?"

"That's a done deal. But I tell you what; I'll get them to give you some business."

"They'll buy some weapons from me? China looking to expand into Ireland?"

She chuckled at the thought.

"No, Mr. Cathery. China's not looking to expand into Ireland or the UK or Europe. We're already here."

He said nothing to that, but a look of fear of something too big for him to understand washed over his face. "One of my guys sold to a Chink...er...sorry, one of you."

She said nothing.

"It must be what you're looking for. It was a big order. Expensive. Unusual.

"When?"

"A long time ago. Maybe a month. Less than two."

"Why so long?"

"I got me ways. But I ain't a miracle worker. And this guy asked for a miracle weapon. It's a specialty item. High profile. I told him it was going to be impossible to get it. I tried to get him to settle for a local piece. We got plenty of varmint poppers out here."

"He had the funds?"

"Oh yeah. He had a stack of green. He paid up. Right then, at the beginning. No half now, half on delivery."

"You said your guy dealt with him?"

He nodded.

"Sounds like you dealt with him."

"No. Not me. Malcolm described the situation to me. Gave me the money already. Of course. He's a good lad. One of my finest."

"Where is this Malcolm now?"

He paused a beat, didn't want to give him up.

"We won't hurt him."

Nothing.

"You know we can find out with or without you."

Cathery nodded and told her where to find him.

"You'd better not warn him when we leave."

"I won't. I don't want him to know you got it from me. Hell, I was gonna go check on him."

"Why?"

"I haven't heard from him."

"How's that?"

He shrugged, said, "The last time I spoke to him was when he picked up the item. Haven't seen him since. Been a week."

She looked at Lu, who stood still, Glock pulled in to his chest.

"What was the gun?"

"It's a sniper rifle called Valkyrie."

"Valkyrie?"

"Yeah. It's an American thing. Really nice. It completely comes apart into several pieces within seconds."

"It disassembles that fast?"

"Yeah. When it came, I thought originally that I had gotten the wrong item. Because it was packed inside a backpack."

"A backpack?"

"It was designed to go in a backpack. The bag had a place for everything. And it changed calibers on the fly."

"On the fly?"

Lu looked at her and said, "He means fast."

She nodded.

"The whole thing is quite impressive. A rifleman could carry it around, and he would look like a normal guy on the street. Could be a college student. Could be full of books."

The woman from Beijing nodded along.

"Of course, I had to press for extra money when I saw it. 'Cause who'd want a weapon like that?"

Assassin was the word that came to her mind. "Did you get the extra?"

"That's why I was going to visit Malcolm today. He's not answering his phone. And he owes me that money."

The woman from Beijing stood up straight. She looked up and down the street. She had no more questions—no more use for Cathery.

"Kill him," she said.

"Wait! What?"

Lu stepped forward and put the Glock to his head. Cathery felt it on the bald spot on his scalp.

"Wait!" he said again.

"Yeah?" she asked.

"Please! I told you what you wanted to know!"

She turned to return to the car. She paused in front of the lights. She turned back, looked down at him, and asked, "Did you see us here today?"

"No. No. I ain't never heard of ya."

She looked at Lu, back down at Cathery.

"You gonna call Malcolm? Try to warn him?"

"No. No. I swear. Besides, he ain't answering. Remember?"

She said something to Lu in Chinese. Then she turned back to the car, closed the umbrella, and got in. She slammed the door and waited.

Lu said, "Close your eyes."

Cathery held his hands up in the air. They shook. He shut his eyes. He repeated the Lord's Prayer. Not on purpose. He was a good ten words into it before he realized it.

He kept his eyes closed and felt the rain beat down on his face.

He waited to die. But the bullet never came. Death never came. He heard tires on cobblestone. Then he heard another thunderclap.

He waited a long minute. He opened his eyes and saw they were gone.

He finished the prayer anyway.

18

FIFTY MILES AWAY, an hour earlier but twenty-one minutes late pulling up to the gate, Widow, Tiller, Rosencrantz, and Guildenstern stepped out of a short hallway leading to the gate and the Cork Airport, which Widow had never been to before and never wanted to come back to again, simply because it was already tainted with hauling around two overpaid body-guards and one CIA agent he still wanted to blacken an eye on.

Tiller had a carry-on bag on wheels that Widow hadn't noticed before. Rosencrantz and Guildenstern both had messenger bags. All three guys wore black suits—no ties among the three of them.

They must've changed during the flight. He was certain Tiller had. Probably in the bathroom on the plane up in the front in first class.

"Come on," Tiller ordered all three men, including Widow. He noted it.

They walked through the airport, past baggage claim, beyond the ticket counters, past signs for car rentals and shuttle buses and a string of guys holding signs for pickups.

Tiller led them straight out to the arrivals and pickups like he had been there before. He walked like he was at home at this airport. He walked like he was in his element.

Widow noted this, too. He chalked it up to the fact that Tiller wasn't known to anybody here. He probably was in his element because he was a literal stranger. Widow could understand that since he had always been undercover, always leading a double life, once upon a time.

It was thrilling.

That had to be what it was.

Tiller had a grin on his face.

Outside in arrivals, they had to cross a catwalk with moving walkways going both to and away from the airport. Passengers were riding them, standing still. There were half as many walking along the regular concrete parts.

Widow wondered if Tiller had used an app on his phone to get them a ride, like Uber or Lyft. He had seen people do that.

When they got to the other side, they ended up in a parking structure, but Tiller stopped on a pass-through stretch of blacktop.

There were cars parked, waiting to pick up people.

Tiller looked left and looked right. He didn't see what he was looking for. He put his hand up and stepped over to Widow.

He said, "We'll wait. We got a ride coming." He looked at an expensive stainless steel watch on his wrist, just poking out of his jacket sleeve. "Five minutes."

They waited.

Eleven minutes passed, not five. A black, polished, and freshly waxed Range Rover drove up an entrance ramp, pulled around several parked cars and cars going the slow speed limit, and jerked to a stop in front of Widow.

The first thing he saw was police light bars, hidden and embedded under the grille guard at the front and under the front plate, and smaller versions around the inside front wheel wells.

Undercover police vehicle. No question.

The driver's side window was tinted and black and virtually impossible to see into. It rolled down. The front passenger door opened, and a big guy stepped out. He stared at Widow from over the top of the vehicle.

The driver was a woman. She spoke in an Irish accent, not too thick. "Tiller?"

"Yep."

"You're with us. Get in." She buzzed her window back up.

The big guy walked around and offered his hand for everyone to shake. He was maybe an inch shorter than Widow was, but beat him out by twenty or thirty pounds. All solid. All muscles.

The guy had small scars on his face. They were combat wounds. That was obvious. This guy had been in a brawl or two or ten. The scars looked like broken bottle gashes. Nothing hideous enough to scare the common man away in fear, but enough to tell a mugger to think twice before trying him as a target.

His hair was buzzed down to a jarhead fashion. He could pass for a Marine, but he wasn't. He looked more Irish than a shamrock, and tough enough to be as hard as an actual rock.

He introduced himself as Gregor. There was no indication if it was the last name or a first name. There was no "Mc" on the front of it, like Widow would have expected.

Gregor popped the cargo space in the back and helped Tiller stuff his bag back there. Rosencrantz and Guildenstern kept their messenger bags on them. Which made Widow think they might have weapons in there. He shook off that thought. No way did they get firearms past security in the airports.

Probably not.

Widow approached the back door, ready to pick his spot in the Range Rover, but Tiller grabbed him by the arm.

"A quick word," he said. He released Widow's good arm and stepped away from the vehicle and onto the sidewalk, a good fifteen feet out of earshot of the others.

Widow said nothing about the arm grab.

Tiller spoke in nearly a whisper. "Remember, we're not here to help them. They're here to help us."

"You don't want me offering intel to them?"

"Of course not."

"What if they're keeping things from us?"

"You think they are?"

Widow nodded, said, "I would. They want to catch this guy. Four guys sent here from the American government, they're going to know we know more than they do."

"Be helpful without being helpful."

Widow said nothing to that.

Tiller turned and went back to the Range Rover.

Widow got in the back, behind the driver, Tiller next to him. Tiller's guys had to pile in behind them in a third, uncomfortable row. They were crammed back inches from the rear door. Widow was grateful to have gotten in before they had the chance to order him to get in the back.

He couldn't see the driver. What he could see was that she was tiny. She had her seat pulled up, probably on the last bit of track. She was virtually on top of the steering wheel.

Widow saw her eyes in the rearview mirror. They were solid blue and bright, like the afternoon sky.

Her hair was thick, pulled back in a no-nonsense ponytail. She wore a brown leather jacket. Widow couldn't see her pants or shoes. He saw a pair of sunglasses folded and left on the dash in front of her. She stared at him in the rearview mirror.

"Mr. Tiller?"

"That's me," Tiller said.

"I'm Nora-Jane Cassidy from Gardaí Special Investigations. This is Gregor."

The guy named Gregor craned his head and looked back. First at Widow, then Tiller. He nodded hello to both.

Tiller introduced only himself and as a state department attaché, which was a typical label for a CIA agent in a foreign land. Like a signal that said, *Don't ask*, to official members of local government.

Gregor picked up on it right away. Maybe he had run into an American attaché before. He turned right around and lost interest, or he was feigning the loss of interest because, like Widow, CIA agents left a bad taste in his mouth.

Cassidy had no experience with the CIA, nor did she pick up on the alias.

Widow saw her eyes light up. A question furrowed her brow.

Cassidy had said she was Gardaí, which was the national police for Ireland. It stood for *An Garda Síochána*, which meant "Guardians of the Peace." Rough translation. Widow wasn't sure if that was the exact Gaelic meaning. For all, he knew it meant "Guardians of the Galaxy."

It was the Irish version of Scotland Yard, only better, any Irishman would argue. They would prefer a comparison to the FBI, only rolled in with Homeland Security. But they'd still argue that the American FBI and Homeland Security would never compare to the greatness of the Gardaí.

The Irish have always had a "we take care of our own" attitude. And for their neighbors in the United Kingdom, they held a "deal with it yourself" attitude. They didn't like outsiders meddling in homeland affairs. In America, the only thing comparable in Widow's mind was that he was from the South. And the South was like that, in a way.

His mom had been a small-town sheriff in Mississippi. He remembered that her department enjoyed handling things in-house. There was no need to call in the state cops or the FBI, not unless it was clearly a matter of regulation.

Texas was also like that.

The big difference was that the Irish had been like that for thousands of years. During WWII, they remained neutral, even though their neighbors were getting bombed.

Cassidy's cop interest in Tiller was showing, but she remained professional. Sort of. She said, "You must be important, Mr. Tiller. Our bosses told us to cooperate fully with you. He said you might help us with our investigation?"

"Maybe. I need to know what I'm dealing with first."

"As far as we know, we got one dead Brit named James Lenny. We sent you the crime scene photos."

"We need to see everything. Hopefully, we'll catch this guy."

"Where are we going first?" she asked.

Tiller looked at Widow.

Widow leaned forward and said, "I'd like to see the video."

Cassidy finally turned around in her seat. The seat belt wrenched with her, and she stared at Widow. He saw her for the first time. She had pale skin, smooth looking. Her lips stood out against her skin's backdrop. They were pink and not too full. Her cheeks were high, as if powerful bones were carefully placed underneath. She was a good-looking woman, right up there out of all the women that Widow had ever seen in his life, but at the tip-top of all cops he had ever seen. She looked like she had missed her calling to be a movie star instead of an inspector for the Gardaí.

He realized at that moment that she was Gregor's superior because he had a struggling look on his face, like he wanted to argue with her, only he couldn't.

Cassidy said, "What video?"

Tiller looked at Widow with the same question on his face.

"The videos, actually. As in more than one. Two, I figure."

"What video? Mister...?"

"Widow. Jack Widow, ma'am. Nice to meet you."

He offered his right hand up and over the console for her to shake.

She stared at it, hesitated for a long second, and then shook it. "And who are you, Mr. Widow?"

"Me? I'm nobody. Just the poor guy that the CIA dug up to solve this thing."

Tiller looked at him with anger on his face that almost felt as good to Widow as when he had punched him.

"The CIA, huh?"

Tiller stayed quiet.

Widow shrugged and said, "What difference does it make? We're offering to help, in exchange for your help."

Cassidy shrugged and said, "I've been ordered to escort you around."

"You mean you've been ordered to take us for a ride?"

Gregor said, "That's what we're doing."

"I mean, take us for a loop. You know? Give us a brush off? Take us around and show us nothing."

Cassidy smiled. Gregor said nothing. And Tiller looked away.

"What videos do you want to see?" she said.

Widow said, "In the photographs you sent us, there are dents in the dirt. Lenny was trying to recapture his glory days. Trying to hit his old shooting record."

She stared at him.

Those blue eyes, he thought. He couldn't imagine a lot of men telling her no. Just with those eyes alone, she'd get far ahead in her organization because every time she interrogated a suspect, she'd get her way. It didn't matter if she was dealing with a man or a woman. No one could resist her.

"You think he videotaped it?"

"I know he did. He used cameras up on tripods, and they're missing from your photographs."

Cassidy smiled again. She asked, "Who are you again? You're not CIA."

"I'm not. Just these guys. I was a special investigator of sorts."

"FBI?"

"Military, ma'am."

"DIA?"

"Something like that."

"If you're not DIA, then some kind of special unit in the Army police?"

He thought for a moment—no reason not to tell her the truth. "NCIS."

"NSIS?"

"N-C-I-S."

"And what's that?"

"Navy version of the FBI."

Gregor said, "Like on TV?"

Cassidy looked at him.

He shrugged.

She turned back to Widow and asked, "You want to see the videos? Fine. There's not much extra there."

"I want to look anyway."

"You got it."

And that was all that was said.

Cassidy took her foot off the brake, and they left the Cork Airport Business Park, went through security exit checkpoints, and swooped off Avenue 2000 and onto the N27, a national primary road in Ireland. They stayed on it for a straight shot that curved every so often until they arrived on Eglinton Street at the Gardaí's Special Investigations Unit office in Cork.

Cassidy went through the police security gate and signed in. The guard insisted on taking a peek into Tiller's bag and the messenger bags of Rosencrantz and Guildenstern. He looked through and approved everything.

Cassidy waited for the guard to punch a button near his window to allow a garage door to open. He waved them through, and they drove down a steep ramp into a garage. She parked the Rover in a slot near the front of the motor pool, like reserved parking, and they all climbed out.

Cassidy was short. Only Widow had been mistaken about how short because he saw her boots were lifted a bit by two-inch heels. She walked in them like she was born with the extra lift, natural.

The boots were tucked underneath a pair of blue jeans. They were faded, no holes. Her age was a mystery. She looked twenty-five, tops, but her rank in a male-dominated field told a different story. Widow watched as she passed the police and fellow inspectors. Everyone showed her nothing less than the respect of a four-star general, everything but the saluting.

He figured four years of university, another five to ten on the job, so she must've been thirty-three to thirty-five.

Gregor noticed Widow staring at her a little too long and shot him a glare.

Widow looked away.

Maybe they were a thing? he thought. *Maybe not. Maybe theirs was just a typical partnership, close to each other.*

Gregor was a big guy with plenty of battle-worn features. Widow figured he might've spent his off-hours in the ring instead of lifting weights in a gym. The guy had a jaw of iron. No question. It looked like if someone threw him an uppercut, his jaw would absorb it and return it to the guy with a hearty laugh.

They walked down corridors and up a short flight of stairs and stopped at an elevator. They took it up two floors. Only Rosencrantz and Guildenstern couldn't follow. The lift wasn't wide enough for all of them to fit. Tiller ordered them to wait in the station's lobby, which was fine by Widow.

They got off the lift and followed Cassidy down another hall—all of it covered in a dreary, gray carpet—to a big corner office. It was shared among four agents, at least.

Two other inspectors sat at desks facing the far wall. The office had a huge set of windows overlooking the east part of Cork. The view comprised a fork in a brown river, a pair of bridges, and a major roadway that was not quite a freeway, like the thousands that Widow was used to traversing.

Cassidy sat in a swivel chair at a neat desk pressed up in the corner against a window.

She spun around and pulled an extra chair up to the desk. She said, "Sit down." She was speaking to Widow.

"Me?" He looked at Tiller.

"You're the investigator."

Widow shrugged and dumped himself down on the seat. It sank under his weight. The wheels were hard to maneuver over the carpet.

He managed, and pulled up close to her.

She keyed the keyboard on a laptop. And it came to life. She took another thirty seconds, clicking through notifications and opening her email browser and thumbing through it for an email she had copied to someone else. Maybe Gregor.

She found it, pulled it up, and clicked on a file. "Here. Look. You're not gonna learn much."

She scooted back a bit and gave Widow room. He grabbed the lip of the desktop and pulled himself forward. The wheels struggled over the carpet.

Tiller saw one of the other inspectors get up and leave his desk. He walked over, took the chair, and pulled it up behind Widow so that he could see the laptop screen.

He didn't ask permission. Cassidy said nothing.

Tiller said, "Go on."

Cassidy reached over and clicked the play button on the video player.

The video started out with Lenny in front of the camera. He had just set it up and clicked the record button.

He wore a hunter-green camo Castro hat and camo pants to match, and a black T-shirt under a dark canvas jacket. A pair of sunglasses sat on his face, covering his eyes in a black tint.

He looked into the lens. Then he stepped around the camera, out of the video. Widow heard sounds of clicking and brushing like his jacket scraped the mic.

The camera's view twisted and moved and faced a plot of grass that was flat from having something laid out on it before.

Lenny came back around the front of the camera. He took off his sunglasses, folded them, and put them into a case.

He knelt on one knee and stared into the camera. Widow saw blue hazel eyes. There was a lot of pain in them, like a man who had lost himself. There was a hint of alcoholism there, too.

Widow had seen it before. Bags under the eyes, stress and pain and a battle to hold back tears, all present, all at once.

Lenny spoke to the camera.

His voice was gruff and worn and strained, like someone who had been recovering from years of smoking hard.

He gave a date, a time, and said his name and last held rank. He said he had been a corporal of horse in the cavalry. He had been an elite sniper. He mentioned his kill record. He mentioned how he had held it for ten years until it was wiped out by some "bloody moose lover."

He claimed that the new record had been a fluke, a joke, an insult. He explained it had beaten his because it had been fired from a high elevation. He talked about how because it was from a mountaintop, fired over a hill, plus the curvature of the Earth's surface, all made it an impossible shot. It was so impossible that it had to be a one out of a million, maybe more, maybe one out of a hundred million. He argued that, therefore; it was only made because of sheer blind luck.

Widow looked over at Cassidy. "How long does he go on like this?"

"I don't know. Five more minutes maybe."

"Let's fast-forward."

Cassidy nodded and reached forward. Widow had to sit all the way back in his seat for her to reach across him. He felt her jacket scrape across his forearm.

She clicked the fast-forward icon and had to stay outstretched across him in order to stop the video.

Widow watched the screen. He saw Lenny reverse his hat, leave the camera, return with a rolled-up sniper mat. He watched Lenny flap it out and lay it down flat. He placed the sunglass case on the edge of the mat. Next, he came out with a box of ammunition, opened one end, and set it down on the mat. Lenny went out of frame again, and then he returned with a rifle, an L115A3 sniper rifle, the same rifle from the photographs in the slide back at Andrews.

Lenny set the rifle up on its bipod and got down on the mat. He took cap covers off the scope and got into a prone position.

Several long minutes later, he had set up the sights on the scope. He got up off the ground several times, moving out of frame.

Tiller asked, "What the hell is he doing?"

"Setting up his shot," Cassidy said.

Tiller said, "Why's he leaving the frame?"

Widow said, "He's using a spotter scope. It's behind him."

Tiller asked, "Why would he do that?"

"Snipers are like weathermen, only more accurate. They record everything. Every piece of data. And they love numbers. He's adding up winds and distance and geometry of the range. He's setting his scope up accordingly."

"Can he do that without an actual spotter to help him?"

Widow didn't look at Tiller. He said, "He's doing it."

Finally, Lenny got down prone. This time Widow noticed he had brand-new boots.

"When's he gonna shoot?" Tiller asked.

Cassidy said, "This time."

Widow saw Lenny turn his feet out, arches flat in the dirt.

Lenny looked through the scope, slowed his breathing, his heart rate. Widow looked at the clock on the lower part of Cassidy's laptop screen. He counted the seconds.

Lenny squeezed the trigger.

The gunshot *cracked!* It was so loud the mic rattled, and they heard basically nothing but crashing static. Then they heard it echo across the landscape and die down to nothing.

Lenny moved his head away from the scope, some irritation in his body language. He seemed to curse to himself.

He'd missed his target.

Then he reacted to something he saw. He stared back through the scope at something. He took his head away again and looked over the rifle to something in the distance. He moved his finger away from the trigger and looked back through the scope.

That's when it happened.

Widow watched.

Tiller gasped.

Cassidy did nothing.

Lenny's head exploded.

19

THEY WATCHED a red mist mushroom around the mess after Lenny's head and the eyeball side of the scope exploded; then the head fell back against the scope and the mist settled to dust and nothingness.

Tiller was covering his mouth.

Cassidy reached forward to turn off the video.

"Wait," Widow said.

She stopped, said, "There's not much else."

"We don't see the killer?"

"Here. Watch." She let the video play.

It played for a long time. Widow saw a dark figure come into frame. It was someone short, a little below average, but taller than Cassidy.

All he saw was below the shoulders. The killer was dressed in all-black —black canvas pants, shirt, and jacket, a black strap on his shoulder.

He watched as the killer stopped and stood beside the bloody remains of Lenny. Then the killer stepped over the body. A bit of a struggle. He stepped close to the camera lens, and then the video went to black.

"He covered the lens," Tiller said.

Widow looked at the video time. It was an hour later.

He asked, "There's nothing after this?"

"No. Just a black screen."

Widow asked, "What about the other camera?"

Cassidy smiled at him. "Other camera?"

"The other camera."

"How did you know?"

"He's trying to prove that he broke the new record here. He's not just going to have one camera pointed at him shooting and not another one synced to the target."

Cassidy smiled and clicked and tracked on the trackpad until she pulled up another file in the same copied email.

A new video played on the screen.

Widow watched.

This one was pointed at a watermelon staked on a pole.

Widow said, "Fast-forward this one."

Cassidy fast-forwarded it until Widow said stop. He had watched the timestamp on the top of the screen, waited for it to match the part where Lenny was killed.

They heard Lenny's shot. The crack. The echo.

Widow counted the seconds from Lenny's shot to the shot of the killer's bullet. They heard one after the other. The camera angle wasn't set up to see the sniper's shot.

Cassidy leaned in close again.

Tiller said, "That's where he died."

Cassidy said, "We'll get a quick glimpse of the sniper walking by, but there's no face."

"Why did you keep this video from us?" Tiller asked.

"I kept nothing from you."

Widow said to Tiller, "Quiet."

Tiller gave him a look like he was acting disobedient, which he was. Technically. But he'd never agreed to treat Tiller as a superior officer.

Just then, they all saw the killer walk back to the camera in a fast stride. Not running, but racing.

Widow asked, "Can we back up?"

Cassidy said, "You can do it yourself."

"It's your computer. I didn't want to touch it."

She reached over and rewound the video for him.

"Pause it. There."

She paused it.

"Can you back up a couple of frames? Till he's in view."

She backed up the video until the killer was in as good a view as he was going to be in. It was still blurry.

This time, Widow saw the same figure from before. No head visible.

Just everything below the shoulder. He studied the image. All black clothing. Jacket. Pants. He assumed boots, but they were off frame in this angle. Maybe the guy wore a hat. He guessed with the sun that high, maybe.

Widow looked hard for a long minute.

Everyone stayed quiet.

He looked at the torso: medium build but probably lean underneath the clothing.

He looked at the waist. Generic black belt. Generic belt buckle. Nothing stuck out.

Then he looked at the guy's hands. Gloved. Black. Empty.

"Can you fast-forward to when he walks back to where he shot from?"

She said, "He never returns. Why would he?"

Twenty seconds later, he leaned forward.

"You see something?" Cassidy asked.

"I do."

"What?

He leaned back in his seat and turned to her, looked at her. "Tell me about the bullet."

"We dug it out of the dirt. The killer took the brass."

Widow nodded. He expected that.

Cassidy said, "It's a C round."

"I'm sure you made a list of all the rifles to fit that caliber?"

"Yes."

Widow moved his chair back. The wheels struggled against the carpet. He looked at her. "Who sold the weapon?"

Cassidy looked past Widow at Gregor. The military experience showed. He was the one with knowledge of firearms.

He came around and said, "We don't know who sold it. Lots of rifles can fire six-point-fives. Nothing particularly special about it."

"Who around here has the power to smuggle a specialty weapon in?"

Gregor said, "There're hundreds of illegal weapons smugglers here. This is Ireland."

"But who could get an illegal weapon? Something very rare?"

Tiller said, "He said there's nothing special about this bullet."

Cassidy said, "It could've been a legally bought weapon. You can get rifles here."

Gregor said, "With a permit."

Cassidy said, "Lenny lived out there in the country."

She pointed north. But Widow was certain that Lenny died to the west.

In her office, the west was the wall. So she pointed north, out that side of the window.

Widow followed her and looked north. Probably a lot of backcountry there too.

Widow said, "Got any of these bullets lying around?"

"We got most of the one from Lenny's skull."

He shook his head.

"You must've bought a box of them. For comparison?"

"Of course."

"Can I see them?"

Cassidy looked back at Gregor and nodded.

He said, "I gotta get them. They're in the crime lab. I'll run and fetch them."

"No. I'll come with you. See them for myself."

Gregor looked at Cassidy for permission.

"No problem. We'll all go."

"Bring the laptop," Widow said.

Cassidy closed the computer and scooped it up. She tucked it under her arm, unintentionally pulling up the break line of the jacket. Widow got a quick glimpse at her service weapon. It had been her unintentional move to show it and his instinctual move to look for it.

It was a Walther P99C, a small nine-millimeter handgun for little hands or just for someone who wants easy concealment. Or both. It was compact, with all the standard configurations of the factory design—all the things you need in a concealed weapon and none of the things you don't.

The weapon was in a shoulder rig, light and well-tailored for her torso. The thing he noted above all else was that she was a left-handed draw.

Widow also saw her badge in a black wallet. One side of it was folded behind her belt, the side with the badge was exposed, facing out.

The badge was gold, with four-star points and four circles. It had writing on it, all in Gaelic. And he couldn't read any of it. But he imagined it matched the sign in the lobby near the elevator that showed she worked in the Special Investigations Unit.

Cassidy walked to the door behind Gregor and Tiller. She stopped, turned, and looked at Widow. "You coming?"

He stood up and followed behind. He took slow strides. He wanted to fall back and walk with her, a little out of earshot. "So, do I call you investigator or detective?"

"Does it matter?"

He shrugged. "To some people."

"Just call me Cassidy."

"What's your official title?"

"You couldn't read it on my badge?"

She had to crane her neck to look up at him. She said, "What? I saw you look."

"I don't read Gaelic."

"It's Detective Cassidy."

"Is it Mrs. Detective Cassidy?"

"Just Detective."

They caught up to Tiller and Gregor, who held the elevator door open with one arm extended.

They got on, rode down one floor, and got off.

The floor opened to one large crime lab. The words "Forensic Labs" were scrolled on the glass, separating many cubicles and lab techs and lab equipment, none of which Widow knew the names of, combined with office machines, all of which he knew the names of. The Navy loved paperwork, and the NCIS was even worse. He was grateful to have been in the field and not behind a desk for most of his Naval and investigation career.

There was no physical security in the lab—no armed guards. No standard desk sergeant signing in visitors, which made him realize he hadn't been given a visitor pass or identifying badge to begin with.

Maybe Cassidy just had that kind of pull. Maybe she was the woman in charge of her unit, like Rachel Cameron had been in charge of the unit he worked in once.

"This way," Gregor said. He led them around more glass windows and glass dividers and one long hallway. No glass there.

They ended up in a windowless room that looked more like a student study room in a university library than a lab.

At the center was a good-sized round table surrounded by chairs. At the center of the table was the same symbol he saw on Cassidy's badge. Same four-pointed stars. Same four circles. Same Gaelic.

He stared at the table and suddenly thought of King Arthur and the Knights of the Round Table. He wondered if any of them had been Irish.

"Take a seat."

Widow sat first, with his back to the only closed-off wall.

Tiller next and then Cassidy. She reopened her laptop.

Gregor left the room through a different door than they'd entered. He was gone a good five minutes. He returned with a box of ammunition and a rifle under one arm. The stock was wood. The scope was enormous.

Gregor set the box of ammunition on the table and slid it over to Widow and left his hand clamped down on top for a long second.

"That's the six-point-five."

Widow looked at the box. It was red with an illustration of a white-tailed deer on it. Packaging designed to call out to hunters to say, *This will get the job done.*

Gregor showed the rifle to them. It was a bolt-action hunter rifle. A German thing that Widow had never heard of. "This is an easy rifle to get here. It was bought easily. The previous owner got it with a license."

Tiller asked a needless question. "What did he do?"

Cassidy said, "He climbed up a bell tower in an old church. Shot four people. And then jumped off the roof."

Tiller said nothing to that.

Gregor said, "He saw it in an American movie."

Widow said, "This is a hunting rifle."

"So?"

"So Lenny was shot from two miles away. He wasn't shot with this."

"We don't know who sold the weapon to the killer. Or how the weapon got into the country. Or even if the guy bought it locally."

"You think he snuck it in?" Widow asked.

"No way!"

Cassidy said, "It's possible that he flew it in legally. Plenty of airlines will allow transportation of rifles with proper paperwork. He could've flown it into London."

"Come on. You guys checked all that stuff already."

Cassidy said nothing.

"Did you find a sniper rifle with that kind of range that will fire this bullet?"

"No. Nothing."

Tiller said, "Maybe he stole it locally?"

Widow said, "He bought it here. He must've waited for it for two weeks or maybe even a whole month."

Gregor placed the rifle down, butt on the floor. He sat in a chair next to it. He asked, "How do you know this for sure?"

"Why are you guys so confrontational about it?"

Cassidy looked at Gregor and said, "We just need to know."

Widow reached his hand out, pointed at the laptop. "Pull up the video from the watermelon again."

"It's still up now."

"Can you see the killer?"

"You know I can. Nothing above the neck. It's a black blur."

Widow said, "What's he wearing?"

"All black."

"Look at the frame."

Cassidy looked down at the screen.

"What's he wearing specifically?"

She studied the black, blurry figure again.

"A black jacket. Maybe canvas. Black shirt underneath. Black pants. I guess black boots."

"What else?"

"Nothing."

"Keep looking."

"No jewelry. Nothing that distinguishes him from anybody else in Ireland. Not based on this video."

"Look carefully. Don't get lost in the exact details. Look for the normal."

She looked again, close.

Gregor scooted his chair over and peered over her shoulder. The rifle moved with him. Tiller scooted back and over around the table. He looked over her other shoulder.

He said, "Just tell us what we're looking for."

Another order, Widow thought. "Keep looking."

"I see nothing, Widow."

Cassidy said, "He's wearing a backpack."

20

He returned to the Irishman who had sold him the weapon. A hard rifle to get in Ireland, but not impossible. Nothing was impossible to get if you know the right people and you have the right dollar amount.

He wasn't from Ireland. He was a foreigner. He was a foreigner every place he went these days. He wasn't returning to his own country.

That was impossible.

But he should've left the country yesterday, after. Any other criminal would've. But why would he? He had unfinished business.

There was more to do.

More people to kill.

He waited behind the trees at the top of a hill about fifteen yards from the old country road. That's when he saw a beat-up country truck coming down it.

The truck was an import, a white import, he liked to think. He distinguished it as white because it came from a Western country and not from an Asian country. Not that he had a thing against Western countries. At least not in manufacturing.

A lot of machines with complicated mechanical parts came from Western countries like America. A lot of good stuff came from America.

This truck wasn't one of them. It was a German thing; he figured. It had a good engine sound, smart design, but was beat up. He could hear the springs rocking on the bumpy road from there. He could hear the gears grinding like the guy was switching them between second and third gear or first and second.

The truck was painted blue. It matched the front side of the driver's house. The house that was fifteen yards away from him.

The house was something he had heard described as a rock cottage. It was small and outdated. If he hadn't seen outside lamps posted below the roof, he would've pegged it as a house straight out of LORD OF THE RINGS, like a hobbit home.

He didn't know which movie he had seen. He only knew it as LORD OF THE RINGS. The copy he had seen was a bootleg. He saw it well over a decade ago in his home country.

The truck slowed, the gears ground, the tires stopped bouncing, and the driver looked around and pulled into the driveway, which was in better condition than the roadway. He pulled the vehicle all the way up, like he was expecting someone else to come home and park behind him.

A girlfriend maybe?

Maybe the guy was expecting a hooker to pay him a visit.

The Foreigner waited, crouched down, stayed out of sight. He took off his backpack, set it down, and unzipped the main compartment. He reached inside, past the disassembled Valkyrie rifle, and grabbed a Heckler & Koch USP. He took it out. It was stuffed in a holster. He drew it and clicked the safety to fire.

He closed the backpack and strapped it on his back.

He waited.

* * *

THE DRIVER of the blue truck parked the vehicle, killed the ignition, and slid out.

The door squeaked behind him.

He walked to the back of the truck and looked around. He stretched and yawned. He had been up all night, driving back along a six-and-a-half-hour drive from Ballyhillin, a town at the northern tip of Ireland. He had spent the last several days there fishing, drinking, and taking in the scenic terrain. It was one of his favorite spots in Ireland to fish. This time of year it was cold, but not as cold as six weeks earlier.

Mostly, he liked it because there was a little-known brothel there where he could get a lot of bang for his buck. And he had just made a lot of bucks lately off the sale of two high-end rifles from America.

The Foreigner walked down the hill and stopped. He saw a figure approaching up the driveway.

The Irishman saw her, too.

He paused by the tailgate of his truck, where he kept a backup shotgun for unwanted visitors.

The girl walking up the drive was young.

She looked younger than the girls he knew from Ballyhillin's brothel. And she was definitely not like them. They were all Irish, and she was not.

She stood five foot one, maybe. She had a nice walk, like a strut that he had seen before. Probably in the brothel. He saw it as an invitation.

What the hell was a girl like her doing way out here?

He took a street cap off his head, an Irish gentleman's acknowledgment of a lady.

"Can I help you?" he asked, with politeness and sensitivity in his voice and his demeanor, but not in his intent.

She had long black hair, jet black. She had nice eyes. Her clothing was standard Irish country garb. There was a jacket for combating the wind, comfortable black pants, good hiking shoes, and a dark shirt under the jacket. She also had a shadowy wool cap to keep her head warm.

She wore no makeup. But she didn't need it.

She spoke in fluent English, which he hadn't expected.

"Hi."

"Hello."

"Are you Malcolm?"

She knew his name.

He looked around and placed his right hand on the lip of the truck's bed, just above the tire. His shotgun was under a tarp, right there. It was already loaded, if he needed it.

"Who are you?" he asked.

"I'm sorry. My name is Sarah," she lied.

"Sarah?"

He hadn't expected that name. It was probably an alias, or just plain fake. Her real name was probably something too hard for people in Ireland to remember.

She nodded. "And who are you? Are you Malcolm?"

"Why?"

"You look like Malcolm. I was told he was a very handsome man who lived here."

"Who sent you?" Malcolm lowered his right hand, slowly, down into the bed of the truck to the edge of the tarp and the shotgun.

"I was sent by Cathery."

Malcolm stopped going for the gun. He looked at her with a puzzled expression.

"He says you deserve a bonus." She smiled at him in the way the girls at the brothel in Ballyhillin did.

"A bonus?"

"He says you do good job. He says that your big client loved the merchandise and paid him bonus. So he sent me."

"You?"

She stepped closer to him. She opened her coat and reached to the bottom of a black shirt underneath and pulled it up.

He saw her stomach. It was flat and tight, a combination of abs and just being a thin girl. Then he saw the bottom of her bra. It was white and clean.

She said, "Bonus. For you." She smiled a big smile, bigger than the girls in the brothel in Ballyhillin.

"A bonus," he said, and he smiled.

She lowered her shirt and gestured that they go inside.

Malcolm didn't argue.

He led the way. Left his truck unlocked, no reason to lock it, not way out here, anyway. He left the tarp where it was. He left the shotgun where it was.

They walked into his hobbit house, and he closed the blue door behind them, locking the dead bolt.

* * *

THIRTEEN MINUTES LATER, the girl unlocked the dead bolt.

The Foreigner stood near the truck. He looked around in all directions. He saw no one.

Malcolm's closest neighbor was a mile away.

The Foreigner walked to the door. He didn't wear gloves. No reason to. No one was going to identify him from his fingerprints. He had never been fingerprinted outside of his own country, and they shared nothing with the outside world.

And he had no need for a suppressor on his sidearm, not way out here.

Out here, people shot guns all the time.

He felt the doorknob. It was cold to the touch. He leaned in close to the door, close to the blue-painted wood, and listened.

He heard low voices, low giggling, a female voice, mostly—the girl's voice.

He grabbed the knob and opened the door, and went inside. The blue door closed softly behind him.

Malcolm's house was small and tight. The Foreigner could've ejected a bullet from the USP and probably hit the refrigerator with it from the living room.

The furniture was old and grimy, like hand-me-downs from his great-great-grandparents who might've been peasant farmers. Not much had changed.

The tiled floor was crisscrossed with white-and-black patterns.

The Foreigner crept through the living room over to an opening that led down a short hallway. He heard the girl giggling louder.

He heard her speak a foreign language, foreign to Ireland. His language. She called out his name. She said, "Are you here? Now is the time."

The Foreigner took three steps, stepped into the open doorway to a bedroom, where Malcolm sat on the edge of his bed, and the young girl was on her knees.

"Bloody shit! What the hell are you doing 'ere!" Malcolm asked.

The Foreigner raised the USP, pointed the muzzle at him.

"Oh, no! No, man!"

The Foreigner smiled, squeezed the trigger. Once. Twice. Three times.

He'd triple-tapped the Irishman.

Malcolm's chest burst open. Three holes exploded, a triangle pattern where his heart was. Blood exploded and sprayed everywhere like blood-packed squibs. It was the short range.

The girl turned on her knees, like she was begging for her life. She stood up.

The Foreigner could see blood splatter across her face and bare chest.

The Foreigner smiled at her.

Slowly, she smiled back.

21

"WHAT DOES a backpack have to do with anything?" Tiller asked.

Widow said, "What does the bullet tell us?"

Cassidy said, "It's common."

Gregor said, "Long-range."

Widow asked, "What else?"

Gregor asked, "Untraceable?"

Widow asked, "What else?"

Gregor shrugged.

Cassidy said, "It had to be fired from a long-range rifle."

Gregor said, "That could be any kind of rifle."

Widow asked, "What does a long-range rifle have to be?"

Cassidy and Gregor looked at each other. No one spoke.

Widow said, "Long."

Cassidy looked at him like she was a kindergarten teacher looking at a student full of smart-ass answers.

Widow said, "This sniper is good. Really, really good. So he knows his rifles. He knows his ammunition."

Cassidy said, "Okay."

"It also means that he's a snob. He's an elitist. An elitist would never use an instrument that was beneath him. He wouldn't use a hunting rifle. No, the weapon we're looking for will be unique. And expensive."

"I'm not following you. What does that have to do with the bullet?"

"Nothing. You guys are focused on the bullet. Why should you look at the rifle?"

Gregor started to say something, but Cassidy put her hand up, pulling rank. She said, "We look at the bullet to match it to the rifle."

Widow said, "That'll never work. Most bullets for sniper rifles can fit multiple guns. You'll never find this kind of weapon that way."

"What do you suggest?"

Widow shrugged and said, "Just look at the rifle."

"How?"

Widow raised his hand, pointed at the laptop screen, at the frozen black figure on the screen.

"There. Look at it. Directly."

They looked at the screen again.

Cassidy said, "Where? There's no rifle."

"Look at his hands."

"I am. They're empty."

"So where's his rifle?"

Tiller said, "He set it down and went back for it."

"No. He didn't. Cassidy already said that he never goes back."

Cassidy's face lit up. She got it. She understood his point. "A snob."

They all looked at her.

"An elitist sniper like him would never leave his rifle behind in the dirt."

Gregor said, "So where is it?"

Widow said, "It's right there. In the frame."

"It's in the backpack," Cassidy said.

Widow nodded.

"He never goes back for it because he already took it apart and set it inside his backpack."

Tiller said, "That backpack is thin. How the hell did he do that?"

Cassidy said, "It looks light. Too light for a rifle."

Widow looked at Gregor.

Gregor said, "It's possible."

"It's not just possible. There's an American company that's already done it."

Cassidy asked, "Would it still fire that far?"

"Sure. It's partially about the caliber, the bullet, and ninety percent the talent behind the rifle."

He had a sudden memory flash. Maybe it was caused by the concussion. Maybe by the man they were after. He went for the pills and the bottle. It was another fumbling with the lid until he swallowed more pills and put it all back into his pocket.

The pills didn't stop the memory flash. Not right then. It came on quickly and left quickly. It was just a flash.

He saw the volcanic eyes again. He saw blood. He saw smoke.

He heard radio chatter in his head. Then it was gone.

He said nothing about it to them.

Cassidy asked, "Who makes this rifle?"

"I don't remember the name of the rifle. But I've seen it before. They were only working on it last I checked. Which was years ago."

"The name of the company?" Gregor asked.

"Nemesis. They probably have a website. Purchase to order. Shipped to your door."

Gregor said, "Only in your America."

"One thing that makes us great."

Cassidy clicked on the trackpad and typed on the keyboard and waited.

"Here," she said and rotated the laptop so that the screen faced Widow.

He looked at it. She had googled the name Nemesis and had gone to their website. This time Widow didn't hesitate. He scrolled his fingers across the trackpad, touching her fingertips briefly. He searched the website for their rifles. It looked as if that was all they made, that and tactical backpacks.

He found the only rifle it could be—their most expensive offer. Just to hold the rifle in his own hands would've cost him five grand.

Gregor let out an exclamation that sounded like "Oh, boy," only it was half in English, and the other half, Widow guessed, was thick Irish.

Cassidy said, "Valkyrie sniper rifle."

The gun had a designation after it, but she didn't read it out loud.

Gregor said, "That's an expensive rifle."

There was a video thumbnail at the center of the page. It led to a YouTube video of the rifle in operation. Widow clicked and played it. The video was short. It showed two guys, American, talking about the rifle. It could change calibers on a dime. It was super lightweight. They claimed all in about ten pounds, with a suppressor.

They showed it assembled, loaded, and fired. Then they repeated the process backward—unloaded and disassembled. They took it apart and set it into a black tactical backpack that could've been the same one the killer carried. It would be unnoticeable in a crowded public square or an airport or a live event or a university campus.

Cassidy said, "This weapon is legal in America?"

"All weapons are legal in America," Gregor said.

Widow stayed quiet.

They weren't wrong.

One commentator on the video said that the Valkyrie took only seconds to put together and to disassemble. Widow counted, and the guy wasn't lying. It wasn't exactly short seconds, but the whole thing could be set up in less than two minutes in the hands of the right operator. Maybe even less than a minute.

Widow stopped the video, went back to the video of Lenny being murdered, and watched it. Then he studied the time stamps. He played the other camera angle from the target, watched the black figure go by again. He studied this time stamp.

He sat back and calculated the timestamps, the time to disassemble the rifle and place it into the backpack and then calculated the yards from the point of the shot to the target, factored in that it took a long time to walk the twenty-seven hundred yards. He used the speed it looked like he was walking and made some rough estimations.

Cassidy said, "What?"

"It took the killer forty-one seconds to take the rifle apart, put it in the bag, and walk across this camera."

22

"Now, tell us who can get this rifle in-country?" Widow asked. "Who would the killer go to for it?"

Cassidy looked at Gregor. The former military. The unit's gun expert.

Gregor said, "The man to get this in Cork would be Cathery."

"Who's he?" Tiller asked.

"He runs a pub at the end of town."

What end? Widow thought.

Cassidy said, "He's the biggest smuggler within two hundred miles."

Widow asked, "Why is he still operating?"

Gregor said, "We haven't been able to touch him."

Cassidy said, "He's got connections to The Cause."

Tiller asked, "The Cause?"

Widow looked at him.

"The IRA."

Cassidy nodded.

"That'd be the one. He's connected."

Gregor said, "Not highly connected. Just enough to keep his nose clean. As long as he doesn't give us any reasons."

Widow nodded. It was the standard balance found in any ecosystem. Every community on the planet had one. There was crime and there was order. And there was always a balance.

Cassidy said, "If the killer used the Valkyrie, that's the man who would've gotten it for him. Let's go see him."

Tiller stood up and said, "I need to use the bathroom or the toilet or whatever you call it."

Gregor nodded and said, "I'll show him. Meet you downstairs."

They all stood up. Cassidy closed her laptop and tucked it under the same arm as earlier, revealing the same Walther P99C in a shoulder rig.

Widow watched.

Gregor escorted Tiller out of the room, down the hall, and to the men's toilet.

Widow followed Cassidy out of the lab and out past the corridor and the glass and to the elevator.

"Let's take the stairs up."

Widow nodded, and they went up the stairs to her office.

The office was empty. They walked in. Cassidy set the closed laptop on her desk and spun around. Widow stayed in the doorway. She walked toward him, stopped at the center of the room.

"You're not one of them," she said.

"One what?"

"One of them."

Widow stayed quiet.

"Be honest, Widow."

Widow stayed quiet.

"You're not with Tiller and those other two guys."

"I came with them. You picked me up at the airport."

"You know what I mean. You're not with the CIA."

"How d'ya figure?"

"You don't look like a CIA agent."

"What does a CIA agent look like?"

She took a breath and said, "Tiller." She paused. "He looks like a spy. Not you."

"I'll take that as a compliment."

Cassidy said, "It is one. Spies don't look like James Bond, you know. Not in real life. James Bond is handsome, dashing, suave. There's nothing suave about Tiller."

Widow said, "I think that's the point. He's not supposed to be memorable."

Cassidy said, "But he is. He's not repulsive, but he's on the same street in a douchey way."

"Douchey? Is that right?"

Cassidy said, "Yeah, like he dresses to impress, but it's all cheap and inauthentic, like a car salesman. He's slimy. He sticks out because he throws his weight around like he owns the place. And he doesn't really give a shit about helping us catch this killer."

I'm not here to help you either, Widow thought. "He's corporate. That's all."

She nodded. "Yeah, he's corporate. He's just a suit."

Widow nodded, said, "You know Bond wasn't originally supposed to be dashing either."

"How's that?"

"Take his name. James Bond."

She stayed quiet.

"It's a plain, forgettable, common name. James Bond. Could be anybody. That's what Ian Fleming intended. He wanted Bond to be a superspy who was forgettable, unnoticeable. A chameleon. Because that's what you gotta be."

She stepped closer to him, closer to the door. She stopped about a foot from him. "Forgettable name, huh? Like Jack Widow?"

"That's my real name."

"Sure it is."

"It is. Given to me by my own mom."

Cassidy nodded and reached past him, switched off the light. She brushed his chest with her hand, on purpose. "Let's go."

Cassidy led him out of the office, down the hall, and back to the elevator. They rode down to the motor pool, where Tiller and Gregor were waiting, but there was no sign of Rosencrantz and Guildenstern.

Tiller and Gregor waited near the same parked Range Rover that Cassidy had used to pick them up at the airport.

Widow stepped over to Tiller and stood there.

Cassidy said, "Where are your guys?"

Tiller said, "They're going to meet with us later."

She shot him a look.

"We'll catch up to them later."

She shrugged, and they got in the Range Rover and took off out of the motor pool.

23

THE FOREIGNER and the young girl walked out of Malcolm's hobbit house with his keys and stepped over to his truck.

The Foreigner walked to the bed of the truck, just over the driver's side tire. He reached in and fumbled around, and found a shotgun. He took it out. It was a Mossberg, no stock. He pumped it twice, ejected a shell. Buckshot.

He reloaded the shell and checked the rest. Then he took the gun into the cab of the truck with him. The young girl opened up the other door and climbed in and shoved a tool bag and a bunch of paper out onto the driveway. She sat down and slammed the door.

The Foreigner smiled at her and slid the Mossberg down in the footwell between them.

"Can I listen to the radio?" she asked in a foreign language.

He responded in the same language.

"Of course."

He smiled at her, and she leaned in and fumbled with the old radio knobs until she found a station that worked. It was Irish music; she guessed. She continued until she found an American country music station. She left it there.

He looked at her.

"I like this music."

He shrugged, started the engine, and backed out of the drive.

"Where to now?"

"We've got another loose end to take care of."

"Does it really matter?"

"Yes. When you're good at something, you have to act professionally."

"But is it professional to kill the guy who sold us the gun we needed?"

He nodded. "It's more professional to protect your identity. We can assume the cops are onto us now. No reason to leave them witnesses."

"Shouldn't we wear gloves then?"

"No need. Our fingerprints won't show up anywhere."

She nodded.

He said, "But in the future, we might have to. On other jobs."

"When we're on the job."

"Yes, when we're on the job. After we get established, then we won't have to kill our allies. Then we can cover our tracks better."

She nodded, like a pupil learning from a master.

"Who's next? Who's the next target?"

"I told you we have to go back to the source and take him out."

"That's the loose end. I mean, who's the next target?"

The Foreigner smiled. "The next target will be fun."

24

THIRTY MINUTES LATER, Widow and Cassidy and Tiller and Gregor sat in the Range Rover. The rain had been a thing all morning.

It reminded Widow of Seattle and of DeGorne. *Cork was like a smaller Seattle*, he thought, which made him think of coffee.

They were parked across and down the street from a pub called Cathery's.

Tiller asked, "Why don't we just go in?"

Gregor looked back from the passenger seat and said, "They don't open until noon."

"So?"

"So he may not be there yet."

"He's probably there."

"Yeah. Maybe. But we can't go giving away our presence. Not yet."

Widow asked, "Why not?"

Cassidy said, "Look, this is how we do things in Ireland. Okay? It's called a stakeout."

Cassidy reached up and adjusted the rearview mirror. She said, "Today's Sunday."

Tiller asked, "What's that mean?"

Widow looked into the mirror at Cassidy's eyes. They were beautiful, hard to take his eyes off, hard to recall whom he had just been thinking about.

He said, "This is Ireland."

Tiller said, "What's that got to do with anything?"

"Cathery is Catholic, deep Catholic. It's before noon on a Sabbath. He won't be there yet."

"What? He's at church?"

Widow shrugged and said, "That's where Catholics go on Sunday."

"Why don't we just go pick him up at church?"

Both Gregor and Cassidy looked back at Tiller.

"We respect the house of God around here, Mr. Tiller," Gregor said.

"Are you serious?"

Widow said, "Relax. He'll come around."

"I thought Catholics don't work on Sunday."

Cassidy said, "He's not that Catholic. He sells weapons that kill people, remember?"

Tiller said, "Plus, he owns a bar. Hello? He sells alcohol to the public. Isn't that a no-no in the Bible? Or whatever?"

Cassidy smiled. "Not in Ireland."

Widow smiled.

They were quiet for five long minutes.

Widow asked, "What time is it?"

Cassidy looked at her watch. Gregor looked for a clock face on the radio, but there was only a digital readout of the radio station, which had the volume turned all the way down.

Cassidy said, "It's a quarter after eleven."

Widow asked, "You guys know what we're missing for a stakeout?"

No one answered.

Widow said, "Coffee."

Cassidy said, "There's a café up the block."

Widow said, "Great. Let's go there. I could eat anyway."

Gregor looked at her. "Someone should stay here."

She nodded.

Tiller said, "I'll stay."

Gregor said, "I'll stay too. You need an official cop here."

"You guys want anything?"

They both shook their heads.

"You keep the Rover," Cassidy said.

Gregor nodded, and she twisted in her seat, looked back at Widow.

"There's an umbrella back there. Behind your seat."

Widow nodded and undid his seat belt and wrenched back, searched with one hand, found the umbrella. It was a long thing, black with a cane handle at the base.

He grabbed it and showed it to her. "Let's go." Widow handed her the umbrella first.

She paused and refused it. "You take it. I can't hold it over your head."

He nodded, and they both stepped out into the pouring rain.

* * *

THE STREETS WERE COBBLESTONE. Widow could hear soft music playing in the distance. It echoed over the alleyways. The rain beat down around them like a thumping chorus to the music. Like soft island drums.

He held the umbrella at the lowest height he could and still cover Cassidy because of the height difference between them. He tried to balance it and still be able to see out from underneath it.

It wasn't working out.

Cassidy noticed. She reached her arms around him, taking him off guard for a moment, but he didn't reject her. She held on to his waist like they were on a honeymoon.

She said, "Relax. I'll guide you."

He relaxed.

"You trust me, right?"

"How can I not? You're the police."

"I am. I could arrest you. If I wanted to."

"For what?"

She was quiet. They walked down the sidewalks, and she stopped him and looked both ways, preparing to guide him across the street.

"Jaywalking?" He followed her lead, across the street, over the cobblestone, though the pouring rain. "Do you have jaywalking here?"

"We've got it."

They continued, turning once, twice more, and crossing another street, all downhills until they made it to a long walk that followed alongside a river.

He asked, "What's this side of town called?"

"We're in Popes Quay. That's the River Lee."

He nodded, which moved the umbrella.

"Here we go."

They stopped, and he raised the umbrella. They went into a café that was more like a New York style coffeehouse. And it was called Book Shelf Café Coffeehouse, which was confusing.

Widow guessed they embraced the hybrid combination of both a café and a coffeehouse. And when they entered, he realized it was also a bookstore. They had books shelved on walls and couches spread out near a fireplace and café tables. There was a long countertop with a glass display of bakery foods and roasts of local coffee stocked in bags to choose from. They could be purchased wholesale or opened and brewed for a single cup, according to a sign on the countertop.

There was no waitstaff. It was "order as you go."

They went to the counter and ordered.

Cassidy picked up a large fruit bowl with heated syrup for dipping and a cappuccino, which came out all neat with foam shaped like an Irish shamrock, a touristy thing. Widow picked up an egg-and-bacon muffin, which they heated, and he ordered coffee, black. No cream. No sugar.

They sat near the last window on the street and ate their breakfasts. After he finished, she spoke.

"So, you're in the NSIS?"

"NCIS."

"I know. It's a joke."

He nodded.

"I'm not in the NCIS. Not anymore."

"But you were?"

"Right. Once upon a time."

"Why are you here? You some kind of expert on snipers?"

He stayed quiet, took a pull from his coffee.

"You're not gonna tell me?"

"I was just wondering."

"What?"

"Are you using your looks to interrogate me?"

"How do you mean?"

"You know you're probably the best-looking woman ever to wear a badge here?"

She was quiet. Stared right at him, unfazed.

"You probably say that all the time."

"You think I'm flirting with you to peel off information?"

"The thought crossed my mind."

"Well, I'm not."

"Okay."

She drank some of her cappuccino, ruining the foam shamrock. He watched her, watched her lips, hoped it wasn't obvious. Then he realized he couldn't care less if she was trying to trick him or not.

"Why are you here?"

"Your department didn't tell you anything?"

She shook her head. "You already know what I know."

"You figured Tiller for CIA."

"That's obvious. What about you?"

"What do you think?"

She said, "You're an ex-cop. Got that. Now you're a private investigator? Hired by Tiller because he needs your skills and, no offense, but he needs someone expendable."

"Gee. Thanks."

"I didn't mean it as an insult. That doesn't mean that you are. Just that's what he thinks of you. I imagine he thinks of ninety-nine-point-nine percent of the world's population as expendable."

Widow nodded.

"So, am I right?"

"About what?"

"Are you a private investigator?"

He shook his head.

"No. Not really."

"So, what do you do?"

"Nothing."

"What?"

"I do nothing."

She paused a beat and stared at him. She said, "Everybody does something."

"You know what a nomad is?"

She nodded.

"That's me."

"You're itinerant?"

He shrugged.

"You don't have a job?"

"Not in"—he stopped and looked up at the ceiling and counted on his fingers—"three-plus years."

She said, "You've been unemployed for three years?"

He nodded, said, "When you say it like that, makes it sound like a bad thing."

"Where do you live?"

"I live right here."

"You live in Ireland?"

"Right now, I do."

"You're pulling my leg."

He shook his head.

"You have no job. You don't live anywhere. So what? You're a drifter?"

"More of a nomad, but yeah. I'm a drifter."

"No home?"

He nodded.

"You're homeless."

He shrugged again, looked out the window. People were walking past: umbrellas, raincoats, couples holding hands, families bundled up together. Then he noticed many of them wore nice clothes, like churchgoers.

He looked back at her and joked, "For me, home is where the homeless is."

She stared at him, didn't laugh or smile, which he had hoped she would.

He asked, "So, what else do you want to know?"

"What's your interest in this?"

He was quiet for a moment. He started thinking about the question, started thinking about the answer.

His arm hurt.

His head hurt.

He reached into his pocket and pulled out the bottle of Tylenol, swallowed a pill, and followed it with another pull of his coffee.

He looked into her eyes, stared at them for a long, long second. The concussion dragged his mind back twelve years into the past. He saw the volcanic eyes again.

She had been thirteen years old.

"Widow?"

"I came to help catch this guy. That's all."

"Why that look?"

"What look?"

"The one on your face."

He shrugged. "It's guilt." He stayed quiet.

"You feel guilty about something." She paused a beat. "Or someone."

Widow took a last drink of the coffee, looked out the window again, saw more churchgoers pass. "Looks like church is out."

Cassidy turned and looked out the window, saw the same nicely dressed people. She nodded, and they finished up and left the coffeehouse.

On the walk back to the stakeout, Cassidy stayed close to Widow, closer than before. Closer than she might have to a man who was nothing more than a guy she was supposed to babysit. That was his impression.

He disregarded it because she was out of his league. He made no mistake about that. Or so he thought. But on the walk back to the Range Rover, she said, "Maybe we can get a drink?"

Widow paused a step, which halted their walk back since he held the umbrella again, and she had one free hand on the small of his back.

"We just had a drink."

"That was coffee. I meant like a drink. You know, at a pub."

"Now?"

"At night. After this is all over."

Widow smiled a big smile for the first time in two days, maybe more, because he still wasn't sure about how long he had been in the hospital after the train wreck. He knew today's date. He had seen it on a calendar back in Cassidy's office, but that didn't help because of his lifestyle. He didn't really keep up with dates. The day of the week, sure, but not particular dates. Calendar dates were for people who had kids, bills, jobs, a mortgage, health insurance, spouses.

He said, "I'd love that."

25

Rosencrantz and Guildenstern, whose real names were Smith and Jahns, had waited in the lobby of the Gardaí Special Unit Headquarters a couple of hours earlier.

They had waited for orders from Tiller. And they got them.

Smith looked at his phone and saw the text messages which Tiller had sent while pretending to need the bathroom upstairs.

Smith told Jahns the messages and the orders, which they had already expected.

They took their messenger bags, which contained a laptop and an external hard drive that contained information. The information would be used as payments for weapons and equipment, including transportation, so that they could drive around Ireland inconspicuously.

They were given a gray panel van with generic markings on the sides. A nonexistent company logo. Some kind of utility company. It sounded real enough. It might even have been real; they had no way of knowing, not without doing some research into the matter. But just like that guy Widow didn't care to know their names, they didn't care to know about the origins of the utility company.

The provider and receiver of their payments was nothing more than a contact that Tiller had provided them. They saw the guy for a whole five minutes in the exchange of the digital information that they had and his giving them a panel van with legal plates and a small bag with illegal sidearms: two Glock 17s and a special handgun loaded with a tranquilizer dart. They had one backup round.

The dart gun was a single-action thing that looked like some kind of modified handgun with a miniature bolt action on it instead of a magazine feed.

They didn't know what was on the laptop or the external hard drives. They figured it must've been something valuable. Probably unrelated to their mission. Presumably some kind of state secrets or other valuable intel that the British government wanted enough to lie about it to the Irish police. Although it wasn't technically lying. It was simply making deals behind their back.

Possibly obstructing justice, but Smith and Jahns couldn't care less about those sentiments. One, they weren't Irish or British. They had no stake in it. And two, they were in the business of breaking laws on foreign soil. They knew they had come there to take the Rainmaker alive. They knew he was too valuable to kill.

They knew what they were dealing with. Tiller had provided intel to them about him. However, the Rainmaker's file was pretty thin. Not much was known about him. Intel out of North Korea had always been scarce.

They knew he was an aging man, probably mid-forties, maybe older. They knew he had survived a rigorous training process since being an orphan, and he had been recruited into it before elementary school.

They knew he was not someone to be trifled with in a long-range firefight.

They weren't sure how he had gotten out of North Korea. No one knew. The file didn't specify if he had escaped or been sent out into the world. It seemed more plausible that he had escaped. And now, he was setting up shop to be a sniper for hire.

That was all fine with the agency. They could just hire him to kill foreign dignitaries that they needed killed. Not a real quandary for the CIA.

That's not what Tiller wanted. He knew that the Rainmaker's knowledge of the top secret North Korean sniper program was far more valuable.

Smith and Jahns parked the panel van around the block at a building that sidelined the street where Cathery's Pub was.

Tiller was certain that the Rainmaker would show up. He would probably take out his loose ends since he had already murdered Lenny.

They waited.

26

THE FOREIGNER SAW the cops for only a moment, staked out on the side street in front of Cathery's Pub. Now, they were parked half in sight, but at a weird angle. The Foreigner could still see the hood of the Range Rover. He saw figures moving behind a small portion of the windshield, but it wasn't enough to see their faces or to shoot them.

Plus, he had no idea how many were in the Rover. He couldn't take the risk of shooting them, not until he had Cathery dead. The cops didn't know who he was. How would they?

Only one target had ever escaped from him before. Only one. He was fairly certain about that.

He watched them for several minutes until he saw a couple coming out of the same alley, holding each other under an umbrella.

Seeing them made him doubt his paranoia, made him doubt their being cops. Why would they park their Range Rover and leave it?

If they were staking out Cathery's Pub, they wouldn't leave their vehicle.

He watched them come out of the alley.

The man was huge. The woman was small. She was struggling to hold on to his waist as they walked off toward the cafés and shops in Popes Quay.

After they came out of the alley, he wasn't sure if the Range Rover had cops after all. He might be paranoid, which was normal for a man trying to branch out on his own as assassin for hire.

The rain hadn't let up for anyone in the city.

Everything was wet. The Range Rover that the couple drove up in. The cobblestone street below. The windowsill of the room he was in.

Only the tip of the suppressor on the rifle was wet. It was wet because he had it assembled and pointed out the window, resting on its bipod on a small, rectangular dining table that came with the room. He was in a small and quaint bed-and-breakfast across the street from Cathery's Pub. It wouldn't be suspicious to Cathery at all because the elderly couple who owned the B&B had been there for forty years before he ever bought the pub down the street.

The Foreigner hadn't rented a room there. That would've been stupid. Renting a room required a face-to-face conversation, a legal passport, a credit card, and a friendly smile. He had none of those things to share with two more witnesses that he would just have to kill. The right way to go about taking out Cathery now was to sneak in through the back in the early morning hours, find an empty room, and wait for the right opportunity.

Of course, when that didn't work, he simply let his protégé use her skill sets to get them into a room. Cathery had never seen her before. So when she walked into his pub late the night before, dressed as a young girl looking for gentlemanly company, all she had to do was wait for the perfect target.

The street was lined with old B&Bs, tourist shops, and one overpriced hotel. They had thought they might get to Cathery the night before, but no luck. When she found a gentleman staying down the street with fetishes for Asian and teenage-looking girls, it wasn't hard to see he was the next best thing.

The guy she found lay dead in the bathtub, about twelve meters from the Foreigner.

The Foreigner watched the rain through his scope.

The rain reminded him of the ridiculous name that the Supreme Leader had given to the sniper program he was in: the Rainmakers.

The story was that the Rainmaker program originated as a fantasy of the Supreme Leader's late father, some kind of throwback to old American movies from the seventies or sixties about snipers and war and bringing hellfire. He supposed the American war phrase of bringing the rain, which had something to do with shooting massive amounts of bullets, like raining bullets, was where the name had come from. Although, the former Supreme Leader also had a predilection for American Western movies, the kind with cowboys and Indians. And he believed a Rainmaker was a kind of Indian holy man.

All of this was speculation. His knowledge of English was decent. Not as good as his protégé's. She spoke impeccable English, a by-product of going to American language schools in South Korea.

The Rainmaker stared out the scope and watched the two men in the Range Rover.

He breathed normally.

His heart rate was normal, which was slower than most people's. He had been rigorously, torturously trained to keep his heart rate slow and steady at all times under the most horrendous strain and stress. Now it was all automatic.

The Rainmaker lay prone, boots off, on the dining table. He was flat and ready to shoot, ready to kill.

He took another deep breath and saw a panel van drive down the block. It was a utility company, something strange about it. He watched it.

It was strange. He saw the drivers. They were cops. He was almost positive. They looked out of place, like cops. They weren't very good at being inconspicuous.

Taking out Irish police was not preferable. Not when he didn't have to, but here they were. They were giving him the opportunity. In his life, in his experience as a sniper, the best thing to do was always take advantage of the opportunities when they presented themselves, especially if the opportunity was to take out the enemy in silence, with no one else knowing about it.

He studied the van.

He read the name of the company. Then he rested the rifle back and grabbed a burner cell phone out of his inside jacket pocket. He pulled it out, fast-dialed one of the few numbers he had.

He paused and waited. The phone rang.

The girl's voice came on the line. She spoke Korean.

He said her name, and then he said, "What's Cathery's status?"

"He's still in the church."

"How much longer?"

She was quiet for a second, and then she said, "Maybe twenty minutes."

"Plus, he has to walk back here."

She said nothing.

He asked, "What's the name of the local utility company?"

She paused for a moment and then told him.

He read the side of the panel van and asked about the name.

She said, "Hold on. I'll google it."

He smiled. Modern technology. One advantage of having her around. One day she'd make a deadly assassin.

She came back on the line and said, "That company went out of business like a year ago."

"Get back here."

"What about Cathery?"

"He'll come straight back after church. Get back here. I need you for something else."

27

Sᴍɪᴛʜ ᴀɴᴅ Jᴀʜɴꜱ had to park the panel van two blocks south, slightly around a bend and back into a short alleyway because they didn't want to risk being seen by Gregor.

Jahns sat in the passenger seat, the tranquilizer gun on his lap.

Smith looked at him. They didn't speak for five minutes and one second until Smith's phone vibrated in his pocket. He undid his seat belt and leaned back against the seat, and fished the phone out of his pocket.

He looked at the phone.

"Tiller?" Jahns asked.

"Yeah. A text message."

"What is it?"

"He says to stay out of sight. He says that Widow and the woman cop went for breakfast."

"Breakfast?"

"Yeah."

"I could eat."

"He said we gotta wait out of sight."

"He say anything else?"

Smith waited and stared at the phone as another text came in, chased by another vibration.

"Just to be on the lookout for the Korean."

Smith tucked the phone away.

Jahns looked down the street, right and then left.

No one was out in the rain. Not on this street.

Another five minutes passed, and then, suddenly, Jahns perked up.

He stared left, in the direction of Cathery's church. He leaned forward in his seat and craned his head and then followed it with his body, his shoulders facing north. He stared out the passenger side window.

Smith said, "What is it?"

Jahns said nothing.

He stared at a small figure walking in the pouring rain, walking straight toward them.

Smith asked again but got no answer again.

He leaned forward to see what Jahns was staring at.

Then he saw it.

Walking straight toward them down the sidewalk was a girl who could've been a teenager. She had fishnet stockings, a short black skirt, knee-high boots, and a white top. She had no purse, only a black backpack.

Her hair, her arms, her legs, the stockings, the boots, and her white top were all soaking wet.

Smith and Jahns stared at her white top. It transfixed them. They couldn't take their eyes off that region of her body.

As she got closer, her expression turned a little vulnerable and a little seductive, a little like she knew what she was doing to the two men.

Jahns was so mesmerized that he reached over with one hand and almost opened the door. Like a man with a plan, like he was going to hop out and ask her if she needed a ride. He had to consciously make himself let go of the handle.

They both watched her. She walked up towards the panel van, stopped on the street corner, stared at them for a moment, smiled, and then she looked right, looked left, and crossed out in front of the van's nose. She passed them by, not fast, not slow, but a steady walk that could have been a saunter.

They both watched her walk away.

Then Jahns stopped for a second, snapped himself out of it.

He asked, "Hey, was she Asian?"

Before Smith answered, he turned back to look at Jahns' face and contemplate the question. Only he never got past the look because right then, he saw another figure standing on the same street corner the girl had passed by.

The figure was a man, average height, a little thin. He stood perfectly still about five feet from the van's nose. He held something in his hand out in front of him. It looked like a Heckler & Koch USP. It looked like it had a suppressor screwed into the barrel.

It turned out that Smith was right, because right then, he saw a puff of smoke come out of the tip of the silencer. Then he saw an explosion of glass and a hole in the windshield.

Jahns saw Smith's forehead blow open. A small, black hole formed in an unrealistic flash like a bad movie edit. Blood exploded out the back of Smith's head and onto the headrest.

Jahns turned fast, panicked. He saw a man standing in front of the van. The man paused and stared at him over the barrel of a gun—smoke plumed out of the tip.

First, Jahns saw the same black clothes he had seen only hours before on Cassidy's laptop video. The same jacket. The same pants.

Then he looked at the man's face.

He had a short but deep white scar across one eye. It cut down like a straight lightning strike. The guy's eye was completely white and foggy, like cigar smoke caught inside a fishbowl.

Jahns had just asked his dead friend if the girl was Asian.

The man standing in front of him was Asian.

The man didn't kill him right away. Instead, he stepped closer, circled around to Jahns's door, stayed back five feet.

Jahns thought about the tranquilizer gun in his lap.

His instincts kicked in and forced him to raise his hands near his face. The universal surrender gesture.

Jahns looked at the guy. His lips were moving inadvertently. The man read his lips. The only word he knew was the English word "Rainmaker."

That told the Rainmaker everything he needed to know. These guys were there for him, cops or not.

He shot Jahns in the center of the forehead, like his friend. Only this time, the blood that exploded out the back of Jahns's head sprayed all over the van's cabin.

The Rainmaker looked around the street, looked through the dreary, pouring rain. No one was there except the girl. She walked back toward the van.

She stopped on the driver's side and looked up at him.

"Who are they?"

The Rainmaker stepped forward, his hands covered this time with his lucky shooting gloves.

He grabbed the passenger door handle and popped it open, stepped back, reached in, grabbed a gun off the dead guy's lap. He stepped back out and showed it to his protégé.

She asked, "Cops?"

Then she looked at the gun. It balanced in the Rainmaker's open palm. It was strange-looking.

The Rainmaker holstered his USP and gripped a small bolt action on the strange gun. He ejected the round, which turned out to be a dart, a tranquilizer gun.

He said, "Not cops. Someone else."

"Who?"

"Americans."

28

THE WOMAN from Beijing sat in the passenger seat of a rental Lexus SUV next to Lu. They were stopped on a dirt road just close enough to see the rundown cottage with the blue door, just close enough to see the local police cruiser out front.

They stayed far enough back to not look suspicious to the cop standing in the driveway.

"What do you think? Was it the Rainmaker?" Lu asked her in Chinese.

"Yep. Got here before us."

"How we going to find him now?"

She was quiet for a long beat.

"We gotta assume this guy, Malcolm, must've told them about Cathery."

Lu nodded.

"If he killed Malcolm for seeing his face. It must be because he's worried someone will track him down by following the weapon he used. Then we gotta go back there and sit on Cathery. Eventually, the Rainmaker will show his face there."

Lu took his foot off the brake and backed up to K-turn back the way they came in, but the road was too narrow.

The woman from Beijing said, "Just drive straight. We can turn around down that way."

Lu nodded, and they drove straight past the lone cop standing in the driveway.

His police cruiser was a compact, old white car. He had the blue lights on. He stood up straight with his cell phone in hand. He was calling the station, she figured.

He looked at them for a brief, suspicious moment, and then he watched them pass.

29

THE RAINMAKER MADE it back to the bed-and-breakfast. He walked in - this time with the ball cap that belonged to the dead guy in the room - cap pulled down, chin tucked in, so the owners wouldn't see his face.

One of them, the wife, he supposed, said a cheery good morning to him. She used the dead guy's name. She probably figured he was the dead guy simply by the process of elimination. The bed-and-breakfast only had so many rooms, and she had only so many guests checked in. She knew every one of them. And she had been serving breakfast to each of them in the dining room, right there near the foyer. He had seen them when he entered. Just a quick glance. Then he turned his back to them and went up the stairs.

He heard the "good morning" behind him and waved back to her over his shoulder without saying a word.

Back in the dead guy's room, the Rainmaker had left the Valkyrie sniper rifle on the dining table pulled up to the open window. He had covered it with a sheet off the bed, which seemed stupid up close, but if someone looked into the window, they would see nothing more than a dining table with something covered on it. Maybe it was a model. Someone's hard work. And the watcher would move on.

The Rainmaker saw himself in a small mirror hung up on the wall near the entrance. He saw his familiar foreign face. Only it wasn't what he always thought of when he saw himself in his mind.

In his mind, he still saw the great young Korean sniper that he had been. He had been among the elite of the Supreme Leader's Royal Guard.

After an event that had happened to him twelve years ago, after he was deemed a failure by the Supreme Leader, instead of being executed, he had been imprisoned, sentenced to hard labor. And then one day, the new Supreme Leader let him out. An act of kindness, he was told.

The Rainmaker saw his whited-out eye, saw the gray in his hair from under the bill of the hat. He took off the hat, threw it onto an empty armchair, and returned to the dining room table. He pulled the sheet off the gun with a flourish, like a magician with a tablecloth at a fancy dinner party.

He slipped off his boots, returned to the rifle, to the prone position, and stared out the scope.

He looked back at Cathery's Pub and waited.

30

Widow and Cassidy returned to the Range Rover. They separated on the way back. Widow gave her the umbrella, said he didn't need it.

She took it and thanked him and walked closer, but couldn't provide him shelter from the pouring rain.

They reached the Range Rover and saw that Tiller had moved to the passenger side front and strapped on his seat belt like he was expecting for them to drive away any moment. Gregor had moved over to the driver's seat.

Without hesitation, Cassidy sat in the back seat. Widow joined her.

"How was your breakfast?" Tiller asked.

Cassidy shot Widow a side glance and said, "It was better than we thought it would be."

Widow nodded.

"Anything happen?" Cassidy asked.

"Not so far."

"Church let out. We should see him any minute."

They sat around, waiting.

After a long minute, Widow noticed Tiller kept looking at his phone. He watched him several times. Tiller kept his phone in hand. He looked down at the home screen, tapped on it, and had an expression of disappointment when he saw nothing there. No notifications. No incoming calls. No voicemails. No unread messages.

"What are you waiting on?" Widow asked.

Tiller looked back at him. "What?"

"You keep looking down at your phone. What are you waiting on?"

"What the hell are you talking about?"

Widow stayed quiet. He looked over at Cassidy. She returned the look, and then she looked straight at Gregor.

Gregor said, "You've looked at that phone several times since they left."

"What? Come on? So what?" Tiller said and shrugged.

Cassidy reached forward and grabbed the seat behind Tiller.

She said, "What's going on?"

Tiller turned flush. He stared down at his phone one more time —instinct.

"You're hiding something," Cassidy said.

Widow said, "Tiller's always hiding something."

"Who you waiting to message you?" Gregor asked.

"No one."

A long moment of silence came over them.

Widow said, "Where are Rosencrantz and Guildenstern?"

"What? Who?"

Cassidy said, "It's from Shakespeare. *Hamlet*." She reached forward and snagged a handful of Tiller's seat belt. Then she ripped it backward, locked him in place. She said, "He's asking where your other guys are."

Widow saw what she was doing, and he reached forward in a fast movement and ripped the phone right out of Tiller's hand while he knew the password was already put in and the phone was unlocked.

"Hey!" Tiller shouted. "What the hell?"

"Shut up!" Gregor said. He reached over and pinned Tiller down from the shoulders.

Tiller struggled and repeated, "What the hell?"

"He told you to shut up," Widow said.

He went through the phone. Skipped the recent calls; that'd be useless. He went straight for the messages.

Widow knew how to use a smartphone. Like every other SEAL, he had to be familiar with modern technology. The world was a technological planet now, and there was no going back.

But he wasn't a fan of cell phones. They were GPS trackers that people carried voluntarily.

He opened the messages and ran through the ones from that day.

"What's it say?" Cassidy asked.

He ignored her and kept reading.

After he was done, he looked up and let the screen on the phone go black.

"What?" Cassidy asked.

"You son of a bitch."

Tiller said, "It's not what you think, Widow."

"What's it say?" Cassidy repeated.

"Widow?" Gregor said.

Widow felt his head pounding again, like a little man with a hammer lived in his skull. Stress triggered his concussion headaches.

He said, "We didn't come here to help you solve this case."

Cassidy said, "No shit. We knew that."

"It's worse than that. We came here to catch this sniper. And Tiller brought his guys to do just that."

"Isn't that a good thing?" Gregor asked.

"No, I mean they're not with us now because they're out there somewhere waiting to black-bag him."

"Black-bag him?" Cassidy asked.

"Rosencrantz and Guildenstern are out here someplace close by, waiting for the chance to grab him and throw him into a van. They've been ordered to take him alive. They're not turning him over to you. They're taking him out of the country. Probably to a CIA black site, I'd guess."

They were quiet.

Widow said, "What the hell do you want with him?"

Tiller fought back, and Gregor let go of his shoulder. Cassidy released his seat belt.

"It's classified. None of you should know any of this."

Widow said, "That's not good enough. What do you want him for?"

Tiller said nothing.

Widow said, "Why haven't your boys messaged you back? It's been what,"—he looked at the times of the last messages—"twenty-seven minutes? That's a lot of time to pass in the middle of an op with radio silence."

Tiller said nothing.

Gregor said, "Does this mean that our sniper is here?"

Widow nodded, said, "He's here somewhere. Tiller's using Cathery as bait. The guy probably wants to kill him to cover his tracks about the rifle. Because it's a specialty weapon, he might be afraid that Cathery will talk about it."

Cassidy said, "Why would that matter?"

Gregor said, "Why not kill him after he got it?"

"He probably didn't know the point of origin. There was probably another salesman between the transactions. Plus, the sniper would want to kill his target first. Can't let anyone get wind of him before he strikes. That's how snipers work. He wouldn't tie up loose ends until the last minute."

Just then, Cassidy looked out the windshield, past Tiller. She pointed and spoke.

"Look."

All four of them looked in that direction.

They saw a man underneath a dark green umbrella coming up the street from Popes Quay's direction. He used the same sidewalk that Widow and Cassidy had used.

They saw his face.

Gregor said, "That's him. That's Cathery."

"Let's take him now." Cassidy let go of Tiller and looked at Widow, then at Tiller. "Mr. Tiller, you're the worst part of agencies like your CIA. You no longer have the support of the Gardaí."

"You can't do that. My support comes from way above your pay grade."

"You know what? I can do that. I'm sure that when my director learns about what you were planning to do, you'll be lucky if we don't detain you."

"For what?"

Widow said, "You've violated about a dozen laws, surely."

Cassidy said, "Obstruction of justice and interference with a police matter will be the first things we charge you with."

Tiller said nothing to that.

"Now, both of you stay here."

Widow nodded.

"We'll let you know what he says."

Cassidy got out, followed Gregor in the rain.

Widow stayed behind with Tiller.

Tiller said, "You work for us. Whose side are you on?"

Widow looked ahead, out the windshield, saw Cassidy and Gregor approach Cathery in the rain, saw them show him their badges. They circled around him. Gregor paced around the back of him, ready to leap in and grab him in case he drew a weapon.

Widow watched for a moment; then he looked at Tiller. He said, "Benico?"

Tiller turned and faced Widow, waiting for the rest of the sentence, which never came. At least, it didn't come as words.

Widow plunged his forearm, his elbow, and his fist back, and jackhammered it forward like a bolt gun. He slammed his fist straight into the good cheek, the good eye, the different side of his face from twelve hours earlier. This time, he crushed Tiller's cheek.

Tiller's face flung forward and to the left like a violent, foul ball in Yankee Stadium.

The Range Rover's factory seat belt comes with a five-star rating. It's truly among the industry's best. This seat belt was put to the test.

The belt's slack went forward with Tiller and locked up and jolted him back. Even though it wasn't designed for in-cabin scenarios, it saved his life, maybe.

The seat belt plus the fact that Widow had long arms and couldn't rear his fist back far enough to throw a punch at over fifty-five percent capabilities. Maybe sixty.

If he had asked Tiller to step out of the car, he probably would've killed him. Maybe. He hadn't intended to kill him, but if he had died from a punch from Widow, it wouldn't have broken anyone's heart.

31

THE RAIN PUMMELED the surrounding cobblestones. The cracks between the stones filled with running rainwater, pooling together in heavy flowing streams. They ran down the middle of the street about forty yards from Cathery's Pub.

Cathery was walking to his tavern. He was getting closer when he first noticed the Range Rover parked in the alley next to his pub. He wondered who the guys were inside. Then he saw a man and a woman come toward him. He wondered who they were, too.

He wasn't armed. He had been under suspicion in the past, and the last thing he needed was to get arrested with an illegal firearm in his pocket. Plus, it was Sunday. He never carried on Sunday, unwritten Irish Catholic rule.

You don't bring your gun to church. He had never done that before. He knew younger, more naive IRA members who had been caught doing that before. If a chief found out, he made sure that they could never carry a gun into a Catholic church again. Not murder, nothing that dramatic. The standard operating procedure usually called for a simple hand breaking. Break a few fingers and some bones in the gun hand, and you would find that the mentioned IRA members wouldn't make the same mistake twice.

Cathery neared the two people. They were headed to talk to him. The woman had a bad poker face. He could see she intended to speak with him.

She didn't have an umbrella. A good Irish lady doesn't get caught in the rain.

As they neared, he figured they were cops.

He was right.

They stopped five feet in front of him. The man circled behind.

The woman said, "John Cathery?"

"Aye. That's me, lass."

The woman reached into an inner pocket of a leather jacket and pulled out a black wallet. *Made for men*, Cathery noted. And she flipped it open to show off a Gardaí badge.

He squinted his eyes to draw it into focus from that distance. "Special Investigations Unit" was what he read. "What do you want?"

"Sir, I'm Nora-Jane Cassidy, and this is my partner, Gregor."

Cathery nodded, didn't care.

Cassidy said, "Questions, Mr. Cathery. We've got questions."

The man circled behind him, staying five feet back. Cathery didn't like that. Usually, if one cop circles behind you, it meant they planned to put you in handcuffs, like they expected him to resist.

"You can come with us on your own volition, or we can talk about the alternative," Cassidy said.

Cathery glanced over his shoulder at Gregor.

"No reason for any violence here. Why the hell would I resist? Where am I gonna go?"

He took his free hand out and shoved it under the pouring rain, out of the dryness of the umbrella, all to illustrate the point.

Cassidy nodded but said, "Still, if it's all the same, we're going to place handcuffs on you."

Cathery said nothing to that.

Gregor stepped forward. He grabbed one of Cathery's arms, the one holding the umbrella, and took out handcuffs, cuffed Cathery's wrist.

Cassidy took possession of the umbrella. Cathery snickered at that. Gregor cuffed the other hand and held them down behind Cathery's back. He pushed him off the sidewalk onto the street and escorted him toward the Range Rover.

Cassidy followed behind them, underneath the umbrella.

32

THE RAINMAKER STARED through the scope. He saw a woman and a man talking to another man. He couldn't identify one man because the guy was under an umbrella, held down low to cover his face from the rain. The other two had just approached him from the Range Rover.

At first, he thought they were the couple he had seen earlier because one of them was a woman, about the same height as the other one. And she appeared to be wearing a leather jacket like the one from the couple, but the man wasn't the same guy he had seen earlier. This guy was tall, but not as tall as the last guy. This guy was maybe six foot nothing. The other one was much taller.

Then he realized his mistake. His first instincts were right. Earlier, he had thought that the Range Rover's occupants were cops. These were definitely cops. The woman took out a badge and showed it to the man under the umbrella. The other man arrested him.

It had to be Cathery. The Rainmaker could only see the back of his head because of the angle. Not that seeing his face would matter anyway, because they had never met. Only his protégé had seen Cathery's face.

He took his good eye away from the scope, grabbed his cell phone, and took out a Bluetooth earpiece. He synced it with the phone and dialed the first number on the call log and rang his protégé.

He returned his good eye to the rifle scope.

She answered, and he said her name in Korean, then he asked, "Are you seeing what's going on?"

"I see it. Are we going to kill the cops?"

"No. We only need to take out the Irishman."

"Okay."

"From where you are, can you see his face yet?"

His protégé was quiet for a moment, and then she said, "Yes."

"Is it him?"

"Yes, but..."

The Rainmaker asked, "But what?"

"There's someone else."

"Who?"

"In their truck. There are two other men. And..."

His protégé went quiet.

"And? What?"

"One of them just punched the other one. Hard. And violent. I think he might've killed him."

"What?"

"Wait. The other guy is getting out."

The Rainmaker peered through the riflescope, readjusted, and looked at the part of the Range Rover in his visible range.

He saw the same man whom he'd thought was the cop's boyfriend earlier. The same walk. The same big stature.

In the back of his mind, he thought he should just kill Cathery and move on. But his curiosity kicked in, and he watched.

His protégé said, "Should we kill them now?"

"No. Let's wait. Stand by."

A hundred forty-five seconds later, the Rainmaker saw the big man's face, recognized him, and wished he had pulled the trigger when he had the chance. He wished he had never seen that man's face again. Because the man he saw in his scope was the only man ever to escape him.

33

Widow GOT out of the Range Rover and cut Cassidy and Gregor off at the pass before they saw what he had done to Tiller.

Before he got out, he pulled Tiller's seat belt from behind, tight enough to pull the guy upright; then he laid Tiller's head back on the headrest. He checked Tiller was still breathing. Which he was.

Widow hadn't intended to kill the guy.

Tiller was out cold.

Widow doubted that Tiller would have any memory of the encounter when he woke up. He'd wake up dazed and confused and with a splitting headache, but not much else. His face was already a little swollen from the punch he'd gotten twelve hours earlier.

Maybe he would piece it together eventually, but what could he do about it?

In case Cassidy or Gregor got a little jazzed by it, he thought it best to delay them from seeing Tiller for as long as possible.

After he confirmed Tiller was alive and breathing, he got out of the Range Rover, pocketed Tiller's smartphone just in case, and took the spare umbrella with him.

He approached them under it.

"What are you doing?" Cassidy asked.

Widow thought for a second and said, "I thought it best to talk out here."

"Why?"

"Don't want Tiller to hear what we hear first."

Gregor nodded and said, "I agree. We can't trust that guy."

Cassidy nodded.

Widow handed the extra umbrella over to Gregor, who let go of Cathery's cuffs and took the umbrella, grateful.

"Hey, what about me?" Cathery asked. "I'm getting soaked here."

"You can stand a cleansing," Gregor said.

Cassidy turned to Cathery. Widow stayed where he was, and Gregor moved to one side of Cathery.

Cassidy spoke first.

"Mr. Cathery. We want to know about one of your clients."

"What clients? I run a successful pub."

Gregor said, "We know you're a weapons dealer."

"'Fraid I don't know what you're talking about."

Cassidy stepped closer to him, kept the umbrella just out of reach and out of range to cover him.

Cathery said, "Shouldn't you guys cover me here?"

He started shivering, which could've been an act, Widow figured.

"Isn't it a violation of my human rights or something?"

"Just answer our questions, and you can go about your business," Cassidy said.

Gregor shot her a look like he didn't think they'd be letting Cathery go.

Cathery looked at her like he also didn't believe it. "If I answer your questions, you'll let me go?"

Cassidy said, "Depends."

"On what? If I admit to something illegal?"

She said, "No. Depends on if you help us out."

Cathery said, "What is this? You guys have been busting my balls for five years. Now you say if I answer some questions, you'll let me go."

Cassidy nodded.

"Even if I admit to illegal activities?"

Cassidy stayed quiet.

Gregor shook his head. "We can't do that. If he admits to something illegal, we gotta take him in."

Cassidy nodded.

Widow said, "I can ask him."

All three of them looked at him.

Cathery said, "Who are you?"

"Let me talk with him, just a few seconds. A couple of guys talking. No big deal."

Cassidy nodded and stepped back casually, nodding at Gregor to follow, which he did. They took the umbrellas and stepped several feet away, just out of earshot because of the pounding rain.

"What the hell is this?"

"Mr. Cathery, I'm not the police."

"You're an American."

Widow nodded, even though it wasn't a question. His cast was getting wet in the rain. He held it close, trying to keep it as dry as he could.

"What do you want?"

"I just want to know about a weapon you sold to someone not from around here."

Cathery stared up at him. The rain pelted one of his eyes. He closed it. Then he looked down at the ground, started shaking his head.

"I knew I should've never sold to that Chinaman."

"Chinaman?"

"Yeah."

"What did you sell?"

Cathery kept staring at the ground.

Finally, he said, "Who did he kill?"

"A former member of the British Army. A war hero."

"Was he Irish?"

"Yes. He was from here," Widow lied.

Cathery shook his head. "I never knew that."

"You knew he wasn't buying an illegal weapon for sports shooting."

Cathery nodded. "I knew he was trouble."

"But he paid you, right?"

"He paid cash. Good money."

"Help me catch him."

"I can't. I can't be implicated in something like this. It'll ruin me. Think anyone will buy from me after? Think the cops here will even let me go if I admit to selling guns?"

"Cathery, I'm not a cop."

Cathery said nothing.

Widow said, "We're not planning to arrest this guy."

Cathery looked at him. "What are you going to do to him?"

"This guy killed someone I knew once. I'm not planning an arrest here."

Cathery looked into Widow's eyes hard. Then he nodded. He said, "I didn't sell him the weapons. So I never actually saw him."

"How did you know he's Chinese?"

"I don't. I know he's Asian is all."

"How?"

"My guy, Malcolm, he dealt with him. I use guys like a sales force. I never deal one-on-one."

"Where's Malcolm now?"

Cathery shrugged and said, "Home. Probably. I haven't seen him for a while."

"You haven't seen him?"

"Or heard from him. He's not answering my calls."

"That unusual?"

Cathery shrugged. "It's not normal. But the Chinaman probably gave him a bonus. He might've taken off. You know, somewhere with a lot of drink and girls."

"You don't seem too upset."

"He'll be back. They always come back. He'll need money."

Widow nodded. "So, you never met the client, but you know the gun?"

Cathery nodded. "Of course. They were tough to get."

Widow looked at him. The rain beat down on Widow's head. The constant pounding on his skull and on the surrounding cobblestones was irritating his concussion. He could feel his head pounding in unison with the rain. Altogether, it sounded like drums in his head.

"You okay?" Cathery asked.

"I'm fine. What do you mean 'they'?"

"What's that?"

"Just now, you said, 'They were tough to get.' Why 'they'?"

Cathery said, "The Asian guy ordered two rifles. Very special. They're called Valkyries."

34

THE WOMAN from Beijing and Lu drove up in the rain to a place that they had already been. They were on the street leading up to Cathery's Pub.

Lu stopped the Lexus and stared ahead. The windshield wipers swiped rain droplets off the glass, creating a monotone rhythm, calming in the conditions in front of them.

"Looks like something's going down."

The woman from Beijing leaned forward and watched. She saw four people: two holding umbrellas, standing off to the side, a man and a woman, and clearly law enforcement. She had been all over the world, and she knew cops when she saw them. "Who are they?"

"Those two are Gardaí."

"Inspectors?"

"That's my guess."

"And the other two guys?" She said and leaned closer, unfastening her seat belt.

"One's Cathery. But..."

"But what?" she asked.

"The other man. I've seen him before." Lu said, "Want me to intervene?"

"No. Let it play out. The Rainmaker is here," she said.

"How come he hasn't killed Cathery yet?"

She didn't answer that. Instead, she said, "Let it play out."

35

WIDOW LOOKED TO HIS RIGHT. He saw a black Lexus SUV stopped at the end of the street at an intersection watching them. *Passersby, maybe,* he thought.

He looked over at Cassidy, who was also looking.

She mouthed him a question: "The Rainmaker?"

He shook his head. Then he looked back at Cathery.

The Rainmaker would make a move to kill Cathery, they had figured. Would this be the move? Would a lone sniper use a guy in a car? Maybe.

Suddenly, right there, Cathery's head blew apart.

The front of Cathery's face blew out of his head, and skull and flesh and half an eyeball and blood sprayed all over Widow's face and chest.

The dead body flung forward. Widow caught it in his arms—no real choice.

Widow held the body for a split second and dropped it. It flopped over, twitching like a chicken with its head cut off.

Widow looked over at Cassidy, who saw it happen.

He shouted, "Sniper!"

She moved, Gregor moved, taking cover in a doorway.

Widow turned, looked back and up. Then he saw a flicker of something, just a quick sparkle, like diamonds in the night. It shimmered in the darkness of an open window above an old Irish bed-and-breakfast down the street from Cathery's Pub.

Then Widow saw the shimmer again, the Rainmaker's scope, staring right at him.

He was next.

Suddenly, a horn blared, loud like a ship in the fog. It cut through the night, through the rain, and saved Widow's life.

He saw a flash from the Rainmaker's rifle muzzle. Instinctively, he dove right, and rolled on the hard cobblestone, just as a rock exploded from the stones a yard to his right.

He landed on his broken arm. He felt the bones. He felt pain. He pushed it down deep, ignored it.

Not now, he thought.

He came up on the balls of his feet. The Lexus driver had blared the horn, unexpected to everyone, including the Rainmaker. His aim jarred a fraction of an inch and he fired the rifle and missed.

No one outruns or dodges bullets; that was all movie make-believe nonsense. Widow knew the only reason that his face didn't look just like Cathery's was because of the Lexus driver.

He didn't wait to give the Rainmaker another shot. He stayed crouched and ducked and weaved and zagged and rolled again until he was down the alley with the Range Rover. The Extra Strength Tylenol bottle that had been in his pocket rolled and bounced, and the lid that never wanted to open for him popped off on its own and pills spilled out of the top all over the cobblestones.

Shit, he thought. It reminded him that his head was still pounding and getting worse.

"Widow!" he heard Cassidy shout. "Widow! Are you hit?"

He checked his body with his hands involuntarily. His hands checked to make sure all the vitals were still intact. Everything was still there. "I'm okay. What about you?"

"Yeah. We're not hit."

Widow looked out on the street at the dead body and bloody mess. Blood was bubbling and pooling near the head from the rain. "Cathery won't make any statements." He yelled it and then felt a little guilty after. Bad timing. Bad joke.

Cassidy asked, "Who's in the car?"

Widow edged to the corner, staying out of sight of the Rainmaker. He pushed his back into the wall. "I don't know."

"Is it Tiller's guys?"

No way, he thought. *They wouldn't be helping him.* He took a quick peek at Tiller. He was still out cold and safe out of the sniper's line of sight. "I don't think so."

"Stay put. We're calling in backup," Cassidy shouted.

He stayed quiet and took out Tiller's phone. He thought maybe he could get Rosencrantz and Guildenstern on the line and get them to help. But it was no use. The phone was passcode protected, and Tiller hadn't given him the passcode. The phone must've had a preset to switch off after so many minutes passed without being used. It was useless.

He slipped back and went to the Range Rover. He popped open Tiller's door and tossed the smartphone onto his lap. No point in keeping it.

Then he patted Tiller down, looking for a gun, which he doubted he'd find.

He looked at the ignition switch. No keys.

Gregor was holding them.

He searched the console, the glove box, under the front seats, and the inside door pockets. He found nothing of use.

Then he ran back to the cargo door, opened it, and found one thing that could help.

He scooped up a bulletproof Kevlar vest, which wouldn't stop a Magnum sniper round, but he wasn't sure what the Rainmaker was using. From what he read about the Valkyrie rifle, it had function capabilities for multiple calibers.

Although, he probably was firing the same rounds he'd used with Lenny. Why change them now?

Widow slid off his bomber jacket and suited the vest up and put the jacket back on over it.

Better safe than sorry.

Widow found nothing else of interest.

He closed the cargo door and returned to the end of the alley, stayed out of sight.

Cassidy called out to him. "Widow?"

"Yeah?"

"Backup's coming."

"How long?" he shouted back.

"I don't know."

Which Widow took to mean five minutes or longer.

They'd be dead in five minutes. Or the Rainmaker would get away.

A thought occurred to him.

He called out to Cassidy, "Cathery said something."

"What?"

"He said that there were two Valkyrie rifles."

Two, he thought.

He leaned out as far as he dared. He saw Cassidy and half of Gregor from where they were perched. They were crammed into a doorway like sardines in a can.

"What does that mean?"

Two, he thought again.

Widow shouted, "Cassidy, there's two of them!"

36

WIDOW'S HEAD POUNDED. It was getting worse and louder and harder. It pounded like a warning bell shoved into his skull. It pounded like someone was inside his head, shooting cannons off a US destroyer.

He shouted out to Cassidy over the cannon-like pounding in his head, over the rain, over his thoughts. He warned her that there were two.

Just then, he saw the flash of a sniper rifle. It came from a rooftop south of him.

He saw the direction the second sniper was aiming. It was down toward the doorway at Cassidy and Gregor.

Gregor took a bullet to the chest. He flew back like leaves under a leaf blower. His body dumped back into the door, and then he toppled forward, falling completely out of cover.

"Cassidy!" Widow shouted.

The Lexus from earlier began honking the horn again violently.

Widow heard the engine rev up and the tires squeal and the suspension bounce on the cobblestone as the SUV sped forward.

Widow saw the second sniper fire again at Cassidy, and again.

The Lexus tore down the street and barreled right alongside the alley.

A woman kicked open the back door and said, "Get in!"

Widow scrambled in, looking back at Tiller once, having a second thought about abandoning him. But he was out of range and out cold. He'd probably be safe. And if not, Widow wouldn't lose sleep about it.

Widow said, "We gotta get the woman!"

He slammed the door behind them, and the woman who had let him in climbed into the front passenger seat, and he realized that she had been half in it. She had folded back half into the back seat to open the door for him.

Now, he only saw the backs of their heads.

The driver hit the gas, and they sped toward Cassidy.

Widow leaned into his door; face pressed into the window's glass. He could see that Gregor was dead. His eyes were lifeless, his face expressionless, and his body didn't move.

Cassidy was squeezing her body deep into the corner of the doorway. Bullets were firing. Pieces of wood from the door and concrete from the old building exploded around her, creating a heavy, wet dust cloud, which might've been saving her life, blinding the second sniper like a smoke grenade.

Widow shouted, "Step on it!"

The back window behind Widow exploded, then a bullet shredded through the metal on the roof. The Rainmaker was shooting at the back of the Lexus.

Widow sucked in and hugged the door.

Another bullet tore through the roof and blew through the car radio and touchscreen navigation system. The bullet hole spider-webbed, and the electronics went dark.

The driver swerved to the right and then the left. He knew how to drive under gunfire. Widow could see that.

The driver swerved the Lexus right into the wall of the building and the doorway that Cassidy was hiding in. Steel and concrete sparked in the rain.

Widow shoved the door and kicked it open.

"Get in!" he shouted at her.

Cassidy dove into the back seat with him. He cradled her close.

The second shooter was firing bullets faster than the Rainmaker—sloppier, more amateurish. Widow recognized it immediately.

The second shooter was firing blind.

Bullets came at them from the side. Slow from being shot out of a bolt-action sniper rifle, but fast enough to scare anyone.

He clenched Cassidy with all his strength. He felt her pull into him like a rescued victim pulled out of deep, choppy seas. She was cold and wet and breathing hard.

He held on to her.

The Lexus driver gunned the SUV and within seconds, and several bullets and bullet holes later, they were out of range.

37

THE POUNDING in Widow's head was becoming unbearable. He felt the skin on his face tightening. He felt his eyeballs swell. They felt like they were as hard as golf balls in their sockets. He felt his breathing getting uncontrollably deep, like he was falling into sedation from anesthesia.

He waited until they were well away from Cathery's Pub, and then he let go of Cassidy and scooped her up so she was seated upright.

He said, "Are you okay?"

She was breathing heavily, nearly hyperventilating. "David. Oh my God, David. We left him."

Widow figured David must've been Gregor's first name. "He's dead," Widow whispered. "Nothing we can do for him now."

"We have to go back. The cops will be there. They're walking into a trap."

Widow shook his head. He whispered to her, "I don't think we're headed back."

"Where? Who are they?" she said back.

Widow squeezed his eyes shut. His left arm hurt. He felt dizzy.

"Widow?"

"I don't know."

Cassidy asked, "Do you think they are friendlies?"

"They saved our lives."

She said, "Ask them."

He stayed quiet. The pain in his arm and the pounding in his head were getting louder and harder.

After several seconds, Cassidy scooted forward and spoke to the strangers.

"Listen, I'm Gardaí. My name is Cassidy. This is Jack Widow. We owe you guys for helping us out."

The strangers in the Lexus said nothing.

Cassidy said, "We need to go back. My cops will be there soon. They can take us."

Nothing.

"The Gardaí will be very grateful to you."

They didn't answer.

"They will pay for your car. I know it."

Nothing.

Cassidy paused a long beat. The Lexus kept driving, turning left, turning right. They ran stop signs and streetlights.

If she didn't know any better, she would've guessed that they were heading to the airport.

She said, "Or you guys can just drop us off on the side of the road."

Widow's vision blurred again.

Cassidy raised her voice. "Listen, I'm Special Investigator Nora-Jane Cassidy, and I demand that you let us out here!"

She reached forward and grabbed the driver's shoulder.

The woman from Beijing twisted in the passenger seat and turned to face them.

Two things struck Widow at that moment.

The first was that she was pointing a Glock 17 at them, mostly at Widow.

The second thing struck him harder than having a gun pointed at him. It struck him harder than the pounding in his head. It struck him harder than a punch to the face. It struck him harder than a bat to the face.

His vision blurred. It got worse and worse. And he thought he must've been hallucinating because he saw a woman staring at him, pointing a gun at him, and she had a familiar face, a face he hadn't seen in twelve years in real life. It was a face that he had seen in his nightmares.

She was the thirteen-year-old Korean girl with the volcanic eyes.

38

THE GIRL with the volcanic eyes, deep and dark and swirling like brown lava inside a volcano, looked up at him from twelve years in the past.

She pointed at him, giggled, and said, "Chicken."

Widow shook his head and smiled down at her.

He moved his MP5SD and let it hang over his shoulder by the strap. He reached out a gloved hand and presented her with an American high five.

The girl with the volcanic eyes spoke in Korean and high-fived him. The other SEALs chuckled along with her.

Widow glanced past Clery, who now stood closest to him , and at Lyn, who was on his radio, about to call for the evac.

Lyn paused, looked back at Widow, and said, "She said she likes you, Chicken."

Widow nodded. "How far are we from the LZ?"

"Two klicks that way," Lyn said and pointed south, past Clery, who was moving out of the way. Clery focused on the road south, like he was scanning it for any more potential threats.

"Now we got wheels," Widow said, and pointed at the Chinese Police SUV.

Lyn said, "Okay. I'll call in and tell 'em to be on the lookout for us."

Widow nodded and went over to the SUV.

Lyn stopped him, grabbed his arm. "Wait."

Widow said "What?"

"We should clean it first."

Widow looked at the SUV. There was blood misted all over the front bench, and the windshield was cracked and too far gone to be repaired on the fly. He said, "Looks fine to me."

Lyn smiled, "The kids, dude."

Widow nodded, said, "I'll do it."

Lyn glanced back at Reyes and Slabin, who were close together, talking. Then he leaned into Widow and said, "Get Reyes and Slabin to do it. They're the bottom of the totem pole."

Widow glanced at the two SEALs and looked back at Lyn. He said, "I'll clean it myself. I can handle it."

"Are you sure?"

"You question my abilities?"

"No offense, but I've seen your quarters."

Widow said, "My quarters are clean to regulations."

"Are they?"

Widow said, "I've cleaned latrines in less than two minutes flat. I can handle a little blood."

"A little?"

Widow shrugged. "A lot of blood. We're not going that far. I'll manage. Just get the chopper flying. Get them to meet us ASAP. I want to get the hell outta here."

"You're the boss," Lyn said and stepped away toward Hollander in the north and made his call.

Widow walked to the vehicle and leaned over the driver side window and looked on the front bench, a quick survey of the damage. He saw the keys still in the ignition, which he had expected because the engine was still running and idling.

The front area was pretty bad. He glanced at the back seat. It was really nothing. Then he backed away and went back to the cargo area. He opened it and found what he needed, two gallons of water and some blankets, not towels, but they would work well enough.

Widow took it all and set it down on the road. He unfolded a blanket and tossed it over the mess, then he hopped in the cabin and levered the seat all the way back and got in. He raised his legs as high as he could and used both feet and kicked violently at the glass. After three hard double kicks, he had kicked out the entire glass and framing.

Widow got back out and pulled the rest down and all off the hood. He grabbed the water and pulled out the blanket. He used both gallons and dumped the water all over the front seats, the upholstery, the console, the steering wheel, and the dashboard. Then he wiped all of it, everything as fast as he could. He used the clean side of one blanket to cover up the wet spots and whatever was left.

He stepped back and looked and nodded. Not as fine a job as a Navy latrine, but good enough.

Widow walked back to the Kweon family and the other SEALs. He led the family away from the SEALs and away from the bank with the dead bodies. The SEALs stayed on the perimeter, scanning and watching out for any threats. Clery kept a watch on Widow. The others scanned the area. Lyn was still on the radio.

Widow helped the Kweon's son pull his mother over to the SUV and place her in the back seat. The son hopped in next to her. Widow signaled for Mr. Kweon to follow suit and have the mom wedged between them.

The girl with the volcanic eyes smiled at him and hopped in the front. She rode in the middle, seated on the console. Not the most comfortable ride, but that's the spot she picked.

Widow leaned in and hauled himself up and sat down behind the steering wheel.

The girl with the volcanic eyes squeezed in close to him. She trembled a little like she was scared, and sitting next to him helped. He stayed quiet about it.

Lyn got off the radio and approached them. He stood five feet from the driver's door and said, "They're coming. We gotta head south."

Widow nodded and stayed quiet.

Lyn said, "Where do you want the rest of us to ride?"

Widow said, "Go around. You ride up front with us. Tell the others to grab on outside where they can."

Lyn nodded and shouted back at the others. He repeated the order. They all acknowledged it and started to the vehicle to find a spot to grab.

Suddenly, Lyn stopped and pointed east into the fog, back toward the dark North Korean side of the frozen river, like he saw something. Widow expected Lyn to go around the hood and get into the SUV so they could be on their way, but that didn't happen.

Widow saw Lyn staring at him one second. And the next second, Lyn's head exploded like a bad special effect from a movie. It was violent and unforgettable and haunting.

Lyn had been standing there with a head; then he was only a body with no head. He looked like a mannequin in a shop somewhere missing its head.

Before anyone could react, a second thunderclap rang out and a quick third. Both gunshots. Both loud and echoing across the landscape.

Widow glanced in the driver side mirror. He could no longer see Reyes and Slabin.

A giant bullet hole had blasted through Reyes's eye sockets. Blood and gore was splattered behind his head and his body had flown back off his feet.

Slabin got it worse than Reyes. He got the same bullet hole in his face, but his body fell and twitched and his arms flapped afterwards, like he was dead only he didn't know it yet.

Clery was the first to react. He shouted at Hollander, only he called him by his first name. Widow saw them in the side mirror. Hollander stood to the north. He was the furthest away. He stood completely still. There was shock stretched across his face as he stared back at his three fallen friends.

Clery repeated his shouts. He shouted, "Glen, let's go!"

Hollander glanced over at Clery, whose back was turned to the gunshots. A bullet ripped through the bottom of Hollander's neck, just above his breastbone. Blood and flesh and tissue sprayed out the exit wound like water from a fire hose.

Clery was left standing there, staring at his dead friend.

"Clery, get in!" Widow shouted out the window.

Clery spun toward the vehicle and ran around the back. He came up on the side and grabbed the passenger door handle. He popped it open and started to hop in. Just then, Clery's head exploded. His body was in midleap into the truck. It flew back out into the snow. His blood sprayed across the inner window pillar, the window, and the side panel. The door swung out and hit the limit of its hinges and bounced back.

Widow stared at the last of his dead teammates in horror and disbelief.

What kind of sniper could make those shots, and so fast?

The Kweon family screamed and wailed and shouted. All in Korean. Widow didn't know what they were saying or which of them was doing the screaming. He had no rearview mirror to take a quick glance at them in the back seat. Nor did he intend to look. He just ripped the gear into reverse, and hit the gas. The SUV flew backward onto the dimly lit highway in partial mist. He was going north and needed to stop and pop the gear into drive and head south.

He hit the brakes. And heard glass explode behind him, right where his head would've been if he hadn't hit the brakes. The bullet fired had his name on it and it barely missed him. That didn't mean it hadn't hit someone else, because it had.

Widow spun around and gazed into the back seat and saw that the Kweon's son was no longer there—not in a sitting position, where he had been. Now, he lay hunched over across his mother. His head was broken open like a busted coconut, but instead of milk seeping out, there was blood, and a lot of it. It covered Kweon's wife's hands. She screamed in shock.

Widow's eyes widened to their extreme limits. He was also in shock. He'd never heard of a sniper this deadly before. No one had.

The girl with the volcanic eyes grabbed at him from the front bench. She was screaming and crying. She shouted at him in Korean. It was the same words over and over. He didn't know it, but she was shouting for him to drive.

Widow froze. He was paralyzed for the first time in his entire military service—in his life—he froze solid.

Suddenly, the sniper claimed a seventh victim. Kweon's wife's chest blew open right in front of them. She was dead instantly. She'd joined her son.

39

THAT RED MIST plumed and clouded outward. It filled the inside of the SUV and sprayed across their faces. Widow saw it all over the face of the girl with the volcanic eyes. There used to be a young, innocent teenage face there. Now it was covered in blood. Her innocence was gone, stolen from her by a sniper's bullet.

Her father's face was covered in blood.

The father was shouting at Widow in Korean.

Widow's body unfroze, and he popped the gear into drive, hit the gas and sped up to the vehicle's top RPMs, doing the one thing he hated to do— leaving his brothers' dead bodies behind.

The SUV exploded into action, and he raced south, down the long dark highway.

Two klicks that way, Lyn had said, pointing south, just moments before his head was blown off.

What kind of sniper can shoot like that? Widow had no idea. He had no time to contemplate the question.

He hoped that the speed and the white mist would help to keep them safe from the elite sniper.

The two living Kweons were shouting at each other, frantic and in shock. The girl with the volcanic eyes was trying to crawl into the back seat. She was trying to grab on to her father. She was trying to hold on to him, trying to hold onto the only family she had left in the world. But he kept pushing her back like he was protecting her.

By context alone, Widow figured the girl with the volcanic eyes was begging to hold her dad. But he was ordering her to stay away, to stay near Widow, where it was safer. She wasn't the target. Kweon was.

They were both crying and shouting and twisting in their seats like they wanted to escape desperately. But where were they going to go?

Widow took one hand off the wheel and nearly punched the switch for the headlights, thinking they were making it easy for the sniper to track them. But then he realized he couldn't. He couldn't maneuver the foreign, curving highway in the gloom, not without the headlights, not in the thick of the white fog.

He drove on.

One klick.

The speedometer was in kilometers. He watched the dial rise higher and higher. His foot pressed all the way down on the accelerator.

He saw a warning sign for a sharp curve.

He hit the brake and released it. He heard another thunderclap gunshot boom in the distance. He swerved the SUV to the right and back to the left, trying desperately to avoid the super-accurate gunfire.

The girl with the volcanic eyes bucked up into the air like a bull rider, and the sniper's bullet skimmed the hood of the SUV.

Suddenly realizing that he was holding his breath, Widow breathed out and drove on.

They were coming up on two klicks.

Widow saw an open field coming up off the shoulder. He saw abandoned playground equipment and abandoned buildings, all brick, two of them missing roofs. The whole complex was an abandoned school.

He swung the SUV off the road toward it.

Widow pulled up as close to the buildings as he could. They could use the brick as cover. He heard the father use an English word. He kept speaking the same phrase in Korean over and over, but there was that one English word in his statements.

Kweon said, "Rainmakers." And he said it with sheer terror in his voice.

Widow slammed the brakes, kicking up snow. He grabbed the girl and shoved her head down, out of the line of sight, out of the line of fire. He turned and looked back at Kweon and said, "We go there."

Kweon was shaking. He said, "No. No. Rainmakers."

"Follow us! Now!" Widow shouted. And he busted open the driver's side door and leaped out. He dragged the girl with him. He pulled her into his body, pushing her head down into his chest to make her profile as small as possible. He used his body to shield hers. He was a much bigger target. He just hoped that he could keep her alive, even if it meant that he'd join his dead teammates in Valhalla She didn't fight him. She cried and clenched his vest.

He leaped out onto the snowy ground. He crouched and shoved his back into the front tire of the SUV.

Kweon was out and opposite them, against the rear tire, but the same side.

He was still trembling and repeating the same Korean with the word *Rainmakers* inserted into his phrases.

Widow pointed at the closest structure and held up three fingers. He said, "On three. We run."

They heard another thunderclap, another gunshot, boom in the distance. The sound was a little more distant than before, but it echoed just as loudly. Almost simultaneously, a bullet slammed into the other side of SUV.

How the hell is he shooting that far? Widow asked himself.

Never in his life had he ever heard of a sniper who could do that. Not at this distance and with this much deadly accuracy.

Widow looked at Kweon. He started counting out loud. "One!"

Kweon looked back at him, shaking. He said, "No. No."

Widow said, "Two!"

Kweon quieted and readied himself to run.

"Three!" he shouted and jumped up in a violent explosion of moving mass. He ran toward the abandoned school with the girl with the volcanic eyes tucked into his chest. He kept his arms tight around her to try to shield her from any bullets.

Another thunderclap gunshot exploded on the horizon. Kweon's chest burst open from the side. He went flying off his feet like a barn door blown off its hinges in a violent twister. He was jerked off his feet and slammed into the dirt.

By the time Kweon landed, he was already dead. Widow glanced back over his shoulder to see Kweon behind him about five yards, saw a huge, gaping hole in his right side. Kweon's face registered nothing.

The girl with the volcanic eyes started screaming again. She let go of Widow and pushed off him. He tried to stop her, but couldn't. She ran back to her dead father.

Widow looked in the direction of the sniper shots.

He saw nothing but faint white mist rolling low over the frozen river's surface, like steaming dry ice. He saw the same faint lights that he had seen earlier from the border wall of North Korea. That's where the sniper was, he figured.

Widow turned and scrambled over to the girl. She was crying over her dead father, clawing at him, trying to make him alive again. Widow snatched her up in a powerful effort that would've dislocated her arms if she hadn't let go of her dead father.

Widow took her and dragged her with him toward safety. She didn't fight back. She just cried and screamed. She came up off her feet. He tucked her into his chest again.

He ran with her clinging to him, through the mist and past the SUV's headlights, which was a mistake. They crossed straight through them. They had to. It was on their path to the nearest building.

His primal brain screamed at him over his mistake. The headlamps had lit them up, only for a moment, but it could be enough. It could be a death sentence.

He turned, but he turned the wrong way, like a bad instinct to check where the sniper was. The girl with the volcanic eyes was clamped to his torso, holding on for protection. Widow heard a bullet whiz through the air, through the mist.

It cut straight into the girl's back, below the left shoulder blade and into where her heart should have been.

The force plowed them off the ground. Widow was flung backward onto his back. He heard another thunderclap gunshot. This one did all the same things. The boom. The echo. But this one missed. They were too close to the ground. Too much in the mist.

The bullet hit the SUV's hood. Metal clanged above him.

There was another boom and a gunshot and echo.

This bullet nailed the passenger side front wheel, and the tire exploded.

Widow held his head up and stared down at the girl. He grabbed her face and pulled her head up. There was blood everywhere. In her hair, on her clothes, on his.

He stared at her eyes to see if she was still alive. He saw nothing, no signs of life.

* * *

TWENTY-ONE MINUTES PASSED.

Widow tried not to think. He tried to fight the immediate guilt he felt. His training told him she was dead. Lyn was dead. His other guys were dead. The Kweons were dead. They were all dead. No one survived. No one was left, but him. There was no reason for heroics. Nothing he could do now.

The only thing he could do to stay alive was to stay still. Stay hidden. Right now, he was invisible. He knew that for sure because if he hadn't been, then he'd already be dead.

Every two minutes, the sniper fired another round at Widow's last known position. The sniper, or the sniper team, knew he was alive. They were searching for him frantically.

The bullets kicked up snow all around him—every single shot and every single time. One hit nearby and kicked snow up into his face. That bullet had nearly hit him. It nearly killed him.

He thought the kill shot that killed the girl with the volcanic eyes was meant for him. It must've been.

The girl with the volcanic eyes had saved his life. He tried to be her human shield, but a bad reflex, a terrible mistake, had made her his. That was something he'd have to live with. It was a deep regret that would later haunt him. Right now, he didn't have time for that. Right now, he had to live, to survive.

Just then, he heard a new sound. It was high above him. It was mechanical.

Then he saw the lights and heard the rotor blades. He heard chatter come on over his earpiece. It was English. It was Americans.

They were calling him. He reached up, slowly, and pressed his throat mic and responded.

The helicopter acknowledged. He heard Tiller's voice. He was on board the chopper. "Widow? What the hell happened?"

Widow said, "They're all dead."

Silence for a long beat.

Tiller asked, "How?"

"A sniper team from the border. Careful, they're still shooting at me."

The helicopter yawed and faced the border.

"Where are you?"

Widow said, "The headlights on the SUV. See them?"

"Yeah."

Widow moved the dead girl and reached down and drew his sidearm. He pointed it at the headlights and shot them out—one after the other.

"I see your gunfire."

"Come get me! Watch for the snipers. They're near the lights on the border wall."

A voice that wasn't Tiller's acknowledged, and the helicopter yawed again and started descending to him.

Widow figured the sniper wouldn't fire on the helicopter because shooting on a US vehicle differed from firing on an unidentified American combatant. The snipers couldn't deny that they knew an American Black Hawk helicopter was American.

The Black Hawk descended, landed twenty feet from the SUV, and waited. It blocked the path of any bullets that might be fired from the border wall.

Widow stood up slowly.

Widow scooped up the dead girl and took her with him. It was automatic. He wasn't thinking it through. He felt the least he could do was see that she had a proper burial, because she had taken a bullet that was meant for him

Two SEALs got out of the helicopter, and Tiller followed. They were all decked out in gear and weapons.

Tiller shouted over the helicopter's loud rotors. He said, "What the hell happened?"

Widow said, "I told you. Snipers."

Tiller's face lit up like it wasn't a surprise. He asked, "From North Korea?"

Widow nodded.

One SEAL saluted him and took the dead girl from him. The other one inspected the bodies and the SUV.

"They're all dead," Widow told him.

Tiller waved him on, and they regrouped at the helicopter.

The SEAL carrying the dead girl put her in the Black Hawk, laid her down, and started looking her over.

Widow climbed into the helicopter's cabin and dumped himself down on a rear bench. He was out of energy.

Tiller got in after him and ordered the SEAL to leave the girl with volcanic eyes behind.

Widow said, "What? No. Take her."

Tiller shouted, "She's dead, Commander. We can't take her."

The SEAL tending to her body looked up, shock on his face. He tried to speak, but Tiller reordered him to dump her.

The SEAL didn't move.

Tiller repeated the order. Right then Naval Command, off the nearest ship, came in over the radio and asked what was holdup was. Tiller explained, and the same order was issued again.

Widow didn't fight back. He had no fight left. He was beaten. He had lost five SEALs and four Korean subjects, including two children. One died in his arms, protecting him. She'd taken a bullet for him. He was done.

Why fight back? What was the purpose?

She was dead. They all were.

The SEALs dumped her out, on Tiller's orders, and the helicopter took off.

Widow remembered learning later that the SEAL who took her in told him something. It was something that he would never forgive himself for. He told Widow she was still breathing before they took off.

40

Widow heard birds chirping. He thought he smelled grits cooking. He knew he was having a case of déjà vu. He came to. His mind wasn't racing in the way it normally might have. Instead, it was more like jumbling. He had a splitting headache from the concussion.

The sounds of birds faded away as he drifted into consciousness. The grits smell also faded.

The motor hum of twin engines replaced the sounds. He recognized the sound immediately. It was the sound of jet engines. He heard the wind. He felt the soft rattle of a finely made aircraft traveling at top speed.

He opened his eyes and saw a blur. Again. But it didn't last as long as the previous day when he woke up in a hospital.

He knew he was seated, leaned back but seated, and buckled in. The chair was something very comfortable, a captain's chair, like at the helm of a spaceship on a 1960s television show.

He craned his head up and looked down at himself and then the chair. He was still in his bomber jacket. The same blue knit long-sleeve shirt underneath. The same pair of pants. Same boots. And the same white cast; only now it looked weeks old rather than one day old because it had been through the wringer. The rain in Ireland. The rolling around on the cobblestone.

His arm hurt.

He knew he was in the cabin of a plane. He tried to focus on the chair and the surrounding cabin. He saw colors right away. The chair was all white, leather, and very comfortable—the most comfortable chair he had ever ridden in on a plane. Then his eyes came more into focus, and he saw white ceilings. He saw glossy walnut paneling and cabinets and dark-gray carpet, thick and comfortable looking. It made him want to slip off his boots and run his toes through the carpet—an intended design by carpet designers, perhaps.

He recognized the plane. It was a Gulfstream jet, maybe a G650 or something like it. Same class.

He was on another plane.

Sick of planes, he thought.

He moved his right hand up to rub his forehead, to cope with the intense feeling of a hangover. He stopped it halfway, expecting to feel the denial of metal clanging to his chair from handcuffs. But there was none.

He was facing a cabin about eight feet wide. He sat in the tail end. He could see a cluster of blurry people seated from the wing and up. Then he saw a cockpit door and a steward service station. No steward on board that he could see.

No one was serving coffee.

He stayed still. He didn't want to alert the other passengers that he was awake yet. He still wasn't sure who they were. Friend or foe?

After he was sure that his senses had returned, he started moving. He sat up in his chair and looked out the window. It was daylight outside. It looked like early morning hours.

The cluster of people stopped talking and looked back at him.

They all stood up and started moving back to sit around him.

There were three people.

The first that he recognized was Cassidy. She was alive and unharmed.

She made her way through the cabin the fastest and leaned over him and hugged him tightly.

"You're okay?" she said into his ear. Not a whisper, but just as intimate as one. He felt her breath in his ear and on his neck.

"Yeah, why wouldn't I be?"

"You blacked out on us," she said, pushing up off him. She stood in front of him, blocking the view of the two others behind her.

He nodded and said, "I got a concussion."

She said nothing, but a questioning look came over her face.

"Long story," he said.

She remained quiet.

"What's going on? How long was I out?"

"You've been waking up on and off all night."

"All night?"

"Yeah. We've been flying for hours."

"I've been out that long? That's not good."

"It's not from blacking out. They gave you a painkiller. You've been asleep from it."

"Painkiller?"

"You don't remember?"

He shook his head.

"You woke up complaining about your head. You asked for your Tylenol. Something about it spilling back in Cork."

Widow looked at her, dumbfounded.

"Wai Lin offered you a painkiller. You took two. She said you'd be out for a long time."

Widow stayed quiet. He didn't remember any of that.

"How do you feel now?"

"Like a million bucks. If it had been run over by a truck and woke up with no memory of how it got on a plane."

She smiled and said, "You're okay." She hugged him again. She whispered one more thing in his ear. "They took my gun."

Widow nodded.

After that, she moved back and sat in the seat next to him.

The two strangers behind her came into view. They stepped up, and Widow stared at them. It was a man and a woman. Both Asian. The man was armed. Widow could see a Glock in a pancake holster on the guy's pants. He wasn't hiding it.

The man wore a thick brown winter coat, open at the front. He took a window seat in the aisle across from Widow.

The woman stayed standing. She stared at Widow like she wanted him to recognize her, like she was an old, long-lost friend.

He looked at her. She wore a dark-green pantsuit with a Chinese collar, notched. The jacket had sleeves pushed up over her elbows. She was a very attractive woman. Nicely built. From effort, not genetics, he figured, because she had a muscular frame like a woman who spent a lot of time in the gym. Not bodybuilder status but like an endurance competitor. If he had to guess, he would have figured that she was one of these busy people who woke up at five thirty every morning to go to CrossFit, lifting and pushing blocks and big tires.

Then he had a flash of recognition. It was her eyes. They were eyes he had seen before. They were dark and swirling and volcanic, like something was brewing under the surface.

She smiled at him. She saw he recognized her.

She spoke in a hushed, low voice. Like she too was seeing an old, long-lost friend. She said, "Hello, Chicken."

41

WIDOW WAS ON HIS FEET. Involuntarily. Unknowingly. Unintentionally. And he wrapped his arms around the girl with the volcanic eyes, tight.

He felt like he was seeing an old, long-lost friend.

She said, "I'm so glad to see you."

He let her go and backed away. "How? How? Is this possible? I thought you were dead? You were shot in the heart?"

She smiled and stepped back. She looked at Lu with more than a look. It was a look asking permission for something.

Lu said, "Show him."

She said, "My name is Wai Lin now."

Widow stayed quiet.

Lin said, "I was shot. Twelve years ago. You know. You were there."

Widow nodded. It was her. No doubt about it. The eyes, the face that had haunted him for years.

Lu repeated, "Just show them."

Lin nodded again, and she backed away, three steps farther. She reached up and took her jacket off, and then unbuttoned her blouse.

Widow stayed quiet.

She untucked the blouse and finished unbuttoning it and took it off. She let it fall into one hand.

She faced Widow and Cassidy, nothing left but the bra.

Widow saw a gold necklace with a locket on it. The locket fell between two breasts, supported by an expensive-looking white bra. Hard for him to look at because instinctively, he still thought of her as a girl he had let die.

Her skin was fair and smooth.

Lin stayed liked that, on display for them for a long second, like she was waiting for them to see something in particular.

Widow didn't know what he was supposed to be looking at. He could see just about everything. So far, she looked like a normal woman. Maybe she was more beautiful than most. Even so, she was normal. Everything was where it was supposed to be.

Lin turned around slowly and revealed a long back.

She craned her head and looked back over her shoulder at them.

She had grown into a beautiful woman, but there was one major thing that set her apart from other topless women that he had seen in the past.

She had a long, thick scar that spider-webbed just underneath her left shoulder blade. It was thick and old. It looked like a pruned, long-dead ocean starfish suctioned onto her back.

It was a scar from the Rainmaker's bullet.

"How did you survive?" Widow asked. He was begging to know.

She turned back around and put her blouse on, buttoned it, and tucked it into her pants. She put her jacket back on.

"I still don't understand. How is this possible?" Widow asked.

Lin stepped over to her right and plopped down in an empty seat next to Lu.

Widow sat back down. "I saw you shot. Through the heart."

"Have you ever heard of situs inversus?" She looked at both Widow and Cassidy.

They both shook their heads.

Widow asked, "What's that?"

"I was born with it. It's a congenital defect where a person is born with some organs flipped."

"Flipped?"

"My organs are reversed. They're mirrored."

Widow stared at her.

She said, "My heart is on the right side of my body. Not the left."

She reached up and touched over her chest.

She said, "The Rainmaker missed. He thought he shot me through the heart. He didn't."

"Still. I thought you were dead. How did you survive?

"The missing police. The helicopter flying in to pick you up. The gunshots. Someone heard it all. I was taken to a hospital. I survived."

Widow stared at her eyes, never looked away. "I'm so sorry. I didn't know. I didn't choose to leave you behind. Any of you."

She stared, shaking her head. "I know. I know. It's okay. None of it was your fault."

He nodded, slowly, reluctantly.

Widow didn't have a lot of regrets in his life. He didn't believe in them. Doubt and regret are killers to a SEAL. But one of the big ones he did have was that night, leaving her behind and going there in the first place. Maybe her family would still be alive.

He wanted to tell her that. But he stayed quiet.

She could see the hurt on his face.

She got up and walked closer to him. Cassidy knew what she was doing and stood up, hopped over to the next seat across from him. Lin sat next to Widow and took his hand.

She said, "Hey. It's okay, Chicken. You saved my life."

He turned to her. A single tear streamed out of his eye. He said nothing. He couldn't.

"Hey. You saved my life," she repeated.

"How?" he asked.

"You just did. That night I was rescued and nursed back to health. The Chinese had a lot of questions. They kept me alive and gave me a life and a purpose."

"What purpose?"

She looked at Lu. "We're MSS."

She meant *Ministry of Security Services*, which was the Chinese equivalent to the CIA, but with six times the budget like the NSA, the style of MI6, and broad powers like the KGB.

"That explains the sweet ride," Widow joked, trying to get off the subject of his regret.

Lin looked around the cabin. "It's a pretty sweet life all around."

"You've done well for yourself."

"That's because of you."

Widow stayed quiet.

"If you hadn't come, my family would still be dead, and so would I."

"How's that?"

"Why do you think Tiller wanted my father?"

She knew Tiller's name. Widow said, "He was a nuclear scientist? We were told to get him out because he knew things about North Korea's nuclear programs, and back in 2007, we wanted to know what he knew."

She shook her head. "No."

"No?"

"My father wasn't a nuclear scientist. He wouldn't know the first thing about nuclear fission if ten thousand kilos of uranium fell on his head."

"Then what the hell was he?"

"The Rainmakers."

"What about them?"

"He was in charge of the program. The Rainmakers are...were a team of the best-skilled snipers in the world. Back then, the former leader of the North, the father, wanted to create a dark force of elite assassins."

Sounds like a comic book, Widow thought. But then he recalled stories of assassinations traced back to the North, with no proof beyond the borders. He recalled the assassination of an estranged brother of the leader killed by an experimental poison. Someone who had the poison smeared on a piece of fabric they were wearing had brushed it against his skin. That simple touch killed him.

Lin said, "He wanted to do this in secret. He thought that a group of mysterious super snipers could put real fear into heads of state."

Widow nodded. It did sound scary.

"These guys were selected as children. They were orphans. My father helped to design the program. It was a combination of twenty-plus years of daily, hourly sniper training, yoga, and medications."

"Yoga?" Cassidy asked.

"What kind of medications?" Widow asked.

"Yoga helps snipers a lot. Teaches them how to breathe, how to remain calm. And so on," Lin said. She turned to Widow. "They took all kinds of meds."

"Narcotics?"

She nodded.

"Just different enhancers and things to keep them in a trancelike state. Over the years, they tried everything on them to see what worked to make them better shooters and what didn't."

Widow said, "That's why they were there that night."

She nodded.

"We weren't running from patrolling guards. They're basically incompetent. We ran that night from the Rainmakers."

Widow nodded, felt good about punching Tiller—twice. Felt bad he hadn't done more.

"Tiller wanted my father for what he knew about the program. He probably wanted to recreate it. Or whatever."

Lu looked out the window.

Widow noticed and stared out with him, saw whiteness in the distance.

Lin said, "After my father was killed, the whole program went to shit. The North Korean leader cancelled the program and jailed the remaining Rainmakers."

"Jailed them?"

She nodded.

Widow felt the jet, felt a short burst of turbulence. "Where are we going?"

Lin said, "Sorry about the jet and surprising you and not speaking up earlier. I didn't know you were you until last night. I swear."

"Where are we going?" he asked again.

Cassidy said, "Let her finish."

"Sorry," he said, "It's my head. It hurts. Making me impatient."

Lin nodded and looked at Lu. "Get him something for that."

Lu nodded and got up and went to the service area in the front.

Lin continued, "He saw them as a failure, and he didn't want them roaming free. They all went to prison. And then several of them got out later."

She paused a beat and said, "We've killed them all...All but one."

"The one we're facing now?"

She nodded.

"The Chinese government is okay with you hunting them down like this?"

"We have an arrangement."

He didn't ask.

Lu came back with two pills in his hand and a bottle of water in the other.

Widow eyeballed them.

"They're good," Lu said.

Widow nodded and took them, swallowed them with the water. He drank nearly the whole bottle, fast. "The one we're after, what's he doing?"

"He was let out of prison after the current leader's father died. The son didn't know who he was or why he was imprisoned. He was let out as some kind of new start. Like a reboot."

Widow nodded and asked, "If he's the last, who was the second shooter?"

"An accomplice. Maybe a trainee."

Widow nodded. "That one wasn't as good as him."

Lin said, "The Rainmaker is old now."

"Was he there that night?"

"Oh yeah. They all were. That's how they got so many shots on us. But I don't know which killed my father.

"I don't have a name for him. Not even sure they gave him one. But now he's out. He escaped North Korea, and he's setting up shop. He made a target list to demonstrate his skill."

"Who's on the list?" Widow asked.

"The top five snipers alive."

Widow drank the rest of the water and crushed the bottle, stuffed it into a cup holder.

"He's already murdered four."

Widow stared at her.

"He has?"

"Yes. He started with the fifth, a Russian, and has been flying around the world, killing the others. Climbing the ladder to the top spot."

"I didn't know that."

Lin shrugged and said, "That's not surprising. Why would you?"

Widow shrugged. "So, where are we going?"

"We're flying to a remote town called Doberman Lake."

"Where is that?"

"It's smack in the middle of Quebec."

"Canada?" Widow asked.

"Yes."

"What for?"

"The Rainmaker will go after the last sniper on his list."

"You know who he is?"

Lin nodded. "We know where he lives. After the Canadian sniper shot the world record, he retired from the Canadian Army."

"I thought he still worked for them?"

She shook her head. "They just say that to have a reason to keep his name anonymous. He lives near the lake, just outside of the city."

"Is it cold there?"

She nodded and said, "Don't worry. We have extra winter coats. You both will get one." She smiled.

Cassidy said, "We should call the Canadian police. We should warn them."

"The Rainmaker is already on his way. We know he's done in Ireland. The police won't help. What can they do?"

"They can go to the last sniper on the list. Warn him. They can give him protection."

She shook her head. "We can't allow that. It'll tip off the Rainmaker. We have to set a trap for him. It's the only way."

Widow nodded, said, "She's right. We gotta catch him. An ambush is the only way."

Lin nodded.

Widow asked, "How do you know he's not already there?"

"He won't get there faster than us. We have a private jet and funding from the Chinese government. He's pretty much on his own."

"He's got funding. The rifles in Ireland, they're expensive."

Cassidy said, "Plus, the flying around the world. And lodging. And the passports he's using. They gotta be fake, and expensive too?"

"He's self-funded."

"You sure?" Cassidy asked.

"We're pretty sure. He stole the money."

"From where?"

"Here and there."

Silence.

Widow said, "When do you expect he'll show?"

"Probably a couple of days. We have to convince the Canadian to stay put with us. Till he shows."

"How are we going to do that?"

She looked at Lu and said, "We have ways."

Widow nodded. She was the little girl he thought had died. But she grew up to be a spook, not like Tiller but not unlike him either.

They were all quiet for a moment, and Lin asked, "Want coffee?"

He looked at her. "I'd love coffee."

"I knew you would."

"How did you know that?"

She got up, started on her way down the aisle to fetch him a coffee. She stopped and turned and said, "I read it in your file."

And she smiled.

42

THE AIRPORT in Doberman had to be one of the smallest, most rinky-dink airports that Widow had ever seen in his life. It was a one-building, one-floor, one-runway thing covered in snow with no visible signs of what most airports call a tower.

They had plowed the runway, so it was the only thing around besides the roads without snow covering it. The good news was it made the runway stick out visibly from the air.

As the Gulfstream jet came in for a landing, Widow saw roads headed away in great, unobstructed distances. The roads were the same plowed dirt.

Along the runway was a long, chain-link fence. Snow hung off it.

He wondered how deep he would have to plunge a leg into the snow before he hit the ground.

The airport was painted blue, also making it unmistakable from the sky.

Widow knew better than to ask about flying with the Chinese MSS over international airspace and landing in a remote airport in Canada. They had made their arrangements prior to reporting the flight path.

But Cassidy was curious, and she asked Wai Lin, who gave her an answer repeated from earlier. She said, "We have our ways."

They landed the jet and parked it, and the pilots came out and joined them at baggage claim, which was a single carousel.

Lu and the pilots carried the luggage, and Widow and Cassidy followed

Lin, who checked in with a guy who looked like part airport manager and part local sheriff, or whatever Canada had in rural areas as their law enforcement. Widow wasn't sure. Was it the Mounties? Or did they have constables?

Walking into the airport, he realized he felt much better than he had when they were in the air. But then he realized he felt a little too good. He wondered what Lin had given him.

Cassidy must've expected his grogginess. She offered to help him stand straight and walk. Truthfully, he wasn't so bad that he needed to be helped to walk, but he didn't tell her. There was no reason to keep a beautiful Irish cop from standing close to him, like the night before, walking in the rain.

He felt her next to him. She was warm, and stronger than she looked.

They walked to the front of the airport and stayed in the arrivals area, which was the same area as departures.

Cassidy finally spoke to him with no one else around. "What do you think?"

"About what?"

"Them? That story she told? Is that true?"

"It's true. I was there."

"What's the rest of it?"

"I'll tell you some other time."

"Seriously? I got to wait?"

"It's not the time. It's a long story. Let's just say it was a mission that went bad. A military op. I watched this sniper and his ilk kill her whole family."

"You actually left her for dead?"

"I didn't know she was alive. And I'm not the one who left her. Tiller ordered it."

Cassidy nodded.

"Anyway, this guy killed my teammates. He's killed your partner. And he killed her family. I say we're due for some payback."

"What about this other sniper in Canada?"

"What about him?"

"He's moved all the way out here. The middle of nowhere. How is he going to feel about Chinese spies and an Irish flatfoot and a homeless man showing up at his door?"

Widow said, "He's a guy like me. He's military. He'll understand. Believe me."

She shrugged.

"Besides, what choice do we have? We're here. Lin seems to know what she's doing."

Lin walked up behind them. She rattled a set of keys in front of them. "We have wheels. Let's go."

They went out to the parking lot and followed Lin to a row of trucks that were identical, just different colors. They were all Ford Explorers, about ten years old but all tough-looking. Weather-tested.

They followed Lin, who hopped in the driver's seat. Lu got in next to her. The rest piled in the back. The pilots sat in the third row of seats. It turned out they weren't just pilots. They were part of Lin's team.

Widow saw them take out Type 05 submachine guns. Chinese military uses them all over the world—their version of MP5s.

They had two of them. They locked and loaded them. Then they pulled out two more and did the same. One magazine each. Each ready for use.

They placed the guns in a black duffle bag.

Widow looked forward over Lin's shoulder.

He said, "You guys got a lot of hardware."

Lu said, "A precaution. We might need it."

"Got any sniper rifles?"

"What for?"

"The Rainmaker and his—whatever, student?—aren't going to be in range of some submachine guns."

Lin said, "If we go up against them with sniper rifles, we'll all be dead in minutes. You know that."

Widow stayed quiet.

Lu said, "It'd be like fighting the Jedi with laser swords. I am not good with a laser sword."

Widow stared at him. The Jedi used lightsabers. At least, that's what he remembered them being called. He didn't correct him.

"Why fight a Jedi on his own terms?" Lu said.

Widow nodded. It made sense.

43

THE HOUSE of the Canadian sniper was like Lin had said. It was north of the middle of nowhere. They drove for only about fifteen minutes to get there, but they covered twenty-plus kilometers because the roads were straight and plowed well enough, and the land was flat, and there were no other vehicles in sight. No speed limit signs posted. No police. Nothing.

Lin slowed the Explorer as she approached a solitary home. She spoke to Lu in Chinese. He listened and looked down at his cell phone.

A GPS map, Widow thought.

Lu spoke English.

"This is it."

They drove up a snowy drive, unplowed and uninviting.

Widow knew they could be seen from the house.

The house was less than a hundred yards down a drive and was on a lake. Which would've made for a very serene home for someone, except the lake was completely frozen over. There were signs posted along the track, warning people not to walk on the ice.

Widow looked out over the lake and said, "Thin ice."

Cassidy squeezed his arm, her tiny hand over his good bicep. He realized she had never let go of it. Not since they left the airport.

She leaned in and whispered in his ear—another intimate breath on his neck and skin. "I'm having second thoughts about this."

He looked at her, didn't whisper. "I am too."

They saw no one on the drive.

The house was a brick colonial, painted white. It blended into the snowy terrain. Widow saw plumes of smoke coming out of one of two chimneys. They stood tall and grand, constructed with thick brick.

"Nice house," Lu said, and he made a whistle at the end.

"One day, maybe you'll get one too," Lin said.

"It looks like something out of a novel," Cassidy said.

"Looks like it's owned by a novelist," Lin said back to her.

Widow stayed quiet.

He checked the windows, checking the rooftop, checking the snowy knolls to the sides of the house. He looked at everything that was good sniper cover.

Once they got past fifty yards, he relaxed. If this Canadian sniper wanted to shoot them, he could've done it long ago.

They got to the end of the driveway and parked on the lakeside. No telling what was a driveway and what was yard because everything was snow.

The house had a couple of huge trees in the front yard, still asleep from winter. No leaves, but there was a tire swing hung from a rope so thick it looked like it came off the anchor of an oil tanker.

No one else seemed to notice it.

There was a truck parked out front. Big, heavy, with big snow tires.

There was a big porch with a swing on it.

They pulled to a stop, and Lin parked and turned off the engine.

She turned to Widow and Cassidy and said, "You guys should go up first."

"Why us?" Cassidy asked.

Lin looked at Widow.

He said, "Because we're white."

Cassidy said nothing.

Widow said, "Four Chinese people who look like government agents—no offense—will cause them some alarm."

"I think they're already alarmed," Cassidy said, and she pointed at the porch.

Widow heard a pair of dogs barking and saw two huge snow dogs running off the porch and to the Explorer. They were huge. Widow didn't know the breed, but they weren't huskies.

Lin said, "Go ahead. Charm them."

Widow smiled.

Then a voice from the porch called out the names of the dogs.

And they went running back.

A man stepped out and let them back into the house. Widow saw someone else shut the door.

The man was about late thirties. He had a good build, athletic, but not a big guy. He had a full beard, the kind that seemed to be popular with young guys. Widow had seen it a lot, traveling across North America.

The man walked off the porch but stayed far enough back from the Explorer. He held a pump shotgun.

"Hello. Who are you?" he called out in a Canadian accent. Not too heavy, but obvious.

"Widow," Lin said.

He got out and walked around the Explorer to greet the man.

"Hello," he said, his hands offered like he was surrendering.

"Hello," the man said back.

Canadians. Even with gun in hand, they were polite. Widow smiled. "Hello," Widow repeated.

"Are you lost?"

"No. We're looking for someone."

"You are? Who?"

"Well, you actually."

"Me? What for?"

"It's complicated."

"Complicated?"

Widow saw a window on the first floor, close to the front door, slide up and open. A figure stood behind it in the shadows.

"Yeah. It's not a shotgun in-hand, standing-out-here kind of story."

The man pumped the shotgun, the international signal for *Make it short.*

"What kind of story would six strangers drive all the way out here to tell?"

Widow glanced back over his shoulder at Cassidy, then back at the man.

"It's the kind of story that six strangers would fly around the world and drive all the way out here *just* to tell."

The man was silent.

"Look, we're not here to hurt you. We're here to save you."

"Save me?" the man said and looked around, endless blue sky, the limitless blankets of white, and then nothing else in sight.

"Yes."

"From what?"

"A man who wants to kill you."

The man was quiet for a moment. Then he said, "I think it's time for you to leave."

Widow said, "Three thousand eight hundred seventy-one yards."

The man was quiet for a beat. He stared at Widow. "What's that supposed to mean?"

"That's the world record for the longest confirmed sniper kill."

The man said nothing.

Widow said, "That's your record."

The man was completely still, completely silent. Widow saw into his eyes and realized he wouldn't shoot him. He realized this man had killed no one in his life. He felt confused.

Then a woman's voice spoke from behind the window. It was followed by a face that came forward and peered out at him.

The voice said, "Better let them in."

44

THE WOMAN from the window opened the front door and walked out onto the porch and welcomed Widow. "Who are your friends?"

"Well, ma'am, it's kind of long story."

The woman was a little younger than the bearded guy. She had blonde hair pulled back; she wore glasses, and she glowed like a woman who smiled a lot. She wore a big winter coat, blue, and far too big for her. Probably the man's, Widow figured.

She walked with a wide stance, like she was carrying something underneath the coat. "Are you good guys or bad guys?" she asked.

Widow looked back at Cassidy and again at the woman in the oversized coat and said, "Good guys."

"Okay then. This is Lawrence. I'm Lara. Gagnon. He's my husband."

The guy named Lawrence smiled and lowered the shotgun.

"Jack Widow, ma'am."

"So get your friends and come on in."

Widow waved back at the Explorer, and everyone got out, followed by slamming doors. The pilots, who were more than pilots, stepped out with the duffle bag.

They all stepped up onto the porch, following Widow and Cassidy, who went into the house first, after Lara Gagnon.

The enormous dogs sat at attention at the base of a grand staircase.

Widow thought, *Like Dobermans. Like the town's name.*

He asked, "Doberman, is that related to the snow dogs?"

Lara said, "You know, everyone who comes here asks that. I don't know. I like it 'cause it's a quiet lake town. Hardly anyone lives here, and the people mind their own business."

"Do you guys have an actual town?"

"Like a downtown?"

He nodded.

"Sure. It's twenty-five kilometers south."

"All we saw was that little airport."

"They built it way out from the town."

"What for?"

She said, "No clue. Hide the town from visitors, I guess."

He shrugged.

The inside of the house was clean and warm and filled with the smell of baking bread.

Widow saw a living room with high ceilings. There were posts and log paneling and brick around a fireplace, and heavy furniture and wood everywhere, surrounded by white walls. The floor was wood with woven rugs.

The main floor was wide open. Widow could see she was cooking something in the kitchen. The dining room table was set for two.

"I'm sorry if we're disturbing your breakfast," he said.

"Don't worry about it. Getting visitors is the most excitement I've had in months."

Lawrence was the last person to step in. He suggested everyone take off their coats and boots and leave them in the mudroom to the side of the entrance.

Widow stepped back in that direction. "Sorry for dragging dirt in."

"Don't worry about it," Lawrence said.

Widow took off the winter coat Lin had given him, and so did Cassidy. Widow kept his bomber jacket on. He had worn it underneath.

Lin and Lu and the pilots took off their winter coats, and Lawrence found a place to hang most of them.

Lawrence kept the shotgun nearby. The pilots kept the duffle bag near as well.

They all sat around a roaring fire on soft, oversized, too-comfortable sofas and armchairs.

But before they did, Lara took off her coat and revealed that she had been carrying something.

She was pregnant.

45

"WHEN ARE YOU DUE?" Widow asked.

"Can't you tell?"

He shook his head.

Cassidy pinched his leg and said, "He was raised in a cave. We think."

"It's okay. I'm due soon."

"Not today?"

"No. Week or two."

"Are you having a home birth?"

"Sure."

"No hospital?"

"My husband is a doctor."

Widow looked at Lawrence, who stayed standing. He was near a substantial white island that acted as part of the kitchen and a bar for the rest of the house. He was on the bar side, shotgun resting across the counter-top. He was drinking coffee. It steamed out of a white mug. If he had offered any to their visitors, Widow would've had one too.

The pilots sat together. Lin and Lu sat in armchairs. And Widow was on a sofa with Cassidy.

"Lawrence is a doctor?"

Lara nodded.

Cassidy said, "That makes you the sniper."

Lara said, "I was in the Canadian Armed Forces."

"JTF2?" Widow asked.

"Yes."

"Amazing."

"Why? Because a woman can't be a soldier?"

Widow shook his head.

"You a soldier?" she asked.

"SEAL. Once."

She nodded. "You've never seen a woman in uniform before?"

Widow shook his head again. "I've known plenty of women who were in the Navy and the Marines. They make damn good sailors and marines and soldiers, I imagine. Better than a lot of men I knew."

"No women SEALs, though?"

"Not yet."

"So why are you surprised?"

"I just never pictured a world-record-breaking soldier being pregnant."

Lara said nothing to that.

"You might be the first. That might be a new record."

Lara asked, "So you figured out I'm the sniper who holds the world record. Why are you here?"

Lawrence said, "You said something about protection."

Lin spoke up. "I'm Wai Lin of the Chinese MSS. We're all here because we have united interests."

"Which are?" Lara asked.

She didn't ask about the MSS. Widow figured she knew about them. He asked, "Have you ever heard of the Rainmakers?"

Lara looked at Widow. Her eyes were wide. She nodded. "I've heard of them."

"They're real." Widow said, "There's one left. He's coming here."

"Why?"

"He's taken it upon himself to eliminate the best of the best."

Lara said nothing.

Lawrence said nothing.

Widow asked, "You know James Lenny?"

"I know him."

"He's dead. Shot from three thousand–plus yards."

She said nothing.

Lin said, "We're here to stop him."

Lawrence stood up and said, "You're here to ambush him."

Lin said, "We are."

"So, what? You want to use my wife as bait?"

Lin said, "That's right."

Lara said, "Lawrence. It's okay. If he's killed Lenny, then he's gotta be stopped."

Lara looked at the duffle bag. "What's in there?"

Lu said, "Type 05 submachine guns, ma'am."

She nodded and said, "That's not gonna help you very much unless you can get close."

"It's what we have," Lu said.

"No. We have more." She stood up and walked past everyone and stopped and looked at Widow. "You coming?"

He nodded and looked at Lin, who nodded to Lu.

Lu followed.

They moved down a hall, passed a bathroom and a study, and stopped at a door with a padlock on it. Lara took out a set of keys and unlocked it.

The room was about the size of a large walk-in closet or a tight bedroom. It had a table in the center of the room with four expensive sniper rifles. They were standing upright in inserts and unloaded.

Lara said, "We might need these."

Widow nodded.

"How long till they get here?"

Widow shrugged.

Lu said, "We think a day or two."

They returned to the living room, and Lin explained the whole story to the Gagnons. She told them her role, her side—everything. She told them about her family. And her medical condition and how it saved her life.

Lawrence Gagnon was familiar with it. He told her she was lucky she hadn't died. Not because of situs inversus. Life expectancy rates with situs inversus are like everyone else. But the bullet wounds, unsterile environment, and delayed treatment sounded like they should have killed her.

Lin ordered the pilots to secure the perimeter. They took their weapons and coats and headed outside to walk the perimeter of the house and the lake and stand guard.

After Lin's version of the story finished, Lawrence stopped eyeballing the shotgun every minute and offered them coffee. Widow was the first to accept. And Lawrence returned with breakfast on plates for his wife and himself. He offered to cook breakfast for Widow and company, but no one wanted anything.

The Gagnons ate, and Widow drank his coffee while telling his side of the story. He told them about the train wreck, the concussion, the broken arm, which they could see, and Lenny and Tiller and the op twelve years ago.

By the afternoon, they all knew everything about what had happened so far.

All but Cassidy's dead partner, which Widow didn't want to bring up, and Cassidy didn't want to talk about.

46

By NIGHTFALL, the pilots were sitting on the porch. They had bottles of water and had split up break times, taking turns going back inside to get warm.

One of them took smoke breaks. His cigarette butts were stuffed into an empty soda can on the porch.

Lu went to check on them every hour, and then he returned to the back of the house, facing the lake.

Occasionally, Widow went outside to have a look. And Lin did the same. Cassidy stayed with Lara. By this time, trust had been earned all the way around, and she had been given her sidearm back.

Lawrence had the shotgun. Lara kept one of the sniper rifles with her, loaded. Widow had no idea why. It wouldn't be much good to her as a close-quarter combat weapon unless she planned to climb up to the roof and use it there.

Lu was armed, of course. The only two people who weren't armed were Widow and Lin, but she had Lu and two other guys for that.

Widow said nothing about it. He knew where the weapons were.

He and Cassidy and Lara and Lin wound up sitting on a deck on the back of the house overlooking the lake.

Just then, they heard a sound in the distance, beyond the lake, echoing over a cluster of snow-covered trees. It sounded like a lawnmower or a Honda Civic that Widow had heard before.

"What's that?" Lin asked.

Lu came running around the side of the house, gun in hand. The noise spooked him.

They saw distant plumes of smoke. And the sound continued.

"Relax," Lara said. "It's a Mosquito."

"A what?" Cassidy asked.

"A Mosquito. It's a one-man helicopter. The neighbors have one."

"You have neighbors?" Lin asked.

"We call them neighbors. They live two kilometers that way."

She pointed across the lake.

"Out here, people have all kinds of hobbies. The Mosquito is Colonel Hardy's hobby."

A second after she said that, Widow saw it. A small black dot on the sky, at first, and then it buzzed the treetops and headed toward them.

Widow felt himself rising to his feet, a precaution. He readied himself to jump over Lara and protect her if he had to.

The black dot grew larger, and he saw a small helicopter, like Lara had said. It flew across the frozen water and buzzed the house.

Widow returned to his seat when he saw the pilot.

He was a short old white man in a wool cap, with goggles over his face. He had a scarf wrapped tightly around his neck.

He took the little chopper close and down to an altitude of maybe forty feet above them, staying clear of one old leafless tree.

He waved down to them.

"I see you got friends," he called out to Lara.

"I do, Colonel," she said and waved back.

The pilots from the front came running through the house to see what was happening. They had their guns out.

The dogs were barking, but not at the Mosquito. They barked at the pilots. They were used to the Mosquito like the old guy flew it over the house every day.

Lin barked orders at the pilots in Chinese, and they quickly hid the Type 05s.

"Well, okay then. Have a good night, Lara," the old guy shouted, and he waved and piloted the tiny helicopter higher and back over the lake.

Lara waved after him.

Widow asked, "Colonel?"

"Yeah. He's retired too."

"Does he know who you are?"

"No. He's just a nice old guy."

Lin asked, "Does he fly that every night?"

"Not every night. Sometimes in the early mornings. He's a widower. Gotta do something out here during the cold months to pass the time."

No one spoke about it after that. The pilots and Lu returned to the front of the house.

* * *

A SHORT WHILE LATER, they were conversing about other things.

Widow said, "I can see why you retired out here."

"Thanks. It's my husband's doing."

"How does he get any work way the hell out here? As a doctor, I mean?"

"He works from the internet."

"How?"

"He started one of those medical diagnostics websites."

Widow stayed quiet.

Cassidy said, "Like WebMD?"

Lara smiled.

"Is it WebMD?"

"I can't say."

"Whoa. Explains the nice house."

Lara smiled. She looked at the sky; the darkness was coming on fast. "Up here, the sun sets so quickly," she said.

Widow said, "Seems like it does that just about everywhere."

The dogs were out running in the backyard through the snow, playing.

Lin said, "Thank you for letting us do this."

Lara said, "Just make sure you get this guy."

Lin nodded.

Widow said, "We don't know how long it'll take him to make a move. I think we'd better take shifts sleeping for now."

"How long will we be out here waiting?" Cassidy asked.

"Not long. He won't wait long. Trust me," Lin said. "Two, three days, tops."

"I'd better call my unit. They have to be worried about me."

Lara said, "No phones out here, and the internet is out again."

Cassidy frowned.

Lara said, "I know how you feel. Lawrence's business depends on the internet. Good thing a lot of it is automated somewhere else."

Widow shrugged and said, "Better to say you're sorry than ask permission."

No one responded to that.

Widow volunteered to take the first shift sleeping, mostly because his head was hurting again.

Lara showed him to a bedroom on the top floor, and he waited until she left and then hit the bed. He slept over the covers. Bomber jacket still on. Pants still on. Everything still on except his boots, which were in the mudroom.

47

Widow didn't dream about the dead girl with the volcanic eyes this time. He didn't have to. She was alive.

Instead, he dreamed about Cassidy. A good dream, except he woke up before it got really good.

He woke up to the same buzzing that he had heard earlier, which made him uneasy. Until he remembered Lara had said the old guy was a widower, and he flew the Mosquito in the early morning sometimes.

He opened his eyes and looked around the room. His head wasn't hurting so much anymore.

The buzzing chopper was far away. It grew a little louder, slowly. After a few minutes, it sounded as if it buzzed around the house once.

He listened.

The buzz came and went and was gone suddenly.

Not a big deal if the guy does that a lot, and Lara had said he does. The dogs weren't barking, which was a good sign.

Still, it bothered him. It bothered him because he didn't hear any commotion from whoever was outside guarding, which he assumed were the pilots and Lu.

Best to check it out anyway, he thought.

He sat up in the bed, knew where he was for the first time in two days right off the bat after waking up. He looked over and saw a tray resting on a nightstand. It had a bowl of cereal on it, covered. For him, he guessed.

He left it and got up, tried not to make a sound. He didn't know the time, but it appeared everyone else was asleep.

No dogs were barking. They were used to the buzzing helicopter, though.

His room didn't have a clock. He walked over to a window and looked out.

The nighttime revealed that this place wasn't so empty. He saw the lights from the neighbor's house across the lake, the old colonel's house.

Widow tried to find the Mosquito. No luck. Not in the dark. Even if it had lights turned on, which it may or may not have, it would've looked like a star, depending on how far away it was.

He looked to the south and saw a bit of light in the sky. Must be downtown Doberman.

The sky was full of stars.

He went out to the hallway. He saw no one around.

A door was ajar, two doors down from him.

He peeked in. It was another bedroom, the Gagnons' master. They were asleep in a king-size bed—the dogs on the floor. One of them looked up at him as he peered in the open door. The dog didn't make a sound.

He left the door and checked out the other rooms, and found Cassidy asleep in one. Her Glock rested within reaching distance on a nightstand. She too slept in her clothes over the covers. Her boots were also in the mudroom.

Next, he found an empty bedroom.

He went downstairs and found Lin asleep on one sofa. The fire was still alive, but glowed less than earlier.

Widow moved to the kitchen and looked around. Nothing of interest, except the coffeepot, which was off. But he looked anyway.

He saw the time on the clock—four in the morning.

A little early for the colonel to be flying that thing, he thought.

He went to the back door and opened it, stepped out onto the deck. The wood was cold under his feet. He went over to the railing and looked around, checked the sky, the cluster of distant trees, the lights from the colonel's house. He saw no sign of the Mosquito.

He also saw no sign of the other MSS men. No Lu. No pilots.

He saw something on the ice. It was on the lake.

He almost stepped off the back deck, but he didn't have his boots on.

He ducked back inside to get them. They were in the front, in the mudroom where he'd left them. He slipped them on and went back through the house, sneaking past Lin.

He realized he'd left the winter coat inside but went outside without it.

The back deck's light was switched off. He left it that way and walked out. He stepped off the deck and into the snow.

Then he saw someone down by the lake. It was one of the pilots. He was smoking a cigarette. As he approached the pilot, he saw the guy trying to see the object on the ice. The pilot took another puff of his cigarette.

Suddenly, his back exploded. A bullet had gone right through his chest. Widow dove for the snow.

He stayed prone and watched. The pilot's cigarette landed in the snow, burned one last time like it was still being puffed, and it lit up the pilot's face, which had an expression of utter shock on it. His eyes were wide open. But he was lifeless.

Widow felt a sudden pain in his arm. He'd landed on top of it—again.

He stayed still.

He saw a figure coming up off the ice—all black.

His eyes came into better focus. He saw the object on the ice was the old colonel's Mosquito. But the man coming up the ice wasn't the old colonel.

This guy looked old, but he wasn't white. And it looked like he had a scar over one eye.

48

Widow saw a USP in the guy's hand, silenced. But he wasn't the one who had shot the pilot. That shot had come from the ice or beyond—a sniper.

Widow guessed it was the Rainmaker that he was looking at because the guy fit the bill. The sniper must've been his protégé. The second shooter. The one who killed Gregor.

The Rainmaker approached the dead body slowly and looked it over once; then he started towards the house.

He wasn't planning to kill Lara with a sniper's bullet. He wanted to do this one up close and personal.

Just then, Widow heard footsteps. He turned and saw Lu and the other pilot coming around the side of the house, investigating.

They saw the figure coming toward them but couldn't identify him.

Then Widow thought, *They don't know about the sniper.*

But it was too late.

Widow saw the other pilot's head explode right in front of Lu.

A faint sound echoed across the ice, a suppressed sniper rifle. It sounded like someone hitting a tree with a board, only softer than that.

Lu's chest burst open in two places, almost at the same second.

The Rainmaker had shot him once, with the USP, and the protégé sniper had shot the other pilot.

Widow had been about to call out to them, to warn them. Again, he was too late.

49

Three men dead right in front of him, four if the old colonel was dead. The Rainmaker and his student had killed them in seconds.

Widow hugged the snow, didn't move.

The Rainmaker walked up to the back deck. He stepped up and entered the house.

It would be seconds before he discovered Lin asleep on the sofa, and everyone else was asleep. Widow had to act, but the student sniper was still out there. Probably on the ice. Maybe they had choppered over together. Or maybe he was on the land, not far beyond the frozen water, near the trees.

If Widow jumped up and ran for the back deck, he would be seen right there. The sniper had nothing else to do—no one else to look at. The house was quiet behind him.

If the second sniper was looking, he'd be seen and killed as soon as he made the first move.

For the first time in twelve years, Widow didn't know what to do.

His head started hurting again.

Not now! He thought.

He closed his eyes, remembered staying still, twelve years ago. Remembered thinking Lin was dead, sprawled out on his chest. He had been stuck then, and he was stuck now—paralyzed.

He had to act.

He couldn't let her die, not again, not twice.

He couldn't let Cassidy die or the Gagnons or the baby on the way.

Widow's life was worth losing if it meant giving them a chance to live.

Seconds passed. He had to act.

Suddenly, Widow got a break, and he was all about taking advantage of the right opportunity. It wouldn't get any better.

Right then, the dogs started barking in the house.

He had to bet that the sniper would watch the upstairs.

He leaped to his feet, stayed crouched, and sprinted as fast as he could, through the snow, up the steps, over the deck, and into the house.

There was no sign of the Rainmaker in the hall or the kitchen.

Then he saw him, standing in the dimming firelight, standing over the girl he'd tried to murder twelve years ago.

The USP in his hand, silenced and held an inch from Lin's head.

Widow exploded into action like he was running in the Olympics, and the starter gun had been fired.

He went through the kitchen, making as much noise as he could. He grabbed the cold coffee pot with his good hand and ran past the bar and into the living room.

The Rainmaker heard him coming and twisted at the waist, ready to shoot the madman running at him with a coffeepot.

Widow was faster and had a longer reach.

He slammed the coffee pot into the Rainmaker's gun hand.

The USP fired as it was knocked free. The bullet slammed into the refrigerator in the kitchen. The gunshot was muted, but the stainless-steel refrigerator door pinged loudly behind him.

The Rainmaker was faster than Widow had thought for an old man. And he was very limber.

He had pulled a K-blade out about as fast as he could draw a gun. He stabbed at Widow with it.

Widow blocked with his left hand. The blade stabbed into his cast, and it got stuck there.

The Rainmaker tried to jerk it out but couldn't. Not before Widow punched him with a fast right hook.

The Rainmaker flew off balance and let go of the knife. The side of his face was red and bloody. Widow had cut his face open somewhere.

Widow went to grab the knife out of his cast, but the Rainmaker scooped up his gun first. He rolled with it and aimed right at Widow's center mass.

He smiled at Widow like he recognized him—the man who got away. He didn't shoot, not yet.

50

THE DOGS BARKED UPSTAIRS, but the Rainmaker didn't seem to care about that. He stared at Widow down the sights of the USP.

Widow should have been dead, but he was still alive.

He spoke first. "Why aren't you shooting me?"

"I no shoot you yet because I know you."

"You know me?"

The Rainmaker nodded. "You the man that night? You escaped me."

Widow nodded, said, "That was you."

"It was me."

"All of them? You were alone?"

The Rainmaker was down on one knee, aiming the gun. It was rock-steady in his hand.

Widow saw that the eye with the scar was completely whited out. He was blind as a bat in it.

"Not alone. But I only one shoot that far. I kill boy. I kill woman. I kill man." He paused a beat and said, "I kill girl."

"What about my team?"

The Rainmaker shook his head.

"Not them. That other sniper. I was reserved for when you got far away."

Widow stayed quiet. He saw Lin moving in the corner of his eye.

"You know what they do when I not kill you?"

Widow said, "Put you in prison?"

The Rainmaker nodded. "You know what that for me was like? It was horror. They kill my wife. They kill my son. They take my eye. Only my daughter left."

Widow nodded.

"She out there. Right now. She getting good. Like me."

His daughter was his student, Widow thought. *A family business.*

Lin moved slowly.

Widow wondered if the Rainmaker couldn't see her because of his eye. He had no peripheral vision on that side of his face.

Widow said, "You're wrong about one thing."

"What?"

"That girl."

The Rainmaker stared at him.

"She lived too."

Lin burst from the sofa, charged at the Rainmaker with a poker from the fireplace. It turned out he saw her moving. He shot her. She went flying back.

Widow shouted, without realizing it.

The dogs were barking loudly now.

Widow attempted to sprint and charge the Rainmaker. But he twisted fast and pointed the USP at Widow again. This time he was going to shoot him. No question.

Talking was over.

This was beyond personal.

Widow jerked the knife all the way out of the cast as he charged. He was ready to die, but the Rainmaker was going to get cut. He wouldn't die without making sure he took that other eye.

A gunshot *boomed!* through the house, and its target exploded.

51

WIDOW FROZE WHERE HE WAS. He had heard a gunshot blasting through the house. It echoed and rang out and quieted down after a long, long second.

The Rainmaker had a silencer on his gun. It wasn't his gun that fired.

And Widow was all in one piece.

The Rainmaker was not so lucky. His head had exploded, like the heads of his victims. A bullet had torn through the back of his head and out his good eye.

Blood was sprayed all over the sofas and across Widow's face and clothes.

Standing at the top of the stairs was a pregnant Lara Gagnon, holding one of her sniper rifles. It was bolt action, and smoke plumed out of the barrel.

It turned out she was pretty good with it at short range, too.

Widow dropped the knife and ran over to Lin.

She was still alive. The Rainmaker had shot her on the left side again, thinking it was her heart. But she was breathing raggedly, and it was still a dangerous wound.

She was conscious. He told her to stay quiet.

Cassidy appeared at the top of the stairs, behind Lara and Lawrence. She had her Glock out.

They all came down the stairs. The dogs too.

The dogs were licking up what was left of the Rainmaker. No one stopped them.

Lawrence took over. Tending to Lin's wounds, he ordered Cassidy to get him water and towels from different rooms.

Widow stood up and grabbed Lara's arm.

"Thank you," he said.

She nodded.

"There's one more thing."

"Yes?"

"You got night vision on that gun?"

She smiled.

They went to the top floor, and she looked out through a window from her bedroom. They left the lights off.

"I see the sniper. It's a girl."

She'd found the protégé, the Rainmaker's daughter. Which he didn't tell her.

"Yeah. How old is she?"

Lara paused and said, "I'd say in her early twenties."

Widow paused.

"Want me to kill her?"

Widow thought for a quick second.

"Hurry, she looks worried. She's shuffling around."

The girl had killed Gregor. She had murdered him in cold blood. And who knew how many others she had killed.

"Do it," he said.

Lara breathed in, held it, and squeezed the trigger.

52

Lawrence kept Lin alive long enough for them to get her into a vehicle and drive to town, where there was a small hospital. He told Widow that she would have to be moved to a better one, which was an hour's drive south, but she should make it just fine.

Widow looked for holes in the ice. He thought about having them dump the bodies in the lake, but he had brought enough problems to the Gagnons.

Lara was a by-the-book type. Mostly.

They wanted to get the authorities out there as soon as possible.

Widow convinced them to wait until Lin was safe and stable in the local hospital. He rode with them to bring her, as did Cassidy. Only the dogs stayed behind in the house.

They arrived in downtown Doberman, and Widow helped them get Lin into the emergency room, which was bigger than Widow expected.

He saw her go in; she was talking. She'd be fine, he figured.

He never said goodbye to her.

He took Cassidy by the hand and fell back with her behind the Gagnons and the nurses and doctors.

They returned to the airport.

She mentioned Tiller one time. Asked Widow if he was going to do anything else about him. Widow responded with a shrug and a "life's too short to worry about an insignificant person like him."

That was all they said on the matter.

They held hands, waiting for two different flights. His was first. He said goodbye to her at the gate and took her business card.

They did the "if you're ever in Ireland again" conversation.

Widow kissed her and boarded a plane to JFK.

In the air, he thought maybe he'd call DeGorne when he landed. Then again, maybe not.

A WORD FROM SCOTT

Thank you for reading THE LAST RAINMAKER. You got this far—I'm guessing that you liked Widow.

The story continues in a fast-paced series that takes Widow (and you) all around the world, solving crimes, righting wrongs.

The tenth book that follows is THE DEVIL'S STOP, which refers to all the places in the USA named after the devil like Hellbent, New Hampshire, a small town that time forgot. First day there, Jack Widow meets a beautiful former Air Force MP who's desperately seeking her husband all while being nearly nine months pregnant. Widow being the man he is means that he's got to help. What starts as a simple missing person soon turns deadly when they uncover that the missing husband was involved in a top-secret government nuclear program and the evil team of dishonored mercenaries who are after it.

Book eleven is BLACK DAYLIGHT. Jack Widow walks a lonely, snowy road at night when he witnesses a heinous crime. The only glimpse of the culprit he gets are taillights that fade into the mist. Widow does all he can to help, but when he does the local South Dakota police and the FBI see him as suspect number one.

What are you waiting for? The fun is just starting. Once you start Widow, you won't be able to stop.

THE SCOTT BLADE BOOK CLUB

Building a relationship with my readers is the very best thing about writing. I occasionally send newsletters with details on new releases, special offers and other bits of news relating to the Jack Widow Series.

If you are new to the series, you can join the Scott Blade Book Club and get the starter kit.

Sign up for exclusive free stories, special offers, access to bonus content, and info on the latest releases, and coming soon Jack Widow novels. Sign up at www.scottblade.com.

THE NOMADVELIST
NOMAD + NOVELIST = NOMADVELIST

Scott Blade is a Nomadvelist, a drifter and author of the breakout Jack Widow series. Scott travels the world, hitchhiking, drinking coffee, and writing.

Jack Widow has sold over a million copies.

Visit @: ScottBlade.com

Contact @: scott@scottblade.com

Follow @:

Facebook.com/ScottBladeAuthor

Bookbub.com/profile/scott-blade

Amazon.com/Scott-Blade/e/B00AU7ZRS8

Manufactured by Amazon.ca
Bolton, ON

34644858R00423